SF   Harlan, Thomas.
HARLAN   The shadow of Ararat

CHIPPEWA RIVER DISTRICT LIBRARY

3 4040 00353 4175

DEC - - 2015

WITHDRAWN

SCL

D1058687

The
SHADOW
of ARARAT

The
SHADOW
of ARARAT

Thomas Harlan

TOR®
fantasy

A TOM DOHERTY ASSOCIATES BOOK

NEW YORK

CHIPPEWA RIVER DISTRICT LIBRARY
Mt. Pleasant, MI
Shepherd Community

This is a work of fiction. All the characters and events portrayed in
this novel are either fictitious or are used fictitiously.

THE SHADOW OF ARARAT

Copyright © 1999 by Thomas Harlan

All rights reserved, including the right to reproduce this book, or
portions thereof, in any form.

This book is printed on acid-free paper.

A Tor Book
Published by Tom Doherty Associates, LLC
175 Fifth Avenue
New York, NY 10010

Tor Books on the World Wide Web:
www.tor.com

Tor® is a registered trademark of Tom Doherty Associates, LLC

Book design by Ellen Cipriano

Library of Congress Cataloging-in-Publication Data

Harlan, Thomas.
    The shadow of Ararat / Thomas Harlan — 1st ed.
        p.   cm.
    ISBN 0-312-86543-0 (hardcover)
    I. Title.
PS3558.A624244S33   1999
813'.54—dc21   99-24484
                                                            CIP

First Edition: July 1999

Printed in the United States of America

0 9 8 7 6 5 4 3 2 1

NOTES ON NOMENCLATURE

The Roman mile is approximately nine-tenths of an
English mile.
A league is approximately three Roman miles in distance.

MAPS

Roma Mater

Oath of Empire,
The Shadow of Ararat

Constantinople

Alexandria

Palmyra

Battle of Emesa (Palmyra vs. Persia)

Battle of Kerenos (Rome vs. Persia)

For me mum and me pop,
Who set me on this long and tortuous road:

Thanks!

ROMA MATER (622 A.D.)

N

Praetorian Camp

FLAMINIAN HILL

The Tomb of Augustus

The Great Clock

SALLUSTII DISTRICT

QUIRINAL HILL

Baths of Diocletian

VIMINAL HILL

CISPIAN HILL

TIBURTINA DISTRICT

Baths of Helen

ASINARIA DISTRICT

Amphitheatre Castrense

Temple of Astarte

Temple of Isis

Baths of Constantine

SUBURA DISTRICT

Baths of Trajan

Colosseum

CAELIAN HILL

The Antonine Baths

The Via Appia Gate

Porticus Octaviae

Forum Romanum

THE PALATINE

Temple of the Divine Claudians

Stadium of Domitian

Pompey's Theatre

Circus Flaminius

Forum Boarium

Circus Maximus

Temple of Asklepios

AVENTINE HILL

Porticus Aemilia

The Ostia Gate

RUBBISH YARDS and CREMATORIUM

The Tomb of Hadrian

ALSIENTINA DISTRICT

TESTACEUS DISTRICT

The Tiber

THE NAUMACHA DISTRICT

Circus Caii

Ianiculum Hill

THE WESTERN
ROMAN EMPIRE

MARE CASPIUM

SARMATIA

KHAZARKHANATE

ALBANIA

(Heraclius, Galen and
Ziebil vs. Shahr-Baraz)

COLCHIS

Mount
Ararat

SLAVS

BOSPORAN
KINGDOM

MOESIA
INFERIOR

VASPURKAN

Van

Tauris

Ganzak
PERSIAN
ARMENIA

*The Sea
of
Darkness*

Trabzon

PONTUS

Odessus

CAPPADOCIA

Amida

Nineveh

R KHANATE

Under
Persian
Control

Ancyra

Samosata

THE PERSIAN EMPIRE

Dastagird

SERDICA

ANATOLIA

CILICIA

CTESIPHON

CONSTANTINOPLE
THRACE

Nicomedia

Propontis

Heraclea

THE LAKHMIDS

BITHNIA

Tyana

Antioch

essalonika

Pergamum

Tarsus

COELESYRIA

PALMYRA

(Zenobia vs. Shahr-Baraz)

Ephesus

LYCIA

Emesa

THE TANUKH

TTICA

Delos

Athens

RHODES

CYPRUS

Tyre

Damascus

Hierosolyma

MARE AEGEUM

PHOENICIA

CRETE

THE EASTERN
ROMAN EMPIRE

ARABIA
PETRAEA

PETRA

ARABIA
FELIX

ARE INTERNUM

Alexandria

Memphis

Arsinoe

CYRENAICEA

AEGYPTUS

SHEBA

SINUS ARABICUS

OATH OF EMPIRE
THE SHADOW OF ARARAT
(622 A.D.)

MEROE

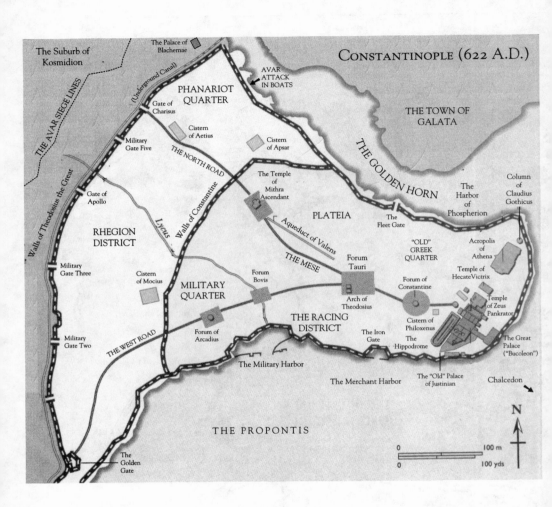

CONSTANTINOPLE (622 A.D.)

The Suburb of
Kosmidion

The Palace of
Blachernae

AVAR
ATTACK
IN BOATS

THE TOWN OF
GALATA

PHANARIOT
QUARTER

Gate of
Charisus

Cistern
of Aetius

Military
Gate Five

Cistern
of Apsar

THE NORTH ROAD

(Underground Canal)

THE AVAR SIEGE LINES

THE GOLDEN HORN

The Temple
of
Mithra
Ascendant

PLATEIA

The Harbor
of
Phospherion

Column
of
Claudius
Gothicus

Gate of
Apollo

Walls of Theodosius the Great

Walls of Constantine

Lycus

Aqueduct of Valens

The
Fleet Gate

"OLD"
GREEK
QUARTER

Acropolis
of
Athena

RHEGION
DISTRICT

THE MESE

Forum
Tauri

Temple of
HecateVictrix

Military
Gate Three

Cistern
of Mocius

MILITARY
QUARTER

Forum
Bovis

Forum of
Constantine

Temple
of Zeus
Pankrator

Arch of
Theodosius

Cistern of
Philoxenus

Military
Gate Two

THE WEST ROAD

Forum of
Arcadius

THE RACING
DISTRICT

The Iron
Gate

The
Hippodrome

The Great
Palace
("Bucoleon")

The Military Harbor

The "Old" Palace
of Justinian

Chalcedon

The Merchant Harbor

THE PROPONTIS

N

The
Golden
Gate

0   100 m

0   100 yds

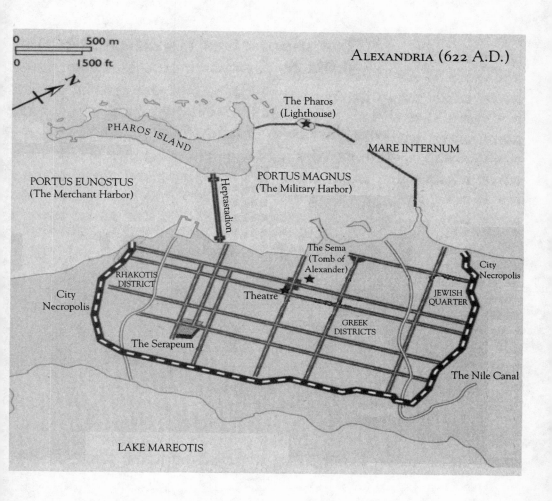

ALEXANDRIA (622 A.D.)

0   500 m
0   1500 ft

N

The Pharos
(Lighthouse)

PHAROS ISLAND

MARE INTERNUM

PORTUS EUNOSTUS
(The Merchant Harbor)

Heptastadion

PORTUS MAGNUS
(The Military Harbor)

The Sema
(Tomb of
Alexander)

City
Necropolis

RHAKOTIS
DISTRICT

City
Necropolis

Theatre

JEWISH
QUARTER

The Serapeum

GREEK
DISTRICTS

The Nile Canal

LAKE MAREOTIS

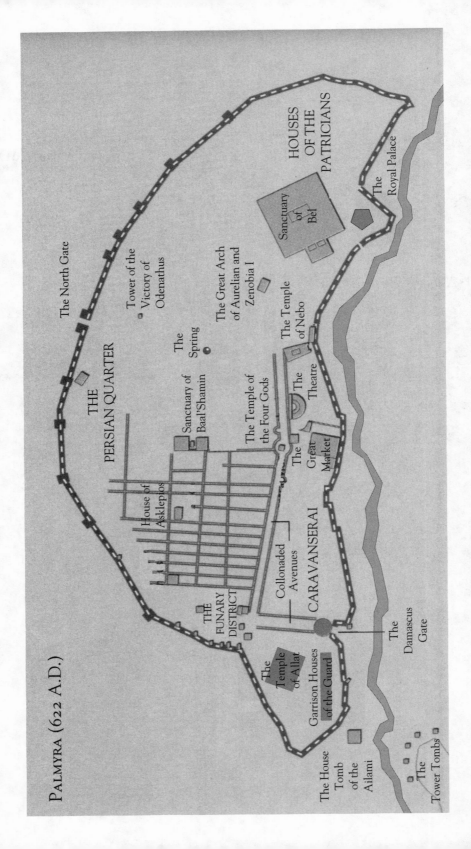

PALMYRA (622 A.D.)

The North Gate

THE PERSIAN QUARTER

Tower of the Victory of Odenathus

The Spring

Sanctuary of Baal'Shamin

House of Asklepios

The Temple of the Four Gods

The Great Arch of Aurelian and Zenobia I

The Temple of Nebo

The Theatre

The Great Market

Collonaded Avenues

CARAVANSERAI

THE FUNARY DISTRICT

The Temple of Allat

Garrison Houses of the Guard

The Damascus Gate

The House Tomb of the Ailami

The Tower Tombs

Sanctuary of Bel

HOUSES OF THE PATRICIANS

The Royal Palace

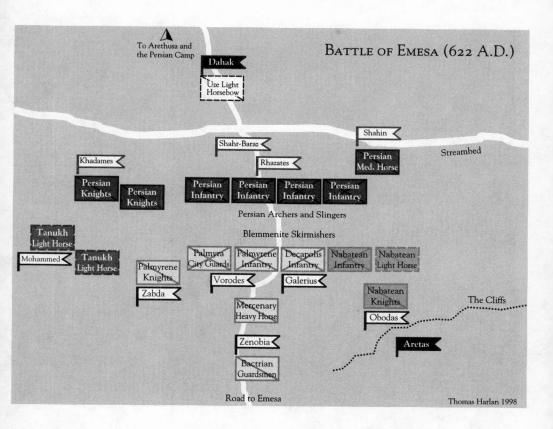

BATTLE OF EMESA (622 A.D.)

To Arethusa and the Persian Camp

Dahak

Üze Light Horsebow

Shahin

Shahr-Baraz

Persian Med. Horse

Streambed

Rhazates

Khadames

Persian Knights

Persian Knights

Persian Infantry

Persian Infantry

Persian Infantry

Persian Infantry

Persian Archers and Slingers

Blemmenite Skirmishers

Tanukh Light Horse

Mohammed

Tanukh Light Horse

Palmyrene Knights

Palmyra City Guards

Palmyrene Infantry

Decapolis Infantry

Nabatean Infantry

Nabatean Light Horse

Zabda

Vorodes

Galerius

Nabatean Knights

The Cliffs

Mercenary Heavy Horse

Obodas

Zenobia

Aretas

Bactrian Guardsmen

Road to Emesa

Thomas Harlan 1998

Battle of Kerenos (622 A.D.)

North,
to Albania
and Khazaria

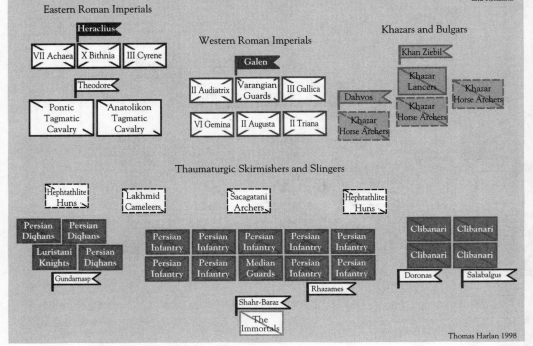

Eastern Roman Imperials

Heraclius

VII Achaea | X Bithnia | III Cyrene

Theodore

Pontic Tagmatic Cavalry | Anatolikon Tagmatic Cavalry

Western Roman Imperials

Galen

II Audiatrix | Varangian Guards | III Gallica

VI Gemina | II Augusta | II Triana

Khazars and Bulgars

Khan Ziebil

Khazar Lancers | Khazar Horse Archers

Dahvos

Khazar Horse Archers | Khazar Horse Archers

Thaumaturgic Skirmishers and Slingers

Hephtathlite Huns | Lakhmid Cameleers | Sacagatani Archers | Hephtathlite Huns

Persian Diqhans | Persian Diqhans

Luristani Knights | Persian Diqhans

Gundarnasp

Persian Infantry | Persian Infantry | Persian Infantry | Persian Infantry | Persian Infantry

Persian Infantry | Persian Infantry | Median Guards | Persian Infantry | Persian Infantry

Rhazames

Shahr-Baraz

The Immortals

Clibanari | Clibanari

Clibanari | Clibanari

Doronas | Salabalgus

Thomas Harlan 1998

The SHADOW of ARARAT

DELPHI, ACHAEA: 710 *AB URBE CONDITA* (31 B.C.)

The Greek woman raised her arms and her face, pale and regal, was revealed as the purple silk veil fell away. Deep-blue eyes flickered in the dimness of the narrow room. A mass of raven hair cascaded down over her pale shoulders. The smokes of the crevice rose up around her as she stood in supplication. Far away, behind her, the low beat of a drum echoed in the sun-baked little plaza in front of the temple. She waited, patient and calm.

Finally, as the irregular drumming settled into her blood and she grew light-headed in the haze of bitter-flavored smoke, a figure stirred in the darkness beyond the glow of the brazier. Strands of long white hair gleamed. Withered fingers brushed against the lip of the corroded bronze tripod. A face appeared in the smoke, and the queen barely managed to keep from flinching back. Unlike the gaudy display at Siwa, here there was no grand chorus of priests in robes of gold and pearl, no vaulting hallway of stupendous granite monoliths, only a dark narrow room in a tiny building on a steeply slanted Grecian hillside. But at Siwa, when the oracle spoke, there had been no stomach-tightening fear.

Here the Sybil was ancient and wizened, her eyes empty of all save a sullen red echo of the flames now leaping in the pit below. The mouth of the crone moved, but no sound emerged. Yet the air trembled and the queen, to her utter horror, felt words come unbidden to her mind, forming themselves pure and whole in her thought. She flinched and staggered back, her hands now clawing at the air in a fruitless attempt to stop the flood of images. She cried out in despair. The empty face faded back into the darkness beyond the tripod and the crevice. The fire sputtered and suddenly died.

The Queen lay, weeping in bitter rage, on the uneven flagstones as her guardsmen entered the chamber to see what had befallen her. The vision had been all that she desired, and more.

)•((

Aboy walked in darkness, his head outlined against the sky by the dim radiance of the River of Milk. His skinny legs were barely covered by a short
kilt of rough cotton homespun. He scrambled to the crest of the dune. Beyond it
the western waste spread before him cold and silver in the moonlight. A chill
wind, fresh with the bitter scent of the desert, ruffled his shirt and blew back the
long braids from his face. Breathing deep, he felt his heart fill with the silence.
He smiled, broad and wide, in the darkness. Laughing, he spread his arms and
spun, letting the huge vault of heaven rotate above him. The great moon, a dazzling white, filled the sky. The river of stars, undimmed by clouds, coursed above
him, the Zodiac forming in its eddies and currents.

He sighed deep and laughed again. He sprinted along the ridge, feeling his
muscles surge and thrust as he hurtled forward. Gaining speed, he lengthened his
stride and kicked off hard as he reached the curling lip of the dune. For a moment,
the wind rushing past, he was suspended in the starry dark. His long braids lashed
back as he fell through deep shadow.

The water was a slapping shock as he struck the surface. He plunged through
broiling murk and felt his feet strike against the sandy bottom. Surging upward,
he breached, throwing his head back. The stars glittered down through the arching
palms, and Dwyrin rolled over and stroked easily to the reed-strewn shore. Gripping a low branch, he pulled himself from the inlet of the Father Nile. He squeezed
muddy water from his braids and coiled them at his shoulder. His tunic, sodden
and caught with long trails of watercress, he stripped off. Cold wind brushed over
him but he did not feel it.

Pushing through the tall cane break at the edge of the inlet, he looked for a
moment out across the broad surface of the Nile. Near a half mile of open water,
running silent under the moon, to the far bank. There he could pick out the lights
of the village, dim and yellow in the night. His right hand checked absently to
see if the oranges were still secure in his cord bag. They were and he took to the
trail leading south along the margin of the river.

Beyond the narrow strip of fields and palms, stones and boulders rose from a
long tongue of hills that arrowed out of the waste into the Nile. Here, where the
river had long ago curved about an outcropping, men of the Old Kingdom had
raised a siege of pillars and great monoliths. Dwyrin clambered up through the
debris that marked the fallen northern wall of the temple. A looming shape hung
over him, ancient face blurred by the desert wind. Swinging over the massive stone
forearm, Dwyrin squeezed through a small space beneath the fallen statue. Within
the ancient temple, long rows of pillars arched above him. The wide stone passages

between them were littered with blown brush and sand. Dwyrin picked his way to the great platform that fronted the temple. From it three great seated figures stared north, down the Nile, to the distant delta and their realm of old.

At the center reigned the bearded king, his arms crossed upon his chest, broken symbols of divinity and rule held in massive sandstone hands. His eyes were dark as he looked to the north and the havens of the sea. To his left sat the languid cat-queen, his patroness, her face still and silent in an ancient smile. One great pointed ear was sheared off, showing dark-grained stone beneath the smooth carving.

Her, Dwyrin avoided, for her long hands were tipped with claws and she always seemed cool and aloof. Instead, he turned to the rightmost statue, that of the mightily thewed man with the head of a hawk. He climbed up, over the pleats of the old god's kilt, and sat in the broad curving lap, his legs swinging over the edge. Beneath him the Nile gurgled quietly.

He sat and peeled his oranges, one by one, and waited for the return of Ra from the underworld. He ate them all, juices staining his fingers and lips. They were tart, and sharply sweet.

Dwyrin reached the edge of the school grounds with his breath coming in long ragged gasps. His sandals, tied around his neck by their thongs, bounced against his back. He vaulted the low fence bordering the vegetable plots without breaking stride and rounded the corner into the stableyard. Distantly, over the whitewashed rooftops of the school, he could hear the morning chanting of the monks. Ra was only just over the horizon, but he had lingered too long at the old temple, skipping broken pieces of shale from the platform into the dark green-brown waters. The stable boys looked up in amusement as he ran across the hard-packed mud of the yard to the rear garden gate.

Sprinting to the wall, he leapt up and caught the top of the bricks with both hands. With a heave, he swung up and over, landing hard on the low grass inside and rolling up. He dodged through the long row of columns that skirted the garden, sliding to a stop at the door to the junior students' dormitory. Within he heard faint grumbling and the snores of the Nubian boy at the end of the bunk line. Glancing both ways down the colonnaded breezeway, he eased the door open and slipped inside. He stripped off the tunic, now dry, and hung his sandals on the pegs by the door.

The thick woven cane door at the far end of the hall swung open and the sharp clack of the journeyman master's cane rapped on the pale rose tiles. Dwyrin froze by the doorway. Master Ahmet, he saw, had turned back to say something in passing to the master of the older boys' section. He had not yet looked fully into the room.

Dwyrin dove to the floor and rolled under the nearest bunk. In it, one of the Galatian students turned over in his sleep. The rapping of the master's cane resumed and the first sharp slap of cane stick on bare foot resounded from the end of the hall. The boy nearest the far door woke, groggily, and rolled out of bed. Dwyrin slid forward under the bunk and on to the next.

Unfortunately, his bed was on the far side of the hall, across the walkway, and halfway down. He slithered forward on his belly, checking the progress of the master's broad feet through the bedposts. Opposite his own bunk, he stole a look down the walkway. The master had turned away from the line of bunks where Dwyrin hid. Dwyrin reached into his rolled tunic and dragged out the rinds of orange within. Heart beating furiously and hands shaking just a little, he waited until the master had turned away again. With a flick of his hand, he skated the rinds down the row of bunks to lodge nearly soundlessly against Kyllun's bunk, where the ball popped apart and spilled its remains in an unsightly pile by the head of the bed.

Dwyrin drew his feet up under him and edged out into the space between the beds. The master reached Kyllun's bunk and gave him a sharp switch on his exposed foot. Then the master paused, dark eyes narrowed, spying the rubbish by the side of the bed. His hand was quick as he turned and grasped the sleep-befuddled Kyllun by one large sun-browned ear.

"So! You are the rascal who has been into the orchards of the holy monks!" Kyllun barely had time to yelp before the cane swatted him sharply across the buttocks. "You'll not be doing so again, my lad!" the master cried, and sharply marched him to the far end of the room, giving him the cane as he went. Kyllun was wailing by the time he and the master reached the end of the room. While the master was turned away, Dwyrin scooted across the gap and into his own bed. Safe.

Kyllun's wailing had roused the rest of the boys now, including Patroclus, whose bunk was next to Dwyrin's. The Sicilian boy eyed Dwyrin with distaste as the Hibernian slid under the thin cotton sheets of his bed and assumed a peaceful expression of sleep.

"You owe me your sweet at dinner," Patroclus hissed as he cast back his own sheets and ran long, thin boned hands through his lank black hair.

"You might as well get up now, everyone else is," he whispered at Dwyrin, who responded with a semi-audible snore and rolled over artistically, his sheets askew and one bare white leg sticking out. Patroclus shook his head and rubbed sleep from his long face with both hands.

The master returned and paused by Dwyrin's bunk, eyeing the Hibernian's recumbent form. One almond-shaped eye, keen and dark, widened a little at the sight of the boy's foot and the cane twitched in his olive hand.

"Lord Dwyrin," he cooed, "it is time to rise and greet holy Ra as he begins his long journey through the heavens." Dwyrin snored again and buried his head underneath the thin straw pillow. "Oh, Dwyrin . . . Get up, you lazy, thieving, treacherous, duplicitous lout!" the master shouted, and caned the backs of Dwyrin's legs fiercely. Dwyrin shot up out of the bed like a porpoise sporting in the Aegean waves. The quick dark hand of the master secured his protruding red, freckled ear and dragged him into the walkway. Dwyrin yelled as the cane was sharply laid across his bottom.

"Young men who sneak out at night," the master growled, "should take pains to clean the grass stains from their feet before they reenter the dormitory!"

"Ow! Ow! Ow!" Dwyrin wailed, as he too was frog-marched to the end of the long room. The other boys stared in amazement as the red-headed boy was dragged into the master's cubicle at the end of the dormitory. The master dismissed Kyllun with a quick motion and the Cilician went quickly, rubbing his ear and glaring sheer hate at the unrepentant Dwyrin.

"Now, young master Dwyrin," the dorm master said as he closed the door behind him, "let me see if I can remember the punishments for stealing, breaking curfew, and causing the unjust punishment of another student."

Dwyrin gulped as the door slammed shut.

Day's end came at last, the ship of Ra dropping once more beyond the western hills to begin its journey through darkness. Dwyrin looked up from the basin at the back of the kitchens to see the sky turn gold and purple, then fade into deepest blue. Two of the cooks came out of the low door, bearing another heavy tray of bowls and cups. Bone weary, his hands red and sore, Dwyrin heaved the copper bucket onto his shoulder and stumbled to the well at the end of the rear court. His hands throbbed as he cranked the wheel around, dropping the bucket and its corded hemp line into the cool darkness below. There was a distant splash and the too-familiar gurgle of the bucket tipping over and filling. Dwyrin leaned on the wheel against the growing weight. His bronze-red hair was gilded by the setting sun. There was laughter from the court within; the junior boys were leaving dinner and going to the night studies.

"Ho! Dwyrin! Thanks for doing the dishes!"

Patroclus and Kyllun leaned over the top of the wall, smug smiles broad upon their faces. Each held an extra sweet, dripping with honey and crumbs. Their self-satisfied faces, Dwyrin thought, were loathsome to look upon. He made the horns at both of them and cranked the wheel back around. The bucket dragged heavy, even against the wheel and its pulleys. The two, hooting with laughter, disappeared from the wall and ran off, sandals slapping on the tiled walkway. Dwyrin cursed silently as he winched the heavy bucket out of the well.

I could have stayed home and done this, he thought bitterly. *Learning to be a thaumaturge sure takes a lot of lifting and carrying . . .*

The curled edge of the bucket bit into his shoulder as he stumped back to the basin. The monks had come again and the basin was filled with cups and bowls and broad wooden serving platters. Dwyrin groaned as he leaned over the edge, spilling fresh water into the curved marble trough.

Holy monks and priests, particularly ones who can call the wind or summon lightning, should be able to clean their own bowls!

The moon was high and clear, well into the sky, when Dwyrin staggered through the corridor to the dormitory. His bed, he thought, would be most sweet. He washed in the cubicle at the end of the dorm, farthest from the master's quarters. His hands were shaking with fatigue, his mind dulled. At last his bed was there and he could slide under the sheets, pulling them up over his head. Buried under the pillow, he allowed himself a whimper. But only one; Patroclus was doubtless listening from the next bunk.

His leg itched. He scratched it. His left side itched. He scratched it. There was something tickling at his belly. He rolled out of bed, his legs beginning to prickle. Turning back the sheets, he grimaced at the nettles and cockleburs liberally strewn within.

Patroclus laughed softly in the next bunk. Dwyrin, after a struggle, mastered himself and did not fall upon the Sicilian with knotted fists. He gathered up the bedding, trying hard not to spill any of the burrs or thistles within, and quietly crept out of the dorm. His hands and shoulder were already throbbing at the thought of drawing another bucket of water. *Things*, he thought as he bent over the washboard at the laundry, *would have to change*.

The masters barely teach us enough to summon a fly, he grumbled to himself. *How can I* . . .

He stopped, a slow wicked smile creeping onto his face. Suddenly he didn't feel so tired.

ROMA MATER, ITALIA

A thin slat of daylight filtered down from above to cast a pall on the face of the young woman in the stained blue robe. Unconcerned with the thick crowd thronging the narrow alleyway, she pushed through mendicants, draymen, butchers with hogs' heads slung over their shoulders, and off-duty *aediles* to finally reach the end of the sweetmeat lane. At the corner, she sneezed in the dust of the wider city street and then quickly crossed between two crowds of chanting priests. Each troupe bore a profusion of banners, small figurines on stands, and a cacophony of drums, trumpets, and rattles. The faithful moved slowly along the street, chanting and singing at the direction of their priests. On the far side, under the awning of a pastry shop, she tucked a loose curl of deep red-gold hair back into the patched hood of the threadbare robe and idly glanced up and down the street.

A half block away, Nikos was looking in her direction, his stubbly face turned up under a broad straw hat. He caught her eye and nodded, then touched the brim of the hat with a thick finger.

From her great height of almost six feet, she could pick him out as he melted into the flow of traffic, pushing steadily in her direction. Distantly, there was a trumpeting sound and the rattle of gongs. It was hot in the Subura district and the air was heavy with a long familiar stench. Thyatis turned the other direction, casting her eye to the opposite side of the avenue. The crowds continued to spill in their disorderly way into the street, blocking traffic and causing the girl to weave her way slowly forward.

The crowd thinned as the road made an inelegant turn into the dye-makers' district. Her sharp nose flared, catching the wretched smell of old urine. She trembled a little, though the sun was hot in the lane, as bitter memories picked at her thoughts. She snorted in disgust and mentally pushed them away. Then her clear gray-blue eyes widened as she caught sight of the Persian.

He stood in the doorway of a tannery, oblivious to the noxious reek that was billowing from the arched windows piercing the wall above the door. He was of a moderate height, only four feet and odd inches. A beaded round brimless hat clung to his head, and a fine watery green robe, bordered with a dull crimson, was draped around his shoulders. He was speaking to a brown-faced man in a brown leather apron, brown cowhide boots, and a sullen brown disposition. As he spoke, the Persian repeatedly pointed across the street to the closed door of a linen shop. Gold bracelets wrapped the Persian's wrists and held back the cuffs of an immaculate white linen shirt.

One of the Roman girl's eyebrows crept up unconsciously as she took in his supple silk pants. She was surprised that the tanner, obviously of old Roman stock, would even trade words with such an obviously decadent Easterner. She turned and pulled back the hood of her robe. A cascade of deep gold-red curls spilled down her back, only barely constrained by two dingy ties of cotton cloth.

Consciously forcing herself to look to the right as she crossed the street, away from the Persian to her left, she loosened the cheap copper clasp of the robe. The robe fell back from her lightly tanned shoulders, drawing the eyes of the tannery workers in the immediate vicinity. She smiled briefly at the nearest one, but the quirk of her plush red lips did not reach her eyes and the young man averted his gaze.

Unseen beneath the robe, one hand loosened the short stabbing sword in the sheath tied to her right leg. Her left hand rose, bunching the flap of the cloak and drawing it across her front. It slid away from her right thigh, revealing a short cotton kilt, a generous expanse of smooth golden-tan leg, high doeskin boots coming almost to her knee, and the loosed sword, clasped lightly in the thumb and forefinger of her right hand. With unhurried steps, she walked up the narrow brick walkway to the front of the tannery. The Persian, gesticulating with his left hand and raising an exasperated voice to the tanner, was utterly unaware.

Something flickered at the edge of her vision.

Only feet from her victim, Thyatis leapt to the left, crashing sideways into two slaves carrying great bales of raw Egyptian cotton. A javelin shattered against the tannery wall, causing the Persian and the tanner to turn in surprise. Snarling, Thyatis surged to her feet, her cloak falling away behind her, the sword darting out like a steel tongue. The Persian, his eyes wide with astonishment over a small mustache and a neat goatee, screamed loudly and bolted past the tanner into the building.

Without sparing a glance for Nikos or her other backup, Thyatis bounded after him. For a moment she rushed forward blind, but then her eyes adjusted and she caught sight of the Persian's green robe fluttering around a corner on a landing at the end of the narrow work-hall. She took the stairs three at a time, then skidded around a corner into a whitewashed room filled with tables, surprised clerks, and clattering shutters as the Persian exited the other side through the window.

Beyond the window, she found a narrow brick balcony looking out over the sprawling yard of the tannery. The space between the buildings was crammed with vats, trestles, and brawny half-naked men laboring to raise stinking hides on long iron-hooked poles from the great barrels. An acrid stench billowed up from the hundreds of vats. She ran lightly along the balcony, ducking under twisted hemp lines strung across the space to hold laundry and rugs. At the far end of the balcony, the Persian staggered to a stop, looked both directions, and then sprang outward, arms outstretched.

The Roman woman sprinted to the end of the balcony and kicked off, her legs flashing in a brief passage of sunlight that had worked its way down between the haphazard brick tenements. Like the Persian, her reaching hand caught a heavy guy-line that was holding up a decrepit banner between the back of the tannery and the building across the alley. For a moment a sea of marveling faces flashed past below her, then she was through a poorly scraped sheepskin window with a loud ripping sound and crashing through a light framework of slats into the room beyond.

She went down in a welter of rough parchment, filthy sheets, and the crushed remains of a flimsy bed. Thyatis rolled up, slashing with the shortsword, but her blade caught nothing. The enormous ebony man that had sprung up from the bed wailed with fear and scuttled backward, toppling a bedside table and an amphora of water. The hanging that served as a door had been ripped from the rod that held it, and Thyatis rolled up and darted through it without a second thought. The dingy walls and reed-scattered floor receded as the edges of her vision clouded with gray. A fierce grin stretched her face, but she was unaware of her appearance.

A hallway filled with tiny doorways flashed past. At the end, a narrow flight of stairs rose up into smoky gloom. Thyatis bounded up the crumbling steps but found them blocked by old chests and empty grain jars. Cursing, she leapt back down the steps four at a time and ran to the one doorway where the hanging was pushed aside. A room occupied by a puzzled-looking naked legionnaire and an irate *lupa* blurred past before she slid the sword back into its sheath and leapt up to grab the sides of the window casement in her hands. With a heave, she hauled herself up and eeled out through the window.

A sloping tile rooftop met her as she spilled out onto it. She tried to get to her feet, but the tiles cracked with a sound like ice breaking and she slithered down the slope of the roof. Flailing wildly, she managed to grab the cornice before pitching off into the garden below. For a moment she swung by one arm, suspended fifteen feet above a confusion of squatters' tents, then managed to hook her foot on the edge of the roof and dragged herself back onto the tiles. Levering herself up, she glanced about. There was no sign of the Persian. Below her, the old widows and immigrant families living in the courtyard of the building stared up at her in amazement.

"Hecate!" she cursed. Teetering, she stood up on the tiles, her eyes running along the windows, rooftops, and disreputable roofs of the nearest buildings. Nothing. She turned back to the window, finding it occupied by the amused faces of the young soldier and the younger prostitute. She grimaced.

The sound of cracking tiles snapped her head around. At the far end of the tile roof, near the back wall of the garden, the Persian had crawled out of a similar window, now without either his hat or his expensive silk robe. He scuttled down the tiles to land heavily on the edge of the garden wall. Thyatis whistled, a long piercing sound that drew the attention of every face in the garden below.

"A handful of denarii for his head," the Roman shouted as she flexed her knees and jumped down into what little clear space was below her. "He cheated me at dice!"

A shout went up in the garden and there was a sudden flurry of movement as out-of-work animal tamers, lazy day laborers, paid mourners and their layabout husbands began running toward the back wall. Thyatis sprinted at an angle across the garden. The Persian, knowing his own business, had ignored her imprecations and was quickly walking along the top of the crumbling mud-brick wall, his arms outstretched for balance. Thyatis reached the corner of the garden wall only an instant behind the Persian. She scrambled up a squishy pile of offal and broken pots to snatch at his heel.

He skipped aside and swung around the side of the building, his hands catching at a series of knock-off Etruscan bas-reliefs that studded the brickline between the floors. Thyatis hissed in rage at missing him and swung up onto the roughly finished wall-top, cutting a long scratch in her leg. Nimble fingers slid a flat-bladed, hiltless knife from her belt, and for a moment she leaned out over the tiny alleyway between the garden wall and the warehouse beyond, gauging the distance for a throw. A shout from behind her caught her attention and she glanced over her shoulder.

A burly man in a striped black and yellow shirt had clambered up onto the wall behind her, and with a start she realized that he was one of the Persians' confederates. He lunged toward her, his knuckles wrapped in leather bindings. The sun glittered off the hooks set into the leather. She swung away out over the alleyway, her left foot wedged against the corner of the wall, her left hand clinging to the embrasure, as his fist flashed past. Her right foot hit the opposite wall of the alley and she pushed off, levering against her grip on the wall to the left. There was a snapping sound as the bronze-shod tip of her boot flashed into the wrestler's throat. Her leg whipped back into a half flex and then she kicked him again in the stomach. Slowly he crumpled at the waist and then pitched backwards off the wall into the refuse pile.

When Thyatis turned, the Persian had almost reached the far end of the tunnellike space between the buildings. Biting back a stream of lurid curses, she reached out for the next bas-relief, praying that the cheap pressed-concrete statuette would hold her weight.

Two streets over, the stocky bald Illyrian, Nikos, dumped the body of the javelin thrower back behind a great pile of crates and other rubbish. Wiping sweat and blood from his hands on ill-treated leggings, he peered out into the crowded street. He had seen Thyatis vanish into the tannery, though he had been preoccupied with rushing the gladiator who had tried to skewer her from behind. Quietly he joined the flow of traffic on the street.

Within minutes he had jogged into the alleyway behind the tannery, seen no sign of either his team leader or the quarry, and then rejoined the bustle on the street of coppersmiths.

Fugitives run in a straight line, he worried as he pushed his way through the throng. *I hope this one knows what he's supposed to do.*

The street ran into a round plaza where it met with two other roads coming in at odd angles. A great religious procession was clogging the intersection, trying to reach the temple of Helios that stood three and a half blocks up the hill to the left. Nikos hissed in fury; there were hundreds of supplicants, priests, and a whole cavalcade of mules, horses, litters, and no less than three elephants. The din was tremendous, between the braying of the animals, the trumpeting of unhappy elephants, and the clashing of gongs and cymbals in the hands of the priests.

The crowd surged and Nikos found himself ground into the brickwork front of a wineshop by the press of bodies. Gasping for breath in the throng, he grasped an awning pole and swung himself up onto the sheet of taut canvas. Sweat ran off his bald pate, stinging his eyes. Standing the heat in the densely packed city was not his forte.

See the greatest city in the world, they said, have an exciting life, they said.

Shaking his head, he scrambled along the narrow lintel over the awnings. From this new height, he could see that there was a commotion halting the procession.

The Persian's booted foot slammed against the side of Thyatis' head and she slid back a foot or more on the back of the elephant. Her feet dangled over the heads of a crowd of angry, shouting priests. The blur of white sparks that clouded her vision passed and she dug in with her boots to climb back up. The Persian staggered in the howdah as the elephant, distressed by Thyatis climbing up his tail, heaved against the heavy iron manacles that bound its feet. The driver, screaming imprecations, lashed at the Persian with his prod, cutting a long gash in the man's arm. The Easterner hauled himself back into the little platform and snatched at the darting metal hook. Seizing it, he slammed it back into the driver's face. There was the crunch of bone and the driver howled in pain before disappearing off the front of the elephant.

Thyatis swung over the side of the howdah and crashed into the Persian, her leg lashing out to cut his feet out from under him. The elephant, frantic, reared up, and the Persian and the Roman were thrown into a tumble at the back of the fragile wicker box. The slats broke away and both spilled out onto the street. Almost unmarked amid all the commotion was the sound of the iron links on the elephants' manacles snapping.

The Roman girl hit the cobblestones in a half crouch and was only partially stunned by the shock. The Persian was not so lucky, falling heavily on his side with a sickening thud. The Helian priests scrambled back, leaving a widening circle around the two and the elephant. Thyatis struggled shakily to her feet and slipped a long knife out of her girdle. The Persian, cradling a broken and bleeding arm, eased up into a crouch, his face streaming with tears of pain. Thyatis started to circle, crouched, the knife in her right hand.

" 'ware!' " came a shout from above, and the sound of a frenzied elephant bellowing cut through Thyatis's concentration. Alarmed, she sprang to the side as the elephant, now berserk, suddenly stampeded in the street. The driver, thrown from his perch, was crushed under massive feet with a despairing scream. The other elephants, hearing the distress of their fellow, also began rearing and trampling. Thyatis, her eyes wide with fear, was frozen for an instant. Then she saw the Persian crawling away from the street, heading for a *taverna* door.

The rampaging elephant now shed the howdah in a cloud of splinters, wicker, and rope and was dancing in an odd circle. It smashed into the shopfronts and hurled supplicants and priests this way and that. Thyatis dodged across the street to snatch up the Persian from the doorway. Grunting with the strain, she hauled him up over her head and into the waiting arms of Nikos.

A moment later Nikos punched in the window of a second-floor room with the Persian's head and tumbled the fugitive and himself into a storeroom filled with baskets, pots, and old cheese wheels. Thyatis followed only moments later. Outside, the screams of the elephants rose and rose, blotting out the din of the city.

In the darkness, Thyatis dragged the Persian up and slammed his broken arm into the wall, raising a cloud of plaster dust. The Easterner started to scream but was cut off by Nikos' scarred fingers closing off his windpipe like a vise-clamp.

The woman's face leaned close to the Persian's, blood trailing down from the cut on her scalp. She smiled, all white teeth in the dim light of the little room. Her fingers dug into his thick dark hair and pulled his head back.

"No man could capture Vologases the Persian," she whispered, "and none did. But *I* did."

A sense of deep contentment filled Thyatis as she stared down at the Persian agent. Nikos' broad hands were busy, binding the Easterner's wrists behind his back. She smoothed her hair back and smiled again. *Well done*, she thought, *very well done*.

THE SCHOOL OF PTHAMES

Dwyrin squatted in the last row of boys in the dim room, his back against a plastered wall. He smirked to himself, watching Kyllun and Patroclus out of the corner of his eye. They had come in late, heads together, and had not noticed him among the other boys.

"Attend me," came a curt voice, cutting across the murmur of the boys talking among themselves. "Today we will consider the ways of *seeing*."

Dwyrin looked up, his hands palm down on his knees. Master Fenops stood in a clear space before the score of boys. He was their instructor in the matter of simple thaumaturgy. His deep voice was out of proportion to his body, which was thin and shriveled with age. Bushy white eyebrows crawled over deepset eyes. Dwyrin paid him close attention, for this was the one thing that brought him joy in this dusty old place.

"Yesterday I discussed the nature of this base matter that is all around us." The teacher stamped a sandaled foot on the packed-earth floor. "I said that it was impermanent, having only the appearance of solidity. You did not believe me, that I saw in each and every face!"

Fenops smiled, briefly showing broad white teeth in beetle-dark gums. "Today I will provide you with a demonstration of the porosity of matter.

"But first, let us consider the nature of man and the nature of animals. What sets a man apart from an animal?"

Fenops' old eyes swept across the boys, seeing their disinterest, their boredom, their incomprehension. He clicked his teeth together sourly and continued.

"You." His gnarled finger stabbed out at one of the boys in the first row. "What sets you apart from a dog?"

The boy, a lank-haired Syrian, stared around him at his fellows, then answered in a truculent voice: "I walk on two legs! I can speak. I know of the gods."

Fenops nodded.

"An ape can go on two legs," he said. "Cats speak, if you know how to listen. The gods . . . enough said of the gods. This answer is passable, but it is not the true difference between men and animals."

Dwyrin sat up a little straighter, trying to see over the heads of the other students.

"The thing that truly sets you, a man, a human being, apart from the animal is your mind. Not solely that you use a tool, or can spark fire, no—you have a mind that can *see* the world."

Fenops rubbed his forehead and pinched the bridge of his nose. "Understand that the eye, the tongue, the hand are organs of flesh and blood. They are physical! They touch, taste, and see things that are material. The eye, in particular, cannot see all that we can touch, or hear, or taste. These organs"—he spread his flat-fingered hands wide and turned, showing his palms to the class—"are *limited*. They do not relay to the mind all that there is to see, or hear, or taste."

Fenops stopped, his face pensive, and studied the faces of the boys in front of him.

"A barbarian with some small wit about him once said that the world that we human beings see is the reflection of another world, a world of perfect forms. He used an analogy of a cave, where the physicality that we feel or see was created by the shadows, or reflections, of these pure forms. His postulation was incorrect, but it was a fair attempt to describe the true world."

Fenops stopped pacing, standing again in front of the Syrian boy. "Stand, my friend. I will demonstrate porosity and impermanence to you and your classmates."

The Syrian boy stood, towering over the teacher. Fenops smiled up at him, taking the boy's right wrist between his fingers. He raised it up, spreading the fingers apart.

"Here is the hand," said Fenops, his voice filled with curiosity. "Through it we feel the solidity of the world. See, it is self-evident that the world around us is solid." He poked his finger into the palm of the boy's hand, pressing hard.

"His hand is solid, my hand is solid. They are material, they have shape, size, weight, dimension. All this could not be clearer!"

Fenops turned to the boys and spread his own hand, fingers wide apart. "But, I tell you, and I will show you, that this is not the truth of the matter. In truth, there is no solidity around you. The world and everything in it is composed of *patterns*, of *shapes*, of *forms*. And these patterns are insubstantial. We exist among great emptiness. When you can truly see, you will see an abyss of light filled with nothing. Even the patterns and forms are insubstantial. See?"

The wizened little man turned and placed his hand on the Syrian's back. For a moment he bowed his head and the air in the room seemed to change, becoming colder. Then Fenops smiled, his eyes distant, and pushed his hand forward, out of the boy's chest.

Dwyrin stopped breathing, seeing the old man's fingers sliding out of the thin cotton shirt that covered the Syrian's chest. The palm followed, then his forearm. Fenops peered over the boy's shoulder, his eyes bright as a raven's, and then the old master stepped through the boy.

In the front row, one of the Roman boys fainted dead away. The Syrian boy stood stock still as the instructor passed through him and then stood, whole and hale, before the assembled boys.

"The spaces between the patterns that make up this boy are so vast that if my own are properly aligned, I can pass through him. He is emptiness, as are we all. A fragile vessel filled only with the will."

Fenops shook out his hands and arms, kinking his shoulders up and then down again. The Syrian boy, trembling, scuttled back to his place in the front row. The old man rubbed his hands together briskly. A tremendous smile flickered on his face. "So! How does one actually see the world as it truly is? Among our order, we use a technique of the mind called the First Opening of Hermes . . ."

A week after the incident of the oranges, Master Ahmet was summoned into the scriptorium by a great outburst of shouting. Pushing though the cluster of boys at the door to that ancient and musty room, he found the junior boys' class in a welter of confusion. Large bees, quite angry ones, were buzzing about the room. The Cilician boy, Kyllun, was receiving the worst of their attentions as he rolled about screaming under a table. Ahmet scowled, and his thin face, normally a dusky olive, turned a remarkable dark red. The boys near him, by the door, caught a glimpse of this and fled with unseemly haste, drawing startled shouts from two monks in the corridor.

Ahmet made two sharp passes in the air with his hand, and the bees quieted, turning in their angry hunt, to swarm and then pass with an audible buzz out the door and into the open air of the great court. Ahmet watched them from the doorway as they spiraled up into the clear blue sky and then turned south before flying over the red tile roof of the main building. The two monks paused in their decade-old argument over the physicality of the gods and looked in astonishment upon Ahmet. The master smiled tightly and bowed to them before closing the heavy cedar doors of the scriptorium.

The boys stood in a short, irregular row between two of the great heavy tables, sweating despite the cool air in the thick-walled room. He turned to the lesser of the two tables. It was strewn with ink pots, quills, decorative paints, sheets of papyrus, and parchment. Under it, lodged against one of the heavy carved feet, was a dented bronze scroll tube. Ahmet picked it up. He shook it slightly, and a narrow chunk of honeycomb fell out onto the tabletop. He ran his finger around the inside of the tube and tasted it.

Then, stilling a smile that had briefly formed, he turned to the five boys who stood before him. All, he noted, were now anointed with red sting marks, the Cilician, Kyllun, worst, but the flame-haired Hibernian, Dwyrin, and the Sicilian, Patroclus, had not escaped without incident. The other two, both Greeks, were sporting only two stings apiece. Ahmet gave all five his best scowling glare and all five paled.

"Sophos, Andrades; go and fetch the physician."

The Greek boys slipped away like shadows. Ahmet studied the remaining three closely. Kyllun looked positively ill, Patroclus and Dwyrin were eyeing each other warily out of the corners of their eyes. Ahmet sighed. It was like this every year.

"The punishment," he said slowly, gaining their complete attention, "for disturbing the studies of your fellow students and for destroying the property of the school"—he tapped the dented scroll case against the edge of the table—"is rather severe." He smiled. "All three of you will suffer it to the fullest extent." He smiled again. All three boys began to look a little faint.

"Ah," Ahmet said, looking to the door, "the physician." He waited with fine patience until the various bites and stings had been salved and anointed, then he took the three boys out of the scriptorium and down the hall.

It was four days before Dwyrin could sit down without wincing, and the laughter and snide remarks of the other boys was worse. Ahmet had taken them into the main dining hall during the evening meal and had them stripped, then he had given each of them a fierce switching until they were bawling like babies. This before the monks, their teachers, and the junior and senior boys. Patroclus, in particular, had taken it badly, Dwyrin thought, and now refused to so much as look at Dwyrin. Kyllun was more subdued, but his desire to beat Dwyrin into a bloody pulp was evident.

The three were denied evening free time, and Dwyrin continued to labor in the kitchens washing the dishes. Days dragged slowly along, and Patroclus and Kyllun began to spend their time together at meals and during studies. Dwyrin paid them no mind, for Master Ahmet was watching him like a hawk, and he felt himself repaid in full by the sight on Kyllun's face when the black bees had boiled out of the scroll tube in a dark angry cloud. Dwyrin studied and even improved at his lessons and pleased his teachers. Dwyrin noted that Kyllun, despite hours hunched over the moldy scrolls and ancient tomes that were the focus of their studies, did perhaps worse than before. Patroclus improved, bending his efforts to besting Dwyrin. Master Ahmet remained watchful, giving none of them time to explore further mischief.

THE PORT OF OSTIA MAXIMA, ITALIA

The heavy oak door of the brick building thudded solidly under the young man's fist. Around him, twilight settled upon the town, the sun sliding into the western sea through a haze of cookfire smoke and the rigging of a thousand ships. From over the high wall of the shipwright's compound, he could hear the waves of the harbor slapping on the stone border of the long slip. Beyond that there was a murmur of thousands of dockworkers, mules, and wagons busy loading and unloading the ships that carried the lifeblood of the Empire.

"Ho!" shouted the young man, his embroidered woolen cloak falling back, a dark green against his broad sun-bronzed shoulders. He had a patrician face, strong nose, and short-cropped black hair in the latest Imperial style. Gloom filled the street around him as the sun drifted down into Poseidon's deeps. There was still no answer.

Puzzled, the noble youth tried the door latch, but it was firmly barred on the far side. He rubbed his clean-shaven face for a moment, then shrugged. He knocked once more, more forcefully, but still there was no footfall within or inquisitive shout over the wall. Idly he glanced in each direction and saw that the street was empty of curious onlookers. He dug in the heavy leather satchel that hung to his waist from a shoulder strap, his quick lean fingers at last finding a small dented copper bell. Blowing lint from the surface of the token, he squinted slightly and shook the bell at chest height by the door.

Within, there was a scraping sound and then the door swung inward. Smiling a little, the young man stepped inside, his calfskin boots making little sound on the tiled floor.

"Dromio? It's Maxian. Hello? Is anyone home?" he whispered into the darkness. There was still no answer.

Now greatly concerned, Maxian fumbled inside the door for a lantern. His fingers found one suspended from an iron hook, and he unhooded it in the dim light of the doorway. Fingertips pinched the tip of the oil wick and it sputtered alight, burning his forefinger. The young man cursed under his breath and raised the lantern high. Its dim yellow light spilled over the tables in the long workshop.

Tools, parchments, rulers, adzes lay in their normal confusion. At the far end of the hall, it widened out into the nave of the boat shed, and a sleek hull stood there, raised up on a great cedarwood frame.

Maxian padded the length of the workshop, his eyes drawn to the smooth sweep of the ship, its high back, the odd tiller that seemingly grew from the rear hull brace like a fin. Standing below it, he wondered at its steering—there were no pilot oars hung from the sides of the ship, nor any sign that they were intended.

"Such a steed as Odysseus could have ridden from the ruin of Troy,"—he sighed to himself—"cleaving a wine-dark sea before its prow."

A door opened behind him, ruddy red light spilling out. Maxian turned, his face lit with delight. A stocky figure stood in the doorway, leaning heavily on the frame.

"My lord Prince?" came a harsh whisper.

Maxian strode forward, switching the lantern to his right hand as his left caught the slumping figure of the shipwright.

"Dromio?" Maxian was horrified to see in the firelight that his friend was wasted and shrunken, his wrinkled skin pulled tight against the bones, his eyes milky white. The shipwright clutched at him, his huge scarred hands weak. The prince gently lowered him to the tiles of the doorway.

"Dromio, what has happened to you? Are you ill, do you have the cough?"

The ancient-seeming man wearily shook his head, his breath coming in short sharp gasps.

"My blood is corrupt," he whispered. "I am cursed. All of my workers are sick as well, even my children." Dromio gestured weakly behind him, into the living quarters at the back of the dry dock. "You will see . . ."

Maxian, his heart filled with unexpected dread, took a few quick steps to the far end of the room, where small doors led into the quarters of the shipwright and his family. In the dim light of the lamp, he saw only a tangle of bare white feet protruding from the darkness like loaves of bread, but his nose—well accustomed to the stench of the Imperial field hospitals and the Subura clinics—told him the rest. The left side of his face twitched as he suppressed his emotions. Quietly he closed the door to the unexpected mortuary. The sight of the dead filled him with revulsion and a sick greasy feeling. Though he had followed the teachings of Asclepius for nine years, he still could not stand the sight and smell of death. It was worse that the victims were a family that he had known for years.

Long ago, when he had been only a child, he had ridden with his father, then the governor of the province of Narbonensis, to see the great undertaking of the Emperor Jaenius Aquila. They had ridden up from the city of Tolosa, where they had lived for three years, through the pine woods and open meadows of the hills above the flowering river valley. Under the green shelter of the pines, they had sat and eaten lunch on a broad granite boulder, their feet in the sun, their heads in the dim greenness. Servants had ridden with them and brought them watered wine, figs, and cooked pies made of lamb, peas and yam. The governor, in his accustomed raiment of rough wool shirt, cotton trousers, and a heavy leather belt, had sat next to his son in companionable quiet. After eating, they sat for a bit, the elder Maxian whittling at a small figurine of Bast with a curved eastern blade.

Behind them, their Gothic bodyguards sat silently in the shadow of the trees, their fair hair bound in mountain flowers that they had gathered from the margin of the road. The long buttery-yellow slats of sunlight cutting through the trees gleamed from their fish-scale armor. The servants retired to the pack mules and lay down in the sun, broad straw hats shading their faces as they took a quick nap. The young Maxian felt safe and at peace. It was not often that his father took him out of the city or even paid attention to him. This was an unexpected treat.

After almost an hour, the governor roused himself from his introspection and turned to his son. His bushy white eyebrows bunched together and he rubbed his nose with a broad hand. For a long time he looked at his youngest son, and then, with a masklike expression, gestured for the boy to get up and follow him. They walked to the horses, now held ready by the servants. The Goths filtered out of the trees after them, weapons now loosened in scabbard, quiver, and belt. Together, the small party rode up the road and down into the narrow valley on the other side.

Maxian shook his head, clearing the memory away. Cautiously he set the lantern on the mantel of the brick fireplace. With quick hands he lit a small fire in the grate and found another lantern to join the first. Dromio remained on the floor, his breath coming in quick, harsh gasps. With the room lit, Maxian sorted through the plates, cups, and bowls on the table. He examined them all, quickly but thoroughly. His eye found no sheen of metallic poisons, his nose no odd, acrid stench. He separated those items containing liquids from those containing solids and made a neat pile of each on the broad sideboard. These things done, he knelt by the side of his friend. Dromio's hand weakly rose up and Maxian took it in both of his.

"Fear not, my friend, I will drive this sickness from you," the Prince whispered.

Dawn came creeping over the tile roofs, pale squares of light trickling in through the deep casement windows set high in the wall above the kitchen table. In time the warm light puddled on the ashen face of the young man who lay slumped over the thick-planked table. Flies woke and slowly droned around the room, lighting at the borders of pools of blood. Drinking deeply, they struggled to resume flight, clumsily flitting toward the meat rotting on the sideboards.

In midflight one large blue-green bottlefly stuttered in the air and then fell with a solid thump to the tabletop. Then another fell. Maxian twitched awake, one hand brushing unconsciously the litter of dead flies from his face. Shaking his head, he half rose from the table. One hand brushed against a pewter goblet, half-melted as from some incredible heat. The goblet struck the floor and collapsed in a spray of sand.

The healer turned around, trying to puzzle out where he might be. His head throbbed with an unceasing din, a great sea of sound like the Circus in full throat. Again he brushed his long hair, now unbound, back from his temples. He started with surprise, then ran a hand through long dark hair that fell over his shoulders in an unkempt sprawl. He came fully awake and looked quickly around him.

A grim scene came hazily into view.

Gods, what I must have drunk last night! What happened to my hair?

The kitchen was a ruin of smashed crockery, crumpled bronze cookpans, cracked floor tiles, and drifts of odd white dust. Dark-red pools, almost black in the early-morning light, covered most of the floor. The walls, once a light-yellow whitewash, were speckled with thousands of tiny red spots. Maxian flinched at the sight, then gagged as he realized that the tabletop behind him was littered with hundreds of bones, some large, most a forest of small finger bones, ribs, and scapulae. Without thinking, he summarized the debris—*three adults, one larger than normal, four children . . .*

The Prince froze, for now the reality of the place forced itself to his conscious mind. The shipyard. The house of Dromio, his wife, brother, and children. The rest of the long and harrowing night came sliding back up out of depths of memory and Maxian doubled over in horror, his hands clawing at the tabletop to hold himself up. The bones rattled and slid as the table tipped over, sighing to dust as they clattered against one another.

THE SCHOOL OF PTHAMES

Near the flood time, when storms came racing out of the desert in fierce squalls and the wind carried the sweet scent of fresh rain striking the dust, Dwyrin was at last released from his dinner chores. He and some of the other boys, Kyllun among them, wheedled the gatekeeper into letting them go out to swim in the river. Ahmet they roused from his afternoon nap to watch over them. The master acceded to their bright eager faces and came, bringing a parasol and some scrolls he had been meaning to read again. The sun was bright, filling the sky, there was a little breeze, and even Ahmet was pleased at the thought of an excursion.

Downhill from the school, a path ran through the palms and thick reeds to the edge of the river. The boys ran in the sun, whooping and yelling, to the bank. A shelf of sand rose up there and ran against the shore, making a shallow, sheltered bay. Ahmet fanned himself as he settled under a palm. The boys were waiting eagerly by the shore. Ahmet looked up and down the river for suspicious logs, particularly those with eyes. He closed his own briefly, then nodded to the boys fidgeting behind him on the trail.

Dwyrin splashed into the water. He had not been swimming like this in a long time, not since his illicit visit to the temple of the Hawk lord. The river was forbidden to the boys, for other than the currents and deep holes, the sacred crocodiles lurked in its depths, always ready to take a sacrifice out of season. Sophos splashed water at him; Dwyrin cupped his hands and squirted back. Sophos yelled and leapt at him. Dwyrin danced aside, laughing.

The boat of Ra settled into the west, its flaming wings touching the thin clouds, marking them with streamers of deep rose and violet. Ahmet looked up from the *Libre Evion* to see Dwyrin hurling through the air at the end of a long rope. At the top of his arc the boy let go and, with a wild whoop, plummeted into the river with a mighty splash. The other boys crowded around at the base of the overreaching palm that held the rope in its crown. Sophos caught the rope as it swung back and ran back up the bank. Ahmet smiled and turned back to the obscure passage he had been considering.

Dwyrin plunged deep into the murky brown water. His feet struck mud at the bottom and slid to a gelatinous stop. Surging upward, he kicked against the clinging mud. His arms thrust back, pushing him up. The mud failed to release him. Dwyrin surged again and felt the thick coils of mud claw up at his legs. He settled deeper. Far above he could see the boat of Ra shimmering through the water. He struggled. The water was cold around him. His arms worked frantically. His throat choked and he struggled to keep from breathing. His limbs were leaden. Water tickled at his nose.

On the bank, Ahmet looked up. There had been a momentary twinge at the edge of the ward that kept the crocodiles at bay. He put the scrolls aside and stood up. Sophos swung past in the air, yelling, and splashed into the water. The other boys jostled each other to catch the rope. Ahmet scanned the waters. Sophos burst up and swam strongly back to shore. The twinge came again. Ahmet reached out with the Eye to encompass the area.

Dwyrin gathered himself again, lungs straining, heart pounding like his father's forge hammer, and thrust down with his arms, his legs hanging limp, trapped in deep mud. Again he strove and sank only deeper. *Gods,* he wailed in his mind, *free me!* A dark haze clouded his mind. His ears were filled with pain and he desperately wanted to breathe in. Fear washed up in him, eroding his concentration. He began reciting the settling meditation. If he would go, he would go at peace.

A dark shape arrowed through the water toward him. Dwyrin swung to face it as it came surging through the thick silt. Ahmet's face appeared out of the dimness and his strong brown arms swept the boy up. Ahmet kicked his legs and the boy came loose, sucking out of the muck like a reed shoot. Together they shot toward the surface.

The office of the master of the school was dark and close, its walls hung with long papyrus scrolls, each unrolled from ceiling to floor. On them gods and goddesses, demons and kings, priests and devils looked down with wide staring eyes. Ahmet knelt on the clean-swept stones, his sandals behind him at the edge of the door. His long dark hair, tied back now in a brass clasp, hung damply over his shoulder. His eyes were fixed on the narrow cracks between the paving stones. His hands rested on his knees.

The headmaster tapped a message scroll bound in twine interwoven with purple string against the edge of the low desk. He was slight, with smoothly carved features. His eyes, tucked back under yellow-white brows, were sharp and bright. His long nose betrayed his Nabatean parentage. His thin hands, veined and spidery, picked idly at the edge of the heavy embossed wax seal on the message tube.

"You felt, then, something brush against the ward. Could this have been someone working against the boy? A rival of his clan? A personal enemy?"

Ahmet looked up, his clear brown eyes calm. "No, master, the boy is of no family of import. Neither ransom nor advantage could be gained from his death or suffering. His father is a blacksmith in distant Hibernia. His family is poor. They would have no enemies here."

The headmaster raised an eyebrow at this. "Poor and a barbarian? How did he come to the school, then?"

Ahmet shrugged, spreading his thin-fingered hands. "Imperial witch-hunters found him. They paid the bounty to his family and sent him here. The Office of Thaumaturgy out of Alexandria pays for his tuition. We have five or six such boys among the younger students."

The master pursed his thin lips and tapped the scroll tube against his chin. His eyes narrowed as he eyed the wall carvings and paintings. He turned back to the dormitory master who knelt before him. A smile briefly creased the deep lines around his eyes. "Someone then, within the school. A jealous student? A local, angered by some slight?" The master pushed the tube into the woven basket at the end of the desk. It would wait.

Ahmet was silent, considering. "The boy, Dwyrin, is not unpopular among his fellows. There is one who might hold a personal grudge, but he is a second-year student as well, with no power to speak of."

The headmaster's eyes narrowed and he leaned forward over the desk, resting his thin arms on the dark fine-grained paneling. "Who holds this 'grudge'? Why have you not informed me of this before?"

"The matter is truly of little import, master. The Hibernian boy slipped out after curfew a few months ago and stole some oranges from the orchards by the river. When he returned he tried to make it seem that one of the other boys was the culprit instead. I caught the Hibernian, of course, but not before I had switched the other boy."

"For this . . . switching . . . the other boy holds a grudge? Who is this other boy?" The headmaster's eyes narrowed. Ahmet looked away, finding the shadowed corners of the room very interesting.

"Speak, Ahmet."

"Kyllun of Cilicia, master."

There was a hiss of breath, almost unheard. Ahmet flinched inwardly.

"The Macedonian praetor's son? By Horus, Ahmet, you were given strict instructions to treat that one with gloves of silk! His father is notorious for his temper. Sending his son here, to our little school, is a mark of favor that we cannot refuse."

The headmaster settled back in his chair, sinking into the deep cotton cushions. His eyes flicked back to the message scroll. "Tell me of these two boys, everything, how are their grades, who is better in the classroom, who is the quickest, everything, Ahmet, everything."

"Well," Ahmet began, "first there are three boys involved, not just two . . ."

Ra had fallen behind the western horizon, carried on his boat of light into the underworld, by the time that Ahmet finished. At last, after a long moment of silence, the headmaster rose from the chair and paced beside the desk, bare feet slapping softly on the dark stones. Ahmet remained kneeling. His hands were damp again. He fought down the urge to wipe them on his kilt.

The headmaster stopped before one of the scrolls showing the tributes given Pharaoh by the princes of Meroe. Gazelles, ibis, hippopotamuses, ibex, and all kinds of creatures paraded across its crinkled surface. He turned to the junior boys' dormitory master, his thin lips pursed. "Tomorrow, Ahmet, you will take the Hibernian boy into the temple, down into the deeps, to the vaults of initiation, and you will elevate him to the second sphere of opening. You will invest him with all the graces and powers that go with such state, you will gift him with the third eye of perception. You will invoke the power that lies sleeping in his heart. You will make him one of us, the illuminated ones."

Ahmet stared, eyes wide with surprise, at the thin figure of the master. The headmaster's voice, thick and heavy, still rippled and throbbed in the air around him.

"Master," he said, almost choking, "the boy is not ready! He is only a second-year student, no better or worse than any of his classmates. He has improved of late, true, but no more than, say, Patroclus of Archimedea. He still has two years to go to be initiated in such a manner!"

"Yes, but you will take him into the deeps of the temple tomorrow and you will make of him a sorcerer of the second order. By my will, I have spoken and you will obey."

Ahmet bowed his head. The master of the school was the master of the school and Ahmet had sworn an oath to obey him. The master gestured for Ahmet to rise and gripped the young man's shoulder with his own gnarled hand.

"If the boy cannot survive the passage to the second sphere his death will be on my head, not yours. I have ordered and you have obeyed. Go with a clear heart, my young friend, and be glad for this youth, who will make such great strides into our world."

The master smiled, eyes crinkling up, lips twitching, but Ahmet did not respond in kind. He bowed and stepped out of the room through the woven reed curtains. His face was still and composed. Outside, Ahmet bowed to the secretary squatting by the doorway, pens and papyrus sheets near to hand.

"Honored Niis, send word to the keepers of the vaults that tomorrow at full sun I will come to them with one who will ascend, Ra and Thoth willing."

The secretary bowed his shaven head and began writing the messages that would have to be sent.

Dwyrin woke, head grainy with fatigue, limbs leaden. He had not slept well, tossing and turning, unable to find his way into the realm of Morpheus. It was very early, the thin dawn light gray in weak bands between the slats of the window coverings. The muted rumbling of snoring boys surrounded him. He rolled over and started, coming fully awake. At the foot of his bed stood a tall figure in a long checkered cloak of red and black. A sun-disk of bronze gleamed in the pale light on the broad smooth chest. The figure's head was curving and black with a long neck and sharp bill. Deep black eyes, shining like marble in water, glittered under the overreaching hood.

Dwyrin's eyes widened and he scooted back in the bed, his flesh crawling at the sight of one of the temple figures come to life.

"Come," a deep sepulchral voice rumbled. "Osiris summons you to the depths of Tuat." The figure extended a hand, wrapped in dark black and gray cloth, ending in a three-fingered claw. "Come, Dwyrin MacDonald." Dwyrin stared in horror at the apparition. His mind refused to work. The figure gestured, its robes making a soft whispering sound. Two shorter forms emerged from the darkness beyond it: squat manlike things, faceless and dark. Their bodies were ebony and patterned with whorls and lines. They grasped Dwyrin by his arms and lifted him silently from his bed. Dwyrin, frozen with fear, could not cry out as they carried him, led by the tall crane-headed figure, out of the dormitory.

In the early dawn the compound of the school was quiet. No birds sang, no chatter of voices came from the kitchens. All lay clear and still under a pale pink sky. The two faceless men carried Dwyrin past the main building and under an arcade of pillars that separated it from the library. Down a flight of steps into the rear gardens, and down a path of flagstones to the rear gate. There, in deep shadows underneath the thick hibiscus and yellowvine, Dwyrin glimpsed a short figure, standing with a tall staff, wrapped in white and pale blue. But then the figure disappeared from view and the thick gate swung open, outward, and the faceless men carried him on, soundlessly, into the scattered brush and trees.

Beyond the belt of palms and brush behind the school the faceless men put Dwyrin down. The crane-headed figure pointed to a trail that led out of the brushland and up, into the jumbled rocks and spires of the hills that crouched behind the narrow river plain. Dwyrin stared up at the crane in concern.

"Go," the deep voice echoed. "Go to the doorways of the dead. We will follow."

Dwyrin looked around. The tumbled red boulders were at last being picked out in gold and saffron as Ra climbed into the eastern sky. In this clearer light, with a cool wind from the west brushing past, Dwyrin saw that the crane-man was richly attired, with golden bracelets on his arms and garments of thick brocade. On his chest hung a bronze sun disk, now gleaming in the pale sunlight. The crane-head was sleek and black, with red stripes running back from the deep-set, gleaming eyes. His skin was dark-hued and polished like mahogany. The hands of the crane were thick and powerful, each with three fingers. One of those now pointed up the trail into the hills. The faceless men had disappeared.

Dwyrin turned and began walking, his bare feet cold on the stones and pebbles. The trail wound up, through a narrow canyon choked with brush and spiny plants. Their branches cut at Dwyrin's legs and the steepness of the ascent made him short of breath. At the top of the canyon, the trail turned left under a rising cliff and slipped between two great boulders, each streaked with red and white in sloping patterns. Dwyrin stepped under the overhang and into a bowl-shape chamber, open to the sky above. In the sky, as Dwyrin looked up, he saw vultures circling and thin streamers of cloud painted pale pink and cream. The roof of the world was brightening.

Before him, on the other side of the bowl, seven tall doors were hewn from the rock. At the side of each an inset carving depicted a creature from the temple. Seven gates with seven gods of old. Dwyrin felt the crane step close behind him.

"Choose," it whispered. "Choose an entrance to your fate."

Dwyrin stepped forward over the tumbled thin plates of shale that littered the floor of the chamber, to the door guarded by the hawk-headed man. Within the shadowed entrance a door of stone swung open. Warm air blew in his face, carrying the smell of thyme, cinnabar, and cinnamon. Figures waited within, with smiling faces and open arms. Dwyrin felt a push at his back and he was among them, stumbling.

The stone door closed silently behind him. Attendants emerged out of the darkness and Dwyrin, in the flickering torchlight, could see that they were men, but their faces were carved into welcoming smiles and the eyes that stared out from the mask were dead and lifeless. Their hands fluttered about him lightly and drew his sleeping tunic away. He spun about, looking for the crane-man, but it was gone. The attendants circled him and nudged him with light fingers toward a great portal that stood on the far side of the hall. To either side, lining the walls, great seated figures loomed in the darkness, fitfully lit by the torches burning at their feet. The smell of incense was strong in the air.

Distantly there was a low wavering chant and the deep boom of drums. Dwyrin shivered, though the air was warm. The attendants urged him onward, through the great doors that stood at the end of the hall. Beyond them, he found himself in a tile-floored room overlooking, through a broad window, a great city of gold roofs and silver buildings and green trees that spread away as far as the eye could see. Dwyrin stopped, stunned by the sight of glittering blue lakes, green lush fields and a full sun high in the heavens.

"That is not for you yet," the deep voice of the crane said from behind him. "This is your path," it said, turning Dwyrin from the vision of the city of gold to a narrow stairway that led down from the room to the left-hand side.

"Here are your servants," the crane said, "to garb you in the raiment of the initiated. They will anoint you with sacred oils, lave your feet, prepare you to descend into the depths." Dwyrin, looking into the deep eyes of the crane, felt the attendants wrap a kilt around his waist, place a tunic across his shoulders, rub his arms and legs with oils and scented water. Thick smokes drifted up around him and he breathed deeply, his head oddly light. A chant began as the crane stepped back.

"Go you down now, into the realm of darkness."

Dwyrin stepped forward to the head of the stairs. Narrow and steep, they wound down into the heart of the earth. He placed his foot on the first step.

"Go you down now, into the realm of the guardians."

The light of the torches passed away, and he descended by feel. The air throbbed around him with the chanting of the attendants and the strong distant voice of the crane.

"Go you down now, beyond light, beyond sight, beyond hearing."

Fumes and vapors rose up around him. The walls fell away on either side.

"Go you down now, into sightlessness, into blindness, into nothingness."

The stair steps ceased and Dwyrin walked in darkness, across a smooth floor covered with fine grains of sand.

"Go you down now, into the heart of the earth."

Darkness was absolute. Hazy veils of light began to shimmer across his vision, but he held his eyes closed now. Bright pinpoints of blue and gold and emerald drifted before him.

"Go you down now, letting body slide away, leaving only *ka*, only *sekhem*."

The floor slipped away and Dwyrin moved forward in a swirling realm of subtle light and form.

"Go you down now, into eternity, into infinity, into nothingness."

Out of the void and chaos of colors and shifting shapes, a throne of basalt rose, and upon it sat a massive, gargantuan figure of a bearded man clad in the symbols of a king.

"Go you down now, into light, into freedom, into all things."

Dwyrin stood before the ancient king in a swirl of colors and light. The king leaned toward him and spoke, but no sound came from that mouth, only colors and shapes and tones of music. They washed over Dwyrin and he felt something suddenly burst within himself. Fire uncoiled in his stomach and rushed out of him in all directions. Crying out, he fell backward, unable to move. Flames leapt from his fingertips, his eyes, from his mouth. His body burned away, leaving only a clear self behind. The giant king settled back in his throne and raised an ankh-scepter before him. Atop it, a great eye opened and Dwyrin's clear self rushed toward it. In his mind, Dwyrin wailed as his ka began to shred away in that mighty wind.

In the distance, beyond the colors, Dwyrin heard the voice of the crane shouting, but he could not make out what it was saying. His self was slipping away, peeled back layer by layer by the great shining eye. Dwyrin began to feel an overbearing fear. *He would be nothing*, his mind shouted, *nothing*! He would be stripped away and there would be oblivion, no Dwyrin left at all.

I am not ruled by fear, he thought, and began to chant the meditation of centering and mind-clearing that they had learned in the school. As he did, the fires in his hands and feet began to burn again, and he faltered, but picked up again. The voice of Ahmet, as from a far place, echoed in himself. *A mind that is free from fear has all power over all things.* The fires burned hotter and Dwyrin despaired, but now the fires drew the swirling light and color into him. His heart leapt and he passed into the meditation of the First Opening of Hermes, that which allowed the students to perceive the dim outlines of the true world.

His body was formed of flame, bright as a star, and the uncoiling thing within him now swirled up his spine and into his head. There was a tearing sensation and Dwyrin felt his forehead, wrapped in flame and light and color, burst open. A golden radiance filled him and the room of the throne. The giant king lowered the scepter and all dissolved into formless chaos, riven with darkness and nothingness.

Dwyrin felt his knees strike a cold stone floor and his arms, strengthless, tumbled before him. His body was shaking. Two strong arms seized him and bore him up. He was clasped to a warm chest and dark scented hair fell about him. Dwyrin sobbed and buried his head in the shoulder of the man. Tears streamed from his face.

"Hush now, lad, you'll be fine," the crane said with the voice of Ahmet, holding him fiercely close. The crane-man rose from the darkened floor, carrying the boy, and retraced his steps through the winding tunnels and passages of the labyrinth.

Ra was full in the sky when Ahmet returned to the garden gate, nudging it open with his foot. The raiment of the crane guide he had returned to its sandalwood chest in the chambers overlooking the city of gold. Dwyrin slept, exhausted, in his arms. Now the morning silence was broken by the clatter of the cooks, the chanting of the novices and their masters in the temple. Unnoticed, the young master strode up the long steps from the garden and into the shadowed passage that led to the master's quarters. His own small cell was lit with dim cool light as he entered. He laid the Hibernian boy on his narrow cot and spread the thin quilt over him. Dwyrin remained deeply asleep. Ahmet looked down upon him with a sad, drawn expression on his face. Shaking his head to clear dark thoughts, Ahmet closed the door and strode off toward the kitchens. Breakfast would be late.

Ahmet sat alone in the long hall that served as the refectory for the masters. The tables were bare and empty, some still gleaming with water from their cleaning after breakfast. He had convinced the cooks to give him a bowl of porridge with figs. An earthenware mug of water stood at his left hand. He spooned the meal, sweetened with honey, into his mouth.

"The boy lives," came a voice from behind him. Ahmet nodded, continuing to eat. There was a shuffling and the creak of the bench as the headmaster sat down next to him. Ahmet could feel the eyes of the old man upon him. He did not turn, draining the mug of water.

"He will sleep two, maybe three, days. Then he will be hale again." Ahmet turned slightly; the old man was looking up at the mural on the ceiling.

"I will have a place prepared for him in the second circle apprentices' quarters," Ahmet said. The master turned then, his eyes shadowed in the dim hall.

"No, that will not be necessary," he said, his voice thin and quiet.

Ahmet rose up slightly, his eyes narrowed, his lips tight.

"What do you mean?" he whispered.

The headmaster reached into his loose robe with a narrow, gnarled hand and drew out a message tube, pale white and bound with a coiling piece of purple and tan twine. He placed it on the tabletop, halfway between himself and Ahmet.

Ahmet nudged it with his finger. "What is this?"

"A letter of request from the exarch of Alexandria to this school, a request for a second-tier sorcerer to complete the levy upon Egypt to satisfy the demands of the Eastern Emperor."

"What? What demands of the Emperor?" Ahmet was incredulous, his voice rising.

"Quiet, quiet, young master. There is no explanation here, only the request that we supply one second tier sorcerer to meet the levy. I have been unable to learn anything more from my colleagues at the Karnak school, or in Alexandria itself. The tribune has made the same demand, in varying degree, upon all of the schools and temples in the province."

The master placed a hand on Ahmet's shoulder, pushing him gently back down onto the bench. "We are neither over- nor underfavored by this, Ahmet. All of the schools have been levied and all are equally unhappy. Unfortunately, ours is one of the smallest schools, with few masters and a limited number of students. I cannot afford to send a journeyman, or even one of the more advanced apprentices."

Now Ahmet did rise up, pushing back the bench, his face flushing with rage.

"So you send a boy, a youth without even a fringe of beard? He will go to the Legions, you know, he will serve with those who are ten or twenty years his senior. He will vanish, swallowed up, consumed alive by fire or sorcery, disease . . ." The master nodded, his face graven with deep lines. Ahmet slumped into the bench, speechless.

"I grieve for the boy, too. But with the trouble that he has caused, and the ramifications for the school, I think that this is the best way, perhaps even for him." The headmaster gripped Ahmet's broad shoulders with his hands, setting him upright.

"You have taught him well, Ahmet. His spirit is strong, he is not untalented in the arts, his mind is quick. I pray he will flourish there, springing up anew in some foreign soil to blossom and prosper."

"No," Ahmet said, his voice low, "he will die, body and mind consumed by some enemies' enchantment. He has barely the skills necessary to perceive the true world, much less manipulate it. In the Legion, he will be overtaxed and burned out like a reed taper. You are sending him to certain death."

With this Ahmet rose, and walked quickly out of the refectory. Behind him, the headmaster bowed his head for a moment and then, squaring his shoulders, rose to return to his own duties.

>·((

Thyatis rubbed one tan finger idly along the partially healed scab that ran just under her hairline. The uneven jouncing of the litter made it difficult, but no more so than walking on the deck of a galley on the open sea. The thick muslin curtains of the litter rustled in the breeze and she nudged the near side open a crack. Beyond the muslin, a light cotton drape embroidered with fanciful octopi and dolphins provided a secondary screen to deny passersby view into her sanctuary. All around her, faint but unmistakable in the late spring air, were the sounds of the greatest city in the world preparing to take the afternoon off. Thyatis' thin nose twitched a little as the breeze caught the shoulder of the nearest Nubian bearer, bringing a musky odor of sweat and cinnamon to her.

I should be walking, she snarled to herself in her mind. *I am not some delicate Palatine daughter to be carted around like a hod of bricks.*

Despite an irrational urge to throw the curtains aside and leap out into the street, she remained in the litter. She smoothed the fine linen dress down over the sleek muscles of her thighs and concentrated on appearing demure and inoffensive.

The litter paused and the lead slave rapped lightly on the recessed oaken door of the house with the bronze-shod head of his walking stick. Thyatis checked the slim knife that she had strapped to the inside of her right thigh. It was secure and invisible. The litter lurched forward again as the door swung wide. She breathed softly and evenly through her nose. No more time for thinking.

This is my patron, she thought, *not an enemy in the warren of the city or a shark in the green waters of Thira. I am in no danger. No danger.*

The architrave of the entrance hall vaulted high above them as the doormen helped her out of the litter. A little stunned by the size of the hallway, Thyatis did not resist as they led her forward, soundlessly, over a vast expanse of seamless sea-foam pale marble. The panels inset in the ceiling were painted with more dolphins, mermaids, eels, and sharks. Watery streams of light fell through blue and green glass panels high on the dome of the atrium. The air seemed to shimmer in the dim light. Pale cream walls rose up, unadorned, to reach the base of the dome. A light current of air brushed over her, stirring her hair. At the end of the entrance hall, lit by slanting beams of afternoon sunlight, a monumental reclining Poseidon took his ease in lightly painted marble. Sea nymphs and porpoises surrounded and supported him as he rested. At the base, waves of stone crashed upward from the massive plinth that supported the entire statue.

Oh, my dear, Thyatis thought, *this is surely not Pater's farm!*

Her eyes widened as the servants preceded her the length of the hall from the atrium to the seat of the sea king. Though the figure was fully three times life size, the artistry of the painters' work was unparalleled. The black curls of his hair seemed to fall so naturally, the pale pink of his skin throbbed with life. The lips of the sea nymphs blushed a pale rose, like the most delicate flowers.

"Magnificent, isn't he?" came a husky voice, breaking the silence. Thyatis turned slowly, nerves taut, her peripheral vision catching the flutter of the servants as they bowed themselves away from her. To the right of the statue, a set of steps descended in broad arcs to an interior garden. A tall woman stood on the topmost step, her raven-dark hair spilling down her back in a glorious cascade of loose curls. Tiny golden pins glittered like stars against the firmament of her hair. A shimmering deep–blue-black dress of silk clung eagerly to her figure. Thin neck-laces of pearl and raw red gold plunged from her neck to vanish in the soft darkness between her breasts. Thyatis suppressed a momentary urge to gape in awe at the expense of such a garment. The raw silk alone would have done to purchase the prov-ince of Pannonia. The lush red lips quirked in amusement, and Thyatis struggled to keep her composure as she realized that her opinion was all too clear to the pair of deep-violet eyes that surveyed her from beneath eyelids lightly dusted with gold.

"Come, my dear, join me in the garden."

The woman turned, showing an alarming expanse of supple white back in the scoop-backed gown. One long-fingered hand gestured idly to the nearest ser-vant and the man disappeared back down the undersea gloom of the hallway. Thya-tis followed the woman down the steps, marveling at her hostess's movement. She seemed to glide, not walk, and though Thyatis accounted herself sure on her feet, she felt clumsy and hesitant beside the monumental self-assurance of the other woman.

Beyond tall glass-paned doors of bronze and silver a low garden lay, subtly lit in the afternoon sun. Tall rowan trees rose above the tile roofs of the building that surrounded it. An almost invisible canopy of thin filmy fabric covered the open sky, muting the light of the sun. A small brook trickled through an immac-ulately kept lawn, guided between carefully placed stones. A tiled walkway led across the stream and into a bower that covered the northern half of the garden. Thyatis crossed the little wooden bridge and paused momentarily, as she suddenly became aware of the light sound of harp strings and the whisper of a lute. An air of peaceful repose lapped around her, languid and warm.

The dark-haired woman settled on a couch that was placed in the bower and gestured for her guest to sit upon cushions laid at the foot of the divan. Thyatis found herself almost frozen in apprehension by the understated but absolutely unmistakable display of vast wealth that surrounded her.

"Come, come, dear. Krista will bring us something light to eat and you and I will talk."

The languid, almost hoarse voice stirred Thyatis from her panicked stillness. With a fierce effort of will, she forced herself to walk to the cushions and settle there, cross-legged, amid them.

The hostess laughed, a cultivated sound, like summer rain on a tile roof. She leaned back on the divan, resting her round white arm on the cushions. "You are in no danger here, my dear, you are under my protection and in my service. I do not harm my servants, particularly ones who do me such good work." The woman smiled, her perfect cheeks dimpling. Against her will, Thyatis found the charm of the woman eating away at her battle tension.

"Forgive me for prattling, but certain things must be clear between us," continued the mistress of the household. "I am the Duchess Anastasia de'Orelio, a lady of the Roman city of Parma. You are Thyatis Julia of the house of Clodia, a hitherto unremarkable clan of Roman landowners. You have been my ward and employee for five years, though we have never conversed before today. I must apologize for taking so long to see you—you are one of my children, under the letter of the law—but it seemed best."

Thyatis bowed her head to cover a start of surprise. She had not realized that she had been adopted into her patron's household. An odd mixture of relief and sadness washed over her. She had a place in the world after all.

Anastasia laughed again, genuinely. "And you are very polite for a young woman of your background and skills."

The Duchess's eyes sharpened as Thyatis looked up with a calm expression. Silver chains composed of hundreds of tiny perfectly formed links rustled on her wrist as the older woman waved a finger around the courtyard and garden.

"This did not come to a silly or stupid person," she said. "It came to me because I was—I am—quick of thought, light of wit, and have a *very* good memory." Thyatis looked up, her mouth twitching in amusement.

"Ah," said the Duchess, "Krista is here at last."

Thyatis turned and observed a young woman crossing the bridge. She wore a simple white shift, though it was of a good fabric and edged with a pale-orange trim. Like Thyatis she was a deep tan, with her dark red-brown hair done up in coiled braids. At first sight, there was something of the Duchess's look to her dark eyes and lips, but Thyatis saw that they were not blood relations. The girl was a slave, marked by a thin jeweled collar and a barely subservient attitude. In her hands, she bore a broad bronze platter filled with cheese, fruit, and bread. Bowing prettily, she placed the food before the Duchess and knelt on the grass. Unbidden, she opened two small ceramic crocks, one of jam and one of fresh butter. Thyatis realized that she was quite hungry. The summons to meet her unseen and unmentioned employer had come at dawn, and breakfast had been a forgotten detail in a busy morning.

"Now, Krista, look at this young lady and tell me if she can be made more attractive than she is already."

Krista did not speak for a moment, completing the preparation of the bread and butter, which she offered first on a porcelain dish to Anastasia, who gravely accepted a single piece, and then to Thyatis, who restrained herself mightily and took only two. The slave sat back on her haunches and appraised the visitor with sharp brown eyes.

"Well, her breasts are large enough, I suppose," she began.

Thyatis was still smarting at the cool commentary of the slave hours later when she at last emerged from the baths that were sequestered under the villa. While she had waited in increasingly furious silence, the slave had detailed all of her obvious and not-so-obvious failings at the prompting and delight of her mistress. After two hours of discussion during which Thyatis felt ever more like an insensate lump, at last they concluded. Anastasia had bidden Krista take her guest to the baths and then make her presentable for evening company. It had taken every scrap of control not to clip the smug little girl behind the knees once they were out of sight of the garden and then ram her perfect little face into the nearest stucco column repeatedly until Thyatis felt better. But she had not, and had suf-fered the attentions of the bath servants in grim silence.

Indeed, Krista had joined the attendants in preparing her hair and anointing her face, arms, and shoulders with subtle powders and dyes. The skilled fingers of the girl were a wonder, and Thyatis at last, grudgingly, felt the tension that had ridden with her all day seep away into the soapy warm water. *At least I have breasts you can see*, she grumbled to herself as the dressing attendants arrayed her in a simple-looking green gown and understated jewelry. One held up a mirror for her and she was amazed to see what looked back out at her. *Maybe, maybe there is something to all this*, she thought.

For a moment, the servants and slaves left her sitting alone on a bench set into a casement window. Velvet pillows edged with seed pearls surrounded her, but the stones were still cold under her hands. Below her, the steep side of the house looked down on rooftops below and a scattering of firelights in the gathering evening gloom. The sky was still flushed with sunset.

So much like Thira at dusk, she thought, thinking of the school she had labored in for four years. She felt very sad and empty for a moment, missing the clear blue wa-ters of the sea around the island and the simple, almost pure life within its marble walls. Her fingers tested the weave of the gown, feeling the lushness of the fabric. Fingertips brushed against the necklace of gold and the jewels that were buried in it.

This dress is the price of Pater's whole farmstead, she thought, and the bleak memory that rose in her mind's eye brought tears to her eyes. The bracelets and rings would buy and sell her brothers and sisters ten times over. *Why did I escape?* She wailed silently to herself.

The moment was broken by a light touch on her shoulder and she looked up into Krista's brown eyes. "Don't cry, mistress," the girl whispered, concern in her voice, "you'll ruin the makeup." Thyatis nodded and stood up. The slave checked her hairpins, the drape of the gown, and anointed her with one last dust of facial powder. "Please follow me, the Duchess is waiting."

Thyatis eased back fractionally from the low table that still held a variety of dishes. Porcelain Chin plates and bowls gleamed under the shuttered lanterns, blue and gold etched designs crawling out from under the remains of roasted grouse, walnut-stuffed dormice, three kinds of grilled fish, two kinds of salad, and the shattered remains of an army of sliced fruits dusted with honey-sugar. For a moment she closed her eyes and savored the subtle taste of the spices in the cream custard she had just finished.

Across the table, Anastasia delicately peeled a plum and sliced it into thin strips with the edge of a fingernail. The Duchess smiled fondly down at Krista, who knelt at her side. Her languid gaze on Thyatis, she idly fed the slices to the girl one by one. Thyatis shuddered as the violet eyes assessed her. She felt alone and close to some unknown danger. Yawning, she stretched and shifted amid the pillows, her right leg sliding out and flexing. Her right hand dropped down to rest on her thigh, only inches from the knife she had managed to keep with her through three changes of clothing and a bath.

Anastasia finished with the plum and waited a moment while the slave washed and dried her hands with a soft towel. This done, the girl gathered up the plates and removed them in almost complete silence. When the last tinkle and clatter had died away, the Duchess stood up and moved to the low wall that separated the dining platform from the edge of the tower wall. Thyatis took the moment to shift again, bringing her feet under her. For a long time the older woman stood at the railing, staring out over the roofs of her own townhouse, its garden, the stables behind it.

Her house stood on the edge of the Quirinal hill, raised up both by nature and man. Below her the city spread away in darkness toward the Tiber. The blaze of lights of the Forum stood to her left beyond the bulk of the mausoleums and temples. The other hills of the city were a sprinkling of lantern lights, bonfires, and torchlight. At last she drew the drapes, closing in the little dining deck that rode atop the highest building in her town estate—no more than seven paces across, a rich wood-lined summer room with a tiled roof and sconces of black iron to hold the torches and lanterns. Despite the season, a cool breeze ruffled the cotton drapes. Anastasia knelt again at the table and poured new wine from the amphora into her cup, and then Thyatis'.

"The city seems so empty now," she said, her voice even and unconcerned. "The plague took so many." She paused. "Of course, the poor suffered the most, and it was before you came to the city."

The Duchess sipped her wine.

"I was newly married then, to the Duke, and he brought me to the city from his estates in the north. He wanted to see the theater and speak with his friends and patrons at the Offices." She drank again.

"He died, of course, when the coughing sickness came. No, that was later. It must have been the bad one that killed him, the one that made you drink and drink yet hold nothing. Yes, he was the one who died in the night, not the day." Thyatis sat very still, her eyes watching her hostess like a hunting bird. The Duchess was speaking dreamily, almost as if the words were spilling from her lips unbidden.

"No matter, as I said, it was before your time in the city. Come, drink with me."

Thyatis raised the cup to her lips, but only wetted them with the dusky red Falernian.

"I remember the first day that you came to the city," Anastasia said, smiling quietly.

Thyatis struggled to keep surprise from her face. She barely remembered that first day—only a confused memory of blinding sun, the crack of a whip, hoarse shouts, horrible fear, and the taste of blood in her mouth.

"You were in a coffle with twenty or thirty others brought in from the provinces, hands bound behind your back, only a slip of a girl in rags. Just one of dozens of children sold to the market to pay the debts of a poor family. You had pretty hair, though of course it was matted and rough. Your legs were strong and you had not surrendered yourself yet. That struck me the most, I think, that you were so new to the chain that you had neither received a brand nor had the life beaten out of your eyes."

Thyatis blinked, coming back from a distant grim memory. In the moment of inattention, Anastasia had moved around the table and now knelt at her side, long fingers running through the younger woman's hair. Thyatis struggled to keep from flinching away.

"Your hair is much nicer now," she said, brushing it back from Thyatis' high cheekbone and neck. "You are better kept." Anastasia rose and returned to the other side of the table. Now she sat, wide awake, no longer dreaming of ancient days. "There is work for you."

The older woman paused, thinking, then continued: "The state has come to a critical period. The Emperor sits easily upon his throne here in Rome, all of his enemies in the West humbled. The people have recovered some of their spirit that was lost in the plagues and the civil war. The fisc, of a wonder, maintains a surplus of coin, and the provinces are beginning to be profitable once again. Despite the unmitigated disasters of the last three hundred years, the Empire has survived and even, now, prospers. It is a dangerous time for the Senate and people of Rome."

Thyatis raised an eyebrow at this last statement. Anastasia nodded, her lips quirking in a quick smile. "No greater trouble has ever come to Rome than under the reign of an Emperor without pressing concerns. It is in such times, when the future seems unlimited and rosy, that grand plans and visions intrude into the business of maintaining a vast state, stretching thousands of miles from the dark forests of Britain to the sands of Africa. Experience shows, again and again, that the hubris of the Emperor—the quest for some unguessable destiny—is a sure road to disaster. We are now at such a point again as faced the Divine Caesar or the great Emperor Trajan or the first Aurelian. It seems like the tide, repeated over and over again."

Anastasia paused, pulling her hair back and binding it in a loose fillet of dark blue silk. In the dim light of the lanterns, and now the moon peeking through the gauze drapes, she seemed burdened by a great weight. Her hair tied, she lay back among the cushions.

"If this is the will of the gods, there is nothing that a mortal can do. But if this is the doing of men, of their ego, of their vanity, then there is much that a mortal woman can do. There is much that I can do. There are things that you can do." Anastasia's voice was a low burr, echoing from the peaked roof of the little room.

"I serve the Emperor, though I have no office. All those who serve me serve him, and through him the Empire itself. We operate outside of the strictures of the law, as you did so recently in the dyers' district. I have known the Emperor for a long time, and he has my complete loyalty. Yet . . ."

She stopped and sat up. Thyatis put down the cup of wine, meeting her gaze.

"What do you know of the Emperor and his brothers?" Anastasia asked.

Thyatis shrugged. "What anyone knows. Galen is Emperor and God. His younger brothers, Aurelian and Maxian, are his left and right arms, extending his reach to all corners of the Empire. In time, when Galen dies, Aurelian will take his place on the Purple and will become a god himself. One presumes that Maxian will serve him as well."

The older woman sighed, shaking her head. "To be expected, I suppose. Let me tell you of them:

"*Primus*, Martius Galen Atreus is our Emperor and God. He is the Emperor of the West, as decreed by the Divine Diocletian in the separation of the greater Empire into two halves. I do not know if your studies covered history, but this was done to resolve problems of rule that the old Empire experienced due to its sheer size. Galen is the son of a regional governor, Sextus Varius Atreus, who was long the administrator of the region of Gallia Narbonensis in southern Gaul. During the most recent civil war, Galen and his brothers were successful in leading the Spanish and African legions against the other pretenders, Vatrix and Lucius Niger, to capture Rome and drive out the Franks and Goths.

Anastasia paused and sighed.

"Even dreadful events can bear good tidings with them. The plague that took so many Romans slaughtered the Frankish and Gothic tribes. Too, the principalities beyond the Rhine frontier have grown strong enough to halt the advance of the tribes farther east. Galen was very lucky in battle to win the Purple. He is, to my experience, wise and cunning. He seems to understand the mechanisms of rule as well as any Emperor in the last two centuries. That he has two capable siblings who have not, yet, conspired against him, bodes well."

"*Secondus*, the next younger brother, Aurelian Octavian Atreus. A brave fellow, though well nigh heedless in battle—some would say the perfect commander of the equites. Well loved of his elder brother. By all accounts and experience, he is utterly loyal to Galen and to the Empire. It is he who will be our next Emperor, for Galen has yet to have any children. Aurelian, on the other hand, has a thriving brood of yelling brats, all as strong as horses and as much like their father as peas in a pod."

Anastasia paused again, her look grim, and she took a long drink from her own cup. A light breeze came up, parting the curtains, and she rose. Pinning the curtains back, she savored the clean night air. From the distance, the sound of bells and gongs echoed from the nearest temple.

"Look," she said, "the priestesses of Astarte are rising to meet the moon."

Thyatis looked out, kneeling next to her patron on the cushions. Far away and below, in the swale at the northeastern end of the Forum Romanum, the domes of the temple of the goddess of the moon were lit by hundreds of candles. All else in that district was quiet and dark, but now the moon had risen high above the Latin hills and the pinpoints of light rose as well, one by one, into the dark sky.

"Ah," Anastasia said, "as pretty as ever." She laid her hand possessively on Thyatis' shoulder. The younger woman trembled a little under the light pressure. Idly, Anastasia stroked her hair. Thyatis grimly kept from leaping to her feet or lashing out with the edge of her hand.

The matron continued, "Aurelian is all that the popular troubadours would have an Emperor be—brave, handsome, kind to children and women in distress. Possessed of a noble bearing and a clear voice. Sadly, he is not the best Emperor for us, for the State, for the Senate and the People. Do you know why, child?"

Thyatis, mute, shook her head no. Anastasia slid the drape of the younger woman's dress off her shoulder. Her long fingers ran over Thyatis' smooth flesh, raising hundreds of tiny goosebumps. Part of Thyatis' hidden mind began to gibber in fear at the intimacy of the delicate fingers. Still, she remained still, though her left hand slid quietly between her thighs.

"Because he has not the sense of one of his beloved horses." The older woman sighed. "He would doubtless ignore the business of the Offices, or hand those paltry details such as the shipment of grain, or the state of the coinage, off to advisors and seek out adventures, glory in battle. He would be slain on some muddy field by a chance-shot arrow, or thrown by a tiring horse, or vomiting his life away in encampment around some Frankish hill-town. Stand, my dear."

Anastasia rose, Thyatis' hand in hers, so that both stood. Thyatis' robe, un-clipped, fell away in a dark puddle at her feet. Anastasia smiled again, her face mostly in shadow. The breeze had snuffed the candles and lamps, leaving only the moonlight to wash over the younger woman's naked body.

"No," the matron continued, "Aurelian will not do. But, *tertius*, Maxian Julius Atreus, now, he is a young man with potential. The potential to be a very fine Emperor. And he is a young man, with a young man's preferences . . . you will please him greatly, I think."

Thyatis flinched at last, as if struck. The Duchess, seeing her fear, laughed softly.

THE SCHOOL OF PTHAMES

Dwyrin woke to semidarkness again, but now there was no crane-headed man looming at the foot of his bed. Instead there was cool dimness and long slats of light falling across the sheets. As he woke, coils of shimmering red and blue light flared quietly around the door frame, ran along the heavy wooden beams of the ceiling, and slithered down the ridges of the cotton quilt. He blinked and they were gone, the stones and beams of the room solid and distinct, even clear in the subdued light.

Dwyrin rose up, expecting to wince at the movement, but there was no pain. He felt oddly calm, like a deep well had opened in him and its strong waters carried through his limbs to his fingers. The room was small, with a low writing table and two chests of burnished dark wood, bound with bronze. Scrolls of the writings of the teachers hung along the walls, revealing portraits of the stars, of diverse animals, of cabalistic signs.

A master's room, he thought. None of the apprentices or students rated a room to themselves. *What has happened to me?* The stones were cold under his bare feet. He tested his arms, his stomach. He remembered flames, being consumed in fire. There were no marks upon him, nothing to indicate the things he half remembered. His stomach growled suddenly and he realized that he was famished.

His tunic and belt were under the low bed, and thus attired he ventured out into the corridor. *How am I going to get breakfast?* he thought. *By the height of Ra it's too late for the students or masters to be eating. The cooks have their eye on me, and no one will have thought to smuggle me food.*

Dwyrin stood in the shadow of the hall, distressed to realize that there was no friend among his fellows that he could truly call upon at this time. Patroclus had been sort of a friend, but the prank with the bees had ended that. He shook his head, trying to clear away the dark thoughts. *I could just wait,* he mused, *but no, I'm too hungry.*

Padding quietly on the smooth tiles, he reached the end of the hallway and looked down from the second story of the masters' quarters into the garden below. Beyond its red brick walls lay the kitchen building and beyond it the students' dormitories. Dwyrin looked warily about and skipped quickly down the wooden steps into the garden. The garden was quiet, with the subdued buzz of bees and flies muted in the sunny morning. Tiptoeing, he passed through a high hedge to reach the rear wall of the garden. Here the bricks of the wall were sheathed in white stucco and covered with ivy and roses. Dwyrin backed up, eyeing the top of the wall and measuring it for his leap. Taking another step, he collided with a solid figure, whose hand settled easily on his right shoulder. Dwyrin froze and the hand spun him easily around. A thin old man, barely his own height, stood there, clad in a simple white kilt and tunic. His head was bare and a rich bronze color. Thick white eyebrows hooded his eyes. The old man smiled, his entire face crinkling up like parchment.

"Apprentice Dwyrin, I am surely pleased to make your acquaintance at last. I am Nephet. Surely you must be hungry now after your interesting experience. Please, come with me."

The little old man's hand was soft on his shoulder, but Dwyrin found himself firmly guided back across the garden and then into the ground floor of the masters' quarters. As they entered the hallway that bisected the main floor, they just missed Ahmet, who came down the stairs into the garden rather quickly and then stood, looking around in concern.

CUMAE, ON THE BAY OF NEAPOLIS

)·((

Maxian trudged up the long pathway from the narrow beach that lay below his brother's Summer House. Though it had once been a rocky trail, filled with washouts and steep inclines, it was now broad and paved with fired tile. A low edging of worked stones capped the seaward side of the trail, and sconces were cut from the rocks to hold torches and lanterns at night. With each step on the cleverly worked pavement, the young Prince grew more and more despondent. Where once the trip down the hillside to the beach had been an adventure, filled with slippery rocks, startled deer, and nettles, now it was an easy afternoon excursion. All of the mysterious edges of the property were gone, carefully smoothed away by an invisible host of gardeners, laborers, and stoneworkers. Even the beach was calmed, the sands carefully raked into a pattern pleasing to the eye. Even the driftwood had been placed by the gardeners before the sun had risen.

At the top of the last switchback in the trail, the Prince turned and stared down into the little cove. The blue-green waters glittered up at him, merry in the high afternoon sun. From the top of the cliff the wire net that closed the mouth of the cove was all but invisible, only an occasional flash off of the green-glass floats that held it up betraying its presence. Maxian fingered the tattered edge of his tunic, feeling the grit of the city under his roughened fingers. His hair was greasy and laid back flat along his scalp. His chin was unshaven, sporting a lumpy three weeks' growth of beard.

He laughed a little, suddenly realizing why the fishermen who guarded the cove had stared at him so, to see the Emperor's younger brother drag in on a leaking ketch to the all but invisible sea-entrance to the Summer House. Though they had recognized him, they must have thought him at the tail end of a horrendous drinking binge. His thought stilled, realizing that this was the first time he had laughed since he had left the charnel house in Ostia.

"Milord?" inquired a soft, even delicate voice from behind him. Maxian slowly turned around, his hand unconsciously brushing back the soot and grease in his hair. A slight woman with her once-blond hair bound up in a bun stood at his side, one hand outstretched in concern. Dressed in a very plain dress with muted red and green embroidery, her wrinkled face was graven deeper than usual with great concern. "Are you well?"

"*Domina.*" He bowed and she smiled at the gesture. "No, not well. How is the house of my brother?"

"In a great state on your account, young master. Though I hazard from your current appearance that you had not heard, your brothers have been raising a great commotion in search of you. I would wager that every praetor and civil governor between Genova and Syracuse is shaking in his boots at the invective issuing from the offices of the Emperor."

"Oh," he said, puzzled at the bemused look on the housekeeper's face. "Have they been looking for me for very long?"

"Only the past ten days. Messengers come and go at all hours, bearing the dire news that you . . . have not been found."

Maxian scratched his head, digging tiny bits of charcoal out of his scalp. "I suppose that they have not happened to mention why they wanted to talk to me?"

The housekeeper shook her head slowly, her bright-blue eyes sparkling with hidden delight. "Not a word."

Now the Prince scratched his beard, finding it equally greasy and thick with minute flecks of soot. "Well, I guess I had better go relieve their concerns. Where, ah, where would they be this afternoon?"

The *domina* turned, looking back over her shoulder. "Where they always are, when they are here together," she said, walking away into the shaded arbor path that wound along the top of the cliff.

Maxian shrugged. He would have to forgo cleaning up, then. Uneasy, he slouched away across the neat lawns that bordered the sprawling marble and granite house that he had grown up in. It was nearly unrecognizable to him now.

The hallways of the servants' quarters of the Summer House were quiet and empty. As Maxian passed the entrance to the vast kitchen, he caught a glimpse of a dozen brawny men quietly eating a lunch of fresh loaves, olives, and cheese. They did not look up as he passed, his boots in his hands. At the back of the great staircase, he opened the door to the tight little stairway that predated the vast mechanism of Aurelian's "Stairway." The dark space under the staircase, crammed with its gears, wheels, and slave benches, was empty. There were no foreign visitors or dignitaries to impress with its smooth gliding ascent to the second floor of the house. At the top of the stairs, he paused to put his boots back on.

When he had been little, the second floor of the Summer House had been the domain of their mother, and it had been filled with women, children, looms, buckets, and a constant bustle of comings and goings. Though dogs and pets of all kinds had been banned, it was filled with a great energy. Now the old hallways and rooms had been torn out and replaced with a stately set of rooms with vaulting ceilings, dark-colored wooden floors, and wall after wall of cunningly painted scenes. Maxian walked through the rooms, filled with furniture, clothing, desks, beds, and the dead eyes of painted figures, with a mounting sense of unease. In his current state of mind, the whispering of the living seemed to bleed from the walls and floor. A sound came from ahead, like the echo of a barking dog, and he spun around.

There was nothing. He shook his head to clear away the phantoms.

Now at the door to the one section of the old house that remained as it always had been, he stopped and cleared his mind. The Meditations of Asklepios came to him and calmed him. His fingers twisted in the air before him. Softly, with a barely audible whisper, the grime, soot, and dried sweat that had been his companions for these last days lifted away from his garments, from his hair, from his skin. Clenching his right fist, the spinning dust cloud coalesced into a hardened black marble, which he plucked from the air and placed in the leather bag at his waist. Taking a breath, he rapped lightly on the door frame.

"Enter!" came a shout from within, and he pushed the heavy sandalwood door open.

His brothers looked up: Galen thin and wiry, clean-shaven, with his short-cut dark hair thinning at the temples, Aurelian tall and broad, with a full dark-red beard. Galen grimaced at the sight of his missing sibling and shook his head. Aurelian turned, his light-brown eyes sparkling with surprise and delight. Maxian rubbed the stubble on the side of his jaw, stepping down the short flight of steps into the map room. The room, never neat, was a tumult of parchments, ledgers, half-empty amphorae of wine, wax writing tablets, and two new things.

First was a great map table, its leaves unfolded to show the entire Empire on its incised and painted panels. All of the chairs, divans, and benches had been pushed to the walls amid stacks of papyrus scrolls and dirty plates to make room. There, on pale wood, lay the breadth of the known world—from icy Scania in the north, to barren Mauritania in the south, from the Island of Dogs in the west, to the uttermost reaches of silk-rich Serica in the east. Tiny cubes and pyramids of red clay littered its surface, clustered around the great port cities of Ostia, Constantinople, and Alexandria.

The Emperor, dressed in a red linen shirt and gray cotton pantaloons in the style of the Hibernian barbarians, stood at the eastern apex of the table, arms akimbo. Opposite him, behind Hispania and the tiny blue-tinted waves of Oceanus Atlanticus, Aurelian was perched on a high stool, one stout leg tucked under the other. One thick-wristed hand was toying with a long ivory stick with a fork at the end.

"There is some trouble afoot?" ventured Maxian, sliding into a low chair pushed against the corner of Africa. A great weariness settled over him now that he was in the safe confines of their father's study.

"I hear tell that you were looking for me. I cannot say that I remember owing either of you a sufficient sum of money . . ." A wry smile played across his features.

"Money, of a wonder, we have enough!" Galen snapped. "What we have lacked these last days is a wayward younger brother of certain useful skills. One that, by all appearances, has been crawling in the gutter with Bacchus for company." The Emperor stepped quickly around the edges of the table, his movement quick and filled with a nervous energy.

Maxian looked up at his brother in surprise; he had not seen him so agitated in a long time. "Gods, brothers, are we at war?"

Aurelian barked with laughter, throwing his head back, teeth bright in the forest of his beard. "Ah, you give the game away, Imperial brother! Little mouse is too sharp eyed not to see your mental state."

Swinging off the stool, Aurelian weaved his way through the tumbled debris to the cool stone and the wine residing in it. Galen, having pulled up at Maxian's exclamation, nervously scratched his head, turning around again. The Emperor went to the inner wall of the room, where a space had been cleared among the benches and a square pedestal set up to hold the second new thing. On the stone block, a drape lay over a round object. Galen drew back the heavy wool covering, revealing a glossy plate, or dish, inscribed with thousands of tiny markings.

"Do you know what this is?" the Emperor muttered, nervous hands folding the coverlet up into neat squares.

"No, I cannot say that I do," the youngest Prince answered. He sipped from the goblet Aurelian had given him, then choked and spit out the vintage on the floor. "Pah! This is terrible!"

He glared at Aurelian, who was blissfully pulling a long draft from his own glass. "You have the wine-taste of a donkey . . ."

"It is a *telecast*," the Emperor said, ignoring the by-play of his siblings.

"It is very old, older than the Pharoahs, brought to Rome by the Republican general Scipio from Egypt when he was governor of that province. It allows a seer, or one with the power, to gain sight over great distances or even conversation if there is such a device where one looks upon." Now the Emperor was very calm, gesturing to his youngest brother. "I need you to make it work."

Galen stepped aside, clearing off the table nearest to the bronze plate. Maxian stared at him in amazement, giving the wineglass back to Aurelian without thinking. Aurelian hiccuped and poured the remaining wine from his brother's glass into his own.

"Ah, brother," Maxian said, "dear brother. I am not a wizard. I am a healer, and not a very powerful one at that. This, this telecast, is the province of the Imperial Thaumaturges, not I."

The Emperor shook his head, leaning back on the edge of the map table. Now his gaze, normally quick to dart about the room, settled on Maxian, and the young man felt the full power of personality that his brother possessed. Maxian shivered, their father had often had such a look upon his face. Galen gestured to the plate again. His will was not to be denied.

Maxian stood up, rubbing his hands on his tunic. Cautiously he approached the device. From a distance, it seemed a plain metal plate, save for the tiny markings. Up close, however, it was revealed to be a series of interlocking bronze rings on a sturdy stand of greenish metal. As the Prince circled it, the rings separated, brushed by the wind of his passage, and slowly spun apart from one another. Maxian pulled up short, becoming utterly still. Behind him, Galen backed slowly away toward the door.

Involuntarily Maxian centered himself and extended his sight, seeking the source of the unfelt wind that now accelerated the rings of the plate into an irregular sphere. As he did so, a dim blue light began to form at the center of the rings. No zephyr drove the whirring sphere of pale incandescence that now gleamed before him. Unconsciously he raised a hand to shield his eyes from a dull flash that he felt building in the device.

It came, filling the room with a blurring glow, and then faded. The Prince stepped forward to the edge of the stone block. Behind him he heard the shuffle of feet as his brothers raised themselves from behind the bench. A tart smell hung in the air, like a summer storm. The spinning rings were gone; now only a blue-white sphere a foot or more across, mottled with green and brown, hung in the air before them. The orb whispered, filling the room with a barely audible hum.

"What is it?" Aurelian whispered, his eyes wide.

"It is the world," both of his brothers answered, their voices as one.

Galen and Maxian turned, staring first at the map table spread out behind them, then back to the slowly rotating globe that was now suspended above the stone block. Half of it stood in shadow, the other half in light. As they watched, they could see white drifts of cloud slowly boil up as they grew over the Mare Internum.

Maxian leaned very close to the device, seeing the coastline of Italia inch past. He looked up at his brother, the Emperor.

"It's going to rain in Puetoli this afternoon," he said.

Galen blinked slowly, his face hardening as he struggled against the fear the device inspired.

"Clever." He sneered. "Show me the Eastern Capital."

Maxian sighed, all too used to Galen's short temper. He backed up and slowly circled the sphere. Out of the corner of his eye, he saw his brothers begin to edge back to the other side of the room. Now started, it continued to spin at an almost unnoticeable rate. Puzzled, the young healer tilted his head, trying to catch the odd thought that was nibbling at the edge of his thought.

Ah, he realized, *the sphere is tilted a little around its center of spin. Odd—why would that be?*

He put the thought aside. In his expanded sight, there was a faint glimmer of energy around the globe and as he approached it, it brightened. Carefully he leaned close to the sphere and concentrated on picking out the city of Constantinople, now the capital of the Eastern Empire.

The surface of the *telecast* swirled and suddenly there was a great rushing sensation. Maxian leapt back in surprise, crying out and cracking his hand against the edge of the map table. A flashing afterimage of seas and lands and city walls hurtling toward him at an impossible speed faded. Behind him, his brothers had scattered at his sudden movement.

"Damn!" Maxian snarled, shaking the pain out of his hand. "That was unexpected."

"What was?" came a muffled question from behind the couches.

"It shows us the city, brothers, but it is not a pretty sight," he answered.

Galen placed a hand on his younger brother's shoulder as he edged up, peering in the murky scene in the surface of the sphere. His face twisted in amusement.

"Ah, my brother Emperor is having an interesting day," the Western Emperor said.

Constantinople was burning.

CONSTANTINOPLE, CAPITAL OF
THE EASTERN ROMAN EMPIRE

)•((

The blow came with a ringing gong sound and a blur of sparkling white light. Stunned, Heraclius fell heavily on his side, all vision gone in his right eye. Booted feet kicked at him and he struggled to roll upright. Nothing but instinct dragged his shield across his body to cover his face and upper torso. A second blow slammed into the leather-and-brass shield, crushing the breath from the Roman's chest. Nerveless, his right hand scrabbled in the muck of blood and rainwater for his sword. Suddenly his fingers caught on the wirebound hilt.

Another blow smashed into the shield, but the Roman surged off of the ground, thrusting up with the short stabbing sword. The tip slid off metal rings and bit into flesh. A man gasped in pain. Heraclius shook his head to clear the blood from his eyes. When he could see again, the line of battle on the parapet had surged back, away from him. Red cloaks swarmed around him now as the Guard crowded forward against the Slavic swordsmen fighting on the walkway between the two towers. There was a high shrieking as the Guardsmen's axes rose and fell, flashing with blood. A monstrous ringing of steel on iron drowned out all other sounds. Rain fell out of the dead gray sky in billowing sheets. Water ran down the side of Heraclius' neck and in the hot armor, that was a blessed feeling for a moment.

Now the melée had run aground on the clutch of grapnels and ladders that the barbarians had managed to lodge on the outer wall. Towers rose up at either end of the rampart, joining the great exterior wall of the city and the lesser wall that fronted the narrow inlet called the Golden Horn. Seeing that the critical moment had passed, Heraclius strode back to the nearest tower.

Sappers in padded leather armor and open-faced helmets were crowding out of the narrow doorway, each carrying thick green-glass jars in frames of cotton batting. Heraclius stood well aside, his back against the low retaining wall that faced the inner wall of the battlement, as they passed. Behind the sappers came slaves in tunics of dirty cotton carrying long brass tubes, ornamented with curling dragon faces. They also had an odd valve slung over their shoulders and heavy leather gloves that reached up to their elbows. Moisture continued to drizzle out of the sky, making the footing difficult on the walkway.

Heraclius struggled to pull the heavy helmet off of his head, finally succeeding. Gasping, he turned his face to the heavens, feeling the hot sweat sluice away in the rain. With one broad hand, he slicked back his hair, the heavy blond curls catching at his fingers. He tucked the helmet under his left arm.

"Brother!" came a shout from the tower above. Heraclius looked up. On the fighting platform twenty feet over his head, Theodore waved at him, sun-browned face creased with a wide smile. "Come up, the Avars are taking to their boats!"

Heraclius turned and surveyed the situation on the battlement. The Guard was kicking the last of the bodies off the walkway onto a great heap in the narrow street below. None of the raiders seemed to have escaped. The grapnels and ladders that they had raised under the cover of the mists and rain had been thrown down or cut away. The sappers were fitting their hoses and pipes to the glass bottles and bronze tubing. In moments, he knew, the battlement would be hellishly hot and tremendously dangerous, particularly half flooded with rainwater as it was. He shouldered his way past a file of slaves and climbed the wooden stairs to the top of the tower.

The waters of the Golden Horn were only partially visible in the gusts of rain. The vast city that stood at his back was clouded by mists and vapors, only the nearest tenements and buildings partially visible through the murk. It seemed that the tower rode in an endless sea of gray, with only ghosts and apparitions for company. Theodore had joined a troop of archers surveying the narrow strand at the base of the walls. Theodore waved his brother over, his own light-blond beard and blue eyes obscured by his helm.

"Brother, dear, I thought that Martina had finally trained you not to wear the Red Boots out into the field." Theodore's pale face was creased by a particularly sly grin.

Heraclius shook his head, answering "It's the garb of a soldier I wore today."

"Ah, then it must be the foundation of your majesty staining them so."

Heraclius glanced down; his riding boots, a plain brown leather pair, were caked with blood from the fight on the walkway, a dark red now fading to black. He cuffed his younger brother on the side of the helmet. "Fool."

"I am no fool!" Theodore said, in feigned outrage. "I am a philosopher, pointing out obvious truths to those too dense to find them for themselves."

Heraclius ignored him with the ease of long practice and stared over the edge of the tower. Fifty feet below him, the narrow beach was swarming with barbarians and hundreds of boats. The Varangians on the lower parapet were shouting insults down and following them with the heads of those of the attackers who had managed to reach the wall.

A piercing whistle cut through the din as the master sapper stood back, waving a green flag. The Guardsmen, hearing the whistle, hurried to the shelter of the far tower. The other soldiers also drew back from the crew of engineers. The leather-clad men hoisted the long bronze tubes over the edge of the wall. Behind them, the slaves hung onto the ends of long poles attached to pump bladders. A second whistle rang out and the slaves dragged down on their handles. Even from the height of the tower, Heraclius shivered in his hot armor at the faint gurgling sound that came as the hand-pumps sucked the black fluid out of the green-glass bottles. The engineers holding the brass tubes leaned out into the embrasures, a slow-match extended on an iron holder. Pitch daubed around the mouthpieces of the tubes flickered into a pale flame. The engineers handed the matchsticks back to a second set of slaves who immediately doused them in buckets of sand held close for such a purpose. The pump slaves dragged down again, and now the canvas tubes flexed as the black liquid pulsed through them.

Heraclius forced himself to look down through the falling rain and mist to the tiny shore. While the barbarians were still swarming about below, many were clambering back onto their makeshift boats. There were thousands of Avars and their Slavic allies on the beach or in the water. Their faces were pale, distant ovals—the Avars marked by a sallow cast and the Slavs by a wealth of red hair. The Emperor felt a hand on his shoulder, and he turned to see the pale face of Theodore.

"You do not have to watch, brother," the Prince whispered. "They chose to come against the great city in arms . . ."

Heraclius gently brushed Theodore's gauntlet aside, saying "I am Emperor, I should look fully upon the works that I set in motion." He turned back.

The first jet of yellow-green flame arced out into the air. For a moment it hung, suspended, almost motionless, above the upturned faces of the barbarians packed into the narrow space between the sea and the foot of the wall. Then another dragon-tongue licked out. Then another, and another. In the misty air, the jets of *phlogiston* began to diffuse as they fell, becoming a blazing cloud of superheated air and incandescent fire. The first cloud drifted onto a great clump of Slavs, struggling to climb onto one of the larger barges. Like a delicate veil, the burning air settled around the men on the boat and in the water. Then it seemed to go out, though men began to scream, and smoke leapt from their hair.

In only a grain, the entire beach burst into raging green-white flame and the tumult of hysterical screaming shot up from below like a signal rocket. Heraclius flinched as the sound of unendurable agony tore at his eardrums. Below him, men writhed in flames that burrowed and tore at their flesh. Hundreds tried to dive into the water to douse the crawling green-gold flames, but the *phlogiston* stuck and hissed and continued to burn, even in the waters. The whole mob surged back and forth in the narrow space, unable to flee, trampling one another, bones cracking under the weight of the frenzied crowd. Air burned away, strangling men the fire had not yet consumed. Flesh bubbled and popped as the fire clawed through holes in armor and eyepieces in helmets. The boats, overloaded, suddenly tipped over, sending hundreds more to a watery embrace in death.

The narrow sea filled with burning boats and the men who had drowned flickered under the water, dying stars that faded, still aflame, into the depths. Shoals of charred limbs clogged the beach.

On the fighting platform, Theodore and Heraclius staggered back as a sudden updraft of air rushed past, bearing the stink of burning flesh and the peculiarly sweet odor of ignited *phlogiston*. The archers who had shared the platform with them scrambled away from the edge, wrapping their dark-blue cloaks around their faces. A vast roar, like a titan enraged, echoed around the tower and through the mists that hung over the city. Green flames lit the low-lying clouds and echoed off the wavetops of the Golden Horn.

Heraclius stood up shakily and made his uneasy way down the stairs into the tower. The attack was over and there was much to do. A soft gagging sound followed him down into the darkness of the tower chamber. Theodore was retching off the back of the platform.

THE SUMMER HOUSE, CUMAE

"Ah," Galen breathed, "well done." He stepped back from the grim scene that still played out in the vision of the *telecast*. "Clever fellows, these Greeks." He turned to his brother, whose brow was marked by extreme concentration. Puzzled, the Emperor of the West stared at Maxian for a long moment, then waved a thin brown hand in front of the healer's face. There was no response.

"Aurelian?" The Emperor turned, an expression of concern on his face. His other brother shrugged in puzzlement as well. Galen turned back, seeing that Maxian's face was becoming more and more drawn. Taking a guess, he gently shook his younger brother's shoulder.

"Maxian? Maxian!"

With a start, the young man suddenly looked around, seemingly bewildered at being in the cluttered room. Galen reached out a hand to accept Aurelian's proffered goblet. Maxian had sat down, rather suddenly, and Galen steadied his shoulder, tipping the wineglass to the pale lips of the young man. Maxian sipped at the wine, then took the goblet in both hands and drained it, throwing his head back. A thin trickle of wine spilled from the edge of his mouth, staining an already matted tunic.

"Ah . . . Thank you, brothers." Maxian held out the goblet to be refilled by the wineskin that Aurelian held at the ready. This too he drained. Now some color was beginning to creep back into his face and hands.

Galen scowled, seeing the toll that the experience had taken upon his sibling.

"It tired you, then?" he asked. "How do you feel? Could you essay the sphere again?"

Aurelian grimaced at his brother. "I think that the lad needs a rest and a bath, brother mine, he is plainly worn out."

Galen's face clouded with anger for a moment, then cleared.

"You are right," he allowed. "See that the slaves take him to the bathhouse and give him a good scrub. We'll talk over dinner." The Emperor turned back to the sphere, but it had collapsed back into the plate of bronze rings. His mood darkened, and he paid no attention to the exit of his brothers, Aurelian holding Maxian up with a broad arm.

Galen brushed his fingertips across the bronze, but nothing happened. He shook his head in disgust, then turned back to the great map. In his mind, he dismissed the *telecast* from his plans and stratagems. The toy had too high a price for him to countenance its regular use. There would be time for it later.

Maxian looked up, smiling, as the slave bent over the back of his couch, pouring rich purple-red wine into his goblet. Shyly the slave smiled back, her long dark hair falling around the delicate oval of her face. Maxian drank, his eyes following her as she passed to Aurelian and refilled his cup as well. Across the low table, Galen smiled a little. He waved the wine slave off when she moved to refill his own glass. The Emperor picked at the scallops in garlic and basil butter that still littered the plate before him.

"Brother," he said, drawing the attention of both Aurelian and Maxian. "Did the fatigue come upon you immediately upon using the *telecast*, or as time passed?"

Maxian frowned, remembering. "At first, it was effortless in response to my command. Then, as we watched the Eastern Emperor fighting on the wall, it became harder and harder to focus. I began to have to strain to keep its vision upon the scene."

Aurelian scratched at his beard. "Perhaps it can only see for so long?"

"Or the focusing upon a scene is more difficult," Galen responded. "Max, did it want to see another scene or just to cease viewing at all?"

Maxian nodded. "That's it! It felt pulled away from what we saw, as if there were some other scene it desired to show." He paused, thinking again, reliving the experience in his mind. He looked up. "Is there another *telecast*?"

Galen smiled. "Yes, the Eastern Emperor has the other of the pair. By the account of the letters that I have received, it stands in his study, as mine does here. The thaumaturges of the East, however, have *not* been able to make it work." The Emperor smoothed back his thinning hair, looking quite pleased. "If, with your help, we can make them work, each in concert with one another, then that will be a vast boon indeed."

Maxian rubbed his chin, his mind turning the ramifications of this development over and examining all sides. At last he said, "A powerful weapon. Better than ten legions. With such a device, or more, if they could be built, each division of the State could act in concert with the other."

Galen rose from his couch, a quiet smile on his face. A slave stepped up and draped a light cape over his shoulders. The Emperor drew it close and the Nubian pinned it closed with a clasp of amethyst and gold. The night breeze off the bay cut through the high windows to the dining court. The tapers and lanterns flickered. Aurelian yawned and stood up as well. Maxian drained the last dregs of wine from his cup and handed it to the nearest slave, which by chance happened to be the dark-haired girl. She smiled and bowed low to receive it, her tunic slipping a little.

"Come," the Emperor said. "Let us view the moon in the bay."

Less than half a moon gleamed in the waters below the Summer House. At the point of the hill that the house sat upon, a circular temple had been built in the

time of Maxian's grandfather. Slim marble columns rose up, a soft white presence
in the moonlight. Below the little temple, the broad sweep of the bay lay before
them. Glittering lights danced upon the water where countless ships rode in the
harbors of Neapolis and Baiae. In the distance, the smooth cone of Vesuvius rose
to cover the stars. The cool breeze was sharper here, and carried the salt tang of
the sea. In this familiar darkness, Maxian felt the unease and worry that had
shadowed him from Ostia melt away. Only a few feet away, Galen was a dark
indistinct shape in his deep crimson robe.

"The weight of the Empire is not upon your shoulders, little brother, so you
cannot know the burden that it is to me." Galen's voice was a whisper in the
gloom. "There are ten thousand details to keep in mind, a hundred interests to
satisfy with every decision. It is not as I had imagined it when we set out from
Saguntum. I am a powerful man; some would say a god. Yet there are so many
things, so many pressing factors over which I have no control."

Galen felt his brother turn and sit on the ledge that ran around the edge of
the temple.

"Each day I struggle, and the thousands of men who are my hands and feet,
spread across all the Empire, struggle. Every day the tide of time and men washes
away a little more of the edifice that we maintain. Every day we pile on more
bricks, more mortar, more blood. And the tide keeps wearing away at the rocks,
the stones, until there is nothing left." Though his words were those of despair,
Maxian could sense no defeat in his brother's voice.

"This can end, my brother. The Empire can know peace again, free from fear
of barbarian invasion, even of civil war." In the darkness, Galen's voice assumed
the cadence of an orator, though it remained low and direct. "After hundreds of
years of strife, the West is at peace. Beyond the Rhenus the Franks and Germans
are quiet. They have at last attained some semblance of civilization. They live in
towns, welcome merchants, till the soil and build homes of stone and wood. To
the west there is only endless ocean, to the south only vast deserts. Only in the
east do enemies remain."

Maxian, sitting quietly in the darkness, stirred. "The barbarians we saw today,
in the vision?"

Galen laughed. "No, the Avars and their subject tribes are an annoyance, not a
threat. They have overrun most of Thrace and Moesia, but they will not hold that
land long. The true enemy, my brothers, waits in the true East, in Persia. Even today,
though we saw it not in the vision, one Persian army is encamped on the eastern
shore of the Propontis, viewing the ancient walls of Constantinople with avaricious
eyes. Another is gathering in northern Syria, preparing to strike at Egypt. By good
luck, my brother Emperor is still in possession of a strong fleet, and the Persians have
none. So they are held at bay—for now."

Maxian spoke. "Then by use of this device, you will coordinate the relief of
the city with Heraclius? Some thousands of men could be sent, I suppose, upon
our fleet to reinforce the city and convince the barbarians to abandon the siege."

"In a way," Galen answered, his voice smiling, "we will convince them to
abandon the siege. But, still, the real enemy is not the horse-riders but Persia. It
is Persia that we must defeat to attain a true peace for the Empire. Peace for both

the East and the West. Your plan is fair, my brother, but far too limited in scope. Heraclius and I, through our letters, have struck upon a permanent solution."

It was quiet in the circle of the temple, though now the moon had settled below the great oak and yew trees. A silver light filled the temple and Maxian could see both of his brothers. The healer suddenly felt cold and there was a sensation much like that which had pervaded the boathouse in Ostia. With slightly trembling fingers he drew his own cape closer and wished for a heavier wrap. The wind died down.

"My brother Emperor proposes, and I agree, that Rome and Constantinople—both Empires—must invade Persia itself and destroy it. Once this is done, there shall be no treaty, no border agreements, no tribute. Persia will be a province of the Empire and will serve us forever. Then there shall be peace."

Maxian coughed, his throat constricted by an unreasoning fear. He spoke, though—unaccountably—it was a struggle to force the words from his lips. "Brother, this is . . . an unwise plan. The West is only beginning to recover from the plagues and the last civil war. Our realm is at peace, true, but the people are still recovering, the army is still rebuilding. An effort to raise the siege of the city of Constantine, yes, I agree it must be done. But to invade Persia itself? That would be mad . . ."

He stopped, coughing. A sense of great pressure surrounded him, more than could be accounted for by the angry look on his brother's face. Maxian held up a hand for a moment, all his attention focused inward. His mind was flooded with confusion and unsettling images, but he managed to calm his conscious thought with the Meditation of Asklepios. Once he began its well-remembered lines the confusion faded and the pressure eased. It did not depart, but now he could feel its boundaries and strength.

With an effort of will, he spoke again: "Persia is vast and its armies uncountable. It has been at peace for decades. Chrosoes is a strong king, ably served by his generals. It is wealthy even by the standards of Rome. To assail it, you would need tens or hundreds of thousands of men. The cities of the West are still half empty from the plague, the cities of the East no better. Where will you find the men to fight for you without baring our throats to the barbarians?"

Galen gave a sharp nod, saying, "A cogent point, brother, and one that Aurelian and I have been pondering for some days. Our most recent calculations show that we can field a temporary army, a *vexillation* if you will, of almost sixty thousand men to fight alongside Heraclius in the East. Ah, now hold your peace, we have thought upon this most carefully."

The Emperor stood and began pacing, his sandals making a light slapping sound on the marble tiles of the temple floor. "In the West, there are currently fourteen legions deployed from Africa to Pannonia to Britain. Beyond these forces, we have many other garrisons scattered about. Too, we count several tribes in Africa and Germania as our allies. By the count of the Office of the Equites, the Western Empire commands just over one hundred thousand men under arms. We are removing none of these legions from their duties; instead we will withdraw select units and cohorts from them. At the same time, we are instituting what Aurelian here, with his penchant for invention, calls a *levy*, to replace all of those men with fresh recruits. While the expedition is in the East, the remaining veterans here in the West will train a whole new army."

Maxian shook his head in amazement, saying, "And where do you expect to find an extra sixty thousand citizens of suitable age and temperament for the legions? Do not forget, brother, that I was at your side on the march from Saguntum to Mediolanum to Rome. I have seen the empty cities and barren fields turning back to forest."

Aurelian coughed expectantly. Galen turned a little to look at him, his face shadowed in the moonlight. He gestured to his brother to proceed. Aurelian clasped his hands before him, then said, "We, ah, we do not intend to induct citizens into the army. We intend to, well, to induct slaves and noncitizens."

Maxian flinched as if struck. A white-hot pain shot through the side of his head as the strange pressure that he had felt all around him in the temple suddenly became unbearable. A vast sense of crushing weight bore down on him, and his mind struggled to resist it. For a long moment of silence, he battled within himself to speak, to regain control of his limbs. As if from a great distance, he looked down upon himself sitting in the little temple, facing his brothers in the darkness. For a brief moment, as his sight hung suspended in the evening air, he caught a glimpse of a vast whirlpool of smoke and dull sullen fire spreading out from the three of them over the land and the sea. In the smoke, faces and phantasms roiled, indistinct.

Then there was a popping sensation and the pressure was gone.

"Slaves?" he croaked, barely able to speak. "The Senate will have a fit to hear of it . . ."

Galen smiled, his teeth glinting in the moonlight. "The prospect of Persian gold and estates and military commands pleases them more than the induction of slaves and noncitizens does. The beauty of Aurelian's plan is that the levy is not voluntary. Each province and city must provide its share, and since the levy is not upon the citizens, they will support it wholeheartedly. Sixty thousand fresh legionnaires in the West will make a great difference, both now and in the future, when they are done with their service."

Maxian shook his head. "I don't understand. What will happen when they are done with their service?"

"Why, then they will become citizens and will receive their grants in land and coin. Those half-empty cities will be filled again, my brother, with a new generation of Romans. Ones who will be loyal to me and to our house."

Maxian snorted in amusement. "The Legions are already loyal and have been from the time of Augustus. The legions in the west are loyal to you, the Emperor, today. You do not have to replace them." He paused, looking at his brothers in the dim moonlight.

"I do not think," he continued, "that this plan of yours and the Eastern Emperor's is a good one. There is more to your effort than meets the eye. The relief of Constantinople would end this fighting in the East. The Persians would go home. Peace would return. If you are so worried about Egypt, you would send your armies directly there."

Galen raised a hand, shaking his head. "Your objection, brother, is noted.

But our plan will proceed. There are great things at stake here, much greater than the simple issue of barbarians or Egypt. I have made up my mind. I will go to the East, to aid Heraclius and to destroy Persia."

Maxian shrugged, seeing only more death to come of it. "Well, then. That is that, I suppose."

ON THE FATHER OF RIVERS

The smile of Ra glittered back from the slow current of the river. The prow of the little ship cut through long troughs of deep-green water, spray falling back in languid waves from the pitted wood and tarred rope dangling from the front of the boat. Dwyrin's legs kicked idly inches from the swirling brown and green surface. The heat of the god was a heavy blanket upon him. His eyes were closed but the meditation of the masters had overtaken him and he saw the land sliding slowly past as a flickering vista of deep russet color and strong deep-blue currents under the earth. One hand rested lightly on a trailing guyline, feeling the sinuous flex of the boat moving through the water flow back into his fingers. The footsteps of the crew on the deck trickled over his hand like rain spilling from the rope, itself a musty deep green.

Three days now the dhow had followed the father of rivers north, winding past the sunken tombs and the deserted, dead cities of the Old Kingdom. League after league of desert paced them, spilling down to the edge of the river, washing around the towns on the eastern bank and the narrow strips of cultivation that supported them.

Two weeks had flown past since the early-morning dream of the crane-headed man, weeks spent in close seclusion with Nephet. The little old man had shown him marvels and delights, ripping back the veils of ritual and ceremony around the path of the sorcerer. Dwyrin had been afraid at first, realizing that he was being inducted into mysteries that were denied to even the journeymen of the school. Secrets of fire, wind, and the slow hard energy of the earth were revealed. There was a constant hissing current of power that ran in the back of his mind now, occasionally leaking into his consciousness like the calling of many invisible birds. During the day he struggled to keep his vision clear of the shimmering coils of power that slithered and shifted within the captain and the sailors. The deck and rigging of the dhow had an unfortunate tendency to melt away, leaving him staring down into the surging blue-green deeps of the river at the flickering bright flashes of the fish within it.

After six days of travel the river began to swell, spreading out. The high hills that had bounded it from the narrows at Tel-Ahshar now fell back to the horizon. The fields grew, reaching back from the river. More boats began to appear, filling the waterway. Sleek long galleys passed them in either direction, the heaving backs of the rowers glittering with sweat under the eye of Ra. Towns grew more frequent and great ruins began to crowd the western bank. Barely a league passed without the stark white bones of palaces, temples or tombs rising above the olive trees and palms.

On the ninth day the dhow pulled ashore for the night just beyond a thriving village on the eastern shore. The captain and the crew tied the boat to a piling of stone jutting from the bank, and all the crew save one went off, laughing, toward the lights of the town. Dwyrin stood on the high raised deck at the back of the dhow, staring after them, seeing them shimmer and waver between the cool purple-blue of the sleeping trees. He blinked and the vision settled back, flickering, to the dimness of the starlight and the thick canebrakes that lined the shore. The sole crewman left behind settled onto a mat near the steering shaft at the end of the deck. Soon he nodded off.

For a long time Dwyrin sat in the darkness, feeling the river and the land breathe around him, his mind and eyes filled with the whispering of the wind, of the rocks and trees that lined the shore, the slow glittering passage of crocodiles in the deep water. As Neket the guardian of night rose in the west, Dwyrin slid entirely out of conscious thought. The thin walls that he had raised up to constrain his vision fell away entirely, leaving his ka floating in air above his now-recumbent body.

The land was filled with dim radiance, the trees, palms, and brushy under-growth damped down by the flight of Ra into the underworld. In the fields beyond the boat, sullen red flames marked the cattle asleep under the swaying trees. Dwyrin spun slowly up into the air, seeing the land in slumber, even the deep currents of the earth muted. The river itself rolled on into the north, filled with green radiance and slow pulses of blue-violet. He turned to the western shore.

There he recoiled, his ka shying back from a cold white radiance. Beyond the line of palms and tall sawgrass on the farther shore a rising mount, crushed in on one side, flickered and burned with a pearlescent light. Around and about the hill a great city lay, outlined in silver and white. Dwyrin garbed himself in the aegis of Athena, his mind tumbling over the weaving spell. Those parts of himself that had begun to fray and slide away in that harsh glare returned. He drifted forward over the river.

At the western shore he paused, the aegis beginning to buckle under the constant pressure of the light. Dwyrin settled within and drew down on the surging current of the river, filling himself with the slow solid power of Hapi, the father. The aegis expanded, blunting the light. In his heart Dwyrin smiled and flexed, surging across the elemental barrier at the edge of the river. He stepped over, halting in shock as his sandaled foot crunched on gravel. He looked down, his hands raised to his face in amazement. Strong and broad, they rose before him. A kilt of pleated white linen was bound around his waist, his feet in fine leather sandals. The heavy weight of a short stabbing sword hung at his waist. He shook his head, feeling long braids fall behind him. He reached back and fingered his hair. It was bound back by a fillet of metal.

Softly he padded forward through the trees and came to a broad avenue.

Startled, he looked back to the river, seeing a broad piling bounded with obelisks running out into the water. He swung back the other way, spying a long curving road rising up toward the slumped mountain. Sphinxes and lions paced the sides of the road, and his feet were swift upon it. He came to a great arch, carved with the faces of kings and gods. He paused under it, his hand pale against the dark golden stone. Beyond the arch, great temples rose up on either side. Between them ran a narrow street of flagstones. Beyond the temples and their vast array of pillars, the slumped mountain now rose up with great clarity. Dwyrin could now see that it was stepped, and rose in tier after tier of hewn granite and sandstone to the summit, where a full third had been caved in, as by some massive stroke.

Dwyrin stepped through the arch and was brought up short. He reeled back, his body stunned by a stinging blow. A figure now stood beyond the gate.

"This is not for you," grated a voice like a millstone. "Go back to the land of the living."

Dwyrin, blinded by the glare seeping from the mountain, shook his head and stepped forward again. The figure raised a huge hand, its fingers curled. The shape of it was indistinct, fuzzed at the edges, but Dwyrin, blinking, made out the head of a wolf and deep burning red eyes. The hand rose, fingers outstretched. There was a slow burring sound and Dwyrin felt himself come apart, limbs dissolving. There was a sharp popping sound.

Dwyrin awoke on the deck of the dhow, the clamor of the sailors harsh in his ears. They had returned from the village, heads thick with wine and fermented corn ale. He rolled aside as their guttering blue flames sprawled around the pale-yellow flow of the decking. Dwyrin shuddered, closing his eyes against the sight. It did no good. No, if anything, his othersight was clearer and stronger. A yellow-blue flame approached him and low musical tones belled from it, hanging in the air like falling rain. Dwyrin groaned and rolled over, his distress spilling to the slow yellow deck in dull purple streams. The yellow-blue flame turned away. Dwyrin lay in the spreading pool of purple.

THE DE'ORELIO RESIDENCE, THE CITY OF ROME

Delicate voices greeted Thyatis as she descended the stairs from the upper chambers of Anastasia's mansion. Below, in the atrium, a choir of young slaves was singing to welcome the visitors to the party. The hall of the Poseidon was thronged with people, their voices and the tinkle of glass and plates rising up like a cloud above them. Thankfully, none of the notables of the city—the bankers, the senators, the Legion officers, their wives, concubines, mistresses, or catamites—paid her the least attention. Anastasia's handmaidens had labored over her for much of the afternoon. Her hair was a sweeping red-gold cloud around her face, tied back near the end with a deep-violet silk tie that trailed down her back. Careful pigments had been applied, bringing forth her lips, her eyes, and the line of her cheekbones.

She wore a new gown, this one modeled upon the silk masterpiece Anastasia had worn that first day. The finest linen, with a gauze drape of silk above it, in a deep green with subtle gold and blue hues. Tiny gold slippers were carefully tied to her feet, with delicate copper wires ornamenting and outlining the curve of her calves. A lapis and dark-gold necklace lay between her breasts. By dexterous sleight of hand, she had secreted her throwing knife and a garrote upon her person without the notice of the slaves who had dressed her. Their solid presence lent her the calmness of mind to navigate the crowd, which spilled down the steps beyond the sea-green hall, through the inner garden, and out into the great garden at the back of the house. Weaving through the chattering throng, she deftly avoided the servants rushing in and out of the kitchen, bearing great platters of candied figs, iced sherbets, sliced up portions of roast on silver skewers, and sugar-coated wrens in aspic.

The trees of the great garden were ablaze with hanging lanterns, and torches were placed along the walkways. Here the younger set of the party had gathered in a brightly attired throng around the ornamental pools. Wine flowed freely from the amphorae carried by the house slaves. Two young men dressed as gladiators, patrician by the cut of their hair and the softness of their hands, brushed past Thyatis on either side. One wayward hand caressed her right breast. Her hand was lightning quick, trapping his thumb as it trailed away. There was a twist and a pop, and the noble youth stumbled into his friend, speechless in pain. Thyatis glided on, ignoring whispered suggestions from the young men and women loitering in the shadows under the pear trees. Beyond the ornamental pool lay a secluded glen in the garden, surrounded by high hedges and trellises of rose and hyacinth. Settled within the glen, Anastasia's gardeners had labored for years to build a Pythagorean maze.

Beyond sight of the house and its merry windows, filled with people and lights, Thyatis relaxed. In the gloom under the waxing moonlight she stepped carefully through the passages in the maze. Around her, softly, came cries and groans. More than once she stepped over half-sheltered couples on the walkway. At last she found the center of the geometry, and there, next to a tiny marble pool surmounted by a bronze faun, were two facing benches. In her time in the house of her mistress, Thyatis had come here often to escape the subtle tensions among the household as well as the training that Anastasia had placed her under.

Finding the bench by feel in the darkness, Thyatis sat, sighing in relief. The sandals were very pretty, but her feet were not used to their tight confinement. She unwound the golden cords from her feet and carefully set them aside. She gently rubbed her feet, hissing in pain at the unexpected blisters. In the quiet darkness, her thoughts fluttered about her head like night moths.

Perhaps I should just leave the city and go far away, somewhere without all this . . .

"I think the same thing, often. Almost every day." The voice was low and deep.

Thyatis froze, then slowly turned. All but invisible in the darkness, a figure sat at the other end of the bench. The hairs on the nape of her neck prickled up and her nostrils flared. She accounted herself uncommonly aware, yet this man had been sitting no more than three feet from her since she had reached the center of the maze and she had not noticed him at all.

"My apologies," she said, "I did not think that I had spoken aloud."

"No matter," he replied, his deep voice easy and tinged with weariness. "If my presence ruins the solitude, I will betake myself away." He moved on the bench, swinging one leg over. Gravel crunched under a boot.

"No," she said, surprising herself, "you do not . . . intrude. There are too many people here for me to be comfortable in the house, or on the lawn."

He laughed—a rich sound like river water. "I hate crowds. Particularly ones like this, filled with all of the people you always see and all of the ones you cannot stand seeing again. The bickering and little games over who has more of this, or more of that. Ah, and the hostess, the dear Lady. A matron of great stature in the . . . community, and of unquenchable appetite."

Unseen, Thyatis smiled. "You know her, then," she said.

"For years! She has always wanted me to be one of her retinue of promising young men. Do your feet hurt?"

Thyatis blinked. "Ah, they're sore from the sandals. They're new and . . . I'm not used to them."

"May I?" came his quiet voice. In the darkness, Thyatis felt two hands, strong and broad, touch her right foot, perched on the edge of the bench. "I have some training in the temple, I can make the pain go away."

"You sound young for a priest," she said, but she swung around as well, placing both of her feet on the bench. Gentle fingers brushed over her toes and slid along her instep.

"When I was younger, I showed some talent for the arts of Asklepios," he said, "so I was enrolled by my mother. I think that she wanted me to avoid the fate of government service that had taken my father. That plan was a failure, I fear. I spend all of my time now on things relating to the Offices." The laugh came again, a pleasant burr in the gloom. Thyatis leaned back against the thick leaves of the hedge. His hands rolled and kneaded her tired muscles.

"This feels wonderful," she said, her voice languid. "Working for the Lady is equally diverting. At first you are told that you will be doing one thing, a thing that you enjoy and show promise and skill at, then the next day another, something that you detest. She is maddening much of the time."

"And gracious and serene the next," he said. "I hope you did not take offense at my description of her before."

"No!" Now she laughed. "All too accurate. She is not happy unless all things around her are in their proper place. The properness, or the placement, may change from day to day . . . Ow!"

The hands paused, then gently probed the aching spot. There was a soft noise, like the hum of a bee, and for a moment a light sparked between his hand and her foot. Thyatis gasped at the tingling shock that traveled through her foot, up her leg, and to the top of her head. In the brief light she caught an image of long dark hair, a small beard, and a strong nose. Then there was darkness, even more complete than before.

"Sorry," he said, his voice a whisper. "You injured your foot long ago? A cut, or stepping on something sharp?"

"Yes. I was in the stableyard and stepped on a horse nail. It was driven all the way through the bottom of my foot." By iron control, she kept from shuddering at the memory of the long days that she had lain in a fever afterward. "Pay it no mind."

"Let me finish what your body started," he said, his voice even.

"How so? It has been healed for years."

A well-trimmed fingernail traced the old wound and then up the back of her calf to her knee. Thyatis hissed at his touch. It tingled through more than her leg.

"See?" he said. "There is still a knot here of old injury. If you will allow it, I can make it go away. You will notice the difference, I assure you. Old wounds linger, even when you cannot see them, disturbing the balance of the body. Odd headaches, dizzy spells, shortness of breath . . ."

Thyatis was quiet for a long time and she drew her knees up to her chest. The priest settled back against the opposite hedge in companionable silence. Even the prospect of a healing magic filled her with dread. Giving up control of her body, particularly to a stranger, even a well-spoken one, was unthinkable. The feel of his hands now reminded her all too much of Anastasia's caresses. At last, with an odd trepidation, she said, "No, thank you. I do not feel it . . . proper."

"No matter, lady, such things are personal."

I am not a lady, she started to say, but the warm orange light of a lantern now spilled into the little clearing around the pool and the faun. Thyatis blinked and picked up her shoes. The priest, now illuminated, squinted up at the slender figure holding the half-shuttered lantern.

"Ai, Krista, it has been awhile since I've had the pleasure of your company."

"My lord," answered Anastasia's handservant, bowing deeply. "My mistress sent me to find you. The dinner is almost ready to be served. She begs your indulgence in joining her at repast."

The young man shook his head in dismay but got up all the same. In the light of the lantern, Thyatis saw that he was tall, with a clean-limbed form, and long dark hair tied back in a fillet. He was dressed in the robes of a philosopher, though he looked more like an athlete. He began to turn to Thyatis, reaching out a hand to assist her up, but Krista slid into the space between them instead. She smiled prettily. "Please, my lord, we mustn't be late."

The priest frowned but allowed himself to be led away. Even as they passed the entrance to the little grotto, Krista was telling him a long story about the candied fruits at the feast. The lantern light flickered on the hedges, then faded away. Darkness crept back in, and the thin moon shone down once more, picking silver highlights off the faun.

Thyatis considered the shoes in her hands, then sat them down on the gravel and began the laborious process of lacing them back up.

Even with nearly a hundred slaves stationed along the walls with fans stirring the air, and all of the windows in the house thrown open, the dining hall was almost unbearably hot. Thyatis stood in an alcove off the passage from the kitchen to the series of chambers that held the throng of dinner guests. From her vantage behind a curtain, she could see the main room, where Anastasia and her coterie of male admirers spilled off a reef of couches. Among them, the young priest was set in the place of honor at the hostess's side. While Thyatis watched, the mistress of the house was making a messy job of feeding him jellied eels. Their laughter rose above the din of the other guests. Thyatis turned away, shaking her head.

"There you are!" Krista stormed into the little alcove, carrying a copper platter burdened with fresh-cut fruit arranged in the shape of a map of Achaea. Her pert features were filled with anger. "You're supposed to be out there, with the mistress, entertaining!"

Thyatis glanced back out through the break in the curtain. "I think the Lady is doing just fine all by herself," she said in a very dry voice.

Krista shifted the platter onto a ledge and rubbed her shoulder.

"The mistress is not supposed to be doing that, you are," she hissed. "You're supposed to be the mysterious niece with a gorgeous dress and plenty to put in it. It should be you being clumsy with the jellied eels and bending over a lot to pick them up."

"Me?" Thyatis said. "I'm dreadful, as the past three weeks have shown, at being coy and alluring. To quote *you*, I'm dense and have no sense of rhythm."

"I'm a slave, you lackwit! I can get the Prince into bed, but I surely can't marry him, now can I?" Krista was spitting mad and the drape of her tunic kept getting out of line. Irritated beyond measure, she slid the shoulder strap back into place again.

Thyatis stared at her in puzzlement. "The Prince?"

Krista rolled her eyes and carefully drew back the curtain, pointing through to the dining chamber and Anastasia's couch.

"Him, you cow, the one that you were in the garden with. You know, for a moment I thought that you had some real flair for this, getting him alone before hardly anyone even knew that he was at the party. But you didn't even know who he was . . ." Krista sat down on a little stool pushed up against the wall, her face a picture of despair.

"Minerva preserve us, you're so . . . so . . . I don't even know what. We show you and show you—but you just don't care!" Krista picked one of the little plums cut into the shape of a tiny Greek temple and began nibbling at it. "This is not going to work well at all."

Thyatis was still staring out into the dining chamber, her mouth hanging open. She turned back to Krista with a look of astonishment on her face. "That's the

Prince? The one that the Lady has been maneuvering for weeks to get to this party so that I can be paraded in front of him like a prize milch cow?"

Krista nodded, saying, "That's one way to put it."

"He's a priest!" Outrage filled Thyatis' voice. "I'm supposed to seduce a priest? That's illegal! They'll lock me up in some pit in the ground and starve me to death."

"Quiet! That only happens to Vestals!" Krista whispered around another of the plums. "Your duty to the mistress is to do whatever she commands. You may be her 'ward' and a member of her family, but you still work for her. Tonight that means that you attract, and hold, the attentions of that young man out there, who will, if things go as the mistress foresees, someday become Emperor. Then you would be Empress, if you manage to get him to marry you, which will be a chore and a half, I can see."

"I don't want to be Empress, you flat-chested conniving little wretch! I want to go back to doing the job I was doing before, the one I liked!"

"Well, Miss Too-good-to-do-the-work, you owe the mistress as big a debt as anyone, so I suggest that you fix your hair, paste a nice smile on your fat peasant face, and get out there before the mistress winds up in an orgy with that bevy of young boys out of boredom waiting for you to show up. Otherwise you'll be on the block again, with a hundred strangers measuring your body with their eyes!"

Thyatis' eyes narrowed and her forearm was a blur ending in Krista pinned to the wall of the alcove. Thyatis leaned close, her teeth bared in a smile.

"Remember what I do for a living, little girl?" she whispered. "Don't threaten me with talk of debts or my past again, or you'll be in the Cloaca Maxima, face-down, with a ticket to the river." Almost gently, she released Krista from the arm lock and put her upright. "Here's your tray. Don't drop it."

Krista frowned and straightened her tunic. For a moment Thyatis thought the smaller woman would attack her, but then the moment passed and Krista shook her head.

"You and the mistress can discuss it," said Krista, her eyes flashing. Then she left.

There was a wicker box of wine jugs on the floor of the alcove. Thyatis bent down and tugged one free of the straw wrappings. She pried the wax seal off the top with a fingernail and took a very long draft. It was thick, resinated Greek wine. She took a second pull on the bottle, then put it aside. She checked her hair, straightened her gown, and made sure that all of the arm bangles and bracelets were still in place. Finally ready, she pulled aside the curtain and stepped back out into the corridor.

Entertain the Prince, she thought. *Attract the Prince. Right.*

THE MOUTH OF THE FATHER OF RIVERS

)•((

Three risings of Ra passed and the dhow passed into the thickly congested waterways of the delta. Hundreds of ships, barges, and rafts passed up and down the great arteries of the Nile. The dhow picked its way between them, nimbly sliding past the huge stone-carrying barges and the three-tiered galleys of the Imperial government. At last, the stultifying heat of midday was broken by a fresh wind from the north carrying the smell of the sea. The dhow captain was well pleased to have made the capital with such speed.

His voice grew harsh with shouted commands to the lazy mob he called a crew. Near dusk the channel of the river widened at the village of Fuwa and the granite lock gates of the Alexandrine canal rose up on the western bank. So late in the day, the locks were clear of traffic and the captain muttered a fervent prayer of thanks to the patron of travelers. His little ship heeled over and ran across the current into the momentary darkness under the vaulting lock gates. The canal diverged from the Nile and ran on a straight course through the center of Alexandria and into the greater, or military, harbor. That passage, however, was restricted to military galleys alone. The captain pursed his lips in thought as he leaned on the tiller, guiding the dhow through the second of the massive lock basins.

His first intent upon reaching the end of such a journey should be to dock at the guild warehouses on the lesser, or merchants', harbor and offload the cargoes he had brought from the South. The boy from the witches' house and his mumbling daze precluded that. The captain scratched his shaven pate and peered thoughtfully at the thick clusters of shacks and crumbling red-brick buildings along the side of the canal. The dhow tacked against the wind, and their progress slowed as the countercurrent from the sea mouth of the canal began to run against them.

The captain handed the tiller off to the mate and clambered down a narrow ladder into the low-roofed cabin under the rear deck. The boy lay there, wrapped in blankets, against the rear wall. His eyes remained open, flickering, unfocused. His skin, as the captain touched his forehead, was damp and hot. The captain shook his head and wiped his fingers on his tunic. His orders from the old witchman were to deliver the boy to the great military citadel overlooking the second, or greater, harbor of Alexandria. Since he could not sail straight into that harbor, he would have to take the cutoff canal to the lesser harbor and then swing around, outside of the two harbors, past the *pharos* and into the military harbor.

He tapped his fingers on the decking. That would take a great deal of time, and he would have to either pay the dock porters more to work late or wait until the morning to unload his cargoes. The captain shook his head to clear his thoughts and looked down with disgust at the trembling boy in the blankets. *There must be some other way*, he thought, and then climbed back onto the deck.

THE SCHOOL OF PTHAMES

Even as Ra slid down through the thick smoke haze over Alexandria, turning the holy disk a ruddy brass, the last rays of the beneficent god crawled slowly down the whitewashed white wall in Ahmet's quarters, far to the south. The young master lay on his narrow cot, feet up on the wooden rail at the bottom. In the dimming light of Ra, his chiseled face was troubled. Liquid dark-brown eyes followed creeping bars of gold down the irregular surface of the wall, but the subtle beauty did nothing to lighten his heavy mood. At last, unable to shake the sensation of tremendous weight that lay on him, he rose.

This used to mean something, he thought to himself, looking around the room. *I used to enjoy this.*

He stood at the window, his hand on the dark old wood of the sill. Ra was now behind the western hills, leaving a splendor of deep purples and reds in the thin clouds and the darkening sky. A few dim stars began to glitter in the darkness. Wind, rising from the desert, brought sweet smell of marjoram and olives to him. Below, in the compound, there was the familiar clatter of the kitchens, and the boys, now released from their studies, ran past in the courtyard to the dining hall.

Ahmet looked down, seeing them flitter past in the deep-blue dimness, the white shapes of their tunics gleaming. The pale-gold light of the tapers in the dining hall met them as they went in. He stood thus for a long time, until the god had entirely passed into the underworld of night and the murmur of the students and masters at dinner indicated that all were within the hall. His thoughts, which had been so troubled, smoothed away and an inevitable conclusion forced itself upon him. After a long time he accepted it, and his mind fell quiet.

The young master turned away, into the darkness of his room. Needing no light, his fingers found the chest of cedarwood his village had sent him when he made the third circle. The knurled bronze clasp came up in his fingers and he began removing the items within. His breathing was even now, and the weight on his shoulders had began to lift.

ALEXANDRIA

)•(

Now in darkness, the dhow glided through the thick waters of the canal, the crewmen standing at bow and stern with long padded poles to keep the ship from the crumbling brickwork that lined the waterway. The city rose around them, the buildings now two or three stories, their lights glittering back from the water. A wash of noise, the sounds of tens of thousands of people, filled the air. The captain stood again at the tiller and his dark face gleamed in the lights of the taverns and public houses that lined the canal. He felt vastly better now that the long stretches of the open desert were behind him.

He had quietly discussed the problem of the witch-boy with his mate, who had proposed a simple solution. At the junction of the military and civil canals was a fortified gate housing the legion detachment tasked with checking the traffic into the military harbor. The boy could most conveniently be left there with his orders, and they would see him to wherever the guard captain saw fit to send him.

Now the dhow captain peered forward through the smoky haze that overlaid the canal and thought he espied the bright torches of the water gate. Indeed, as the dhow eased around a barge moored at the side of the canal, the twin towers and high wall of the gate rose up before him, brightly lit with torches and a brazier set on the dock beside it. The gate itself was now shut, its oiled iron portcullis closed.

" 'ware the dock," the mate shouted to the pole men. The other crewmen bent to the backing oars, straining against the weight of the dhow. There was a grinding crunch as it struck the fore end of the dock with a glancing blow, and then the pole men steadied the craft. The captain stepped to the gunwale and then off onto the mossy corroded stones of the dock.

Beyond the brazier and a little open space some ten feet long stood a guard-house jutting from the massive plinth of the eastern tower. Two legionnaires, their maroon cloaks cast aside, sat upon three-legged stools under one of the brighter torches. They looked up, eyes hooded in the guttering light, their beards full and twisted into long braids. The leftmost one rose as the dhow captain approached and loomed massive in the flickering light. His arms were like the pillars of a temple, massive and sharply defined. The *legionarius* stood forward a step and grunted a challenge.

"Greetings, noble legionnaire," the dhow captain answered in his best Greek.

The legionnaire grunted again and cocked his head to one side. The dhow captain swore under his breath. Couldn't the Empire post soldiers to Alexandria who at least spoke some kind of civilized tongue? A long passage of hand waving, pantomime and, finally, shouting passed before the guards got the idea that the dhow captain had something in his boat for them.

The mate, meanwhile, had gone through Dwyrin's cloak and traveling bag, stealing the food therein and anything else of value. This crucial task accomplished, he bundled the boy up in the blanket and carried him up on to the dock. By this time the dhow captain was at his wits' end. The two blond giants were laughing and shouting back at him. The mate came up with the boy and the captain handed him off to the larger of the two, waving the packet of travel orders in their faces.

Saemund, *ouragos* of the II Triana Legion, stared in surprise at the backs of the two little dark men who had come from the boat. At first he had thought that they were native merchants trying to sell him something, but they had not understood his plain speaking when he told them that he had lost all of his money at dice the night before. He shook his shaggy head in amazement and unwrapped the large, clumsy bundle they had given him. At his side, Throfgar, his battle brother, turned the papyrus sheets this way and that, trying to make head or tail of the spindly runes marked on them.

"Ach, brother," Saemund exclaimed as he turned back the motheaten blanket to expose Dwyrin's flushed and sweating face, "they've left us a foundling!"

Throfgar stared over in surprise, for the long red-gold braid of the youth marked him as a northerner like himself. He scratched the fleas in his beard in thought.

"Could he be the son of one of the other fighters?" he ventured.

"None that I have seen," Saemund answered as he carried the sick boy into the guardroom. There he gently placed the boy onto the duty cot at the back of the small, smoke-blackened room. He turned the blanket out and laid it over the boy, tucking it in under his feet. Then he turned to Throfgar with a puzzled expression, cracking his large knuckles.

"We should report this to the *tetrarchos*," he said. "I'll stand the watch here, you go and tell Tapezos what has happened."

Throfgar nodded in agreement and tossed the packet of papyrus sheets into the kindling box next to the small, narrow fireplace. He went to the back of the guardroom, where a narrow passageway led up a flight of steps to a stout wooden door. He pounded on the thick striated panels for a moment. Then a narrow metal cover turned back from a slit in the door at eye level.

"Ho, Tapezos," Throfgar rumbled, "tell the *tetrarchos* that we've got a visitor for him."

Tapezos muttered something on the other side of the door and slammed the viewport closed. Throfgar shrugged and ambled back down the stairs. Saemund had returned to his post on the dockside. Throfgar checked the boy, who moaned slightly as the German turned back his eyelids, and then joined his battle brother on the watch.

A few moments later there was a clattering sound as the inner door opened and Michel Pelos stumbled out, yawning, and walked out onto the quayside. Throfgar and Saemund grinned broadly at the Greek, who had drunk overmuch for his stomach the night before. Michel rubbed one side of his lean, scarred, face and hitched his sword-belt up.

"What in Hades is the matter with you two grinning idiots?" he snarled in poor Latin.

Saemund pointed back into the little watch-room. "There's a package for you," he said.

Michel grimaced at the two Scandians. He went back inside, then they heard him cursing. He came back out. He was not amused. "A funny joke. I may be Greek, but that does not mean that I like little boys."

Throfgar laughed again, braying like a camel. Saemund smiled too, though he had noticed that the tetrarchos was becoming an odd reddish color in the face. He hit his battle brother in the arm to shut him up and told the tetrarchos what had happened.

"Huh." Michel pondered the situation. "A foundling, but probably not a citizen. And sick to boot. Well, there isn't much we can do for him here. I'll send a runner to the centurion and see what he wants to do."

Several hours later two camp physicians came and carried the boy away. He was still flushed and sweating, his eyes unseeing. Saemund and Throfgar had finished their watch by then and did not see him go. The next pair of guardsmen on duty lit a fire in the little oven with the papyrus sheets.

THE VILLA OF SWANS

Anastasia groaned theatrically and waved for her handmaiden to lay another chilled cloth on her forehead. "The heat is terrible." She moaned. "Like the forges of Vulcan."

Thyatis, sitting on a low stool next to her, eyed the slave Krista out of the corner of one eye. Krista knelt at Anastasia's side. The slave rolled her eyes while deftly picking a second cloth out of the chilled ewer. Another slave, this a handsome Nubian lad in a short tunic, slowly waved a fan over the recumbent form of the mistress of the house.

At last, Anastasia sat up and Krista plumped the pillows behind her so that she might rest more easily. A small plate of freshly pitted cherries was placed near the Lady's hand, in case she desired refreshment. Having come from the Offices only moments before, Anastasia was dressed in a regal yet subdued outfit. Somber colors, showing very little skin, and restrained makeup. In the dim light of the sitting room, under the frescoes of forest creatures, nymphs, and centaurs, she seemed to Thyatis to show her true age. There was a drained look about her eyes that the carefully applied powders could not disguise. Thyatis sat straighter and composed herself as Anastasia's languid gaze fell upon her.

The Duchess shook her head slowly, picking up a cherry from the little porcelain bowl. "I fear that I made a mistake with you, my dear. One of the first things that my late husband told me when he decided to accept me as a partner and equal in his business here in the city was: to each tool a proper purpose."

Inwardly Thyatis quailed in fear. The moderate-seeming disaster of the dinner party for the Prince now assumed much larger character. It was a struggle to keep from breaking into tears, yet she managed. *It was not fair! I tried my best . . . it's not my fault I don't know how to be coy!*

Anastasia leaned a little closer, her eyes intent upon Thyatis. "I apologize for misusing you."

The words took a long tick of the water-clock to make themselves known in Thyatis' conscious thought. When they did, she smiled in relief and quickly composed herself again. Anastasia nodded, picking one of the cherries off the plate and rolling it between her long fingertips.

"You have tremendous skills for one so young—skills that I value very highly—but not the ones that I attempted to foster in you for this *one* purpose. At the time, the throw seemed worth the risk. However, the tactics of seduction and pleasant intrigue are not what I have had you trained in for five years. Your talents so obviously lie in direct action. It was a mistake on my part, one that I will not make again. I confess that I was tremendously angry at the outcome of that night."

She glared at Krista, who prostrated herself to the floor. As the slave girl put her forehead to the pale rose tiles, Thyatis caught the edge of a self-satisfied smirk, like the little cat Bastet lapping up fresh cream. Anastasia continued, "When one manages—after weeks of effort—to get a Prince of the Empire to spend the night in one's house, it should be in the bed of the intended, not with some minx of a slave girl." The Duchess sighed.

"No matter, he left hung over and satisfied. At that point, it was as good an outcome as I could hope for."

Thyatis bowed her head as well, in contrition and to hide her relief that she would not be forced to undergo the awful prospect of trying to seduce a young man of high station in front of twenty or thirty of his peers and acquaintances. Only the evident discomfiture of the Prince and the timely intervention of Krista with an artfully spilled tray of fresh-cut fruit had saved her from fleeing the dining hall in shame and utter embarrassment.

Anastasia sighed, leaning back in the divan, her eyes narrowed in thought. Krista, still prostrate, slowly crept back out of sight of her mistress. The Duchess twirled one of her long dark curls around an elegant finger for a moment, then tucked it back into place. By her face, Thyatis saw that she had come to some decision.

"Today," Anastasia began in a businesslike voice, "the Emperor summoned me to the Offices and laid out before me his . . . requests . . . for me and those who serve me. He is undertaking a daring campaign to assist the Emperor of the East. He has requested that I provide him with persons of certain abilities to serve on his staff during this expedition. Among them, I believe that I shall send you,

Thyatis, along with your faithful Nikos, as . . . hmm . . . couriers would suit you best. I expect that you will be rather out of place in precincts that are usually the domain of men, but I believe that you will prosper."

Thyatis was slowly overcome by a sense of giddy relief and anticipation. *She was going to resume her previous work, and with Nikos at her side, no less!* The prospect of having a well-wrapped sword-hilt in her hand and boots on her feet washed over her like an exquisite wine. *No more wretched perfumes or troublesome garments! No more house servants fluttering around her like distraught moths when she did not sit properly . . .*

Anastasia shook her head, smiling, at the joy apparent in her young ward. She wagged an admonishing finger at the seventeen-year-old. "Calm yourself, my dear. You will be in Constantinople soon enough."

THE WINE-DARK SEA, NORTH OF ALEXANDRIA

The creaking of a sail and the slap of bare feet on planking woke Dwyrin from part of his fever dream. Darkness and a terrible fetid smell surrounded him. He was very thirsty. The storm of colors that had clouded his vision for so long had begun to recede from his sight. Distantly he knew that the privations his body had been subjected to were beginning to focus his mind as the body failed. Weakly he tried to sit up. There was the clink of chains and he caught his throat on a stiff metal band. He fell back, hitting his head on rough wooden planks. Around him, there was a murmur of sleeping men. He raised a hand gingerly to his neck and found that there was a collar around it. A heavy chain ran through a ring welded to the outside of the collar. Above, in the darkness, there was the shouting of men, and beyond that, the rush of the sea. An incredibly foul miasma assaulted his nose.

Macha save me! His mind wailed. *This is a slave ship!*

The lights began to creep back into the edges of his vision, and the darkness in the hold around him assumed strange and fantastic shapes. The sleeping men slowly became outlined first in gold, then deep blue, and finally a shimmering red. So too did the chain and the links of it. Dwyrin struggled to clear his sight, focusing on the meditations and the rituals that Nephet had taught him. For a moment, it worked, and he could suddenly see with the "clear sight" that the teachers at the school had drilled into them over and over. The links of the chain in his hands became completely clear, perfectly distinct. His thin fingers ran over them, suddenly catching on a discolored link.

It is not in harmony with the others, he thought. He pressed against the iron of the link with his thought and the ragged purple scar that ran across it in his clear sight sparked, then flared up for a moment. The iron splintered in his hand. Suddenly fearful of discovery, Dwyrin slowly passed the chain through the ring on the neck collar one link at a time. In a moment it was gone.

Free, he stood up. Hundreds of other captives lay all around him, sleeping tightly packed together. Ten or fifteen feet away, a raised walkway ran down the center of the hold. There was a carpet of bodies between him and the walkway. Behind him, the hull was solid oak planking. Above, however, were the timbers of the main deck. A series of tie-hooks were screwed into the beams.

Gauging his spring, he leapt up and snatched at the first one. One hand laid hold, the other scrabbled at the splintery planks. For a moment he swung there, his arm trembling with effort. Then his other hand caught the next tie-hook. His feet he drew up in a curl. Panting with the effort, he let go of the first hook and swung out, grabbing for the next. By luck he caught it on the first try and immediately let go of the previous one. The momentum carried him to the fourth and then he dropped lightly onto the walkway. The ship creaked as it rode over a swell, groaning along its full length.

Dwyrin panted, crouched on the walkway in the darkness. His arms trembled and he felt light-headed. Regardless, after a moment, he stood up and quickly ran to the end of the hold. A ladder led up to the deck, and now he could spy an edge of stars through the hatchway and past the square sails that caught the wind to send the ship northward. He crept up the stairs.

Cautiously, he raised his head above the hatchway and looked about. The rear of the ship rose up in front of him, a high stern castle with two great steering oars mounted on either side. On the steering deck, a lantern guttered in a green-glass holder. Low voices drifted down on the night wind. Dwyrin looked back up the main deck, seeing little, only great piles of goods, tied down with netting. As quietly as he could manage, he crept out of the hold stair and to the near edge of the ship. Beyond it the sea rushed past, a vast depth shot with blue flames and violet clouds. The wavetops glittered with pale-blue fire. Colors began to spill out of the corners of his eyes, blinding him.

Unsteady, he climbed up onto the gunnel, gripping one of the ropes that ran from the edge of the ship to the nearest mast. Below him an abyss of light and shadow convulsed as he stared down into the infinite depths. Vast sea creatures writhed in the void, intricate and complex beyond all imagining. A sensation of falling gripped him and he clung tight to the rope. Distantly, like an echo in a dream, he heard someone shouting. At last he managed to relax his hand enough to let go of the rope.

Hands seized him, rough and callused, dragging him back onto the deck. Sounds rushed past, but he could not understand them. He struggled, striking out with weak fists. Something fast smashed into the side of his face and the pain cleared his vision again. The faces of brutal men crowded above him. One held more chains, another a sack whose dark opening yawned like a hungry mouth. Dwyrin cried out in fear, and focused his thought against the hands holding him down. There was another bright flash and then a horrid wailing. The man who had been holding him down leapt back, his head wreathed in bright white flame. Soundlessly he tried to scream, but the flame burrowing into his chest consumed all of the air in his lungs. The other sailors scattered in horror. The burning man fell backward against the gunnel, his limbs thrashing in extreme pain.

Dwyrin scuttled to one side, seeking safety in one of the great bales tied to the decking. An iron hand suddenly gripped his throat. Still weak, he struggled to tear the talonlike fingers from his windpipe. It was no use, and after an endless passage of trying to breathe a giddy darkness swallowed his mind.

THE OFFICES, THE PALATINE HILL, ROMA MATER

Unlike the isolated detachment of the Summer House in Cumae, the Offices of the Palace were crowded shoulder to shoulder with bureaucrats, lictors, patrons of all sizes and shapes, Imperial officers, Praetorians in their red cloaks, foreigners and hundreds of slaves.

Maxian stood for a moment on the steps of what had once been the Temple of the Black Stone, built off the north side of the Palatine Hill on a great raised platform. Now the temple was the venue of the various embassies, both from foreign states and from cities and provinces within the Empire. A constant stream of people swarmed up and down the steps, hurrying across the narrow way to the vaulted arch and gate that led into the Imperial Offices themselves. The young healer, dressed in a nondescript cloak and tunic, leaned back into the tiny bit of shade the column provided him. The air was heavy and hot, thick with the miasma of thousands of sweaty people going about their business in a great hurry. He continued to peer over the heads of those on the lower steps, looking for the man he had come to see. Though armed with a good description—tall, sandy blond hair, crooked nose—he still failed to pick him out.

The heat of the day did not better his temper, which had been worn of late. Dreams of the night in Ostia continued to haunt him, now intertwined with memories of the vision he had experienced in the little temple at Cumae. A recurring sense of familiarity linked the two events, and he had been spending long, and late, hours in the Imperial Archives to try to find out what could have caused the deaths of Dromio and his whole family in such a way. Too, he still held serious reservations about his brother's plan to aid the Eastern Empire. He rubbed tired eyes with an ink-stained hand. *Where was this Briton?*

Old Petronus, at the library tucked into the back of the Baths of Caracalla, had suggested this foreigner to him and had, supposedly, arranged this meeting. Odd that the Briton, Mordius, required a meeting in a public square—it would have been far more comfortable to meet in an inn or banquet house. *No matter,* the Prince thought, *if he has answers . . .*

"My lord?" Maxian looked up. A tall northerner stood on the step below his, though his height easily raised him to an equal eye level with Maxian. Sure enough, he had a nose once broken and now crooked, long blond hair tied back in braids, and he was dressed in trousers and a light cotton shirt. A small, neat beard completed the picture.

Maxian squinted at him. "You are Mordius? A Briton?"

The man smiled. "Aye, my lord, the very same. Petronus sent a message that I should meet a young, tired-looking Roman with long dark hair here. Are you he?"

Maxian smiled back. "I am. Let us go someplace dark and cool, with wine . . ."

An hour later, in the recesses of a tavern in a narrow street just north of the Coliseum, Maxian thought he had a good mark on this barbarian. As Mordius had explained over an amphora and a half of middling Tibertinan wine, he was a man sent to Rome to make money for his investors in distant Londonium. He had been in the city for six years, first to handle shipments of ceramics and glass back north to Britain, then handling a growing traffic of wool, lumber, amber, iron, coal, and tin from the icy northern islands to the ever-hungry markets of Italia. He was married to a Roman woman now and had a young son. Two of his cousins had come to join him; they handled the warehousing and traffic of goods. Mordius had a new objective—to make more money with the money that he controlled in Rome itself.

None of this surprised Maxian. Foreigners had been coming to the Eternal City for centuries, looking for work, looking for riches. Some few found it; many more failed and went home or became refuse in the streets of the Subura. Others passed onward, always looking for a new Elysium. This one, however, had stuck and from the restrained richness of his clothes, from his accent and his bearing, the Prince thought that he had become successful.

"It is impossible to be successful in Rome if one does not follow proper custom," Mordius was saying. "One requires a patron, both to represent your interests in the courts and to help you navigate the intricacies of the State and the will of the people. I account myself lucky to have made the acquaintance, even the friendship, of Gregorius Auricus."

Maxian looked up in surprise. "The one they call Gregorius Magnus? He is a powerful man in the Senate and the city."

Mordius bowed his head in assent. "Just so. Without his friendship, all of my efforts here would be dust. I would doubtless be back in Britain, digging stumps out of fields." He paused and raised the earthenware cup he was drinking from. "Even this poor vintage would be acclaimed throughout Londonium as an exemplar of the vintners' art. I drink to Rome, the Roman sun, and fine wine." He drained the cup. Maxian joined him, then put the cup down on the table between them. "Petronus, at the baths, said that you had encountered a difficulty with a business deal. He told me this after I had related to him a problem that I had with a business arrangement of my own. It seems, and I say seems, that the two troubles might be related."

Mordius refilled his cup, then offered the amphora to Maxian, who declined, turning his cup over. It joined a confusion of old wine stains on the tabletop.

"A difficulty, yes," the Briton said, his face growing still and grim. "Almost seventy thousand sesterces in investment, gone. A man who had become a good friend, gone. Nothing to indicate an enemy, a business rival. All ashes within a day."

"A fire?" Maxian asked, disappointed. Petronus had hinted at more than that.

"The fire came after," Mordius replied. "Joseph and his family were dead before then. I will tell you what I know, what I heard, what I saw." The Briton sat up a little straighter on the bench and the cadence of his voice changed. Maxian wondered if the man had trained as an orator in his youth.

"Two of the businesses that I represent are the importation of lumber, which is cut into planks for building in the city, and wool, particularly to be made into heavy cloaks. As such I see the foremen of both the lumber mills and the weavers on a daily basis. Five months ago each man told me an odd story about a silversmith, a Jew, who had come to them to ask them for their refuse. To the mill he had come and asked for the dust that comes from the saws when they are cutting the logs. To the weaver he had asked for their old scraps of linen. This intrigued me, for I can smell business, particularly new business, from miles away. I asked around, spent a few coppers, and found the silversmith. His name was Joseph and his shop was down in the Alsienita, across the Tiber. A poor neighborhood, but cheap enough for him to afford a workshop without too many bribes.

"The day that I went in to talk to Joseph about his sawdust and linen rags he was despondent. He had been spending all of his time on his new project, and his wife was beside herself at the state of their jewelry business. His sons and daughters were spending all of their time making a terrible mess in the back of the shop with his oddments, while customers went waiting at the door, and then did not come at all.

"Needless to say, it seemed a reasonable business opportunity—not as if I were setting his house afire and then buying it from him in the street . . . I had some silver in my bag and I gladly pressed it into his hand in exchange for his story. He looked hopeful, and I know that he was more open with me, a fellow foreigner, than with some—pardon me, my lord—snobbish Roman. So he told me the tale and it pricked my ears right up.

"Joseph had a brother, Menacius, who was a scribe and made a good living in the shops down behind the Portica Aemilla copying scrolls and letters and what-not. I know the kind of living a good scribe makes, I've paid my share of gold to them. Still, this Menacius was very successful, for he was blessed with three sons, all with good eyes and steady hands. The three of them were like peas in a pod and this suited Menacius very well, for their letters were all but indistinguishable from one another. He could set all three of them to one book and each would take a section. Three working instead of one makes quick work. The sesterces were wheeling themselves up to the door—that's how good it was. Now, like most good things, this came to an end.

"One of the sons fell sick, and then another ran off with a snake-dancer from Liburnium. To make things worse for Menacius, he had just caught a deal with the Office of the Mint for no less than seventy copies of the Regulation of the Coinage. A very good sum he stood to make from that too, no doubt, but to win the deal he had to agree to a tight delivery schedule. Now, with only one scribe, he was in a terrible state. Being a man of family, he had gone to see Joseph and poured out his tale of woe. Joseph, who was a fellow good with his hands and clever to boot, thought about it for a time and then struck upon a solution.

"If there were not three sons, then make one son do the work of three. Their strength came from their handwriting being steady, firm, and clear. So he struck, so to say, upon this." Mordius opened a small leather bag and removed a tiny object, pressing it into the Prince's hand.

Maxian turned over the little piece of lead in his hand. A square bolt, no more than a little finger's bone in length. Flat at one end with two notches, one on each side, bumpy on the other. He looked up in puzzlement at the Briton, who was grinning broadly.

"A bit of lead?" Maxian asked. The Briton nodded, taking it back. With one scarred hand, he cleared a space on the tabletop. Then he carefully took the bit of lead and dipped it in his wine cup. Even more carefully, he then pressed the bumpy end into the tabletop.

"Look," Mordius said, moving his hand away. Maxian leaned over and squinted down at the table in the poor light.

"An alpha," he said. A tiny, almost perfect, letter was scribed on the tabletop in dark wine.

The Briton nodded.

"Joseph and his sons made hundreds of them from lead scrap, all of the letters of the alphabet, even all the numbers. Each little peg was scored at the flat base, so that they could slide into a copper slat to hold them straight. Seventy slats per frame, each frame made of wood with a backing. Each frame a whole page of letters." The Briton paused a moment, watching Maxian's face closely.

Maxian stared at him in dumbfounded astonishment. After just a moment fear replaced astonishment, and then a universe of possibilities unfolded before him. He sat back stunned, unable to speak. Mordius reached out, turned over the wine-cup, and then filled it. The Briton pushed it toward Maxian's hand, which of itself moved, took the cup, and brought it to his lips.

After a time, Maxian could speak. "And then what happened?"

The Briton shrugged. "There were troubles, of course. Papyrus was no good to use with the frames; the scrolls kept splitting when they were pressed against it. None of the inks used with a brush or quill would stick right to the lead and they smeared anyway. The frames were awkward and really no faster than a trained scribe to use. Joseph and Menacius and their families labored for weeks to solve the problems. That was what had led Joseph to the mill and the weavers. He was looking for something that would make a better writing surface than papyrus. His sons had found that there were fine-grained woods that would hold the ink and fine linens that were flexible enough not to split when the frames were pressed upon them.

"By this time I was a partner in the enterprise, though they kept the details to themselves. The deal that I struck was for the right to use the frame-scribe for my own business and to export books made with it to the north. A scroll is like gold there, there are so few, so I knew that my fortune was assured. One copy of

Plato or Sophocles could become a thousand copies, each easy to transport and worth a hundred times its own weight in silver.

"Only a month ago one of Joseph's sons came to me at the warehouse and bade me come and visit the shop that night. His father had finally solved the last puzzle. They were determined to make a clean copy of the Regulations that very night and do the rest of the lot over the following days. The deadline was very close and I know they must have been overjoyed.

"But when I arrived that night, the shop was shuttered and dark. I knocked and knocked, but no one came to the door. At last a neighbor saw me in the street and told me that they had all gathered for a late-afternoon meal and none had gone out. Fearing that something was wrong, I forced the door—no easy task at a jeweler's shop!—and went inside. I was back out again in minutes, gagging at the smell and the sights I saw within. They, of course, were all dead amid the clutter of their meal."

Maxian, unbidden, felt a great pressure upon him, seemingly from the air all around him. For a moment he was back in the dim kitchen in Ostia, dragging Dromio onto the table, pleading for his friend to hold on just a little longer. Trembling, he drank again from his cup. The eyes of the Briton, hooded, were on him.

"I have seen much the same," the Prince said, his voice weak. "Like loaves of bread."

"The neighbor saw me, of course," Mordius continued, "and ran out of his house. I gasped something about them all being dead and the smell. He thought it was the plague and ran off shouting. Within minutes half of the neighborhood was in the street with buckets and torches. The *vigiles* came, but could not reach the house for the press of the crowd. The shout of *plague, plague* was like a drumbeat. They burned it, the whole house and the ones on either side, to keep the plague from them. I fled, knowing that I would be next on that pyre.

"I went back a few days ago. There was nothing left, only the burned-out shell of the house and, in the ashes, a few of those, unmelted. I took that one as a souvenir, but nothing else. I account myself lucky that my visits were few and I knew little of their work. I am alive."

Maxian stared at the little lead token on the table. He scratched his beard. That odd feeling was back, tickling at the edge of his perception. "No one else now, save you and I, know of what they had devised. No other scribes, no officials?"

Mordius nodded. "I thought the same thing. But these Jews are a secretive lot and they do not talk to strangers, particularly Roman ones. Someone killed them, but who I cannot say. There would have been many who cursed their names, if they had been successful, but now they are unknown."

"What are you going to do?"

The Briton snorted, putting his cup down. "Leave. Go back to Britain and dig in the fields, I suppose. Fight with my father and my half brothers. The city has a cold feeling to it now, more so that I've told you. No good will come of this, I fear. Thank you for the wine." The gangly foreigner stood up, bending his head to avoid the low timbers of the ceiling.

"Thank you for telling me this," Maxian said, standing up straight. He dug in his purse and brought out two solidi, which he pressed into the Briton's hand. Mordius raised an eyebrow at the weight of the coins, then bowed. "My lord." Then he was gone, out into the sunshine in the street. Maxian stood by the table for a long time, looking down at the little lead slug. Finally, he picked it up and put it in his purse before going out himself.

As Maxian entered the great suite of rooms that formed the office of the Emperor of the West, an unaccustomed sound echoed over his head. The courtiers and supplicants who crowded the chambers arranged in front of the octagonal chamber that housed the secretary were nervous, shuffling their feet and talking in low tones. Passing by the pair of Praetorians at the doors of the octagonal room, he was startled to realize that one of the voices, raised in anger, was that of his brother, the Emperor. In the octagon, the Secretary was absent and all of the scribes were warily watching the half-open set of double doors that led into the inner chambers.

Maxian stopped and made a half turn. The nearest of the Praetorians turned his head a fraction, his eyes questioning. Maxian nodded at the doors to the waiting rooms. The two guards immediately closed them with a heavy thud. At this the scribes looked up, then hurried to resume work. Maxian walked among them, idly looking over the papers and scrolls that littered their desks. After a moment he found the senior man. Dredging at his memory, he recovered the man's name.

"Prixus, everyone here can take a break to the triniculum and get a late meal. Go on."

Prixus bobbed his head and began putting away his pens, ink stone and other assorted items. The other scribes, seeing him, began to do likewise. Maxian continued to the double doors, quietly closing them behind him after he had entered. Within, a cluster of men blocked his view of the apartment that Galen used as his office, but another voice, strong and clear, had joined the argument.

"Caesar, I disagree. This policy of recruitment is open to abuse at all levels. Here before you stand loyal men who can raise as many legionnaires as this levy at half the cost, and these men are already trained in war."

Maxian edged around the back of the room. At least twenty men, all senators or knights crowded the chamber, and many were officers in the Legions. This was unexpected—after seven centuries the ban remained, barring the Legions from the precincts of the capital. In the middle of the room stood an elderly figure: Gregorius Auricus, the man known as "the Great." Garbed in a clean white toga of fine wool, the magnate looked every inch the Senator that he was by right of birth. A mane of fine white hair was combed behind his head, and his craggy face was calm and composed. Across the green Tarpetian marble desk from him, Galen stood as well, his face clouded with anger. The Emperor had chosen to wear the light garb of a Legion commander, a deep-maroon tunic with gold edging, laced-up boots, and a worn leather belt. The gladius that usually hung from that belt was on the desk, pushed to one side by a great collection of scrolls, counting tokens, and pens.

"What you propose, Gregorius, is against the laws of the Empire, the Senate, and the people." Galen's words were clipped and short—a sure sign of anger. "The relation of the Empire to the *fedoratii* is well defined, and they are used only as *auxillia*, not as Legion-strength units. It has never been the practice of the Empire, nor will it be mine, to bring foreign armies, whole, into the service of the state. Further, you have stated, here and on the floor of the Senate, your opposition to the levy. I respect your position, but it is the will of the Empire to proceed in this manner."

Gregorius shook his head, turning to declaim to the nobles and officers who looked on from the edges of the room. "My friends, colleagues. This levy is a dangerous act. Its offer of manumission to any able-bodied slave or foreigner in the Empire in exchange for a mere ten years of service is a blow to the very foundations of the state. There are other ways to provide for the defense of the Empire in this dangerous time. I urge you to support me in pursuing these other means."

Galen stepped around the desk, and Gregorius stepped back, halting his incipient oration. The Emperor slowly surveyed the faces of all those assembled in the room. If he spied Maxian at the back of the room, he made no sign of it. At last, he turned back to the magnate, who had been a firm supporter of his rule since that blustery day in Saguntum nine years before. The two men locked gazes, and the tension in the room built a little higher.

Maxian continued to work his way around the periphery, for he had finally made out his brother Aurelian standing in a doorway on the far side. Galen began speaking again:

"We are here, Senators and officers, to discuss an expedition that has already been set in motion, to plan, to prepare for victory. The Senate has already voted to allocate funds for the relief of the Eastern Empire. This expedition is crucial, not only to the beleaguered East, but to ourselves as well."

A mutter went up in the back of the room, though Maxian only caught a fragment: ". . . the East rot!"

Galen heard the whole statement, and his face darkened further.

"We speak of a Roman East, fool. Half the extent of our great Empire, the half that holds nearly two-thirds of the citizens of our realm. It is easy for us in the West to forget the long watch the East has kept, holding back the Persians and their allies, providing grain to the great cities of Italia. While we struggled in the West to drive back the Franks and the Germans, the East stood by us. Gold, men, and arms came to us. Now they are at the precipice. Persia seeks not just tribute but conquest, to drive their frontier to the Mare Internum, to seize Egypt itself."

Another murmur rose, this one at the edge of laughter. Galen slapped his hand on the green tabletop, the sound echoing like a slingshot.

"Do you venerate the memories of your fathers? Do you sacrifice to the gods of your household?" He turned, his gaze baleful and filled with venom. "You dismiss the Persians as 'trouser-wearing sybarites,' unfit to take the field of honor against a Roman army. You do not think they threaten us. You are twice the fools to count a man a coward and a weakling because he wears pants of silk. The Persian has smashed four Roman armies in the past three years. He stands at the brink of success, all brought by his strength of arms.

"But I think he has heard your insults. Yes, even in the East, the nonsensical maundering of the Senate is dissected and considered. Our enemy has found new friends to help him against us. The King of Persia accounts necromancers, sorcerers, dead-talkers, and alchemists among the tools that he raises against us."

The room suddenly grew very quiet. Maxian paused. He had never heard this before.

"Yes," Galen said, a grim smile on his face. "This time, when the Persian comes, he will come with dark powers at his command. Ever before the Persian Kings acted with honor, eschewing the malignant tools of the magi. Now he cares only for one thing—victory and the defeat of Rome. The tombs of your fathers will be despoiled and broken open. You will fight against your dead brothers, and their cold hands will clutch at your throat . . ."

Maxian tuned out the polemic of his brother, finally shouldering his way past two pasty-faced regional governors to reach Aurelian's side. His brother clapped him fondly on the shoulder and nodded toward the closed door that stood behind him. Maxian nodded in agreement and the two slipped through into the private chamber. The door, a heavy oak panel carved with a two-part scene of the victory of Septimus Severus over the Arabs, closed with a muffled thud. Blessedly, it cut off the angry rhetoric from the council room.

"Ah!" Aurelian sighed in delight, collapsing into a pile of cushions and pillows on the couch against the opposite wall of the little room. "Is there any wine left in that basket?" he asked. Maxian poked through the wicker basket set on the little marble ledge inside the door. Afternoon light slanted through the triangular panes of the high window set into the wall to the right.

"No, only some bread, cheese, and a sausage." While he talked, Maxian's nimble fingers had found a knife and were cutting a circular hole in the end of the loaf. Cheese followed, and chunks of sausage, to fill up the cavity he gouged out. When he was done, he cut the loaf in half and tossed the lesser piece to his brother on the couch.

"Piglet!" Aurelian laughed. "You've taken the larger."

Maxian nodded, though his mouth was too busy biting the end off the loaf to speak. He felt exhausted and hungry, though he had eaten several hours before, when he had left his apartment in the palace on the southern side of the hill. Despite this, Aurelian was licking crumbs off his fingers before Maxian was even half done. Finished at last and thirsty, Maxian stood up and walked to a bronze flute that stood up from the floor near the door. He uncapped the end and shouted down it, "Wine!" When the flute-pipe made an unintelligible muttering back at him, he recapped it. Then he took up the other couch, opposite Aurelian.

"So," Aurelian said, with a knowing look on his face, "I hear from reliable sources that you spent the night, not so long ago, with a certain raven-haired Duchess. Was she as magnificent as all reports indicate?"

Maxian stared at his brother for a moment, digesting this statement, then he laughed.

"After the party at De'Orelio's? She was quite entertaining that night, true, but I did not sample her myself. The wine was of exceptional quality and I arrived tired, so a slave helped me to bed and to sleep. The Duchess and I have gone over that ground before—though I mean no disrespect to the Lady, she is really too old for my taste."

"You slept?" Aurelian asked in disgust. "The reports in the Forum are far more entertaining than you, piglet. By the account of reliable, sober and upstanding Senators, you were engaged in an orgiastic celebration with no less than the Duchess, her ward, and a tangle of every other lad, lass, and goat in the villa. Why, old Stefronius assured me that the decadence of the notorious Elagabalgus was as nothing compared to your soldiering among the youth of the city . . ."

Aurelian was laughing so hard that he could not even dodge the heavy pillow that Maxian threw at him. Maxian sighed and leaned back on the couch.

"What is Galen arguing with Gregorius about?" he asked, hoping to divert the gossip-hungry Aurelian from the subject at hand.

"Oh, the levy, the supplies for the expedition to Constantinople, the weather, everything. They've been at it for three hours now. Neither is willing to budge a finger's worth—and *worse*, each is absolutely sure that he is in the right."

"Why not just issue the edicts and be done with it? The Emperor has proposed, the Senate has voted . . ."

Aurelian threw the pillow back, though Maxian neatly caught it with one hand and tucked it behind his head. His brother fluffed his beard with one hand, thinking a moment. Then:

"Galen, despite the good state of the fisc, does not want to bear the cost of the expedition solely from the coffers of the state. He summoned all those 'well-respected' men out there to extort from them the coin, the bread, the arms, the armor, and most important, the *ships* to carry his sixty thousand veterans to the East. Gregorius knows that, and knows that as he is the richest man in Rome, if he refuses to pay then Galen is in a tight spot. He wants an *arrangement*, but it is not one that Galen will give."

Maxian looked perplexed, saying "Gregorius has always supported us, he was a friend of father's, for Apollo's sake. What would he want that Galen cannot give?"

"Not 'cannot,' piglet, but 'will not.' Gregorius wants to arrange grants of citizenship for some of his clients—the ones who have made him so rich. He also wants to 'help' out with the expedition by mustering his own Legions, six of them to be exact, from those same clients. He is even, in his graciousness, willing to arm, equip, and train the lot of them."

Now Maxian was even more amazed than he had been earlier in the afternoon.

"Gregorius has enough money to field almost fifty thousand legionnaires?" He sputtered. "Where in Hades did he find that many able men in the Empire? Galen has had to hatch this dubious levy to get that many in arms!"

Aurelian nodded slowly then said, "Gregorius is not considering just men in the Empire."

Maxian's head snapped up, a look of suspicion on his face. "And where *does* he intend to get these men?"

Aurelian nodded to the north, past the pale-green reeds and marsh-doves painted on the walls. "From the tribes still beyond the border, those that have not settled in their own principates, towns, cities, and duchies. To join their fellows who live among us now."

"The *Goths?*" Maxian found himself on his feet, shouting. Aurelian remained recumbent on the sofa, nodding. "And the Lombards, and Franks, and a bevy of other footless bands, all looking for a slice off of the big wheel of cheese. Gregorius argues, and here it is hard to fault him, that the Goths are staunch friends and allies of the state. They have fought at our side for almost a hundred years, but by the same treaties that bind them to us, and we to them, they are *not* Roman citizens. They hold lands in the name of the Emperor, but they are a subject state. Many of the Gothic Princes are welcomed at Gregorius' house and they repay him, and his patronage in the city, with an easy way beyond the frontier. Gregorius Magnus did not become as rich as he is by ignoring opportunities, but I think, as does Galen, that he is beginning to run out of favors to pay them off with. Now they want to become citizens, and this is one way for them to get that."

"They could serve, individually, in the Legions and gain the same status," Maxian pointed out.

"Many do, but more want to serve together, which has been against the law for over eight hundred years. And if fifty thousand of them showed up at once, we wouldn't be recruiting them, we'd be fighting them and Gregorius would be Emperor instead of our beloved brother. Gregorius thinks that together they are invincible in battle."

Maxian sniffed at that, but Aurelian held up an admonishing finger. "Check the rolls of the Legion sometime, piglet. Almost half of our current soldiers are German or Gothic. They are fierce fighters and they can be very loyal."

"The Legions have always been loyal to the state," Maxian shot back.

"True. But Galen does not want to test that proverb. That is another reason why he wants to install the levy—to gain more legionnaires who are *not* German."

Maxian's retort was lost in the oak door opening and a slave entering with the wine. A pretty brunette in a short tunic, she placed the amphora on the marble ledge and took the wicker basket away. After she was gone, Maxian realized that his brother was laughing again.

"You need a wife, or better, a bevy of concubines, piglet. I'd swear that you didn't hear a single word I said while she was in this room."

Maxian blushed and snarled something unintelligible at his brother. He got up and poured two goblets of wine, this a dusky red Neapolitan by the smell. He swirled the grape in the goblet and tasted it—excellent! He passed the other glass to Aurelian, who drank it straight off. Maxian sighed at the indifference of his brother to the subtlety of the vintage. The door opened again, and this time Galen entered, slamming the heavy panel behind him. The two younger brothers watched in silence as the Emperor paced icily from one end of the little room to the other.

Finally, after almost ten minutes, he looked up and seemed surprised to find the two of them in the chamber with him.

"Oh. I wondered where the two of you had gotten to. My apologies. Is there any wine?"

Maxian poured another glass and handed it over to his brother. Galen's high temper was visibly ebbing as he finally sat down and drank the wine in two short swallows. Maxian and Aurelian both continued to sit, their faces impassive as the Emperor sorted through his thoughts in the quiet.

Galen put the glass back on the ledge, turning to Aurelian. "Aurelian, as we had discussed before, the Senate is voting you to hold the office of Consul while I am gone. Nerva Licius Commodus, who is holding the other consular office, will be going with me, so we shall fill the other with Maxian here. I trust both of you, though not necessarily anyone else in the city, so be careful. The Senators are a little restless over this campaign in the East and will doubtless bend the ears of both of you while I am gone."

Aurelian nodded in agreement, though his open face showed how pleased he was at the prospect.

Galen smiled, a little tight smile, and ran a hand through his short hair. "Maxian, you are the linchpin of this whole effort in the East. I had considered taking you with me—a campaign would be beneficial to your education—but someone has to maintain the *telecast* here so that I can be informed of any developments in the West. The device will be brought up from the Summer House within the next week, in secret, and installed in my rooms. Aurelian will handle the day-to-day business, but you need to keep an eye on the men who were in that room with me."

Maxian rubbed his face, feeling the beard stubble. He did not like his brother's emphasis on the word *education*, for it implied that his long period of freedom was at an end. For the last six years, since they had come to the city in triumph, his brothers had carefully excluded him from the business of the state. This had been the wish of both their mother and their father, who saw for him a different path, that of the healer-priest. With Galen in the East, such liberty was at an end. Oddly, he did not feel outraged or angry at the presumption of his brother, but rather more comfortable, like a familiar cloak had been draped, at last, around his shoulders.

"Brother, if I do not mistake you, you want me to take over the network of informers and spies maintained by the Offices? Is this not the domain of the Duchess de'Orelio?"

Galen looked at his younger brother for a moment, his face pensive. "De'Orelio has always supported us, little brother, as has Gregorius and the other nobles. But in times such as these, when great events are in motion, the solid earth may be sand, the old friend an enemy. Given these things, I desire that you should begin assembling a separate set of informers and spies loyal to us."

Maxian bowed his head in acceptance. Galen continued to brood, his face grim and his manner distant.

"Within the month," he said, "the Legions in Spain and southern Gaul will arrive at Ostia Maxima and I will join them. I shall sail east with them, and join the others at Constantinople. Then Heraclius and I will begin our expedition. We shall have victory, and peace."

Maxian shook his head in puzzlement, saying, "Again you mention that *peace* shall come of this, brother. You are taking a great gamble, to throw yourself and the Emperor of the East into the heart of Persia. Even with this great army you may still be defeated. You may die. Both halves of the Empire may lose their Emperors. This will not be peace but civil war again, and the barbarians will still storm against the walls of Constantinople. Would it not be more prudent to clear the invaders from Thrace, Greece, and Macedonia? Then the full weight of the Empire could turn against the Persians in Syria and Palestine."

Galen laughed and his eyes were bright with some secret knowledge. "Cautious! So cautious, piglet. You are right, such a campaign would restore the borders of the Empire and drive the enemy back. But that is what the 'cautious' Emperors of Rome have done since the time of the Divine Augustus. None of their efforts has brought peace, only a little delay in the next war. The great Emperors—Julius Caesar, Trajan, Septimus Severus—they won peace by the destruction of their enemies. We will do them one better, we will take nearly a hundred thousand Romans into the heart of our ancient enemy and destroy not only their capital but their state. Persia, all of Persia, will become a Roman domain, not just an edge of it, but all. Then, then there will be a true peace in the East and over the whole of the world."

Galen paused, and now he seemed refreshed, even ebullient again. The grim and distant manner was gone; instead he poured more wine for all three of them.

"Nike!" he said, raising his cup to the goddess of victory. "And a Roman peace."

Maxian drained his cup, but there was no peace in his heart.

Though he had lived in the sprawling maze of the Palatine for six years, Maxian was still unable to find the offices of the Duchess, though he thought that they were somewhere in one of the buildings on the northern face of the hill. At last, having wound up again in the sunken garden on the eastern side of the hill, he approached one of the gardeners laboring over the replacement of tiles. The garden, built over five hundred years ago by the reviled emperor Domitian, was laid out in the shape of a race course. Great bushes, carefully tended, were crafted into the shape of rearing horses and chariots. At the north end there was a pool and around it ancient tiles, now cracked. The gardener, dressed in a muddy tunic and laced-up cotton leggings, was half in and half out of the pool, wrestling a replacement tile into place. Maxian paused and bent down at the edge of the tile border. The gardener, grunting, heaved at his pry bar and the tile, backed with concrete, at last shifted with a grinding sound and slid into place. The workman leaned heavily on the length of iron and looked up, his eyes shrouded by bushy white eyebrows.

"Friend, if you have a moment, I've a question," the Prince said. "I'm seeking the offices of the Duchess de'Orelio."

The gardener frowned and spit into the pool. "You're far off course," he said.

"The Duchess, though a generous woman to the less fortunate, is of a questionable position in the offices. Though she visits often, she has no 'place' here. If you wish to speak to her, you'll have to go to her townhouse over by the Aquae Virgo. Do you know the way?"

Maxian stood up, brushing leaves and dirt from his knees. "I do," he said. "Many thanks."

Back in the maze of hallways, Maxian made his way south, finally reaching the long curving arcade that ran along the southern face of the Palatine. Here the way was thronged with officials, scribes, and slaves. Here too was the office of the chamberlain of the palace, and Maxian strode in with a confident air. Of all of the palace officials, Temrys knew him by sight. Apparently, so did the chamberlain's secretary, who paused in his instruction to two other scribes at the appearance of the Prince.

"Milord! Do you need to see the chamberlain?" The secretary's face was a study in surprise and not a little apprehension. Inwardly, this evidence of power cheered Maxian.

"If he is not overly busy," Maxian said, clasping his hands behind his back.

"One moment, sir." The secretary bustled away, back into the maze of cubicles and tiny rooms that were the warren and domain of Temrys and his minions. The two junior scribes, at last making out the profile of the visitor and the cut of his garb, sidled away and disappeared. Maxian smiled after them. A moment later the secretary reappeared and bowed to the Prince, indicating the way into the rear rooms.

Temrys' private office was only twice the size of that of his subordinates, though he had it to himself rather than sharing as they did. The chamberlain rose as the secretary showed Maxian into the low-ceilinged room. Of middling height and lean in body, the Greek was most notable for his pockmarked face and general air of sullen resignation. Today, Maxian noted, he was dressed in a dark-gray and charcoal-black tunic with a muddy brown belt and boots. Coupled with thinning gray hair and narrow lips, he did not make a dashing figure.

"Lord Prince," the chamberlain muttered, gesturing to a low backless chair that sat at the side of his desk. Temrys sat, hunching in his own curule chair, his face blank.

Maxian removed a pile of scrolls and placed them on the floor. He too sat, smiling genially at the older man. "Chamberlain Temrys. My esteemed eldest brother has directed me to assist my older brother in the governance of the state during the coming absence of the Emperor. I find that I do not have the facilities, that is—an office and a secretary—to undertake these tasks. So I come to you, the most knowledgeable and experienced of the civil service to provide these things to me."

Temrys' frown deepened for a moment, then, unaccountably, lightened. He straightened up a little in his chair, cocking his head at the Prince. "An office? Space can certainly be provided to you. I am puzzled, however, that your brother, the Caesar Aurelian, will not be using the Augustorum and you, in turn, his own offices. They come well equipped, I assure you, with scribes, secretaries, slaves, messengers, all manner of staff."

"I know! I need something more . . . private. Something out of the way, where things are quieter and more at ease."

Temrys almost smiled at that, but the mask of his face did not slip. "Of course, my lord, it will be done at once. I know the perfect place. It will take some days to prepare. Shall I send a messenger to you when it is ready?"

Maxian stood, smiling again, and bowed very slightly to the chamberlain.

"That would be perfect," he said. "Thank you."

Walking out, with the now-unctuous Chamberlain at his elbow, Maxian noted the sidelong glances of the secretaries and scribes in the warren of rooms. *How can anyone work in such a place*, he wondered to himself, *with every eye watching you at all times?*

He stopped at the door, thanking Temrys, and then strode off down the hallway. His lips quirked in amusement. *I will never use those offices*, he thought, *but it will divert attention for a little while.*

Cool water closed with a sharp splash over Maxian's head as he dove into the great pool that graced the open-air *notatio*. Dolphinlike he darted through the water, turning over and seeing, for a moment, the wavering light of the sun far above, through the water. The cunningly tiled floor of the pool flashed past as well, all porpoises and mermaids in blue and green and pale yellow. A moment later his head broke the surface at the far end of the pool. He climbed out, exhilarated. Around him, dozens of other swimmers splashed in the cool blue waters or sat talking on the benches under the arches. He stood, dripping, on the mosaic floor and pondered whether to return to the pool and swim laps or to seek a masseuse for a scrape and a rubdown.

"Sir?" One of the *balanei* had come up. Maxian nodded in greeting at the boy, seeing that he was dressed in the attire of the bath attendants.

"A distinguished gentleman begs a moment of your time, if you will join him in the steam room?"

"All right," Maxian said, a little wary. "Can you summon a *tractator* to join us as well? My shoulders are still sore and tight."

The slave bowed and hurried off. Maxian made his way to the *caldarium* across the great vaulting central chamber of the bath building. Above him doves and wrens flitted in the vast open space under the roof of the *cella soliaris*. He passed through an atrium occupied by arguing Greeks and their attendants. Within, the air was thick with moisture and heat. He paused for a moment in the dimness. The huge room, barrel shaped, soared above him. The air was filled with billowing steam, making it almost impossible to see.

"Over here," came a voice from the back of the room. Maxian descended the short flight of steps onto the raised wooden floor. Steam hissed up from the floor below as water flowed in from pipes under the platform. The heat felt delightful after the chilly pool. Sitting on a bare step at the back of the chamber was a familiar figure, even wreathed in steam. A conspicuous space had been cleared around the old man, though the *caldarium* was so large that there was no lack of benches.

"Ave, Gregorius Auricus," Maxian said, settling into the warm seat.

"Ave, Maxian Caesar," the magnate replied, dipping his head in greeting. Maxian frowned at the honorific. Gregorius, his eyes bright even in the gloom, nodded. "It is one of your titles now, you will have to get used to it."

"I suppose. It does not seem to be right, somehow, that I should bear the titles of my brothers. Not fitting, in a way."

Gregorius sighed, rubbing his thin arms. "Your brothers have taken a great deal of trouble, over the past years, to follow the wishes of your mother. They have carried the burden of the Empire themselves, letting you follow the path that your gifts led you on." He reached out and took Maxian's hand, turning it over, running his callused old fingers over the Prince's young, smooth palm and thumb.

"If Lucian Pius Augustus had not been stricken by the plague, you would be the most revered member of your family today. And you would still be in Narbonensis, doubtless spending your days walking from mountain village to mountain village, tending to the sick and the poor, as your mother hoped."

Maxian smiled at the pastoral image. "I would like that," he said.

Gregorius shook his head, saying, "You will never see it. You have a different purpose now. I caught sight of you the other day, when your esteemed brother and I were arguing in the Offices. I heard afterward that the Senate had acclaimed you Caesar and Consul, to rule at your brother Aurelian's side while the Augustus Martius Galen is away, in the East."

"It is so," Maxian said slowly, wondering what favor or proposition the old man would put to him now.

Gregorius smiled slowly at him. "You must learn to guard your expression more closely, young Caesar, I can all but read the thought in your look. No, I do not want anything from you today. What I want is but a moment of your time. I have known you, your brothers, your family, for many years. I do not know if you remember, but when you were young and your father came to the city, he would ofttime stay with me in my family's house on the Coelian Hill. On at least one occasion, he brought you to see the Circus, I believe. The ostriches frightened you. Your father was a friend of mine, and you know well that I supported your brother in his campaign against the pretenders.

"I say this to you not to gain your favor but to show you that I have always supported your family, your father, your brother. Martius Galen is a good Emperor. Perhaps the best we have been blessed with in the West since the Divine Constantine. He is cautious in his policies, frugal with the assets of the state. He is just and impartial in his judgments. He appoints with an eye to merit and not to wealth or personal gain. He does not confiscate the estates or possessions of the Senators. In all, a most able and practical ruler. The temples are well blessed with his presence."

Gregorius paused, sighing deeply. His old face was lined with concern. "Yet at the same time, he is a man, and men are often blind in some manner. I know that you must have remarked yourself from time to time on the precariousness of the Western Empire. Our population is scant following the plague. Our own people are weak, given to idleness and sloth. Have you not noticed, in your work, how

frail our people seem, in comparison to the German, the Briton, or the Goth?"
Gregorius waved at the mist and the other men taking their ease in the baths.

"In a crowd of a hundred, you can tell each man's nation by his appearance—
the Roman is short, with poor skin and an unhealthy pallor. The Briton is tall
and fair, abrim with health. The German the same, the Goth another, save gifted
with great strength. I have many clients, as you doubtless know. They come to
me to discuss their troubles and their successes. First among the lament of the
Roman is the death of his children, his heirs, from disease, or weakness or accident.
The Goth deplores the state of his finances but rejoices in the strong children
born to him. It is a terrible shame, but I have had to repopulate whole farms, or
fabricae here in the city, with freedmen of Briton or German blood."

Maxian stared at him in undisguised horror. The bloodlines of the rural patricians were as jealously guarded as the Vestals.

"Yes, I see the look on your face—yet there was no other way! The blood of
my cousins had grown too weak to sustain itself. It pained my senatorial heart to
adopt these people from beyond Italy as my sons and daughters. I am old and I
have seen a great deal in my life, but this frightens me the most, the deterioration
of the Roman people. The state cannot hope to stand when there are none to
support it. New blood must be inducted to the body of the people, to sustain the
Empire. Is this not so in the East?

"There are many different nations given citizenship there. Here the boon of
citizenship is so carefully guarded . . . What I have asked of your brother is nothing
less than accepting the Gothic people, and the friendly Germans, and the loyal
Britons, into our state as equals. I have spoken to many, many of their dukes,
headmen, and chiefs. They are a loyal people—have they not fought beside Rome
for the last three centuries? They should be rewarded for that, at least."

Maxian pursed his lips, considering the issue. Gregorius had a valid point. At
last he said, "Each man may seek his own way into the service of the Empire and
thence to citizenship. Such has it been for a long time."

Gregorius nodded in acknowledgment but replied, "So it has always been, but
that is no longer a suitable response. What of the carpenter who labors for the
state? What of the matron whose husband has died, yet she struggles on, raising
ten children by herself? The children in turn may serve the state and become
citizens, yet she cannot. Is there justice in this? When the Romans were a strong
people, it made good sense; now it does not. I know that I cannot convince your
brother of this, and rest easy, I shall give him the ships, the money, the supplies
that he needs. I agree that the Eastern Empire must be aided. There will always
be disagreements, even among friends."

The *tractator* arrived and Maxian signaled to him. Turning to the Senator,
he said: "Thank you for your words, and thank you for supporting our family in
the past. It means a great deal to me, as it did to my father. So that you understand
clearly, I do not always agree with my brother, but I will always support him. Good
day, sir."

Gregorius nodded, with a little smile on his face, resting his hands on the
head of his walking stick.

"A good day to you as well, young Maxian. Oh, one thing before you go. A client of mine, a Briton named Mordius Arthyrrson, came to see me yesterday. He said that he was returning home and giving up his share of his family's business here in the city. This was troubling to me, though I wished him well. He was a fellow of good promise. He also said that he had talked to you about what had happened. I did not press him about it, for other of my men had told me the tale already. I think that you should know that this is not the first time that this sort of thing has happened."

Maxian stared at the old man for a moment, then nodded and went out.

OSTIA MAXIMA, THE COAST OF LATIUM

The staccato of drums echoed off the brick buildings facing the great harbor of Trajan. Thyatis turned, shading her eyes against the late-afternoon sun as it slanted in golden beams through the remains of the rainclouds. Hundreds of ships, riding at anchor in the mile-wide hexagon of the Imperial Harbor, lit up, their colored sails gleaming in the perfect light. Seagulls circled overhead in the cool rain-washed air, cawing. Apollo and his chariot were preparing to descend beyond the western rim of the world in glorious display. The rainclouds were lit with purple and gold and reds in a thousand hues. A fresh breeze had sprung up, carrying the deep smell of the sea to her. The funk of the harbor was blown away, and with it the stinks of the city behind her.

"A beautiful sunset," Anastasia said from the comfort of her litter.

"It is," Thyatis said as she knelt on the pier next to her patron. She fingered the hilt of her sword, thinking of the endless leagues that would soon be between her and her patron. Beyond the handful of men that she was taking with her, she would be entirely alone in the East. She looked up, seeing the calm violet eyes of her mistress. Only confidence and strength were reflected there. Thyatis' spirits rose and a core of determination began to accrete within her.

"Your supplies are already loaded?" the Duchess asked.

"Yes, milady, everything that Nikos and I could think of, plus more besides. The men are already aboard, most sleeping or reading."

Anastasia smiled. "They are soldiers, after all."

Gently she took the hand of the young woman. Seeing her now, clad in dull raiment, a heavy cloak, and worn boots, with her hair tied back and with no makeup, Anastasia realized that she had begun to grow attached to her ward. This troubled her greatly, for she had long considered the last daughter of the Clodians to be only a possibly useful tool. The remnants of her anger over the failure of her stratagem to ensnare the youngest Atrean Prince passed away. Laughing a little, she let go of Thyatis' hand.

"Go with good fortune," she said, making the sign of Artemis to bid her well.

Thyatis rose, bowing. "And you, my Lady." Then she turned, her hair glittering in the last rays of the sun, and went aboard the ship. Anastasia watched her ascend the gangplank and go forward to speak to the captain. The sailors began to untie the mooring ropes and unfurl the sail. The tide was beginning to run out.

At last, with the purple of night spilling over the harbor, the Duchess tapped on the top of the litter, indicating it was time to go.

Krista blinked and stirred beside her. "Time to go home, mistress?" Her voice was sleepy.

"Yes, dear, time to go home."

The slaves had roused themselves as well and picked up the litter poles with well-practiced ease, sliding it easily aloft. Then they trotted off down the street. The western horizon was a long smear of deep rose and streaks of gold. In the litter, Anastasia leaned against the frame, staring out at the dark houses as they jogged past on the road to the city. One long finger folded the corner of her shawl over and over, running the sharp edge against her thumb.

I hope she comes home alive, she thought, letting a dram of the sadness that filled her seep out.

THE PALATINE HILL, ROMA MATER

It was full dark when Maxian returned from the Forum. He was tired and his temper had not improved with a long afternoon spent listening to Senators droning on about the will of the gods and the assurances of the oracles that the Emperor's campaign in the East would go well. Of late, he had been sleeping badly, with strange dreams troubling his few hours of rest. Despite his eldest brother's admonitions to take up the burden previously carried by de'Orelio, he had not done so.

As he had planned, he had visited the offices provided him by Temrys twice, smiled at their ostentatious décor and then left. The official staff and their careful watchfulness made the rooms useless for his task. He knew that Aurelian expected his aid and assistance, but instead his thought returned again and again to the dead craftsmen. He fingered the little lead slug in his pocket as he climbed the stairs to his apartments. He was accustomed to leaning heavily on the undefined "feelings" that were the tool-in-trade of the healer and the sorcerer. The feel of the matter of the scribes reminded him too much of both that dreadful night in Ostia and the experience in the temple at Cumae.

There were forces at work beyond normal sight. He could almost discern them, walking in these ancient hallways. When the palace was almost deserted, as it was now with the Emperor and much of his court gone to Ostia and the great fleet, with only the sputter of the lanterns and the occasional sight of a slave dusting or mopping the floors, Maxian could feel the weight of the years and the tragedies that had occurred here. From the corner of his eye, if he was careful not to look, the shades of those that had lived here and died here could almost be seen. When he had been younger and had first come here, they had been welcome; the dim outlines of old men, clean-shaven, fierce and proud. Those were the strongest, those who had ruled here in the long centuries of the Empire. Now, with his skills grown and matured, he could sometimes see the others—those who had died in violence, those who had died in childbirth, those who had wept, or laughed, or loved here. Even the stones whispered, trying to tell their stories.

He stopped at the entrance to his apartments; a thin slat of pale-yellow light showed under the door. He had left with the dawn to accompany his brothers to the Forum; no taper or lantern had been lit then. He calmed himself, reaching inside to find the Opening of Hermes. Once he had done so, he drew the power of the nearest lamps to him, causing them to sputter and die. He placed a hand on the wall, feeling the room beyond. Three people waited within, none near the door. The room beyond was watchful, but not filled with anger or hostility. He tilted his head to one side, willing the sight away. It receded and he opened the door.

"Gentlemen," he said to the three people within. "I trust you have something of importance to say to me. It is late, and I am tired."

Gregorius Auricus nodded, standing to bow. At his side were two others; another of equal age, who Maxian realized with a start was the woman once known as Queen Theodelinda of the short-lived Lombard state. The Emperor Tiberianus had perished trying to drive her out of northern Italy. The other he did not know.

Gregorius gestured to his two companions, "the lady Theodelinda, an old friend of mine, and Nomeric, a fellow merchant, though he lives in Aquilea on the Mare Adriaticum."

Maxian nodded in greeting at each in turn. Theodelinda bowed and Nomeric nodded. The Prince put up his cloak and hat on pegs by the door and went into the small kitchen off the sitting room. The palace servants had delivered a tray of cold sliced meats, flat bread, cheese, and some little dried fish. A stoppered bottle of wine completed the dinner. Maxian picked up the tray and returned to the main room. Once he had seated himself and taken a draft of the wine, he picked up one of the fish and began chewing it. He gestured to Gregorius Magnus to have his say.

"Well, my lord Caesar, I apologize for intruding on your solitude here, but some things had occurred to me since our discussion at the baths and I thought that I should share them with you. We shall not take a great deal of your time. Theode' and Nomeric I brought so that you would know the extent of the trouble that is brewing. I account them both good friends, though as you see, neither is a citizen. Theode' was spared in the destruction of the Lombard state, accepting an amnesty and taking up residence in the hill-town of Florentia. I made her acquaintance through letters. Nomeric at one time was the chancellor of the *feodoratica* of Magna Gothica in upper Pannonia."

Maxian raised an eyebrow at this, for it was generally ill advised for members of the Imperial Household to be meeting at night in their chambers with high-ranking members of subject states, particularly Gothic ones. Gregorius, however, seemed to think that it was perfectly acceptable.

"Nomeric, of course," the old magnate continued, "no longer serves the Gothic king, having retired from that duty. He is a, well, how to put it . . . an ambassador without credentials to the Empire." Nomeric, who had been carefully saying nothing, his face placid, cracked a tiny smile at this.

Gregorius leaned forward on his walking stick. "I cannot expect that you will not pursue the matter of which we spoke earlier. In the course of such an investigation, you may find that you have need of monies that do not come from the Imperial purse. You may find that you need assistance, or help, or even protection. I have spoken with the lady, and with the gentleman, and they—and I—are willing to offer your our assistance, help, protection, and funds, if you will accept them."

Maxian finished the last of the cheese, putting down the little paring knife. He wiped his lips on the sleeve of his tunic and cocked his head, saying, "And in return, you expect that I will do what? Show you favors? Influence the law? Be the voice of your business concerns, your peoples, in the court? My brothers and I do not look favorably on those who attempt to bribe the officials of the state. Why, in fact, do you think that I will need help beyond that of the state?"

Gregorius stood up, hobbling a little on his ancient legs, and walked quickly to the door. For a long time he stood next to it, listening. Then suddenly he opened it and stepped out into the corridor. He looked both ways, then returned to his seat, shutting the door. Tiny beads of sweat dotted his brow. "My apologies, my lord Caesar, but I am overly cautious. Theode', tell him what you think is afoot."

Theodelinda glanced at Gregorius in concern, then turned back to Maxian. She had deep-blue eyes, almost the color of peat. Maxian struggled to focus his attention on her words rather than the thought of what she had looked like when young.

"My lord," she said, "after the death of my husband Agilulph at the battle of Padua, I was among the captives taken by the Emperor. We all expected to be slain out of hand or sold into slavery, but Martius Galen Augustus came among us and made an offer of amnesty to each man and woman that would forswear arms and reprisal against the state. Our gratitude was great, for we had come to your land as invaders and had hoped nothing less than to conquer Italy and make it our own. That the Emperor should show us some mercy made a great effect on me, even with the blood of my husband soaking my dresses. I took myself, along with those of my household who would follow me, and settled, as the venerable Gregorius has said, in the town of Florentia.

"It may surprise you, lord, but Florentia, while small, is a center of trade and manufacture. In particular we are very proud of our textiles and weaving. My people are clever with their hands and I was able to start anew, as the matron of a business rather than the ruler of a people. We have prospered. We are not citizens, but we believe deeply in the just law of the Empire. Our fathers were barbarians, living in wood and forest, but that is not what we want for our children.

"A strange thing has come to my attention, however. When we came to Florentia the textile *fabricae* there was not overly large, but it was doing well. The town bustled with business. Our settlement there, and our new business, only added to that. In the last years, however, we have attempted to better ourselves again, by adopting new practices suggested by my sons and daughters. All of these efforts have failed. Of my eleven sons and daughters, only two remain alive, and one is crippled by the fall of stones from the construction of the temple of Hephaestus.

"For a long time I was sure that these 'accidents' were the work of our rivals in the dyeing and weaving trades. But then I learned that the same kind of accidents had befallen the other families as well. At last, driven to extremes by the calamities, I went into the hills and sought out a wise woman who tends a shrine at Duricum. I spoke to her of our plight and she laughed, saying that I should go home and worship the gods in the manner of the fathers of the city. When I pressed her to explain, she pointed to my garments and said that if I dressed in the manner of the founders of the city, the accidents would stop."

Theodelinda halted for a moment and reached into a carrying bag that lay at her feet. From it she withdrew a length of cloth and passed it over to Maxian, who took it with interest. It was amazingly supple, with the finest weave that he had ever seen. A delicate pattern of images was worked into it. Unlike the moderately rough woolen gown and robe that the Lombard lady now wore, this was almost like silk.

"What is it?" Maxian asked, laying the cloth out over his knees. The feel of the fabric drew his fingers irresistibly.

"We call it *sericanum*, it is a weave and a fabric that my daughters devised after I managed to procure, with the help of Gregorius here, several bolts of finished silk. It is marvelously smooth, is it not? Almost like silk, but not quite. Of course, it is made from wool and flax rather than the dew caught in the leaves of the mulberry tree."

Maxian glanced up at the jest but saw that Theodelinda's eyes were filled with pain rather than humor.

"Your daughters are dead, then," the Prince said. The elderly lady nodded. "If I understand the thrust of this conversation, all of those who participated in the manufacture of this cloth are dead. Leaving you with almost nothing of what you started."

A great pain washed over Theodelina's face, but she said, "Only gold remains. I am still rich, though my house is empty."

"Is this all that remains of the cloth?" the Prince asked.

"No," said the quiet raspy voice of Nomeric. "That is from a new bolt of cloth. It was woven no less than four weeks ago. The weavers, at the last report, are still alive, even hale and hearty."

Maxian slowly turned, his eyebrow raised in question. The half-completed theory that he had been slowly working on shuddered in his mind, and various bricks threatened to fall out of it. "How, may I ask, did you accomplish that?"

Nomeric smiled and deferred to Gregorius. The old man coughed, then shook his head.

Nomeric steepled his fingers, gazing at the Prince over them. "The manufacture is in a holding of my family in Siscia. In Magna Gothica."

Maxian turned to Gregorius in puzzlement, saying, "I fail to see the connection."

Gregorius nodded and cleared his throat. "Siscia is the city the Goths built as their capital after the peace of Theodosius. It is a Gothic city, under Gothic rule, with Gothic law. It is, so to say, not a *Roman* city. There is no . . . Imperial presence there. Do you see my meaning?"

Maxian leaned back on his couch, rubbing the side of his face. With his other hand, he toyed with the length of cloth. He thought now that he saw what Gregorius was driving at. "By your logic, then, if the investment that our mutual British friend had made had been undertaken outside the borders of the Empire, it would have been . . . successful."

Gregorius nodded, tapping his walking stick on the mosaic floor in excitement. "That has been my thought for some time! You see then, my young friend, why you may need help from outside the state?"

Maxian nodded, lost in thought.

Gregorius and his companions left long after midnight. Maxian was even more exhausted than before, and now he sat on the edge of his bed, the room lit only by the light of a solitary wax candle. On the little writing desk next to the bed lay a package of items that he had gathered. He knew that he should wait until the next day, after he had slept, but the curiosity that had been gnawing at him would not let him wait. He unwrapped the cloth of the package; inside were several items—a swatch of the *sericanum* that Theodelinda had left, the tiny lead slug from the house of the scribes, a boat nail from Dromio's workshed in Ostia. Each thing he placed on the floor at the foot of the bed in an equal triangle, then he settled himself on a quilted rug from the chest. He considered calling for a servant to summon Aurelian to watch over him while he was meditating, but then put the thought away—his brother was busy enough and Maxian, really, had nothing to tell him yet.

He arranged himself, sitting cross-legged, and then began breathing carefully, in the manner that he had learned at the school in Pergamum. After a moment the room began to recede from his vision, then there was a sense of slippage and the vision of coarse stone and wood was gone. In its place dim shadows of the wall, the bed, the door remained, but each was an abyssal distance filled with the hurrying lights of infinitely minuscule fires. Maxian calmed himself further, letting his mind discard the illusions that his conscious mind forced upon the true face of the world.

All sense of matter was shed, leaving only these tiny rivers of fire tracing at impossible speeds the outlines of the chair, the writing desk, and the three things on the void-surface of the floor. Maxian focused his sight upon them, seeking to find their resonance. The lead slug expanded in his sight, becoming impossibly large. The whirling motes that formed its surface, to his first sight so heavy and solid, to his second a ghost, and now, to the third, nothing but emptiness filled with a cloud of fire, parted. There was a sudden sense of dissipation, and Maxian stumbled in that strange realm. Something beyond the matrix of the lead slug was suddenly drawing him, tugging at his perception and even his essential self.

Maxian willed his sight to fall back, to resume the greater vision apart from the distracting detail that formed the slug. Now he could see the resonance that echoed and impinged upon the tiny weight of lead. Wonder at first, and then a numbing horror, pervaded his consciousness. The slug, the cloth, the nail were the center of a maelstrom of forces. Dark energies of corruption and dissolution spiraled out from them, flaying at everything they touched. Now that he was aware, Maxian felt them pricking at his own core of being, like a cancer, eating away at his own strength and vitality.

A curse, he thought wildly, *some malefic power summoned by a great sorcerer! I must destroy these things immediately!* The urge was so strong that he almost cast off the meditation right there and ran with the objects out of the room. But his inner calm held, and Maxian realized with a start that his own thought and will were being bent by the forces that were collecting in the room. *Destroy them*, the vortex whispered, *smash them, burn them up*.

With a great effort, he called up the Shield of Athena, as had been taught him in his first days at the school of Asklepios in Pergamum. By this means, all dire forces could be turned away from the body of healers, allowing them to engage a diseased or corrupted form and perhaps, if they were very lucky and skilled, drive from it the deadly humors that arose in men and ate away at them from within. A shining band of blue-white flickered into being around him, struggling against and finally severing the tendrils of night-black that had been digging into his self. Immediately he felt better, his mind clearer, his thoughts ordered and his own again.

Now he made a curious discovery, seeing the strength arrayed against him. The three objects on the floor were not the source of the corrosion that still flashed and burned against the flickering blue-white shield. Rather they had drawn it, like a shark is drawn to blood in water or the wolf to the wounded in the flock. As he watched the weave of the cloth began to unravel, breaking down into single strands, then to wisps of fabric. *It will be utterly gone in a day or two*, the Prince thought, marveling at the power of this curse. Even the lead of the slug and the iron of the nail were deforming under the crushing power of the black tendrils. *What can give it such awesome strength?* A feeling of familiarity tugged at his thought, something he had seen before . . .

Ignoring the three tokens for the moment, Maxian gave his thought flight and rose up in vision through the wooden timbers that made the roof of his apartments, through the floors above and then into the night sky over the Palatine and the city. From this vantage, the city was a pulsing sea of light—the people, the buildings, the river, all shimmering with their own rivers of hidden fire. And through it all, Maxian was stunned to see the blue-black power rise, swirling around his rooms at the palace like a whirlpool. The curse rose from the very stones of the city, from the sleeping people, from the statues of the Forum and the sand on the floor of the Circus.

It is the city! he realized in awe. *The city is purging itself of an enemy, of a . . . a disease.*

That was what he had seen before in the third sight, the body collapsing upon a cancer and destroying it. *An invader, something inimical to the body.* His vision collapsed then, suddenly, and in less than a grain, he was lying on the floor of his room, bathed in sweat, his palms and forehead so hot as to burn.

THE ISLAND OF DELOS, THE AEGEAN THEME

Dwyrin woke to the wailing of slaves and the crack of the lash. His head had a strange, light feeling to it, but the riot of colors and space-bending distortions of vision were absent. He lay back on a smooth marble bench, feeling fully awake for the first time. His stomach growled with hunger and his mouth was parched, but he could think and see. A low vaulted ceiling stained with soot stood above him. Sore, he tried to move, but iron chains were shackled around his arms and legs. *This is not good*, he thought, peering around the room. A high window stood at the left, letting a shaft of sunlight in to light up the far wall. Through the window, he could see clear azure sky.

Other than the marble bench, the chains and the single door, the room was unremarkable. The window let in the echo of a busy marketplace, though to Dwyrin's ear there came no sound of animals, only a multitude of voices, most raised in despair and sorrow. Coupled with the regular sound of the lash, he realized that he had not dreamed the slave ship. *I have been sold into slavery*, he thought dully. *How will I finish my training? I have to escape from here.*

There was a rattle as the bar slid from its socket, and the door swung outward. Two men entered the small chamber, one a stout, muscular tub of a man in the leggings and tunic of a sailor. The other wore a toga and sandals, tall and thin with a crown of white hair plastered against his skull. The patrician came to stand by the marble bench and looked down upon Dwyrin with limpid blue eyes, almost the color of the sky through the window. His face was as lean as his body, with a delicate nose and eyebrows that wicked up against his forehead. Carefully the white-haired man examined Dwyrin's limbs, rolling back his eyelids and poking and prodding his extremities. The patrician kept his hands away from Dwyrin's mouth and was very cautious. When he was done, he stepped away from the bench and rubbed his chin thoughtfully.

"In good health, Amochis, though your finger marks are still on his neck. The drug is still in him, so he is safe to hold here for the moment. I see no sign, not that I truly expect it, of any 'magical' powers."

The sailor flushed at the dry sarcasm in the doctor's voice. "I saw what I saw, master, he threw fire from his hands and it killed one of my crew. Burned his head right off, it did, even under water." The sailor's voice was not angry yet but that was bubbling under the surface of his calm expression.

The doctor smiled, his thin lips creasing a little. "Do not take offense. I merely meant that I cannot write a certificate verifying that this boy is possessed of special *talents* beyond a pretty face and red hair."

Amochis frowned at this and hooked his thumbs into his belt strap, saying, "To prove it, you'd have to let the drug wear off, and then it might be you that has no head."

The doctor shrugged, having given his opinion.

"I will pass on my report to the Master of Merchandise, though I expect that you will only be able to sell him as a link-boy or house slave. As it stands, you should move him to one of the pens. It will be cheaper than keeping him here . . ." A thin-boned hand with carefully trimmed nails gestured to the bare walls.

So saying, the doctor left, ducking under the lintel of the door. Amochis stood for a moment in the center of the room, glaring at Dwyrin, who had not moved or spoken during the examination. Finally Amochis shook his head as if to clear the cloud of anger that was gathering around him and stomped out, muttering. Dwyrin caught a fragment about money. The door swung shut with a heavy clang and then the scrape of the bar being shoved home. Some time passed and the slat of light from the high window drifted across the far wall, creeping up until at last it disappeared and darkness filled the chamber. In all that time Dwyrin had lain still, listening to the constant murmur of people outside of the window. With a sick feeling in his stomach, he realized that there must be thousands of slaves outside, and hundreds of overseers.

He had heard of this place, at the school and before, when he was taken on the Imperial ship from his distant homeland to Egypt. He had come, by dreadful circumstance, to the island of Delos. The human stockyard of both the Eastern and Western empires. A tiny, almost barren island off the shore of Achaea, consisting entirely of the single largest slave market in the world. *Ten thousand slaves bought and sold per day*, part of his mind gibbered, *and you only the latest of them.* The slavers would never believe that he was part of the Emperor's levy. If they did believe the sailor, that he was a magician, he would either be killed out of hand as too dangerous to sell or auctioned to the powerful as a freak or an ornament. Tears forced themselves out the corners of his eyelids. If only he could summon the meditations or the entrance of Hermes, he could take these shackles off. But nothing came, the preternatural lightness in his head kept coming between his groping thought and the remembered shape of the power. Night deepened and at last he fell asleep, famished and exhausted.

When the light in the window brightened again, Dwyrin woke, groggy and with a splitting headache. The lightness in his mind was gone, however, and he fumbled to bring the meditations into focus. Hunger kept intruding on his thoughts and distracting him. At last, by digging a fingernail into his palm, he managed to focus enough to bring the first entrance into focus. It wavered, though, and his concentration kept slipping away, into realms of roasted lamb, or fresh grapes plucked from the vines in the village, or tart olives fresh from the brine. He struggled through this, finally managing to reach the clarity of vision that had allowed him to see the chain link on the ship. Slowly, with many stops and starts, he began examining each link in the chains that held him to the table. His neck throbbed with pain at the strain of keeping his head up so that he could see the heavy iron bands. None of them evinced the discoloration that the one on the ship had. He collapsed back onto the hard marble, gasping with effort.

Ra had crept up to almost the window itself when the door rattled and opened again. To Dwyrin a cold blast of ... something ... came through it. His skin flushed with goosebumps and he turned his head, almost afraid to see what had stepped so lightly through the doorway. In his partially restored over-sight he watched in fear as the timbre of the light flexed and dimmed. Strange flows of power licked around the room, crawling on the walls like indistinct spiders. A man entered the chamber, with Amochis in tow. He was gray, and of middling height. He was plainly dressed, in a small dark-colored felt cap, a long cape and shirt, with a dark-brown tunic below. His face was a narrow triangle with heavily lidded eyes. Dwyrin flinched away from the crumbly chalklike skin, the pale eyes, almost the color of lead. Sickly white currents of power glided under and over his skin and garments like caressing snakes. He had no smell.

"This is the slave I spoke of, master," Amochis said in a quiet voice. Over the dead man's shoulder, Dwyrin could see that the sailor was almost paralyzed by fear. The acrid smell of his sweat filled the room.

"Pretty, very pretty," the dead man whispered with a voice like dry bones tumbling into the bottom of a well. "I see promise in him, buried like a hot coal. You were right to bring him to my attention, Master Amochis." Feather-light fingers drifted over Dwyrin's face, almost touching him, but never quite making contact. The dead man leaned over the Hibernian, his face close to Dwyrin's chest. Dwyrin shuddered at the intimacy as the dead man began sniffing him. Up close, Dwyrin could see the tiny line of stitches that ran from the man's neck up his throat and around the back of his skull. A scream began to bubble in his throat and he scraped himself as far away from the breathless exhalation of the dead man as he could.

The dead man smiled, the muscles of his cheek twitching like earthworms to compose his face. A narrow hand was laid on Dwyrin's shoulder like a grave cloth settling on the newly dead.

"No, no, my young friend, do not be afraid. I shall not harm you. Lie still and think of pleasant things. I will take you away from this place, to somewhere you will be greatly appreciated."

The smile came again, and this time the muscles were quicker to respond to the ancient will that swam in the deep-black pools of its eyes. Dwyrin froze like a rabbit in the face of a wolf. The dark pools became deeper and deeper, like a lake draining into whirlpool. Frantically he tried to summon the Meditation of

Serapis to hold his mind inviolate against the pull of that darkness. He failed, and consciousness left him again.

Dwyrin woke again in almost darkness, though now no chains lay upon him. Another ship creaked around him, and the groaning sound of ropes rubbing against the sides of the ship filled the air. A sheet covered him; by its feel against his skin it was cotton. He shuddered at the thought of being naked, either physically or mentally, in the presence of the creature that had leaned over him in the slave cell. The air around him seemed oppressive and his skin crawled with a sense of imminent danger. Very cautiously he opened his eyes and looked around. This time the chamber was not belowdecks in the hold, but it was small, low-ceilinged, and occupied only by the cot upon which he lay, a bucket, and a curved door. The wall the cot was built out from was curved as well, and Dwyrin realized that he must be in a small room wedged into the corner of a ship hull. A dim blue light shone from the edges of the door, giving him what light there was to see.

Carefully he checked his limbs, finding no shackles or chains. His clothes were gone, and he seemed unharmed. At his neck, however, there was a thin cord of metal. Delicately he tested its strength and its feel in his hands suggested that it was unbreakable by regular means. He slowed his breathing and attempted the First Entrance. After a moment he stopped. The power, the passage that had always been there before was simply gone. Despite his best effort, despite running through the entire litany of the meditations, nothing unfolded in his mind to lead him into the overworld of forms. He fingered the cord around his neck again, puzzling at its sudden warmth.

The creak of the door and a flood of blue-white light into the room interrupted further ruminations. Squinting and raising a hand to shield his eyes, Dwyrin quailed to see that the figure outlined in that harsh glare could only be the dead man.

"Come, my young friend, dinner is set upon the table." The half-hidden mockery present in that dust-dry voice did nothing to assuage Dwyrin's fears. Still, there was nothing else to be done at the moment. Wearily, for his body seemed very weak, he levered himself off the bed and crouched down to crawl out of the tiny space. Beyond, a cabin held a table bolted to the floor, a profusion of carpets and bric-a-brac, two chairs, and a number of plates and bowls. The smell of dinner slithered across the Hibernian like a snake, the prospect of food twisting his stomach but the subtle smell of carrion clogged his throat. Dwyrin took the smaller of the two seats gingerly, clinging to the side of the table as the ship rolled a little.

Even as the Hibernian seated himself, the dead man was already composed in his larger chair. A spidery hand lifted a pale-white bowl and drew back a cloth laid over it, offering it to Dwyrin.

"Bread?" the voice whispered from its bone-filled well. "You should start easy, do not take too much at once." The bowl was placed at the side of the platter in front of Dwyrin. The boy took a piece of one of the cut-up loaves. It looked and smelled like way-bread, heavy and solid. It was not fresh. He bit at it gingerly, his tongue checking for the small fragments of stone that often survived the sifting at the end of the milling process. The bread was nine or ten days old, but still it was edible. He chewed slowly. His host watched him with interest.

"You may call me Khiron," said the dead man, drawing a bronze goblet toward him. "You are my or, rather, my master's property. You seem an intelligent youth, the more so for having spent time in one of the myriad Egyptian schools." The thin black line of an eyebrow quirked up at Dwyrin's sullen gaze. "The signs upon you are quite unmistakable, you know. The calluses of the fingers, caused by a reed pen. The inkstains on the same hands, obviously of an Egyptian source. The meditations that you summon to calm yourself, to try the exert your will over the hidden world. All of these things point to such a conclusion."

Dwyrin did not respond, continuing to slowly chew the bread. Khiron looked away for a moment, his thoughts composing themselves. His profile was that of a hawk, with a sharp nose and deeply hooded eyes. For all his appearance, however, Dwyrin was unaccountably sure that he was not Egyptian. With his othersight gone, Dwyrin had to look very closely to see any of the signs that had convinced him before that this creature was a dead man. The skin was pale, but not with the chalky texture and graininess that it had shown in his true-sight. The long dark hair, lank and a little oily, still hung down from his shoulders, but now it did not coil with the glowing worms of power that it had before. His dark eyes were still pools of vitriol, but now they did not swim with living darkness. In his lips, there was the slightest trace of a rose blush. Then the creature smiled at him, and Dwyrin shuddered to see the pure malice and hatred in the thing for him, a living being.

"We will be in the great city in another three days," Khiron said, "and my master will take you into his House. You will be well cared for there. You shall not want for food, or drink, or attention of any kind." The dead man leaned a little closer over the table. "But you will not have your precious freedom, though you may walk freely in the city. No, the master will be delighted to add you to his collection." Khiron drank again from the goblet, and Dwyrin felt a chill settle over him as the touch of rose in the dead man's lips flushed and began to spread into his cheeks.

"Eat and drink, my young friend, there is more than enough for both of us. Delos is always most accommodating in providing me with provisions." Now the creature laughed. The sound was like babies' skulls being crushed between iron fingers, one by one.

Dwyrin continued to chew the bread.

The ship rolled up over another swell, its sails filled with a southern wind. North it drove, through a dark sea, its oars shipped, only the hands of dead men upon the tiller.

CONSTANTINOPLE

))·((

Thyatis stood on the bow of the *Mikitis*, the north wind in her face, her hair, loose, streaming behind her in a gold cloud. Though the wind off the Sea of Darkness was chill, the Aegean sun was hot, and she had stripped down to a short leather vest and a thigh-high skirt. Her normally fair skin had bronzed under the Mare Internum sun, and she ignored the sidelong glances of the ship's crew as she had for the three weeks of their journey from Ostia. Nikos was watching her back, a silent presence on the foredeck where he sat, sharpening one of his many knives. Like a knife itself, the sleek merchantman that the Duchess retained for her "work" sliced through the deep-blue waters of the Propontis. Around her the narrow sea was broad and open, its waves gentle. Before her, between twin dikes run out from the towering walls of the capital of the Eastern Empire, the military harbor was a great confusion of sails, masts, ships, and longboats.

The *Mikitis* banked over and the crew ran to furl the main sail. The steering oars bit the water, and the ship shivered as the captain lined up to pass between the two hulking towers that stood watch on the entrance to the harbor. Beyond the profusion of sails and rigging, the granite walls of Constantinople rose up: height upon height topped with sharp-toothed crenellations and the jutting shapes of massive towers. Even from the deck of the ship, one hand holding easily to the forward guyline, Thyatis felt the brooding power of the fortresses. Beyond them she knew from the Duchess's notes, a thriving city of close to two million souls bustled about its daily business. All this despite the six-month-old siege of the Avar barbarians and their Slavic and Gepid allies. Coming up the Propontis the signs of the nomads had been clear on the northern shore—burned-out farms and distant pillars of smoke. Now the *Mikitis* entered the harbor and the walls loomed even greater above her.

With a practiced eye, she surveyed the flotillas of short-oared galleys, crimson sails furled, drawn up on the slips of the harbor, their bronze beaked prows gleaming in the afternoon sun. Hundreds of merchantmen crowded the harbor as well, swarming with sailors, laborers, and a vast confusion of supplies, materiel, and men. Under the aegis of the walls, the wind died and the sailors aboard the *Mikitis* unshipped the long oars. The splashing of their first strokes was overborne by the sudden beat of a deep-voiced drum. Thyatis swung around on her perch and saw one of the galleys nose out of a shed built on the western rim of the harbor. Like a great hunting cat, it surged forth from concealment, a hundred oars on each side flashing in the sun like a thicket of spears. The drum beat a sharp tattoo and the ship leapt ahead as the oars, rising and falling as one, cut into the water.

The galley strode across the low chop of the harbor like a great water spider, each beat of the drum a stroke. The wicked shape, the glaring eyes on the prow, the unison of the rowers brought a lump to Thyatis' throat. *To command such a creature of war!* she exulted. *To be like a god, speeding across the waters* . . . In too few moments the galley had crabbed out of the harbor and into the open waters of the Propontis. Sadly she gazed after it.

Within the half hour the *Mikitis* had slid into its assigned space at dock, and Nikos and the other men in Thyatis' command were unloading all of their gear with practiced ease and speed. Thyatis had changed back into her nondescript garb, with the voluminous hood of her heavy cloak brought up, though now she had added a shirt of closely woven iron links underneath her other garb. The weight on her torso, and the close feeling of the padded cotton doublet that underlay it, gave her a comfortable feeling. Now that they were on land, she rationalized that its weight would not be a detriment. Besides, this was an unknown city—at least to her, though Nikos had been here before—and that meant it was more than usually dangerous. She moved through the crowd of men, speaking to them individually, double-checking that no one had forgotten anything.

Finishing her inspection brought her to the landward end of the dock and a young Imperial officer in a light boiled leather cuirass, a red cloak, and strapped leather boots. He wore a short fringe of beard in the eastern manner, though his hair was cropped short. He was peering down the dock while fidgeting nervously. A message pouch was slung over his shoulder and a bored-looking horse was tied up to a post on the dockside.

"Can I help you?" asked Thyatis, guessing that he had to be their guide into the city.

"Ah, well, perhaps . . . I'm looking for the centurion commanding this, ah, detachment. I have orders for him as well as quarters for his men." He continued to peer past her, though she had moved to place herself directly in front of him. He suddenly turned to her, apparently seeing her for the first time. "Do you know which one he is? They all look kind of, well, scruffy."

Thyatis smiled and pulled a leather orders pouch from one of the pockets on the inside of her cape. She handed it to him, flipping back the waxed cover. The sun flashed for a moment on the Imperial Seal and the smaller, though no less ornate, blazon of the house of Orelio.

"We all look scruffy, Optimate, it's our job. I'm the centurion in command, Thyatis Julia Clodia."

The optimate stared at her, the mill wheels in his head obviously jammed for the moment. His mouth opened, then closed. Then he shook his head and he made a short salute. "My pardon, lady, my brief did not include the gender of the commander. I apologize for any insult I may have given."

Thyatis looked him up and down for a moment, then shook her head. "I'm not in the mood for a duel today, and getting to quarters sounds pretty good. I've got twelve men instead of ten, will that be a problem?"

The optimate shook his head, relieved to have avoided a problem with the odd-looking Western officer. His tribune had taken great pains to impress upon him the necessity of keeping a steady ship with all the new crew aboard. Getting on the wrong side of a "special" unit was a quick way back to the farm with his head on a platter. He looked over the Western crew as they hauled what seemed to be an inordinate amount of kit up to the end of the dock. Their appearance did nothing to allay his sinking feeling that the junior officer had gotten the biggest hassle in this muster. None of the men was well kept at all; their beards were straggly or far too long. Their clothes were a jumble of rag pickings and armor, without any semblance of uniform. All of them had a villainous look, none more so than a quartet of short, bandy-legged men with long mustaches and slanting eyes. With a start the optimate realized that they were Huns, or at least Sarmatians.

Looking around, he realized that there was a serious problem. He turned partially away from the crew standing around behind the young woman, gesturing for her attention.

"Milady, I'm afraid that I was told that this was an infantry detachment—I didn't think to bring any horse transport, or wagons, and your men have far too much to carry. Can I beg your indulgence to wait here for an hour or so while I round up something to carry your gear in?"

Thyatis tugged at one ear, glancing back over her shoulder at Nikos, who drifted toward them in his customary, silent manner.

"Well . . ." she said, dragging it out, "all this kit is awfully heavy to carry. I wouldn't want to wear my men out, they have too much drinking and wenching to do later."

She gently took the optimate by his elbow, her thumb digging into the pressure point behind it just enough to get his attention. Then she leaned close and whispered into his ear. "My men and I can carry this gear twenty miles in the hot sun without animals. Your city is barely *two* miles across. I think that we can make it. Now, if you're too busy to give us directions, I'll just let them follow their noses—they do have an instinct for finding someplace to stay, whether the locals like it or not."

The optimate did not flinch, which bought him a point of favor with Nikos, who had come up on his other side. The Greek idly removed the orders from the waxed leather pouch at the young under-officer's side and began leafing through them.

"Ah . . . milady," the optimate said, struggling to keep his voice even, "you misunderstand. My orders are to give you and your men all assistance in getting to your quarters and you to the staff meeting this evening. If you want to walk all the way to the . . ."

". . . Palace of Justinian," Nikos said, finishing his sentence. "The royal treatment, as it were."

Thyatis grimaced at her second.

"What is it now," she said, "a prison? Fallen down in ruins? They're not going to put us up in a palace, for Hermes' sake." Nikos grinned and passed her the orders tablet. She read it over and shook her head in amazement, handing it back to him. The optimate sighed in relief as she let go of his elbow.

"We'd really better walk then," Thyatis said with a resigned tone in her voice. "Best to get everyone settled down before they start breaking things."

• • •

Martius Galen Atreus, Augustus Caesar Occidens, stood in the window embrasure of the suite of rooms that he occupied while in the Eastern capital. From the third floor of the Palace of Justinian, now commonly referred to as the "Other Palace," he could see out over the rooftops of the Imperial precincts. The bulk of the "Great" Palace loomed almost due north, blotting out the skyline save for, beyond it in turn, the huge dome of the Temple of Sol Invictus. To the west the gardens filled the space between Justinian's old brickwork palace and the rising wall of the Hippodrome. Beyond that was the city, a vast teeming hive of people, three-, four-, and five-story apartment buildings, forums crowded with merchants, the great Mile Stone, and the rest of the sprawl of the Eastern capital. Leaning against the sill, Galen was stricken by an unaccustomed despair. By the count of his secretaries the precincts of Constantinople held almost as many people as lived in Rome, Ostia, and their surrounding provinces. The plague had devastated Italy, but it seemed to have barely touched the East.

A polite cough behind him heralded the entrance of his aide. Galen turned, taking care to show a slight smile and betray nothing of the sadness that now filled him.

"Ave, Augustus," Aetius said, bowing slightly. The boy was still a little stiff in his presence, a tendency made worse by the ritual of the Eastern court. Galen shook his head in dismay; had anyone ever been so young? Romulus Aetius Valens was the scion of one of the few patrician families left in Rome that still boasted numbers of sons. Nomerus Valens, the patriarch of the family, had been smugly pleased to obtain the appointment for his son, but from Galen's point of view there had been a paltry number of suitable candidates put forward. Of them Aetius was the best, even if his instinct was to bow at any occasion.

"Aetius, I am only a man, not a god. You need not bow and scrape before me." Galen's voice was gentle and filled with wry amusement. Aetius looked up and saluted again.

"Stand at ease, lad, and tell me the news."

Aetius saluted again, standing straight. His short brown hair was cropped in a severe line above his brows and his usually pale skin was beginning to brown in the Greek sun. He pulled two wax tablets from under his arm, placing them on the writing desk that stood between them. Galen sat down in his camp stool and perused the tablets. While he did so, Aetius reported:

"Augustus, the third and sixth cohorts of the Seventh Augusta, the equites of the Sixth Gemina, and four thousand Gothic auxillia have landed today at the harbor. With these men, the numbers of the Western vexillation here in the capital have grown to twenty-five thousand men. The quartermaster has requested that I inform you that we are out of places to put more troops. If, perhaps, you could discuss this with the Emperor Heraclius . . ."

Galen waved off the rest of the statement. His men could double or triple bunk for the short time that the army would be in the Eastern capital. Now that both he and the Eastern Emperor were in the same place and able to meet face to face, the coordination of the great expedition had vastly improved. The use of the *telecast* had been intermittent and tremendously tiring to the sorcerers maintaining the link. The ancient devices still tended to lose focus and drift to other scenes or faraway lands. Though they had shown great promise, they were not a reliable mechanism. Galen had been forced to dismiss them from his calculations save as a means of emergency communications. The trouble now was not on the part of the Western Empire, but rather the East, for Heraclius was engaged in a power struggle with the great landowners that supplied the majority of his fighting men.

"Go on, what other news?"

"Resupply of the ships continues apace, though it seems backward that we should come here to bring on supplies when all of the supplies in the city are already brought in by boat." Aetius paused, but Galen did not respond to the implied question. Gamely the youth continued, "The word from the chamberlain of the palace is that the Khazar embassy has still not shown up, delaying that meeting and a letter came by messenger from the Duchess de'Orelio."

Galen raised an eyebrow at this last and put down the tablet. "Where is the letter?"

"In the hands of the messenger, Augustus. She informed me that she had been directed to deliver it in person." The boy, if anything, became stiffer. Galen shook his head—he was afraid that the boy's reaction would only be a small reflection of the trouble to come with the Easterners.

"She is here, then?"

Aetius nodded.

"Show her in then, lad, and stop looking like you'd swallowed a prune pit."

"Ave, Augustus!"

Aetius turned on his heel and marched to the door. A moment later the messenger entered and Galen raised an eyebrow in surprise. Rumor had held for some months that the notorious and "oriental" Duchess had finally decided to bring her mysterious ward out into the open. Though Anastasia had been the Imperial spymaster for three Emperors and had never given Galen any indication that she was anything but utterly loyal to the state, he was pleased to see some indication that she was mortal.

An Emperor required many spies and informers to serve his will and be his eyes throughout his domain. Over the last eleven years, the de'Orelio faction had gathered nearly all of those resources to themselves—first when the old Duke had been the spider, now that his widow was. Galen had taken pains in the last year to establish his own sources of information, ones that were not beholden to Orelio, but it was slow work. Most damnably, he had not found any *man* who could execute the covert strategies of the state as well as the Duchess. It galled him, though he felt no ill will toward de'Orelio, that she was so obviously his superior in this area.

The messenger planted her feet and stood at parade rest before the writing desk. Galen noted with interest that she was both as young as had been reported and as beautiful. Too, she wore simple garb, most reminiscent of a Legion scout. Tall worn leather boots, light-green cotton breeches in the Gothic style, a loose tunic of weathered brown with piping at the collar and cuffs. A dark-gray cloak was pulled back a little off broad shoulders. Her hair, a rich gold-red, was braided back from her head. Gray-green eyes surveyed him calmly, even as he looked upon her.

"Ave, Augustus Caesar. Thyatis Julia Clodia, centurion, Legio Second Italia, at your service," she said, handing him a scroll tube. "Greetings from my mistress, the Duchess Anastasia de'Orelio. She hopes that you are well and that your venture is blessed with success. I am to tell you that if there are any questions, I am to answer them."

Galen nodded at the politeness, breaking the thick wax seal at the end of the tube. Within were thick sheaves of finely rolled papyrus sheets. They were covered with the spidery writing, in dark ink, that de'Orelio favored. He began reading but put the report aside after the first page. Much of it was routine business and the other he would go over in private. The messenger interested him more than the message. He gestured that she should sit on one of the stools facing the desk. With only a minute hesitation, she did so.

"Aetius, could you go and get something for me to eat. Something light. And wine, but not the Greek, something we brought with us."

The boy bowed and hurried out, closing the door behind him. Galen smiled again and scratched his ear, looking sidelong at the young woman sitting across from him. *How to approach this?* He realized with a rueful chagrin that he had never had a "business" conversation with a woman save the Duchess. De'Orelio had always made him nervous, though she did not give him heart palpitations as she did the Senate. Galen realized that the foremost reason he trusted the Duchess was the effect she had on the senatorial class.

He shook his head slightly, then decided to dispense with the usual politeness that obtained between women and men in his social circles. This was one of his officers, for all that she was a woman, and he had work for her to do. Being polite and following convention would not speed things up or make them more efficient.

"Clodia, you are a bit of a puzzle for me, given that you are, to my knowledge, the only woman officer that I have on this expedition, indeed, the only woman soldier that I have in my army. I have discussed you and your situation, and your talents, with the Duchess on more than one occasion and I will be blunt. I did not think that you could do the work that she set you to. In fact, I was entirely opposed to the concept of this . . . 'special' . . . *contubernia* when she proposed it to me."

Thyatis was very still, not even blinking. Galen paused a moment, seeing if he could gauge her reaction. She waited patiently, so he continued.

"I did not interfere, however, when she pressed ahead with your team on her own initiative, and I understand from her reports that you have been successful. She took great pleasure in relating to me the events of your pursuit in the Subura. I am, I was, pleased by your success. You have proved your ability enough to win you and your men a place here, on this expedition."

Now the girl cracked the smallest of smiles. Galen did not smile back; he was not finished.

"Our situation here is different. I have noted in my admittedly limited time here in the city that the Eastern officers are even more traditionally minded, more constrained in their thinking than mine. I do not believe that you are going to be useful here in an . . . open way."

Galen held up a hand to still the young woman's incipient protest.

"In the rolls of the expedition, you are listed as one of my couriers, a member of my staff. I am uneasy at bringing you to the general meeting tonight, but I do not want you to be unfamiliar with the other officers. I put this question to you. Can your *optio*, Nikos, go in your stead?"

Storm clouds gathered in Thyatis' gray eyes. Only the ceaselessly drummed lessons of Krista and Anastasia kept her from launching into a stream of invective suitable to a sailor. Instead, she breathed deeply and seriously considered the Emperor's request. "Augustus Caesar, Nikos is a steady man with many useful skills, but he is not the leader of my team, I am. The men follow me because I have won their respect and fear. If he goes in my stead, then my authority will be challenged and I will lose that respect. I urge you to reconsider your decision."

Galen frowned. The girl, no—the *centurion*—was all too right. He would not undermine the authority of any of his other officers in such a way. Though it would cause trouble with the Eastern officers, he could see no way to avoid taking the minotaur by the horns.

"I don't suppose you can be unobtrusive?" he asked, resigned to an even longer and more contentious staff meeting than usual. *If she proves too much trouble*, he thought, *I'll send her back to Italia.*

Thyatis suddenly smiled and the room, to Galen's surprise, seemed suddenly brighter.

"Imperator," she said, "you won't even notice that I'm there."

True to Thyatis' suspicion, the quarters that she and her men were assigned were in no way "royal." Beneath the Palace of Justinian were a series of great vaulted cisterns, now long dry and replaced in function by the cistern of Philoxenus, beyond the Hippodrome. Now they were crowded with engineers, servants, great heaps of equipment, wicker baskets of grain, and other goods. At the back of the far chamber, in stuffy darkness, she found Nikos and the rest of her detachment. The rest of the interview had gone well, the Emperor finally becoming just a harried and overburdened army commander to her rather than a suspicious near enemy. Unlike some who had gone before, this Emperor was irritated by the practices of the court and seemed more of a provincial landowner like one of her uncles than a living god.

She couldn't help grinning to herself. Her right hand flexed unconsciously and drifted to the hilt of her sword. The mechanics of a plan, the hundreds of options and possibilities inherent to violent action, swam in her mind, rising and falling in a lake of possibilities. As they had always done since she was a little girl, her thoughts coalesced into a strategy and intent. She slapped her hand against her thigh in delight.

Nikos had not been idle, waiting for her return. The men were quartered behind a great pile of wicker baskets in a corner of the vast room. Most were inspecting their gear for rust or broken links when she walked up; the others were huddled in a corner of the little camp, engrossed in the rattle of dice. The *optio* looked up, then cleared off the overturned crate that he had been using to fletch arrows on. Thyatis grunted and slid the whole smoked ham off her left shoulder. It made a meaty *thwack* on the wood.

Nikos grinned. "Been to the kitchens, I see. Was there wine as well?" His dark eyes glittered in the light of the nearest lamp.

Thyatis snorted in amusement. "By the example of the Divine Julius, the favored drink of the legionnaire is vinegar."

Nikos rolled his eyes and pulled a wineskin from under the crate. "No matter, I've my own. Was there trouble at the commander's office?"

Thyatis shook her head. "No, we got along fine. He was concerned that my delicate nature would be offended by attending the general staff meeting tonight, with the officers in the Eastern army. He wanted you to go instead."

Nikos paled. The prospect of hobnobbing with more than a hundred officers, nearly all of them of noble birth, filled him with dread. Better a thousand scream-ing woad-blue Picts charging your position than a general staff meeting. Thyatis was still smiling though, so it couldn't be that bad.

"Settle down," she said, pulling a knife from her belt and spinning the blade around its point on the top of the crate. "I disagreed, politely, and promised to be unobtrusive. There seems to be trouble brewing between the two armies. He doesn't want to rock the galley right now."

Nikos rubbed his nose, thinking.

"How are you going to avoid notice?" he asked, thinking of her with her looks and hair and attitude among the bearded nobles of the East or the stiff-backed Western officers. There was surely going to be trouble of it. The word that the Legion commanders were at each other's throats was all over the city. Brawling between the soldiers only one incident away. Though neither Heraclius nor Galen had affected to notice it yet did not make it go away.

Much of the problem sprang from the simple fact that while the Western Empire had clung tenaciously to the military organization of the early Empire, the East had not. Where the Western forces were in the numerical minority, they had a clearly defined chain of command. The Eastern army that was gathering was more a collection of personal retainers, each under its own warlord, than a pro-fessional army. The Western officers expected there to be a single overall com-mander, preferably their own Emperor, while the Eastern lords all demanded a voice in the course of the expedition. The Western troops and officers spoke Latin, the Easterners Greek or Aramaic. This was just the beginning of the difficulties, mused Nikos, watching his commander with a worried eye.

How will they accept her? he wondered. *We accept her, even though she is younger than most of us, save Tycho, and a woman besides. Why is that?* he questioned himself. *We follow her without question, she is our commander, yet by no precedent should that be so . . .* He shook the thought away. It was not germane to the situation. She was his commander. Even when he had first met her, it seemed only natural that she should lead and he should follow. *Her shoulders are broad enough to carry us,* he thought, and nodded to himself.

Thyatis had turned away from her lieutenant and threw an apple core at the crowd of gamblers in the corner. It bounced off the partially turbaned head of a Syrian. The Syrian looked up, scandalized, but his handsome face cleared when he saw who had thrown it.

"Anagathios, get your perfumed buttocks over here. I've a question."

The Syrian gathered up the pile of coin in front of him, pocketed the dice, and sauntered over to the little desk. He knelt on the floor next to Thyatis and prostrated himself with a great flourish.

Thyatis grinned but cuffed him on the side of his head. "Stop trying to look up my dress, I'm not wearing one." She grabbed on his ears and dragged his head up. He put on a pained expression, and his mouth dragged down in a doleful grimace. He spread his hands wide in supplication.

Thyatis leaned close. "Do you still have your box of mummers' paints?"

Anagathios nodded in the affirmative and pointed off into the pile of bedrolls and kit.

"Go get it," she said, slapping the side of his head affectionately. "I've work for you to do before evening comes."

The Syrian sprang up from his crouch and then fairly bounded away into the gloom to the rows of packs. Thyatis shook her head in amusement. She turned back to Nikos, but her face was concerned now. He knew that face: It was the mission face.

"Do we have anyone that speaks Walach well? I mean really well."

Heraclius, Augustus Caesar Oriens, looked down the long marble table with something akin to disgust in his heart. Though his impassive face showed none of the growing rage within him, his eyes were beginning to betray his temper. Theodore, sitting at his side and a little lower, nudged his arm gently and shook his head. Heraclius sighed; his impetuous younger brother was the one he was supposed to keep in check, not the other way around. To his left hand, in watchful silence, sat the Western Emperor, Galen, his Legion commanders, and a few underofficers and couriers. To his right, in loud confusion, milled the thematic commanders, their aides, in two cases their concubines, and a constant procession of underlings. Of them, only Mikos Andrades, the *drungaros* of the fleet, showed any sign of organization or respect.

At last, Heraclius rose, his face carefully ordered, and tapped loudly on the tabletop with the hilt of his dagger. The sharp sound rang off the marble and through the whole long chamber. Some of the Eastern commanders looked around and, grudgingly, began seating themselves. After almost ten minutes there was something approaching quiet in the room. Heraclius looked them over slowly.

The comparison between the richly attired and bejeweled Eastern commanders, each a Duke or better, commanding thematic provinces from Egypt to Anatolia, with their beards and long curled hair, and the little collection of Romans on the opposite side of the table grated on Heraclius. The Eastern Empire had not been ravaged with plague, invasion, and civil war like the West, yet for all the robust survival of the East, the Western officers carried themselves better, were politer, and more . . . Roman . . . than the rabble that Heraclius had struggled to lead for the last five years.

"Gentlemen," he said at last, "today we are to discuss the planning and execution of the greatest Roman military expedition in almost two hundred years. The specifics of our intent have been discussed with all of you separately, either in person or by letter, so I will not belabor them.

"I will, however, formally introduce my counterpart in the west, the Augustus Martius Galen Atreus, who stands together with me today as no Emperors of East and West have done since the time of Constantine the Great. We are of like mind, we see that a bold stroke is necessary to resolve the threats to the Eastern Empire . . ."

This was too much for one of the Dukes, and Theophanes surged to his feet, shouting.

"Bold! Reckless and suicidal is more like it! What of Thrace and Achaea, which lie under the Avar yoke? What of the army of barbarians that besiege this city? What of the Persian army encamped within sight of this palace, across the waters in Chalcedon? You have had bold plans before, Augustus Caesar, but they have been failures, expensive failures!"

Heraclius surveyed the crowd of nobles and officers, ignoring the ranting of the Thracian duke for the moment. Theophanes was right; past efforts to drive back both the Persians and the Avars had been disasters. In his heart, Heraclius wondered if the entire Eastern Empire was cursed, or if, at least, he was. His support among the remaining nobles was very slim, which was only one of many reasons that he was very glad that Galen and the Westerners were in the city. Not only did Galen's Legions give him troops that would support him personally, but also they showed the citizens of the city, as well as the nobles, that he was still Emperor.

"Lord Theophanes, sit. I know what has happened before. I know the setbacks we have suffered. But the state of affairs remains this: The Avars cannot take the city unless they can bring a fleet against us. They have neither the skills nor the facilities to build ships to match ours. This means that the only way they can take the city is if the Persians are able to cross the Propontis. The only way to cross the Propontis is if the Persians have a fleet. Though the Royal Boar sits in Chalcedon in my Summer Palace, eating figs from my orchards and drinking wine from my vineyards, he does not have a fleet. If, however, the Persians take Antioch, or Tyre, or Alexandria from us, then they could build one. So, the Persians are the true enemy. If they are defeated, then we can turn against the Avars and run them back into Dacia with their tails between their legs."

Theophanes was still standing, but the vehemence in Heraclius' voice had stilled him, and his courtiers, in low whispers, urged him back to his seat. Eventually, with the air of bestowing a great favor, he did so. *Well*, Heraclius thought sourly, *that is past at least* . . . He tapped Theodore on the shoulder. The Prince rose, bowed to the Western Emperor, nodded to the Legion officers and ignored the Eastern nobles. With the assistance of one of his aides, he unfolded a long parchment map on a wooden frame, then took his place beside it.

"My lords, this is the eastern half of the Empire, from Pontus Polemoniacus in the north on the Sea of Darkness to Arabia Felix in the south on the Sinus Arabicus. As my brother has alluded, the Persians have thrown their armies forward to Chalcedon in the west and Antioch in the south. By good fortune their advance south against Palestina and thence to Egypt has been halted for the past nine months by the presence of the Shahr-Baraz here, beyond the Propontis. We expect, however, for this to change soon. Luckily for the continued grain supply of the city, the approaches to Egypt are blocked by our allies, the kingdoms of Palmyra and Nabatea."

Theodore paused and glanced aside at his brother. Heraclius shook his head minusculely and the Prince skipped forward over that part of the plan. "Our forces have almost completed gathering here, in the western end of the Eastern Empire. Once the muster is complete, we will leave the city by ship under the cover of darkness. Now, our spies in Chalcedon and the ports of the East have circulated that our intent is to sail an expedition north, into the Sea of Darkness, past Sinope, to Trapezus. From there, this purported expedition will march south, gathering the support of the Armenians and cutting off the Persian armies that are still to the west of this line of advance. By this means we could force the Persians to abandon all of Anatolia and Cilicia."

The Eastern lords were abuzz now, for this very plan had already been related to them by their spies as well as by various officers of the Imperial Court. It had made good sense, and for this reason they had agreed to meet with the Emperor. Now it seemed that the plan would be changed. None stood, however, to put the question to the Prince.

Theodore waited until they subsided before continuing. "This will *not* be our plan. Despite the long alliances that the Empire has held with the kingdoms of Armenia and Lazica, they are unwilling to join us in this campaign. The state, frankly, is too poor to bribe them, and we do not have the men to spare in fighting our way through the mountains. We will use a different axis of attack. Both Emperors are united in the belief that the only way to defeat the Persians is to strike against their heartland, the provinces between their capital at Ctesiphon and the city of Rayy. It is not enough to defeat their armies, though we will surely have to do that as well, but we must capture their centers of religious and political power."

Theodore turned again to Heraclius, who now stood. He surveyed the assembled nobles and officers with a gimlet eye. He needed these men, their troops and their gold, to carry out his plan. In a moment of odd clarity, he understood that they were as surely his enemies as the Persians or the Avars, the more dangerous because he had to rely on them. In their faces he saw, in varying degrees, treachery in the desire for power, for gold, for dominance over their fellow men. For the moment, and only for the moment, he was their master. Slowly he took a battered iron dagger out of the folds of his brocaded robe and placed it on the tabletop.

"This is the blade of my father," he said. "What you will now be told must remain in strict confidence among those assembled in this room. The plan that my brother has outlined is what we desire the Persians to learn, but what he will now tell you is what they must not learn. The betrayal of this confidence will earn you death, by my hand, by this blade. Do you swear secrecy in this?"

There was a moment of silence, and then the Western Emperor rose, his face stern, like a statue cut from Minoan marble. His men rose at his back.

"I, Martius Galen Atreus, Augustus Caesar Occidens, so swear."

His men, as one voice, echoed their master. The Western contingent sat. Heraclius turned his gaze to the easterners. They were eyeing one another, uncertain of this new tack. At last, the *drungaros* of the fleet stood. He was a thick-bodied man with a thick black beard and beetling eyebrows. His garb was plain, a cotton tunic with the emblem of the fleet upon it, a mail shirt underneath. Alone among the commanders of the East, he had been elevated to his position by means of ability and skill. He turned to Heraclius.

"I, Mikos Andrades, *drungaros* of the fleet of the Eastern Empire, so swear."

With some reluctance, the other nobles swore as well, finally sitting.

Theodore resumed.

"The fleet will sail south, rather than north, first to Cyprus and then to the port of Tarsus. We know that the Persians hold Tarsus only lightly, and the army will seize it. From this port the army will disembark the fleet and then march with good speed northeast to Samosata on the old border with the province of Osrhoene. If our reports are to the good, the Persian army that had been encamped at Antioch will have already marched away south, to capture Heliopolis and then Damascus on its way to Egypt. Engaged as it is against the Palmyrenes and Nabateans, this army will then be unable to prevent the movement of our force deep into southern Armenia, to the Persian city of Tauris, beyond Lake Thospitis.

"At or before Tauris, our armies shall meet our allies in this expedition, the forces of the Khazar *Kagan*. From Tauris we shall strike farther east, towards Rayy in Tabaristan, before turning south to come down upon Ecbatana and Khermanshah before striking at Ctesiphon not from the west, as we have always done, but from the north. In this way the Persians will be cut off from their traditional retreat into the highlands. Their capital shall fall and their Empire with it."

The Eastern lords looked on with a variety of sour expressions. Heraclius could see that they felt the plan far too ambitious. *No matter*, he thought, *we will win this time or the East will fall into the same darkness that almost consumed the West*.

Theophanes rose again, with a considering look upon his face. The Thracian glanced up and down the Eastern side of the table speculatively. "Now, *Avtokrator*, this is a bold plan indeed, and I can see that there is both the possibility of victory as well as the possibility of considerable loot to be had. No Roman army has ever gone beyond Ctesiphon; the lands beyond it must be rich indeed. The Khazars are well feared for their horsemen. I agree that this is the plan to follow. I have only one small question."

Heraclius sat up a little in his seat; he suspected what the Thracian would ask next, and inwardly he smiled in anticipation. He motioned for Theophanes to go ahead.

"Who will lead this expedition? Which general, which lord will carry out your plan?"

The shouting began immediately and Heraclius settled back in his high-backed chair to watch with interest as the great lords bickered with one another. On the left side of the table the Westerners, who already knew what Heraclius had decided, had called for wine and something to eat. It was going to take awhile at this rate. The Eastern Emperor let them argue among themselves for a time, carefully gauging who thought himself the strongest, who had the alliance of whom. At last he tired of the game and rapped on the tabletop again. He was ignored, so he nodded to Theodore. Theodore stood, took a breath, and then thundered, in his best battlefield voice:

"The Emperor would speak!"

Echoes died and the lords of the Eastern Empire slowly turned to their nominal master. Remaining seated, Heraclius toyed with the dagger for a moment, then he said simply: "I will take personal command of the expedition."

For more than a mere moment, silence absolute reigned around the table. The faces of the thematic lords were studies in puzzlement, alarm, and outright fear. No Emperor had essayed to lead the armies of the Eastern Empire to battle in over two hundred and thirty years. The very thought that the Emperor should stand on the field of battle at the side of the fighting men was unthinkable. Heraclius glanced over at Galen, who smiled a little, and spoke again.

"These are desperate times, as has been repeatedly pointed out. The legionnaires, the people, expect their Emperor to defend them and their families. I can think of no better way to show that I mean nothing but victory than to go myself. It also resolves the question of who will lead, for Galen and I will command the armies of the Empire, as it was in the beginning."

Behind Galen, the Western underofficers stood forward from the wall, raising their arms in salute.

"Ave! Ave Caesar! Thou conquerest!"

The Eastern lords stared back at them in puzzlement; in some the sense that a new and unexpected factor was forcing itself upon them began to grow. Theodore rolled up his map and, with his aides in tow, departed the room. The other lords milled about but then began to disperse as well. Heraclius continued to sit, watching their faces as they left. At his side, Andrades remained until all of the others were gone save the Western Emperor and two of his aides. The room was quiet and a servant entered and began blowing the lamps out.

"*Avtokrator*," Andrades said quietly, "your oath was stirring, but I doubt that these words will stay in confidence for more than a day or pair of days."

Heraclius nodded and looked to Galen and the two young men who stood behind him. The Western Emperor smiled.

"*Drungaros* Andrades, sometimes it is necessary to set bait to find the fox. So we have done tonight. My hunters"—he gestured at the blond youth with only a trace of beard on his left—"are waiting to see what is flushed."

Andrades stroked his beard, still lush though now shot with streaks of white, considering the poised young man at the western Emperor's side. Then he eyed Heraclius. "A risk, *Avtokrator*. What if the Persians get wind of it? What if someone escapes the net? The Boar has at least one sorcerer in his camp across the water. They could send a message to Chrosoes in Ctesiphon and a new army could be raised to meet you in the highlands as you march to Tauris. There would be nowhere to retreat to."

"The Persians will know sooner or later," Heraclius answered. "Our ploy here is to see who in the city is in the pay of the Avars or their Persian allies. Despite the speed of a wizard, Shahr-Baraz still has to march himself and his men back to Syria. Our fleet is vastly faster. We can beat him to any location on the coast that he tries to reach. I am more concerned with treachery here, at home, than with the Persian army."

Andrades nodded glumly, seeing the truth of it. More troubles had come from Roman fighting Roman over the past thirty years than from the invasions of the Avars or the Persians. More trouble could come of it now.

"*Avtokrator*, who will command the defense of the city while you are gone?"

Heraclius frowned. This was a thorny issue that he had been struggling with himself. He had found no good answer. Any lord he left behind would be well tempted to seize the Empire for himself if things went awry for the army in the field. Heraclius had sent armies against the Persians twice before; each had been soundly defeated. This was his last throw of the dice.

Seeing no answer from the Emperor, Andrades cleared his throat. "A suggestion, if you would not take it ill. The priest Bonus, of the temple of Sol Invictus, is a man of good character and wit. He was, if I remember rightly, a centurion in his youth before entering the temple, so he knows the way of war. The people would support him, and as a priest of the god, I doubt that he would want the Purple."

Heraclius considered, biting his lower lip. Galen, now sitting beside him, nodded in agreement with the *drungaros*. The Eastern Emperor nodded as well. "A good suggestion. So it shall be."

THE HOUSE OF DRACUL, NEAR
THE HIPPODROME, CONSTANTINOPLE

Dwyrin was thrown to a tiled floor, landing heavily. The bag over his head was untied and pulled off with ungentle fingers, allowing fresh air, at last, to reach him. He gagged and tried to spit to clear his mouth, but there was no moisture left in him. The tiles under his hands were small and worked into a mosaic. The sharp scent of incense came to him, though the pain of his right wrist was overriding all other senses. A clammy hand dragged him up by the scruff of his neck. A warm white light from a hundred candles filled the room, banishing even the smallest of shadows. Dwyrin knelt at the edge of a great rug; an opulent room surrounded him, filled with rich lacquers and wood, hung with silk and brocade. A sizable wooden desk was set a little off to one side, and before it sat a sturdy-looking man in a light-colored shirt and dark breeches.

The man bent forward a little and gestured to Khiron to bring Dwyrin closer.

The dead man hoisted the boy up by his arms and dragged him forward, dropping him on the carpet at the end of the desk.

"Now, Khiron, don't be harsh to the boy. He's young. Not used to rough treatment."

The voice was thick with the burr of an accent, but not one that Dwyrin had heard before. Still queasy at Khiron's touch, Dwyrin looked up, meeting the eyes of his owner. They were a merry blue, twinkling in the light of the lanterns. The man's face was broad and rather plain, but creased with the beginnings of a smile. A light-blond beard edged his chin, and he showed the signs of incipient fat. His whole body was broad, like a cart, as were his hands. A gentle finger brushed Dwyrin's forehead, tracing the line of his forebraid.

"Pretty young thing, isn't he?" The voice was cheerful, but despite all appearances Dwyrin shrank from the man. For all his jollity, this was Khiron's master. The time with the dead man was still a blur of horror and despair. Even this place, wherever it was, was better than the boat with Khiron and his captives.

"Oh, aye, master. The very paradigm of vitality. Does he please you?"

The rich voice laughed again, saying, "Well, not yet! But there is promise here. How did you come by him, dear Khiron?"

"In my travels, master, I came by chance to Delos and decided to take to shore to acquire provisions for my voyage. While perusing the cattle, I was approached by a nervous Egyptian slavemaster who said he had something special to sell. I am not unknown on Delos, so I presumed that it was some exotic frippery. Instead, there was this sweet boy, all drugged and beaten. But I could smell the power in him, so I purchased him for a pittance, sure that he could find some use here, in your house."

The stout man laughed, a deep bubbling sound, like a spring in the mountains.

"He has the Power, does he? Have you seen it? What expression of that art does he own?"

Khiron placed a thin-fingered hand on Dwyrin's shoulder. "Master, he brings forth fire by the tale of the slavemaster, who lost one of his men when the boy attempted to escape from the slave ship in the waters off Alexandria. The man, by the account, was utterly consumed while leaving not so much as a char mark on the decking."

A talonlike fingertip hooked under the thin metal chain that ran around Dwyrin's neck.

"As you see, I have a ban upon him so that I do not suffer a similar fate . . . The fire is strong in him, though, like water building behind a dam."

"A fire-bringer." The stout man's voice oozed with pleasure. "Many uses for such a talented young man. You wound me, Khiron, bringing me such a pleasant dinner companion and then telling me this! Stand him up."

Hands like iron set Dwyrin upright. The stout man stood as well, and Dwyrin was surprised to see that he was only a little taller. The stout man placed his hands on his hips and stared into the Hibernian's eyes. Dwyrin sagged against Khiron's claw-grip but fought to match the stout man gaze for gaze. Lanterns hissed quietly in the background, then the stout man blinked and looked away.

"Know, young man, that I am the Bygar Dracul, the master of this house and all that exist within it. You are my property now, a slave. If you serve me well, you will be treated well. Otherwise, there are more torments than the lash to be found here. Khiron, take him below, into the pits, and see that he is safely put away. But he is to be kept whole, until I call for him again."

The dead man took Dwyrin from the office of the Bygar and down through a maze of corridors, all lit by lantern or lamp. Dwyrin dimly sensed that they were now belowground. The rock walls were no longer covered with tapestries and hangings. They descended a long flight of stairs that doubled back upon themselves once, then twice. Now the walls were damp with seepage. They passed through a solid oak door, which Khiron carefully closed behind them, muttering the while. Now the corridor was dark and ill lit. Only one fitful lamp guttered in an invisible breeze. A strange tang filled the air, like rotten lemon. Khiron drew his cloak back from his shoulders and pushed Dwyrin ahead of him.

"Walk, boy, and stay at the center of the corridor." The dead man's voice was thready and low, like a whisper caught in the wind.

So they walked for a time. Dwyrin felt the grade of the corridor descend again, and now dark spaces opened on either side of them. Some of the openings seemed to have worked lintels and walls, others were gouged from the raw stone. A cold exhalation crept from most of them. At last they came to another door, though this one was of iron, and studded with bolts and spikes. Khiron reached over Dwyrin's shoulder, though so quietly that Dwyrin had to focus hard to see his hand in the gloom. There was a clicking sound, and the door suddenly split in the middle. Golden light spilled out, blinding the boy. Khiron pushed him ahead, again, into the room.

The cell was small, and lit only by the reflected brilliance of the lamps and candles that Khiron maintained in his own chamber. A sturdy door of iron bars separated Dwyrin and his tiny space from the rest of the dead man's domain. Dwyrin spent his time curled up with his back against the smooth stone wall of the cell. There was a thin blanket of scratchy wool to lie upon and a ewer of water to drink from. Beyond the bars, Khiron paced restlessly in a room filled with lamps and candles, such that no corner was cast in shadow, no wall darkened by the lack of light. A narrow cot and a small stand completed the furnishings. The cot was covered with another blanket and a straw tick, but Khiron lay on it only rarely. Though Dwyrin woke, slept, woke, and slept again, the dead man only paced endlessly around the lighted room.

The stand held a pair of candles and a small icon, though the face of it was turned away and Dwyrin could not see what it represented. The dead man muttered as he walked, and after six wakings, Dwyrin began to make out the words of his captor. They were a jumble, single words repeated over and over, short phrases, a long rambling internal monologue. On the seventh waking, Dwyrin's mind had cleared enough that his body could weakly tell him that it was ravenous with hunger. Too, he was aware enough to realize that Khiron was reminding himself, over and over, of all the things that he had seen or done when he was alive.

"K-kk-hiron . . ." Dwyrin's voice stumbled. His tongue felt enormous, choking the breath from him. ". . . hungry . . ."

The dead man paused in his endless pacing and turned, hooded eyes focusing on the boy behind the tiny grate. Khiron moved closer, a dark bird, head bobbing as it turned sideways and peered into the little cell. A simulacrum of a smile fleeted over his face, a mask put on and then taken off. A bone-pale hand reached out and touched the bars.

"Hungry? Why, I had all but forgotten you, little mouse. Your belly must be quite empty now. It would not do for you to starve or waste away. Food you shall have."

Khiron straightened and his body was tensed with energy now. He passed to the door, a gray cloud in the butter-yellow light of the room. In a moment the room was empty, the door shut. Dwyrin crouched at the entrance to his cell, a thin arm snaked through the grate and groping around the outside. His fingers found the sconce of a candleholder, rusting and ancient to his touch. Stretching upward he managed to catch the dripping wax on his fingertip. The heat of the hot wax flashed through his arm and, for a moment, sight threatened to return. For a bare instant the room flared unimaginably brighter as Dwyrin's eyes took in the radiance of both the candlelight and the shimmering power that coiled endlessly behind the physical light.

Then the thin band of metal around his throat turned freezing cold and his head snapped back in a howl of pain. The burning ice around his neck choked off all thought, all breath, and plunged him into an abyss of cold, filled with grinding ice and a bottomless black lake.

"Food . . ." a distant voice hissed. There was a clanging sound and hands like spiders clawed at him, dragging him out of the warm cocoon of unconsciousness that had been wrapped around him. His throat still burned with the cold fire, though it was greatly muted now. A bowl filled with some sweet-smelling porridge was pushed into his hands. Trembling, he ate from it with his fingers. The porridge was thick and had chopped nuts and figs in it. There was more water in the ewer. After cleaning the bowl, he looked up, exhausted with the effort. Khiron was crouched before him, long cape lying in a puddle of storm-gray around him. The dead man's head was cocked to one side again and his deep-yellow eyes surveyed the starving boy curiously. Dwyrin bowed his head and pushed the empty bowl away. Weariness filled his body from his feet to the top of his head.

"Sleep . . ." said Khiron, his voice growing distant even in the space of that word.

The cell door rattled and swung open. Khiron crouched outside again, snaking a long arm in to drag the boy out. Dwyrin shook his head to clear the muzziness of sleep. The sharp smell of the dead man tickled at his nose and he woke fully.

"Time to go upstairs," Khiron growled, his voice and body equally tense. He shoved a bundle of clothing into Dwyrin's hands. "Dress in this."

Dwyrin stripped out of his tunic and breeches. The new clothing was a wadded lump. In it were trousers, a shirt, a cloth belt, and a felt cap. The fabric was plain and gray, with a little embroidery at the cuffs and hems. It was a little too large for him, particularly in his current state. The dead man watched him closely but without overt malice for the time it took him to dress. Flat-bottomed sandals completed the garb. Done, Khiron surveyed him up and down before pushing him toward the iron door.

"No time to dawdle," he rasped—his voice tighter than usual.

They ascended the long passageway again, returning to the office filled with candles. The stout man, the Bygar, was still seated at his desk, but now two others joined him. Khiron guided Dwyrin to the side of the desk, facing the two new men. Dwyrin felt the dead man recede to the edge of the room, but he did not leave, he merely became less obtrusive. The men in the room had been speaking but had fallen silent upon the arrival of the boy. Now they surveyed him, and he them. The first of the two men was large, taller than Khiron, with a bristling beard and great whiskers. His black hair was curled and fell in ringlets past his broad shoulders. His arms were thick and corded with muscle. He was clad in heavy woolen garments, like a merchant, but they sat uneasily upon him. Dark piercing eyes scanned Dwyrin up and down, then the chin lifted in appraisal, a hand adorned with many rings stroking the lushness of his beard.

"Barely a sprig of a boy." Whiskers's voice was like a trumpet, echoing in the confined space of the office. "He should still be watching the sheep, not about on a man's work."

The other man was well built too, but next to his companion, he seemed a sapling to an ancient oak. Where Whiskers wore his clothes like a stone, this one was dressed in a flowing black robe of some shining material, with dark cotton trousers and arms graced by many bands of dark gold and red and amber. He too had dark hair, but it hung long and straight on his back, bound back by a silver fillet. His face too was long and straight, with arching eyebrows and a sharp nose. He was clean-shaven, without even the shadow of a beard. Whiskers exuded an aura of strength and vitality, almost abrim with energy. This one was cold and distant, like the ice on a mountaintop. Looking upon him, Dwyrin met his eyes for an instant and quailed away. They were deep pools of darkness, filled with horror and suffering.

Dwyrin felt faint, realizing that if the othersight were still upon him, the true shape of the creature across from him might be revealed, and that knowledge might destroy his mind. Being trapped in the same room with this monster and Khiron seemed to drain all air from the space. Dwyrin could now dimly sense the tightly controlled fear in both the Bygar and, behind him, Khiron. The school and the sun on the bricks in front of the dining hall seemed infinitely far away.

"He has potential, Dracul." The voice of the creature in black was smooth and cultured. His Greek was flawless and filled with an ironic lilt. "Your servant has done well. You make our journey not only profitable but pleasant as well."

Dracul made a half bow in his chair, acknowledging the compliment.

"Your presence is a boon as well, Lord Dahak. I know that you are a collector of rare items and so I thought of you when this young man was brought to me. He carries Power within him, waiting to be channeled, tapped, used."

Dahak nodded, his eyes flickering in the candlelight. "Show us."

The Bygar nodded to Khiron, who stepped up behind Dwyrin and rested his bony hands on the boy's shoulders. The dead man leaned close, his gray presence blotting out the candlelight in the room.

"Now, dear boy, I will lift the ban from you a little. I want you to call fire from the stone." A gnarled finger drew Dwyrin's chin around and pointed to a stand of bronze set against the wall beside the entry. Upon it sat an oblong of dark flint. The wall hangings had been taken down, the carpets rolled back from the foot of the stand.

"Not too much, now. Just enough to show our guests."

A fingernail slid between the chain around Dwyrin's neck and his skin. The edge, so sharp, cut into his neck, drawing a bead of blood. The veil that had lain over Dwyrin lifted a little, revealing the room awash in a swirl of dark purple, midnight blue, and a nameless color. By utter effort, Dwyrin kept from looking to his left, where Dahak lounged on a divan. The echo of his presence in the room was enough to distort the flow of power around him, drawing it into himself. The flint block was inert, not so much as a spark of its ancestral fire remaining within it.

"Bring the fire . . ." Khiron crooned in his ear.

Dwyrin stumbled through the Opening of Hermes, failing to reach the level of calm needed to exert his will. Khiron's fingernail dug into his neck. The pain sharpened his focus and he was able to complete the Meditation of Thoth. Now the power in the room, in the bronze stand, even buried deep in the innermost heart of the flint began to expose itself to him. With a deep breath he focused on the block as he had done on the ship, drawing power, first in a tiny thread, then in a surge from the candles, the rugs, the wall, the floor. A bright white-hot point suddenly danced into view in the heart of the flint. Dwyrin fanned it with the flood of power he was drawing from the appurtenances in the room. It began to glow.

Even Dahak flinched back when the flint oblong suddenly flashed into flame, burned white-hot and then shattered with a booming crack, scattering shards of flint across the room. Many bounced back from a sudden, wavering wall of power raised by Dahak's languid hand. There was a pattering sound as they rained down onto the floor and tabletop. Flames licked at the wall and the bronze stand collapsed, riven into shattered bits. Dwyrin fell forward onto the carpet, his head spinning with the power.

With Khiron's hand gone from the chain around his neck, the flood of sensations cut off. The room seemed terribly dark.

Dahak laughed, a terrible sound like graves opening. "He will do, my dear Dracul. He will be magnificent."

The Bygar smiled and gestured to Khiron to take the prize away.

Maxian sat amid roses on a mossy stone bench, his face drawn with exhaustion. Despite the calm peace that pervaded the gardens built on the downriver side of the Temple of the Healers, his mind was unquiet. Darkness seemed to hang over the city now, with a flickering dissonance in the shadows under the buildings or along the wharves that lined the river. Since the night that Gregorius had come to him with the two barbarians, the prince had not slept in his rooms on the Palatine. The whispering of the stones had grown too loud. Now he wondered if he could even bear to remain within the precincts of the city.

Here, in the domain of the priests, he found that there was some peace. Whatever power it was that had invaded the city, and was now so obviously crushing the life from its citizens, the god of healing had the power to keep it from his doors. Maxian rubbed the side of his head, trying to relieve the knots of strain that bunched in his shoulders and neck. He snorted to himself, thinking of how little use he was to his brother.

To his great credit, Aurelian had seemed to know that something was weighing on his little brother's mind and had quietly reassigned all of the tasks that Galen had intended for Maxian. In a way, this made it worse, for now Maxian felt useless. The power that gnawed at the vitals of the people of Rome was so strong that he could not even budge it from a single stone. He was unwilling to bend his thought to dealing with the bureaucracy as his brother needed him to. He groaned aloud and buried his head in his hands.

"So bad, is it?" came a soft basso voice like an echo of thunder. Maxian looked up, and his drawn, pale face lightened for a moment at the sight of the stout man who now stood by the bench.

"Tarsus!" he said in delight, and stood. The two men embraced and Maxian felt much of the weight of responsibility lift from his shoulders. Then he stood back and looked on his old friend with glad eyes. Tarsus met his gaze with solemn brown eyes and then laughed, hugging the young man close to his massive chest.

"You're too young to have such a care-worn face, my friend," the priest of Asklepios rumbled. "I've not seen you since I came to the city, so tell me your troubles."

Maxian sat again, though now he looked up, where long ribbons of cloud marked the sky like a race course. Tarsus sat down as well, leaning back against the willow tree that butted up against the end of the bench. The Prince turned a little to see him.

"I've come upon a serious problem," the Prince began, "one that threatens, or afflicts, everyone in the city. You are new come here, from Pergamum, you must have seen the sickliness of the citizens!"

Tarsus nodded, his craggy face falling into its own lines of care and worry.

"Too many dead babies, or mothers dead in the birthing chair. Wizened old men and women of thirty and forty. Bones too brittle to knit properly. Summer colds that become the coughing death . . ." The healer regarded the Prince gravely.

"You've found something causing this?" Tarsus asked.

Maxian nodded, then paused, shaking his head. "I . . . I *might* have found something that *could* be causing this. I . . . don't know. My skill in the otherworld is not strong enough to see the whole shape of the situation." The Prince turned pleading eyes to his teacher. "I don't know enough of the kind of sorcery that could cause such a thing to say . . . I've found a . . ."

Maxian paused, suddenly loath to relate the vision of the city drowning in darkness to his old friend. A dreadful thought formed unbidden in his mind. If the curse afflicted things that were outside of its purview, like the new cloth, or the ship at Ostia, then if he told what he knew to Tarsus, or to Aurelian, then they would be at risk as well. Though Tarsus was an exemplary doctor, surgeon, administrator, and teacher, he did not have the power over the otherworld that Maxian owned as an accident of birth. He could not protect himself from the tide of corrosion that permeated the city outside of the island.

Maxian looked away from the concerned eyes of the priest. He felt sick. "I can't tell you now. I need to find out if I'm right . . . It is very dangerous, Tarsus. If I could tell you and keep you safe, I would."

The Prince stood up and walked quickly out of the garden. Behind him, the old priest watched him with grave concern. After a moment, Tarsus shook his head as if to clear it of worry and got up to return to his duties in the sickward of the temple.

Maxian climbed the long ramp of narrow steps that ascended the southern side of the Coelian Hill. At the summit, he paused for breath. His tunic was damp with sweat from the exertion. At the top of the steps, there was a small square, and on the western side, a little circular Temple of Jupiter. In the midday heat, the streets radiating out from the square were empty and the lackluster chuckling of the fountain on the northern side was a lonely sound. He crossed the square and went up the broad steps into the dim coolness of the temple.

Within, a marble statue of the god dominated the circular nave, his arm raised to hold a pair of bronze thunderbolts. Beyond that there was a column-lined porch overlooking the sweep of the city. Maxian hauled himself over the low wall and sat, his feet dangling over the edge, and surveyed the thousands of roofs that now lay below him. The white shapes of temples rose like ships in a sea of red tile that descended in steps and a slope to the banks of the Tiber. To his right, upstream from the island that held the calm garden of Asklepios, he could make out the broad open space of the Campus Martius, now all but abandoned with the departure of the Praetorian Guard with the Emperor to the east.

Sitting in the shade, he felt a great fondness for the weathered old city. It had sheltered the art, civilization, and culture of the entire world for centuries. Now it was almost beaten down, its once-proud monuments chipped and cracked, many in ruins. High up here, above the stink and the crowds, he could see the sweep of the city and feel the breadth of Empire that it represented. He thought, his face twisted in regret, of all of the old ghosts he had seen in the palace. Each of them had laid down his whole life for the dream of a world Empire that would sustain civilization forever. A faded glory now. He rubbed his eyes, feeling terribly sad for a moment.

Under the hot sun, the city lay somnolent in the late afternoon. Maxian restrained himself from seeing the city, knowing that eddies of corrosive power were lapping even around this temple. The problem presented by Tarsus, or his brother, occupied his mind. How could he defeat this curse upon the city if he could not tell anyone else? He was far too weak to break the spell, or spells, that anchored it to the city. He needed powerful help. Another sorcerer, someone who was a master of the art, someone who could supplement his own meager skills.

Another thought occurred to him as he sat with his back against the cool marble pillar. He needed help that was not *Roman*. By constant vigilance he held the curse from his own mind and body with the Shield of Athena, but in some way it was a part of him as well. He could feel a vestige of it slipping and sliding through his arteries and veins. Another Roman wizard, brought into such an enterprise, could well be overwhelmed and destroyed—like the *sericanum* had been consumed—before he could defend himself. The Prince rubbed the stubble that had come during the last few days. *I need to shave*, he remarked to himself. *And I need to find a foreigner who is strong enough to help me . . .*

Feeling vastly better that he had at least the beginnings of a plan, he left the temple, striding down into the narrow streets and alleys of the Subura district.

THE GREAT PALACE OF
CONSTANTINE, THE EASTERN CAPITAL

The flood of servants ebbed back at last, leaving the small dining chamber on the top floor of Heraclius' palace at last inhabited only by himself, Theodore, the Western Emperor Galen, and the ambassadors from Nabatea and Palmyra. Heraclius poured the latest round of wine himself, careful to avoid spilling more of the fine Miletean vintage onto the thick carpets that filled the room. All of the diners were well full, having demolished a nearly endless series of courses. Galen, as seemed to be his wont, had eaten moderately and drunk even less. His dry wit, and Western accent, had greatly amused the two ambassadors.

Adathus, the Palmyrene, leaned over and picked two perfect grapes from the remains of the bunch. His aquiline face was creased by a slight smile. His garments were rich, embroidered with tiny jewels and pearls. His hands were well adorned with rings, and the brocade of his shirt was an intricate wonder. Beside him the Nabatean, Malichus Obodas, seemed plain in comparison, though Malichus was dressed in an elegant sea-green silk robe and girdle. Both men had spent vast sums upon their attire, but was that not expected when one visited the court of the Emperor of the East?

"So," Adathus said, "what blessing brings us the attention of the two most powerful men in the world?" His words were flattering, but his eyes were not, for they calmly considered both of the Romans before him. Galen was attired in his customary costume, the field garb of a legion commander: white tunic with a red cape, a heavy leather belt, and lashed-up boots. Heraclius much the same, though he had forgone the cape and settled for a tunic of heavier material, edged with gold. As the Palmyrene had expected, both were calm and possessed of a tremendous confidence. Even with the sad state of the Eastern capital on this day, both of the ambassadors could count ships in the harbor and see that strength was flowing to the Roman hand.

Heraclius helped himself to a peeled apricot dusted with sugar. He took a bite and savored the play of flavors on his tongue. Then he put it aside on the little silver tray by his dining couch.

"The wind is turning in the East," he said, his voice calm. "In short time the Persians will be blown back to Ctesiphon by it. The barbarians who are camped before my walls will be destroyed or chased back to their grasslands. The Boar will be hunted down with long spears and skewered. These things will transpire, regardless of what we discuss this evening."

Malichus rubbed his sharp chin with a well-trimmed fingernail. "If this is so, and I do not doubt it, great lord, why summon us to your presence?"

"We intend more than the simple chasing off the Persians," answered Heraclius. "We intend to deal them such a defeat as they have not suffered in almost a thousand years. We have the men and the will. All we need are the pieces put into the proper motion. For that, frankly, we need the aid of both of your states."

Adathus stole a look at his companion, then arched an eyebrow, saying: "Even now the armies of both our cities, as allies of Eternal Rome, have forestalled the advance of the Persians from Antioch southward. We protect Damascus and thence the road to Alexandria. What more can we do to bring about the defeat of the Persians?"

Heraclius nodded in agreement. "This is so. However, the Persian army at Antioch will soon be marching south, intending to capture Palestine and then Egypt. There will be battle in Syria Coele somewhere. Our plans are already in motion, as are Shahr-Baraz's. It is vital that the Persian army in Antioch remains south of the Orontes river, preferably diverted to a siege of Damascus or some other strong city. This state of affairs need not pertain for long, no more than a few months. This will give us time to complete our part of the evolution."

Adathus leaned back in his couch, his brow furrowed in thought.

"And what evolution would that be?" he asked, clearly suspicious.

Heraclius rang a spoon against the pewter goblet he had been drinking from. Servants entered the chamber and cleared away the platters and other dishes. The last servant gathered up the dining cloth that had covered the table used to serve the four men. Beneath it, the surface of the wooden table was inlaid with a map of the Eastern Empire in tiny, carefully crafted mosaic.

"The Persian armies are four," Heraclius began, using his dining tine as a pointer. First he pointed to the narrow strip of blue between the Mare Aegeaum and the Sea of Darkness. "Shahr-Baraz stands across the Propontis in my Summer House with a swift force of cavalry. Though he daily bites his thumb at me, he holds no more land there than the width of his lances."

The tine moved south and east, across the brown shape of Anatolia, to the eastern edge of the Mare Internum, where the Levantine coast ran up to meet the body of Asia Minor.

"The nearest true Persian army is at Antioch, under the command of his cousin, Shahin. This is the army that will threaten Egypt as soon as it can. Beyond those two armies, the main force of the Persians is at Ctesiphon, under the command of the Shahanshah himself. A fourth army is currently in the uttermost East, campaigning along the Oxus.

"We desire to defeat the Persians one at a time, so we have let rumor slip that our army will sail north from Constantinople and land at Trapezus." The tine slid north across Anatolia to the verge of the Sea of Darkness, and then east along that coastline to the mountains that ran down to the dark waters. "From there that army will advance south through Armenia and Luristan, to threaten the Persian heartland. To counter this, the Boar will take his horsemen back east, across Anatolia, to join up with Chrosoes' army from the heartland."

The Palmyrene broke in, eyeing the map. "But that is not your true plan then."

"No." Heraclius smiled and pointed to the plain of Issus to the northwest of Antioch. "Our army will land here instead and march inland to Samosata. We will be between the Boar, to the north in the mountains, and the main Persian army to the south at Ctesiphon. But our situation will be very precarious if Shahin and his army at Antioch are not already engaged in campaign."

"So we are to occupy their attention," Malichus commented, frowning. "Our armies are equipped for border skirmishes, for fighting bandits and policing the desert. We do not have the heavy infantry or horsemen to face Shahin and his *clibanari*. They would roll right over us in the first standup fight."

"I know," Heraclius said with a grim look on his face, "your generals will have to be careful and draw him southward with the promise of battle. One legion of Eastern troops and one of Western will be coming up the coast from Alexandria to join you. If you can keep Shahin's attention and fall back to meet them, then you will have the fighting men to fight him on even terms. But . . . that is not the plan either."

Malichus and Adathus looked up from the map in concern.

Heraclius took a deep breath, steeling himself for the next words. "By the time you would come to that battle, our armies will have engaged and defeated Chrosoes' main army somewhere between Samosata and Tauris. Then we will turn south to assail the Persian capital. Shahin will know our movements by then for sure, so he will be forced to turn back to defend their heartland. When that time comes, your forces, and those of the two Legions that have come up from Egypt, will be well placed to press him as he retreats back across the Euphrates."

Now the two border chieftains glanced at each other and smiled. An army in retreat would be easy prey for the swift horsemen and raiders that their principalities commanded. There would be rich loot to be had as well from the fleeing baggage train. At little cost or even risk if the Persians could be denied battle . . .

From his chair, Galen watched the by-play between the two ambassadors, and saw their native caution warring with naked avarice.

Adathus pursed his lips and stroked his mustaches with a long, olive-toned finger. "This plan has promise, great lord. Still, it is risky if Shahin should manage to trap one of our forces and bring us to battle. Our peoples are not great in number and we husband our fighting men carefully—what assurances can you offer me that the Legions from Egypt will arrive on time? What restitution will you make us for the losses as the Persians march through our lands?"

Heraclius fought to keep his face impassive. The haggling had begun. He nodded solemnly. "War is a terrible business, and Palmyra, in particular, may suffer greatly. To this end I propose that in recognition of the aid and assistance you give us, as you have given in the past, the Queen shall be proclaimed Tribune for her part in this defense of the East."

The eyebrow of the Palmyrene ambassador inched upward in surprise. Within the hierarchy of the Empire, a Tribune stood just below a Caesar in rule, only two steps from the Purple itself. Such honors were not bestowed lightly, and never upon the head of an allied state. *The Eastern Emperor is both tremendously assured and in a grave situation*, he thought, *to make such an offer*.

Heraclius turned to the Nabatean, his face serious. "Our friends in Nabatea have long stood by our side as well. Your state handles the vast majority of the sea trade from Axum and Sinope, your ports on the Sinus Arabicus are thronged with ships carrying our goods and the goods of others, destined for Rome and Constantinople. Your frontier patrols restrain the nomads of Arabia. We have been remiss in not acknowledging your aid and assistance. It seems to us, if you join in this endeavor, that Petra and Bostra should be treated as Roman cities henceforth."

Now the Nabatean roused himself from his languid air of detachment. The alliance between Bostra and Palmyra was old, and loosely fitting, but traditionally the Northerners had taken the lead in dealing with the Empire. The Nabateans had long been more than content to count the coin that spilled into their coffers from the vast flow of trade between the Empire, India, and distant Serica. Still, as an allied state, they were forced to pay a hefty toll when the goods actually passed into Imperial lands. Were Bostra and Petra to be proclaimed *urbes*, true Roman cities, then nearly a third of that toll would be removed. Great sums were to be made from such a change in tax status.

Malichus nodded involuntarily.

Heraclius smiled genially. "Let us drink, then, friends, and discuss the more mundane details of such a joint effort."

The moon rose huge and yellow-orange over the spires and towers of the city. Galen stood on an embrasure of the palace overlooking the waters of the Propontis. To the east, across the band of dark water, he could make out the twinkle of bonfires on the farther shore. A cool wind blew out of the north from the great open waters of the Sea of Darkness. He turned to his companion.

"A nice ploy with the desert chieftains," he said in a quiet voice.

Heraclius nodded somberly, leaning on the still-warm stone of the crenellation. Even in the soft light of the moon, Galen could see that his brother Emperor was troubled.

"I think that it will work as we have planned," the Eastern Emperor said. "Their greed will lead them to battle and defeat at Shahin's hands."

"Do you doubt your stratagem now? Do you wish to discard it? We can still split off the Sixth Gemina and enough Germans to make another Legion-strength auxillia band to prop them up."

Heraclius pushed away from the wall and hooked his thumbs into his belt. "No, we are committed. I do not want to face the Boar with twenty thousand fewer men than I could. Sending those troops to fight in Syria would be a waste. Besides"—and now the Emperor smiled—"both of those cities are rich enough to take the loss."

Galen frowned, tapping his fingers on the stone. "Petra and Palmyra have been allies of the Empire for hundreds of years—are you sure you want to expend them in such a manner? It does not seem particularly honorable."

Heraclius laughed, a grim sound. "That bastard Chrosoes was surely honorable when he violated the treaty and attacked me five years ago. This is not an honorable war, my friend, this is survival. I will repay him insult for insult. I *am* the Emperor of the East."

"True," Galen said, shaking his head a little at the venom in the Eastern Emperor's voice, "but what of afterward, when we have won? The desert frontier will still have to be defended—and the men of these cities will be dead."

"There is nothing to defend against," Heraclius said, dismissing the subject. "Chrosoes is the enemy. He will pay for his treachery and his pretensions to my throne."

Galen was silent, balancing the good of the Empire as whole against the devastation that would be visited upon the distant cities in his mind. He was still standing by the wall, looking out on the dark bulk of Asia, beyond the moonlit waters, when Heraclius went back inside.

THE VIA APPIA, SOUTH OF ROME

)•(

The moon rode lower now, a great orange melon in the sky. Clouds obscured part of its face and cast the road into a deep gloom. Maxian nudged his horse forward to keep up with the lead rider. The clip-clop of the horses' hooves echoed from the metaled surface of the Via Appia, but the sound was swallowed by the hedgerows that bounded the road on either side. Beyond the hedges, unkempt fields were scattered with small buildings and raised mounds. Almost three miles behind the Prince, the guardtowers of the city wall at the Porta Appia could barely be made out, marked by gleaming lanterns and torches. The guide halted and raised his lantern. A black opening yawned on the right side of the road, marked by two pale white columns. The lantern lowered as the man leaned down from his horse to make out the inscription on the pillar.

An owl hooted softly in a nearby tree, then there was a rustle of leaves as it took flight.

Maxian, his face shrouded by a deep hood, fingered a gold coin. It was a double aureus, with the face of his brother on one side. Freshly minted, almost sharp-edged. He sighed and put the coin back in the pocket of his tunic. At his side, the old Nabatean laughed softly.

"Soon, soon, my lord, you shall have the lever that you need."

Maxian had rapped sharply on the overhung door with the head of his walking stick. Late afternoon was sliding quickly to night, and the narrow streets of the trans-Tiburtina were growing dim. People were walking quicker, trying to get home before full dark. The sky, what of it could be seen, was a deep purple streaked with rose-colored clouds. Maxian rapped again, faintly hearing movement within the residence. The door was unremarkable, marked only with a small sigil of two raised horns around a trapezoid. He had come here, to a stinking alley in the "foreign" district, on the recommendation of the last wizard he had visited. Though he had begun his search for assistance with a grim determination, now he was bone tired and ready to give up and go home.

The sorcerers and wizards he had approached, particularly those on the Street of the Magi in the Forum Boarium, had either refused to speak to him outright or had sent him away when he began to explain that the city was infused with some terrible power that could kill men or corrode metal. The last, a Jewish numerologist, had listened patiently to him for over an hour, then spread his hands and said that he had no experience in such matters. But, he continued, there was a man known to him, a Nabatean, who might be able to help.

And so Maxian was here, at this darkened oak door, at nightfall.

The sound of a sliding bolt rasped through the thickness of the door, then another noise, like a pin being drawn out of a metal socket. The door creaked open a crack, and a startling blue eye gleamed out at the Prince.

"Good evening," Maxian said in a very polite voice. "I seek the wise man, Abdmachus, who lives here. I am Maxian Atreus. I seek assistance in a delicate matter."

The eye disappeared and the door opened the rest of the way, revealing a short, thin man with a wisp of white hair showing from underneath a small felt cap. The fellow was dressed in a trailing robe of narrow blue-and-white stripes, bound at his waist with a dark-green sash.

"Come in, young master. I am Abdmachus. Welcome to my house."

The house of the Nabatean was long and narrow in its plan, wedged between two larger buildings. The tiny front room was bare with a tile floor. A second, heavy door led from the atrium into the rest of the house. It had no lock, but Maxian felt a tugging sensation as he passed through it. Beyond that portal there was a sitting room with a small fire in a brazier. Unlike the homes of the poor, the smoke was well behaved, swirling into a corner of the ceiling and vanishing up a partially exposed pipe of fired clay. The floor was thick with heavy rugs, all in muted browns and reds. Two low couches faced each other, making a triangle with the brazier at the head of each.

Abdmachus gestured Maxian to the rightmost couch and settled himself on the other. Maxian chose to sit rather than recline. The olive-skinned foreigner continued to regard him steadily.

Maxian coughed, clearing his throat. "Sir, I am in need of assistance. I understand from a fellow I met yesterday that you may be able to help me. Are you familiar with the, well, the unseen?"

Abdmachus cocked his head to one side, regarding the young man.

"If you mean," said the old man, "am I of the *magi*, then yes, I am experienced with the unseen world. I am confused, however, by your coming to me. You show unmistakable signs of being possessed of power as well, of the ability to see the unseen. I can feel the pattern of defense you have raised around you even now. Why have you come to me?"

Maxian raised an eyebrow; the elderly man was no fool, and well skilled to boot.

"I am not a sorcerer," he said in reply, "I am a priest of Asklepios. I have found something, however, that is far too strong for me to affect with my own powers. I need the advice, perhaps the help, of someone more . . . experienced."

Abdmachus smiled, showing small white teeth.

"Ah, experience I have," the old man said. "I no longer have the strength of youth such as you possess. But I do know a trick or two that gets me by in my dotage. I am no longer as strong as I once was—but as the Greek said, with a long-enough lever one might move the world! Now, this thing that you have found—it is a dangerous thing, and something that you have come across in your work? But if you are a priest of the healing art and you have not been able to defeat it, it must not be a disease, but something . . . something that causes disease?"

Maxian spread his hands, his face even grimmer than before. "Master Abdmachus, I beg you to hear me out fully before you make up your mind. I have gone to other wizards before you, and all of them, save Simon the Numerologist, have turned me away or told me that I am insane. There is an affliction upon this city that only I, as best I can tell, can see. A corruption and a bane that brings disease, death, insanity upon the inhabitants. Now that I have perceived it, I see it everywhere—in the broken stones of the street, upon the faces of the people in the markets, all around us. I know this sounds absurd, but it is as if a terrible curse has been laid upon the city of Rome."

The old man, much to Maxian's surprise, laughed softly, his eyes twinkling. Maxian's face clouded with anger; he had expected better of the Nabatean. He stood up.

The old man stopped laughing and held up a wizened hand.

"Wait, wait, my impetuous guest. I am not laughing at your theory. I am laughing at myself, for wasting so much time of my own. I believe you. I think that I know what you speak of. Sit, sit."

Maxian returned to the couch, not sure that he believed the old man.

"What you *see*," the old man said, "is like a tide of dark power, one that pervades the city, all unseen, almost unnoticed unless one knows what to look for. It is subtle and powerful, and it is so prevalent that to one raised here, or a long-term resident, it would seem . . . natural. Yes?"

Maxian nodded. "Yes, but it is inimical, deadly. Do you know what curse has spawned it?"

Abdmachus laughed again and shook his head slowly.

"It is no curse, young master, it is a blessing, a boon to Rome."

"How can you say this?" Maxian sputtered. "It has caused the deaths of eleven people that I know of! I have seen its ability to destroy, to erode and deform even metal, with my own eyes!"

Abdmachus shook his head again and stood up, going to the opposite wall of the room. There he passed his hand over a section of the brickwork, and it folded silently out to reveal a hidden space. From this space, he took a leather bag of coins. He returned to the couch and carefully removed a single golden coin from the bag.

"Look, young sir. This is a coin I accepted in payment yesterday from a noble of the city, a patrician, an officer of the state. Only now have I touched it, and only long enough to show it to you and to place it here."

The old man placed the coin on the small table that lay between the two couches. The pale gold gleamed in the firelight.

"The last man to touch it was this officer, who came to me seeking a favor. He is still *close* to the coin and it is still *close* to him. It is freshly minted, so almost entirely clean of the impressions of others, only his *shape* is upon it. Do you understand my meaning?"

Maxian nodded. The school in Pergamum had touched upon the theories of contagion and similarity, though more in the light of mending broken limbs and curing fevers than working power upon a hale person.

Abdmachus put the bag of coins behind his couch and leaned over the single coin. He looked closely at Maxian. "Now, I know that maintaining the pattern of defense is draining, so I shall make a new one, one that encompasses both of us. When I am done, please lower your own so that they do not interfere with one another."

Maxian nodded and almost without thought his sight expanded to fill the room. Now he could see the trembling aura around the old man, a stolid, burnished bronze color. The rest of the room was a tracery of fine blue lines of fire. His own shield glittered in the air between him and the Nabatean. The old man too was still and quiet. For a moment nothing happened, and then the blue fire began to wick up into the air. The brazier sputtered and went out, though Maxian could still see clearly in the darkness. The walls, floor and ceiling gave up their energy to a coalescing sphere that spun out, slowly, from the figure of the old man to pass over Maxian and then halt just beyond him. The blue fires slid, glutinously, to the sphere and at last it was complete.

The Prince relaxed for the first time in days, and his own shield flared and went out. He slumped backward on the couch, the low-level headache that he had been fighting while the shield was up passing away.

"Better, is it not?" the old man whispered, his eyes still closed in concentration. "Now I will show you the blessing of Rome . . . but be prepared to raise your pattern again at an instant. This will be quite dangerous."

The Nabatean reached out a thin hand and plucked at the air above the gold coin. Bidden by his hand, it rose up to spin slowly in the air between the old man and the prince.

"By the *shape* of the man who held this coin, I can influence him for good or ill. I can harm him, so . . ."

The old man twisted his hand in the air, and a virulent crimson tendril sparked in the air in front of him. Maxian sat up straighter, his own hand raised in an involuntary ward. The tendril of fire crept through the air and twisted around the coin. The air around the coin flexed, becoming cloudy, and for a moment the image of a stern, patrician face appeared around the coin.

"Easy, easy, young master, I will not actually harm the officer, but look, beyond the pattern of defense . . ."

Maxian turned his attention outward and his face froze at the sight beyond the pale-blue barrier. Acidic darkness surged against the blue sphere, filled with deep-purple fire and an eye-dizzying eddy of contorting shapes. The power that lay throughout the city, in the stones, in the air, in the war, englobed them and hissed and spit against the blue wall.

"You see the blessing? As I raise evil intent against a steward of the state, against an officer who is a very pillar of the Empire, the blessing moves against me. The pressure upon the pattern is incredible . . . even here, in a place where I have lived for many years and invested much power, it is almost enough to overcome me. I withdraw the threat."

The crimson tendril faded away and the coin spun gently down to rattle on the tabletop. Abdmachus opened his eyes, breathing heavily. Beyond the flickering blue wall, the darkness surged and spun about, beating against the invisible wall. Then slowly, inch by inch, it receded and flowed back into the walls, into the air, into the earth. Maxian let out a long slow breath when the last vestiges were gone.

The old man also slumped against the back of the divan in exhaustion, but his eyes were still bright. "It has always puzzled me that no Roman mage has written of this effect, or that the Empire has not trumpeted its protection to the four corners of the world. But seeing you here, now, with an equally puzzled expression tells me that no *Roman* has ever come athwart it and lived to tell of it to another."

Maxian pursed his lips and slowly nodded.

"Any who provoked the power," the Prince said, "would be destroyed were they not ready. No one would know . . ." He looked up sharply at the old man. "Then how did I survive discovering it? How did you survive discovering it?"

Abdmachus ignored the question for a moment, wearily levering himself up from the couch and disappearing behind a curtain at the back of the room. He returned in a few moments with jugs of wine and water and two broad-mouthed cups. He poured the heavy wine and then added a liberal dose of water to each. After he had drained the cup, he spoke.

"When I first came to the city, I was . . . so to say . . . not officially welcomed. I sought no license to practice my craft and I did not make myself well known. I took these rooms and set about assiduously minding my own business. I was younger, but still careful, so when first I essayed a commission such as I just demonstrated, I took many extra precautions."

He paused and poured another cup of wine, motioning to Maxian to drink himself. The Prince sniffed the wine and put forth a small fraction of his ability to see if it was safe. It was, and so he drank.

"It is common knowledge among the practitioners of the craft, at least it is outside of Rome, that the Empire is all but inviolate to sorcery and magic of all kinds. The widespread presumption is that the Imperial thaumaturges are so powerful that they detect or repel all attempts to do ill to the state. But my time here in the city has told me otherwise. Your sorcerers are strong, true, but they could not do this.

"Has it never struck you, or any other Roman, that your enemies have not slain your Kings or Emperors by magic? That the priest-kings of Persia or the witchmen of the Germans have not shriven your armies to ruin in the field of battle? These enemies can summon horrific powers and, I assure you, have done so in the past. But their efforts were for nothing. Such an attempt is a sure path to ruin for the practitioner. And this, what we have seen this evening, is why."

Maxian put the empty cup down. By parts he was greatly relieved that he had found someone who not only believed him but had considered the same problem himself. The perspective that he brought, however, was disquieting. He rubbed his face again, trying to urge his mind to motion. Abdmachus saw this and smiled again, though the young man did not see.

"Young master, you are gravely tired. There is nothing that can be done tonight about this. If you would care to, you may sleep here tonight. Here, at least, you can sleep free of troubling dreams and the effects of the power."

Great cypress trees folded over the top of the lane as they turned off the Via Appia. A suffocating darkness surrounded Maxian, and he shivered though the summer night was still warm. He could smell the richness of the fields on either side of the hedgerows. The lane descended and then turned to the left. The lantern ahead jogged to the right and the horsemen entered a small clearing.

The moon had passed through the clouds and now loomed large over a small temple on the far side of the clearing. Silver light lay upon the stones at the entrance to the tomb. Abdmachus swung spryly down from his horse, as did the two attendants who had led them to this place. Maxian looked around, surprised that the burial place of the Julians would seem so insignificant. Then he too dismounted. The Nabatean stepped to his side, carrying one of the two hooded lanterns they had brought.

"Light your lantern," he said, his voice low.

Maxian nodded and lifted the heavy bundle from the saddlebag on his horse. Praetor whickered at him and nudged his shoulder with a great soft nose. Maxian smiled in the darkness and dug in his pocket for a carrot. The stallion accepted the bribe with a gracious air and allowed himself to be tied off to a tree near the entrance to the temple. This done, Maxian unwrapped the lantern and sparked the wick to light with a snap of his fingers. Abdmachus had lighted his as well. The Nabatean turned to the two attendants and bade them sit in the cover of the trees and watch the entrance of the tomb and the lane.

"You've the other tools?" Abdmachus asked, turning back to the Prince.

Maxian hefted the leather bag he had slung over his shoulder; there was a clank of metal from within. In the moonlight, the Nabatean's head bobbed in acknowledgment.

"Then let us go," he said, his voice still low.

The door to the temple was a heavy iron grate, ornamented with a heavy cruciform lock. The bars were closely set and very thick. Abdmachus knelt next to the lock and carefully felt it with his fingertips. After a moment he began chanting in a very low voice, almost inaudible, yet Maxian could feel the shape of the words clearly. The air around the two men changed, becoming oppressively heavy, then there was the sound of rusted gears and rods scraping and the lock clicked open. Abdmachus stood and breathed out a shuddering breath. He wiped his forehead, then pushed the door gingerly open.

"It's been too long since I practiced that," the Nabatean said, his voice wry.

Within, a long narrow room led to the back of the building. The walls on either side were lined with deep-set niches, each holding a portrait bust. At the end of the room was a curved wall and a small altar. Behind the altar stood the mossy statue of a woman. Maxian stepped close and could barely make out the visage of a grim-faced goddess. *Minerva*, he thought to himself. Behind him, the Nabatean was rooting about in the heavy bag.

"Here," Abdmachus whispered, "there should be a circular hole in the side of the altar." He handed Maxian an iron rod, sixteen inches in length, with a handle at the end. The Prince knelt by the side of the marble block that comprised the altar. He felt along the side in the gloom; the lanterns were almost completely shuttered to prevent their lights from betraying them to passersby. His fingers found a smooth-sided hole, and he guided the bolt into the receptacle. On the other side of the block, Abdmachus had done the same. The Nabatean peeked up over the stone.

"Are you ready?" he asked. Maxian nodded. "Then on the count of two."

"One, then two . . . heave!"

The Prince grunted as he put his shoulder into dragging at the handle. Between the two of them, they managed to dislodge the block, revealing a dark opening under the altar and a draft of icy air. A smell of dampness and decay rose from the pit as well. Abdmachus shifted the hood on his lantern and peered down into the darkness.

"Excellent!" he breathed. "There is still a ladder."

Maxian laughed softly.

"You've done this before, I see," he said to his companion.

Abdmachus' white teeth flashed in the light of the lantern. "My family was poor, and the hills around my home city of Petra are riddled with the tombs of the nobility . . . sometimes an apprentice magi must make do with what he has. It has been some time, but one does remember some things."

The Nabatean tied off a line on the handle of his lantern, then leaned over the pit and lowered it slowly down. When it rested at the bottom of the pit, he swung his legs over the lip and onto the first rung of the ladder. Maxian watched while the old man's head disappeared into the shaft, then took one last look around. The empty eyes of the ancient heads gazed curiously back at him from the funereal niches. He shook his head in amazement at the desecration he and the old man were about to perform. *No matter*, he thought, *the dead care nothing. I need a tool, and many who would die will live because of what we do.*

Maxian had fallen asleep within moments of his head hitting the thin pillow. The little storeroom behind the sitting room was crowded with bags of herbs and odd-smelling boxes, but the Prince had paid no notice. He was snoring within a minute, the thin blanket pulled tight around him.

Abdmachus stood in the doorway for a little while, his hands warmed by the copper lantern he held before him. The old Nabatean considered the young man carefully. The Roman was exhausted and emotionally drained.

Why, after all these years, should such an opportunity fall to me? he wondered. He had come to enjoy living in the barbarian city, even if his dress was mocked by the laborers who frequented the taverna on the corner. His brow furrowed in concentration and he raised a single finger, quickly tracing the glyph for *friend* in the air before him.

On the cot, Maxian moaned a little and turned over, hiding his face.

•   •   •

The tunnels of the catacombs were narrow and low-roofed. Abdmachus led the way with his lantern, now unhooded, while Maxian carried the bag of tools and the other light. The air was fresh and a soft breeze blew into his face as they clambered through chambers strewn with bones, skulls, and decaying burial goods. After fifteen minutes the Prince realized that they were tending downward. Tunnel after tunnel branched off to the side of their path. A huge warren of narrow holes, pits, and cavities filled with skulls had been dug under the tomb of the Julians. A fine drift of finger bones crunched under his boots as they walked.

"Master Abdmachus, how big *is* this place?" Maxian asked at last as they descended another ladder.

The Nabatean laughed and stopped at the bottom of a corroded wooden ladder, steadying it as the Roman came down. "This valley has been the burial place of Rome for over a thousand years, my young friend. All of those millions of bodies have to go somewhere. Worry not, we are almost there."

At the bottom of another ladder, unaccountably, the tunnel veered sharply left and climbed steeply. Maxian scrambled in the loose dirt to climb up, then caught hold of a firm edge of stone. He pulled himself up and found that it was a marble step. A staircase now ascended, and the light of Abdmachus' lantern was far ahead. It was easier going than the loose dirt but still difficult as the steps were tilted sharply to the left. After a moment they joined a wall with a smooth marble facing. Maxian paused, staring in amazement at the bas-relief carved into the marble. A Roman family sat around a table, raising wine-cups in the blessing of the fall harvest. The face of Bacchus was graven above them, laughing from a wreath of holly leaves.

"Come, my friend." Abdmachus' voice echoed from ahead. "This is the place."

At the top of the tilted staircase, Maxian crawled out into a large chamber. High above, a rough earth ceiling showed the twisted roots of trees. The floor was uneven and loosely packed with gravel and dirt. By the light of the two lanterns, three tomb-houses jutted from the floor and walls. Dirt spilled around their marble doorways, but they were unmistakably of the vintage of the temple they had entered through. The Prince stared around in amazement.

"How . . . ?" His voice faltered.

Abdmachus looked up from where he was squatting by the door of the middle tomb-house. "As I said, young master, the people of the city have been burying their dead here for over a thousand years—once the valley that we rode through was not flat and level, but a long, low swale running south from the city. Hundreds of tombs like these dotted that valley. There was, if Cassius Dio is to be believed, a Temple of the Magna Mater, not too far from where we entered. Then, when during the glory of the Republic it was decided that the Via Appia should be built, the Claudians filled in the valley, burying all of those tombs, temples, and monuments. Like these . . ."

Abdmachus turned back to the door of the tomb-house. His long fingers traced an inscription cut into the door, brushing dirt away. He grunted noncommittally as Maxian leaned close with the other lantern. The inscription was shallow and hard to read.

"I think that this is the one. The patterns coalesce around it in the right way."

The Nabatean looked up at the Prince, his eyes shadowed in the lanternlight. "The door is sealed in such a way that I cannot open it. You must, and it will be difficult. The body within was lain here after a long journey, and the men who buried it feared that it would not rest well—not unexpected from a man foully murdered by his supposed friends. A working was laid on this tomb, particularly upon this door, and it has only grown stronger with age, not weaker. It will take plain force to overcome it in the time available to us."

Maxian nodded and laid the bag of tools down at his side. Abdmachus moved aside, and the Prince knelt in the loamy dirt before the door with his hands on his thighs. He calmed himself and then silently chanted the Opening of Hermes. After taking a circlet of twisted yew branches from the bag, Abdmachus settled the crown on the Prince's head. The darkness of the cavern seemed to close in on Maxian for a moment, but then his sight blossomed.

The door to the tomb-house was a deep viridian abyss. Trickling currents of fire crawled across the marble facing and descended into unguessable depths. For a moment he quailed before the strength of the door ward. Then he centered again and reached out to draw power from the crusty loam of the floor and the tree roots high above.

There was an instant of emptiness as the Prince drew on the fabric of the unseen world around him, then a stunning rush of power burst to him from the walls, the floor, from the litter of bones that were scattered about the cavern. Blinding white-hot energy coursed through the corridors of his mind.

In the dark cavern, Abdmachus had closed down all of his othersight and sat, cross-legged, at the side of the young man, his fingertips laid lightly on the pulse at Maxian's neck. The body of the Prince stiffened suddenly, and Abdmachus struggled to keep from laughing out loud in triumph. The boy twitched and his body convulsed, but his pulse—though it began to race—stayed strong. The Nabatean began a low chant, placing his fingertips lightly on either temple of the Prince. Around him, the detritus of bones trembled in the ground and then each femur, skull, and scapula began to twist itself free of the earth. Finger bones scrabbled in the dirt, then began to rise into the air. Clavicles rose and joined the slowly spinning array of bones. The door of the tomb-house began to flicker with a tremendously deep blue, almost black.

One of the skulls, already missing a quarter of the forehead, suddenly disintegrated in midair with a loud crack as the power Maxian was drawing from the remains of the dead took its physical integrity. There was a rapid popping sound as the smaller fibula and ribs pulverized. The other remains began to erode as an invisible wind lashed across them, spinning them faster and faster around the old man and the Prince.

Maxian felt and saw and heard none of this. His attention was utterly filled by the snarling whirlwind of power that had rushed into him like a mountain torrent. Something in the back of his mind gibbered in fear at the sleeting fire that channeled through his body. But his intellect was soaring on a godlike wave of ability. He directed his will against the tomb door and the ancient ward rang like a porcelain plate as the vast power smote it. The viridian abyss flexed under the assault and then deformed, suddenly becoming an almost silver mirror, throwing back a contorted reflection of the Prince. Then it broke apart in a shower of tiny green flecks. Maxian's intellect stormed into the tomb-house, greedily swallowing up the long-dormant energies of those buried within. At the center of the tomb, his rush slowed and then stopped. The body of a man lay on a simple bier. The body, long decayed and shriveled to a bundle of dry sticks, was dressed in the tattered remains of a formal white toga. Once leather-bound sandals had attired his feet, but they were only scraps now.

Maxian struggled to stop the avalanche of power that his initial attempts to draw on the rocks and stones had precipitated. At the edge of his perception, he could sense that the roof of the tomb, the walls, even the floor was beginning to erode. If he did not halt the effect, even the body before him, the lever that Abdmachus had promised him, would be destroyed. Grimly he tried to recenter his thought, and after a seemingly endless period of raging against the dissolution that was tearing at him, he succeeded. Though he could no longer feel it, his body was soaked with sweat and had collapsed in Abdmachus' arms.

Maxian's spirit hovered over the ancient body. His *shape* body was filled with what seemed to be an almost infinite power, burning white-hot at the core of his form. Mentally he flexed his healing talent and found that it had subtly changed. Before it was a delicate skein, capable of settling with utmost precision into damaged flesh or a wounded organ. Now it throbbed with a visceral power, capable of reforming shattered bones from chips, of reconstructing whole bodies. He wondered with delight at the vision of transformation it showed him. His thought turned back to the body. *This will work!* He exulted.

He placed his hands, shimmering in and out of mortal sight, on the withered body. He muttered a low chant and dust puffed from the floor into a great cloud that filled the chamber. He spoke again, strange inhuman words, and the dust congealed into the visage of a dull red heart suspended over the body of the dead man. Stiff fingers sank into the chest of the corpse, peeling back dry leathery skin to expose the corroded organs. The dust-heart began to beat, stiffly at first, but then filling with blood. The organ steamed and smoked. Maxian seized it from the air and crushed it in his invisible fingers. Hot blood, almost boiling, spurted between his fingers and flooded into the exposed cavity.

Maxian steeled himself, bringing the words of an old spell to his mind. Abdmachus had shown him the crumbling parchment and he had labored to make out the words, crudely scribed in the tongue of ancient Thessaly, but now they were clear and bright in his mind. Ghostly lips moved, saying:

"O Furies and horrors of hell! Dread Chaos, eager to destroy countless worlds! O Ruler of the underworld, who suffers for endless centuries because the death of the gods above cannot come too soon! Persephone, who hates and reviles her own mother in heaven! Hecate, goodness of the dark moon, who grants me silent speech with the dead! O Custodian, who feeds the snake-crowned Dog with human flesh! Ancient ferryman who labors to bring souls back to me on his ship of bones! Heed my prayer!"

The blood, steaming and hot, settled in the inner cavity of the body, soaking into long-closed arteries and veins. A sucking sound filled the dank chamber and the corpse trembled, filling with the burning liquid.

"If these lips of mine that call you have been tainted enough with hideous crimes, if I have always eaten human flesh before chanting such spells, if I have cut open the breasts of new mothers and washed them out with warm brains, if any baby could have lived, once his head and organs were placed in your temple—grant me my desire!"

The corpse, its lips flushed a pale rose by the blood curdling within it, did not move.

"Tisiphone and Megara! Are you listening to me? Will you not use your savage whips, studded with hooks and teeth, to drive this ancient wretch from the wasteland of Erebus? Shall I conjure your true names to call you forth into dreadful light? Shall I follow you over graves and burial grounds, driving you away from every tomb and urn? You, Hecate, shall I drag you before the gods in heaven and show them your true aspect, pale and morbid, always hidden behind artifice? Shall I tell the gods, O Persephone, what kind of dear food it is that keeps you under the earth, what bond of love unites you with the gloomy king of night, what defilement you welcomed that makes your mother deny you?"

The stones of the tomb echoed with the violence in Maxian's shout. The air crawled with strange lights and shuddering darkness. Still, the body on the slab did not move, though now wisps of steam and smoke issued forth from its eyes and mouth.

"Upon you, you lowest rulers of the world, shall I focus the sun—breaking open your caves—and daylight shall strike you. Will you obey my will? Or must I call him who makes the earth tremble when his name is invoked, who can look upon the Gorgon unveiled, who lashes a frightened Fury with her own whip, who dwells in the depth of Tartarus that is hidden even from your view, for whom you are the 'gods above,' who commits perjury in the name of Styx?"

The clotted blood, thick and viscous in the open wounds of the body, suddenly boiled up again. The limbs of the corpse twitched as it circulated, reaching the extremities. Flooded with the black liquid, the tissues in the cold breast began to vibrate, new life stealing into organs long unaccustomed to it, struggling with death. Every limb began to shake, the sinews stretching, the tendons popping. Eyelids flickered open, revealing dead white orbs. Stiff lips twitched and the chest, its gaping wounds closed and puckered, heaved with breath.

Maxian was giddy with triumph, seeing life and vitality flow throughout his creation. His head began to spin and he clutched at the stone lip of the table. His ghostly fingers fell through the platform.

In the cavern, Abdmachus stared up at the ceiling with near terror. The whirlwind of bones was gone, all of the remains consumed by the young master. The roots that anchored the roof were gone as well, and a steady trickle of gravel and stones rained down onto the floor of the chamber. The tomb door was gone, dissolved into dust, and a strange wind now blew into the open tomb. For all his long years scrabbling in the earth of graveyards, ossuaries and among the remains of the dead, the Nabatean harbored a carefully concealed fear of close spaces. The earth groaned around him as abused stones shifted. He cowered over the body of the young man, his own talents extended to the utmost to hold up the pattern of protection that kept *him* from being consumed.

The body of the young Roman twitched in his hands, and suddenly a scraping sound came from the open door of the tomb. The Nabatean twitched around to face the opening, his mind gibbering to him of cold-eyed ghouls and the other denizens of the dead places. In the ruddy orange light of the remaining lantern, the hand that suddenly came out of the darkness and gripped the door frame was smeared with red blood. Abdmachus flinched back and scuttled away from the body of the Prince. Another hand joined the first, and then the naked body of an elderly man heaved itself out of the doorway. He was almost bald, with thinning gray hair and a strong, patrician nose. His body was well muscled yet showing age despite an active life. A welter of scars marked his chest and the side of his neck. The dead man sneered, seeing the little oriental cowering in the dirt before him.

"Get up," the man snarled in an archaic accent. "Bring me clothing."

Abdmachus crept across the floor to the bag of tools and began rummaging in it, one eye on the dead man. The corpse pushed away from the wall and shook its head like a dog shedding water. It raised its hands and turned them over, seeing their pale flesh. It felt its chest and traced the scars and old wounds. At last it looked down on the unconscious body of the Prince.

"This is the one who has given me life again?" the dead man rasped.

Abdmachus looked up from the tunic, boots, undershirt, and cowled robe that he had removed from the tool bag. "Yes," he said, "he is your master now."

The dead man snorted and dust puffed from his nose. Puzzled, he dug a bony finger into each nostril and dragged out dirt and the desiccated remains of worms.

"Pfaugh!" The dead man cursed and tried to spit. A fine cloud of white powder drifted out of his open mouth. "Have you any wine?" it asked in a querulous voice.

"No," answered Abdmachus, handing the corpse the undershirt. "Put this on."

The corpse dragged the cotton shirt over his head and patted it down. It looked down at the Prince lying at its feet. "I could break his neck right now, while he sleeps. Then I would be my own master."

Abdmachus shook his head slowly, saying, "If he dies, you go back to the worms. While he lives, and wills it, you live."

The corpse accepted the tunic with a wry smile. Its dead eyes turned to Abdmachus.

"Then he should live a long time, shouldn't he . . . Persian?"

THE CISTERNS OF THEODOSIUS, CONSTANTINOPLE

The slow gurgle of water slid past under the bow of the long boat. Thyatis crouched in darkness, her head just above the lip of the hull. She could barely hear the soft sounds of men breathing at her side or the faint swish of oars in water. Like Nikos and the two Turks that were rowing, she was clad in loose-fitting black robes with soot blackening her face and hair. The darkness around them was only fitfully broken by the light of a shuttered lantern that danced over the water ahead of them.

Thyatis squinted, trying to make out the features of the men they were following. It was too dark and the light of the lantern too intermittent. She bit at her lip nervously. The chase was long and slow, wearing on her nerves. At first it had seemed it would be an easy operation—follow two of the Eastern lords who had slipped out of the Great Palace to their presumed meeting with Persian spies, then swoop down and bag the whole lot. She had not expected the quarry to descend into the depths of the half-abandoned cistern system that burrowed under the hill holding the palaces.

The sound of the oars of the other boat echoed off the high ceiling. Intermittently, the murmur of a man speaking carried to Thyatis, but she could not make out the words. Behind her own craft, two more shallow-drafted boats carried the rest of her men.

Around them, great pillars rose out of the cold waters, passing overhead like the branches of great stone trees. The air was chill, for the waters were fresh from springs in the hills beyond the city. Despite the Avar "siege" of the city, the aqueducts that fed the great public cisterns remained open and full. Nikos gently touched Thyatis' elbow. The boat ahead had pulled up to a jetty of stone jutting from one wall of the vast chamber. The distant lantern brightened as the man carrying it slid the hood aside and a set of steps were revealed, leading up into darkness. The thump of the boat coming to the jetty slithered across the water.

Thyatis held up her hand and the two Turks gently backed their oars. The other two boats glided silently to a stop in the partial cover of one of the towering pillars. The Roman girl watched and waited as two men got out of the boat at the jetty and climbed up the stairs, leaving one man in the boat with a second lantern. After a few minutes there was a distant *clang* of metal and the last traces of the lantern the two men were carrying disappeared from the steps. Thyatis turned and her hand flickered in quiet-talk to Nikos. Go, she signed, *quietly and take the boat.*

Nikos nodded and shed his cloak and shirt. Barefoot, he eased over the side of the boat. Thyatis and the two Turks subtly adjusted their seating so that the boat did not rock and make a noise as the Illyrian slipped into the dark water.

Taking a long breath, he submerged and the water closed over him with barely a ripple.

For a time, the men and woman in the three boats waited. Thyatis sat, still and quiet, watching, feeling the air around her and the breathing of her men. At last she felt the soft breath of Jochi as he breathed in and pushed his bow away from him, bringing the string taut. Ahead, in the pale light of the lantern on the jetty, she saw the dark waters part near the end of the boat and a lithe, stocky figure emerge. Nikos' hand blurred and the boatman's throat was suddenly crushed by iron fingers. The knife in the other hand slid through cloth and flesh with a whisper, and the body of the boatman jerked. There was no sound, but the boatman crumpled into the bottom of the boat. Nikos crouched over him, staring up the stairs.

No sound came, no shouts of alarm. Nikos climbed out of the water onto the jetty. Moving quickly, he picked up the lantern and moved it to the bottom of the steps, pointing upward. On the lead boat, Thyatis motioned her men forward. Jochi reslung his bow and took up his oar. The three boats slid forward over the dark water to the dock.

Dwyrin was curled into as small a space as he could manage, well back in the little recess on the side of the chamber of candles. He practiced being invisible, his breathing faint, his thoughts concentrated on stone, rock, and tile. In the chamber, the dead man Khiron was sitting quietly, staring at the little table and the items upon it. From time to time he would reach out a gray hand and shuffle the items about, making little tinkling sounds. So he had been since Dwyrin had awoken. The air in the chamber seemed close and heavy. The dead man had not taunted the boy, or brought him any food or water. The ache in Dwyrin's stomach was growing, but there was nothing to be done about it. Dwyrin watched the dead man out of the corner of his eye.

Suddenly Khiron stood, brushing his long cloak back from the little chair. He strode to the heavy doorway that led outside, to the long corridor, and paused as if listening. When he turned back, his face was drawn and grim. Then suddenly it stretched into the rictus of a smile.

"An arrangement has been made for you, boy," he said, his voice gravelly.

A tremor of fear rippled through Dwyrin and his eyes began to smart with tears. He scrunched himself smaller and pressed against the rough stone at the back of the recess. Khiron ignored this and unlocked the grate, reaching in and dragging the boy out with a long arm. He stood the Hibernian up and dusted him off.

"I will miss you, little mouse," the dead man said, his voice light, like flayed skin flapping in the wind.

"Come, it is time to meet your new master."

At the top of the long flight of stairs from the cistern, Nikos and Thyatis stood on opposite sides of the iron-bound door that closed off the top of the steps. One of the men, Ulfgar, stood before the door, carefully attired in the garb of the dead boatman. Anagathios had finished daubing color on his face and carefully smearing it to make an even surface. Done, the Syrian packed his small wooden case with precise, unhurried motions and then slipped back down the stairs. Thyatis nodded at Ulfgar and then quietly unshipped her shortsword from the sheath slung over her back. With the blade free in her left hand, she drew the fine-meshed silk veil of her hood over her face with her right. On the other side of the door, Nikos shook out a length of wire that had been threaded through a medium-length copper tube with knurled ends. His head, too, was shrouded in a hood of fine black silk.

Ulfgar swallowed and then rapped sharply on the door. There was no answer. He rapped again, louder. A few grains passed and then there was a metallic scraping sound beyond the door and a small window swung open. A smoky yellow light shone through and Ulfgar raised his own lantern, illuminating his face.

"What is it?" a heavy voice snarled in Walach. Through the edge of the small window, Thyatis could see part of a small room, lit by more than one lantern. A murmur of voices echoed off the walls—two, perhaps three more men.

"Let me in," Ulfgar said, his voice sounding tired and worn. "I'm tired of sitting in this cold pit."

The man in the window sneered and rubbed the top of his bald head, saying: "Too bad for you. You're supposed to stay with the boat."

Ulfgar scratched the side of his eye with a finger of the hand holding the lantern and raised an amphora of wine with the other.

"I'd rather not drink this alone," he said, mouth twisted to the side in a half grin. The eyebrows of the guard inside raised. Some kind of thought pattered through his head and he came to a decision.

"Pass that through and we'll take care of it," he said, smiling.

Ulfgar snorted and tucked the amphora under his arm. "Alone and cold I may be, but I'm not stupid." He turned and began making his way down the steps. The guard in the window looked after him and sighed.

"All right!" he called, laughing after the retreating back of the Saxon. "You and your wine are welcome!" There was a sliding sound of metal on metal, then the door opened a crack and the guard inside stepped partway out into the little landing at the top of the stairs.

Nikos was quick, like a snake, and the wire loop was over the guard's head, around his throat, and being dragged savagely tight before the Walach could as much as take a breath. Nikos held the copper tube in one hand and had yanked the end of the wire, which was wrapped around a short crosspiece of old oak, with the other. Thyatis blurred past the choking guard with the crushed trachea and the blood bubbling out of his nose and was into the guardroom before the three men seated around the stone table could more than look up in mild amusement at the antics of their friend.

The nearest one was looking over his shoulder at the doorway. His eyes widened as she rushed in. Her shortsword speared through his half-open mouth, cracked its point through the back of his skull, and then whipped back out like a bloody snake. He was still sliding sideways out of his chair, his spinal cord cut neatly in half and his mouth in ruins, when she ran past the man seated on the right side of the table and rotated her torso. The blade, spattering blood and white bits of bone across the room, rotated with her and sheared through the throat of the second man, carrying him and his chair over backward to sprawl across the floor with a clatter of wood.

The third man had sprung up out of his campstool and had lunged toward the spears on a wooden rack next to the rear door of the guardroom. Thyatis, nearly turned all the way to her right by the follow-through of her swordstroke, plucked a throwing knife from the bandoleer at her belt with her free right hand, cocked and threw in one smooth, effortless motion. The heavy-tipped blade sank into his back below his right shoulder, hilt deep, even as two black-fletched arrows, fired through the doorway, punched into the side of his chest from the opposite angle. He crashed into the wooden frame holding the spears and other gear. It collapsed with a great clatter of wood and metal.

Thyatis leapt over the body at her feet and to the far door. It was bolted on her side, which gave her pause for a thousandth of a second, and then she slammed the bolt open and rolled out into the passageway beyond. It was dark, and broad, with a musty smell. She glanced each direction and saw and heard nothing. The two Turks scuttled through the doorway behind her and took up positions facing each direction. Thyatis stepped back inside the guardroom.

Anagathios and one of the Greeks were dragging the bodies of the dead guardsmen out of the room as she entered. Nikos had cleaned off his strangling loop and had slid the copper tube back into the holder slung over his back.

Anything? he signed.

No, she answered, also in finger-talk, *a crossways corridor, empty and dark. We must be in the cellars of the building. Take your team and find the roof or a window. Alert the Imperials and then head for the fighting. I'll take my team into the main part of the building and find the Persian agent.*

Nikos nodded and then gathered the three Greeks, Anagathios, and Ulfgar to him. After a moment of silent discussion they faded off into the corridor outside and headed off to the left. Thyatis took stock of the room and then joined her team, comprised of the two Turks, a Yueh-Chu exile named Timur, and a hulking Goth named Fredric.

Can you smell a kitchen? she signed at Jochi.

The Turk smiled broadly, revealing a mouth filled with snaggly yellow teeth under a lank black mustache. He pointed to the right and up.

Let's go, she gestured. The two Turks led off, their bows out and arrows on the string. Thyatis followed, with Timur behind her and Fredric at the rear. They trotted up the corridor.

This time, when Khiron dragged the foul-smelling leather bag off Dwyrin's head, they were not in the study. Instead they stood on a raised wooden deck that overlooked a garden of pale-white flowers and dark bushes with long narrow leaves. Above them arched a roof of iron slats with mottled glass between each support.

A huge yellow-green moon wavered down through the glass. A heady scent filled the air. Dwyrin knelt on a thick rug. Sitting in wicker-backed chairs were the Bygar, the whiskered man, and the dark thing in flesh. Again, Khiron stood just behind Dwyrin and to one side, the fingers of one hand resting lightly on the boy's shoulder.

The remains of a meal lay between the Bygar and Whiskers. The Lord Dahak had only a partially full glass of wine in front of him. The smell of roast lamb, chickpeas, fresh bread, and resinated wine tickled at Dwyrin's nose. His hunger began to wake up, clawing at his stomach. It grumbled, loudly, and Whiskers laughed at the sound.

The Easterner turned to the Bygar. "Ai, friend, do not deliver merchandise in such poor condition! At least a scrap of bread for the boy. He is thin enough already."

The Bygar smiled and made a little half bow in his chair.

"I fear that my servant may have forgotten his charge," said the Walach.

Khiron knelt on one knee, his head low. "Forgive me, master, I did forget. Shall I call for the servants to bring him a meal?"

The Bygar glanced at Dahak, who was observing Dwyrin with lidded eyes. The Eastern sorcerer looked back and shrugged. It was of little import to him. The Walach nodded to Khiron, saying, "Yes, the boy should eat before he leaves my house for his new home."

Dwyrin quailed at the implication and sank lower on the rug. Fear filled his mind at the thought of departing from even the minimal sanctuary of Khiron's chambers to be with this . . . creature. Dahak smoothed back his long hair and stood, pacing over to the Hibernian. Khiron slunk away at the approach of the Easterner and then went off through the moon-flowers and bushes to find a servant. The sorcerer ran his hand just over Dwyrin's head, and the closeness of his touch was like standing in a frost-gale. Dwyrin shuddered and collapsed into a tightly curled ball on the floor.

Dahak laughed, and the moon-flowers wilted and closed at the sound of his voice. "Your pardon, Bygar. I did not mean to spoil the display of your flowers."

The Easterner bowed to his host. While he did so, there was a sudden fall of light through the windows in the roof. White and orange sparkled in the sky for a moment, and the shadows danced across the deck. The Bygar looked up with puzzlement, but Whiskers stood quickly and dragged his cape, hat, and a longsword encased in battered leather wrapping from behind his chair.

"An Imperial signal rocket," Whiskers rasped as he jammed the hat onto his head. "It is time to leave, my lords."

Dahak spun slowly around on his heel, his brow furrowed in mild concentration. Dwyrin was forgotten at his feet.

"There is nothing outside . . ." he began, then he rocked back as a black-fletched arrow sunk into his chest with a meaty *thwack*. For just an instant the Easterner stared down in puzzlement at the long shaft of the bolt, his hand raised to touch it. Then two more feathered into him, and he fell backward with a grunting sound.

Dwyrin rolled away from the falling sorcerer and off the decking. He fell heavily into a moon-flower bush by the side of the deck, crying out as thorns in the underbrush tore at him. There was a sound of running feet as a group of men charged out of the dimness. The Bygar shouted an alarm and then vaulted over the back of the deck and into the darkness of the garden. Whiskers, on the other hand, snatched up his cloak and spun it around his left arm. His right held a gleaming three-foot blade that had seemingly materialized there. He too shouted and sprang down the steps of the deck and into the midst of the charging men.

To Whiskers's great surprise, his lopping overhand stroke was parried by a flicker-bright length of steel in the hands of the lead attacker. He danced back as the assailant, dressed from head to toe in black, lashed out at him, nearly catching the elbow of his left arm. He lunged back in and for a moment the air was a flutter of steel in the moonlight and the spark of clanging arms. The other two attackers split off, the largest bounding up onto the deck itself, while the other dashed left into the brush of the garden.

Dwyrin rolled over and clawed at the thin metal chain around his neck. It flashed cold and seemed to constrict around his throat, but this time he knew what would happen and fought to open his mind to the othersight. Then, suddenly, there was a huge booming sound and the assailant who had charged up onto the deck was blown backward by a gout of white-hot lightning. The attacker sailed back across the garden and smashed into a wooden wall, breaking the timbers even as every bone in the man's body was crushed to a pulp of blood and bone meal. The nimbus of the lightning stroke hung in the air, etching a blast that arced across the great chamber.

On the deck, Dahak staggered to his feet, a halo of blue-white sparks leaping from his flesh and the remains of his clothing. The wooden shafts of the three arrows caught fire and smoked as they were consumed. Thunder boomed and echoed through the enclosed space like the rampage of the gods. High above, the glass panes shattered as the shock wave of the blast struck them and they came raining down in a thousand fragments.

Dwyrin had been blown back as well, but the rush of power in the garden had torn at the ban around his neck as well and now he ripped it from his neck. His othersight flooded in and the great space of the room was a maelstrom of unleashed energies. The creature Dahak stood at the center of a vortex of rippling lighting and fire. The lines of force that crisscrossed the great city began to give up their power to the Easterner and a wall of lightning suddenly rushed out from him.

To Thyatis, the world suddenly went pure white and there was a sound so large that it smashed into her like a wave. Her sword fight with the whiskered man was forgotten as she was flung backward into the ornamental pool of the garden. The foreigner was blown forward too, and he tumbled into the shallow water beside her. Distantly, part of Thyatis' brain was screaming *sorcerer sorcerer!* Still stunned, she stared at the ceiling above her in amazement as the thousands of glass fragments that had been raining down into the garden were thrown back into the sky like tiny comets. The wooden walls of the garden chamber caught fire.

Dwyrin staggered up, the pearly white of a Shield of Athena glittering in the air around him. The powers uncorked in the room were flooding into him as well, for he had no training to hold them out. Instinctively his mind grasped at the flames and the burning red torrent that surged in the earth under his feet. Fire lit from his hands and he turned sideways to throw it. Like a live thing, it leapt from his hands to tear at the flickering sphere of lightning around the creature hiding in human flesh.

Dahak staggered as a white-hot bolt of flame savaged the lightning wall he had raised around himself. He whirled and saw through the inferno that the fire-bringing power in the boy was running wild. Desperately the Easterner drew down the latent energy in the stormclouds hanging over the city and wove a tighter wall of defense before him. The building was fully aflame now, and choking smoke was filling the garden. In the distance, there were more screams and the sound of fighting. Dahak cursed and cast around for his companion. The Boar was crawling away from the firestorm, his sopping-wet cloak thrown over his body.

Three arrows suddenly flared into ash in front of Dahak, burned to a crisp by the flames raging against the lightning wall. More of the attackers were coming and trying to bring him down. *Enough*, he swore at himself, *we must leave*. He summoned wind and suddenly rose into the air.

Thyatis, who had scrambled out of the pool even as the wash of flames from the maelstrom around the deck swept across it, bolted for the doorway to the kitchens. Jochi and the other Turk were there, firing their bows as quickly as they could into the raging fire and lightning storm behind her.

"Save it," she barked at them as she dashed through the door. "No arrow will get through that."

The roof above them groaned and Thyatis realized that the entire building was now afire.

"Out! Out!" she shouted at the two Turks. "Get everybody out of here."

Behind her, there was a terrible roar and the roof above the garden collapsed in a gout of flame, coming down with a crash. Dust and smoke billowed out of the door, and Thyatis and the remainder of her men fled into the hallway.

Dahak soared through the storm clouds, ringed by thunder and the ghosts of lightning. Power burned in him, his body failing, ravaged by the forces it conducted. The Boar, clutched close in his wiry arms, screamed as the electrical surges that coursed through Dahak's body tore at his nervous system. Below them the house of the Bygar collapsed in a great pyre of flame. Smoke and soot billowed up hundreds of feet to lick at the low clouds. The streets around the old brick building were swarming with Imperial guardsmen, firemen, and the citizens of the neighborhood. Rain had begun to fall, but bucket brigades were in full force, trying to save the warehouses on either side of the old mansion.

Dahak cared nothing for this, bending all of his will to reaching safety on the far side of the Propontis. They hurtled low over the wavetops of the waterway. The sorcerer could barely make out the far shore. The last spark of static electricity fled him, and for a moment the two of them rushed through the night air, then the dark waters suddenly snatched up at them, catching Dahak's trailing foot. The water was icy cold and a sharp shock as it smashed into them, then swallowed them up. The sorcerer struggled in the surging water for a moment, then consciousness left him and there was only the weight of the Boar, dragging him down.

Dwyrin sat on a narrow stone bench in a narrow little hallway, fidgeting. He picked at the scabs on the side of his face and his lower arms. The rosebush had torn him up pretty badly when he fell off the decking in the garden room. The Illyrian, Nikos, who was sitting on his left, nudged him to keep still. To his right, Timur, who seemed to be Turkish or Sarmatian, was sleeping, or pretending to sleep. The hallway was hot and filled with clerks, soldiers, and couriers, who pushed past the three sitting on the bench. Dwyrin tugged at the bandage over his right ear. It itched.

The last thing Dwyrin had seen in the house of the Bygar had been the blossoming flame of his own fire-cast raging against the swirling blue-white wall of lightning. The voice of the Eastern sorcerer had been huge, like a thunderstorm filling the sky, but then there had been fire and smoke. Strong arms, wiry and corded with muscle, had scooped him up and dragged him out of the burning building. Dwyrin had passed out, his throat filled with the bite of woodsmoke. He had woken in a crowded barracks, lying on a thin pallet of straw behind a great heap of barrels. Overhead, a series of stone ribs held up a soot-stained brick ceiling. An evil face with sallow skin, pinched eyes, and long, greasy, mustaches had been crouched over him. Dwyrin had stared back in astonishment, but the man had smiled and given him bread, cheese, and weak wine.

Dwyrin gathered that Timur was a soldier, though not a legionnaire. A mercenary drawn to the service of Rome by the smell of gold, doubtless. He and his fellows were a footloose band that was living in a basement of one of the lesser palaces. Their chief seemed to be the Illyrian, Nikos, who had looked the battered Dwyrin over after the boy was strong enough to sit.

"You say you had papers, lad?"

Dwyrin nodded. He remembered the master of the school pressing them into his hands. Where they were now? Who knew? But he did remember his purpose.

"They were orders to report to the prefecture in Alexandria, to enter the Thaumaturgic Legion. To serve the Emperor in the great war."

Nikos had shaken his head in disgust at the thought of the young boy before him being drawn into the toils of the Imperial military machine. It was bad enough that he had fallen afoul of slavers, but the Legion? Timur, leaning against the nearest wicker crate, had chuckled at the expression on Nikos' face.

"Are you sure of this, lad? Being a twenty-year man is no light load. You'll be gray when you get out, mark me." Nikos jerked a thumb over his shoulder at the crowd of men playing dice at the entrance to the area claimed by the other members of his squad. "Look at these fellows. With your training, you could take up a soft life in the city, become rich. Have servants."

Dwyrin had shaken his head. He had given old Nephet his word that he would carry out the task set him. His honor depended on it. Nikos and Timur had argued with him for another hour, but it was to no avail. So, the next morning, they had trooped with the boy up to the quartermaster's billet in the "new" palace.

A door opened in the hallway and a slightly built clerk with a frizz of white hair looked out.

"Dwyrin MacDonald, enlistee?" The man's voice was devoid of emotion, but it carried to where the three were sitting.

Dwyrin jerked awake and stood up.

Nikos stood as well and tousled his hair. The stocky Illyrian smiled, his stubbly square face lighting for an instant. "Be careful, lad. Don't take any extra duty and never, ever volunteer. Remember that!"

Timur stood as well, easing up on his bad leg, and fingered his mustaches. He looked down at the boy for a long moment, his face a mask. Then he smiled a little too and pressed a worn leather knife scabbard into the boy's hand. It was grimy and nicked, and the hilt of the knife was wrapped in leather so black with age and sweat that it seemed like obsidian. Dwyrin smiled back and bowed, taking the leave-present. He turned and entered the room set aside for the oathtaking.

Outside, Nikos glared at the closed door. Timur leaned against the wall at his side.

"We should have convinced him to stay with us," Nikos said, his voice tight with disappointment. Timur snickered.

"He's too young for you, optio." Nikos ignored him.

"The centurion will skin me for letting a fire-caster get away," he continued. Timur shrugged. The boy was gone. Nikos stalked off down the hallway, ignoring the clerks and bureaucrats who got in his way. Timur followed close after, though his leg was hurting him again.

In the room, there was only a desk with a camp stool behind it. On the stool sat a lean-faced man with dark brown hair. He wore the tunic, short cloak, and leggings of a senior centurion. At his right breast, a small golden eagle was pinned to hold back the folds of his cloak. He had a muster roll open on the desk in front of him. The clerk, having shown Dwyrin in, retreated to the wall by the door. The centurion did not smile and looked the Hibernian up and down, his lips pursed in disapproval.

"Name?" he asked.

"Dwyrin MacDonald, sir."

The centurion carefully checked through the roll. At last, he shook his head slightly.

"There is no record of your levy, MacDonald," he said.

Dwyrin nodded, saying, "I was supposed to report to the prefect in Alexandria, sir, but I became sick and was sold to slavers. During that time I lost my travel and assignment papers, sir."

The centurion continued to regard him, his light-brown eyes cold. "Do you know which unit, or legion, you were assigned to, MacDonald?"

"Yes, sir, the Third Ars Magica."

An eyelid of the senior centurion flickered. He put the main muster roll aside and unfolded a smaller one. He checked through it, his long fingers rustling through the rolls of papyrus. He looked up. "Here you are. You are to report to a unit that was to muster at Alexandria. Have you taken the oath of enlistment?"

"No, sir."

The senior centurion sighed and gestured to the servant at the back of the room. The white-haired man crossed to another door and returned with a tall wooden pole surmounted by a bronze eagle with downswept wings. Beneath the eagle were two cross-plates, each inscribed with letters. The servant knelt and held the standard in a firm grip. Another servant entered through the same door, with a smoking copper brazier and a wooden-handled object. The senior centurion and the new servant fussed with the brazier. Finally it was ready. The centurion turned and motioned for Dwyrin to kneel.

"Take off your tunic," he said, his voice level. Dwyrin obeyed. The centurion stood over him. Dwyrin stared at the floor, wondering what the oath entailed.

"You are Dwyrin MacDonald, of the house MacDonald. Son of Aeren."

"I am," the boy answered.

"You pledge yourself to the service, in war, of the people and the Senate and the Emperor of the city of Rome?"

"I do," Dwyrin answered.

"Do you swear to uphold the state with your very life, under the auspices of the gods?"

"I do," Dwyrin said. Now an odd feeling stole over him, a prickling along his skin. For a moment he was tempted to assume the entrance of Hermes and see if some fey power had entered the room, all invisible. But he did not. The centurion continued to speak, his voice rising.

"I so swear," Dwyrin finished. The centurion pulled the wooden-handled rod out of the fire in the brazier. Before Dwyrin could flinch away, the two servants seized his arms and bent them back. The centurion, his eyes glinting in the reflection of the fire, pressed the white-hot brand against the pale white shoulder of the boy.

At the top of the steps at the far end of the corridor that led away from the quartermaster's offices, Timur heard the echoing wail of pain. He smoothed his mustaches and his hand slid into the light shirt he wore. His fingers ran lightly over the ritual scarring that decorated his chest and abdomen. He smiled and then made his way down the stairs. They were narrow and steep and well worn by the passage of thousands of feet.

THE SUBURA DISTRICT, ROME

"Gods, what a pit!" The dead man sneered, his leathery face twisted into a grimace. He and Abdmachus rode down a narrow way behind the Forum. The alley was choked with garbage, broken furniture, and the rotting corpses of dead animals. The little Persian led, while the dead man had the young Prince thrown over the front of his saddle. A gray cape had been added to the clothes Abdmachus had given him in the tomb. The motheaten hood was pulled forward, shading the man's extremely pale complexion. The Persian nudged his horse right and they turned into a little courtyard behind the brick edifice of a four-story insula. The dead man looked around carefully, his face a mask, while the Persian swung off his horse and made his way up a flight of broken steps to bang on the door at the back of the block of flats.

A sound rose, echoing from the pale brick faces of the buildings, a great murmur like the sea against a steep shore. The dead man turned around on his horse, looking for the source of the noise. Off to the south he saw a great cliff of marble rising over the red tile roofs. A forest of banners and pennons surmounted it. Smoke rose around it, curdling against the soaring wall and collecting in the arched openings that ringed the top of the edifice. He scratched his nose, then held his hand up in the morning light. It seemed odd for it to be so bleached and pale, very like the belly of a fish.

A man in a dirty yellow smock opened the door and nodded to the Persian. Abdmachus stumbled down the steps and came up to his horse.

"What is that?" The dead man pointed at the building looming over the rooftops.

Abdmachus turned, his fingers busy untying the straps that held the Prince to the horse. He squinted into the sun.

"Oh," the Persian said, "it's the Colosseum. There must be games today."

They had entered the city through the Porta Ostiensis gate, by the river, at dawn. A great throng of merchants and draymen had already clogged the artery leading into the city from the southwest. The Persian had shown his papers to the overworked guards at the gate, and they had entered without incident. The dead man was, by turns, troubled at the wan pallor evident on the faces of the people and stunned by the vast size of the city and the crumbling monuments therein. Cutting across the city toward the bowl of the Subura, they had passed through ancient gates, triumphal ways, and skirted the palace-clogged magnificence of the Palatine. As they rode through the thronging crowds, the Persian could hear the dead man muttering to himself.

The Prince owned an *insulae* on the southern side of the Subura, and the

Persian and the dead man carried his body up the steps, down a rank hallway, and through a stout wooden door into a bare apartment. Only a few sticks of furniture were about, but there was a bed made of pine boards and crisscrossed leather straps. They lay him there and the Persian bustled off to find water and make an infusion. The dead man crossed the bare dusty room to the windows set into the south wall and, putting his shoulder to them, opened the shutters. Brilliant sunlight flooded the room, cutting long sparkling trails through the dusty air.

"Ai, no strength in these limbs," the dead man mused to himself. He clenched his fists and frowned at the sound of muscles cracking.

Beyond the windows, the temples and pillars of the Forum rose up over the tiled roofs of the buildings across the street. The way below was crowded with morning shoppers. The little door fronts were crammed with goods: fruits, slabs of meat, bushels of grain, carefully bundled feathers. The noise from the street echoed off the roof in the apartment. The dead man half closed the shutters. Abdmachus returned to the room with a steaming pot of water. The sharp smell of mint and sage rose from it.

"What is that great cylinder?" the dead man asked, pointing out the window.

Abdmachus glanced up, then said, "The triumph of Trajan. A long bas-relief depicts his conquest of the Dacians."

The dead man snorted and rubbed the side of his long face. Dust and grit came off under his fingers. He smiled.

"Dacia . . . always troublesome. How long was I in the ground, Persian?"

Abdmachus tipped the lip of the pot to Maxian's lips and spilled a little of the brew. The young man twitched and the Persian managed to get more of the brew down him. The Prince groaned and his eyelids fluttered.

"Over six centuries," the Persian answered absently, his attention focused on the pulse and color of the Prince.

"Six centuries and the Republic winds up looking like a pigsty?" The dead man came to the other side of the bed and gazed down on the long-limbed youth who lay between them. "Six centuries and the city is a crumbling ruin, filled with plague victims and lepers? Is there no order? I see that the administrative skills of the Senate have not improved . . ."

Abdmachus looked up briefly but said nothing. The Prince stirred, his eyes opening.

"Are we in the city?" Maxian's voice was faint.

The Persian rolled back each of the young man's eyelids and pursed his lips in concern. "Lie still, lad, you're still shaken up. The effects of the spell were rather stronger than I expected."

Maxian smiled weakly. "Feels like my skin has been scrubbed off and then put back on, wet."

With a great effort he turned his head to look at the dead man. "Welcome back to the land of living."

The dead man scowled and looked over his shoulder at the partial view of the city from the window. "Not much to see. How many have died from the plague?"

The Persian and the Prince exchanged puzzled glances. Abdmachus cleared his throat. "My lord, this is twice you've referred to the plague. We don't understand."

The dead man stared at each of them in turn, his face a picture of incredulity.

"Out there"—he pointed out the window—"the people on the street. They look ghastly . . . the only time I've seen such deprivation in an unbesieged city was during the outbreak of the plague in Thapsos when I was a young man."

Maxian coughed, then managed to clear his throat. "It is no plague, my friend, it is the common state of the Roman citizen in these days. Those men and women are as healthy as they're liable to get."

The dead man shook his head in disbelief, then took quick steps to the window. He looked out for a long time. Then he said: "They are like the walking dead. Each face is cut with terrible weariness and pain. The citizens are . . . diminished, frail almost."

Abdmachus exchanged a knowing glance with the prince, then said: "It is why we have brought you back, my lord. There is a . . . a curse upon the city. We need your help to break it. But be warned, it is very strong. We believe that it is, in part, the doing of your nephew."

"Who?" The dead man was puzzled. His face creased in thought. "I have—I *had*—no nephews. All of my children are dead."

Maxian struggled to rise and managed to get up far enough to lean against the plaster wall. "The *Histories* say that he was adopted by you, made your heir. He used your name, in part, to make himself Dictator of the city. You must remember him—Gaius Octavius. Your sister's daughter's son."

The dead man stared at Maxian with something like shock on his face. He rubbed the back of his head, then turned around and paced to the window. There he turned back again, his hands on his hips. "Octavian? That mousy little sycophant claimed to be my heir? A colorless, mewling senatorial lickspittle? All he did was follow around on my heels, snooping. I surely left no will naming him my heir . . ."

Abdmachus laughed. The dead man was beside himself with disgust. Maxian was more serious. The dead man continued to curse luridly, until at last he ran out of epithets.

"Whether you made out that will or not, it was presented to the Senate in your name. After a civil war he became Emperor," the Prince continued with a weak voice. "The first of many. Under his supreme rule, the Republic became a shell, and the Empire came to rule the world. It was in his time that this curse that you see reflected on the faces of the citizens began. We think, Abdmachus and I, that it was intended to protect and sustain the state and that for a long time it did. But the world is changing and the state, because of this curse, cannot change with it. The people are the ones who are suffering. The state remains, but it is becoming more and more rotten. Great changes must be made to cure this ill."

The dead man had barely heard anything that Maxian had said. "But what happened to Marcus Antonius? What happened to my supporters? Marcus should have followed me as Dictator—he was well beloved of the people! The Senate would not stand for an Emperor . . . did the wars continue, did Rome bleed still more?"

Maxian sighed. It was going to take a long time to bring the dead man up to date on the doings of the city and the Empire . . . If only his head did not feel like it was being crushed in a vise. The dead man began pacing restlessly. The nervous energy in that spare frame only made the pain in the Prince's head worse.

THE SPICE ROAD, NEAR
THE WADI MUSA, THEME OF ARABIA FELIX

The tall Egyptian was walking along the bottom of a streambed when a bandit came rushing out of the deep purple shadows under the rocks.

A steep-sided valley soared on either side of him, littered with giant red sandstone boulders, bigger than houses. The sun was setting behind him as he trudged up the long incline, filling the western sky with a vast swathe of gold and saffron. In the wild hills of the Ed'Deir night fell quickly, replacing the searing heat of the day with chill cold. Sand and gravel, as red as the sky behind him, crunched under his feet. Ahmet had come a long way, from the upper Nile, to Alexandria, then by *felucca* to the Nabatean port of Aelana. The port was bustling with merchants and traders shipping cargoes from the Sinus Arabicus—that narrow sea that bounded Egypt on the east. The few coins that remained in his wallet after the trip from Alexandria were insufficient to purchase a camel in that bustling port. So he had walked.

He knew that he was only hours from the "hidden" city of Petra, nestled in these barren hills in a close valley. But he had not gotten there yet. His mind was weary and he did not recognize the slap of sandals on the smooth sandstone until it was almost too late.

The bandit was swathed in dark cloth and only his eyes glittered out of the head wrappings. He swung a long staff tipped with a nine-inch iron blade. Ahmet sprang back and the iron rang on the stones. The bandit said nothing but slashed again with the pole-arm. Ahmet dodged to the left, gasping for breath. His blood filled with the rush of fear; the narrow canyon and the lambent sky receded from his vision. Only the sharp tip of the spear filled it. The bandit lunged again, and Ahmet darted to the right. The bandit cut low and the iron bit into the side of the Egyptian's leg. Pain sparked and there was a roaring sensation in the priest's mind. He jumped inside the reach of the spear and lashed out with a knotted fist.

The blow took the bandit in the side of the head, rocking him back. Ahmet followed with a kick to the stomach and then wrenched the spear away from the man as he fell back with a choking cry. Without thinking the priest reversed the pole-arm in one motion and struck downward, all his weary rage behind the blow. The iron sank deep into the bandit's chest, like a knife into heavy bread, and then grated against the stones. The bandit twitched and spasmed around the blade pinning him to the sandy floor of the streambed. Grimacing, Ahmet jerked the blade out of the man. Blood sluiced from the weapon, spattering on the ground.

The priest stepped back, the spear raised, and he looked around. The air, now filling with the dim of twilight, seemed preternaturally clear. Shuddering, he took a series of deep breaths and calmed his heart. His racing pulse subsided. *He might have friends*, he thought. His focus turned inward for a moment, and he let his awareness expand to cover the great stones, the walls of the canyon, the scrubby gorse and bent little trees. There was no one else. A mournful owl called in the distance, hunting for its prey.

Ahmet shook his head and bent down over the dead man. He said a prayer to guide the soul of the bandit to the Great River and the Judges. Then he took the knife and wallet the man had at his waist and strapped them to his own kit. The body he rolled up in the desert robes and carried into the deep shadows. He found a crevice in the rocks and pushed the body into it. He gathered rocks in the darkness and piled them at the entrance. There was a little flash of soft light as he placed a ward to keep animals away from the body and ensure its rest.

Then he continued up the canyon. Above him, in the arc of sky that was not obscured by canyon walls, the firmament of heaven was filled with a thousand stars, all bright as jewels.

Two hours after full darkness, Ahmet climbed the last switchback of the trail at the head of the Ed'Deir and came over a lip of rock and into the valley of the city of Petra. The valley rose up in a bowl, away from him, filled with the lights of lanterns and torches. Hundreds of houses climbed up the terraces of the city before him. Above them the crags of the mountains rose, a great palisade of stone cupping the city in stony fists. There was no moon, and the gleam of the house lights cast a soft glow into the haze that hung over the city. He stood at the entrance of the canyon, leaning against his staff. From a great height off to his right, there was a blaze of firelight on the mountaintop. As he stood in the darkness at the edge of the city, he could hear the murmur of thousands of voices raised in song. The citizens were singing in the High Place.

The streets were empty and the houses shuttered and locked. Ahmet wandered for another hour before, on the far side of the city, past the dark and empty amphitheater, he found a caravansary. Beyond the squat stone buildings, a dark cleft opened in the mountains and a stream flowed out, gurgling and chuckling to itself in the darkness. Ahmet rapped on the door with the head of his staff. Eventually a small slot opened and a tired-looking man with mussed dark hair and a pale, angular face stared out.

"Good evening," Ahmet said. "Do you have room for one more traveler tonight?"

The innkeeper looked him up and down, then peered out of the slot up and down the street. It was empty and a lone man, dressed in the garb of an Egyptian priest, stood before him. The man shut the covering over the view-slot and slid back the bolts on the door. Ahmet bowed and stepped inside. The innkeeper rubbed sleep from his eyes and led the Egyptian into the common room on the right side of the atrium.

"Rooms we have," he said, over his shoulder, "a solidus a night. There's cold stew on the fire and water in the bucket. Wine is a copper a mug, if you want it."

"Thank you, no," Ahmet said. "I do not drink wine."

The innkeeper grunted and pointed up a flight of stairs on the far side of the common room. "The third door on the right, past the landing. You've it to yourself for tonight."

Ahmet nodded his thanks and shrugged off his shoulder bag and parcels onto a table near the fireplace. He counted out a solidus in copper from his wallet and gave it to the innkeeper. Then he drew out the scabbarded knife that he had taken from the bandit and gave it to the innkeeper.

"A bandit attacked me in the canyon outside of town. Only one. This was his. Perhaps the civil authorities should check into it."

The innkeeper raised an eyebrow and examined the blade, turning it over in his hands. "He dead?"

Ahmet nodded and took his bowl and a spoon made of carved horn out of his satchel. He went to the fire and began scooping cold lamb stew out of the iron pot.

The innkeeper put the blade back among the priest's things. "I'll tell the prefect in the morning. If the fellow is dead, there's little use of rousing anyone tonight."

The innkeeper went back to bed, turning down the wick on the one lamp near the entry door. Ahmet sat and ate his stew in quiet solitude. The water was tepid and smelled of smoke, but he drank deep from the bucket as well. After he was done, he said a short prayer to the hearth gods for finding safe haven for the night.

"Are you a priest?" A sleepy voice came out of the dimness on the other side of the bulk of the fireplace. Ahmet turned slightly. A man had sat up from lying on the bench behind the other table.

"Yes, of the order of Hermes Trismegistus. I am Ahmet, of the School of Pthames."

Even in the dim light of the single lantern and the embers of the fire, Ahmet could see the flash of strong white teeth nestled in a dark beard. The middle-aged stranger swung off the bench and came to sit opposite the priest on the other bench. He was dark-skinned, whether by the sun or birth could not be told. He had a strong nose and a noble chin and forehead. A neatly trimmed beard and mustaches graced his face. Long dark hair was tied back behind his head. He was dressed in the tan-and-white linen robes of the desert tribes south of the Nabatean frontier.

"I am Mohammed of the Bani Hashim Quraysh. I am a merchant on my way to Damascus."

Ahmet smiled back. He did not need his othersight to see that the merchant was a bundle of barely repressed energy. His handshake was firm and direct. "Well met, Mohammed of the Quraysh. I am also on my way to Damascus."

Again the smile in the darkness. "To many men, I would say that traveling alone on these desert roads is a chancy business But I heard you speak with the innkeeper and you seem a man capable of taking care of himself. I wonder . . ."

"What?" Ahmet said, his voice filled with amusement. It seemed clear to him that the Southerner had been watching and waiting in the darkness, making up his mind about what he was going to say. Despite the Arab's direct, even rude, approach, he found himself liking the irrepressible fellow.

"I wonder if a priest that is quick with his hands, and wit, would consider traveling with a merchant on his way to Damascus. By the look of your cloak and sandals, you've no camel or horse. You're walking and it's a very long road to Damascus from here."

Ahmet nodded, impressed at the keen eye of the merchant. "I just came from Aelana. It has been slow going."

Mohammed nodded, quite pleased with himself. He reached into his robes and pulled out a finely tooled leather pouch. Tiny ivory clasps held it closed. He unsnapped the top and shook out several silver coins into his palm. "Ten solidii— if you will accompany me and my men to Damascus and help protect the caravan. Before you ask, I will tell you—a priest is good luck and these are dangerous times, particularly on this road."

Ahmet eyed the coins on the tabletop as if they were asps. His vows with the order urged poverty and a simple, even rustic, life upon the priests.

You've already broken those vows once, said a little voice in his head, *coming here, looking for the boy.*

He reached out and turned one of the Roman coins over. It was newly minted. On the face, the stern visage of the Emperor Heraclius, on the obverse, the sigil of the mint of Palmyra and a smaller inset of a woman in a crown. He picked up four of the coins and pushed the others back.

"I will accompany you as far as Gerasa—I am looking for a missing friend, and I do not know if they have gone as far as Damascus."

"Good enough for me," the merchant said. The Southerner pushed his chair back and gathered up the other coins. "You're tired, I think, so sleep in. We won't leave until late afternoon tomorrow at the earliest. I have a cargo of myrrh to load and pottery to sell. Ask the innkeeper where I am, he'll know."

Ahmet nodded his thanks and put the heavy coins in his wallet. The merchant gathered up some things from the other table, one of them a heavy papyrus scroll. Ahmet raised an eyebrow at the sight.

"What are you reading?" he asked as the merchant finished gathering his things.

Mohammed looked down and laughed softly. "A gift from a friend. You will find that I am a questioning man—always wondering about this thing or another. I was pestering him with questions about the way of things in the world and he gave me this. To my thinking, he hopes that I will read it and bother him no more. He calls it the *torah*. It is a holy book of his people."

"He is a priest, then," Ahmet said.

Mohammed nodded. "He calls himself a teacher, but I think that you are right." He looked down at the scroll case. "It was a princely gift. I will have to find something as good, or better, to give back to him when I return to the south."

Ahmet rose as well, his supper done.

"Good night, Mohammed," he said. "Perhaps on the road to Gerasa, we can discuss the way of things."

The merchant nodded, smiling, and went up to his room.

Morning came and with it a great racket in the street. Ahmet dragged himself from the soft bed with great reluctance. After four days of sleeping on stones in the wilderness, the comforts of the caravansary were welcome indeed. He rubbed at the stubble on his chin and pushed the shutter on the deep window embrasure open. In the street below, hundreds of men and horses were milling about.

Soldiers, he thought. *A cavalry regiment.*

They were dressed in desert garb and light armor, with lances and bows. Eventually order was imposed on the unruly lot and they trotted away up the narrow canyon that the stream came out of.

When he had reached Alexandria on the trail of the boy, Dwyrin, Ahmet had found the Greek city in an equal uproar. The canals and harbor were clogged with barges, dhows, and great triremes. The Roman Legion that was stationed in Egypt was being withdrawn to fight against the Persians, and tens of thousands of men were on the move. It had taken almost three days to find and see the quartermaster in charge of the levy of new troops. Then Ahmet, to his dismay, had learned that the boy had not reported in at all.

Much of his small store of coin was expended in getting the chief scribe at the prefect's offices in the New Palace to find out where Dwyrin's unit was heading; the Third Ars Magica, a component of the Third Cyrenaicea Legion, was being loaded aboard ship to sail to Sidon on the coast of Phoenicia. If the boy was not on the rolls in Alexandria, perhaps he had met with his unit already and was well away from the city. Non-Imperial shipping to the embattled coast of Syria was nonexistent, and he could not well take passage on a troop transport. He had made his way back to the inn on the southern canal. Several sailors had been in the common room, and discussions with them had led Ahmet to take a ship back down the Nile to Heliopolis and then go by camel to the burgeoning port of Clysma on the Sinus Arabicus. Everywhere he had traveled in the lower delta, the Roman army and its auxillia was on the move.

So too here, in Petra. After shaving and performing his morning rituals, Ahmet went downstairs and found that the cavalrymen had eaten all of the breakfast save a few day-old rolls and a little porridge. He sat in the corner, where the Arab merchant had sat the night before, and ate the spare meal. After he was done, the innkeeper stopped by his table.

"Master Mohammed left a message for you. He is busy all day but will return in the evening and hopes to depart at first light tomorrow."

"Thank you," Ahmet said. "If it is not impolite to ask, where are the soldiers going?"

The innkeeper grimaced. His son was among the regiment that had finally marched away after leaving the common room and the grounds littered with debris. The worry the departure caused was doing him and his nervous stomach no good at all. "There is fighting in the north, in Syria Coele. The Persians are going to try to take Damascus. So all of the 'allies' of the Eastern Empire are sending men to fight at Damascus and stop them."

Ahmet cocked his head to one side; the townsman seemed displeased by this. "Stopping the Eastern devils would protect all of Arabia and Petra, would it not?"

The innkeeper snorted derisively. "You mean keep it safe for Roman taxation and Roman law! There is a Roman peace, true, but it is a cruel peace if you ask me. We are an 'ally' of the Empire, yet their tax collectors pinch us as fiercely as any Imperial province. Their gods are placed over ours, their language at the expense of our own. The young people—they think of themselves as Romans, not Nabateans."

Ahmet nodded politely. It would be the same if Persia conquered the Arabian provinces, save that with the Persians rode darkness. He shuddered in the cool, dim room. The priests of Hermes Trismegistus hewed to a moral code—one fiercely enforced by the masters of each school—and were very careful in their exercise of the powers of the unseen world. But the stories out of the East, from the Persian capital at Ctesiphon and beyond, did not relate any such restraint. The *mobehedan* of the Sassanid Empire consorted with demons and devils; they indulged in the necromantic defilement of the dead, they sought power at the expense of their own souls. Even in the placid sun of upper Egypt, the masters of the order would often wake, trembling, at the dark of the moon as the distant echoes of horrific practices in the East troubled the ether.

No matter; he would find the boy and return to the school. Though Ahmet thought that he understood his own purposes well, in truth his mind was a whirl of conflicting desires and intents. He really did not know why he had fled the school, simply that it was no longer the place for him.

It was three days before Mohammed completed his business in the city. All that time, more men, horses, and supplies continued to flow out of the Nabatean capital and up the Wadi Musa to the road to Jerash and the north. Ahmet continued to sit in the caravansary, watching columns of light archers and more horsemen pass by. Long trains of wagons, laden with barrels and crates, followed. On the afternoon of the third day, the priest considered what he had seen—close to fifteen thousand men had headed north. Given the thin population of the Nabatean hinterland, all desert plain and rocky mountains, nearly every able man and animal in the principality had been committed. If this same effort was repeated in the other cities of the Empire, the coming war would be great indeed.

There was something odd, too, about the citizens of the city of stone. To the unaware eye, they were a common-looking people—worn thin by the desert, browned by the sun, with dark hair and eyes. To the Egyptian, though, they seemed furtive. They talked little to strangers, or even among themselves. The nightly ceremonies on the mountaintop, on the Ad'deir—the high place—were closed to outsiders, and the chanting was indistinct to his ears in the valley below. There was an undercurrent of power in the city as well, something that constantly tickled at the back of his mind, though there was nothing to be perceived if he put his mind to searching it out.

Mohammed bustled in, followed by two of his men. They were swarthy fellows, with a grim look about them. Ornamented knives and short curved swords were thrust into their sashes. They were clad in robes of tan and rust. Mohammed sat down on the bench opposite the priest. His smile flickered on, then off. The merchant was tired.

"Are you ready to travel?"

Ahmet arched an eyebrow. He had been ready to travel for three days. The rest had done his legs good, though; they felt as if they had recovered from the trek up the desert valleys from Aelana. He would be well pleased to be gone from this city that crouched amid the red hills.

"When you give the word, Master Mohammed."

The merchant slapped a broad hand on the tabletop. "Good. We're leaving."

THE PALATINE HILL, ROMA MATER

T wo Praetorians, bulky in their red cloaks and plumed helmets, closed the heavy door behind Aurelian. It made a solid sound, sliding closed, and the acting Emperor sighed in relief. It was late at night, near the midnight hour, and he had just finished the day's business. Rubbing tired eyes with the heel of his right hand, Aurelian tugged his cloak off and threw it on a backless chair by the door. The dark-purple garment joined a haphazard pile of shirts, tunics, and other cloaks. The rest of the outer chamber was littered with dirty plates and moldy half-eaten fruit.

Aurelian snorted at the sight but ignored it. At home, on his estate northeast of the city, his wife and her legion of servants would have dealt with all of his mess much more effectively. Here, in the city, in the palace, however, he had banned everyone from his rooms, for they were his one small refuge of peace and quiet amid the chaos of the Imperial Court. Even his bath slaves waited outside the door until he was ready to go to the Baths.

As he did nearly every night, he thought of calling for one of his brother's concubines to soothe him to sleep with gentle hands and a soft, warm body. As he did every night, he shook the thought away. He was too tired to consider anything but the rumpled sanctuary of his bed. He kicked his sandals off, bending the copper clasps that held them closed, and sat down on the side of the large, elevated bed that dominated the inner chamber.

"Hello, brother."

Aurelian flinched at the soft voice and half turned, his right hand holding a bare dagger, reflexively pulled from its sheath at his belt. Maxian sat in a low chair by the window, a dark-gray cloak draped around his thin shoulders.

Aurelian raised one bushy red eyebrow—his delinquent brother looked even more exhausted and worn down than he did. "Are you all right?"

Maxian raised an eyebrow of his own. He had been thinking the same thing about his older brother.

"Yes," the youngest Atrean Prince said. "Do I look like you do?"

Aurelian gave a weak laugh and fell backward into the thick cotton and wool blankets on the bed.

"Gods," he said, rubbing his eyes again. "Galen makes this look so easy! I thought I was helping him before, but there are daily crises that I've never even heard of before. No wonder they divided the old Empire—I cannot conceive of trying to run a state twice the size of ours."

"I am sorry," Maxian said, guilt plain on his face. "I am supposed to be helping you."

Aurelian raised his head up enough to give his little brother a good glare, then fell back again, groaning. "No matter, piglet. Even I can tell that something serious is bothering you. What is it?"

Maxian stood slowly and limped to the door of the outer chamber. He ran his hands over the join at the center of the panels and along the sides. Then he returned to the chair and closed the window shutter, making the same motion over its surface. This done, he settled in the chair, uncorked a heavy wine bottle, and drank a long draft.

"Give here," Aurelian said, rolling over on the bed and taking the amphora from his brother. "You don't drink much, and never bring your own, so it must be very serious. Who is she?"

"Huh!" Maxian laughed, while his brother took a long swallow. "Not a woman like that. A friend died and I took it harder than I should have. It has taken me awhile to shake it off—I must apologize again—you needed my help and I didn't give it."

"Oh, I'll live." Aurelian smiled, his cheerful disposition beginning to show through the weariness. "I'll occupy my spare hours thinking of ways for you to pay me back."

Maxian nodded ruefully; he was sure that Aurelian would devise some particularly fitting revenge for this dereliction of duty. He scratched his forehead.

"I have work to do," Maxian said, meeting his brother's eye with equanimity, though his stomach was fluttering. "Galen's work. This business with the Duchess . . . do you remember?"

Aurelian nodded, putting his hands behind his head.

"Oh, yes," he said, "I see her every day—every day, my brother—and she scares me and impresses me at the same time. She seems to know *everything* that goes on. Never once have I put a question to her that she could not answer."

Aurelian got up, rubbing his nose and taking another swallow from the amphora. "I have no idea whether she tells me the truth or not, piglet. She could be concealing anything behind those dusky violet eyes. Each day I have to rely on her more, and that makes me very nervous. I know—*I know*—that Father trusted her implicitly. She and Mother were close . . . but, by the gods, I cannot bring myself to do the same."

Aurelian stopped, looking a little surprised at the depths of his feeling. Maxian nodded and took the amphora back, popping the cork back into the spout.

"I'll have to disappear for a while," he said, stowing the jug. "I'm watched all the time now, you know, just like you are. A month or two should do it— when I resurface, I should have some alternative sources of information for you and Galen."

The acting Emperor looked up at his younger brother, a half smile on his broad, bearded face. Maxian drew his cloak on and stepped to the window.

"I know," Aurelian said. "You've always made us very proud."

Maxian stopped, his hand on the shutter.

"Max, the day you came home from school with that caduceus on your cloak, that was about the happiest day of Mother's life. Pater was fit to bust too. I'm sorry Galen and I have to ask this of you now, but—well, you know how it is."

"I know, Ars," Maxian said, still looking away. "I hope you'll be proud of this too."

The shutter clattered on the frame and the young Prince was gone.

<hr>

THE PORT OF THEODOSIUS, CONSTANTINOPLE

D wyrin scrambled aside from the bulk of a ship crane. Men shouted around him as a great siege engine swung out over the dock, ropes and cables straining to control the weight of the iron-and-wood machine. Thirty men leaned into the lines that guided the engine down into the hold of the great merchant-man. The day was clear and the sky a brilliant blue. A crisp wind off the waters of the Propontis cut the heat on the deck of the ship. Dwyrin climbed up into the rigging, his bare feet and hands quick on the tarred ropes.

From his new vantage he could see much of the harbor under the city walls. Hundreds of ships were jammed into the dockside and the quays of the military harbor. The dockside was a multicolored swarm of soldiers, sutlers, engineers, heavily burdened laborers, and officers. It seemed that the two sloping roads that led down from the towering walls of the city were crammed shoulder to shoulder with an endless stream of men, horses, and wagons. Mules and horses raised their voices in protest, filling the air with a great noise. The transport to which Dwyrin had been assigned also held two companies of siege engineers and one of auxillia. The Gothic mercenaries were helping the engineers load, their broad-muscled backs gleaming with sweat under the bright sun. Their long pigtails were wrapped around their heads like blond crowns. The engineer centurion bellowed orders through a bronze horn. The engine slowly descended into the darkness of the hold.

Dwyrin climbed higher and found a spar to sit upon. His bare legs, finally browned rather than burned by the sun, dangled over the deck thirty feet below. His right arm still throbbed with the pain of the Legion brand. He gingerly fingered it. The pain had been incredible, though now he felt an odd sense of security and belonging. This troubled him, as he had not even met any of his fellow legionnaires. He had been passed from hand to hand until an optio of the quartermaster's corps had dumped him on this ship with his papers and kit. All he knew was that the ship would leave tonight, and in days or weeks it would reach a place called Taurus, and he would find his unit.

The breeze tousled his pale-red hair, grown even longer now that he was escaped from the strictures of the school. For some reason the Legion had not demanded that he adopt the short cut of the legionnaires that he saw on the deck of the ship or on the quayside. He hooked one leg around a rope to steady himself and began braiding his hair back. Around him, the great port of Theodosius continued to swarm with activity like a kicked-over anthill.

"Get your backs into it, you lazy whoresons! Pull, you bastards, pull!"

Thyatis stalked up the line of sun-bronzed sweating men. The tan linen tunic and kilt that she favored clung to her, soaked with perspiration. Her temper was foul, and had been for days since the disaster at the Walach's house. Nikos, Timur, and the other men hauled for all they were worth. The wagon, laden with supplies and heavy ironbound chests, creaked slowly up the ramp onto the ship. Thyatis cracked her baton on the side of the wagon, inches from Jochi's head. The sharp sound galvanized the men.

They shouted. "Heave! Ho!"

The wagon advanced another inch.

"Pull, you mangy bitches! Pull!" Thyatis' voice cut the air like a whip.

"Heave! Ho!"

The wagon advanced again, two inches this time. The front wheel crunched into the lip of the ramp. The men shouted again, muscles bunching and straining.

"Ball-less priests! You are weak! Pull!"

"Heave!" came the answering shout. "Ho!"

The front wheel trembled against the lip of the ramp, then there was a groaning sound and it tipped up and over. The wagon rolled forward onto the deck. Men ran up and slid chocks under the front wheel to keep it from rolling forward into the gaping maw of the open hold. Thyatis stepped up onto a giant wooden block that formed part of the main mast. The rest of her detachment, now expanded to two tent parties, or twelve men, hustled onto the ship to secure the wagon. Only two more to go. She slapped her thigh with the heavy baton, ignoring the stab of pain.

The day after the debacle of the raid, she had been summoned to the personal quarters of the Western Emperor. She had sat in a low chair in the center of his study, back straight, eyes front. Though she was consumed with anger at the failure of her mission, her face was a carefully composed mask. This much, at least, the ladies in the House of de'Orelio had taught her. The Emperor, Galen, had met her privately, with only a young Eastern Empire officer in attendance. He was short, but broad-shouldered, with the look of a cavalryman about him. She remembered him from the staff meeting—Theodore was his name. The rest of the face clicked into place; he was the younger brother of the Eastern Emperor.

"So, Centurion, two of your men dead, four injured. A block of the city lost to fire, and the traitors, whoever they were, escaped. To balance this, you recovered an Imperial recruit who was being held captive in the house."

Thyatis flinched. The scorn in the Emperor's voice was clear. She cleared her throat. "We wounded the Persian sorcerer, sir."

Galen's eyes flashed. "You _think_ that you wounded the sorcerer. But witnesses in the street observed him flying away to the east, out over the harbor. Further, he was carrying someone. This does not strike me as being particularly wounded."

"He was very strong, sir. He nearly killed all of us."

Galen nodded, his face a mask equal to hers. "And we know little more than we did before. We know that the Walach, Dracul, was negotiating with the Persians. We know that the traitors did go to his house that night. We know that a Persian sorcerer was in the city—even though none of the thaumaturges in the service of the Eastern or Western Emperors detected him. This went ill, Centurion. Our entire plan may be compromised."

"Yes sir."

Galen sat in thought, his face pensive. Thyatis fought hard against fidgeting. At last, the Emperor looked up again, his eyes troubled. "Not much time passed between the arrival of the traitors and the start of the fighting in the house. You rushed the men in the garden room within what, fifteen grains? of entering the house. It may be that they did not have time to meet and discuss what they had learned in the Palace. One of the servants that we questioned said that there were _two_ Persians who had come to meet with Dracul. If this is so, then maybe the passenger the sorcerer was carrying was the other Persian and our plan is still safe."

He glowered at Thyatis. He stood up and stalked to the window, his anger palpable. Thyatis continued to stare straight ahead, though from the corner of her eye she could see that Prince Theodore had winked at her. Was he trying to reassure her? Galen drummed his fingers on the window ledge. When he turned back, he seemed to have reached a decision.

"You were lucky, Centurion. If the captive boy had not been a fire-caster, you and all of your men would have been dead. I do not hold the outcome against you, though it is in no way pleasing to me. The fleet is leaving within the next four days and we are now completely unsure as to the state of our enemies. More to the point, the failure of your mission has caused me a loss of respect in the eyes of the Eastern commanders. I was counting on your mission being carried off flawlessly."

Thyatis felt her stomach curl up and shrivel into something the size of a dried fig. This was going to be very bad. By sheer will, she kept her head up and her eyes clear.

The Emperor paced behind the desk. "I had intended to keep you close to hand and use you and your men on the campaign as scouts, couriers; whenever I needed something carried out quietly. Now I see no option but to accept the services of the Eastern scouts and to remove you from an obvious position on the playing board."

He stopped and leaned forward on the desk. His eyes bored into hers, fierce and still angry. "I am sending you into the East, ahead of the army. You get the short straw, Centurion. You and your men are being detached from my staff and the army as a whole."

He picked up an oilskin packet from the desk. She stood and accepted the heavy package. The Emperor regarded her for a long time. Then he said, "The packet contains orders for a mission into the high country beyond the old frontier. You are being sent by a roundabout way to deep in Persian lands. There is a timetable for when and where we expect to meet you again. I hope that I will have the pleasure, Centurion. Dismissed."

She spun on her heel and walked out. Her stomach was fluttering around her ears now. They weren't going to be disbanded! She still had her command and what seemed to be a particularly desperate and dangerous mission. The clerks in the outer chambers stared after her in surprise, for she was grinning from ear to ear as she hustled out.

Full dark had settled over the city when the sound of men chanting and the creak of the great sweep oars on the side of the ship woke Dwyrin. The lanterns that had hung from the mast and on iron hooks by the doors to the fore and aft cabins were dark. A thin sliver of moon gleamed above the eastern horizon, but it barely shed enough light to pick out the rigging. The ship was away from the dock and passing between the twin towers that guarded the entrance to the military harbor. He peered over the side of the ship, his blanket wrapped around him. Below, a sleek lateen-rigged coaster, not even half the size of the transport, was plowing through the waves at their side. Unlike the transport, it was lit with lanterns fore and aft.

Beyond the breakwater, the waters of the Propontis opened before them. The sailors scrambled aloft and began running up the great square sail. From his perspective on the foredeck, Dwyrin stared up in puzzlement. The sail was dark, almost as black as the sky. Still, no lanterns were lit, the sailors working in darkness. The coaster peeled away from their course as the prow of the ship bit into deeper waters. Still lit by its lanterns, it curved away to the northeast, heading for the Sea of Darkness. The merchantman, still running dark, headed south. Clouds gathered in the east, driven by winds off the distant steppes. The moon was soon obscured and utter darkness covered the waters. Behind them Dwyrin could see the lights of the city walls in the distance. Long trails of torches sparkled along the stone roads leading down from the city to the harbor. The army of the Empire continued to move, even in night.

Again Thyatis stood on the railing at the sharp beak of the *Mikitis*. Clouds swallowed the eastern horizon, a darker blot against the night sky. Above, cold stars gleamed down. A chill wind cut out of the north and filled the sails of the sleek ship. One hand was wrapped in a guyline, the other steadying herself on the prow. Wind rushed past her and the ship seemed to soar across the waters. The hiss of the waves was loud. Before her, across the Sea of Darkness, lay Trapezus and the beginning of their mission. She smiled in the darkness. This was far more than she had ever dreamed of. She wondered how things were faring for the Duchess, so far away to the west.

The *Mikitis* rode onward, dark sails fresh with the wind. To the south, the Anatolian shore passed away in the night, only sparsely lit by the lights of farmhouses.

THE PLAIN OF JERASH, THE THEME OF ARABIA MAGNA

A hmet walked back into the camp, his staff making a faint *tap-tap* sound on the cold ground. Night was upon the plain and the sky above was a vast dome of stars. The moon, narrow, rode over his left shoulder. One of the Bani Hashim guards stirred as he approached, then settled back into the velvet shadow of the boulder that he was leaning against. On the other side of the stones, the dim light of a fire barely illuminated the tents of the caravan guards. The priest picked his way among the tent ropes to where Mohammed sat on a folding canvas chair. The merchant looked up as he approached, putting aside the heavy scroll that he had been squinting at in the light of a candle stub.

The caravan had been traveling north for six days from the city in the hills. The dusty metropolises of Philadelphia and Gerasa were behind them. In each place the signs of the mobilization of the Nabatean state were apparent. They had passed two bands of infantrymen sitting by the side of the road outside of Gerasa the day before. This whole day they had climbed up a long rocky slope that led up from the valley of the stream called the Jerash. The sun had beaten at them like a smith in the forge. With the fall of night, there was a little relief from the heat, though the stones continued to be warm to the touch for hours after sunset.

Ahmet was a little awed by the open desolation of the countryside. Endless leagues of towering rocky hills and barren plains had passed as they rode north. Stinging winds cut at them from the deserts to the south and east. Intermittently tribesmen appeared out of the heat haze with flocks of sheep or goats. Widely separated oases offered some hope of water and relief from the sun. When he had said as much to Mohammed, the Southerner sneered.

"This is easy land," he replied, his hand light on the reins of the chestnut mare he favored. "In the south, beyond the An'Nafud, the land is harsher. There my people live, on the edges of the great sand. There it takes skill to survive."

It was a long way from the fertile valley of the Father of Rivers. Ahmet had shaken his head and urged his camel onward. Night fell and they were still far from the nearest rest house. Mohammed led the caravan into a low saddle between two hills where the rise of the land offered a little shelter and had them make camp.

Ahmet sat down next to the merchant, folding his legs under him.

"What do you believe?" he asked the man sitting next to him.

The merchant stirred. "I do not know," he said. "My people believe in many gods. There are four goddesses who rule the heavens and the seasons. The god Hubal, who dwells in the stone house at the well of Zam-Zam, is said to be the first among these gods. I have seen his shrine, and it is unremarkable save for the black stone that is the altar there. The priests say that it fell from the sky, bearing the blessing of Hubal. There are other gods too, but I do not know all of their names."

"My homeland is possessed of ten thousand gods," Ahmet said. His voice showed the shadow of his homesickness for the green olive groves and palms of the school.

"What do you believe, priest? Do you believe in this Hermes Trismegistus?"

Ahmet laughed softly. "Hermes Trismegistus is not a god, my friend. He is a symbol of what man may accomplish. The doctrine of my faith is that though there are gods like Set and Apollo-Ra and the others, the focus of man's existence is upon his own betterment. Hermes Trismegistus was the first teacher of our sect, a powerful sorcerer who first learned how to see beyond the world of the eye and the nose and the mouth."

Ahmet motioned to the stars, the tents, the camp. "All of these things that you see are only reflections of what the ancients call a true form. Like shadows on a wall. Even you and I are not what we appear to be. We are echoes of our true selves, what my people call the *ka*, or the Jews the soul."

Mohammed carefully rolled up the scroll and slid it back into the case. "I have been reading this book, the *torah*. It speaks of a pair of gods, one male and one female, who made the world and all of the things in it. It says that man is the final creation of these gods, who are not named. Does your Trismegistus believe that?"

Ahmet shook his head, though the motion was almost undetectable in the dim light of the fire. "No. Trismegistus teaches us that the totality of existence was created a very long time ago by a single force. There was a breath of creation that made all that is, but not in the forms that we see now, around us. This one force is the only true god, the creator. Every race of men knows that some power beyond them created the world and gave it shape and meaning. Trismegistus teaches that all of the gods that men worship are reflections of the ultimate form of this first, true creator. In my land we call the first creator Ptah. All other gods sprang from Ptah. Trismegistus would say that all other gods are reflections of the true god."

Mohammed grunted and combed his beard with his fingers. "How do you worship, then, this god without a face? Are there no idols to give it form?"

"No," Ahmet answered, "we do not believe in idols. The mind of man, we believe, is the temple of this god of creation. Of all creatures only man is blessed with the knowledge of god and the ability to apprehend the magnificence of the god. We live simple lives, we do not collect goods or riches. We give ourselves up, in a way, to the apprehension of god in all the works that it has formed."

"But where did man arise, then . . ."

They sat by the dying, then dead, fire for long hours, talking. Above them, the wheel of stars turned in its course until, finally, the eastern horizon began to lighten.

ROMA MATER

Maxian rubbed his eyes. They were weary from days of poring over hundreds of account books and histories that he and Gaius Julius had recovered from the Imperial archives or purchased from booksellers in the city. He was attacking the problem of the curse from the viewpoint of a physician. Something, some event or carrier, had started the contagion upon the people and the city. It had a source of infection. If that could be discovered, it could be lanced or burned away. Then, perhaps, the city and the people would be able to recover. Exhausted, the Prince rose from the stiff-backed chair and walked to the counter built into the wall of the apartment room. He poured a glass of wine from the amphora there.

At the far end of the room, the little Persian was working too. Unlike Gaius Julius, he did not read Latin well, but he had a more pressing task. Soon after the three men had taken up residence in the apartment, odd things had begun to happen. Things fell over and broke or caught fire suddenly. After a week of an increasing series of disturbances, Abdmachus had taken it upon himself to open his awareness and keep watch, both in the physical world and in the unseen world, for a day and a night. When he roused himself at last he reported to a grim Maxian and an unconcerned Gaius Julius what the Prince had suspected from the beginning.

The contagion was collecting, like rainwater in low ground, around the building. The Prince seemed to be the focus. Careful examination of the walls, floors, and other rooms then revealed a subtle, but swiftly acting, corrosion of the plaster, the wood of the walls, the tiles of the floor. The dark tide was washing up around the building and wearing it away.

So today, like the days before, Abdmachus slowly worked along the walls of the rooms that they used, muttering and chanting. Pots of paints lay by his side, and from them he daubed a constant series of sigils and glyphs upon the cracking, eroded plaster. Maxian looked around in mild disbelief. Every surface—wall, floor, and ceiling—was etched with ten thousand signs of warding and protection. To the hidden eye, the rooms were filled with a flickering blue glow, shining forth from the writing on the walls. Now it was safe to work within the rooms, though the tension of the quiet siege wore on all three of them.

The back door of the flat banged open and Gaius Julius sauntered in. Now he wore a toga of soft white wool, with a dashing light-blue half-cape and hood thrown over one shoulder. He bore a great load of new books, parchments, and scrolls that he unceremoniously unloaded with a great clatter on the one piece of bare table in the main room.

"What ho, citizen! Still drudging about, I see, Persian. Perhaps you could pick up around the place and sweep while you're kneeling down there?"

Maxian put the glass of wine aside, untasted, and stepped up to the dead man. There was something odd about him today, and not just his good humor. That had surfaced only a few days after their return to the city. Compared to the Prince's restrained demeanor or Abdmachus' polite quietude, the dead man was a veritable volcano. Maxian eyed him closely while the dead man stacked the new acquisitions into different piles. Suddenly, the Prince seized the dead man's shoulder and spun him around. Gaius Julius' hot retort died to see the naked fury on the Prince's face.

"What have you done?" the Prince hissed. "Abdmachus, come here!"

The little Persian carefully put down his paints, brushed his hands off, and joined the Prince, who had the dead man by the ear and was checking his pulse with the other hand. "What is it, my lord?"

Maxian pinched the cheek of the dead man, his voice harsh. "Look at the flesh; it's warm and flexible. See the pulse of blood at his throat, the texture of his hair. Our dead friend has been up to something. What have you been doing, Gaius?"

The dead man stepped back, rubbing his ear. "Nothing of note, priest. I do admit that I feel better than I have in . . . well, centuries!"

Maxian scowled at the easy laughter of the dead man. He turned aside to the Persian, keeping his voice low. "He's becoming more alive each day—what could cause this? Is there some way for the dead to restore themselves to full health once they are raised?"

The Persian squinted at the dead man, who had shaken his head in disbelief at the concerns of the living and was unloading fresh apples and pears from the pockets of his cloak.

Abdmachus turned back to the Prince. "I hesitate to bring up the possibility, my lord, but I have read in some of the older tomes that the risen dead can restore vitality to their corrupted bodies by the ingestion of the fluids of the living . . ."

"By drinking their blood?" The Prince's eyes widened in shock. This was fast becoming some Greek tragedy. He turned back to the dead man, who was leaning against the big table, noisily crunching an apple between broad white teeth. "Gaius Julius, what have you been up to? I want you to tell me everything you did today, and I do mean everything . . ."

The dead man leered at Maxian, saying, "Everything? I'm surprised that such a young man would need to resort to the voyeurism of the old!"

Maxian's hand twitched and his fingers formed a brief, quickly traced sign in the air at his side. The dead man suddenly staggered, the apple dropping from his hand, half eaten. Gaius Julius' face trembled and a shockingly rapid white pallor flooded his flesh. He bent over, moaning in terrible pain, collapsing to the floor on his hands and knees.

"In another place and time, old man, your levity would be welcome. But right now, with very little room for error, we cannot afford it."

Maxian bent down and dragged the dead man's head up with one hand. Drool spilled from his mouth. The Prince leaned close. "Tell me everything that you did. Now."

Gaius Julius rolled over on his side, gasping, as the Prince restored some of the necromantic energy that sustained life and thought in his ancient limbs. "Pax! Pax! I will tell you.

"I left in the morning with a sullen disposition, as I'm sure you noticed. These dreary rooms wear on me. I went to the Palatine and renewed my acquaintance with the master of the archives. After a few cups of wine and some silver, he allowed me to search through the old Legion and city militia records. After several hours of digging in the dust and sneezing, I took a break to have lunch. I had gathered almost all of those items on the table.

"Ah, the sun served to lighten my spirits tremendously. I purchased a meat pastry with pepper and a cup of weak wine from one of the vendors on the square of Eglabalgus and found a place to sit in the garden on the north side of the hill, not too far from the archives. While I was sitting, I happened to catch the eye of a young lady on an errand and, by some fine words, convinced her to sit with me a while and share my wine."

A tremendous smirk flitted across the face of the dead man.

"She was a fine beauty—long legs, tousled raven hair, the disposition of a minx. Not so much chest, but I am rather fond of such a woman. No matter. We passed some enjoyable time together and then I shooed her out of the archives and went back to work. The master of the archives was taking a nap, so I thought it might be best if I brought the things that I had found back here, rather than spending the rest of my failing eyesight copying them.

"Oh, and I purchased some pears and apples from the stall at the end of the street."

Abdmachus, who had returned to his paints and chanting, looked up, his brush poised only inches from the wall. He and Maxian exchanged glances. The Prince's face was cloudy with tremendous anger. His fists clenched and unclenched unconsciously at his side. Abdmachus felt the ambient power level in the room rise.

"Old man, what did you tell this stripling of a girl about your work?"

Gaius Julius spread his hands. "Nothing, nothing at all. We chatted about inconsequential things."

"Did you tell her your name?"

"Of course, I introduced myself quite politely."

"Did she recognize it?"

Gaius Julius smiled broadly. "Of course, but it is a common name, she had no inkling of who I truly am. Doubtless, if she thinks of it at all, she will assume that my family is of poor nature but great ambitions. Really, my Prince, who is going to think of me being *me?*"

Maxian shook his head sharply. "Did she tell you *her* name? Was she, perhaps, a slave in the garb of one of the great houses?"

Gaius Julius paused, thinking. It was evident that he had not thought it important to remember the cognomen of his afternoon's dalliance. By the wall, Abdmachus muttered something under his breath as he resumed painting.

Maxian had caught it, though, and repeated it aloud, his grim humor melting a little. "Husband to all the wives, and wife to all the husbands."

"I have it," said the dead man, now sitting up. "It was Christina, or Christiane, or something like that."

Maxian snarled, his face contorted with rage. "Not Christina, but Krista. She wore an emblem of three flowers intertwined with the head of a ram. Her hair is wavy with curls and it falls just past her shoulder. She has deep-green eyes. She is a slave."

Gaius Julius blinked in surprise. "That is the very woman!"

Maxian dragged the dead man up off the floor as if he weighed nothing. There was a blur of dim radiance along his arm, and he threw the dead man against the nearest wall. Gaius Julius, his mouth open in an O of surprise, crashed heavily against it and then slid down with a sickening crunch to the floor. The Prince stalked across to where the dead man lay, gasping, on the ground.

"Fool! You would bugger your way into our common destruction! That slip of a girl, all breezy ways and innocent desire, is the agent, the very eyes, of the mistress of the Imperial Office of the Barbarians!"

Abdmachus caught his breath and turned his full attention, at last, to the confrontation between the two men. Maxian had seemingly grown in the last little while. His rage was palpable in the room and the barely harnessed power that the Persian had tricked out of him in the tomb under the Via Appia was leaking into the air around him. The scrolls on the table rustled and glass tinkled in the other room. Despite the late-afternoon sun outside, within the long narrow room it had grown dark. Gaius Julius cringed on the floor, seeing his final and utter dissolution reflected in the enraged eyes of the Prince.

"Office . . . Office of Barbarians?" he wheezed.

"Yes," Maxian bit off. "Her mistress, well known to me, is Anastasia de'Orelio, the so-called Duchess of Parma. She sits in the shadows behind the Emperor and pulls many strings. Though I have long accounted her a friend, both personally and politically, she knows *nothing* of what I have discovered and is unlikely to apprehend it even if I did tell her. Further, since I have accepted the assistance of our Persian compatriot here, I could now be well accounted a traitor. Coupled with my mysterious absence of several weeks, I expect that she has her agents about, quietly looking for me."

Gaius Julius flinched away from the Prince and his scathing voice but pulled himself back to his feet, leaning against the wall. His voice was quiet, showing restored composure. "Enough. I am no stranger to plots and politics, boy. You can destroy me, but then you will not have my skills or service or *leverage*. If this de'Orelio is on the lookout for us, then we will have to move, disappear. I can deal with anyone, man or girl, that is watching us."

Maxian continued to stare at him, anger smoldering in him.

Gaius Julius stepped away from the wall and made a little, hesitant half bow. "Apologies, Prince Maxian, I did not mean to endanger our enterprise. I will make sure that it does not happen again."

Abdmachus held his breath for a moment, but then the Prince nodded and turned away, going back to the books on the table. Gaius Julius looked after him for a moment, then shrugged. He had plenty of perspective on the matter; he had already been dead once.

"Ah, my lord," Abdmachus said.

Maxian looked up, his face a rigid mask.

"My lord, Gaius Julius—for all his faults—is right about one thing. We must move from these rooms. Not immediately, but surely within the week."

"Why so?" the Prince growled, but his anger was beginning to fade.

"Here, my lord." Abdmachus brushed the section of wall behind him. The symbols that he had been drawing were pale and faded. Under his fingertips, the plaster shaled away from the wall in a big chunk, clattering to the floor. Behind it, the lathes of the wall were revealed, corroded and eaten by termites and worms.

"You see? The building itself is being eroded by the power of the curse. Soon the walls and ceiling will collapse. I have checked the upper floors—they are no longer safe to walk on. There is a sewer main under the northern corner of the house. I fear that the mortar of its walls is weakening as well. If we remain, the building may soon collapse."

Maxian sighed and slumped back in his chair. The weight of the effort was telling upon him. Each day some new complication arose, and still they had found nothing of note in the old books and records. The public histories of the early Empire were filled with nothing but praise for the first Emperor. The other records were all horrifically mundane—the daily accounts of clerks and scribes. Any books of sorcery or magic from the dawn of the Empire were well hidden away by the thaumaturges of the time or their current contemporaries. Maxian was sure that a single circumstance had precipitated this chain of events, but so far there was no sign of it. Further, there must be some mechanism, or several, that promulgated the curse through the centuries. Again, there was nothing that had stood out from the reams of dry parchments and papyrus.

"Then we will have to move. Where to?" The Prince's voice was exhausted.

Abdmachus frowned now; this was an important consideration. Slowly he spoke. "Someplace near the city, but not within it. The curse is too strong within the walls. Someplace that is free from this influence . . . I don't know. The suburbs are unknown to me."

Gaius Julius, still rubbing the knot on the back of his head, spoke up. "If I understand you, magician, it should be a place that was not built by Romans. Perhaps someplace where the owner used imported laborers?"

Maxian slowly turned and stared at the dead man for a long moment. Then he smiled a little. "Abdmachus, our dead friend has the right of it. We need a villa or a summer house outside of the city, one built by a foreign ambassador, or merchant, or exile. Somebody that wanted a taste of home in their new surroundings. But it will have to be built by foreign hands, perhaps even with materials from beyond Italy or at least Latium. Can you find such a place while I pack the books and other materials?"

Gaius Julius raised a hand. "I will find the place, Prince. Abdmachus has important chanting and mumbling to get to. I will start this very evening."

Maxian nodded. They needed a safe haven.

"I feel three and a half kinds of a fool, Prince Maxian," Gaius Julius said as the two of them topped the rise on their horses. Maxian was riding a dappled chestnut he had borrowed from the stables maintained by his brother. The dead man was riding a skittish black stallion. Though he was obviously a masterful rider, the horse was tremendously nervous around him. Behind and below them, the vast sprawl of the city filled the valley of the Tiber. They were northeast of the city, not too far from the famous estate of the Emperor Hadrian at Tivoli. Here, low rolling hills rose up from the swampy bottomlands toward the distant spine of the Apennines.

The road they followed was in poor repair. The stone blocks were ridged by grass and some trees had sprouted at the edge of the road, cracking the carefully fitted stones. Still, the air was clear and the smell of orange trees filled the air with a heady scent. Maxian felt better already, just being out of the city. The contagion exerted ever more pressure on him now, and he felt it as a bone-deep weariness. They came to a high dark-green hedge and followed it through a tunnel of overarching trees to an ancient gate. Maxian pulled up, surprised to see that there were two sphinxes flanking the gateway.

Gaius halted as well and turned his horse. The corners of his eyes were crinkled up in amusement. He gestured at the gateway. "I felt the fool first for forgetting that this place was here at all. Second, for forgetting that I had paid for it. Third, for forgetting that I had urged its construction and a half for being addled enough to bring her here, to the city."

Maxian shook his head, puzzled by the rueful look on the face of the old man. "Who?"

Gaius laughed and spurred his horse through the gate. "Who? Don't they teach that story to the young rich men anymore? A scandal indeed. She was a Greek all right, she came as a gift and nearly walked away with the whole party."

Maxian followed and they rode up a short lane that ended in a circular garden. Beyond the garden, now overgrown with flowering shrubs and tall grass, stood a striking building. Twin lines of pillars flanked the central entrance on the opposite side of the garden. At the end of each line of pillars, a slab-sided obelisk rose. Two facing statues guarded the doorway, their half-man, half-beast bodies facing one another. Beyond this a flat-topped building rose up with two floors. Though perfectly situated on the grounds and within the context of the hills and the long slope behind it, it seemed an unexpected foreigner found—startlingly—at a family gathering.

"The Summer House of the last of the Ptolemies: Kleopatra, Pharaoh of Egypt. Built by Egyptian and Phoenician craftsmen imported months in advance of her arrival in the city at my side. The stone was shipped by barge from the Upper Nile to Alexandria and thence to Ostia. Five hundred stonemasons, carpenters, architects, and laborers came with it. It took them six months to raise this, after they had flattened the ground and built a berm down there to keep the slope from slipping."

Gaius Julius pointed downslope, where a ridge was now overgrown with saplings and oak trees.

"Here she held court, while I muddled about in the politics of the city and prepared for my great expedition. It was a house of beauty, Prince, filled with scholars and philosophers. No real Roman, of course, no *Senator*, would come within miles of the place. Look around; they still do not build close to here. They felt that she was the very devil-temptress of the East. A harbinger of an 'oriental despotism.' And see what Octavian gave them . . . he who cursed her name the loudest."

"Huh" was all Maxian said, staring around at the grand edifice. Even over long years, it still stood, an exemplar of the craftsmen that had built it. "Who owns it now?"

"Why," Gaius Julius said with a grin, "you do, my lord. Or, rather, your brother owns it. It is a property of the state, but a forgotten one. We should be quite undisturbed here."

Maxian swung himself down off his horse. He walked up the broad sandstone stairs to the first level of the house. The front portico was apparently solely for show; the pillars enclosed a long arcade on either side of the garden and shaded the front of the house. The roof was pocked with holes where stones and lumber had decayed and fallen down. He picked his way across the entryway and into the first room. In the dimness, he fumbled along the wall, then stopped, cursing himself. Gaius Julius, after hobbling the horses, joined him.

Maxian muttered and a pale-yellow light sprang up from his raised hand. Gaius Julius hissed in surprise.

"I had forgotten this was here," the dead man said, looking past the Prince into the house.

The sorcerous light had revealed a half-circle of a room. The walls were marble and the floor a great mosaic of many colors. A great deal of litter, blown in from the garden, lay in drifts across the floor, but the ceiling was still intact and in the facing circle of the chamber, on a broad marble pedestal, stood a statue of a man. He was tall, taller in stone than in life, and nearly naked, though a breastplate and leather kilt had been cunningly carved upon his torso. In one hand he leaned upon a tall spear and the other reached toward the viewer. Curly hair graced his head, and the artisan—from life or more than life—had made him handsome. At his feet the figures of men, much smaller than he, bowed before him or lay dead. The sculptor had been a man of surpassing skill, for the personality of the figure was like a stunning blow to Maxian.

"Alexander . . ." breathed the Prince.

At his side, Gaius Julius snorted with disdain. "You paid attention to least one of your pedagogues, I see. It has suffered through the long years. A pity, it was quite a work of art when it still had paint on it. She was obsessed with him, you know. Often she would try to convince herself that I was his spirit, invested in flesh once more."

Maxian turned. The dead man's voice had an odd, almost haunted quality to it. "What do you mean?"

Gaius Julius sighed. "I don't know. Near the end I think that I was under her spell. I believed it too, that I would be the new Alexander. They killed me over the cost of the appropriations for my expedition, you know. I was emptying the treasury of every last coin."

Maxian shook his head. "I don't remember that. I thought you were preparing a campaign against the Dacians. That's what my tutors said, anyway."

The dead man snorted, waving his hand in negation. "I read that history too. Written by someone ninety years after the fact of the matter. No, I had a grander plan than that, my young friend. I intended nothing less than the conquest of Persia—even as Alexander had done—and then to swing north and conquer the Scythian lands north of the Sea of Darkness and fall upon Dacia upon my return, from behind."

Maxian stared at the old man in shock, his eyes suddenly widening in apprehension.

Gaius Julius looked back at him with puzzlement. "What is it, Prince?"

Maxian shook his head. "Nothing, just something I had heard before. Let us look at the rest of this house and see if we can use it."

The girl, brown and quiet as a deer, crouched in the rhododendrons on the hillside. Below her, in the old house, she could hear the faint voices of the two men as they moved from room to room. Her long dark hair was tied back in a braid and stuffed down the back of the light cotton tunic she wore. Her feet, tucked under her, were wrapped in leather and sandals. A light leather girdle circled her narrow waist. From it hung two pouches, a hard leather case, and, in the small of her back, a thin dagger in a plain scabbard.

Behind her, the brush rustled quietly.

"Sigurd." The girl hissed, not bothering to look back. "Quit staring at my butt and get back to the horses. Take them over the hill, out of the wind, so that the ones down in the garden don't smell them and say hello."

The brush whispered again and Krista felt the sensation of being watched recede.

Men, she thought, *mighty easy to distract . . . It's a wonder they get anything done.*

Below, the voices suddenly became clearer as the two men walked out onto the rear porch of the villa. More exposed to nature on the open slope, it was in much worse shape than the front, and they picked their way carefully across a band of broken tile and collapsed fountain drains.

". . . do, old man. Arrange for wagons to bring all of the materials from the insula up here. I'll begin moving in immediately, and I'll fix the water mains so that it's livable, at least."

Krista parted the brush enough to get a clear look. Then she grimaced. She recognized both men. This was very interesting, much more interesting than either she or her mistress had anticipated. Quietly she returned the brush to its original position and slipped away up the hillside. Time to return to the city. There was more work to do.

TRAPEZUS, THE EASTERN THEME OF PONTUS

A bitterly cold wind cut across the deck of the *Mikitis*. Thyatis and Nikos, wrapped in all of the cold-weather gear they had, huddled in the lee of the forward deckhouse, staring across the choppy waters of the bay at the shore. A steep headland plunged down to the sea, leaving only a narrow margin of black-sand beach at the waterline. The sky was gray, the color of old pipe. The ship was anchored a quarter mile from the harbor quay. Rain spattered out of the sky at random intervals.

Nikos, bundled up in a fur-lined coat he had browbeaten out of one of the Turks, muttered something unintelligible at Thyatis' side.

She turned her face away from the wind. "What? I didn't catch that."

Nikos pointed up in the sky. Black birds with broad wings were soaring above the ship on the gusts of wind from the north.

"Colchis," he said. "The cormorants."

Thyatis shook her head. "I don't understand."

Nikos turned away from the barren shore as well, his arms crossed over his chest. He leaned close. "In the tale of the Argolid—the sailors came to Colchis, a barren and dreadful shore, and the birds would have attacked them if they had not made a great noise by beating on their shields."

Thyatis shook her head. She did not understand the reference.

Nikos looked sideways at her and sighed. "The benefits of a classical education, Centurion. A band of Greek pirates under their captain, Jason, came here looking for a fleece of gold. They put ashore, legend has it, here and made common cause with the daughter of the King. They murdered her father and took the gold. When they got home, they were heroes."

Thyatis grimaced. "A parricide doesn't sound very heroic to me."

Nikos smiled. "I think you'd like her, the Princess in the story. She was strong and beautiful and knew her own mind. Later her husband is unfaithful, so she feeds his children to him in a stew."

Thyatis smiled at that. "You think I would kill an unfaithful husband?"

Nikos shrugged, he had never thought of his commander in that light.

"I think," she said, "that I would just leave. If he was dishonest, then there is no reason to stay. I can make my own way in the world—a man would have to be a companion, not a lord."

The wind dropped a little. Boats put out from the harbor, though the heavy sea made it rough going. She gestured toward the boats. "Play it low key with the customs officers. The ship will draw enough attention in these waters without some run-in with the local prefect. I'm going to go below and get into my demure-daughter-of-nobility outfit."

Nikos nodded, wondering if she would be able to carry through and not cold-cock some minor official for getting fresh with her. He smiled at the thought of his commander in a dress—it was true she looked great, but she did hate it so. He too scrambled down onto the lower deck and shouted for Arastus and Jochi to join him. There were palms to grease.

The town of Trapezus was built on a broad shelf of land above the cliffs of the harbor. In ancient days, a road had been cut from the harbor shore and the black-stone quays to the plateau. Trapezus was built to the edge of the cliffs, all white-washed buildings with dark streets. The houses were covered with vines and ivy with little pearly flowers. Here, under the looming massif of the Tatus Mountains, the rain was plentiful and the growing season long. The main road south out of the city was ancient too, with mile markers far older than the coming of Rome. The dark pine and spruce forests that clung to the mountainside had seen kingdoms rise and fall on the narrow plain between them and the sea.

Nikos scratched at his new beard. It was scraggly and grew in irregular tufts. He did not like it, but it was necessary. He jammed the colorful triangular hat back on his head and settled the leather vest that he now wore over his tunic. Even in summer it was nippy here in early morning, under the shadow of the mountains. He pushed open the stableyard gate. Behind him Jochi and his brother, Kurak, urged the two mules forward. The wagon rolled out of the back of the inn and the other members of the detachment mounted their horses.

The Sarmatians could not be happier; they had purchased some good horseflesh with Thyatis' coin back in Constantinople and had suffered with their beloved charges all through the sea voyage to Trapezus. Now they were mounted again and seemed, at last, to be happy. They cantered off down the road, whooping with joy.

The others either rode in the wagon, now with clapboard sides advertising the traveling show, or walked behind. All of their gear was in the wagon or on their backs. Nikos was not particularly pleased that the centurion had elected to have them travel in the guise of players, but it did mean that they were both beneath the contempt and the attention of all but the meanest officials that they might encounter.

Thyatis was still in her demure-daughter outfit, though now she was riding on the top of the wagon, with her boots hooked into the back of the wooden seat that the two Turks were sitting on. Hidden by the top of the clapboard sides, she had a bow and her shortsword by her side. Nikos scrambled onto his own horse, a bay stallion with a gentle disposition. He urged the horse ahead to the turn in the lane that led into the back of the inn. The cock had barely crowed, so the street was empty. He waved an all-clear back to the wagon and the whole troop set out. It was a long road to the south, and the first days were a hard pitch up the passes of the Tatus.

Thyatis sat in the shade on a mossy boulder by the side of the road. The oilskin packet that the Emperor had given her was open in her lap. She spread the vellum map out, carefully creasing down the corners. Ravens complained in the pines just up the slope from her. The shade fell from the steep side of the canyon and the granite cliffs that loomed at either side of the road. Here there was a narrow verge by the side of the road, and the little caravan was stopped in a grassy area. The other side of the road was edged with worked stones and a swift stream rushed past at the bottom of the canyon. One of the Greeks, Tyrus, had stopped by while she was reading over the orders and had left her a lunch of bread, dried meat and cheese. She idly picked at the cheese.

Above her the looming cliff sheltered a thin four-story building wedged into a flat ledge above the trees. Empty windows stared down at the road. Parts of the brick walls were crumbling or covered with the thick wild ivy that grew in the mountains. The peasants in the valley below said that it was haunted and that it had been a temple in the time of their fathers' fathers. Crows and ravens roosted in it now, and owls hunted from it at night. Thyatis had scrutinized it when the party had stopped for lunch, but it did not have an ill-feeling.

A pebble bounced past her from upslope. She turned slightly to see that Nikos was descending from the trees. He cursed as he waded through a thicket of gorse and blueberry bushes. There were trailing streaks of blood on his chest and arms as he reached the boulder and clambered up its side. He had abandoned the tunic and vest that he had affected as the master of ceremonies for the traveling company. He wore loose, baggy, checkered pants and heavy boots. His torso, corded with muscle and etched with old scars, was brown with the sun. Thyatis smiled at him as he sat down. Tiny scratches covered most of his body. He rearranged the shortsword and the brace of heavy knives that he favored.

"A beautiful day," he said, looking up at the swatch of pure blue sky showing between the cliffs. "A pity to be about a dirty business with such nice weather."

"Yes," she said, leafing through the papers, "a pleasant holiday. How are the men?"

Nikos grimaced, saying "They're getting used to riding again. All of that city work took the edge off everyone, I think."

Thyatis nodded and the smile was gone from her face. A shadow of doubt crossed it. "Once we are out of these mountains, we'll be in territory neither friendly nor easy. High desert valleys, rough mountains, clans and tribes hostile to both the Empire and to Persia. We've a long way to go as well. Our first waypoint is to meet with an Imperial agent at the city of Van, on the eastern shore of Lake

Thospitis. By my reckoning, that lies almost four hundred miles from where we now sit."

Nikos nodded, saying "Three, maybe four weeks, with the wagon and the weather. Half that if we were just on horses."

"Without the wagon, we'll just look like what we are—a suspicious group of hard-assed characters that look like they belong in prison with one innocent girl among them."

Nikos laughed, but he watched her face closely too. The orders, which she had not discussed with him, troubled her. He figured that she counted their chances of getting out of this alive to be very low. Nikos had been in one army or another for almost thirty years, and he had long ago come to terms with sudden death. Each day was only as it was.

He poked at the bread. "You should finish eating that, you'll need it."

Thyatis grimaced back at him. "It tastes like dirt. Couldn't you steal anything fresher?"

"The best kind of bread is free. Are you going to tell me what we're lolly-gaging around up here in the high country for, or shall I guess?"

Thyatis did not answer right away. She gathered up the papers and the map and packed them away in the oilskin again. Then she ate the rest of the bread and the cheese. The meat she tucked into one of the pockets of her shirt. After they had left the last of the valley towns, she had shucked the dress and had Anagathios pack it away with the rest of the actor's apparel. She had gone back to the dark-burgundy linen shirt and baggy woolen pants that she favored for cooler weather. Not the raiment of a Roman lady—the pants alone would have caused a riot in the Forum—but it wore well on the road. She checked each of the weapons that she was carrying—long dagger on her thigh, short sword in a case sheath on her back.

Nikos sat, patient as a stone, saying nothing.

"All right," she said at last, after she had unbraided and rebraided her hair. Two small braids now framed her face, glittering red with gold highlights in the sun reflected off the water. The rest was woven back behind her head.

"At Van we meet this agent, and he makes sure that we get over the mountains into Persia proper. Two hundred miles and a mighty mountain range east of Van is the Persian city of Tauris. It sits like a cork in a bottle at the end of a long valley that runs north toward the Mare Caspium. About a month after we're supposed to have arrived, all unnoticed, in Tauris, the entire Roman army is supposed to show up at the south end of the valley, below the city. Maybe at the same time, and maybe not, a mothering great host of Khazar horsemen are supposed to show up at the north end of the valley. Now, these barbarians have said that they'll join up and help beat the living daylights out of the Persians—whom they hate—but unless Tauris is in Roman hands, it's not going to be easy."

Nikos held up a hand, then carefully counted the men sleeping on the grass next to the wagon, or cleaning their gear, or standing watch at the ends of the canyon. "Ah, Commander, I count that we have a grand total of fourteen men to hand—including yourself. There is no way that we're going to capture some Persian fortress in the back of beyond by ourselves."

Thyatis shook her head. "That's not what our orders say. They say that we're to have Tauris secured when the two Emperors arrive."

"They say how?"

Thyatis gave him a lopsided grin. "That's to the discretion of the commanding officer."

Nikos sighed, seeing the delight hiding under his centurion's tanned features. "I don't suppose that you read any Greek poets when you were younger?"

"No," Thyatis said, her face showing a flicker of old pain, "my education came late in life. I learned to read and to write, but no poet suitable for a young lady."

Nikos cocked his head. Thyatis' past was an unopened book—though it was hotly discussed in private among the men who served her. "What did you read from?"

Thyatis shook her head and stood up, brushing pine needles and leaves from her pants. "That doesn't matter now. What poet did you want to quote?"

"Homer," he said, looking up at her. "Odysseus to Achilles, before Troy, 'a noble death does not bring victory—only victory brings an end to death.' "

Thyatis smiled, but it was wintry. "My poet says: 'when on desperate ground, fight.' "

THE EGYPTIAN HOUSE, LATIUM

The pipe made a groaning sound, like a soul in torment in Hades, then quivered and finally, after another long moan, spit muddy water. Maxian, his face, arms, and hands covered with grime, bits of leaf, and plain old dirt, stepped back, smiling in delight. The water flowed murky for a few minutes and then, finally, clear. The cistern at the top of the house echoed as the water fell into its depths. The Prince rubbed his eyes with the edge of his tunic, trying to get the dirt and sweat out of them. After making an even greater mess of his clothing, he gathered up the lengths of copper pipe that he had scavenged, the hammer and tong-shaped grippers, and set off down the brushy slope.

Inside the house, he piled all of the scrap and tools in a heap inside the back garden door. He stripped off the fouled tunic and threw it into a basin that stood inside the door. Farther into the house, he came upon Abdmachus and two of his servants who had come up from the city to assist their master. The Persian was carefully measuring the length of the main hall in the villa.

"We'll have running water in the house within the afternoon," he said in passing.

Abdmachus grunted and continued to carefully spool out the length of twine that he was using to mark distance. The two servants followed along, making marks in colored chalk at regular intervals. Maxian shook his head in amusement. He went up the steps to the upper floor, a grand stair flanked with statues of ibis-headed maidens and hawks. In the upper rooms, another two of the Persians' servants were mopping the floor and carrying away the debris that had blown in through the windows. Gaius Julius was lounging on a couch that had been brought up from the city. Sets of papyrus scrolls were laid out on a low table next to him. He was ignoring them and eating part of a roast pheasant.

"We'll have water soon," Maxian said as he opened the hamper containing the picnic lunch that the dead man had brought with him on his latest return from the city. "The Baths might even work if we have the servants clean them out."

Gaius Julius nodded appreciatively. He was a good Roman.

"It's not a proper house without a bath," he said, picking bits of bird out of his teeth.

Maxian set down on the other couch and began cutting slices of cheese off the wheel he had found in the basket. There were black grapes as well, and a jug of wine. The Prince sniffed it and wrinkled up his nose. "For a dead man, you have odd tastes in wine."

Gaius Julius shrugged. "These modern wines have a foul taste to my palate. This Gaulish wine is the best I've found. There's vinegar in that other jug, if you need your thirst quenched."

Maxian shook his head and picked up a wine-cup left over from the night before. He stood and cleaned it out with a cloth. "I'd rather water than that piss! And thanks to my hard work, we have it."

He went out of the room and down the hall to a little private room with a marble privy seat. Built into the wall next to the bench was a shallow bowl. Above it, a corroded green bronze handle in the shape of a dolphin was set into the wall over a spigot. The Prince tapped on the dolphin with the handle of his knife and it squeaked a little. He dragged on the handle and the pipe complained and gurgled. Water spilled out and he caught it in the wine-cup. After three cupfuls it ran clean.

Abdmachus was sitting on the other couch when he returned to the room overlooking the back garden. The Persian had a wax tablet covered with markings from his survey. He looked up at Maxian's entrance. "My lord, this house is almost thaumaturgically correct—following Egyptian practices. I think that we've finally gotten the blessing of the gods on our pro . . . is something wrong?"

Maxian had halted suddenly and was staring at the cup of water in his hand. His face was a confusion of emotions. He looked up and thrust the cup at Abdmachus. "Drink this, and tell me what you taste!"

Confused, the Persian took the cup and drank.

"It tastes like water, milord, good water at that. Fresh from the spring. A little coppery."

Maxian handed the cup across the table to Gaius Julius. "Drink!"

"Faugh! I hate water," the dead man said, but he drank anyway. "Huh. Sweet and cold. Not like that crap we drink . . ." The dead man looked up, his face startled. ". . . in the city."

Maxian nodded, his face both grim and filled with exultation. "One way or another, everyone in the city drinks water—either straight, or in soup, or mixed with wine." The Prince's voice was filled with utter certainty. "They bathe in it, they wash their clothes in it. But they don't drink it out of the river anymore, the Tiber is too foul for that. And many of the little springs that used to provide the Hill districts with water are dry. Not all, but most. And where does everyone get the water they drink?" Maxian turned to the Persian.

Abdmachus frowned at him, then the sun rose in his mind. "The aqueducts! Nearly all of the water in the city comes from the eleven aqueducts. All are controlled by the Imperial Offices—they're critical to the function of the city. A spell placed upon them would affect the waters and, through the waters, every person in the city . . ."

Maxian nodded sharply. "Here is what we're going to do, then." He began speaking rapidly. Abdmachus began taking notes on his wax tablet.

A hundred yards up the hillside from the Egyptian house, in a thicket of rowan trees, two figures sat quietly, their backs to the largest of the trees. From their vantage, they could see down both the overgrown lane that wound up the hillside to the house and into the front garden. Early-morning dew sparkled on the leaves of the bushes and trees around them, but both were thickly bundled in woolen cloaks and blankets against the night chill. The larger was snoring softly, his head at an angle. The smaller was awake, her sharp ears having caught the creak of a wagon and the whickering of horses on the still morning air.

To the east, the sky was a slowly spreading pink and violet. The sun would soon rise over the mountains and wash the land below with light. For the moment, there was a calm stillness as the land still slept, but the dawn crept in on light feet. The dark-haired girl sat up a little and doffed the straw hat that she had been covering her head with. There was a wagon in the lane, with two drivers. They clip-clopped past on the road below and turned into the garden path. Quietly enough to keep from waking her companion, she slid out of the scratchy wool blankets and slunk off down the slope, flitting from tree to tree.

The two men, one gray-haired, the other with a dark mane, pulled the wagon around to the back garden entrance and unloaded two heavy kegs—filled with wine or water by the apparent weight of them. They rolled the kegs inside the house, raising a clatter on the tile floors. Indistinct voices echoed in the empty hallways. The girl crept lower on the hillside on her hands and knees. Now the wagon was only thirty feet away, across the little side road that ran around the house. The horses were patiently waiting in the traces. The voices continued to echo in the house, though now they receded. The girl looked left and then right. Predawn stillness continued to cover the land.

She waited a moment, but no new movement came from inside the house. Crouching low, she scuttled across to the side of the wagon and paused, peering under the heavy wooden bed. She could just make out the steps on the other side, but no one was on them. Her nose wrinkled up; there was a foul odor seeping from the wagon, like rotten meat. *Oog . . . what are you doing, pretty Prince?* Krista swallowed, suppressing the sudden desire to throw up. There was still no noise from the house, so she crept around the end of the wagon and peered inside the bed.

There were two long shapes, wrapped in ancient, dirty canvas. The smell was thicker now, but she steeled herself and reached into the back of the wagon to twitch the nearest edge of canvas aside. Her face flickered with revulsion at the sight of a gray-black foot protruding from the bundle. It was scabrous and the toes were swollen. Nitrous dirt clung to it in clumps. The smell was worse, like a fist in the face, and she had to sit down behind the wagon, gagging.

The clatter of boots echoed on the stone steps at the back of the house. Krista started, then realized that she was trapped behind the wagon. Carefully she drew her legs up under her and edged beneath the wooden bed. From underneath the rough boards, she saw two sets of sandaled feet tromp down from the house and go to the back of the wagon.

"Gods, that is a foul stench . . . like rotten butter." That was the Prince.

"Huh, you're an ill-experienced pup. I don't even note it anymore."

They bumped around in the wagon and then there was a sliding sound as they dragged the first of the two bodies out. She heard Maxian grunt as he took the weight, then the older man jumped down and took up the rest of the burden.

"Watch the steps," the older man said, and then they staggered off with the body between them. Krista peered from under the wagon until they had entered the house, then she slipped out from under it and darted off into the shelter of the woods. Twenty minutes later she was back on the hillside, shaking Sigurd's shoulder. He came awake, only slightly muzzy from sleep.

"Come on, we've got to go back to the city immediately."

The dreadful sickly sweet odor still hung in the air, but Maxian had grown inured to it. His medical training had taken over and now he gazed down upon the two bodies—secretly dug from potters' fields south of the city and now spread open with clamps and tongs—with a detached air. Gaius Julius loitered behind him, leaning against the wall of the basement of the Egyptian house. The older man wore a butcher's apron and heavy leather gloves, spattered with dark fluid. Maxian placed his hands on either side of the first body's head and began to breathe carefully.

Perception fell away as his flesh relinquished control of his view of the world. The hidden world blossomed, an infinitely textured flower opening in his mind. Detail flooded his mind like a swift mountain torrent, and he struggled for a moment to compose and order it. He bent over the body of the ancient man, dead now for weeks. His fingers moved in the body cavity, sliding over the glutinous remains of liver, spleen, and lungs. His fingers, so used to the work, were his anchor and focus now as his awareness plunged into the recesses of the decaying body. Flesh parted before him, and the innermost secrets of the organs were revealed.

Against the wall, Gaius Julius watched with apprehension. He had seen more than his share of death, and it was no stranger. But the air in the tomblike basement seemed chill and noisome compared to a battlefield. Too, the work of the past nights, of trolling the alleys of the Subura and Aventine slums for suitable bodies, had been grim. The poverty and dissolution of the lower classes of the city that he still, after centuries, loved shook him. In his previous life, he could remember thinking of the people of the lower city, below the hills, as nothing but useful tools in his quest for power. Now the decay of the city and its people struck him cruelly in the heart. He knew that during the short period in which he had the power to revise the workings of the Republic or the customs that supported it, he had done little or nothing. And what now? Had he, somehow, caused all of this to come to pass?

An hour passed, grains trickling through the glass. Maxian suddenly shuddered and stepped back from the first body. Sweat trickled down his face and he looked exhausted. The dead man stepped quickly to his side and helped him to a chair next to the wall. Gaius Julius squatted, peering at his young master. The lad's eyes were flickering, unfocused. His right hand was clenched in a death grip. Gaius Julius stood and brought him back some wine. Maxian shied away from the cup, but the dead man gripped the Prince's head in his free hand and forced him to drink. After the first taste, the young man took the cup in his own hands and drank deeply.

"How do you feel?" Gaius held Maxian's head up in his hands, staring at his eyes.

"Exhausted. I may have to wait until tomorrow to examine the other body."

"Can Abdmachus do it?"

The Prince shook his head, too weary for words. Gaius Julius lifted the Prince's clenched hand up, so that the boy could see it. Maxian had trouble focusing, but when he did, he frowned. "Odd. Why is my hand doing that?"

Gaius Julius pried the fingers back and revealed a small, irregular clump of pale-gray metal in the Prince's palm. He plucked it out and rolled it in his fingers. An eyebrow rose. "It looks and feels like a slinger's bullet. Was it in the body? I saw no wound like this would have made—had he carried it for a long time?"

Maxian, still terribly weary, shook his head *no*. Then his head rolled back against the wall and he began snoring. Gaius Julius sighed and put the odd ball of metal on the end of the table. This done, he carefully lifted up the Prince and, straining with the effort, carried the boy up the stairs to the main floor of the house.

Anastasia de'Orelio, Duchess of Parma, looked up in irritation at the sound of rapping on the door to her private study. Sighing at the latest interruption, she put down the letter she was reading and composed her hair.

"Enter," she said, her voice tired and on the edge of open irritation. She sighed again inwardly when Krista entered the chamber and knelt by the side of the desk. Perhaps it had been a mistake to begin using the girl in the field. She was quick and usually circumspect, it was true, and rarely drew attention to herself—she was a slave, after all.

"Yes, my dear, what is it?"

"We kept watch on the Egyptian house in the hills, mistress, until the

Prince and his servant returned. They came back very early this morning and they had two bodies, fresh ones, in a wagon. They took them inside the building and we came back to the city to warn you. The Prince is up to something dreadful up there! We should inform the aediles, or the prefect, and stop him."

Krista was almost breathless. She and Sigurd had hastened back to the city as fast as they could.

Anastasia sighed and looked down at the girl, still kneeling at her side, panting. *Youth!* she thought to herself, rubbing the graininess from her eyes. Too many late nights, now that the Emperor was gone from the city, and too little sleep were wearing her down.

"My dear, the Prince may be a little odd, but this news is nothing untoward. Remember, he is a healer of the Temple of Asklepios. Though it is not particularly pleasant that he may traffic in the bodies of the dead, it is his profession to understand the workings of the human body. The other watchers in the city reported to me earlier today that two bodies were purchased from the burial temple on the road south of the city. The families, I suppose, would be upset, but they are dead, you know.

"You must learn to see the whole picture, Krista, if you are going to be of use to me. It is good, even, that the Prince has decided to undertake his medical investigations outside of the city. If it were discovered that he was carting bodies around in the wee hours, it would reflect badly on the Emperor."

Krista gave her mistress a frowning look but quickly schooled her features into calm acceptance and polite attentiveness.

The Lady d'Orelio continued: "The Prince has a project that is consuming all of his attention—which is a welcome change from his previous lassitude. Though I surely appreciated his pursuit of the available women in the city, this is far better for him. His brother, I know, is worried about his apparent disappearance, but I'll have a talk with him tomorrow. In the meantime, you need to return to your previous duties here. I will send Sigurd and Antonius to watch the Egyptian house."

For a moment, Krista considered telling her mistress what she felt about that in a loud and angry voice, but the memory of previous, very short-lived arguments with the Duchess quelled that impulse. Instead she bowed her head to the tiles and retreated demurely from the room. In the hallway, after closing the door, she cursed—entirely silently—for fifteen minutes before, shaking with anger, she stalked off to her own cell in the servants' quarters.

Pigheaded old woman, she snarled to herself in the safety of her thoughts. *The pretty Prince may be a healer and all, but he and that old man are up to something evil.*

But she could see no way to do anything about it if she wanted to continue living. Disobedient slaves were treated harshly in Rome.

"It's lead." Maxian spilled the remains of the metal shavings into a cup on the long wooden table. The air in the basement was still fetid and stank of corruption. Two days of sweaty work in the darkness had not freshened the air any. Abdmachus was perched on a stool they had scavenged from one of the outbuildings of the house. Gaius Julius, fresh from dragging the body of the young black man out to the crematorium in the back garden, was sitting on the steps down from the main floor, drinking deep from a flagon of watered wine.

"Lead?" Abdmachus' voice was filled with curiosity. "Did he eat it?"

"I don't know . . . It permeated his whole body, in minute fragments, much smaller than can be seen with the naked eye. His liver held most of it, though his kidneys and stomach lining had some. When I started drawing it out, there was a great deal suspended in his blood as well." Maxian's voice was still weary, but he had begun to recover from his second examination.

"Gaius Julius." The Prince turned to the old man. "This man was a longtime resident of the city, yes?"

The dead man nodded and wiped his mouth before saying: "By the report of the aediles in his district, he had lived there almost his whole life, fifty-two years. He was the oldest man in the area, or at least the oldest recently dead. It's lucky he had no relatives to pay the burial tax, or they would have cremated him before I got there."

"So, a Roman citizen of fifty years. He probably never left the city in his life, unless to visit the gardens outside of the city on a holiday. Somehow he ingested a large quantity of lead. Now, the other man, he was not long in the city?"

"No more than a month," Gaius Julius said, "a Mauretanian slave who angered his master. Clubbed on the head with a pewter mug and left to die in the alley behind the master's house. The street sweepers picked him up. Just fresh the morning we brought him here."

Maxian nodded, pensive. "He is reasonably healthy, foreign, and he has no lead to speak of in his body, though there were minute traces in his stomach."

Abdmachus raised an eyebrow at this. "Then he was exposed as well to something common that carries the metal."

Maxian picked up the fragment ball and crushed it between his fingers. The particulate metal collapsed easily into a powder at the bottom of the cup. He rubbed his fingers clean on a cloth.

"I have lead in my body too," the Prince said, his face calm and considering. "I checked after I examined the African boy. Far less than the old man but more than the slave. We were all three exposed to the metal, and I think that I know how."

Abdmachus cocked his head, staring at the Prince.

Gaius Julius spoke into the moment of silence before Maxian, however. "The aqueducts again. I remember reading in the logbooks of the Imperial architects that the pipes that carry water from the stone channels to the public fountains and insulae are made of lead. Is it the taste in the water that you noticed before?"

Maxian turned and his face was dark, turned away from the lantern light. "Yes. Subtle and almost unnoticeable—unremarked by anyone because Romans do not, as a matter of course, drink their water straight. Anyone who did notice the taste would assume that it was river water. So! Another piece of the puzzle."

Gaius Julius stood up and stretched, groaning at the ache in his old bones. "Not the whole answer then? Is lead poisonous? Would it cause these things that you see?"

Abdmachus cleared his throat. "I doubt not that this much lead in a man's organs is cause for concern and may have hastened his death, but the thing that we are seeking is sorcerous in its base nature. Lead, my dear general, is most assuredly inimical to sorcery."

"He's right, Gaius. Generally when you desire to prevent sorcery from affecting something you wrap it or stop it up with lead. It is a neutral metal, neither positive nor negative in influence. The unseen powers slide off of it like water off glass."

Gaius Julius' answer was interrupted by a sudden bark of laughter from Abdmachus. Both the Prince and the dead man turned, their faces puzzled, to look at the Persian.

"All this time . . ." Abdmachus put his hands to his face, though his body shook with laughter. "All this time, we wondered and argued and plagued the gods with our pleas for knowledge . . ."

"All this time—what?" Gaius Julius snapped.

Abdmachus held up a hand and pinched his nose to stop giggling. "All this time, my dear fellow, the Kings of Persia have made one unceasing demand upon the *magi*—why is the Roman Legion immune to sorcery? Have you not considered it yourselves? Rome marches out without sorcery and nearly conquers the world—smashing Egypt, a veritable den of wizards—crushing the remains of Alexander's empire, breaking the backs of the Gaels and their druids, the Germans and their witchmen. Who thinks of a *Roman* sorcerer?"

"No one!" Gaius Julius huffed. "Sorcery is the work of weak Easterners and Greeks. Roman spirit conquered the world!"

Maxian laid a hand on the dead man's shoulder and shook his head slightly.

"You think that each soldier marched out from Rome with a belly full of lead," he said quietly, watching the little Persian. "Each man carried, all unknowing, a puissant shield against the wizardry of his enemies."

"Yes," Abdmachus said, his face weary. "Workings and patterns that could lay waste to whole nations of warriors fail or falter when directed at the ranks of a Roman army. I am a fool not to think of it before. Even some of your weapons are made of lead . . . all innocently impervious."

The dead man rubbed the stubble of beard that had accumulated while he had been passing on sleep and rest for the pleasures of digging in body yards and rubbish dumps. "Well, all that aside, do the bodies show the influence of this 'dark power' that you two can see pervading the city?"

Maxian breathed deep and sat down in the high-backed chair again. His head was splitting again, this time with a fatigue-induced ache. Though he felt stronger than ever after the ill-remembered events in the Appian tomb, the kind of detail work that he had done with the two bodies carried its own price.

"The old man's body carries it like a mother cat her kittens. It hides in his blood and crawls, unseen, along his bones. It seems . . . it seems to be almost a part of him. The African has none of it. He is a clean slate."

"Again, something tied to the city, to Rome," Abdmachus said. "And you? Could you find it in you as well?"

"Yes," Maxian said, his face drawn with fatigue. "As strong, or stronger, than the old man. It seems to be quiescent now, but I fear that it is waiting for the opportune moment to come out and destroy me somehow. I could try removing it from my body, perhaps here, where it is attenuated by this foreign building. I could succeed . . ." He shook his head to try to dispel the gloom that threatened to overwhelm him.

"Odd," the Persian said. He picked up his note tablets and began shuffling through them. "Pardon me if I pry, but you were born in the provincial city of Narbo, if I remember correctly. You have come only recently to Rome—no more than, what, twelve years ago? Yet you say that you show as much effect of this curse as a man who has lived in the city all his life. This augurs that the curse is not borne by something specific to the city of Rome at all."

Maxian considered this—it could be true. But if so, then what carried the curse? Something that affected men thousands of miles apart, yet possibly only within the confines of the Empire. What commonality did they hold that subjected them to this?

He and Abdmachus continued talking and the afternoon whiled itself away. Gaius Julius took the opportunity to slip away and sleep in the shade of the cedar trees in the garden. They would argue for hours, he knew, and never realize that he was absent. The sun was hot, and the afternoon still and quiet. He yawned mightily. *Even a six-hundred-and-forty-year-old needs a nap now and then*, he thought.

Krista crept through the wild irises and lilies that grew on the northern side of the house like a slinking cat. She had traded her bright shift for a dusty gray tunic, nondescript and already worn. Her feet were bare, though the calluses that she had acquired on the hard floors of the house of de'Orelio served her well as she moved through the overgrown bower. Her long hair was tied back behind her head. She had left the broad-brimmed straw hat she favored for going out in the sun back at the tree line. Coming to an old aisle in the garden, she peered out from the high grass. There was no one to be seen, or heard. She darted across to the foundation wall that held up the northern end of the portico.

Again she paused, listening. Very faintly from inside the house, she could hear the banging of a hammer and chisel on stone. *Well, that's at least one of them*, she muttered to herself, under her breath. Fear churned slowly in her belly—fear not only of being caught by the men here at the house but also of what would happen to her if she was not able to complete this excursion before the Duchess noticed that she had been on her trip to the flower market in the Forum Boarium for a very long time. Luckily, no one had bothered to tell the stable master that she was no longer taking the white pony out to the hills with Sigurd. It was tied off to a tree in a field almost a half mile away, downhill.

The prospect of being seriously whipped or even losing a foot for running away did not please her at all, but she was bone-certain that the pretty Prince and his foreign companions were up to something dangerous. She had wrestled with her feelings for the Prince on the long ride up from the city and had come to the sobering conclusion that though he was quite nice, for a Prince of the Empire, and seemed to like her quite a bit, if he was up to something that would hurt the

Duchess, then he would have to pay for it. This digging up of bodies and carting them about secretly put her on edge. That and the odd feeling she had gotten about the old man she had waylaid in the Archives. He looked like a grandfather, but he had been far too active in their little tryst than he had a right to be. His eyes and skin were funny too. She had dreamed bad dreams about him for a week after that.

She pattered down the line of the portico wall, keeping her head low, to the end. There she peeked out and saw that the back garden was also empty. The sharp *crack-crack* of the chisel continued to echo from inside. She glanced around again. *Twenty steps and she could get up the stairs and inside, or maybe she should climb this little wall and go in through the portico?*

An iron clamp suddenly closed on her left arm and a heavy hand, smelling of freshly turned dirt and worse, closed over her mouth. She nearly screamed, but twisted aside instead and lashed out with a long brown leg. Her heel caught something soft and fleshy and there was a sharp grunting sound behind her. The clamp released on her arm and she darted away from the wall. Her heart pounding with fear and her veins afire, she sprinted off down the hill, leaping over the broken fountains and the scattered bushes.

A rock, thrown with a keen eye, clipped her on the side of the head as she vaulted the crumbling brick wall at the bottom of the garden, and she tumbled, senseless, down the hillside to crash into a rosebush. The last thing she heard were boots clattering over the wall.

"Your friend is quick," Gaius Julius said sorely, sitting on the steps to the upper floor and kneading his inner thigh to try to get the knot out of the muscle. "Another two fingers to the right and I'd have been puking my guts out while she made like Diana into the woods."

Maxian ignored the dead man, all of his concentration was focused on the deep wound on the side of the girl's head. The rock the old man had brought her down with had cracked her behind the ear and left a bad cut. Little sharp fragments of the stone had been driven into her scalp and the fleshy part at the top of her ear. The power buzzed and trembled in his hands, flickering a faint green while he worked. Under his gentle fingers, the slivers of stone trembled and then slowly eased themselves out of the flesh with a liquid *pop*. Skin knit closed behind them and shattered veins closed up.

After fifteen grains, he smoothed back her long hair and the flap of skin settled back into place, becoming one with its fellows. There would be no scar. Maxian smiled and felt in himself a simple joy that he had not felt in a long time. For just a moment, his mind was clear of the heavy dread of his burden. He gently turned her face back up and raised her head to slide a brocade pillow under it.

"Known her long?" Gaius Julius' voice was carefully neutral. Maxian looked up, his eyes narrowed. Abdmachus, sitting in the background, turned away a little and concentrated on his notes and writings. The dead man regarded the Prince with a level eye.

"Two years," Maxian said, his voice cold.

"What are you going to do with her? By your account she is the servant of a possible enemy of ours. By her presence I'd say that she had been spying on us for quite some time. I've checked the hillsides both above us and below us. There are places on the upper hill where two people have been regularly watching the house. This Duchess of yours, she knows that we're here. She might even know what we've been doing."

Gaius Julius' voice was calm and mildly curious. With a start, Maxian realized that the dead man really didn't care that he had just nearly killed a sixteen-year-old girl—but he was concerned about the effect she would have on their tactical situation. For a moment the Prince was fully conscious of the vast gulf between the old man, who had done more than his share of terrible things in the name of the old Republic, and himself. Then he shook his head and reminded himself that the margin they trod was very narrow and, sometimes, for the good of the people, some few might have to be expended.

"We are not going to do anything with her, beyond keeping her here. You're right, the Duchess may know. If we assume so, then we have to move again. How soon do you think we'll have to go?"

Abdmachus coughed quietly, and Maxian turned away from the dead man. The Persian was standing on the other side of the table that the Prince had used for his impromptu surgery, gazing down at the unconscious girl with a quizzical look on his face.

"What is it?" Maxian asked.

"My lord . . . please do not take this amiss, but when you were working on her wound, did you feel the curse within her?"

Maxian paused for a moment, reconstructing memories of his work in his mind.

"No," he said, shaking his head, "I felt the lead in her body, of which there is more than a little, but not the contagion."

"Has she lived in the city her whole life, then? Or is she another import, like the Mauretanian?"

Maxian considered—though he had spent more than one enjoyable afternoon or evening, or even night, in the house of de'Orelio in the company of the slave girl, their conversation had rarely turned to herself. With a little start, the Prince realized that he had told the witty green-eyed girl far more than he had ever intended about himself and his brothers.

"I don't remember it well, but I think that she was raised in the house of the Duchess. The daughter of house slaves, probably."

Abdmachus scratched his head in puzzlement. "So she has lived in the city for—what?—sixteen years? Yet she is not afflicted. You have lived here for only twelve years and you carry as much of the curse as that old man of fifty. I think, my lord, that what we seek is not tied to the city at all. The lead, surely, is as much an affliction to the people of the city as the coughing sickness in winter. This is something else, something that is tied up in the Empire. It only manifests itself in the city so strongly because so much of the effort of the Empire is concentrated there."

The Prince nodded slowly, as his mind broke apart the Persian's argument and turned it around and about, examining it from all angles. He rubbed his nose, deep in thought.

"The old man," he said at last. "What do you know of his life, Gaius Julius? What was his occupation? Did he always live in that district, or did he come from somewhere else? What did he *do?*"

The dead man spread his hands.

"Well," he said, "to hear the neighbors tell of it, he had always lived there, in a top-floor apartment with a bad view. He did tinker's work—repairing shoes, leather goods, pots, pans, things like that. He drank his share of wine, didn't make any trouble, and kept out of the way of politics and crime. By my view, quite a respectable citizen. You probably know him better, having been in his guts and seen what he ate and shit the last day of his life.

"But I know one thing that they seem to have forgotten. I wager he never mentioned it, less he was dead drunk and the wine wasn't enough to keep his memories at bay. He was a citizen—a twenty-year man, by the Legion brand on his shoulder and the discharge mark."

Maxian turned back to look down on Krista's recumbent form. Her chest rose and fell slowly under the grubby cotton tunic she was wearing. Without thinking of it, he checked the pulse at her neck and wrist. She was sleeping easily now. He ran his hand over her face and the sleep deepened. When she woke, she would feel no pain or aftereffects of the blow.

"A citizen. I am a citizen, by birth and action. The slaves are not . . ."

Something tickled at the edge of his thought, something from his youth in Narbonensis, something about . . .

". . . the children of citizens, or citizens themselves. I remember a herdsman on my father's estates in Narbo, he said that the young of a strong bull are stronger than the offspring of a weak bull. The blood of the father and the mother affects the child." His voice sharpened.

"This contagion is carried by those who are citizens or the children of citizens of the state. It must be passed by blood from generation to generation."

Abdmachus rose from his chair and joined Maxian by the table.

"Eventually," the Persian said, speculatively, "it would affect the majority of the population, save those whose were never citizens or whose parents had always been slaves. It might even get stronger with each generation."

"A pretty theory," Gaius Julius said from the steps, "but how did it afflict the citizens of the city in the first place? The lead didn't carry it if what you say is true. I somehow doubt that a wizard wandered around the city, bespelling everyone. Someone would have noticed. So, how did it first happen? And, more to the point, is it still happening now?"

Abdmachus sighed and returned to his chair. He was growing weary of the strain of all this. He devoutly wished that he could slip away and find a ship to take him back home. It was nearly a decade since he had last seen the green hills of his homeland or ridden under night skies familiar from boyhood. He had trouble understanding merchants from home now, and he continually caught himself thinking in Latin. Sadly, he put those thoughts away and wrote down the latest conclusions in short-stroked characters on the wax tablet that he carried with him always.

"My lord," he said when he had finished, "this is a strong spell to maintain such durability. I've been a sorcerer for nearly all my life, and the thought of constructing such a thing makes me feel a little ill. There are two kinds of things I can think of that would make such a thing work; first, that a sacrifice of blood be made when the working was done. Second, that the subject be permanently marked or forced to ingest something that fixed the pattern to them. These things make me think that perhaps . . . perhaps it is a religious ceremony. Something that each citizen undergoes upon coming of age? I am not familiar with those kinds of customs among your people . . ."

Gaius Julius shook his head, grimacing. "No, there's the little ceremony when you come of age—but that's just wine and grain on the family altar and a party. I suppose excessive drinking might cause it . . . that would explain much of the last six centuries. But then it must be past my time, since I don't show its effects. . . . What?"

Maxian was staring at the dead man.

"Show me your arms," the Prince said.

Gaius Julius stared at the Prince for a moment, then shrugged out of his tunic. He showed first one arm and then the other, front and back sides. Maxian grunted and turned away, lost in thought.

"Well?" the dead man asked as he pulled the tunic back on. "You want to explain that?"

"You served in the Legions?"

"Yes, though from the reading I've been doing, not the Legions that you have now! My troops were either my personal followers or citizens called up when the city was threatened. No, let me take that back. My men were professionals—I suppose the last of the citizen-soldiers were in my grandfather's time. What of it?"

"You don't have a brand, or mark, on your arm."

Gaius Julius laughed; a sharp bark of amusement. "No, boy, I was a political officer! The brands are for the men who enlisted or were levied—they had to serve a long term—six to twenty years—and you don't want them to desert, now do you? I would never be branded, nor would any officer of the equites. We served out of choice, to further our political careers. This Augustus, this 'son' of mine, seems to have reorganized the Legions and instituted new programs—the branding, the issuance of a certificate of enlistment, an identity badge stamped from tin." He paused. "So much changed after I died."

The dead man looked old suddenly; truly old, not just his appearance, but his spirit and will, for a moment, seemed to be as ancient as his body. Enough of his new world was the same, or similar, that the things that had changed—like the wine, or the size of the city, or the abject poverty of the poor and the rampant excesses of the rich—struck him hard. Maxian looked at him with sympathy just for an instant and then forced his mind to remember that the old man was *dead* and a tool, little more. A lever, perhaps, to move a mountain.

Abdmachus had been shuffling through the notes that he and Maxian had made, and he pulled out a parchment book, complete with a leather binding. He opened it and turned to the third or fourth page. Clearing his throat, he read aloud in a carrying voice: "To the Republic of Rome, to the Senate, to the People and to the Law of the City of Rome, I swear that I will serve faithfully, to obey my officers, to follow commands, to keep ranks and to stand when others may flee. Upon my honor, the honor of my family and my blood I do so swear."

He put down the book and nodded his head slightly, paging forward through the chapter of the *Annals Militatum*. Maxian frowned.

"This is the oath," the Persian said, "that Augustus instituted during his reorganization of the army in the sixteenth year of his reign as *princeps* of the Republic. The previous oath, by my notes here, was taken to an individual Legion and hence to the commander of that Legion. With this change and oath, made before the standard of the Legion as tutelary representative of the city and the state, Augustus attempted to impress upon the troops that their responsibility was to the Republic, to the Senate, and to the Emperor rather than their own commanders."

"Did it work?" Gaius Julius asked in an envious voice.

Abdmachus shrugged, saying "I have not read the military histories of the Empire, but the discipline and élan of the Roman army is known throughout the whole world. In battle they stand fast against terrible odds. They have rarely mutinied and they do not pillage or rape their own lands."

Maxian spoke, his voice thoughtful. "The oath is followed by the branding— it might be enough to fix the ritual upon the mind and body of the soldier. Hundreds of thousands, perhaps millions, of Roman citizens must have taken the oath throughout the history of the Empire. Many are given grants of land, spreading them willy-nilly throughout the Empire. They have children, and their children must carry the oath-binding down through the generations as well . . ."

Abdmachus flipped to another set of pages and read: "The sons of the man who has completed his service, and accepted either the grant of land or the payment of cash monies to begin business for himself, are compelled as well to take service with the Army of the Republic after the passing of their sixteenth birthday. To those who complete their service as well, these same benefits and exemptions will accrue."

The Persian closed the book, his fingers tapping on the binding.

"Many generations might take the oath, then," he said, "with each one becoming more firmly fixed than the one before. Over hundreds of years, the minuscule talent for the power that lies in each man and woman, bound by this oath, would accumulate and feed into the thing that we know today. Each stone that they laid, each cloak that they weave, even the wine that they ferment—all are touched by a little bit of the power and it grows, it grows monstrous . . ."

Maxian sat down heavily in the chair. His mind whirled to accommodate the prospect of a pattern of sorcery grown, man by man, woman by woman, over six hundred years. Millions of citizens living and dying, each adding to its power. Growing like a fungus in the darkness under the shade of the state, until it swallowed the world. *My gods, the raw strength inherent in such a structure of forms!* A voice in the back of his mind gibbered in fear—there was no way that he could overturn such a power!

He shook his head sharply and stood. "Bring me more bodies—these ones alive. I would know the strength of this thing."

On the cold table, Krista moaned slightly and turned over, away from the Prince.

Maxian ignored her. "Gaius Julius, I need soldiers, both those newly inducted—if there are any left in the city, and those who have served their term as well. The sooner the better."

OUTSIDE OF THE CITY OF
VAN, PERSIAN-OCCUPIED ARMENIA

"Ah, bugger the lot of them." Thyatis slid the long-glass back into the leather case it rode in and slid off of the crest of the rocky slope. Nikos and Timur, who were lying up under the shade of a boulder at the bottom of the dry streambed, looked up as she crawled into their little shelter. She fit herself into the last free bit of shade under the overhang. Nikos passed her a wineskin filled with brackish water from the last well. She drank deeply, spilling a little water on her chin and chest. Wiping it away left a trail of tan mud.

"Pah!" She snarled and rubbed the mud away. "A desolate country. Well, my loyal followers, there's too much to see and too little to do about it. There must be five or six thousand Persians between us and the gates of the city. Either of you have any suggestions about how we're supposed to get in there?"

Timur laid back against the cool stone and closed his eyes. He was only a scout; this was a matter for the commanders to hash out. The wind whistled through the high chalky walls of the streambed and cooled them a little with its hot breath as they sat in the shade. Timur was filled with a sense of homecoming, though he knew that it was false. This high plain, dry and desolate save around the fringes of the great lake that crouched at its center, was only enough like his homeland to inspire memory, not to reveal to opened eyes the towering peaks of the Altai or the Khir Sâhr. His leg ached, another sign that he was not home. If his leg had been good, would he be here?

"Are you sure that we have to meet this fellow in the city?"

Thyatis nodded, her face filled with disgust. "Yes, I've only the passcode to identify myself to him, not to his contacts in Tauris. Without him, we'll have to try to get into Tauris by ourselves without any local assistance. We need to get in there and find this man. If he's already dead, or fled from the city, then we can break off and head south to meet the army, but if the chance remains, we take it."

Nikos nodded. "How do we get in, then? This is some barren countryside—we won't be able to sneak up close to the walls. We haven't even seen a local, so there's no one to take a message inside or show us some secret way into the city. We know nothing about the Persian commanders, so unless you're willing to take the time to scout them out, we can't try faking our way past their patrols to get within a throw of the city."

"True . . . I do love your optimistic nature, Nikos. Timur, open your eyes and answer me some questions. You were out for hours last night—what did you find?"

Timur's dark eyelashes fluttered and he blinked a little.

"*Beki jegun*, there are two *wadi*," he said, "dry streambeds like this one—that run down from the hills to the lakeshore on either side of the town. The southern one is larger and deeper. It seems to run close to the south wall of the city, so—perhaps—some few of us could make our way down it to the point closest to the walls. From there a brave man might be able to make it to the wall and over, if the city men do not spear you as you attempt to climb the rampart."

"That's not a very good chance," Nikos said. "There might be a commotion and we don't want either the defenders of the city or the Persians to know that we're here. We have to get in, and out, quietly with this guy. If no one knows we were here, I'll call it successful."

Timur shook his head. "*Beki arban*, that is a fool's hope. The land is dry and the sky clear. Eventually the Persian scouts will cross our path and see the wagon tracks. Then they'll know we were here. Then they will hunt for us."

Thyatis slapped her thigh, causing a cloud of dust to puff up. "Both of you are fools and so am I. There's a perfect way into the city—sitting right there, bright and blue as the sky. The lake. We can take a boat into the lakeside part of the town after full darkness."

"A boat?" Nikos sputtered. "Where are we going to get a boat in this wasteland? The townspeople won't be leaving them around for the Persians to use for day picnics. There's neither wood nor time to build one."

Thyatis laughed and crawled out of the overhang into the sun. It was on its downward course but still high in the sky. She squinted at it and estimated the time to dark before fitting the broad flat-brimmed straw hat back on her head. She strode off down the *wadi* at a brisk pace. Behind her Timur groaned and slowly crawled out of the shade. The ache in his leg was killing him these days. Nikos ran off to catch up with the centurion. Timur looked after the two of them with concern—it wasn't a good idea to run around in the heat when it was like this.

The sky above was a blue-white bowl. Not even the wisp of a cloud marred its perfection.

"Is this why we've been dragging this thrice-damned wagon all over creation?" Nikos was whispering in the darkness and Thyatis had trouble picking out his voice from the soft slap of the lake water on the rocky shore. Each of them had hold of one side of the collapsible hide boat that the Sarmatians had been carrying in their gear in the wagon. A change of clothes and their weapons rode in the bottom.

Carefully they picked their way down the beach to the water's edge. The waves of Lake Thospitis were a bare ripple compared to the tides on the Sea of Darkness, but they had scoured off a bit of a strand. Uphill, in the cluster of trees that sheltered the wagon and the other men, there was the long-drawn-out hoot of a nesting owl. Immediately Thyatis and Nikos went to ground, carefully touching the boat down so as not to make a noise. Around them the night air was quiet, filled only with the sound of the water slapping against the shore and the nearly inaudible squeak of bats.

Thyatis rolled over so that she could see up the beach in either direction. There were no lights, or the clatter of horses' hooves on stone. Ten or twenty grains passed and she began to feel better, but there was still no all-clear signal. The moon had not risen yet, so the shore was black as pitch. She could hear Nikos breathing.

A cry of pain suddenly cut the night and there was the unmistakable ring of steel on steel from the copse of trees. A fire shot up, lighting the treetops, and against it Thyatis could see running men. There was shouting and she stood, frozen with indecision. An arrow whickered through the air and plunged into the lake behind them.

"Ai, come on," Nikos hissed, and began dragging the boat toward the water as fast as he could. "It's too late now to do ought but get away!" Another arrow came out of the night and slapped into the rear bowsprit of the boat. Thyatis woke up and spun to dash after Nikos, who was in the water and pushing the boat farther out. She splashed into the water, high-stepping, and then darted sideways at a faint sound behind her.

A spear clove into the water with a hiss, and a man cursed within feet of her. In the darkness, now only feebly lit by the fire raging in the crown of the dry trees, she could barely make out the shape of a hulking figure. The gleam of firelight off the man's longsword, that she could see. He stepped in, slashing overhand with the blade, and her arm rang to the joint as she slapped the blade away on the flat. She jumped up out of the water, furious with herself for leaving her own blade in the boat, and kicked at the weaving head of her assailant. There was a ringing *crack* as the iron hobnails on her boot caught the edge of the man's helmet.

She dropped back down with a splash onto both feet as the attacker stumbled back.

In the darkness, Nikos was shouting for her. She ran through the shallow water in the opposite direction, away from the man. Within thirty feet he was gone in the darkness, and she swerved into deeper water. More feet were running on the beach, and voices were shouting commands. Up the hill, the sound of steel had faded and the roar of juniper trees combusting filled the air. In their light, she could see dozens of men in armor running down the hill to the beach.

Oh, Timur, she thought, you were far too right for your own good!

She waded back into the lake until only her nose and eyes were above the water. Then she began paddling slowly, keeping her arms underwater, back in the direction Nikos had been with the boat. On the shore, men with lanterns and torches were beginning to spread out, searching the waterline.

Nikos, you half-Greek half-Illyrian who-knows-what-else bastard, you'd better not have run out on me. . . .

The boat, low in the water with its burden, rocked gently from side to side. Nikos lay in the bottom, a partially drawn bow with arrow to hand across him. Over the water he could hear the cussing of Persian sergeants as they ordered their men to spread out and quarter the beach. Too, there was the splashing of men entering the water with lanterns and spears. With the trickiness of sound over water, he could not tell if they were close by or far away. For the moment he did not dare risk looking over the side at the beach lest he betray some reflection.

Instead, he whistled, the long cry of a night-jar. Forty heartbeats later, he whistled again.

There was a sudden shout up the beach, the cry of men on the hunt catching sight of their prey. Officers' whistles cut the night and the light on the shore began to run north. In the boat, Nikos half sat up, forgetting his earlier vow. The clusters of running torches seemed like fireflies across the water. Now there was shouting again, and the rasping sound of steel on iron. The torches bunched and men shouted angrily. Nikos sat up farther, but he could see nothing more. His heart was filled with agony—if not his commander, that was at least one of his men, brought to bay.

The boat rocked fiercely, and a voice thickened by exhaustion said: "Idiot! Get down and balance the boat before you fall out."

Nikos sat down on the opposite side of the boat and grasped Thyatis' wrist as she hauled herself over the side. She was soaked through and still wore the light iron mail shirt she had donned when they first came into sight of the embattled city. Gasping for breath, she lay in the bottom of the boat in a pool of water.

"Row." She snarled, her voice filled with anger and loss. "Get us out of here."

On the shore, the sound of fighting halted and there was a commotion among the hunters. Nikos dipped the paddle into the dark waters and stroked away. The little hide boat began to move through the night. Thyatis, utterly drained, lay in the bottom of the boat, quietly weeping.

THE EGYPTIAN HOUSE

"Hey! Hello!" The shout echoed down the corridor, ringing off of the mossy stones. "Anyone! Hey, you motherless bastards! Hello!" Krista hung from the bars of the cell that she had woken in, feet on the bottom rung of the door, shouting at the top of her lungs. Her hair was a tangle of mud and dried blood, one arm was badly scratched, and the side of her head and face was very tender. The cell had some blankets and straw on the floor as well as two buckets.

"Let me out! Let me out or you'll be in some deep shit!"

Disgusted and hoarse from shouting, she jumped down onto the floor again. Restless, she prowled around the little room. It was small and mean, and all too obviously a cell.

The old bastard can sure throw, she muttered to herself, seething with anger at having been caught. *The mistress isn't going to be very pleased with me.*

Her jewelry and belt were gone, along with her sandals and the leather thongs she used to tie her hair up. Krista guessed that she had been thoroughly searched before being dumped like a sack of millet on the floor of the room.

Footsteps echoed in the hallway and she turned and curled up on the floor, facing the barred door. In a moment her breathing was even and steady and a soft snore escaped her lips. A haggard figured stopped at the entrance to the cell and leaned on the bars, exhausted.

"Ai, poor girl. What am I going to do with you?" The Prince's voice was faint, burned out by exhaustion and terribly long hours of unremitting effort. He wore a heavy butcher's apron, deeply stained by blood and crusted with dried gore. His leggings were spattered too, and there was a faint charnel stink around him like an invisible mist. Krista was horrified by his appearance, watching him from between almost closed eyelids. His hands, too, were dark with dried fluids.

"Let me go," she whispered. *Who knew where that old man was, or the little Orientals she had seen coming and going from the house?* "I didn't mean to spy, I was only curious . . ."

Maxian raised his head and, through a blur of exhaustion, could make out that she had raised her head, catlike, from the floor to look at him. A wave of relief swept through him, leaving him giddy, that she was all right and that his work on her head wound had not been in vain. He suddenly realized that he was tremendously tired and should sleep.

"That's a good idea," Krista said, for the Prince had spoken his thought aloud. "If you let me out, I'll help you back upstairs. You need a bath too."

Maxian looked down at himself and staggered a little to see how gruesome a sight he was. For a moment his mind spun in all directions, as he comprehended how much blood there was on him and how old some of the stains were. Memories began to crowd back into his waking mind, a hurried procession of subjects—some live, some dead, some near death—coming to the examination table. The grating vibration of a saw cutting into bone. The crack of a limb breaking open in the vise. First the buzz of the power in his hands, cleaving into the organs of a still-thrashing body, then the howl and the lightning as he split open the skull of a long-dead general and the power of the corpse flooded into him.

A terrible howl of anguish tore out of him and filled the corridor. Krista clapped her hands over her ears and rolled up into a tiny ball at the back of the cell, far from the shuddering thing that crouched at the door to her cell. Then it began to weep, its body racked with great heaving sobs. She crept forward and a lithe hand snaked out to lift a ring of keys from the back of the stiff apron. One of them fit the door and it swung inward. Krista stepped out, gazing down in pity at the man on all fours, grinding his head against the stones. The door at the end of the hallway was open.

"Please," came from behind her as she slipped up the steps, "please don't leave me . . ."

She half turned, looking back down the dark corridor.

Downhill from the bulk of the house, in a grove of cypress trees, there was a crude shrine to Jupiter. Maxian knelt in the brick building before a rude altar. Thick ivy covered the outside of the little building and filled the tiny windows. The Prince had placed two tallow candles on the altar, one at each end. Once there had been a small statue of the god in the recess behind the altar, but it had long since vanished. He reached out, placing two pieces of tin on the grimy stones.

"O lord of justice, forgive me. I have defiled the bodies of two of your servants—these men, Aurus Antonios Sabeinos and Julius Terentius—who served the state and the Emperor and did not do ill. I have desecrated their bodies and cut them up into pieces. I beg you to let them enter the peace of your afterlife and to ascend, whole, into your heaven to be rightly judged."

The Prince's hand trembled slightly as he spilled wine into a shallow ewer placed on the ground before the altar. He sprinkled crystallized honey and grain, taken from two small bowls, into the ewer. His whole body hurt, savaged by the power he had drawn upon to examine the bodies dragged into his basement room. Odd whorls of light and shadow fluttered before his eyes. He would not have been able to reach the little building down the hill without Krista's help.

"O Mithras, he who judges and assesses all that is man, forgive me for these acts. I seek to help the many, the People and the Senate, and for this, some few must die. I take this sin upon myself, I accept the responsibility, both now and in the time after life, for these actions."

Maxian bent his head to the floor of the temple, pressing his forehead into the soft loamy soil. His mind, at least, was clear. After his collapse in the hallway in front of Krista's cell, he had been bedridden for three days, barely able to feed himself. His body, pressed beyond its own limits, had finally revolted, refusing to support his demands. Also, he had realized that he had committed, in the fury of his work, dreadful crimes. He raised his head from the floor, tears dripping from his eyes. He struggled to put revulsion at his acts aside, hearing the cold calm voice of Gaius Julius in his mind: *Lad, a good commander must be willing to spend the lives of a few to secure victory and the safety of all.*

"O lord Mithras, accept my offering, please, please forgive me . . ."

A pinpoint of sunlight, golden and warm, crept slowly along Thyatis' cheek-bone. Unmindful of the dirt and the thin tracks cut by tears, it danced along the line of her jaw and down across her clavicle. There it disappeared into the top of her ragged tunic along the line of her breast. But another came, lighting the tumble of curls that pillowed her face and drifted across her eyelid. She twitched a little and yawned. Dust clouded up from the tattered woolen cloak that lay over her and she sneezed. Coming fully awake, she lay still, feeling the rock of the boat and the brush of wind off the water. The regular *slap-sluice* sound of a single man rowing reached her. Gingerly she drew back the cloak.

Nikos, wearing her straw hat to shade his face, was sitting in the stern of the hide boat, his arms rising and falling as he dipped the blade-shaped paddle from side to side. The boat cruised through the deep-blue waters, foam hissing away from its sides. Seeing that she was awake, he smiled and nudged a woven straw bag toward her with his foot.

"A little food left," he said, his voice weary, "and plenty of water."

She levered herself up from the flexible floor of the boat. She looked around, seeing the lake as a broad sheet of tourmaline blue. Tiny waves rose and fell on its quiet surface, picked up by the wind. The sun was still rising in the heavens—it seemed to be about three hours after sunrise. Away to the northeast, she could make out the dull brown line of the shore and low hills rising behind it. To the north, dead ahead of the boat, she could see a vast blue line of mountains rising up out of the heat haze that marked the plain beyond the shore. She pointed.

"You're making for the passes of the Ala?"

Nikos nodded, resting the paddle on his thighs for a moment. His arms felt like lead weights after rowing for the past twelve hours. He sighed and rubbed his face, feeling the skin dried and cracking under the relentless sunlight beating up at him off the water.

"Yes," he croaked from a parched throat. He paused and took a long swallow from the waterskin that lay between his legs. "By the map you had, there's a stream that comes down to the lake dead ahead. I figured we could get ashore there and maybe find something to eat before we strike north."

Thyatis turned around, her hands busy in the straw bag. She found some cheese and strips of dried meat. There was no bread left. She found another waterskin as well and drank from it. The meat was hard and she tucked it into the corner of her mouth to soften. She did not eat any of the cheese yet. Her mouth was too dry.

"North? You figure that we'll be far enough away from the Persians at Van?"

Nikos nodded. "By the map it's nearly thirty miles from the city, so their patrols should be intermittent at best. We can follow the stream north to cut across this headland that we're headed toward. Beyond the peninsula, we can make for the road that goes north across the Ala into the valley under the eaves of Ararat."

Thyatis wiped her mouth clean and stoppered up the waterskin again. She squinted north, her hand shading her face, looking at the distant blue mountains. Going north to Mount Ararat and the valley of the Araxes was the second way across the great mountains to the east—they would come into the valley that contained Tauris from the north, rather than from the west on the main road. Fewer Persians, fewer questions, but a long delay. They would be weeks late getting to the city. She looked back at Nikos, who shrugged. He had thought of the same things.

She chewed on the tough meat. It would be a long way to go. She did not think of the dead men she had left behind on the shore, or the stranger in Van who would wait fruitlessly for them.

Thyatis crouched in the thorn bushes, her cloak held over her head to break up her outline. Only feet away, the hard pack of the road slashed across the hillside and then down into the little river valley they had spent the morning climbing up out of. The sun burned against the back of her neck—adding another layer of bronze to her already dusky skin. There was the faintest breath of a breeze and it turned again, bringing the *clip-clop* of horses to her ear. Nikos had heard it first as they had turned the switchback on the long tawny hill that led up toward the distant line of blue-green pine trees. Looking back, they had seen two riders on the road behind them, more than two miles away. In the still air, the sound of their passing over the ancient arched stone bridge that spanned the stream in the valley had just reached them. The two fugitives had faded off of the road then and now crouched on opposite sides of the track.

Nikos was behind two low trees bent over from the weather, about forty paces up the road, as it turned to double back on itself. Thyatis was lower down, with the steep slope of the hill dropping off behind her. The jingle of riding tackle and the voices of two men reached her. She tested her grip on her shortsword, wishing briefly for a long spear or another bow. *No matter now*, she thought as the first of the two riders trotted around the lower bend in the road. From their embroidered riding cloaks and swept-back hats, they were Persian dispatch riders. *But not in a hurry*, she wondered, her eyes bare slits in the frugal shade of her cloak.

They passed her and she slid the cloak off into the brush. She paused, waiting, one hand on the branch of thorn that she would have to push past to reach the road. Behind the screen of trees, Nikos pushed the bowstave away from him and sighted down the length of the black-fletched arrow at the jouncing shape of the rider on the horse with a splash of white on its face. He breathed out with an unheard *huh!* And the arrow leapt away from him to bury itself in the chest of the leading post rider.

The man was still gaping down at the three-foot shaft protruding from his torso, watching dark blood bubble out of his chest, when Thyatis sprinted up the road behind the second rider. The second man was still asking his friend what was wrong when Thyatis sprang up and snaked an arm around his neck. The bay-colored steed, quite startled, reared with an outraged whinny and the man was thrown back into the air. Thyatis twisted into the angle of the horse as he fell and put her shoulder into it. The post rider flew a dozen feet down the road and smashed into the ground with a cracking sound. Thyatis dodged aside from the horse, which had turned and snapped at her.

The other man had slumped over on his horse and it was prancing in a circle as his dead weight cut at its mouth with the bit. Nikos sidled up it, speaking softly to it. Thyatis circled the nervous bay.

"Nice horsy. Nice horsy. Horse want apple? Nice apple."

Nikos collared the first one and tugged the bridle out of the dead man's hand. A good push sent the post rider to the ground in a tumble of limbs. Nikos led the horse away, toward the little straggle of junipers on the side of the road. When he trotted back, Thyatis had calmed the other horse as well.

"Check him," he said, taking the reins of the horse from her.

Thyatis nodded, she had not forgotten the second post rider. She slipped her shortsword back into its sheath and sidled up to the man lying sprawled in the dust and rocks of the road. He was still alive, though his eyes were glazed over with shock and blood was slowly oozing out of the corner of his mouth. She slapped him lightly on the cheek and his eyes wandered back into focus. She had turned up the hood of her cloak and the sky was bright behind her.

"Soldier, where are you going?" she asked in her poor Persian, voice sweet and deep.

"Ah!" He moaned and tried to turn over. Thyatis held him down, gently. By her guess, his neck was broken and he was bleeding inside. "We're . . . to Dogu-bayazit . . . to the headman . . ."

He began coughing and his mouth filled with blood. Thyatis grimaced and drove a thin dagger into his eyesocket. Her sad face was the last thing he saw with one good eye. Afterward she wiped off the knife on his shirt and then, as Nikos was doing just up the road, stripped him of everything but the bloody shirt and his loincloth. They rolled the bodies into a crease in the side of the hill, no more than a place for water to run when it rained. Mounted, they continued on, to the north. Nikos watched the young woman out of the corner of his eye. There were still tiny spots of blood on her cheek, but she had not bothered to wipe them away.

Sun-bright snow gleamed off the top of the mountain, a spearhead of glittering white even at thirty miles distance. Thyatis shaded her eyes, looking across the gulf of the valley of Dogubayazit, through thin air, at the massive pyramid shape of Ararat. It rose, solitary, from the valley floor, first a dun brown on the lower slopes, then banded with the green of pines and spruces, then another band of gray rock above the trees that ran into a mantle of snow. Clouds clung to the flanks of the mountain and crowned it. The bay post horse whickered at her and she patted its neck. It didn't like standing in the snow. The horse picked its way down the snowy slope, back to the narrow track that they had followed up the granite slopes of Tendürük.

For two days they had ridden higher and higher into the mountains ringing the basin of Lake Thospitis, leaving the tiny mountain villages behind. In the last one they had passed through quickly, for they wore the cloaks and emblems of the Persian dispatch riders. The eyes of the village men had been on them constantly, dark and glittering in the afternoon light. Beyond that village, the road became a trail through flower-strewn alpine meadows and thick stands of spruce. The air was cool and becoming chill as they labored ever higher into the peaks.

Today, though, they had come up the last snowy reach and broken out in the pass under the snowy bulk of the mountain to their left. Lesser peaks fell away to the east, on their right, and Thyatis pointed that way now. Ragged ranges of bare stone and icefields receded before them to the horizon. Beyond the range that they had climbed, a great wall of mountains rose up to the southeast, behind them.

"Persia," she said. "Beyond those mountains is Tauris." She turned and pointed northeast; there the wall ended and plunged down into a broad valley, visible even from here, that cut between the blue wall and the pyramid of Ararat to the north. "The valley of the Zangmar; it will lead us into the highlands north of Tauris and then to the city."

Nikos shivered. The wind bit at his exposed face, and he pulled up the cloth that in lesser elevations he had worn to keep the dust from his nose and mouth. Now it kept his nose from freezing off. Thyatis did not seem to feel it, though, and she rode with her face and hair exposed now that they were beyond the habitations of men. He followed her down the rocky trail that curled off the pass and plunged into a steep canyon that wound toward the valley below Ararat.

"Are we going to go into the town?" he asked, once they were below the pass and the trail had widened a little.

Thyatis shook her head. "Even in this disguise, I will not risk it. The rider said that he was going to see the headman of Dogubayazit—not the garrison commander. I think that the valley ahead is free of either Roman or Persian troops. You saw the way the last village looked at us. We might receive a fine welcome, or we might not live past the night. We have supplies enough now with their rations, and we know which way to go."

Nikos spurred ahead a little, so that they were even on the road.

"We've been out of touch for six days," he essayed. "We should get some kind of news—anything at all might be helpful. The war might already have begun!"

She turned to look at him, and her gray eyes were cold like the sea. "We have only three more weeks before the Emperor is before Tauris. I will not be late."

East of Dogubayazit, the old road turned away from the river to the north and climbed up a hill onto a broad plateau studded with stands of trees and high grass. Nikos was in the lead since they had crossed the sluggish river that ran west toward the town. Thyatis rode behind, lost in thought, her cloak hood pulled up to cover the color of her hair and the broad hat nodding over her eyes. They had swung wide around the town, leaving the trail down from Tendürük as soon as possible to cut across the foothills—through gorse bracken and myriad sharp ravines—to reach the river well east of habitation. Much of the previous day had been spent searching for a ford across the river, but they had not found one until early this morning. They had swum the horses across in the predawn darkness, hanging to their saddle straps.

Only two hours ago they had reached the road and turned onto it. By the rough map that Thyatis retained from the oilskin pouch, it ran east alongside the river to another plateau and thence to the Zangmar. It should be deserted for much of its length. Soon they would be past the last of the trees clinging to the fringe of the river and be in highland plain again. Nikos suddenly whistled and held up his hand. He was looking back down the road toward the town. She reined to a stop at his side.

"Look," he said, pointing behind them to where a curve on the road rose up beyond the grass and trees. There was a line of mounted men descending the hill. The afternoon sun glinted off their spearpoints and flickered from helmets and mail. "It must be a Persian patrol."

"Off the road," Thyatis said, spurring her horse into the trees. "Let's make for the next ravine and lay up until they pass." She goosed the horse with her heels, and it broke into a trot through the high waving grass. Nikos followed close behind, though he turned in the saddle to see if they had been spotted, letting his horse follow the one ahead.

They had crossed the grassy slope that slid down from the road and were urging their mounts up the far side of the streambed when horns sounded from the southeast.

"Hi-ya!" Thyatis shouted, and the horses bolted up the slope. Nikos turned and looked over his shoulder, rising up in the saddle. Behind them, on the road, scouts riding in advance of the main body of horsemen were winding their horns and pointing in their direction. One rose up in his saddle, a long horse bow drawn from the saddle scabbard.

"Weave!" he shouted at Thyatis as they topped the rise. The air thrummed as one shaft blurred past in the air, then another. "They've mounted bowmen!" She broke left and he right as they thundered down the far slope of the hill. It was thick with high brush and low trees. Nikos reached the next streambed and turned right, putting his heels to the horse. Minutes later he had reached the head of the little draw.

Behind him the first of the riders from the road had topped the hill in pursuit and was coaxing his horse down the nearer side, through the spiny bushes. Nikos slipped his own bow out of the saddle rest and strung it in one motion. All of his time spent with the Sarmatian brothers had not been wasted. He found a long-shafted flight arrow by touch in his quiver and fitted it to the bow. On the other slope, another rider had joined the first in following their trail. They were leaning over their saddle horns, examining the ground. The one on the right suddenly jerked and slipped forward off his horse. The arrow had punched right through him and out the other side into a tree. Nikos smiled, a shark's smile, as he nudged the horse back into the cover of the brush.

Seconds later he stopped smiling as twenty or thirty armored riders topped the ridge. Horns sounded to his east and south as well. *Hades' infernal bollocks*, he snarled to himself as he trotted the horse forward through deeper brush in the next ravine. *It's an entire bloody army!*

The bay horse whickered softly at Thyatis and nudged her head with its nose. Despite the tension of the chase, she rubbed the soft rubbery snout that was checking her ear to see if there were any carrots in there. The horse quieted as the ravine echoed with the clatter of hooves on stone. Three of the Persian scouts appeared briefly in a break in the scrubby trees that clogged the downstream end of the ravine. Thyatis rose up a little, readying herself for action. She could hear them pushing their horses through the brush down the slope from her. She half drew the short horse bow that the ambushed post rider had slung in a lacquered wooden case at his saddle horn. Four short-shafted arrows with tan fletching were pegged, headfirst, into the ground in front of her. They were only hunting arrows, but she would make do with what she had.

She was shielded ahead and on the left side by a heavy gray-blue bush with spearpoint leaves and a sweet odor. To her right, the rocky course of the tiny stream that had gouged the ravine out of the lower slopes of Ararat wound down toward the distant plain of Dogubayazit. Thirty feet below her, where the Persians were crashing through the brush, the streambed kinked to the left side of the ravine and ran under an enormous thorn tree with a thick base. The walls of the ravine, cut from decayed lava and sediment, rose up nearly twenty feet and were crowned with long grass. A patch of blue sky, now interrupted by scudding clouds, made a roof of this little space.

The first scout crawled out from under the overhanging branches of the thorn tree and stood up, a spear ready to hand. He looked about with care. The ground before him was rocky and poor for tracks. There was some sand, but it was all disturbed, perhaps by animals passing along the ravine. Thyatis remained utterly still, and the bay, feeling her waiting tension, did so as well.

"Anything?" called one of the two scouts on the other side of the thorn tree. His accent was thick with the glottal sound of the eastern Persian highlands.

The lead scout sniffed the air and surveyed the ground once more.

"Nothing clear," he called back. "I think they did go up this way, though. Let's press on."

The two on the other side agreed and the lead man began hacking at the thorn tree with his longsword to clear it enough to pass the horses through. After a moment, though, he found what Thyatis had found, that one flexible branch held back much of the brush on the right side of the tree. Putting his shoulder to it, which earned him two long scratches and countless little ones, he bent it back. The other two men urged their horses through the gap.

When the last man was almost past the tree, Thyatis bent, plucked an arrow from the ground, fitted it to the bow, drew and let fly in one smooth motion.

Another arrow was on the wing as well, even as the first sank nine inches deep into the exposed side of the lead scout's head. Blood gouted from his mouth and filmed his eyes as the heavy-headed bolt punched through the side of his skull with a *crack!* right above the ear. He toppled and the heavy branch whipped back into its original position, lashing at the horse and the face of the third scout. Tangled, the man screamed in fear as hundreds of thorns cut and tore at him. The horse screamed too and shied away suddenly. The cut man wrestled to regain control but the horse, its own face and nose cut by the thorns, bolted.

The other arrow flashed past the face of the second scout, who had turned at the last moment to say something to the lead scout, and smashed itself against the dark wall of the ravine. He spun back and spurred his horse forward with a shout. Thyatis abandoned the bow and snatched up a hunting spear from its rest against the gray bush. The Persian rushed past her position, slashing down with a slightly curved longsword. She took the stroke on the spear-haft and the wood splintered but held the blow. Half of the spear hung limply, nearly cut through. She hurled it at the man's face as he curvetted his horse around for a second try. He leaned nimbly to one side and the crude missile spun past him.

With a ringing "Ha!" he spurred forward again, his blade out and ready to strike. The longsword in the scabbard on the bay horse rasped as it slithered out into Thyatis' hand. She crouched and then scuttled behind the nervous bay and into the clear space beyond the horse. The Persian turned as well, edging his horse forward with good knee work. The ravine was a tight fit for a man trying to fight on a horse, particularly with all of the brush to hand. Thyatis lashed out, cutting for the face of the horse. The Persian and the horse, moving as one, pranced aside, and she barely recovered her guard in time to fend off a ringing overhand blow.

Cursing, she skipped farther right, clearing away from the wall. Her right hand, free, clawed a long knife out of her belt scabbard.

The Persian rushed his horse forward a little while he slashed with the long-sword, trying to pin her with the shoulder of the horse against the crumbling rock of the ravine wall. Steel rang loud in the enclosed space as she beat back his attack fiercely. In a half a breath, she lashed out with a boot against the horse's leg and it shied away. In the moment of opening, she darted left past the head of the horse and the long knife slashed, glittering.

The Persian kneed the horse hard, trying to spin it around to follow her, but the saddle strap, cut through, gave way and he spilled himself and then the horse onto the gravel and stones of the ravine floor. Thyatis rushed in, weaving past the kicking horse, and the tip of her sword sank into the man's throat. There was a fountain of dark red that covered his face and doublet. Thyatis staggered back, her blood afire with the rush of battle. The horse whinnied in distress and then man-aged to stand up. Thyatis spun, gravel spitting from under her boot.

The lead scout lay dead under the thorn tree, the arrow standing up from the side of his head like a gruesome signpost. The other scout, the one trapped behind the tree, was nowhere to be seen. The lead scout's horse was nudging him with its nose, blowing softly. Thyatis grimaced and walked up carefully by the side of the horse and took it in hand. It was confused, but she led it back to her own horse and introduced them. Flies began to buzz about the bodies of the dead.

Thyatis mounted, feeling a twinge in her left arm. Wincing, she peeled back part of her shirt—there was a gash on her upper arm, running diagonally down from the shoulder. Blood curdled from it. *How did I get that?* she wondered. With the two other horses roped in behind her, she nudged the bay to a trot up the ravine. Somewhere ahead the ravine would reach a break in the ridge, she hoped, and she could cut across the slope of the mountain. Night was coming quickly.

Running on foot, Nikos crashed through a stand of cattails at the edge of a pond. The call of horns echoed off the wooded hills to his left, up toward the slope of the mountain, and again to the rear. He splashed quickly along the edge of the pond, stirring up a roil of muddy water and torn seagrass. The sky was growing dark and the land under the mountain was falling into shadow. The horns came again, much closer, though farther up the slope. Nikos plunged into the deeper water of the pool and began to half wade, half swim toward the far bank.

Horses snorted close behind him and he slid soundlessly down into the water. The western sky was a boil of hot orange, violet, and deep blue-purple. Clouds had gathered in the late day over Tendürük and now the sun had plunged into them, filling the vault of heaven with all the blood of its passing. The pond lay in twilight shadow now, deep gray and muffled blue-black. Nikos lay back in the water, only eyes showing, and slowly moved backward toward the far bank. The shore he had abandoned he watched carefully. Two men, perhaps more, were moving there on horses. He could make out bare glints of their movement as they searched the shoreline.

Indistinct voices carried over the water to him; there were at least three men there now. A horn sounded in the woods behind them, clear and ringing in the twilight. Others answered it from the woods above and more men began to gather on the shore. Nikos cursed all the gods and the fates that had brought him to this point—particularly the one who had snatched the horse and all of his equipment from him two miles back along the trail. His hands found the hard-packed mud of the bank.

Someone struck a flint and a spark of light guttered among the men gathering under the eaves of the trees. A lantern was lit and helms and bright mail glinted in the warm light. Thirty or forty men had come out of the forest now, faces lean and marked with narrow beards and mustaches. Some wore red tunics over their armor; others wore tall *spangenhelms*. A voice of command boomed among them and the crowd shifted, focusing on someone whom Nikos could not see over the confusion of men and horses. He slid beneath the jutting root of an ancient and gnarled tree.

The men on the far shore listened while the booming voice rose and fell, then they began to break up into smaller bands. Some mounted and rode off into the woods, others quartered the area around the shore, gathering firewood and unpacking baggage from the horses. A single figure remained standing by the pond, staring across it into darkness. In the light of the torches and lanterns, Nikos could see that the man was exceptionally broad of shoulder and possessed of a mighty beard. The Illyrian crawled carefully up the bank, keeping the old tree between him and the watching man, then he jogged away into the darkness.

Breath hissed from clenched teeth as Thyatis dragged a length of tattered cloth around her wounded arm. The bleeding had grown worse as she had pushed herself and the three horses to make distance across the flank of Ararat. Always, she had heard the horns of the Persians away and below her, but sometimes they grew nearer. Following the game trails across the mountainside was hard going. Rocky canyons cut the slope, forcing her into long detours. She had made only a few miles since she had left the ravine where she had killed the two men. She had come down a dizzying slope of loose shale and talus to reach the bottom of a broad canyon. For a little while she had made good time, but then the canyon had dropped away in a broad glassy lip of stone that spilled a trickle of water over a sixty-foot drop.

Full darkness had caught up with her, and beyond a sliver of moon, there was little light in the canyon. Attempting to find a way down around the cliffs was a useless effort at night, so she had denned up in an overhang upstream from the waterfall. A tiny fire guttered at her feet and the faces of the horses loomed at her out of the darkness. The horses had her water and the last of the grain from the saddlebags. Her fire was only twigs backed up against a small boulder. There was a bit of cast-up wood at the edge of the overhang as well.

She wrapped the length of cloth around her upper arm again and tied it off with one hand and her teeth. When she could see clearly again, it was a ragged edge of the night, stars peeking in around the overhang of the rock shelter. The fire was still flickering and the scant light picked out figures carved into the rock above her head—lions, gazelles, and a fat figure of a woman with a beehive. They glittered and sparkled in the darkness. Thyatis closed her eyes, all unaware that sleep had stolen up upon her.

Nikos jogged on, his legs still moving even though they seemed to drag through mud with each stride. His clothes, soaked by the trip through the pond, were dry again and rasped against his skin. The rocky plain, cut with odd mounds and sculpted towers of black stone, stretched ahead of him. His foot hit a rock and nearly turned his ankle. He stopped. Running on unknown ground under almost no moon was unwise. Stopping was a mistake, though, for his arms were leaden and he slumped against the nearest outcropping. The stone, brittle and spongelike with tiny razor edges and a crumbling nature, cut at his hand though it seemed to take a very long time for the pain to reach his consciousness. He staggered back, wiping the blood off on his leggings.

He walked on, picking his way through the eroded lava field with mindless care. Exhaustion crept up upon him, and when he started awake, he was lying, curled up, between two pitted stones in a tiny patch of sand. The boat of the moon had crossed most of the sky. He levered himself up and continued on.

A mile past the lavafield, he reached a shallow *wadi*, dry as a bone. He slid down the side of it, but found, once he had trudged across the sandy bottom, that he was too tired to climb up the farther bank. He began walking up the bottom of the *wadi*. The river of milk hung over his head, and in the starlight, the mountain loomed enormous ahead of him, gleaming pale white under the moon.

The ringing of clear bells woke Thyatis. Her eyes opened and she saw a roof of burnished dark cedarwood above her. Sunlight, filtered dim by golden curtains, fell at the edges of the platform that she rested on. A great murmur of people carried on the air to her. She felt strange; her hands and feet would not move to her will. The roof rocked back and forth, and she realized that she was on something that was rolling forward on an uneven road. Incense traced trails in the air and slowly drifted away behind her. A heavy cloth of soft silk lay over her, and a diadem of silver leaves was upon her brow.

Her eyes, at least, she could move, and from their corners she could make out pillars of gold placed around the platform that held her bed. The capitals of the pillars were worked into a deep flourish of leaves and carefully cut flowers. Rich paints anointed the carving with deep greens and yellow highlights. She could smell flowers too, and guessed that the bed of the great platform that she lay upon was deep with them. The bells rang again, tinkling silver, as the wagon stopped. The sound of the crowd rose, and there was the basso shouting of men.

Incense pooled in the still air under the roof beams. Voices rose and fell, though the sound of chanting halted—all-pervasive and unnoticeable until, as now, it was gone. The golden curtains to the left side of the bier parted, carefully brushed aside by a gloved hand. Thyatis struggled to rise, but her limbs, heavy, refused to move. The face of a man rose into view, looking down upon her with sad eyes. He was elderly, with short graying hair and an intelligent brow. He wore a rich burgundy cloak, bound with clasps of silver and gold over a linen shirt of deep purple. His beard was neat and short, shot through with veins of white hair. Gently the man placed a hand on Thyatis' forehead and bowed his own.

Tears fell from his eyes, sparkling in the dusty sunlight. The old man's shoulders shook slightly, and Thyatis blinked the salty water away, but he was trapped in his own grief and did not see the slight movement. When at last he looked up, he had composed himself. He leaned close, close enough for Thyatis to catch the smell of clean fabric and a muskiness of coriander and thyme. His lips brushed her forehead and then he stood fully. The shadow of the roof fell across his face. He was the king once more.

"Good-bye, brother," he said, his strong voice subdued. "I will take you to your true home and build you a monument to last a thousand years." Then he turned and went out through the golden curtains. The voices raised, soldiers chanting a name, as he emerged into the sunlight. Thyatis strained to catch it, but now the world was receding into a dark funnel of rushing lights. The clamor of the people faded and sleep overcame her again.

.   .   .   .

The sound of a boot crunching on rock and gravel filtered into Nikos' dreaming sleep. He lay still and opened on eye a bare fraction. A pair of heavy leather riding boots was within his field of view, standing on light sand and scattered rocks, and another pair beyond them. The snort of horses broke the silence. He continued to breathe evenly, though he was sure that the time for subterfuge was long past. Something sharp pricked his ear, and he twitched.

"You know," came a voice in Persian, in a slow burr, "this fellow might be awake already."

Two more sharp pinpricks came to rest between his shoulders. Nikos opened one eye and moved his head slightly. Three Persian cavalrymen were arrayed around him. The closest, kneeling, had a long dagger in his hand and its point rested lightly against the side of his head. The man, almost clean-shaven his beard was so closely cut, smiled down at him and traced the end of the knife across his cheek to rest against the skin of his throat. Nikos swallowed to moisten his tongue.

"I'll not run," he said. "Let me rise and you can take my weapons."

"A reasonable fellow," one of the other Persians commented. The two spears and the knife withdrew enough for him to stand, though the alertness of their wielders did not waver. Nikos climbed to his feet, the rush of adrenaline in his blood cutting through the muzziness of sleep broken too early. The cluster of brush that he had crawled into when the sun had begun to lighten the eastern sky seemed much smaller and sparser than it had in the night. Another Persian was on horseback, a distance from the litter of brush, a bow and notched arrow in his hands. Nikos turned slowly around, catching sight of the great bulk of the mountain to the northwest and another two horsemen. He clasped his hands on the top of his head. There was nothing to be done now.

The man with the dagger deftly removed the Illyrian's shortsword, cooking knife, and the dagger he wore on his left leg. Quick fingers checked the folds of his shirt and his pants. Satisfied, the Persian handed the weapons off to one of his juniors and drew out a length of rope.

"Turn," the sergeant said. "Hands behind your back."

Nikos did as he was told. The sun was bright, cutting through banks of clouds. It might rain in the foothills of the mountains. He stared at the snowcap of Ararat.

Luck of the gods with you, girl, he thought.

After binding his hands, the Persians helped him onto the back of one of their remounts and then the whole band galloped away to the south, leaving a cloud of dry white dust to mark their passing. The tight cords bit into Nikos' wrists. His hands were already becoming numb.

There was a weight on her chest when Thyatis woke. She shifted a little, off a rock lodged under her shoulder blade. A hiss stilled her, and then she felt muscular coils shifting between her breasts. She lay back, completely still, and slowly opened her eyes. A triangular head with beady black eyes stared back at her. A heavy, scaled body lay coiled across her chest and trailed down onto her belly. Thyatis barely breathed, testing her hands and feet. She could move them again. The head of the asp danced from side to side, its pale pink tongue tasting the air. It drew its tail in with a slithering rasp. It was under her tunic, close to her warm skin. She could feel the coolness along her cheek where its own head had lain against her neck.

Oddly, for she was in dreadful danger, she did not panic or scream. She watched the snake as it curled its muscular body up out of her shirt and down off her shoulder. It was long—two or three feet in length—and its center was a tight bundle of muscle like the arm of a strong man. At last the tail tickled across the upper curve of her left breast and it was gone. She let out a long breath, still soundless, and turned her head to follow its passage.

It was gone. The dry dust of the overhang floor was unmarked, save for her own footprints. The three horses were cropping quietly at the leaves of the broad-leaf trees they were tethered to. She did feel as exhausted as she had expected, and sat up. The sun was high, shining down into the bottom of the canyon outside. A little tumble of ashy coals marked where her fire had been. Echoes of the strange dream were still ringing in her head. The man who had stared down at her seemed familiar to her—in a way, though he had not looked anything like him, he reminded her of her father. Thyatis shook her head wryly; there no sense in puzzling over it.

The horses were happy to see her, though she had no apples or biscuit to give them. She untied them, one by one, and led them down to the little stream to drink. The sun was high—it was nearly noon. She drank deeply from one of the rock pools in the stream and washed her face and hair. Looking in the shallow water, she grimaced at the peeling skin on her forehead and ears. The sun had never been her friend, her complexion was too pale, but her arms, legs, and stomach, at least, were tan enough to stand the sun.

Breakfast was hearty, culled from the rations in the riding packs of the two Persians she had killed the previous day. She sat on a broad, flat rock that jutted out over the stream near the overhang, in the shade of a broadleaf tree with white and tan bark. The personal belongings of the two dead men were spread out around her. Little amulets, knives, leather pouches of coin, wadded-up bits of cloth, flint, straw bound up in a knot, buckles, beads on a string, and last a crude map on poorly cured parchment. The map, compared to her own, showed the area around the city of Tauris. She wondered why scouts would have such a map.

They must, she thought, have been truly coming from the west rather than the east. The outriders of a larger force. An army, then, was making its way into the valley she sought, not from the south or east, as she would have expected, but from behind her, from the west. Some Persian force that had been harrying the plateaus of Anatolia, she guessed, called home. Nikos must have been right, the war has begun and the enemy is moving.

She finished chewing the strips of marinated lamb and drank most of the water in the skin. Then she refilled it. When her gear was repacked and the horses had their fill of the stream, she mounted again and gently kicked the bay into motion. If there was a good way out of this canyon, it was upstream, not down. Tauris was still far away, and now she was alone.

)•((

Abell tinkled in the darkness, a clear silver note.
Anastasia's violet eyes flickered open. A sliver of moonlight fell
through the gauze curtains of the broad window across the room, only barely
illuminating the furniture and the thick rugs that covered the floors. The lady
sighed silently and raised herself up. Silk sheets slipped away from her body, ex-
posing smooth bare skin to the cool night air.

"Yes?" she said into the darkness. Her voice was thick with fatigue, and she
ran a hand through the unruly pile of curls on her head. At the sound of her
voice, a shape stirred by the door and there was a clicking sound as the bar was
drawn back.

"Mistress?" The door opened slightly, letting a ray of lantern light cut the
darkness in the room. "The lord Prince requests a moment of your time." The
tentative voice was Betia's, her new handmaiden. The little blond girl was still
tremendously nervous around her mistress. The servants were sure that the "mysterious" disappearance of Krista had been the result of disobeying the mistress of
the house.

Anastasia blinked twice and drew the sheets back up over her chest with one
arm. The light from the lantern had fallen across her breasts and half of her face.
"Lord Aurelian, or Lord Maxian?"

"The Caesar Maxian, my lady. He is waiting downstairs."

Anastasia sighed—some nights seemed to have no end. "Oh, bother. Well,
send the young man up."

"Here?" Betia squeaked, her voice filled with astonishment. "The bedroom?"

"Yes, dear," Anastasia said dryly, "we mustn't keep the Prince waiting."

Betia scampered away, her little feet making a pitter-patter on the tiles of the
hallway. Anastasia fluffed her hair with her hands and then rearranged the pillows
on the bed to make a backrest. Sighing again, for she was very tired, she pushed
the quilts off the bed, leaving only a single, almost sheer, sheet to cover herself.

"Tros," she said to the slave standing in the shadows behind the door. "Be a
dear and light half of the lanterns."

The slave, a hulking Islander with long black hair, moved from lantern to
lantern, lighting them with a smoldering punk. Anastasia lay back among the
pillows, adjusting them slightly to better present herself. Footsteps fell in the hallway, the sound of heavy boots and a man's tread.

"Hsst!" Anastasia motioned for the slave to leave. With an inscrutable look
upon his face, the Islander slipped out the doors leading onto the balcony, drawing

his *gladius* while he did so. The Duchess moistened her lips and raised an eyebrow as the door opened.

"Lady de'Orelio," Maxian said, turning to close the door firmly behind him. "I apologize for the lateness of the hour . . ." He turned around and stopped, his next sentence forgotten. To cover the flush of red that brushed over his face, he bowed deeply. "Pardon me, my lady, I did not know that you had retired already."

"Oh," Anastasia said, her voice low, "think nothing of it. I have often thought of entertaining you late at night."

Maxian's nostrils flared at the laughter hiding in her voice, but he kept his face expressionless. The room was lit by low warm lights placed about the periphery, beeswax candles by the hue of the light. The Duchess looked magnificent in the dim light and the shimmer of the flimsy cover that lay over her body. He looked away and picked up a chair by the window, moving it to the foot of the bed.

"Given the hour, and your inconvenience, I will be blunt. I have something of yours, something that you've mislaid. I apologize for not returning it promptly, but I was occupied with other matters."

The Duchess sat up straighter, cocking her head to one side. Maxian swallowed as the sheet slipped very low, only being caught by one fine white hand at the last moment. She drew up one leg, pointing the toe. "I must profess ignorance, my Lord Caesar, I did not realize that I was missing anything. What, pray tell, is it?"

Maxian settled back in the low chair, crossing his right leg over his left leg. He met her eyes steadily, feeling a subtle change in the tension between the two of them. In the warm light, her pale-violet eyes seemed quite large. He bit his tongue.

"One of your servants, lady, was found lost on a property of mine. My own guardsmen took her into their custody but neglected to inform me of this for a time."

"Krista?" An edge of anger crept into the Duchess's voice, and she sat up fully, drawing her legs underneath her. The sheet pulled tight under her hand, clinging to the curve of her stomach like a skin of oil. "Did you punish her? If you have not done so, I surely will if you return her."

Maxian smiled a little, seeing the spark in Anastasia's eye. *Ah, so she went off without permission . . . A reckless slave, and I do not think she understands what we are about!*

"Truth to tell, Duchess," he said, standing up and smoothing his tunic down, "I was rather pleased to see her when she was brought to my attention. I had neglected to bring any servants with me from the palace and she has done wonders for my household." He walked to the side of the bed and sat down, catching the edge of the sheet with his hip. The Duchess's eyes widened a bit.

"I am pleased that she . . . satisfies you, my lord." The sheet crept out of Anastasia's hand, inch by inch. Maxian swung his right leg up onto the bed and the movement made the last bit of fabric slip out of the Duchess's hand. She hissed softly at the touch of cold air.

"I cannot say," Maxian said, leaning closer to Anastasia, "that I have ever had anything but complete satisfaction in my dealings with the House de'Orelio. Indeed, the thought moves me to a proposition."

"Really?" Duchess the purred, turning her face toward him. Her right hand fell to rest on his thigh. "What do you desire of the House de'Orelio tonight?"

"I would like to keep this servant, my lady. A well-run household is worth a great deal to me. What will you take for her, coin or trade?" Maxian gathered the edge of the fallen sheet in his hand, feeling the silk slide over her skin as he covered her stomach and breast again. She was very warm under his palm.

"Oh, trade will do, my lord. But at such an hour, you will have to offer a great deal to make it worth my while."

His mouth covered hers and she fell back, her fingernails digging into his shoulder.

THE PORT OF SOLI,
THEME OF CILICIA, THE EASTERN EMPIRE

"Third Cyrenaicea, Fourth Maniple? That's a mounted unit. Drago! Where's that lackwit?" The centurion had a shout like a boar in heat. His voice boomed over the tumult of the port of Soli. Close to sixty men were crowded into the stifling tent, pressed up against a flimsy wooden divider. A granite-faced quartermaster centurion sat on a triangular camp stool next to the folding table behind the barrier. Soldiers in half mail with arms like tree trunks held back the press of men. The legionnaires shouted and shoved, trying to get to the front of the tent.

"Drago!" The senior centurion scowled. A flap at the back of the tent opened, spilling in a white-hot glare of Mare Internum sun. A Greek with a bad complexion stuck his head in the opening. "Where the Hades have you been, you insufferable catamite?" The Greek grinned.

"This boy," the quartermaster said, pointing a stubby finger at Dwyrin, who was standing in the tiny free space between the press of hot, angry men and the table. "This boy needs a horse and kit so he can catch up with his unit. They already pushed off for Samosata three weeks ago. Take him over to the stables and get him whatever they can spare, then get your backside back over here!"

Hundreds of tents surrounded them in a classic Legion encampment grown monstrously out of control. The port of Soli, where the combined armies of the Eastern and Western empires were busily unloading from the Imperial fleet, had been a sleepy fishing village before the Emperor Galen and his advance elements had landed four weeks ago. A half-moon of shallow bay, barely enough to allow a ship to reach the rickety wooden quay, on an open shore had marked it. The village behind the quay was composed of mud-brick buildings and flimsy wooden structures.

Galen had landed two thousand infantrymen in the surf of the beach and seized the town. The villagers had mostly fled when the black fleet had appeared offshore. Those who had failed to flee, or had come back for personal belongings, had been taken and impressed into work gangs. Three hundred engineers, stonemasons, and craftsmen had come ashore in longboats at the wharf. Within two days they had torn down the village and extended the quay by fifty feet using the brick, wood and fieldstone from the buildings. Galen had come ashore then, with five hundred Sarmatian light horse and his bodyguard. The Sarmatians, under the command of Prince Theodore, had pushed inland to secure the nominally Roman city of Tarsus, eighteen miles to the northeast.

By the time Dwyrin's ship had reached the port, after a twelve-day voyage from Constantinople, the Western Emperor had put ashore the fifteen thousand men who had sailed with the initial fleet. Theodore and his light horse had secured Tarsus and all of the drayage that they could lay their hands on. Bands of auxillia roamed the countryside, confiscating horses, mules, wagons—all that and every bit of portable food and fodder they could lay their hands on. The one quay in the old harbor had been joined by two more—one composed of purposely sunken merchantmen, the other of brick and soil carved out of the hill behind the town.

The initial camp had doubled and then tripled in size, gaining a new ditch and palisade with each expansion. The Western Emperor, the army general staff, and Galen's personal guardsmen and servants now occupied the first, innermost camp. The three western Legions—the Sixth Gemina and Second Triana and the Third Augusta—that had landed with Galen occupied the next layer of the camp, and the barbarians the outermost ring. Outside of the outermost ditch, a great mustering yard of corrals, barns, and feedlots had been thrown up to hold the thousands of horses, mules, and donkeys destined to carry the logistical tail of the Roman army.

More ships arrived each day, offloading supplies, materials, and men—in whole formations, in *banda*, and as singletons, like Dwyrin. The Western officers were furiously trying to match men to units and unsnarl the traffic jam that clogged the port from dawn to dusk.

"Quite a commotion, isn't it?" Drago pulled Dwyrin roughly aside from the clatter of a heavy wagon laden with sheaves of arrows. Mud spattered on Dwyrin's legs. It hadn't rained recently, but the lowlands around Soli were very close to the water table. Drago sniffed at the muck that passed for streets in the camp. "Nothing like eastern mud—thick as tar and yellow as bile!"

Dwyrin stared around in awe as they passed through the middle camp—thousands of canvas tents were arrayed in neat rows, each block marked by the standard of the Legion and maniple housed there. Hundreds of legionnaires hurried to and fro in the camp; work details were cutting the ditch lower and reinforcing the inner palisade. Others marched past in formation, dust caking their legs and armor. There was a tremendous sense of barely controlled chaos and energy in the air.

"Huh." The Greek watched as a maniple of legionnaires entered the gate from the outer camp, heavy bags of water slung over their shoulders. "Keeping them busy, I see. Come on, we've still a ways to walk. Now, your chit says that you're for the Third C, in the thaumaturgic battalion—you get a standard kit, no armor, but a horse. I'll tell you now, you're not getting any kind of a good horse. All the good horseflesh is either in the field already with Prince Theo or being reserved for the Eastern army. They as are too good to set foot on common dirt, or walk!"

Dwyrin was lugging a heavy bag of personal effects: cooking gear, a bedroll, and a bundled cloak. A leather harness hung, doubled, at his waist. A short-sword that, for him, was a heavy weight and a knife hung from it. He had passed on the javelins—his unit did not use them. Hardtack and dried meat with cheese and some rolls were in a cloth bag as well. A waterskin hung off his other shoulder. In all, nearly seventy pounds of gear—he could barely stand with it all on him. So he kept walking lest he fall down from the weight.

A bridge of logs crossed to the outer camp, over a ditch filled with hundreds of men stripped to the waist digging with shovels and picks. Ramps of tamped earth led up to the outer rim to carry the dirt away. At the eastern end of the ditch a dam had been built to hold back the waters of the Efrenk River. The river cut close to the eastern side of the camp and, in previous days, had provided the town with water. Now it was going to be rerouted into the ditches to fill them.

"Are the Persians going to attack us?" Dwyrin asked as they crossed the corduroy bridge into the clamor of the outer camp. This belt was a vast morass of mud, horsehair tents, and gangs of outlander *auxillia*. The road to the outer gate was straight and properly Roman, but the camps and enclaves of the foreigners were anything but. Long-haired Huns, Sarmatians in tattoos and ritual scars, red-haired Goths, Alans, blue-painted Celts, blond Scandians, black Africans from beyond Mauritania—the detritus of the frontier. All arguing, fighting, gambling, cleaning weapons, sleeping. All waiting for the order to move north.

"No," Drago answered with a grimace. "The nearest Persian army is over two hundred miles away, on the other side of the bay of Issus." He pointed off to the southeast, across the broad blue waters of the Mare Internum. "The latest that I heard, from the captain of a coaster out of Cyprus, is that the great Prince Shahin commands that force and that he is preparing to march against Damascus in the south. All this effort that you see is to keep the men busy until the army is ready to move out. Most of the Western troops will be gone within the week, to march up to Tarsus and join the blessed Prince Theodore. In another month only a garrison will remain here."

The Greek led Dwyrin out of the barbarian camp and then turned right. The corrals were lodged against the bank of the Efrenk to allow for easy watering of the animals. A troop of cavalry cantered past as they approached the tents at the gate of the maze of corrals. Dwyrin gazed after them; they were white men with long dark beards and cloaks of gold and brass. They held lances in leather cups at the sides of their saddles.

Drago pushed aside the flap of the biggest tent and ducked inside. Dwyrin followed and blinked in the dim light. It was another room filled with little tables and annoyed men. Drago bantered with a thin-looking Sicilian at the end table. Dwyrin looked around and took the opportunity to shed his gear into a bare patch at the edge of the tent. The air was close and stuffy, but the break from the sun was welcome.

The Greek tapped him on the shoulder and handed him a set of badly cured parchment papers. "Your travel orders, lad. They'll get you a nag to carry you. The latest report is that the Third left Tarsus in advance of Theodore and is on the road to the city of Samosata. That'll be the jumping off point for the whole army. He says"—Drago gestured idly at the man he had been talking to—"that the road is clear between here and wherever the Third is camped."

Dwyrin tucked the papers into his tunic and clasped the Greek's shoulder in return. "Many thanks, Drago. I'll be on my way, then."

Though of poor color and given to fits of eye-rolling, the horse that Dwyrin rode out of Solis was no nag. It was a stout little steppe pony that had been gathered up in the sweep for suitable horses in the province. Dwyrin named it Macha in hopes that the spirit of the goddess would fill it and give its stocky legs more speed. It was a fruitless hope—the pony clopped along at a steady pace for hour after hour, but it refused to canter, much less break into a gallop. Still, it had a mild nature and rarely bit.

The road from the port to the inland city of Tarsus was crowded with legionnaires moving in both directions as well as trains of heavily laden mules and wagons. Tarsus, a sprawl of red brick buildings and dusty-tan edifices of poor-quality marble, was swarming with Eastern officers and cavalrymen. Dwyrin slept in a barn on the eastern side of the city; no lodgings were to be had in the town with the press of army billeting. He ate a sparse breakfast and watered Macha at a well on the eastern edge of the city. The citizens, drawing water for their homes, held forth that Prince Theodore was preparing to advance east into Persian lands without the support of the rest of the army, which was still held up unloading at Solis. The great triple-spanned bridge across the river beyond Tarsus was blocked when Dwyrin reached it. He waited for an hour behind a press of Gothic horsemen and bands of Cyrenaican archers.

At the far end of the span, a wagon had lost an axle. The northern horsemen were hooting and laughing at the efforts of a troop of Roman engineers to clear the wagon, but it had been loaded with baskets of lead shot and heavy, precut timbers. The Cyrene troops were squatting in a long line along the side of the bridge, talking in low tones. Their patterned tan cloaks and dark, burnished skin stood out in stark contrast to the sunburned faces of the Goths and their heavy, grease-slicked blond and red hair. Dwyrin managed to edge his pony around the upstream side of the wreck, drawing the curses of the centurion in charge of the gang trying to move the wagon. It was overloaded and too heavy to push. The engineers began shouting at one another.

Dwyrin rode on, now that the road was clear. Another smaller camp had been thrown up on the far bank of the river. The garrison troops, a clean-shaven lot of dark-haired Celts, looked on with amusement as the Hibernian rode past, almost swallowed in his red cloak and gear.

"Don't be home late for dinner!" they shouted after him, laughing.

He waved and rode onward. Before him, the flat plain of Adana stretched out, a fertile valley of olive groves, vineyards, whitewashed mud-brick houses, stands of cedar and spruce trees. Beyond it, a low range of mountains rose in the east, running from the sea north to the vast escarpment of the Taurus Mountains. Even through the humid air, Dwyrin could see the snow-crowned peaks off to his left glitter in the afternoon sun. Clouds were gathering among them, but for now the sun was bright and the air clear. Tiny red birds sang in the trees along the road. It was quiet and peaceful, the clamor of the army left far behind.

He urged Macha to go faster; it was a long road to Samosata.

Cold wind howled out of the north, driving a fine spray of grit and dust against the Hibernian. Dwyrin leaned into the gusts, his cloak, now pale with dust, wrapped tight around his head and shoulders. Gravel, whipped by the wind, stung at his legs as he struggled forward through the wind. Macha, her head low, trudged along behind him at the end of the bridle. The pleasant valleys that drew up to the coast were well behind him now, and he had crossed a bleak range of rocky hills and barren mountains to come out onto an endless plain of dried mud and broad dry streambeds. The Tauruses still towered on the northern horizon, cool and distant, but the old Roman road that he was following slashed almost due east across the headwaters of an enormous river plain.

Every ten miles a waymarker rose from the barren soil to mark the road, most of which was covered with blown drifts of dirt and sand. The stele, once deeply graven with the sigil of Rome and the Emperors who had raised them, were worn and chipped by the weather. The road ran straight, but the stones at its verge were tumbled and broken. Off the road, in the distance, he could sometimes see villages, or perhaps the ruins of villages. Short grass peeked from between the stones at the edge of the road, but the low hills were dry and yellow, barren of trees or cultivation. Even the Legion night camps, dug out of the baked mud only weeks before, seemed empty for long years, already half filled with windblown sand and fallen-in walls.

The wind had struck him as soon as he had come out of the hills above the abandoned city of Gaziantep four days ago. It did not let up, even in the night when the temperature of the plain—hot as a baker's oven in the day—plunged to near freezing. His eyes were nearly glued shut with grime and dust. His hair and nose were coated with a thick layer of yellow matter. Still, he kept trudging east, keeping to the road, sleeping in the bare hollows of the land where there was some respite from the wind. Every third waymarker, there was a house of stone or brick built at the side of the road. In the shelter of these crumbling dwellings, cisterns had been cut into the earth and lined with stones. Usually there was water at the bottom of the shallow pits. He kept on, though most days the sun was only a brassy disk in the sky, burning down through heavy air.

He had begun to get nervous. Though his othersight no longer overwhelmed him as it had on the voyage on the Father of Rivers, little things still leaked through to his consciousness. The endless flat plain seemed to affect his mind, emptying it of trivial things, paring down his thoughts until they were little more than the desire to put one foot in front of the other. The drone of flies was constant. The power was very deep in the earth here, hidden and dim. Sometimes as he crossed one of the shallow valleys, he could feel the water in the ground, running cold and distant, but it did not come near the surface. Other things trickled around the edge of sight. Voices seemed to call in the darkness, and the land felt watched and angry.

One night, as he lay sleeping in the lee of an ancient masonry wall, he woke to see the figures of four men standing beyond the pale ring of his campfire. Macha was sleeping, leaning against the wall, her breathing heavy and slow. The pale men stared down at him with shadowed faces. They were dressed in long robes, worked with crosshatched patterns and flat-topped helmets of fluted brass. Their beards were curled and painted, but they were so dim that he could see the gleam of stars in the pits of their eyes. He moved to rise, and they faded, but the echoes of their anger and hatred lingered. That night he broke camp before dawn and pressed on in the darkness, eager to leave that place.

Four days onto the plain, he topped a rise that he had not even noticed climbing, so gentle was its slope, and looked down onto a ribbon of pale green and the broad surface of a great river. The road turned and ran down the slope below him, to a small village and a great bridge of stone pilings and a wooden truss. In the distance, he could see men in red cloaks standing watch on the circular stone towers at either end of the span. The river was easily two hundred paces across and a deep blue, rushing swift under the sandstone pilings of the bridge. Macha whinnied, smelling the water and the greenery. Dwyrin smiled and urged her down the slope with his knees.

A dead man lay in the shadow of one of the outlying buildings. Dwyrin rode up the road slowly and stopped thirty feet from the entrance to the village. The place was quiet, the only sound the idle rattle of a shutter in the wind. He could smell the dead man from the road and see that the outthrust arm was puffy and discolored. Scratching his chin, he shrugged the Legion cloak back, off his arms, and rode slowly forward. In his mind, a flurry of thoughts scattered and a point of calm formed, oil on the waters, and he extended his perception out to the sun-heated walls and the cool shadows of the doorways.

At the center of the village, there was a square of bare earth fronting a dilapidated temple with four pillars of brick, faced with carved wooden slats painted to approximate marble. Other buildings crowded the plaza, their doors dark and empty. Dwyrin skirted the center of the space, angling to the left, toward the towers by the bridge. As he passed opposite the temple, he could see the bare legs of two bodies—man or woman, he could not tell—lying on the portico. Flies buzzed in the still air at the center of the village. A door rattled, but he had felt the wind move against it, and he was not distracted.

Dwyrin muttered to himself, raising the first defense, the shield of Athena, around him. To his partially opened othersight, he could see the wan blue veil fall between him and the sun. The power of the river was close, a rolling green wave, and he reached out to tap into the eddy of it as it broke and curled against the bridge supports. A hot spark began to flicker in the back of his mind. Macha moseyed on, never in a hurry, past the dead square and into the lane beyond.

Here the houses were a little better built—fieldstone with plaster facings. Down the street, on his left, a garden wall jutted out from a house, ornamented by a trailing vine sporting little blue-and-white flowers. Dwyrin became uneasy; a sense of cold and hunger was seeping in around the edges of the shield. He loosened the shortsword in its scabbard on his right hip. The street was empty as he rode on, the echoes of hooves sounding thin to his ear. Past the houses, there was a bank of palms and part of a garden field. As he rode by the last house—tightly shuttered, with a painted door in muted red—he twitched, looking to the right, into the field. *Something* . . .

A crack like thunder knocked him off the horse and slammed him into the ground. The Shield of Athena blazed into full strength as he rolled away on the ground. Macha wailed in pain and toppled over, most of her hindquarters burned away. Dwyrin was partially blinded, the etched zigzag of a bright blue-white light searing his retinas. The hot spark in his mind exploded and his hands danced in the Invocation of Geb, the stone of the earth. Through a blur of tears, he saw men rushing forward out of the palms on the left side of the road. Facing them, he stabbed his hand out, loosing the dammed up power that he had drawn from the earth and the river.

A bolt of scarlet flame ripped across the road and slashed through the gang of running men. The lead two men, clad in desert robes and light chain mail, flashed to ash in the torrent of fire. The men behind them screamed in horror as the wall of flame washed over them, clawing at their clothes with bright fingers. Dwyrin staggered forward, a halo of blazing white flame roaring around him. The remains of the faithful horse smoked and then burst alight, filling the air with greasy smoke. Nine men howled in despair on the ground, their muscle and fat sizzling away in the heat of the fire that he had summoned. Contorted limbs thrashed, as they crisped to a reddish black and finally lay still.

The Hibernian, sick, finished the last man off with his sword. The twisted features, eyeless and locked in an endless scream, mocked him from the ashy ground. The palm trees were ablaze as well, sending pillars of white smoke into the air. Dwyrin turned around, stunned at the devastation that he had wrought. The field was burning too, and the nearest houses were black with smoke. Flames licked at the eaves. The othersight surged in his mind and the physical world was washed away in a torrent of colors and living sound. He fell to his knees, clawing at his face. His mouth was open, gasping for air, but he could not scream.

Smoke, faintly lit by fire, smudged the night sky. It drifted in long streamers across the arc of heaven, obscuring the stars and the fattening moon. Beyond the smoke and the dim red light of the fires, it was dark as pitch. Dwyrin groaned and blinked. His eyes were gritty. He sat up, and a thin layer of ash flaked off him to settle to the ground around him in a white cloud. The world was solid again, the earth firm under his feet instead of an infinite abyss of minuscule fires and strobing adamantine forces. The sky was close and filled with the comfortable light of stars, not a dizzying unguessable depth congested with millions of whirling spherical fires, packed so closely that they left no room between them.

The grove of palms had burned down to the ground, and the nearest houses sagged, roofs gone, windows black scars with trails of smoke along the whitewash. The bodies of the dead still lay around him, along with the poor horse. There were scuttling sounds in the night as scorpions and other scavengers retreated from his movement. He stood, though he felt weak, and tiredly brushed the ash off himself. All of his kit on the horse was gone. He checked his belt and cursed aloud.

"Mother of storms! Grave robbers . . ."

While he had lain unconscious, someone had crept up and lifted his pouch, his knife, his sword, everything but the woolen shirt, his leggings, the cloak he had lain upon, and, thankfully, his boots. He checked the pouch on a thong around his neck and was vastly relieved to find that his orders and identification disk were still there. He rubbed the tin disk and felt better, knowing that as soon as he reached some kind of Legion outpost, he would be home again, of a sort. He bent over the body of the horse and chanted soft words. After he had made the prayer of the dead, he cupped his hands and blew into them. A little white spark guttered there after a moment and then it became a pale cold light. He set it in the air before him, where it bobbed and weaved, lighting his path. Then he walked on, heading for the bridge over the river. If his eyes had not deceived him, there had been Roman soldiers there.

The bridge was deserted. The remains of a camp lay at the end toward the village, but the soldiers were gone. The coals in the cook-pit were cold and Dwyrin searched fruitlessly in the tents for any personal effects that he might use. He did find a spear behind one of the tents, which he took to use as a walking stick. The tiny mite of glowing light attracted itself to the head of the spear and, after fluttering around it, came to rest. The river gurgled softly to itself under the bridge as he crossed. When he reached the other end, he stopped.

The air was silent. The wind had died down. He looked back across the long span of the bridge, gleaming palely under the light of the moon. Something had attacked him in the village with a storm-power. Only his aegis had saved him. He could feel nothing in the ether of the night. The land was sleeping; only the river was still awake, running green and quiet in its bed. He turned away and walked down onto the hard road. At the edge of his vision, there was a flicker of hidden warmth. Ignoring it, he continued along the road, though he turned his head slightly to see if he could catch sight of it out of the corner of his eye.

A man was crouched in the shadow of the last support of the bridge on the eastern bank. Only a muffled outline marked him, though now that he was aware and focused, Dwyrin could see the patterns of heat that rippled in his blood and bones. The boy turned, facing the man, and leaned on the spear.

"I'll not bite," he said, his voice squeaking unexpectedly. Dwyrin paused, disgusted with himself. He had meant to sound strong and assured, adult. Instead he was certain that he sounded like a tired sixteen-year-old boy. "Come out. Are you a Roman?"

The figure shifted and then stood up. A dark cloak fell away from a naked blade, but that vanished with a scraping sound into a scabbard. A man stepped gingerly out of the darkness to the edge of the pale cold light that shone from the spearpoint. He was older, with a stubby beard and lank brown hair. His face was creased with furrows cut by years under sun and wind. His eyes were deep-set and glittered in the dim light. He wore the cloak of a Roman soldier, with a mail shirt of heavy round links and hard leather straps. A battered leather bag was slung over his shoulder, and the shortsword was accompanied by two long knives and a short stabbing spear. The man cautiously slid sideways, putting himself away from the bridge.

"Who are you?" he asked, his voice deep and rough with hard use. "Did you come out of the village?"

Dwyrin nodded wearily. He did not move; the man was ready to bolt into the night at any provocation.

"I came over the hill this afternoon, but someone attacked me in the village and I had to defend myself. I was overcome, though, and . . . well I fainted, I think. When I woke up, it was dark. Were you stationed in the camp?"

The man nodded, but he did not relax. He shifted the spear in his hand, passing it to his right.

"I'm Colonna," said the man. "*Ouragos* for the Fourth *Lochaghai* of the Sixth *Banda* of the Third Cyrene. What's your name?"

"Dwyrin MacDonald," said Dwyrin, "I'm a recruit for the Ars Magica of the Third. I was late getting to Constantinople and I've been trying to catch up ever since."

Colonna snorted and swung the spear over his shoulder in an easy manner. He stepped closer and looked Dwyrin over closely. "A wonder-worker? You seem mighty damned young to be a hell-caster."

Dwyrin stared back, his face set. His ears were burning though. The man had moved from cautious fear to insolence in record time. The ill-hidden sneer on the man's face was far too familiar to Dwyrin—the bullies in the village were no different from this fellow.

"What happened here?" Now Dwyrin's voice was steady.

Colonna shrugged. "Bandits attacked the village yesterday. Fifty or sixty of them on horses and camels. There was a fight among the houses and the *lochagos* decided that we should fall back to the bridge. Most everyone was killed on the bridge, but the bandits were pretty badly beat up. I fell in the river and took my time getting back. Everyone else was dead by then. I hid out down by the edge of the fields, keeping an eye on things."

The soldier pointed back across the bridge.

"Today they set up shop in the village, with some of them on the bridge in the cloaks of the dead men. I moved up under the bridge to listen—most of them left about noon with the people from the village. Raiders down from the north, looking for easy pickings now that the war has started. I lifted what was left of my gear from the camp when the big show started in the village."

Dwyrin quirked an eyebrow up. "Big show?"

"Yeah, the thunderbolts and pillars of fire. Flattened most of the village, so I decided I should cross the river and keep an eye on things from the far bank. Quieted down quick, though. The last of the bandits scattered right after, but it didn't seem too safe to go back. I figured that I'd wait a day and see what turned up. And I got you . . ."

"You got me," Dwyrin answered. "Unless you've got some horses hidden around somewhere, we should go. How far is Samosata?"

Colonna flipped the spear around the back of his head, shoulder to shoulder, considering the boy. Then he swung it down and tapped the butt against the stones of the road. Dwyrin waited with weary patience. Finally the soldier shrugged again and adjusted the bag on his back.

"It's about three days, kid. On foot. You sure you don't want to wait it out here? Another supply convoy or column will be through pretty quick. This is some empty country, traveling all alone."

"No." Dwyrin started walking. He had no stomach to remain in this place.

"This is dangerous land," Colonna said, as they topped a rise and began hiking down a long grade toward, at last, a valley littered with green orchards and fields. Both the older man and the youth wore hats of plaited reed and grass, gathered from the banks of the last dry watercourse they had crossed. Dwyrin ignored the muttering of the Sicilian. After three days of traveling with the *ouragos*, he spent more and more time in his own head, wondering what the teachers at the school were doing. The lessons that they had tried so hard to drum into his unreceptive mind were filtering back up now, but whole in some way, complete. He practiced them while they walked.

"The sun will roast a man in his breastplate. The natives are of an evil disposition and will murder the man found alone, away from his unit. The nights are cold enough to freeze. The water is poor and will give you the runs."

Colonna went on and on, his voice grating against Dwyrin's ears with an endless litany of complaints. In some sense, Dwyrin thought, the old soldier was trying to help him by unburdening himself of observations made in decades of service. It made Dwyrin's head hurt. He hoped that the city ahead was Samosata and they would, at last, part company.

"Poison asps crawl under the rocks and will creep into your bedroll while you sleep. You wake to the feel of their fangs piercing your skin. The fodder for horses is sparse and bitter—those animals not raised here will soon sicken and some will perish. The land hates men, so long has it . . ."

Dwyrin shut out the voice. He felt cold, despite the burning heat of the day. There was something in the dead rocks and parched soil around them that disturbed him. The city seemed far away, shimmering in the heat haze of the middle day. He stopped in the middle of the road and turned around, staring back up the road that wound out of the hills. He felt uneasy, a prickling sensation rippled along his arms. Something was watching them from the ridge behind.

Colonna had stopped too and was leaning on his walking stick. The soldier seemed old and weary. Dwyrin completed his slow circuit of the horizon. There was nothing.

"Funny feeling?" the older man asked.

"Yes, like hidden eyes watching us."

Colonna nodded. "I feel that way most of the time. They *are* watching up there somewhere in the rocks. Remember, the land hates us, and so do the people who live here. They only wait for a chance to murder us without cost to themselves."

They continued onward, though now Dwyrin looked out on the barren tablelands and sparse vegetation crouched in the folds and crevices of the land as if he were adrift in a hostile sea. Dark intent slid along under the surface, waiting for a chance to rise out of the depths with crushing teeth. The sun, unrelenting, filled the brassy white bowl of the sky with fire. At the edges of his othersight, dim greens and sullen red crept in at the edges of the road. In the flat, between fields of dusty tan plantings, they passed a broken building. White pillars, cracked and worn by the wind, leaned drunkenly, broken teeth in the raw red gums of the soil. Dwyrin shuddered as they passed the temple, moving to the far side of the road and keeping Colonna between him and the well of despair collected among the scattered bricks.

Colonna stopped talking.

Samosata was a sullen maze of empty streets. Native guardsmen passed them in through the western gate of the city without a word. The local men were wrapped in long turbans that covered their faces, leaving only dark crevices for their eyes. They had long spears and curved swords hung from jeweled harness and scabbard. Even their hands were covered with wrappings. No one could be seen on the streets. The houses were blank, gray-white walls with shuttered rose-red windows. There was a close, hot feeling to the squares that they crossed.

They stopped at the far edge of the city, having seen no one, but edgy with the sense of anticipation that had slowly filled the air around them like water seeping through a pinhole into a bladder. A plaza, barely thirty feet across, butted up to the eastern wall of the city. Three-story buildings of heavily plastered mud brick pressed against the open space. A gate with two square towers cut the wall. There were no guardsmen to be seen on the wall or in the shadow of the gate embrasure itself. Colonna stopped at a well in the southeast corner of the square. Dwyrin stood behind him while the soldier drew up the bucket, facing back toward the narrow alley they had come out of.

Only the scrape and jangle of the bucket and the rope that secured it broke the empty silence in the square. Dwyrin leaned against his staff, hood drawn over most of his face. His eyes were closed and within the quiet of his mind, he felt the hidden air around them trembling with violence. The hot spark that always seemed to glow at the back of his mind sputtered and flame licked against the tinder of his fear.

"Keep easy, lad," came Colonna's voice in a whisper. The so-familiar nasal whine was gone, his voice quiet and professional. "I feel it too. Just wait." The bucket rattled on the edge of the stone wall that cupped the well. Colonna thumbed the top off his waterskin and carefully poured the cold water into the grimy mouth. When he had filled the skin and stoppered it again, he raised the bucket and drank thirstily from it. Water spilled around the corners of his mouth, soaking the front of his cloak and pattering to the ground. Done, he passed the bucket to Dwyrin.

The boy took it, a heavy wooden thing, with a bent copper handle and bolts. It was almost empty, but he drank from it, heedless of the mud swirling at the bottom. The air leached any moisture from man or beast, making the taste of water an elixir. He put the bucket down. Two figures had appeared in the mouth of a street across the square. Dwyrin turned to face them.

Like the citizens of the city, they were completely covered by long desert robes—though these were pale baize and white. They bore no open weapons, but a sense of menace flowed forward from them like a fog. Dwyrin felt Colonna slide in behind him, and there was a *tink* of sound as the soldier swung his spear up. The desert men stepped out of the street, into the square, and stood aside from the opening. There was a sense of darkness there, filling the street. Dwyrin hissed in surprise.

"What is it?" Colonna whispered. "There's something there?"

Dwyrin raised a hand. There was something in the shadow of the street. Something lame and crippled but filled with bile and a seething, dark power. A hint of the smell of burned flesh reached the two Romans, even across the length of the square.

"Aiii . . . that doesn't smell good." Colonna shifted his stance, raising the spear into a throwing position. Dwyrin angled his own walking stick downward toward the flagstones of the square. Brittle red-black power trickled among the stones, and there was more in the deep blue-green of the well at his back. Using the staff as a focus, he began teasing the stones to yield to his will. It would not be much, but more than nothing.

The something in the street crept closer, its hate beating against Dwyrin like the heat from a bonfire. More of the desert men appeared. The power in the stones and the air and the water suddenly shifted its pattern, bending toward the mouth of the street like filings to a lodestone. Dwyrin began to sweat. The thing coming along the shadows of the street was very, very strong. He prepared to let go the fire-spark that had swollen to an incandescent fury in his heart.

"Get ready," he croaked at Colonna. "Cover your eyes and hide behind me."

The rattle of a heavy chain falling, link by link, through a brass housing broke the tense silence in the square. The gate between the towers creaked and began to open. City men in dusky brown robes came out of the dark openings at the base of the towers and dragged the massive wooden doors apart. Dwyrin's eyes twitched back to the opening to the shadowed street. The desert men had faded back and were disappearing at a trot into the other byways opening onto the square. The bitter hatred of the lamed creature receded as well. There was the clatter of hooves on flagstones.

"Mithras bless us!" Colonna breathed, making the sign of the bull. A troop of Roman cavalry in short red cloaks and leather armor cantered into the square through the open gate. They were Eastern troops, with light bows at their backs and long spears set into leather holsters at their feet. The lead officer, a swarthy fellow with a bushy black beard, reined his horse in before the well. Dwyrin looked up at him, face pale and drained. For a moment the fire in his mind threatened to leap out and consume the officer staring down at him with a puzzled look on his face, but then, with an audible groan, the boy swallowed the whirlpool of flame and sagged to his knees in exhaustion.

Colonna grabbed his shoulder as he fell and propped him up. He smiled broadly at the officer and saluted. "Not used to the heat, sir, he'll be right with some more water."

DAMASCUS, THE THEME OF SYRIA MAGNA

Ahmet sat in the shade of an olive tree, his hat turned upside down in his lap. It was late afternoon on the hillside, and of all of Mohammed's men, only he was still awake. The others, even the guards, were sleeping in the shade under the trees in the grove. The camels and horses were grazing on the low grass between the trees. Even the flies were quiet, only a few buzzing around the Egyptian's head, and they were slow and lazy. He was eating an orange and putting the peels in his hat. From his vantage, he could see down the slope of the low hill to the gates of the great city. A pall of dust and smoke shrouded the road from the south. Ahmet finished peeling the fruit and popped a section into his mouth. Strong white teeth bit down and he savored the taste.

A river, broad and swift, lay between the hills and the walls of Damascus. Drovers on the road the previous day had named it the Baradas. Twin bridges, long wooden spans on great pilings of gray stone, arched over it, carrying the elevated road to the gates. A great bastion of towers and gates met the bridge there and gave entrance to the teeming streets of the city. Marshlands and water gardens surrounded the city on the southern and eastern sides, channeling all traffic onto the three raised roads that came to the gates from those directions. Ahmet was not impressed. Alexandria was ten times larger than this provincial town.

The road leading to the river remained a confused snarl, as it had been the night before. A constant stream of people was leaking out of the fastness of Damascus, heading south by foot, by camel, by horse, by litter, and by wagon. At the

same time, bands of fighting men on horse and afoot were trying to move north.
As Ahmet watched, another column of horsemen with brightly pennoned lance
tips trotted past the base of the hill, forcing their way down the crowded road. A
distant murmur of voices raised in anger drifted on the slow afternoon air. The
armies of the Eastern princes were trying to get north of the barrier of the Baradas.
Even the noblemen were backed up at the bridge.

Near dusk, the men roused themselves and began gathering wood for a fire.
Ahmet stood at the edge of the grove, his hands clasped behind him, looking
across the shallow valley toward the lights of the city. Great black and silver clouds
of birds rose from the marshes and wheeled away across the sky, hunting for insects
before nightfall. With the gloom of twilight creeping across the valley, the Egyptian could see the lights of encampments along the northern and western roads to
the city as well. The pale sandstone walls of the old city were joined by new,
bustling suburbs of canvas and wood.

Stars had begun to show in the darkening sky over the peaks of the mountains
to the west of the city when Mohammed at last returned. He labored up the slope
to the olive grove with a heavily laden horse in tow behind him and two bags
thrown over his own shoulders.

"Ho, priest!" Mohammed said, wheezing with effort. "Take a poor working
man's burden." He swung one of the bags off his shoulder and Ahmet caught it,
grunting with effort. It was very heavy. Some of Mohammed's cousins ran up to
take the other and the reins of the horse. The merchant straightened up and
stretched his back.

"Ah, better, better! It's Shaitan's own pit of torments in there, I'll tell you.
The place is a madhouse." Mohammed looked around, counting noses. Satisfied
that everyone was present, he shooed his men away and crooked a finger at Ahmet.
They walked together, away from the camp, up the slope to the top of the hill.
A tumble of stones crowned the summit. Mohammed sat down on a flat rock and
began unlacing his sandals. Ahmet sat nearby, his shape muted in the dim light.

"I looked for your friend," the southerner said, kneading his sore foot between
powerful fingers. "But there are no Roman legionnaires in the city. There's every
other kind of fighting man in the eastern half of the Empire down there, but no
Romans. There are Arabs, Syrians, Palmyrenes—a whole host of Palmyrenes—
Nabateans, Palestinians, Goths, Turks, Ethiops—but no Roman Imperial troops."
Mohammed paused, looking off into the night, toward the bridge over the Baradas.

"If I knew no better, I'd say the city was a mutiny against the Empire waiting
to happen, but every man's voice is raised against Chrosoes of Persia. I spoke with
everyone I knew from the times I've been here before, and not one of them said
that there were any Roman troops in the city. The governor maintains a civil
guard, but— ıd this from my friend Barsames the glassworker—the two cohorts
of the Secon Triana that had been stationed in the city were withdrawn to Tyre
on the coast almost a month ago."

Ahmet shook his head in puzzlement. "I don't understand," he said. "The
quartermaster in Alexandria was quite specific that the Third had been sent to
Damascus, along with another Legion."

Mohammed shrugged. "No matter, my friend, this man you seek is not here now. These Legions may arrive soon—that is a common rumor in the markets—but until then . . ."

Ahmet stood, his face filled with confusion. He paced around the cairn of rocks.

"I shall go to the coast then," he said at last. "To Tyre, or wherever the Legions are."

Mohammed turned a little to keep his friend in view. "This fellow, you are certain you must find him? Do you owe him so much?"

"Yes," Ahmet said in a sad voice, "I owe him a great deal. I doubt, no, I am sure that he does not know that I am seeking to find him. But I cannot countenance what was done to him, not and remain an honorable man."

Mohammed spread his hands questioningly.

Ahmet sighed and sat down, his head in his hands. "Weeks ago now I was a priest-teacher at a school in Upper Egypt. A school devoted to teaching the works and philosophies of Hermes Trismegistus and the other ancient savants. This school is moderately well known, and many rich families send their sons to learn the techniques and practices of the art of sight and power. I was the youngest master of the school, a teacher.

"Then one day a message came from the father temple in Alexandria that we had to answer an Imperial levy—a sorcerer of the third order must be sent to the muster of the Legions. The master of the school chose to send Dwyrin Mac-Donald, one of my students, to fulfill this obligation. I protested this decision, but Dwyrin was sent anyway."

Mohammed raised an eyebrow; he had guessed bits and pieces of his quiet Egyptian friend's background from the way that he spoke and how he thought, but he had never realized that he had been traveling in the company of a man who commanded the hidden powers. Inwardly he chuckled; he could not have chosen a better companion for the road!

"Did this Dwyrin not want to go? What did he think of it?"

Ahmet snorted in disgust. "I am sure that Dwyrin was elated to be so chosen—but, my friend, Dwyrin is, or was, a sorcerer of the third order in only the most flimsy legal sense. He is not even the best of my students! A boy of sixteen—with talent, yes—but nothing of the discipline of a master. Ah, I should have gone in his stead to begin with."

"You have masters of the art that are sixteen?" Mohammed's voice was confused.

"No!" Ahmet exclaimed in horror. "When the master of the school received the notice of the levy, he bade me take the boy to the hidden temple and initiate him into the mysteries of the third order—but he has not the training for it, not the discipline, not the patience! He has been opened to a world he cannot properly see, or control. He is still a child—a troublesome child—one the master of the school felt it best to be rid of, lest he cause more problems, but that is no excuse to offer him up as a sacrifice to the gods of war. He may already be dead."

Ahmet stared off, into the night, with blank eyes.

Mohammed clapped him gently on his shoulder. "So, you abandoned your position at the school to find him, then? What will you do if you do find him?"

"Take his place, I suppose." Ahmet's voice was low and filled with fatigue. "Join him and teach him what I can if they will not release him from his duty to the state. He was, he is, my student. I am responsible for him, for all his cheerful tricks and irreverence. He had promise, my friend, promise to be a fine young man with a good talent. He could have done many worthy things. I am sick to think of him dead in a field, entrails pecked by crows, because the master of the school found it convenient to dispose of a possible political problem without getting his hands dirty."

Mohammed laughed silently in the darkness. *Was that not the way of the world?*

"There is no more difficult path than that of an honorable man," he said in a portentous voice. "Ahmet, tomorrow we will take the caravan into the city and turn the glasswares and pottery over to the warehouse my wife's cousin's brother owns. Then my business will be done for this venture. I think that we should then make inquiries at the citadel to see if the Roman authorities there know the whereabouts of the Third Cyrene. Then you and I, if you will have my companionship on the road, will go and find your student and see about getting your honor back."

Ahmet glanced up. "A fine offer made to a man that you've barely known three weeks. Why would you do such a thing?"

Mohammed sighed, clasping his hands together in front of him. "You are driven by honor and your duty as a teacher. I am not driven by anything. I have a fine wife and a rich family in my home city. I could while my days away, and I have, in reading and philosophy. I have spent my time in the saddle too, raiding the oases and villages of the enemies of my tribe. I could play the merchant on the road, journeying to distant lands and cities, and this too I have done. My heart is hungry, and I have not found the thing to fill it. I am restless, my friend, and I want to understand all of this." He waved a hand to encompass the sky, the grove, the ground beneath their feet.

"I miss the comfort of my wife and our household, but something is still missing. So, I will come with you and see something, at least, that I have not seen before. Perhaps I will find what I am looking for! One never knows where he'll end up, setting out on an unknown road. Truth might lie around the next bend, or over the next hill."

In peaceful days, the markets of Damascus were filled with a raucous throng of thousands coming and going along the narrow, covered ways. Now, with tens of thousands of troops camped around, or in, the city, it was worse. It took Ahmet three hours of pushing through congested streets filled with bands of armed men, rickety stalls, and the citizens of the city to reach the broad square surrounded by mighty temples and buildings of the state that marked the center of the ancient town. Once on the square, Ahmet was able to breathe again and walk at a normal pace. He headed for the imposingly porticoed front of the Temple of Zeus, which

made itself unmistakable by towering over the entire square and every other building adjoining it.

He mounted the long tier of steps at the front of the temple, passing by
fountains set into the broad front that fed a series of shallow ornamental pools at
the base of the building. The footsteps of many priests and penitents echoed off
the high ceilings as he made his way into the dim recesses at the side of the central
nave. There were a number of small offices there, and he walked along them after
asking directions of a slave at the front of the temple. At the end, in a rather
barren cell, he found the man he wanted to see.

"Master Monimus?" A slight man with only a trace of hair remaining on his
head looked up from a low desk. Wooden scroll cases surrounded him like honeycombs, filled with burnished brass handles and well-worn wooden pegs. The
priest's eyes were a merry blue, and his face, though deeply lined with age, seemed
open and pleasant.

"I am Monimus," he said in a clear tenor voice. "Please sit. There is wine, if
you are thirsty."

"Thank you, master. I am Ahmet of the School of Pthames in Egypt. I also
serve Hermes Trismegistus."

Monimus bowed, still sitting, and poured two shallow cups of wine from an
ancient red-black amphora. He passed one of the *krater* to Ahmet and sipped
politely from the other. Ahmet sipped as well, then placed the ancient drinking
bowl on the edge of the table. Monimus waited with the calm that all of the
masters of the order seemed to assume as a matter of course. Ahmet cleared his
throat, not sure how to begin, but he thought of how Mohammed would handle
this and decided to plunge straight in.

"Master Monimus, I must beg your indulgence and ask two favors of you and
your house here. I am on a long journey and I am afraid that I have not pleased
the master of my school overmuch. He did not give me leave to undertake such
an absence, and he may be most displeased with my hasty departure. Despite this,
I feel that I should tell him where I am and where I am going, and why I left in
such a precipitous manner."

Ahmet opened the heavy cloth bag that he had purchased in Gerasa and
drew out a letter written on poor papyrus. He placed it on the desk between himself
and the master. "If you could see that this letter reaches Master Nephet of the
School of Pthames, near Panopolis in Upper Egypt, I would be grateful. My second
favor is more pressing, though you may not know the answer. Has any news of
the Imperial Legion called the Third Cyrenaicea reached you? I must find a man
who is serving with it, but my last report held that it was coming here, and it has
not done so."

Monimus sat quietly for a little while, his blue eyes considering Ahmet. The
young Egyptian began to feel very nervous at the examination, but he remained
still and did not fidget. After a time the Syrian priest sighed and picked up the
letter from where it had lain on the desk.

"Of course I will see that this letter reaches your superior in Panopolis. I
believe that I know this Nephet from my time at the sanctuary of the Order in
Ephesus. He is a stern man, if memory serves, but he does care about his charges,

and forgives. Of your second request, I can say nothing, for I know nothing of the matter. Every tongue in the city has the matter of the war against Persia upon it, but I have heard nothing that would indicate that the Imperials are coming here. Are you determined to find this man?"

Ahmet nodded.

The older priest picked at the edge of the letter, his face troubled. "You know of the levy upon the orders, of course?"

Ahmet nodded again, and something of the anger he felt must have shown through.

"Yes, an evil business," said Monimus, his voice quieting to a whisper. "Little good can come of it—yet it is a desperate necessity. You may not feel the tremors and echoes in far Egypt, but here, so close to the border, we feel the workings of the Persian *mobehedan* often—almost daily in the last months. The walls between our world and the others are strained and pinched. We tremble at the approach of each darkness of the moon, for then it is worse. They are desperate for victory. They are paying a terrible cost for strength to bring against Rome.

"If you go north or east, tread lightly. There are foul powers on the hunt in those lands."

Ahmet nodded again. He had been feeling a growing unease the farther north he had come with the caravan. The air seemed brittle and thin, the sun dimmer than usual. In his othersight, odd flickerings and half-heard voices filled the empty spaces of the desert. Lines of unexpected tension and force were gathering in the unseen world.

"Master, I will be careful in my travels." Ahmet bowed, his head almost touching the tiled floor.

Monimus made the sign of the god and watched the young man go. The sense of unease did not leave him. He turned back to the rolls of the Temple and the order for timbers to begin construction of a new lodging house behind the main building.

Mohammed was waiting in the shade of the great entrance hallway to the sanctuary of the Temple of Zeus, staring up at the giant marble figure of the god of storms. The Zeus reclined on poorly carved clouds, but his body was well cut, standing forth from the rock. One arm supported the god against the clouds and held a cluster of bronze thunderbolts, the other raised a torch of stone. Oil-fire gleamed on that sconce, casting flickering light on the ceiling of the temple. Under the wavering light, the skin tones and painted hair of the statue seemed close to life. Ahmet coughed politely.

Mohammed shook his head and looked around at his friend. Though his face was properly solemn for such a place, Ahmet could see that a huge grin was threatening to break out under the brushy black mustaches.

"Come," the merchant whispered in a voice quiet as a shout, "I've done well this morning!"

Outside, Mohammed fairly bounced down the steps. Ahmet lengthened his stride to keep up. The merchant bustled across the square, stopping only to purchase a wooden skewer with roasted meat on it. Chewing, he began talking to Ahmet.

"There will be a council of the chieftains and Princes tonight, my friend, in the Roman citadel. All of the lords who were summoned have arrived as of last night, and the governor has called this meeting to lay out the plans of campaign. There is no better way to find out where the Third is stationed, and where it is *going* to be stationed, than at this meeting. Everyone will be there, even the Princes of Nabatea and Palmyra."

"And how," Ahmet asked with asperity, "are *we* going to get into this conclave of the great?"

"Ah, my friend, that is the beauty of the thing. You are traveling with *me*, so these things are possible! As luck would have it, one of the bands of lancers that have been hired by the Palmyrenes are cousins of my wife's brother's wife's uncle. I convinced their war captain—an old rascal named Amr ibn'Adi of the Tanukh—that we should ride with them, and just by the by, attend the conference tonight as his aides."

"Oh," Ahmet said. "Do you usually get your friends into this much trouble?"

Mohammed laughed aloud at that. "Nay! All of my friends take great joy in my company—all of them say that I am the most interesting of men to be around! Besides, Amr ibn'Adi does not speak Latin or Greek—so you and I will have to translate for him."

Night in the streets of the city was almost as bright as day. Thousands of lanterns hung from the entrances of the market stalls and over the doorways of the houses. Torches ornamented the walls that enclosed private gardens. Parties of men, led by link-boys with burning wicks, moved through the streets, slowly converging upon the gates of the Roman camp that lay near the northernmost of the city's eight gates. The light glowed off low clouds that had gathered over the city in the late afternoon, bringing a cool rain to wash the streets.

Ahmet and Mohammed were among those who approached the gates, in the party of the desert chieftain Amr ibn'Adi. The sheykh was a villainous rogue with long curling mustaches and a salt-and-pepper beard who affected a ragged cloak and hood over his rich garments. His three bodyguards—the most allowed by the governor—held no such flimsy disguise. They were stout men with broad shoulders, plain weatherworn cloaks, and well-used armor and weapons. Mohammed, in turn, was dressed in a subdued red shirt, dark pants, and long cloak of white-and-green stripes. Ahmet, who did not account himself one for fashion, thought that his friend looked rather dashing in the outfit—obviously his best, carried in a small trunk for just such an occasion. Ahmet owned no pretense such as this; he had cleaned his simple white tunic and robe before entering the city. He had his staff and the leather book bag that he habitually wore at his waist. He had tied back his long raven-black hair with two braids and a silver clasp.

The residence of the Roman governor was no more than a fortified Legion camp carved out of the buildings of the northwest corner of the city. Stout wooden and iron gates barred the way into the camp, watched by a band of slightly overweight men in ill-fitting armor. Ibn'Adi's party was halted by their commander, an elderly man with close-cropped white hair and a scarred face. The retired legionnaire searched them, even Ahmet's bag and staff, before waving them through into the camp.

Ahmet looked around curiously at the fired brick buildings, arranged in neat rows, with paved streets between them. Though there was every sign of the regular presence of a strong garrison in the city, it was obvious that all of these residences had been carefully closed up, their owners departed. Mohammed was looking around too, with a slightly puzzled look on his face. The broad street that led down the middle of the camp was busy, though, with parties of chieftains and their retainers in a broad array of desert robes, silks, linens, and partially hidden armor.

"Why have all these chiefs come to fight for Rome?" the Egyptian asked as he and Mohammed trailed along after ibn'Adi's ruffians. "Most seem to be bandits or vagabonds. I thought that the men of the frontier were at odds with the Empire."

Mohammed nodded, his face creasing in a sharp smile. "Few here love Rome, if any do, my friend. But near every man here knows that Persia is not better and perhaps worse. Under Roman rule, or Roman 'protection,' there is law of a sort. Under this King of Kings, this Chrosoes, there is no law. These chiefs are here to protect the rights and usages that they own today. With Rome, the way that things are done has not changed in hundreds of years. If Persia conquers these lands, everything will be different."

Ahmet nodded at this, then said, "So none of them see an opportunity to better themselves by siding with Persia? To my mind, that would seem a good way to dispose of rivals and make oneself stronger at their expense."

The Southerner laughed, but softly, for one of the guards with ibn'Adi had turned a little, trying to catch their conversation while they walked into the inner camp. They passed through another vaulted gate, but these walls were of worked stone. Four towering men in mail shirts and boiled-leather *pteruges* stood in the shadows of the passage. They were red-haired and taller by two hands than any man that passed between them. Longswords were hung at their belts, and they wore many rings and bracelets on their arms. Ahmet returned the steely gaze of the nearest one as he passed. *Germanii*, he thought to himself as they entered the governor's camp.

"The men that have made that calculation, my friend, and have chosen to side with the King of Kings are not at this meeting tonight. No, they have already ridden north to Antioch, to join the army of the great Prince Shahin." Mohammed's voice was low and clear. He had drifted a little behind Ahmet, though he walked close by.

"These are men who have made themselves and their tribes strong under the tutelage of the Empire. If it is driven out, they will suffer by it. These are the men who have ruined their enemies by naming them traitors, or heretics, or taxless. Chiefs like these, whose families have held power for generations under the eye of Rome, are the creatures of the Empire. They use that patronage to control the best trade routes, and to drive out the smaller clans or break them to their will."

Ahmet glanced back; Mohammed's voice was verging into bitter anger. "Do you hate Rome, then? Have these things happened to your family?"

Mohammed blinked, apparently unaware of his tone. "Hate Rome? No, I do not hate the Empire. It is as it is. I hate those that oppress the weak, those that drive out the less favored, but the Empire is like a boulder on a mountainside. If it is urged to motion, it cares not what it crushes in passing. The nature of a boulder is to ignore the things that are insignificant to it. A man like you, or I, is immaterial to the boulder. We are too small to harm it. But I do not love Rome either. How can I? It does not love me."

Ahead of them, ibn'Adi and his men stopped at the bottom of a set of steps that led up to a broad veranda. Guardsmen stood in the shadows between pools of warm light cast by lanterns hung from iron sconces bolted to the wall. The sheykh turned and motioned to Mohammed, who moved forward and made a small half bow. Ahmet leaned closer as well.

"Remember, my new friends, that I speak none of these barbarian tongues favored by our hosts." Ibn'Adi's voice was deep and very strong, like a high wind on the desert. Ahmet could understand him well, though Aramaic was not his best language. "Al'Quraysh, you will speak for me, while your Egyptian friend will translate what others say. Speak softly, priest; I hear well and I know that others of the chieftains will not have this small advantage that the Lord of the Sky has given me. Let us not give away rams for free, eh? Also, keep your weapons handy. There are those who may cause trouble, and if such comes, we must be ready. But do not draw steel unless I command it!"

Mohammed and Ahmet both bowed. The sheykh looked them over, lingering a long time on Mohammed, who assumed a pleasant and inoffensive expression. The old man smiled at last and turned to go inside. As he mounted the steps, he seemed to shrink, one leg seemingly weaker than the other, and he leaned more heavily on his staff. Mohammed caught Ahmet's eye and winked.

Within the wooden house was a high-vaulted room with wooden beams supporting a roof of slate tiles. Fifty or sixty men had already gathered in the room, where many couches and divans had been arranged in a rough circle. Tables had been pushed back against the walls, clearing this space. At the far end of the room from the door a raised dais stood with an altar of light-colored stone upon it. Behind it, on the wall, was the cast image of a bull in corroded greenish bronze. Two rows of fluted wooden columns ran the length of the room. The old chieftain, rather than pushing forward through the men clustered at the center of the room, moved through the crowd to the right, taking up his position in front of one of the pillars with Mohammed just in front of him and Ahmet to his left. The three guards settled in behind the pillar.

Lanterns were hung along the beams overhead and there were tapers in copper holders on the pillars. The vaulted space above the beams was already filling with dim smoke, but high above Ahmet saw that there were openings covered with latticework to let the smoke out. Men continued to enter the chamber, and now noise rose from the center of the room as men jostled for position among the couches. Ahmet remained still, for the sheykh was apparently at complete ease leaning against the pillar. Mohammed too was content with his view.

Between the men standing in front of him, Ahmet could make out that at the end of the circle of couches away from the door, three divans—more ornate than the rest—were still unoccupied. He was about to ask Mohammed who the assembly was waiting for when there was a commotion at the door. Men's heads turned and they fell silent.

A party of men in very dark-red clothing entered—long capes with deep hoods and glittering silver bracelets and necklaces. Four such men, with narrow, hawklike faces, entered in a wedge, and the desert chieftains and their retainers parted before them like the tide off a rocky shore. Between them walked a man of middling height with dark-olive skin and a neatly trimmed beard. His cheekbones were sharp and he wore very little jewelry, only a ring of gold on each hand and a thin circlet of fine silver metal at his brow. He wore a simple tunic of pale rose-colored silk, bound with a black belt. As they passed, Ahmet felt a wave of controlled power roll over him like a soft breeze. A *sorcerer*, he thought, his other senses pricking fully awake for the first time in many days.

He centered and allowed his vision to expand slightly. The four men in the hoods smoldered with purple-black flame, like the fire that danced at the edge of a hot forge. Ahmet shuddered a little, realizing that each man—obviously the servants of the man in rose—had a spirit bound to it, some hellish imp drawn from the cracks and crevices that sometimes disgorged tormented and dreadful beings into the realm of man. At the center, the man in rose gleamed with concealed strength, like a strong light beheld through a colored glass or through ice. He turned at the couch on the left of the three and took his ease there. The four hooded men arranged themselves behind him, making no sound. Ahmet wondered if they could sense him as well.

"This is Aretas, the ninth of his noble line," ibn'Adi said from behind the Egyptian in a quiet voice. "He is the Prince of the city of Petra in the south. He styles himself the King of the Nabateans, though they are more rightly the subjects of the Governor of the Roman province of Arabia Minimis. He is a vain and dangerous man."

The Petran had seated himself and accepted a cut crystal cup of wine, when the doors to the room opened again and all of the men turned again to see who had entered. Beside the restrained menace of the Nabatean and his minions, the man who entered struck Ahmet as an inoffensive clerk late to a business meeting of his master. He was tall and thin, balding, with a hooked nose, and his white tunic—though richly hemmed—hung from his frame like a sheet. Four of the red-haired guardsmen flanked him, however, and when he took the center couch, Ahmet knew that he must be the governor of the province of Phoenicia.

"The Roman Lucius Ulpius Sulpicius, as dry a man as ever birthed by the loins of the Roman wolf. Though his seat of rule is at Tyre on the coast, Damascus is his responsibility." Ibn'Adi's voice was tinged with wry respect for the gawky man that now settled, uncomfortably, onto the center couch. His Germans cleared a broad space around him, pushing aside some of the Arabs who had been edging closer to where Aretas was sitting.

Lucius cleared his throat and then rapped on the arm of his couch with a bony hand. "Friends, our company is gathered, all but one, but it already grows late and there is much to discuss, so we will begin. I will be brief and blunt—the Empire thanks you for your friendship, shown so well by coming here today and gathering those men you command to the standard. It will be rewarded and the Empire will mark those who came when called and who did not."

Mohammed turned the slightest bit and whispered to Ahmet, "Ah, Constantinople will remember those who came to lick its hands and kiss its boot when called, like dogs . . ." Ibn'Adi stilled the younger man with a fierce scowl. Ahmet finished his translation of the governor's Latin and ibn'Adi nodded.

"An invasion is upon us," the governor continued, "one that will bring sure disaster to us all if it is not stopped, and stopped well short of Damascus or Tyre. The enemy is strong. The latest report from the north counts his number at nearly sixty thousand men."

A current of whispering rushed around the room, and Ahmet saw that many of the men around him were startled by the size of the Persian army. He wondered how many lances the chieftains in this room commanded. The sheykh did not seem concerned, however, when Ahmet related this to him. Rather the old man seemed to be more interested in the reactions of the other captains and warlords.

"Do not be alarmed," the governor said, pressing on through the murmur of his audience. "The count of our own army is equal to that, or greater. Within three days the rest of our forces will have completed the muster here and we shall march north across the mountains to Emesa to meet the invaders. Our will is strong and we will defeat the Persians, driving them back beyond the Euphrates."

"With what?" One of the chiefs, dressed in a heavy brocade robe and bareheaded, stood from his couch. He sported a thick dark beard that had been carefully braided at the ends, with small jewels bound into it. "I see many brave men here, but the forces we can put to the field are lancers and bowmen on horseback. I hear fine words from Constantinople, but I see no Roman soldiers here. Where are the Legions? My men and I rode six days from Gerasa and I saw none upon the road. My cousins tell me that the Legion camps at Bostra and Lejjun are empty. I see no Legions here either. Where is Rome? Where is the Emperor of the East?"

Lucius remained seated, his face calm. "The Legions have been sent to the coast, to Tyre, to receive reinforcements from Egypt and the Western Empire. They will meet us at Emesa, having marched up the coastal road. Three legions— the Third Cyrenaicea, the Second Triana, and the Sixth Ferrata—will join us there. With those men, and the *auxillia* they command, our army will number no less than eighty thousand men to stand against the Persians."

"I do not believe you!" the Gerasan chief shouted, his face reddening with anger. "When the Iron Hats come at us, there will be no Romans there, only us, with our light mail and bows to stop them. This is a bootless venture! Any man who goes north"—the Gerasan turned about, his gaze challenging the crowd— "will be a dead man."

"This is not so!" Lucius stood at last, his pale face dark with rage. "Rome will not abandon you. The honor of the Empire stands with you, as will its soldiers on the field!"

"Lies!" the Gerasan shouted back, shaking his fist at the governor. "Rome whores us like it does its daughters on the steps of the Forum!" His men began shouting too, and the German guardsmen rushed forward to stand between the Southerners and their patron. The room filled with noise, and the men in front of Ahmet pressed forward to see if there would be a fight. Ahmet stepped back, out of the way, and hurriedly related the lurid insults that the Gerasan was defaming the governor with. The edge of ibn'Adi's lip twitched a little, almost into a smile. His guardsmen closed up, hands on their weapons.

It was impossible to see over the heads of the shouting and gesticulating men in front of them and Ahmet stepped back, running into someone standing behind him. He turned, an apology on his lips, and stopped, unable to speak.

A woman stood behind him, her hand on his shoulder. At first, all that he was aware of were her eyes—a cobalt bluer than the open sky—with heavy dark lashes in a delicate oval face. They smiled at him and he felt the shock of that personality all the way to his stomach. She pressed him gently aside with a murmured "Your pardon, holy one," and he had a blurred impression of a cloud of lustrous black curls ornamenting a graceful alabaster neck. Then a very solid-looking breastplate of bronze workings on steel interposed itself and Ahmet could feel the hands of Mohammed and the sheykh holding him up from behind. A phalanx of ebony-skinned men clad in solid armor and heavy links of mail from head to toe pressed through the crowd behind the spear point of the woman. Belatedly Ahmet remembered to breathe.

"And I say," the Gerasan roared over the tumult of the crowd, "that I shall not lead my men north to battle unless the Turtlebacks stand with us! No matter your honor, Lucius Ulpius, my duty is to my people, not to the tax coffers of Constantinople and Rome! I do not come so cheap!"

"Your father swore to stand with the Empire in the test," the governor hissed back, his fists clenched, "and so did you, when I stood with you beside his funeral bier. Are you renouncing that oath, then? Do you turn your back on your father? Your honor?"

The Gerasan snarled something unintelligible and the sound of steel rasping from a copper sheath cut across the pandemonium in the room. In the crowded space between the ring of couches, the factions of men formed up behind the governor and the Prince of Jerash froze. Everyone held his breath as the prince's blade flashed in the air in front of him. Lucius Ulpius' face drained of color, his eyes fixed on the point of the knife, dancing only a foot from his sternum. The Gerasan, his face flushed, stepped forward and his dagger lurched into the creamy white chest of the woman with the mane of raven hair as she stepped in front of the governor. A tiny pinpoint of blood sprang up where the razor-sharp tip cut into her skin.

"You would murder me, Zamanes?" Her voice cut across the room, reaching every man, though its tone was private, even intimate. "Would you murder the trust between the Empire and the cities of the Decapolis?"

The Gerasan Prince, his eyes wide in utter shock, stepped back, his dagger falling away to one side. One of his servants lifted it from his nerveless fingers and tucked it away in his robes. The woman turned, ignoring the governor, who had also stepped back into the safety of his guardsmen, and stepped up onto the couch next to him.

Ahmet, at the back of the room, forgot to breathe again as she rose up above the heads of the men crowded into the hall. She was slightly built but tall for a woman, about five and a half feet high, and in her presence all other things seemed diminished. The blue lightning spark of her eyes, even across the hall, struck Ahmet like a blow. Her hair, a cascade of heavy curls, swept across her bare white shoulders and down her back. A net of gold wire and pearls held it back away from her smooth forehead and face. She was clad in a deep-purple gown with embroidered traceries of minute roses and lilies along the hems. She was not a heavily endowed woman, but the curve of her breasts against the silk seemed the most perfect shape imaginable to the Egyptian. The tiny spot of blood remained, like a ruby set between them. Her voice was the purr of a languid cat, but it was strong, strong enough to reach clear to the back of the room.

"Rome called us," she said, her voice ringing like a bell, "but we did not come here for Rome. We came because we are all threatened. We came because, at last, this is our time. The Empire has suffered too grievously to stand alone as our shield against the Persians any longer. It is time for us, the peoples of the Decapolis, of Petra and of Palmyra, to stand apart from our parent and defend ourselves as adults. I will stand against the mad King, Chrosoes. Alone, if need be, as did my namesake. Will you stand with me?"

Ahmet turned and stared into the face of ibn'Adi, who was smiling a long, slow smile like a hunting lion that prepares to feast well.

"Who . . . ?" he whispered.

"Our Queen," the old chieftain proudly answered. "Zenobia of Palmyra. The Silk Empress."

Pale-gold dawn was creeping across the eastern sky when, at last, the conclave of the chiefs broke up. Ahmet, who had spent most of the night in meditation, came fully awake. The desert men were filing out, speaking in low tones among themselves. The lanterns had guttered down to only a dim flame at most, and some had gone out entirely. The tapers and the tallow candles that had replaced them were done as well. The Egyptian rose from his place by the wall, out of the way, and walked amid the couches, strewn with emptied jugs and dirty plates. The air was still heavy with smoke and the tang of many men in an enclosed space. Mohammed, who had stayed up, in the thick of the discussion, sat on the edge of the couch that the Roman governor had occupied, holding his head in his hands.

Ahmet paused, standing at his shoulder, and gently tugged the Southerner's ear. Mohammed looked up, his face drawn with weariness. The Egyptian smiled down at him and placed fingers on either temple. In his mind he chanted a little lullaby that his mother had once sung over the wicker cradle he had slept in as a baby. Mohammed's eyelids flickered and then closed. He fell backward with a snore escaping his lips. Ahmet arranged him on the couch.

"Can you work such magic for me as well, holy one?"

Her voice was no longer so clear and strong, now it was immensely tired and rough, barely audible. Ahmet turned and settled by her on one knee. Her gown was creased and spattered at the lower hem with food and stains of wine. Her hair had escaped most of the delicate net of gold and now was simply tucked back in a single braid behind her head. The luminous face was still, quiet in extreme exhaustion. Her eyes still held him, though, even in weariness. He met them without freezing, so in a way he had the better of it.

"Milady, I can make you sleep, but you should return to your camp first. If I understand aright, you will have many enemies after the doings of this night. And . . . I am not a holy one. My name is Ahmet, once of the School of Pthames. Any pretense I maintained to being a priest is long gone now."

Zenobia brushed his excuse aside with a delicate wrist flip. She levered herself up from the couch and took his hand. Her eyes met his and they were, for a moment, vulnerable and wholly human—not the distant imperious presence she had maintained throughout the night.

"Take me to my camp, Ahmet, and make me sleep. I cannot otherwise. I will pace and pace and scheme and plot until at last exhaustion overcomes me. Then I will sleep a dozen hours, when only a handful are wise to take."

She laid a hand on his cheek; it was cold as ice. Ahmet shivered at the touch but took her hand between his.

"You're warm," she said, smiling up at him, and leaned her head against his chest. Reflexively he gathered her into his arms. She nestled against him, warm and close, content in the day. Without hurry, he lifted her up and walked out of the temple house of the Romans. Outside, as he walked toward the gate, he began to sing in a soft voice that only she could hear.

THE EGYPTIAN HOUSE, OUTSIDE OF ROME

T hunder growled in a dark sky. Lightning flashed between clouds pregnant with rain. In the face of the storm, a cold wind gusted across the arcades of the veranda around the house, driving leaves and straw before it. The trees on the hill above the house bent in the wind, and the grass on the hillside below the garden rippled in long waves with each gust. Inside, a fire burned in every room— in bronze braziers, in grates built against the outer walls, in a deep brick-lined pit that had been excavated in the floor of the basement room. In the buried room, cylinders were suspended from the ceiling, holding captive a harsh white light that shone down upon smooth stone moist with blood and salty water. In the unseen world below the stones of the house, a river of power surged blue-black, grinding against the restraint of the earth.

Fierce tentacles of blue fire rippled against a glittering shield of rose-colored light that encompassed the house and the basement. Around the periphery of that invisible barrier, grass crisped and shriveled. Trees that had stood for two hundred years rotted away, leaving only a husk of bark and limb. Leaves that touched the ground smoked into ash, never bursting alight. Stones cracked to gravel and gravel ground to dust. Five miles away the inhabitants of the house of Junius Alpicius Niger were all struck dumb in their sleep and rose to find every animal—domesticated or not—within the grounds of their estate dead upon the ground. The sky, anguished, vomited lightning and rolling thunder against the house in the hills. The rose-colored shield held, turning aside the stabbing fingers of lightning that grasped and tore at it. The stones shuddered in time with the leaping blasts of light. In the front foyer, the face of the Alexander was constantly lit by the strobe of each strike. In that hellish light, it seemed that he smiled.

Maxian screamed aloud in torment, his fingers half buried in the chest of a small, thrashing body. Energy surged over his body like a second skin of pulsing red and deep purple. The muscles of his face, his chest, his legs twitched uncontrollably with each surge. A great triangle had been carefully cut into the stone of the floor and filled with aconite and silver. It was etched within a greater circle of worked gold. Maxian stood at one vertex, while Abdmachus and Gaius Julius shuddered in pain at the other two. Each had stripped to only pale cotton loincloths, and each lay within a three-ringed circle of colored chalk and gold wire. Snakes of ultraviolet fire hissed from their bodies, crackling and snapping. The power flooded the air and sluiced into his body through a tattoo of an inverted pyramid that had been cut into Maxian's chest.

Within the mewling body of the tiny child, squirming in a pool of blood, urine, and feces, Maxian's fingers danced frantically. The power he drew from the earth, from the sky, and from the dead man and all that he represented warred inside that tiny frame with a bubbling black corruption that tore and gouged at the child's internal organs. Maxian's face was chalky and dry, he had sweated out all the water his body could yield sixty grains ago, but despite a nearly blinding headache that sent clouds of white sparks across his vision, he continued to battle the contagion. It would not die, no matter how thoroughly he tried to drive it out. He had rebuilt entire organs from the soup of bone, blood, and tissue that churned in the child's torso, but each one, no sooner than he had sketched it anew, began to corrupt and decay.

One hundred and sixteen grains after he had started, Maxian staggered back from a flash of black light, edged with corroded red, and collapsed to the ground. Falling, his body cut across the edge of the triangle and with a thunderclap that shook a great burst of dust from the stones of the room and broke every glass, jug, and plate in the house, the chain of ultraviolet fire collapsed into nothing. In the silence that followed even the raging storm above seemed muted and distant. Maxian moaned and rolled over, his body convulsing with the aftereffects of the procedure. On the table, the body of the infant corrupted with a slick sucking sound into a spreading pool of black-green bile. It puddled and then began to run off the edges of the table, spattering against the floor.

Still within his circle of protection, Abdmachus quivered, his mouth drooling and his eyes glazed over with pain. Gaius Julius twitched once like a gaffed river pike and then lay still. After a moment his eyes flickered open and cleared. The pain that had racked him like a lash was gone. Stiffly he sat up, his head turning jerkily from side to side. Dust puffed from his bare skin. Absently he brushed it off, leaving only clotted trails where his old wounds were damp with new blood. He looked carefully around, though he was having trouble seeing, and marked the position of the prince. The dead man considered the steps up to the house. His master was unconscious at least, perhaps dying. He could believe that the Persian was wrong, that he could have a life without the power flickering dimly in the young man, or he might collapse to dust and bones as he rode away over the hill.

Sighing, he gingerly crossed the circle and bent down over the Prince. The boy's left pupil was huge, filling his whole eye. His breathing was very shallow and intermittent. His hands and arms were red and cracked as if they had been plunged into a fire. The Prince's lips were blue and his pulse was thready. Gaius Julius sighed again and hoisted the boy up in his arms. When he turned toward the stairs, something sharp pricked his neck.

"An admirable choice, old man." Krista kept the spring-gun close to his neck. "Just take the boy Prince upstairs and I'll see to him. You get to clean up down here. Make sure the Easterner doesn't drown in his own vomit."

Gaius Julius grunted, his left eye twitching in suppressed anger. The girl, dressed now in a simple black tunic and a midlength gray skirt, slid past him and out of his line of sight. The razor-sharp iron tip of the spring-dart traced a line along the folds of skin at his neck. *I never should have caught her that day*, the dead man growled to himself. *I should have let her go . . .*

Upstairs, the rain had settled into a steady downpour, intermittently lit by the rumble and crack of lightning in the hills around the villa. The dead man carried the Prince to the north bedroom and lay him in a bed that had been carted up from the city a week before at Krista's command. Gaius Julius pulled heavy quilts over the trembling figure of the boy, while the girl relit the fires in the grate and the braziers near the windows. The heavy shutters had blown open; now she closed them again, securing bronze wheel latches shaped like asps. The sound of the storm receded and Gaius Julius suddenly felt weak himself. His hands shook as he sat down. The boy's color had grown worse.

Krista caught the dead man's eye and nodded.

"You will die as he dies," she said. "I saw you thinking, down there, that you might be free. You won't. If he dies, you go back to the worms. Do you want that?"

Gaius Julius did not answer. She met his gaze.

Finally he shook his head. "No. I want to live."

"Then go and bring strong wine, whatever broth or soup you can find, and more firewood."

Krista searched the other upstairs rooms while the dead man was gone, finding two more blankets and another brazier. She dragged the heavy thing, ornamented with legs carved like dolphins, their mouths holding up the corners of a fluted shell, back to the bedchamber. Her fingers were quick to sprinkle oil over the dead coals and then to strike flint. Little flames curled up and she blew gently on them. When Gaius Julius returned, laden with a stewpot, two amphorae, and three stout logs, the room was lit with a cheerful glow.

Krista broke the seal on the jugs of wine and poured the thick burgundy fluid into a shallow copper bowl placed over the nearest brazier. It steamed as it hit the hot metal. After a moment she lifted the bowl off the flames and poured it into a heavy mug of dark-green glass. A ladle of the soup broth followed. Crouching on the side of the bed, the girl peeled back the eyelids of the Prince. His skin was chalky and his breath was very faint. To her delicate touch, his face was cold as stone. Hissing in despair, she pried his teeth apart and spilled the warm mixture into his mouth. He twitched and nearly knocked the glass from her hand, but she stroked the side of his throat with her fingers.

His throat muscles convulsed and he swallowed the broth. Krista held his head up, making sure that he could take it down without choking on it. This done, she poured more into his mouth. A faint blush began to tint his lips.

"Make more," she said to the dead man. "We give him as much as he can take." Gaius Julius nodded and began heating more wine in the copper bowl.

Outside, the mutter of the storm continued and the streams that flowed from the hills rose steadily toward their banks, clogged with the pale corpses of fish and frogs.

Krista and the dead man sat in the bedchamber. The girl was under the covers, holding the sleeping body of the Prince close. He was still cold, but the dreadful pall had left his face and hands. A small black cat with sleek fur was curled up next to her on the pillows. Gaius Julius was sitting next to the fire, feeding small sticks into the steady flame of the logs. The twigs snapped and crackled as they were consumed. A light piney smoke drifted up from the lip of the grate. By a clever trick, the heat of the blaze radiated out into the room, warming the dead man's cold bones, while clay pipes took the smoke away and out of the roof of the house.

"Why haven't you left?" Gaius Julius' voice was quiet with exhaustion and the fragile peace that had settled over the firelit room. "There've been no lack of chances since that day I caught you on the stairs."

Krista considered for a moment, then said, "The day after you caught me and locked me back up, the Prince came down to see me in my cell. He told me that he and the Persian had discovered that a terrible curse lay upon everyone in the city. Only he and the Persian could know of it and live by their powers. He said that he would not tell anyone, even his brother, of what he had found unless he could lift the curse. I didn't understand, so he unlocked the door of the cell and took me upstairs.

"There was a wicker box on the garden porch with a pigeon in it. The Prince said it had come from the city just that day, from the palace. He wrote a little note on a scrap of paper and put it in a little tube on the pigeon's leg. The pigeon flew from his hands, out over the garden. Do you know what happened to it?"

Gaius Julius stood, his hands stretched out to the fire. The shutters rattled a little as thunder boomed over the dark hills.

"No," he said. "What happened to the pigeon?"

Krista curled closer to the Prince, wrapping her arms around his shoulders. "When it flew out of the garden, there was a dark flash, like a great bird striking. Then there was nothing but a cloud of feathers falling out of the sky. I said that an owl must have seen it, but the Prince took me to the edge of the garden, where the Persian had put those piles of stones. The pigeon was there, or what was left of it. It was already rotten with worms and fly eggs.

" 'See?' he said. 'Everything that knows this secret dies unless it is protected. The house is safe; you are safe if you are with me or with Abdmachus. There is no better cell than this knowledge.' So, old man, I stay here, because there is nowhere to go. It is the same for you, or for the servants."

Gaius Julius stood in the darkness by the window. He had feared as much. The confusion of plans and stratagems that had been fermenting in his mind for the last two weeks condensed, a dewdrop trickling down off a leaf to drop, a pure sphere, into a pool of still water. He turned toward her.

"There is only one thing to do, then," he said. "If either of us are to escape this, we must do everything we can to help the boy destroy this curse."

Krista opened one sleepy eye and peered at the old man. "Are you saying, confused old man, that we're not doing everything we could to help him?"

Gaius Julius smiled, the firelight throwing deep canyons onto his face. "No, child, we haven't done *everything* we could. If I understand this aright, we've only just started doing *everything* that we could do."

Krista sniffed and pulled the quilt over her head. It was very late and she was very tired.

The old man sat for a time thinking, feeding the last of the twigs into the fire. He realized that this was the first time that he could remember since he had been a boy that he had actually been alone, in as safe a place as he could reasonably expect, with the time to think. The first time in many years of his memory the pressure of his dreams did not trap him. He started and stood up suddenly.

He did not dream!

Gaius Julius grinned in the dark room, a wide smile, from ear to ear. He thought back to the first moment of his new life, sprung from the moldy earth of the tomb, and realized that he had not dreamed, not once. Weeks had passed and when he closed his tired eyes, only an abyssal blackness waited, free of voices and portents.

"I *am* free," he said aloud, but Krista was asleep and the small black cat only yawned, showing a pink tongue and white fangs before tucking its nose under its tail and going back to sleep.

The narrow valley led up onto a barren ridge. Wind whipped across the rocky summit and the Gothic bodyguards drew their cloaks tightly around them. Maxian wheeled his horse, staring out over a vast landscape of pinnacles and rounded, rocky mountains. Clouds and fog filled the canyons between the peaks, making them helmets of unseen soldiers rising from a sea of white froth. Maxian's father ignored the cold, though it blew his fine white hair into a faint halo around his head. He pointed west, across a valley filled with smoke. Maxian turned and saw, as he had as a boy, the citadel of Montsegur, aflame.

The fortress rose, a tumble of white stone and square towers above a vast granite plug that cut into the sky. The peak it crowned was rugged and steep-sided. Only one winding trail clawed its way up the southern face, and that trail was overhung at many points by the walls high above. Montsegur rode in the sky, seemingly inviolate, but on this day it was wrapped in flame. A great tower of black smoke rose above the burning castle, and even from where he stood, a good two and a half miles away, Maxian could see the tongues of flame roaring from the windows of the towers and the central basilica.

Between the bare ridge that they stood upon and the walls of the dying fortress the air was as clear as the finest glass. Maxian could see tiny figures, each wrapped in a yellow-red corona, leaping from the walls of the citadel. Trailing smoke, they plunged down into the bosom of the clouds that swirled around the mount, vanishing like sparks into the sea. The air above the inferno shimmered with the waves of heat billowing off the limestone walls.

The elder Atreus grunted as one of the towers, outthrust from the southern wall, suddenly cracked at its base and slid, with dreadful majesty, off into the abyss. For a moment, as the entire seventy-foot structure fell, it held its shape, but then it struck the side of the cliff and exploded with a booming sound that could be heard clear across the valley. Maxian flinched back from the sound, for the volume of the noise it represented staggered him. The echoes came back a minute later from the walls of the canyons.

"Come, my son, and see the work of the Emperor." The elder Atreus urged his horse forward, and they descended a trail of stones that cut down the mountainside across a long slope of broken shale and small round boulders.

Under the clouds the valley below Montsegur was a hive of activity. Thousands of men had hewn a sprawling encampment out of the poor soil and scrubby trees. Maxian followed his father through the camp and marveled at the standards he passed. Four of the Legions of the Army of the West were here, each with a camp placed equidistant around the base of the peak. A road had been built across the valley and then up the flank of the mountain. As they rode through the rows of tents, gangs of workmen were raising tall posts by the side of the road, lining it on either side. Each post had a crossbar of rough-hewn pine across the top.

At the base of the peak, a raised ditch had been dug all the way around the mountain, with a parapet behind it. A palisade fence of pine logs marked the top of the earthen berm. It ran off into the rainy mist in either direction. Legionnaires manned watchtowers placed along its length. The soldiers in the towers that they rode past to reach the mountain road looked down upon them, eyes impassive in the shadows of their helmets.

As they neared the base of the mountain, now wholly hidden by the low-lying clouds, Maxian could hear a rumble of fire and cracking stone echo down from the heavens. Between the cliffs and the circumvallation was a stretch of barren soil and tufted grass. Bodies were strewn about it, some already pecked by crows. The inner face of the gate was adorned with the bodies of two men, each nailed up to the crossbars. Maxian turned his head, unable to stomach the sight of their decayed faces. The road rose up sharply on a long ramp of packed earth. The ramp cut past the first three switchbacks of the old road.

They rode up the ramp in silence. Maxian stared around in fear. The clouds were very low now, like a wavering gray roof above them. The elder Atreus rode on, though, and Maxian kicked his horse forward to follow. The passage through the clouds was strange—the mist clutched at them, leaving trails of water on their faces. Strange sounds echoed in it and Maxian's heart thudded with the sudden fear that he would never find his way out of the twilight world that he had ridden into. After a time the mist began to brighten, and they ascended the second switchback above the ramp. A moaning sound filled the air, and there was the rattle of metal.

Ahead, the elder Atreus turned aside from the road and halted on the inner edge. Maxian followed suit, as did the three Goths. Within moments figures appeared in the mist, rising like the bodies of the dead from a disturbed pool. A long line of men and women, stripped naked, their necks bound with wire collars and tied in a coffle, staggered past. Legionnaires trotted alongside in soot-stained armor, swinging spiked truncheons, urging their charges forward with the crunch of the club or a kick if they faltered. The feet of the captives were bloody and the roadway was puddled with crimson when they had passed.

Maxian stared after them as they disappeared into the mist. "Father, won't they ruin the value with such treatment?"

The elder Atreus laughed and looked over his shoulder. "They have no value, boy, they are heading straight for the crucifix. Within the day they will all be dead, ornamenting the road from here to Narbo. More will come too, so close your heart to them."

"Father, who are these people? Are they rebels? Barbarians?"

The governor snorted, then clucked at his horse and cantered up the road. Maxian, his face red with embarrassment, followed after.

The road became a track and Maxian and his father were forced to halt six more times before they reached the end of it. Long gangs of captives passed them, bloody, burned, their eyes vacant and desolate. Many showed grievous wounds and the bite of the lash and the truncheon. Maxian quailed away from the dead eyes that stared at him as they stumbled past. At the top of the trail, a great tower of pale limestone blocks rose up from the dark stones. The massive shape was pierced by a long tunnel, ill-lighted and slippery. At the mouth, soldiers were hauling bodies of men out of wagons and throwing them down the mountainside. A gutter cut into the rock of the road at the lip of that black mouth was chuckling merrily with a stream of frothy red water. Bones floated past as the horses stepped over it. Maxian's horse balked at the smell of the tunnel, but he could not allow that, so he lashed it with his riding crop and it cantered forward into the darkness.

Pale sunlight etched the courtyard beyond. The elder Atreus had pulled his horse aside and sat upon it, unmoved by the carnage that filled the space between the gate tower and the central building. Here there was no distant air to attenuate the crackling roar of the flames that consumed the basilica. Squads of soldiers in blackened armor jogged past into the tunnel, weapons crusted with gore slung over their shoulders. A centurion trotted past after the men and raised his arm in salute as he came abreast of the governor. Maxian stared up at the flames leaping from the windows of the house.

A deep grinding sound came, and then the entire upper story of the building caved in with a roar. The ground trembled at the shock, and a great burst of sparks and new smoke flew out of the top of the ruin to join the black pall that blocked out the sky. Maxian covered his face, for now hot coals were raining out of the sky and the air was thick and hard to breathe. The elder Atreus took his son's bridle and kneed his horse forward again. The gray mare high-stepped through the twisted piles of dead that were scattered around the courtyard, and they climbed a stone ramp on the side of the outer wall to a platform that stood on the side of the rampart.

All around them clouds and smoke billowed. The rest of the castle was aflame, with Roman soldiers running through the smoke, carrying what loot they had scavenged from the dead. The clouds had grown dark and were rising, obscuring the top of the trail and closing upon the gate. Maxian looked out over a sea of white foam, with the hot breath of the dying castle blowing past him. His father got down and tied his horse off on a broken stub of wood at the top of the stone ramp.

"Do you understand this, son?"

Maxian swayed on his horse, near to tears. "No, Father, I don't understand. Who were these people? Why did they have to be slaughtered in such a way? Were they rebels against the Emperor?"

The elder Atreus stared up at his son, his face bleak. "No, son, they weren't rebels. All they desired was to live in their villages and practice their faith in peace. They harmed no one, they did good works, they raised their children to fear the gods and to be honest with men. In all Gaul and Hispania they were respected and welcomed wherever they went."

Maxian began to cry, his voice breaking as he tried to speak. "Then why did they die? Were they bad? Why were they punished?"

The governor stepped to the withers of the horse and reached up to take his son down. The boy clung to him and cried. The horrors of the day were too much for him.

The elder Atreus stroked his son's hair and held him close. "Son, they died because they would not make the proper sacrifice at the altar of the Emperor. They called him a man, and not a god, so not deserving of their faith. They held to a belief that only their twin gods were worthy of the respect of worship. But the Emperor or the state cannot countenance what they did.

"You see, the Empire is like a family, and the Emperor stands at the head of the table, the leader and the protector. All look to him for guidance, for judgment. Like the father of the family, the Emperor protects the people from the barbarians and from civil disorder. Like the father, the Emperor provides an example to the young peoples who are under his protection. The Emperor judges when there are no other judges. The Emperor brings life, providing seed for each new generation. In all of this, he must be respected. He sits, as the father does at the head of the table, between man and the gods.

"But without respect, without the filial duty of his children—his subjects— the Emperor cannot govern. The father who does not have the respect of his children is weak and the family divided. The sons fight among themselves and the daughters are their prizes. There is civil disorder in the cities and mutiny in the countryside. In this matter of faith, the Empire has always been a loving father— forgiving and accepting—allowing each race of peoples under its protection to worship their own gods in their own way. But for the health and the prosperity of the family, each man and woman must also pay their respects—in the temple or the home—to their father, the Emperor.

"These men," he said, his free hand indicating the ruined citadel, "though all judge them goodly men, refused this. They refused to respect and honor the Emperor. They refused, even when put to terrible pain, to venerate his name. They met in secret and urged others to follow their path. In them, in all seeming piety, was worse faithlessness than in any man. In their temples there was no respect, only the slighting of the Emperor's name. This cannot be countenanced. You see their end. One that will only be whispered of in time to come. A final judgment upon them and their Persian creed."

Maxian could not stop crying and burrowed deeper into the warm shelter of his father. The old man stood on the parapet for a long time, holding his son. The limestone walls and pillars of the ruined temple hissed with green flame and the pyre of black smoke rose higher and higher, into the darkening sky.

Krista knelt on muddy ground among the high bushes of the side garden. The day was cold and gusty, so she had tied her hair back with a scarf and wore a pair of knit breeches she had stolen from the old man. They were made of wool, dyed a dark green, and they stopped the wind far better than some flimsy tunic. She had cut an oblong hole five or six hands long out of the ground with a sharp-bladed shovel and carefully placed the turf aside. Into the little muddy hole she placed a bundle wrapped in cotton batting and string. Then she unscrewed the top of a heavy ceramic jar she had borrowed from the basement and carefully sprinkled the gray-green dust inside over the top of the bundle. There was a very sharp smell and she turned her face away while she finished. She closed the top of the jar and put it aside, then she covered the bundle with rocks.

The turf went back on over the rocks and she tamped the grass back down. Still crouching over the hole, she cleaned up the rest of her mess and put the shovel and jar back into her carrying bag. She sighed and leaned over the hidden place.

"Rest easy, little brother," she said, and made the sign of farewell and blessing. Though the grass would soon grow back over the cut turf, she sprinkled wine and wheat grains over the grave. She hoped that the little boy's spirit would find its way to the green fields beyond the Lethe. Then she slipped off through the bushes, heading for the front of the house. This time no one saw her.

· · ·

"I fear that I am a poor commander for this desperate venture," Maxian said, his voice still hoarse. He sat in a wooden chair with upswept arms, covered with a quilt. His face was still pale, though he had nearly recovered all of his strength. While he still looked young, there was some shadow around his eyes that made him look far older than he had the week before. Krista sat behind him, on the edge of the bed, with the little black cat on her lap. The dead man and the Persian sat in the other chairs, but only Abdmachus seemed comfortable in them. He was sitting cross-legged after the fashion of his people.

"I have put us all at risk with a very ill-considered approach at dealing with this problem. I was thinking of this . . . thing . . . as a contagion, a disease. It is not, it is a curse, a construction of forms and patterns in the unseen world. It must be dealt with as such." Maxian raised his hand to stop Abdmachus, who started to speak.

"I know, my friend, that many other sorcerers have gnawed at the edges and come away empty-handed or dead, but this thing operates within boundaries and rules of its own. It is *not* a disease and I do not believe that it can be treated like one, a single patient at a time. Everything that this is fits together, like a puzzle, or the stones of a bridge. If the one keystone can be removed, properly removed, the entire edifice will come apart. I believe that if we can effect that, the entire curse will be lifted."

Abdmachus stirred, his white eyebrows perking up. "What, Lord Prince, is the keystone?"

Maxian smiled, but he did not answer. His face twisted a little then, becoming grimmer. "I also know that regardless of how much you might praise my current powers, they are wholly insignificant in the face of what will be required. I must have access to a vast reservoir of power, far more than is contained within mere rocks and stones, or even in the three of us. Where can I get it?"

The Persian quailed at the hard stare he received from the Prince. He looked to Gaius Julius, but the dead man was smiling genially and only raised an eyebrow in question. Krista was ignoring the men entirely, for the little black cat had rolled on its back and was batting at her braids with its paws. It caught one and bit at the end of the hairs.

Abdmachus turned back to face the Prince, who was still staring at him with an almost hungry gaze. "O Prince, I . . . I do not know of such a power! The exhumed dead are repositories of strength, as you have seen from your experiences in the tomb. You see the pool of necromantic energy that Gaius here provides. I do not know! Perhaps another Emperor, as well loved as he? Perhaps we could find the body of Augustus Octavian and . . ."

"Bah!" Gaius Julius' voice was harsh in the close room. "No one makes a pilgrimage to *his* temple! There are no parades on the day of *his* birth. Do I ken you, Prince, that you need the very power of the gods? That you need enough strength to topple a mountain by pulling out the single stone at its heart?"

"Yes," Maxian whispered, his eyes still fixed on the Persian, who was beginning to tremble a little. The Easterner raised a hand to his mouth and wiped sweat from his lip. "Yes, Gaius, I need the power of a god."

"Well, then," the dead man said, rising from his chair and circling behind Abdmachus, who looked up at him fearfully, "barring that we storm the gates of Olympus and drag Jupiter out by his short hairs to serve us, we must find the next best thing. Persian, you *do* know what that is, don't you? And I'll wager from the palsy in your hands that you know *where* it is as well."

"What do you mean?" Abdmachus' voice was a strangled whisper. A terrible fear had begun to blossom on his face.

"I mean," Gaius Julius said, gently placing his hands on either side of the little Persian's neck, "that I have read the *Histories*. I know that the Tomb is empty, that it has been empty since the disaster of the Emperor Valerian's capture by Shapur of Persia three hundred and sixty years ago. I know what price Rome paid for his ransom. What I don't know is, where is the Sarcophagus? Can you tell me that? Can you tell me where the King of Kings, this Shapur the Young, hid it?"

"No, no! I do not know such things! They are forbidden! The *mobehedan* are the only ones who know such secrets! I am only a low *moghan*, not one of the great ones!"

Gaius Julius' fingers, ancient and weathered like the roots of oaks, dug into the little Persian's neck. Abdmachus squirmed as the nails cut into the nerves, but he did not have the breath to scream. The dead man leaned close, his mouth close to the little Persian's ear. "They trusted you enough to send you here, to the heart of the enemy. They trusted you to carry their plan into the house of the enemy. You are strong enough to build the ward that holds this house safe from what must be the strongest power in the world, save the gods themselves."

The fingers began to crush the little man's windpipe, fractions at a time. Abdmachus struggled desperately to breathe, but there were only little gulps of air to be had.

"Where is the Sarcophagus? Tell me!"

Gaius Julius released the chokehold, suddenly, for Maxian had made a small gesture with his left hand. The Persian gasped for air. When he had recovered, the Prince gestured again and Gaius Julius, with an unpleasant smile, gave him a glass of wine. Abdmachus drank deeply and then put it aside. He glanced fearfully at the dead man but then focused on the Prince.

"Lord Prince, please, surely this is not necessary? I have served you faithfully! I am Persian, yes. I was sent here as a spy in the capital of the enemy. But I am your friend, I have thrown my lot with you! Please do not ask these things of me!"

Maxian leaned forward, his face in shadow. His voice grated like stones crushing the bones of the dead. "Abdmachus, you are faithful, but there is no way out of the trap save victory. If you do not give me freely what I need, then I will draw it from your dead skull. Gaius Julius will take great pleasure in killing you and I will raise you up again, only wholly my creature, and your secrets will be mine. If you serve me freely, and me only, then you will live and have free will. But you must choose, and you must choose now."

Abdmachus quailed away from the face of the Prince, but there was no respite from his will. During the Prince's speech, the dead man had drawn out a wire-wrapped cord and now held it ready behind the Persian's head. Krista looked up from playing with the cat, frowned, and gathered up the little creature before leaving the room.

"Lord Prince . . ." Abdmachus started to speak but then stopped. Fear, cunning, and despair flitted across his face, but in the end there was only hopeless resignation. "Yes, I will do as you say."

Maxian smiled, but there was no laughter in his eyes. He rose from the chair and put aside the patterned quilt. He leaned down and took Abdmachus' head in his hands, raising it up so that he could meet the Persian's eyes. A hum rose in the room, like a hive of bees, and the Persian twitched suddenly. Maxian released him and smoothed the tousled gray hair back.

"Where," said the Prince, "is this Sarcophagus?"

Abdmachus groaned and fell on his knees to the floor. A trembling hand went to his forehead and then flinched back, finding a mark there. Though he could not see it, it was that of an inverted pyramid and bound to his flesh more surely than any tattoo. Tears dripped from his eyes as he knelt before the Prince, forehead to the floor.

"I have heard that the great King Shapur took the Sarcophagus to the *mobadan-mobad*. The high priest had demanded it of the King of Kings as recompense for the murder of Shapur's brothers. The Sarcophagus was taken to the East, to a hidden place, for the *magi* feared that their enemies would seize it from them." Abdmachus halted, his voice weak with fear. "They built a new tomb of gold and lead to hold it, for none could open the Sarcophagus, though many tried. The greatest of the *mobehedan* died trying to unlock its secrets. I do not know where the great *magi* hid it, only that it is somewhere deep in Persia . . . Please, it cannot be found!"

Gaius Julius smiled now and fondly patted the head of the traitorous Persian. "Boy, nothing is impossible if a man puts his mind to it." He looked at Maxian, who was slouched in the chair again, exhausted from his small effort. "That Sarcophagus contains all the power you need, Prince. All we have to do is find it and retrieve it."

The dead man idly toyed with his knife. It was quite old; he had purchased it from a dealer in rare objects in the city. Now he drew the blade and the rasping sound of iron on bronze brought a sickly smile to the Persian's face.

"Where might we find someone who knows where the old wizards took this body, Persian friend?" Gaius Julius' bald head gleamed in the firelight as he bent close to the little Easterner.

Abdmachus swallowed and cringed away from the dead man. "Please, Lord Prince! This thing is a great secret. It is spoken of only in the barest whispers among my people. The agents of the *mobehedan* would murder any man in Persia who ever spoke of such a thing!"

"Then," Gaius Julius said, sliding the flat of the blade along the Persian's chin, "perhaps someone who is not Persian might know? An Egyptian? A Chaldean?" The point of the blade pricked at the corner of Abdmachus' eye.

"Aaah! Please . . . there is a man, a man in Constantinople. He collects rare things: books, objects of art, secrets! He may know where the Sarcophagus was taken. Aaa!"

Blood oozed from around the tip of the dagger and the dead man grinned in delight.

"I have met this man before! Please, I will take you to him. If you have gold or secrets to sell, you can get anything you want from him!"

"Enough." Maxian was tired of the game. "Abdmachus, go and see that the rooms in the cellar are cleaned up."

Gaius Julius stared after the little Persian as he scurried out. He whistled a merry tune.

Maxian looked up, his tired eyes half lidded. The dead man was excited, even eager. This was a new thing, and something that bore watching.

"What is the body in that casket to you, Gaius Julius? It will only be old bones and dust by now."

"I was only bones and dust, Prince, before you came and raised me up. If we can steal the body of the Conqueror, then you can return him to life as well. Is this not so?"

Maxian nodded, his face guarded. The dead man was in an unaccustomed state—he was trying to be earnest.

"Please understand, Prince, that all my life I dreamed of the Conqueror—of being him, of bestriding the world like a giant. My adult life was the execution of that dream. In the end, it destroyed me. Now, past death, those cares have passed from me, but this . . . this I want. I want to see him, alive. I want to speak to him. I want to stand at his side in battle."

Gaius Julius paused, seeing the troubled look on the Prince's face.

"Yes," the dead man said slowly, "in battle. You know that this can only end in a struggle, one that will be fiercer than any that has gone before. A war that you will have to win if you are to succeed. But think! Think of having *him* to command your armies! There can be no better weapon in all the world."

Maxian held up a hand to still the words. He stood, tired and thin, and wrapped the quilt around him. He stared at the old man for a moment, then spoke. "In the morning, take Abdmachus and go to the old port of Ostia. Find a ship, a swift one. We must be on our way to the East as soon as possible. The servants and I will prepare the house for departure. Oh, and make sure that my Imperial brother does not know that we are leaving or where we are going. Be quick about it."

Gaius Julius bowed, another unaccustomed thing for him, and left the room. Maxian went to the grate and stared down into the fire. He felt cold and empty. The struggle with the contagion had drained him terribly. His own talent flickered through his body and told the same tale that Krista had—he had come very close to death. Only her quick thinking had saved him. He wondered what he could do about that.

The patter of small paws made him turn. The little black cat darted into the room and jumped up onto the bed. It yawned at him, all teeth and yellow eyes, before burrowing under the covers. He smiled and shuffled back to the chair.

"Hello, Krista," he said as he lowered himself into the cradle of hard wood.

"Master." She came into the room, a dark ghost in black and gray. She had brushed her hair away from her face and it fell behind her in a cloud.

"Come and sit," he said. She drifted into the room and folded herself onto the couch opposite.

"We will leave soon, for the East. Gaius Julius will go to the port tomorrow . . ."

"I heard."

He paused; she was not well pleased. He decided to be blunter than he preferred.

"I owe you my life," he said, "and I want to reward you, but those gifts that I can give are lacking. I have thought of purchasing you from the Duchess and freeing you, but since you know what we are about and what has happened, that would be freedom in name only. Until the contagion can be defeated, there is no freedom for any of us. You are bound to me, or to Abdmachus, until this is done."

Krista's eyes narrowed. She had already come to the same conclusions.

"So I come with you to the East," she said in an angry voice, "and what am I? Still a slave? Half a free woman? I think—I am still a slave and will always be one. You did not have to tell me *anything* about what you were doing here. You could have sent me away or let me escape. You didn't. It's my duty to be obliging. I'm here because you fancy my company, in bed and out. Your gratitude means nothing to a slave, for it's the gratitude of an owner to a dog that has done well in the hunt—forgotten in the morning."

Maxian's nostrils flared, but he did not otherwise react. Instead, he sighed and looked away. "True. I do want your company. I do not trust the old man or the Persian. Gaius Julius would have me his slave in an instant if he thought that he could maneuver such a thing. Abdmachus—well, before tonight he thought that he was the master of the situation; now he is my creature. I desperately need someone to talk to, to trust. I hope that would be you, if you will still come with me."

"I have no choice," Krista said in a resigned voice. "Outside of the barrier that you and the Persian provide, I'm dead. I want to live, so, yes; I will come with you. I don't think that you will ever think of me as a free woman, but life is better than death."

Inside, Maxian felt a sharp pain at her rejection. *Why didn't she understand that he wanted to help her? He just couldn't. Not right now. But soon he would!*

He turned away and climbed into the bed himself, careful to avoid the little black cat. Krista closed the fire grate part way and then disrobed. The house was silent, the only noise a patter of rain on the slate roof.

A bay mare walked along a dirt road shaded by cypresses. Her rider dozed in the saddle, a broad-brimmed straw hat pulled low over her eyes and a disreputable gray cloak thrown over a muddy brown tunic and leggings. Only a stray curl of reddish-gold hair betrayed anything amiss. Another horse followed close behind on a lead. The road wound down in a lazy path from the foothills of the great mountains behind, heading into a broad valley filled with streams, vineyards, farms, and the distant sparkle of a river. Beyond the river rust-red cliffs rose up in an escarpment backed by great volcanic cones. The horse kept to the left side of the road, for there it was shadier and much of the center of the track had been badly torn up by the passage of many horses and wagons.

The road turned and plunged down the side of a hill, angling toward thicker stands of cypress clustered along the banks of the river. A broad field of high grass and brilliant yellow flowers lay between the hill and the riverbank. As she descended the hill, Thyatis caught sight of a band of mounted men cantering out of the trees into the field; their lance tips sparkled in the sun, and there was a flutter of blue and red banners among them.

Thyatis cursed evilly, turned her horse off the road, and cut across the face of the hill through heavy brush. A hundred feet from the road, she stopped and slid off the bay. She tied her mount to the nearest tree and hurriedly pulled its feedbag from the packhorse. A handful of grain quieted the horse. Thyatis untied a hunting spear from the back of the bay and slipped off into the brush in the direction of the road.

Thirty or forty feet off the road, the side of the hill boasted a thick stand of juniper. Thyatis had noticed them as she had come down the hill—they offered good cover in full view of the road—and now she crept down to them from uphill. She could hear the jangle of bit and bridle on the approaching horsemen. They would turn the corner of the road and begin climbing the hill within moments. She sprinted the last fifteen feet into the stand of juniper and threw herself down behind the bole of the largest tree she could see. Cautiously she peered around the trunk.

Three horsemen cantered around the bend: tall men dressed in russet and tan riding leathers and tunics. They rode past swiftly, shouting at one another.

Must be racing to the top of the hill, she thought.

The rest of the band followed more sedately, thirty in number. They were well armed and richly attired and equipped. Thyatis counted spears, bows, long curved swords among their armament. But they had no water bags and no signs of heavier equipment, or anything to make a camp. *A patrol*, she thought. *The city must be close.*

At the end of the column, riding a little back, was a heavyset man with a large full black beard. Slung over his left shoulder was a round shield painted with the face of a tusked boar in brown and black and white. His horse ambled along, taking its time up the hill. The Persian's eyes seemed heavy with sleep, idle in the late-afternoon sun. Thyatis stilled herself, slowing even her breathing, and did her best to settle all the way into the leaf-strewn soil. The Persian rode with his bow athwart the shoulders of the horse, an arrow laid across it. Thyatis waited a long time after the Persians had passed away over the hill before she relaxed and rolled over to put her back against the trunk of the big juniper.

"He's a quiet one, isn't he?"

Thyatis froze, her ears twitching at the quiet voice. The brush and leaves to her left and right rustled slightly and she started—inwardly—in astonishment as three men in motley brown, tan, and green cloaks appeared around her. They wore half masks of wood carved in the appearance of men with short beards and slanting eyes. The two on the left bore long knives with handles of bone and iron-headed spears, while the man on the right, who had spoken, was armed with a long bow of yellow wood with a countercurve at the top and bottom. The bowman settled to his haunches and laid the weapon down on the leafy ground.

"Greetings," he said in oddly accented Greek. "My friends and I are hospitable."

Thyatis drew her feet up under her, her ears straining for any noise that indicated more men in the band of woods than these three. She could hear nothing, yet she had not heard these men either, even when they were only feet away from her.

"Who are you?" she asked in her own rather poor Greek. One of the men to the left hissed in surprise. It was difficult to keep them all in view at once, so she stared straight ahead, keeping each in her peripheral vision. The man on the right raised a gloved hand for silence.

"I am Dahvos. These are my brothers, Jusuf and Sahul." His voice was low and muffled by the mask, and did not carry much past Thyatis. "Well met, fellow traveler."

Thyatis watched them in silence. The masks were odd; they must be difficult to see out of in these woods. Their boots were made for riding, so horses must lie hidden nearby. They wore light-colored shirts with intricate embroidery on the sleeves and at the neck. One of the men on the left had a heavy silver bracelet wrapped around his forearm. They remained quiet, waiting for her to respond.

At length, she said, "I am Thyatis. Greetings."

The men looked at each other and nodded. The one on the right, who seemed to be their leader, took off his wooden mask with a sigh and stowed it away in a cloth bag at his side. Behind it, he was young and fair-skinned, with blue eyes and regular clean-shaven features. He pulled back the hood of his cloak, showing long braids of red hair tied with strips of colored cloth. Thyatis tilted her head to one side, seeing out of the corner of her eye that the other two had taken off their masks as well. It struck her odd that none of the three wore beards, though the eldest of the three was showing signs of stubble. He was shorter and stouter than the other two men, with streaks of gray in his sandy blond hair, and watchful watery blue eyes. Thyatis could make out a familial resemblance between the two younger men, but this one, he was much older and had a markedly different facial structure.

"You are odd-looking fellows," she said, glancing around at the trees and thick brush. "Why did you shave your beards?"

The young leader, with the bright blue eyes, smiled a little, his gaze flickering over the other two.

"Because," he said, "we are Romans. It is well known that Romans go clean-shaven."

Thyatis snorted in barely repressed laughter.

"You," she said, "are the sorriest-looking set of Romans I've ever seen."

"And you would know?" shot back the blue-eyed one.

Thyatis grinned, showing fine white teeth.

"My acquaintance with Rome is a long and profitable one," she retorted. "Better yet, I am a Roman, my fine barbarian friends, so my experience is unquestioned. You see, I have no beard at all. Now, why are you sneaking around avoiding Persian patrols pretending to be Romans with no beards?"

It was the older man's turn to snort in laughter, and he picked up the knife that he had laid down at the beginning of the parley with a flip and faded off into the brush. The other brother, the one with brown eyes, shrugged and settled back against a tree. With his cloak wrapped around him and a preternatural stillness, he seemed to fade into the mottled bark and leaves.

Dahvos grimaced and toyed with the handle of his knife. "We've come down from the north, just to see what there is to see."

Thyatis quirked up an eyebrow—she began to remember some of the long-ago briefing in Constantinople. She smiled a little at the barbarian.

"You," she said slowly, "are Khazar nomads, scouts belike, come down the valley of the Araxes from the steppes in advance of the army of the *Kagan* Ziebil."

"We are not Khazars!" Dahvos hissed in disgust. "We are Bulgars of the Onoghundur! We are twice as brave as a Khazar, we father three times the sons! Our arrows fly farther, our lances are keener! Bah! The Khazars are our children."

Thyatis spared a glance at the other man, Jusuf she guessed. He was rolling his eyes.

"Pleased to meet you, brave Bulgars who serve a Khazar lord. How long have you been in the valley? How many Persians have you seen? Have you touched the wood of the gate of the city to prove your bravery?"

Dahvos bristled at the implication of cowardice. "We have, Roman. We— and others—have been here for a hand and a half of days. We have seen . . ." He paused to think. "Twenty hundreds of Iron Hats on the road, and many more in the city. They are all riding south to the city. Jusuf has been to the city, for he speaks their language, while I do not. They are busy there, like a hive of bees poked with a spear."

Thyatis considered this, then picked up a little stick and cleared off some of the dirt in the space between them. She scratched an oblong on one side, then a winding line running away from it.

"You have seen the lake?" she said, pointing at the oblong. The two men nodded. Jusuf inched closer so that he could see clearly. "This squiggle is the Talkeh River, which feeds into the lake. This square is the city of Tauris, to our south." A box joined the picture a little distance up the river from the lake. "Have you been south of the city?"

"No," Dahvos said, looking to his brother for confirmation, "there are great marshes between the city and the lake—impassable to horses and wagons. The road skirts them and runs right through the city over a bridge of red bricks. On the other side of the city are cliffs, very rough and bad for the hooves." He picked his own stick and drew a curving line behind the box of the city, showing the escarpment.

"The *Kagan*," he continued, "will come from the north on this road and reach the city. But there are many Iron Hats there, and the walls are strong. The people will not be able to cross the river if the Iron Hats are in the city."

Thyatis nodded; that was as she had been told. Well, it was her business to make it easier for the Roman army to meet up with its allies, so that she would do. These seemed likely fellows for what she had in mind. She smiled at each of them in turn.

"My liege lord, the Emperor of the Romans, is coming here too. I have sworn to my chief that I will ensure that the city of the Iron Hats falls easily to him when he comes before its walls. This is why I am here. If you desire to do a brave thing, come with me to the south. I am going to sneak into the city without the Iron Hats noticing. Are you that brave?"

The two brothers looked at each other, then back at her.

Dahvos was the first to answer, his grin bright in the shade of the junipers. "Milady—I will gladly go with you. You will see that the Bulgars are the bravest of men!"

Jusuf stared at his brother and shook his head in silent dismay, then he too nodded, but his face was long with worry. Thyatis looked over her shoulder to make sure that the road was clear, then got up and dusted off her breeches. Dahvos sprang to his feet and slung his bow over his back. Thyatis looked down at Jusuf, who was still sitting with his back to the tree, and offered him a hand up. He took it, though he eyed her as if she were a snake.

"Then," she said, "let's be about it."

Clouds had come up after sunset, covering the moon and the stars. Well after midnight, Thyatis and Sahul returned to the tiny dry camp the Bulgar scouts had made in the hills behind the city. In the complete darkness, even Sahul had gotten lost and they had spent the better part of an hour stumbling around in a maze of fields and irrigation canals before reaching the hills. Thyatis was sore and tired, but she ducked into the little felt tent that the scouts had put up with a determined look on her face. Inside, Dahvos and Jusuf squeezed aside to let their older brother and the Roman woman in.

A single tallow candle was suspended in a little copper holder near the apex of the tent. A circular hole, edged with leather stitches, let the smoke out the top. In the dim, flickering light Thyatis surveyed the faces of her companions. In the darkness outside, another six Bulgars were sleeping.

So, she thought, *I command men again.*

It was odd, though she had never really marked it before, that these men would accept her leadership with so little qualm. She supposed that she was like a spirit suddenly come among them. The thought of a woman skilled in war, so far from her home and family, was already so incredible that the thought of her command was equally acceptable.

"Sahul and I went to the walls by the river. We saw a sizable camp of horsemen—tents and stake lines for the horses—on the plain to the north of the city. The city is strong. Its walls are new and well reinforced. Many men were on the walls, and we saw three patrols while we were making our way back along the water."

While she talked, she arranged some twigs and leaves into a map on the rug that made a floor of the tent. The men leaned close, filling her nostrils with the smell of horses, sweat, and leather. Sahul grunted and made a downward gesture with his hand.

"Yes," she said, "we saw one other thing. The banner that flies above the gates of the city is the same blazon as I saw on the shield of the horseman two days ago. I believe that it is the mark of the Persian general Shahr-Baraz—he who is called the King's Boar. If this is so, then the city will be very difficult to take. Shahr-Baraz commands the Immortals of the King of Kings, their finest warriors."

Dahvos coughed and tapped a grass stem on the little map of the city. "Do we run away, then?"

Thyatis grunted in turn, sharing a wry glance with Sahul. *Young men!* she thought. *They'll be the death of me yet.* Sahul shrugged, his face impassive. His eyes glinted with merriment, though.

"No, we will have to be very careful. The first thing that we need to do is find a local who is willing to help us—we have to find out something about the layout of the city. Then we get inside and then we see about bringing about the ruin of the Boar."

The discussion continued for a little while and then Sahul excused himself. Thyatis blinked when he was gone. The oldest brother moved like a ghost. Dahvos yawned hugely and made a show of leaving, but dallied for at least ten grains before Jusuf pushed him out the tent. The middle brother bowed as he closed up the door. Thyatis sat alone in the dimness, feeling the quiet close around her. The tent had been a gift of Sahul's on the first night she had spent with the Bulgars in the valley of Tauris. The nomad never said anything, even in the guttural language of the steppes, but his meaning was clear—if a woman traveled with them, then she would be treated well.

Thyatis was in no mood to dispute him. The trip from Ararat had been grueling without a companion to watch her back. Sleeping again among men who could stand watch in the darkness was a relief, though she never slept deeply. A wind began to pick up outside, blowing from the east before the rising, still invisible sun. Thyatis snuffed the candle out and lay down, her head on a rolled blanket. The Bulgars amused her; for scouts in hostile land, they carried an inordinate amount of baggage. Still, they were the finest woodsmen and trackers she had ever met. Even better than Nikos or the Sarmatians.

Thinking of her men, particularly of Nikos' broad brown face, tore at her self-control. She wanted to mourn them, but there was no time and these strangers might not understand her grief, or take it wrongly. With an effort, she turned her thoughts from the dead and back to the efforts of the days to come.

She had almost fallen asleep when a light scratching came at the tent flap. She opened one eye and peered up at the little circle of stars she could see above. Night was almost done. Sighing, she whispered "enter" to the darkness.

Jusuf slid into the tent, a lean dark shape against the wall of felt. Thyatis felt sleepy surprise; she had been almost certain that it would be Dahvos that came calling first.

"Your pardon," he said, in better Greek than his younger brother had, "I wanted to talk to you." His voice was a deep timbre, reminding Thyatis of dim forest and massive trees. He sat, cross-legged, next to the door. She sat up quietly and waited for him to speak.

"Sahul and I have discussed you, and . . ."

Thyatis covered her mouth in embarrassment; she had not intended to laugh.

"Sahul speaks?" she said, her voice bubbling with amusement. She felt Jusuf smile in the darkness. Her heart warmed a little for him, he seemed so humorless most of the time.

"Yes," Jusuf said judiciously, "on occasion. When he feels that it is warranted. Also, sometimes he sings, but only upon important days, or festivals. He has a beautiful voice."

"Go on," Thyatis said, "I need *some* sleep before we move on in the morning."

"Even so. Again, I apologize for the intrusion, but Sahul and I are concerned. You come out of the woods like Diana, hunting, with death in your face. You say that you are Roman and that you are oathbound to enter this city, Tauris, and prepare for the coming of your Emperor. You say nothing of how you came here. Dahvos, who by tradition commands this band, is smitten with you and follows you like a boy after his first woman. We are here to offer him counsel and advice, so that he might learn from our experience. Yet he does not command now, you lead us. We wonder, Sahul and I, whether you came alone and where might your own men be."

"Dead," Thyatis said with a dull voice. "Killed by the Persians on the shores of the great lake or lost on the road since then. Only I escaped—their sacrifice bought me that much, at least."

"I feared so," Jusuf said. In the darkness, Thyatis sensed that he made some gesture, but she could not see what it was. "Sahul would say that a raven rides on your shoulder, carrying the smell of death. We see that you wear command like an old cloak. Know this, O Roman lady, that we will follow you while Dahvos follows you—he is the *bagatur*—but should he die or have a change of heart, then we will take our own counsel."

"You think that I will bring your deaths?"

"Roman lady, I know that you bring my death. I care for Sahul and the others. Do not spend them needlessly to feed your grief."

With that, Jusuf rose and crawled out of the tent, leaving Thyatis alone again. Weariness overcame her and she slept.

Thyatis shaded her eyes, her gloved hands cutting the light of the late-afternoon sun. Across the blue-green of the river, the walls of Tauris rose like sandstone cliffs. Banners of gold and red fluttered over the parapet in the northerly breeze. She and the Bulgars were crouched on a sandy bluff west of the river in a stand of larches and hazel. Jusuf and one of the others had gone down to the river to scout the banks. While they waited, Thyatis was counting the men on the walls and the horses in the encampments under the city walls.

Sahul touched her shoulder and she turned in time to see Jusuf push his way through the screen of trees. He shoved a short brown man in front of him. Sahul took a step into the direct line between Thyatis and the stranger. Jusuf pushed the brown man down to his knees, and then knelt himself. He was winded and sporting a bruise on his cheek.

"Trouble?" Thyatis asked quietly, looking the captive over.

Jusuf shook his head. "I was down by the bank, in the high reeds, and I saw a *banda* of Iron Hats bathing in one of the streams that empty into the river. I swung around upwind of them, which was upstream, and found this fine fellow taking a piss in the water. So I convinced him to come along to see you."

Thyatis grinned. The stranger was looking around, sizing up the green and brown men among the trees, their manner and their weapons. He was short, just four feet tall, with curly dark-brown hair. His beard was short and neatly trimmed, and he wore a baggy gray shirt with stitching at the collar and the cuffs. His boots were very well made but scuffed with long use. Dark-red woolen pants completed his outfit. Jusuf laid a bag, a bow, a quiver of arrows, and two daggers against the nearest tree. Thyatis smiled at the stranger, but he answered only with a scowl.

"You speak Greek?" she ventured. "Latin? Aramaic?"

Their captive looked around again and then crossed his legs and sat down rather than kneeling.

"I speak little Greek," he said in a very bad accent.

"I am Thyatis," she said, taking a way-loaf out of her bag and breaking it. She placed one-half of the thick biscuit in front of him and bit off an edge herself. "I greet you in peace and offer you the hospitality of my house." She pulled the wax plug from the mouth of her wineskin with her teeth and drank a swallow before offering it to him.

The man stared at the biscuit on the ground, at her, and again at the Bulgars, most of whom had disappeared back into the brush while Thyatis was speaking. Gingerly he picked up the biscuit and bit a piece off. He chewed it, made a face, and took the wine. He drank a long draft from the skin, squeezing the bottom to squirt it into his mouth from a distance. Done, he wiped his mouth on his sleeve and belched loudly. Thyatis finished her biscuit. It tasted awful.

"I am Bagratuni," said the brown man. "I accept your hospitality."

"Welcome, Bagratuni," Thyatis said. "Do you like the Persians?" She pointed across the river at the walls of the city.

The man laughed, a short, sharp, barking sound.

"I piss on the lowlanders," he said, making a gesture that Thyatis assumed was obscene. "Do you come to fight them?" He pointed at Jusuf's sword and bow, then at her own.

Thyatis looked at him and cocked her head to one side. She had a feeling about this little man, but how much to trust him?

"We hunt the lowlanders," she said, indicating herself and the invisible Bulgars. "They make fine sport. Can you help us hunt them? Have you been inside the city?"

Bagratuni slapped his leg, smiling in delight. He rubbed his nose, thinking. "The city is a bad place to hunt the lowlanders. There are no free True People inside—all lowlanders and their women. Very dangerous to go there."

Thyatis' eyes narrowed. "You say no *free* True People, what about slaves? Are there many True People slaves in the city?"

Bagratuni nodded, his grin fading.

"Yes," he said more slowly, "there are many True People who serve the lowlanders in the city. Many True People die when the lowlanders come to build the city. Many work on city, but no food, no rest. Only death. The lowlanders, they put bones of children in brick mortar. Then they laugh."

"Bagratuni, can you get us into the city?" Thyatis leaned a little forward. "Not all of us, only a few need go."

The brown man rocked back on his heels. He made a clucking sound with his lips.

"Maybe," he said, speaking slowly. "If you let me go, I will come back and lead you into the city by a secret way. But I have business to attend to, so I must go quickly."

Thyatis glanced at Sahul, who remained as impassive as ever, and at Jusuf, who shook his head glumly. She looked back at the brown man and smiled a little. "Honored guest, I would not think of keeping you at my hearth if you are late in your travels."

She stood up, careful to keep a screen of hazel between her and the distant city. Bagratuni rose as well, though his face was puzzled.

"Go in peace," she said, and motioned to Jusuf to give the little man his weapons back. Bagratuni buckled his sword and daggers onto his belt again, bowed sharply, and crashed off through the brush. Thyatis jerked her head after him at Sahul. The elderly Bulgar nodded and glided off into the trees, barely a leaf stirring in the wake of his passage. She turned to Jusuf, who was leaning on his spear with a disgusted look on his long face.

"You want a local—I find one, a perfectly good one, even healthy. His teeth are good, hardly worn down at all! And you let him go."

Thyatis gave him a hard look and he straightened up.

"Leave a man here to watch for his return—with or without friends. Everyone else moves camp with me. If he is not back by sunset, we go across the river my way."

Jusuf nodded and slipped off between the trees. Thyatis turned, staring across the river. *How much time do I have?* No news of the advance of the Roman army had come to her. The Bulgars knew nothing, and she couldn't wait like the Boar, if it was he sitting over there in the city of tan and gold.

THE OLD PORT OF OSTIA, LATIUM

Ziusudra smiled broadly, spreading his muscular arms wide. "You see, my lord, did I not say she was beautiful?"

Gaius Julius swung up over the side of the ship. He was quite impressed, though he took pains to keep his face even and calm, showing no particular emotion.

"She is swift, like the wind over the water, and light, like a young girl dancing."

Gaius Julius raised an eyebrow and surveyed the broad teak deck of the *Nisir*. The long ship was clean and spartan, its ropes and line tied up in neat bundles. High walls rose up on either side of the deck, and two masts rose out of the polished wood of the foredeck. A high prow curled up at the front, painted in gray and dark blue. Two tall steering oars flanked a steering deck at the back of the ship. None of the Tyrean crewmen was in evidence, leaving Gaius Julius and Ziusudra standing alone under the tall masts.

"She seems sound," the Roman said, testing the weave on one of the ropes tied off to the main mast. "How long would it take you to reach Alexandria, say, or Tingis on the coast of Mauretania?"

The Tyrean smiled, his strong white teeth gleaming amongst the bushy red beard. "My love is swift and sure—I can plot a course by the light of the stars. I have made course from Ostia to Alexandria in eight days, Cadiz on the coast of Hispania in four. *Nisir* will take you anywhere you desire to go, like the chariots of the sky gods."

Gaius Julius shook his head in amusement—no ship captain on the Inner Sea would say any less. He rubbed the side of his long nose, considering the captain, the ship, the strength of the timbers under his feet.

"I understand that you have had . . . some ill luck of late."

Ziusudra's eyes narrowed, seeing a slight smile on the patrician's face. "There was some . . . trouble . . . with a cargo of eels a month ago. But it was the fault of the shipper! We made our run in plenty of time!"

"The eels," Gaius Julius said slowly, "got loose and escaped through the bilge hatches, my good Tyrean friend. Two of your men had to go to the surgeon to have the creatures detached from their bodies. A terrible calamity. My sympathies. I wonder, then, if it is safe to carry precious cargo on your ship."

The Tyrean glared back at Gaius, his hands on his hips. If he had been a pot of hot water, he would have been boiling over. "Those baskets were supposed to be eel-proof! Ah, and the stench! It took a week of scrubbing to get it out of the planking. You're not looking to move rare and precious animals, are you?"

"No," Gaius said, relenting at last and cracking a smile. "Only some tourists—but, my friend, this is a private voyage, so no other passengers will be allowed aboard. Oh, and no cargo either, just me and my *friends*."

"No cargo!" Ziusudra was outraged. "How shall I make a profit then? I have notes to pay, my lord. I must turn some shekels with this voyage!"

"No matter," Gaius said, pulling a plain wooden scroll case out of his tunic. "I took the liberty of acquiring your notes from Zuscis the banker. He was quite pleased and so am I. This seems a fine ship to own."

Gaius Julius grinned, showing his own even white teeth to the Tyrean. Ziusudra glared back at him with beetling brows.

"If you do well, then you shall have the *Nisir* back when we are done."

OUTSIDE OF SAMOSATA,
THE NORTHERN EUPHRATES PLAIN

Dwyrin woke with cold water sluicing over his head. He gasped and sputtered, blowing water out of his nose. A rough hand dragged him up from the water trough that he had been held over. He shook his head, feeling cool water spill down inside of his shirt. Against the hot air around him, it felt blessed.

"Wake up, lad!" a familiar voice growled. The nervous whine that had marked it for so many days was gone now. "Back to the land of the living!"

Blinking his eyes clear of the stinging water, Dwyrin looked around. Another Imperial camp surrounded him, filled with tents and, above them, a rampart of hastily packed earth. He was standing by the side of a large tent with a wooden frame rising behind it. The frame supported one side of a broad canvas sunshade a good thirty feet on a side. The sunshade covered a camp within the camp, shielding it from the westering sun.

Colonna peered into his eyes, holding back the lid with his thumb.

"Huh," the soldier said, "you're in good shape now. You faint a lot?"

Dwyrin pushed his hand away and stood up. His knees felt weak. "Where's my unit? I have to report."

"Well . . ." Colonna said, scratching at his beard and staring off into the distance. "Why don't we have something to eat first, and then we'll go see the Tribune. You're a little late as it is, so waiting a mite more won't hurt."

Dwyrin considered, and his stomach voted for him. Dinner it was.

A large tent had been pitched near the middle of the camp for the cooks. Unlike the carefully laid out pattern of the camp at the port, this one was a jumble of tents, ditches, and the low wall. Many sunburned barbarians with long blond hair and tattoos were present, sitting under the flaps of their hide or horsehair tents. Colonna held aside the canvas door of the big tent and Dwyrin passed in. There were no tables, only a series of big pots filled with stew. Colonna handed the boy a battered tin bowl and a spoon carved out of horn.

"Don't forget to give it back, lad, it's my only extra."

Dwyrin nodded and held out the bowl for a grizzled legionnaire with a missing arm to ladle some dark-brown slop with chunks of unrecognizable meat into. Colonna was right behind him, holding out a bigger bowl for his share.

They ate outside. Colonna stood against the wall of the mess tent and shoveled food into his mouth with his own spoon, a bent copper thing. Dwyrin squatted on the ground. He was too tired to stand. The meat might have been goat, or maybe pig, but he really didn't care. When they were done, Colonna made him wash it down with sour tasting water. When he took the first gulp, he coughed and nearly spit it out.

The soldier slapped him on the back, making him cough more.

"The Legion's drink, lad, watered vinegar. Quenches the thirst, they say. Hate it myself, but you'd better get used to it."

It was nearly full dark when Colonna took Dwyrin to see the tribune. The inner camp was surrounded by a fence of wands driven into the ground, each about a foot apart. A single guard sat on a triangular stool just inside the one opening into the domain of the sorcerers. He was dressed in a plain tunic and boots. Colonna identified himself and Dwyrin and each showed the man their identification disks. Dim lights gleamed among the tents within the paling. As they passed through the fence, Dwyrin felt a chill pass over him, and he looked around. The guard laughed and pointed them toward the tribune's tent.

The great sunshade that had blocked the afternoon sun now served as a great roof over the center of the wizard's camp. A cheery orange-red fire blazed in a ring of stones directly beneath it. The light flickered off the underside of the shade. There was no one to be seen, only empty, poorly lighted streets between the tents. Dwyrin felt unsettled by the quiet of the inner camp, the more so since passing the wands he could no longer hear the grunting of camels and the voices of men in the outer camp. A standard was placed before a single tent, set a little apart from the others. It was quite similar to the standard Legion eagle, but it bore a single disk, marked with the eye of Horus, rather than the civitas and the laurels. There was no list of battles suspended from it either.

"Tribune Quintus Metelus Pius?" The trace of a whine had crept back into Colonna's voice.

"Enter," came a gruff, distracted, voice from within the tent.

Colonna entered, followed by Dwyrin. A brass lamp illuminated the interior of the tent, casting an odd, even white light over the bed and table. The tribune was sitting behind the table on a camp stool, bent over a profusion of small metal pieces laid out on a cloth. Dwyrin started when he realized that the lamp did not contain a flame but rather a sphere of glass holding some kind of a sprite. Looking closer, he could make out a tiny face pressed against the glass and a blur of wings. The creature stared back at him, its golden eyes enormous and filled with terrible pain.

"*Ouragos* Colonna of the Fourth of the Sixth of the Third, Tribune." Colonna saluted.

The tribune looked up, his watery blue eyes barely glancing over the soldier and Dwyrin before his attention returned to the clutter of metal springs and gears on his desk.

"Your business?" the tribune said in a disinterested voice. Colonna stood straighter.

"This lad, Dwyrin MacDonald, is reporting for duty, sir. He had orders to travel from Constantinople to join up with your unit, sir. He was delayed and has only just arrived."

"Oh," the tribune said, carefully fitting a toothed gear onto a tiny greased post fixed to the side of what looked like an egg made of tin. "Well, take him to Blanco and get him squared away. I think there are some empty bunks in *insula* four. You may go."

Colonna paused and looked over his shoulder at Dwyrin, who was almost asleep on his feet. The confrontation in the town had been terribly draining. "Ah, sir, there is a minor problem, if I may . . ."

The tribune looked up and finally put down the collection of metal parts in his hands. He ran a greasy hand though his short-cropped red hair, leaving a streak of oil and soot through one side. In the steady white light, his face was solid and handsome in a restrained way. He was not pretty, but there was something respectable about him. Dwyrin had a fleeting impression of a stolid cow with big ears in a field of hay, but pushed it away.

"Go on," the tribune said, looking Dwyrin over at last. He raised an eyebrow at the tattered cloak with burned edges as well as the dust and grime from the road that covered the rest of the Hibernian's clothing.

Colonna coughed and said, "The lad was attacked on the road, at the bridge over the Euphrates, and his horse and kit were lost. Can he draw new gear from stores?"

A wintry smile flickered across the tribune's face and he leaned back from the table. "Not much to choose from, *Ouragos*, only castoffs and dead men's kits. But the boy needs clothing and gear, so yes, I'll make out a chit for it."

The tribune reached under the little table and there was a clattering sound. He drew a piece of broken pottery out of a bucket and scratched something on it with a pointed metal tool from the table. Colonna accepted the chit and saluted again. Dwyrin remembered to salute as well. The *ouragos* hustled him out of the tent.

"Not bad," the soldier said as they walked through the lane between the tents. "You can get your kit, at least."

They stopped near the gate and Colonna turned Dwyrin around to face him.

"When you report to your centurion tomorrow, it will not go so easily. I know the centurion in charge of the detachment here—he's a hard-ass named Blanco. The punishment for losing your kit is severe, but if you follow his rules, you'll make it through. Now, tent four is over there."

Colonna pressed the piece of pottery into Dwyrin's hand. "I've got to go make my report to the infantry tribune, so you go grab some sack time."

The Sicilian hurried off down the lane, lit by drifting sparks of light, and Dwyrin turned away to stumble off to the fourth tent. He was home, he thought, at last.

Dwyrin stood quite still, the numb feeling in his legs sliding up into his hands. The centurion looked up. "Is there a problem, MacDonald?"

Dwyrin swallowed. His throat was dry and filled with dust. "I have no gear sir, it was stolen when my horse was killed."

Blanco nodded and sighed, his broad chest stretching at the light tunic that he wore. He waved toward the bunk across from the little table. "Sit down."

Dwyrin sat.

"Did Colonna take you to the tribune already?"

"Yessir."

"What did the tribune say to you, or to Colonna, about your gear, your kit? Did he say anything?"

Dwyrin flushed and felt a hot spark kindle in his head. The patient, mocking tones of the masters he had heard many times at the academy. He hated being treated like a child, even if he was so young.

"Sir, he said that I should draw a new kit, sir, from Stores and that I should be assigned, sir, to the . . ."

Dwyrin's throat choked shut. Blanco had clenched his hand and Dwyrin's muscles contracted in a spasm. His head swam and white-hot lights began to sparkle at the edge of vision. Blood trickled into his mouth from his lip as he bit down. Power surged in the ether around him. Dwyrin's hands ground into the bunk.

Blanco shook his head.

"No," the centurion said, "mouthing off."

Dwyrin's head filled with a sharp buzzing sound, like a stone saw on marble. He struggled to breathe. The hot spark sputtered in his head and guttered out. Dimly he perceived the surging green trail that wrapped his neck and danced at the slight movements of the centurion's meaty fist.

Don't think. Colonna's voice echoed in the buzzing sound.

Dwyrin fell limp and dropped his mind back into the beginning meditation. Vision curved and folded away from him. The light of the tallow candle spun out into the fire-form of its raw element.

"You're slow, much too slow . . ." he heard echoing as consciousness suddenly left him.

The gargling cry of a camel he heard first, then as his eyes opened stones and gravel heaved past. Tight hands gripped him at arm and thigh. Dwyrin saw dim blue sky flash past, then the edge of a post cracked against his forehead. Old blood was in his mouth. Another pair of hands dragged his arm up and into a heavy leather thong. His eyes suddenly focused on his other hand as it too was bound into a heavy black leather loop. Beyond it he saw the great roof of the mess tent and the other pavilions. A cold wind slid between his bare legs.

Two boys not much past his age stood at either side of the wooden frame he now hung from. To his left a short, tan, black-haired boy with a long face and thin nose, dressed in plain white shirt and trousers, was staring at him with guarded dark eyes. To his right he glimpsed a shorter and broader boy, also in plain white, with a broad round face and short blond hair. He too wore a closed look on his face, though otherwise he had the look of a merry fellow.

One of his legs was dragged back and a wire-cored rope flipped around it three times. Dwyrin felt fear fill his body and corrode what passed for his returning consciousness.

He knew what was going to happen next. The centurion hadn't been kidding. He was on a whipping frame, and soon some twenty-year veteran with arms like tree trunks was going to come out with a snake-lash studded with metal hasps and give him thirty or forty full strokes and his back and legs would disappear in a red mist. He gagged and a small groan escaped him.

A sharp slap brought his head around, eyes wide. A young woman stood close to him, dragging his head back with a dark tan hand.

"Shut up," she hissed. Her hair was dark and thick as pitch and tied back in a dull red fillet around her head. Her face, like that of the boy on the left, was thin and lean. Her eyes were a dark brown, with graceful black eyebrows above. She shook him again, her white shift falling back from a firm tan arm, and pushed his head back against the edge of the frame.

"If you squeal like a pig, Celt, I'll make sure you never have a moment's peace here, see? You're in our five now, and if you make us look bad, I'll skin you myself."

The girl pushed him back and then squatted down to tie his other leg to the frame. Across the little space behind the mess tent, Blanco and Colonna were sitting on a bench, drinking from heavy earthenware cups. Two wooden plates sat next to them on the bench, the remains of their morning gruel clinging to the edges. They were deep in some discussion, heads bent close.

Above the tents and the patchwork quilt of ropes, wires and threaded nets and cloth that depended from them, Dwyrin glimpsed the high peaks of the Tauris. The sun glinted from broad spearheads of snow and ice. The wind from the east bore their chill. There was a coughing sound.

Dwyrin forced his eyes to remain open, his head to turn, slowly, to the sound of crunching gravel that heralded someone's approach. The dark-haired girl stepped back from the frame, to the side of the boys, now drawn together in a knot.

Blanco and Colonna put down their mugs and stood up, saluting as the tribune paced into the little square. As the night before, he wore stained trousers and a rumpled shirt. His spectacles lent him a distracted air. He returned the salutes.

The tribune glanced around at the preparations and sniffed. He walked to the back of the mess tent and banged on the doorpost with his fist. One of the cooks stuck his head out the canvas flap.

"Something hot, lad," the tribune said. He turned around then, leaning against the post. He signed to Blanco and then settled back.

Blanco stepped out into the square, hands behind his back, and cleared his throat. "The legionarius Dwyrin MacDonald, having failed to maintain his issued kit, gear and horse in good order and condition, must abide by the law, wherein five and twenty strokes of the lash will suffice to maintain discipline," he intoned.

Then he stepped back and signed to the girl in the bound hair. She stepped to the side of the frame and back a little, and shook out a long length of rawhide thong, weighted at the end, and showed it to a pale Dwyrin with a peculiarly ritualized motion. Then she went around to the back of the frame.

Dwyrin gritted his teeth and tensed his back.

Behind him, he heard the lash slither out, shaken free from the girl's hand. Its tip rattled across the stones and gravel. Then he felt it gathered up again in her hand. Her feet shifted on the gravel. Dwyrin's mind began yammering prayers. His hands were sweaty in the loops at the end of the ropes. The wind slid across his skin, raising goosebumps.

"One." Blanco rumbled.

Dwyrin flinched.

The lash rapped hard against his back and the side of his neck, then lifted away. Dwyrin rebounded from the end of the ropes.

"Two."

Dwyrin gasped, the trail of fire across his back now lit and surged through him. The second stroke fell and his teeth ground down. Muscles and nerves howled in pain. He gasped again, fighting against the enormous scream that was rising up within his body.

"Three."

A long gargling cry slid between his teeth, and Dwyrin felt the disgusted eyes of the girl on him.

Blood hissed in his ears as the lash lifted up, whistling, from his naked back. Again he flung forward against the ropes. A long, mewling cry bubbled from his lips and he bit down on it. His tongue spiked with pain. The hot spark at the back of his brain spun and flashed. Across the little sandy square Blanco looked up from the bench with interest. At his side the two young boys tensed, greyhounds at the leash. From the edge of his vision, in the flickering gray haze, he could catch their forms shifting in and out of awareness, first a sharp green and then a pale blue.

The girl flipped the snake back in her hand and adjusted the leather strap on her forearm. Sweat beaded under the red fillet. She tossed her hair back out of her eyes. She squinted. The sun had now risen fully over the peaks of the Tauris and slanting rays spilled across the camp. Tentpoles and banners were picked out in the hot light.

Dwyrin hung limp, eyes filled with tears.

Gods, don't let her see me cry, he raged at his body. It trembled and twitched at every sound. His mind scrabbled at nerves and muscles, willing them to be still. He heard the scrape of gravel under the girl's foot as her shoulder rolled back to propel the braided snake against his raw back.

The spark roiled and spun in darkness, drawing red rage into its heart. Blanco spread his feet and balanced himself, now poised at the edge of the circle. Colonna was sitting again, a slow smile creeping across his face. The cook appeared at the back door of the kitchens and scattered the mess boys back to their duties. Then she too leaned there, her face in shadow still under the plain lintel of the door. Her dress was blue and long, Dwyrin saw through the rippling pain, bordered with curling red and yellow flowers. The details seemed clear and fine in his sight.

"Five," Blanco growled from the bench. Dwyrin's body betrayed him again, tensing forward, flexing the lines, and then it cast back. The lash was across his back in a bar of white fire. This time the girl had put her shoulder into the blow. The spark whistled down now into inner darkness, growing huge in his mind. Nerves screamed, grating raw stone and branch across him.

"Six."

"Seven."

His voice, distantly, was a high, girlish scream, but his heart was black and filled with darkness. Blanco was smiling now, his eyes half closed, rocking back and forth on the balls of his feet. And Colonna was leaning back against the dull gray planks of the kitchen wall, his eyes sparkling.

"Eight." Blanco started whistling, a little tune that ran along the scales, up and down again. Dwyrin's right eye failed, consumed by a white-hot blur of sparks only he could see. Only his left remained, filled with the sight of cracked white teeth in Colonna's mouth. He saw the centurion turn and say something to the Sicilian. The other laughed and slapped his knee. Dwyrin snarled in rage, spittle trailing from his mouth.

"Nine."

"Ten."

"Eleven." The girl was pausing now, drawing out each stroke. The disgust of her gaze sank into the raw blood on his back, and he could feel the quiet laughter of the two boys. Spinning hot, the spark suddenly consumed his left eye as well and he saw nothing but staccato white and orange, shot with green and purple. Dwyrin suddenly felt his body snap away, lost in black and red pain. His mind recoiled free and he plunged into the world of forms without meditation, without trance. Power coursed, brilliant flows and patterns turned and wheeled around him. Familiar analogies and themes failed him. A shifting pattern of nothingness trapped him in a confined space. Vortices of form spun in the void around him. The familiar patterns of earth flow and life energy could not be discerned. He grasped futilely for the meditations, for his center, but there was nothing but the spinning spark, shuddering and flaking at the edges.

A ghost rose up before him in the void of forms, each layer rotating in counter to those below; it flexed and bunched, then power leapt and cast from it. Dimly Dwyrin grasped that the girl was laying the lash against him, yet the bands of cerulean and rose that extended from the ghost did not touch him but disrupted against the nothingness. His heart expanded and the spark annihilated the nothingness. The void shattered and broke into mirrored fragments. The surging coil of the earth flow gripped him.

His form solidified in the void. Suddenly the glowing snake shapes of the girl behind him and the boys to either side sprang into focus from the writhing maelstrom of ether. The narrow darkness of the lash flicked toward him and the hot spark flared, consuming it. Dwyrin howled soundlessly, hot yellow light rushing out from him, crashing against the pale-blue geometries that sprang into being between him and the lithe coil of the two boys.

The ghost girl lunged, her spirit-fists red-hot with power as they smashed into him. The spark whirled and turned in his mind, shedding layers of light. Dwyrin steadied himself and lanced back, deep green-black power flowing from the earth below him. Shining brightly he gripped the dull fires of the wooden frame and leached them into his arrow-bright attack.

The girl ghost spun and darted, her dragon coil shading and swallowing his stroke. The two boys attacked simultaneously against the counterspin of the sphere that Dwyrin coalesced around himself. The sphere cracked in a rippling line and the girl struck through it. Dwyrin shuddered, his form collapsing around the pinpoint hole that knifed into him. The three were like quicksilver, gliding away from his attack, tearing long strips out of his defense. He leached the earth, but the currents of power there were far too deep to reach. Stones yielded their hearts to him and burst into powder at his feet. Lightning rippled and he sought to bind the two boy ghosts with a feint; one he caught and held in contest a moment, but the girl swept away the remainder of the sphere and knifed into the red-hot core of his being. The second boy followed her attack, shredding his connection with the earth. Darkness collapsed and left nothing.

Gasping, Dwyrin's true eyes stared into the sun. The swirling disk of Ra now rode in the sky, moments from passing into the clutter of stays, guides, and lines that suspended the woven net above the inner camp. A face obscured the sky. Dwyrin blinked. The girl's face resolved itself, sweat dripping from the side of her nose. Her eyes were slits. She thumbed back his eyelids in turn and slapped the side of his face lightly. Dwyrin choked and tried to sit up. Movement drew ragged pain across his back. Tears welled from his eyes, blinding him.

"He's fine," he heard. "No worse than most. Some salve and a week and he'll be done."

Gentle hands slid under Dwyrin as he gasped, and lifted him up. He blinked furiously, catching sight of a tent roof occluding the pale sky, before he was lain into a stretched canvas bunk. The sound of clinking coins echoed from the roof

down to him. The two boys slid quietly into the corners of his vision. The blond
one smiled encouragingly, the corner of his mouth stained with red juice.

"Pomegranate?" he ventured. The other boy scowled, thick dark hair inching
down over his eyes. He brushed it back as he leaned closer. Dwyrin turned a little toward him. The dark boy reached out of sight and brought a leather canteen with a
knurled bronze lip to Dwyrin's mouth. Cool water spilled across his lips and he drank
hungrily. The throb of his back was growing greater in his mind. Even before, on the
frame, it had not itched so much. The blond boy broke a little of the pomegranate off
and pushed it into Dwyrin's mouth. He bit down on the bitter seeds and felt them
squeak aside before breaking. Sharp-tasting juice filled his mouth.

"You were lucky," the blond one confided, chewing on the rest of the pomegranate. "Usually they finish the lashing, even if you pass out."

"He's right," the dark-eyed boy asserted, "I lost a mule once, got fifteen, each
accounted for and measured." Both boys nodded in agreement.

"Lucky," they said, as Dwyrin slipped first into a gray haze and then nothing.

▣◗)•(◗▣

THE ROMAN CAMP OF

DENABA, SOUTHERN SYRIA MAGNA

)•((

"Empty," Zenobia shouted as she galloped down the via principalis of the encampment. A dry wind whistled through the streets, blowing thistles and trash
in front of it. At the center, before the broad brick front of the headquarters, she
pulled up and turned the midnight-black stallion that she had taken to riding to
face her companions. Ahmet, Mohammed, and the others cantered up to meet
her. The square in front of the commandery was of hard-packed earth and flat
stones. The building behind Zenobia was shuttered and empty, its doors barred.
Around them the camp lay deserted; hundreds of fired-brick buildings stood in
neat rows with dirt streets between them. The barrel-vaulted roof of the baths
stood off to one side of the square, and Ahmet could see that its doors stood ajar,
with sand blown into the doorway.

"Not so much as a chicken or a pig left," the Palmyrene Queen continued,
leaning forward in the saddle and scratching the ears of her mount. "So like a
Roman, leave nothing, take everything. Al'Quraysh, have your scouts found anything in the vicinity?"

Mohammed shook his head. The sheykh Amr ibn'Adi nominally commanded
the motley collection of tribesmen, Palmyrenes, Syrians and Nabatean levies who
formed the light horse attached to the army. Mohammed was their leader, however, and ibn'Adi spent much of his time as one of Zenobia's close circle of advisors
instead. Ahmet had not seen the Southerner happier since they had begun traveling together.

"No, Empress, the hills around us are deserted and even the dwellings of the camp followers are abandoned. Some of my men report that there is a good place to set up camp down the stream three or four miles. Shall we move on and camp there?"

Zenobia laughed, her dark hair a wave of ebony around her head. "What? And waste this perfectly good camp? If we are to do Rome's work, then we will take Rome's privileges! We camp here tonight, and for the next week or two. My brother will be coming soon to meet us here with the rest of the army of the city. Quarter the men, send out foraging parties, and repair any defenses that have fallen into disuse. Go!"

Mohammed made a half bow in the saddle and then galloped off, his robes flying out behind him. The other commanders—Zabda, who commanded the *cataphracti* of the army, drawn chiefly from the heavily armed and armored nobles of the Decapolis, Nabatea, and Syria; and Akhimos Galerius, who led the massed infantry cohorts of the cities—bowed as well and rode off to see to their commands. Zenobia watched them go and sighed once they were out of earshot. She turned her horse again and surveyed those men who remained with her in the square.

"When Vorodes arrives with my infantry, we shall take some time to prepare before we march north." The Queen motioned to ibn'Adi, who was seemingly sleeping on his horse, for his eyes were closed and a soft snore was fluttering his white mustaches.

"Old Father, when you wake up, go around and find those men who are familiar with these hills. Set them out to watch the roads from all directions. Should any man come, I would know of it sooner than a raven could bring it to me."

Ibn'Adi cracked an eye open and nodded, then nudged his horse and they ambled off together toward the road from the south where the army was busily snarling itself in a half-mile-wide mob as detachments attempted to move to their allotted areas of the camp.

The Nabatean Prince, Aretas, watched the old chieftain go and laughed mirthlessly. "That one never sleeps, sister."

Zenobia answered his cold smile with one of her own. "Brother," she said, with only the faintest hint of sarcasm, "I will work out of the headquarters, if you and your priests would prefer the *praetorium* for your quarters. Will you see that the temple fires are lit and the proper accommodations made to the gods?"

Aretas inclined his head, saying: "We would be honored to occupy the house of the commander of the camp, and we will see that the army is not disturbed by ill omens or unchaste spirits."

The Prince gestured and his guardsmen, dressed like he in dark-burgundy tabards and enameled armor, rode up to join him. He graced the other men still with the Queen with a flicker of a cold smile and rode off to find his baggage train and the cohorts of heavy horse that he had maintained for his own service. Ahmet felt a sense of unease lift from him as the Petran rode away. The King of the Southern Highlands was not well loved, nor did he care. He had given up nearly all of his army to the service of Zenobia, but he remained aloof from the discussions among the commanders and kept his own counsel. He seemed content to follow Zenobia's lead in all things.

The Queen sidestepped her horse close to Ahmet's and smiled. "Son of Egypt, will you take charge of the hospital and the baths? I can think of no better man to undertake such an important task. Find cousin Zabbai in that confusion at the gate and move the cooks, quartermasters, and doctors into the hospital. There must be a spring to bring water to such a large camp. Find it as well and see that there is water within the walls. We will be here for a time, and such comforts as can be garnered shall be."

"Yes, milady," Ahmet said, bowing a little.

The Queen smiled, her voice softening. "When you are done, come and find me, I will be in the commandery. If it pleases you, take quarters near to mine. I would like to talk to you later."

Ahmet nodded, though he felt a little dizzy from the blood rushing to his head. Zenobia turned away, taking those brilliant eyes and flawless face with her. He shook his head to clear the vision away and turned his horse. There was a great deal of work to be done.

Ahmet and a crew of Syrian stonemasons who had been enlisted in the army to satisfy the honor of their city put their backs into a lever and groaned, straining against it. The stone that they were trying to break out of the wall of the cistern trembled and then slipped aside with a grinding noise. Water, dark and cold, spurted into the round chamber.

"Up the rope! Up the rope!" Ahmet shouted as the water flooded over him, knocking him to the ground. The stonemasons shouted in fear as one of the torches, knocked loose, hissed out in the water swirling around the floor of the room. Above them, in the square opening cut into the side of the rock cistern, the other men threw down ropes to the men at the bottom of the well. Ahmet struggled in the water, forcing himself to his feet. The stone that had sealed the old pipe from the aqueduct gave a peculiar groaning sound and then suddenly broke free in the rush of water. The Egyptian splashed aside, his heart thudding with fear, as the heavy block of basalt crashed into the thigh-deep water where they had been standing. The water was rising quickly. He looked up.

The stonemasons had scampered up the ropes like a band of monkeys and were crawling out through the hole. The men outside were dragging them through the opening as quickly as they could manage. Ahmet snared one of the ropes and wedged his foot into a crack between the stones that made the wall. The water tugged at him as the cistern filled, but he too scrambled up the wall and many rough, callused hands were waiting to hoist him through the opening.

"When it fills to the marker stone"—he gasped—"open the sluice gate so that the baths fill."

Then he fell backward on the mosaic floor of the caldarium, his limbs trembling with the closeness of death. Through the raised floor, he could feel the rush of waters into the well like a stampede of bulls. *Close, very close*, he thought, and then rolled over on the sea-green tiles and got up.

• • •

Torches guttered in the hallways of the *principia*, the headquarters of the camp, filling the air with the sharp smell of juniper resin. Ahmet limped into the atrium that lay before the offices of the camp commander. Zenobia's guardsmen, a crew of fierce-looking Bactrians with high turbans, hooked noses, and beards plaited into two jutting points, stopped him and looked him over. The Bactrians were only one group of thousands of mercenaries that the Silk Empress had summoned to her standard. The camp outside was filled with more of them—Blemmyenite archers, Axumite spearmen, Arabic light horse, Indians, Sogdian horse archers and swordsmen, the masses of the Tanukh, and even Persian heavy horse, or *cataphracti*, drawn by the lure of the Queen's gold. Among them, the Nabatean cavalry and heavy infantry seemed out of place, too well ordered to fit in well with the riot of the other tribes. Satisfied that he was inoffensive, the Bactrians allowed Ahmet to enter the tribune's offices.

Zenobia looked up from behind a heavy marble bench she was using as a desk and smiled. Her hair was braided back out of the way. Her secretaries and scribes sat at small portable desks along the walls of the chamber, and two of the maidens who served her were sitting on cushions, sewing. The Queen had shed the heavy silk robes that she favored for riding and wore a simple cotton tunic with linen leggings. The heavy torque of gold that she wore as the symbol of her rule was laid aside as well. There was a smudge of ink on her left cheek. Ahmet bowed and noticed that his kilt was torn and muddy.

"It should not be proper," she said with a lilting amusement in her voice, "for a mere priest to bathe before a Queen." The timbre of her voice shifted. "Did you escape injury?"

"Yes," he said, brushing at the clods of mud that had somehow affixed themselves to his tunic. "The hospital is occupied and nearly ready. The baths are hot, and there is water in the cisterns. The Romans had blocked up the end of the aqueduct. It was little trouble to remove the stones."

Zenobia nodded, her head tilted to one side. Her dark eyes were grave as she looked him over. Then she shook her head and pushed a pair of papyrus scrolls across the bench toward him. The rings, too, were gone from her fingers—delicate settings of lapis and emerald. Her nails were short, but trimmed, for she often rode with gloves.

"It would please me if you read these dispatches over—I understand that you know Latin as well as Greek and Egyptian. I believe that I understand them well enough, but I would be sure. Come back when you are done, but no sooner than the second watch change. I have much to do before then."

Ahmet felt one of his eyebrows raise; the second watch was near midnight. Regardless, he bowed and took his leave. Despite her jest, he thought that he would avail himself of the baths and a good scraping, now that they had hot water.

After the bell that sounded the change of the second watch, Ahmet came again to the offices of the commander of the camp. Only two of the Bactrians were on guard, but they let him pass without qualm, standing quiet and watchful in the shadows of the entranceway. The clerks and scribes were gone too, leaving the Queen sitting alone at her desk, the only sound the scratching of her pen on the rough paper.

Save for the watchmen, the camp slept heavily, exhausted from the hard march north from Damascus. The army had been slow to move with each contingent stopping and starting at its own schedule. Three days forth from the city, Zenobia had launched into a whirlwind of reorganization that had delayed them again. Now the army was divided into four main *banda*, as the Eastern Empire would name them—the light horse, regardless of their tribe or affiliation, was under the command of ibn'Adi, and Mohammed was his chief lieutenant. The *cataphracts* and *clibanari*, those noblemen with heavy armor for themselves and their mounts, armed with lances, maces, and long swords, were led by the queen's cousin, Zabda of the house of Odenathus. The masses of foot archers, spearmen and slingers were the command of Akhimos Galerius, a Syrian Prince who had served in the armies of the Eastern Empire. The Nabateans remained the sole sore point—Aretas had utterly refused to give up his personal guardsmen, who numbered no less than two thousand heavy horse in full armor. Zenobia had, perforce, made him commander of the reserve, which also consisted of her personal household troops and a contingent of Persian knights from the far southeast of Iran. Another of Zenobia's cousins, Zabbai, was custodian of the baggage train and the hospital.

Ahmet sat quietly, placing the two scrolls in front of him, and waited for the Queen's notice.

She wrote quickly, in a strong hand, with neat letters. In profile, her face was strong. Her brow was high and traced by the delicate arch of her eyebrows. Her neck, cast in partial shadow by the candles that lighted the desk, was smooth and supple. Tiny gold earrings with ruby centerpieces hung from her ears. Her upper arms were adorned with gold circlets fashioned in the shape of asps. Their eyes were sparks of jet. Something tickled in the back of Ahmet's memory, seeing that and how her hair was arranged in a golden net. When he focused on it, it escaped him.

At last she finished the document and sprinkled fine sand over its surface. Looking up, she smiled at him briefly while she rolled the blotter across the surface. Her seal, in purple wax, completed the document.

"Done," she said, sighing in weariness. "You have read the dispatches?"

Ahmet nodded.

She stood, bracing herself against him as he stepped to assist her. She shook her left foot, trying to restore circulation. "Behind this room is a stairway that leads to the roof. Let us go there."

She picked up a lantern that had been set by the end of the bench, along with a smoldering taper. Bending down, she lit the oil wick and then raised it to her shoulder. The Queen drew aside a drape that hung in a doorway at the back of the office. In the hallway beyond, a narrow staircase rose up to the right side, and after a moment of climbing worn stone steps, they came to the roof. A triangular vault capped each of the rooms below, and these made valleys in the rooftop. Zenobia walked forward carefully, picking her way along the tops of the walls, avoiding the slate roofs or the expanses of curved red tile. At last they came to the side of the *principia* that faced the baths. A narrow, dark alleyway divided the two buildings. From this vantage, few of the lights of the camp could be made out. It was dark and the sky seemed crowded with stars.

Zenobia sat and leaned against the sloping wall behind her.

"Sit," she said, and pinched out the wick of the lantern. Ahmet settled beside her in the dark and found, to his surprise, that a thick woolen blanket had been laid there. A breeze drifted in from the hills, and he could smell the spices and perfume in her hair. The Queen drew another blanket around herself and the priest, settling in close to him. Seemingly of its own will Ahmet's arm circled her waist and drew her closer. She sighed softly and laid her head on his chest. Her own hand, small and delicate, found his.

After a time, when he had thought that she had fallen asleep and the moon had ridden up over the barren hills, she stirred and squeezed his hand.

"Did you read the dispatches?" she said in a sleepy voice.

"Yes." His own voice was husky. Her warmth was disconcerting in the chill of evening.

"What do you think?"

It was his turn to sigh. The reports sent by Palmyrene merchants in the ports of Alexandria, Tyre, Sidon, and—most damning—Caesarea Maritima told the same grim story. Though at first he had scarcely dared credit it, now it seemed undeniable.

"I think that your man in Caesarea has the right of it. The three Legions that the Empire withdrew to the coast are not returning. The two Legions that the Emperors promised your man Adathus are nowhere to be found. We are alone, with Shahin's army at Antioch ready to overwhelm the whole coast. Are you going to press on, into the north?"

Zenobia shifted in his arms, sliding into his lap. For a moment, his brain turned off entirely, but when it worked again, she was leaning back against his chest with his arms crossed over her breasts, her hair tickling his nose.

"Almost four hundred years ago, a King of Palmyra faced worse odds. He smashed the Persians in open battle at Nicephorum when the Empire was divided in civil war. The Emperor Gallienus rewarded him with the titles of *dux Romanorum* and *restitutor totius Orientis*. Since those days the Kings and Queens of Palmyra have stood by the Empire as a shield against Persia. My namesake, the first Queen Zenobia, married the Emperor Aurelian, giving up her throne to a cousin, Timolaus. It is my duty to protect these lands from the invaders."

"Even," Ahmet said into the soft cloud of her hair, "when Rome does not stand with you?"

She laughed, but it was a bitter sound. "Rome assumes, but it does not ensure. Because we have always stood at the side of the Empire, they think that we will always stand by them. Aretas reminds me of this with each new sun. Yet . . . Heraclius is a wise king, and cunning. If he has withdrawn his forces from Syria, it must be to gather them for some other strategy. I *know* that he will not abandon these provinces. If nothing else, he is Roman, and the taxes are too rich to give up! We have some part, unrevealed, to play in that stratagem. If we can play it out to our favor, then things will go well indeed."

"Your chiefs seem to fear battle with Persia," Ahmet said slowly. "They are unsure, they waver. If they knew that Rome was not coming, then they would flee into the desert."

Zenobia snorted in disgust. "I know them. They are weak. They talk among themselves of grand dreams and great plans, yet when the hounds corner the stag, they balk and fall back from the kill. I will have to drive the spear into its heart, even in the face of sharp horns! If I lead, they will follow—for what better moves a man than his pride? If I, a woman, will dare the Tiger of Persia, how can they say that they were any less brave? I will go north, and they will follow. Shahin's army is great, but the Boar is not with him, and I am Shahin's master."

Ahmet laughed and squeezed her close. She turned, smiling up at him.

"Thou conquerest, Empress, thou conquerest."

She wrinkled her pert nose at him but lay back again, weary.

"You are making fun of me," she said. "I shall have your head cut off for it."

Ahmet made as to shudder, then said: "And who would sing you to sleep, then, Princess of the Sand?"

"No one." Her voice was sad. "I would be alone again."

They sat in silence for a long time, watching the stars wheel overhead. The moon began to set at last. The night was passing. A colder wind began to blow off the desert.

"Do not take it amiss, lady, but why have you favored me so? I am neither the handsomest of men nor rich. My birth is poor and my vocation obscure. The favor you show me must plague you in this volatile mix of tribes and chieftains you have assembled. Aretas, for one, rarely looks at me with less than venom in his eyes."

Zenobia laughed, and her small hand snaked out of the blankets to pinch his nose. "What a man you are! You are the most insecure of creatures. All these things are points in your favor, silly man. No one, even the dour Aretas, considers you more than a summer dalliance for me—the mysterious Egyptian priest, caught in the toils of a cunning woman. They say, when they speak of it around their campfires, that I curry the favor of the old gods to consort with you. The Princes and lords sniff and make catty comments about my low taste in men. None of them consider you the least impediment to their plans for me."

Ahmet frowned. "How can you exist amid such a state?"

"I was born to it," she answered calmly, "it has always been so for me. The sole daughter of the house of Septimus Palmyrene is either a prize above all others or the victor who takes the prize herself. My earliest memory is of two of my aunts fighting over their position in my mother's funeral procession. So it has been, so it shall be. I favor you because you have a good heart and know little of me. In you there is some hope that I can be solely myself—not the Queen, not the schemer, not the pivot that the fate of Empires turn upon—but Zenobia, the woman. The failed poet. The scholar."

Ahmet nodded, thinking that he understood.

"There is only one thing that I ask of you, Ahmet. It grates on me to do so, but I see no alternative." She shifted around to face him and her face was grave. "Soon there will be battle and I will lead my men into the thick of it. When that day comes, if you could be at my side to protect me, I would count it a great favor."

"Protect you? I am no warrior!" He stared back at her, puzzled.

She gave him a sad half smile. "Yes you are, my friend. The most precious kind. Persia will come against us with more than their fighting men; they will come with sorcery and dreadful summonings. That is what I need desperately from you, to hold back whatever dark arts they bring to bear upon me."

"But," he said, "I thought that Aretas . . ."

Zenobia shook her head and placed a finger on his lips. "If I were to fall in the battle, Aretas would command. He and his sorcerers are to protect the army as a whole and I believe that they will, but the Persians are not fools, they know whom they face. I will be the focus of all the might they can array against me. Please, stand by my side."

The pleading look in her face was too much for what resolve remained to him.

"Of course," he said, "I will stand by you."

The lost student was forgotten.

Four days after Zenobia's army had occupied Denaba, Ahmet and Mohammed were sitting in the quarters in the *principia* that they had taken for themselves, playing a game that the priest had been given as a gift by one of the Indian officers. Mohammed advanced one of his horsemen along the right-hand side of the board. Ahmet frowned; the Arab played very aggressively, and Ahmet was still trying to divine the patterns of movement the pieces made among the red and black squares of the board. He moved an elephant to the right, to close off the lane of attack that the horseman represented.

Mohammed was surveying the board when there was a sharp rapping sound at the door. Both men turned and one of the Tanukh scouts, still dusty from the road, fell to his knees and bent his head to the concrete tiles of the room.

"Blessings and greetings!" the man barked, "I bring tidings from the north. The Persian army has been sighted crossing the Orontes at Arethusa."

Mohammed stood up, forgetting the game. "How many men? Is the Boar with them? Do they have any elephants?"

The scout settled back on his heels. His face was flushed with the effort of his ride. "The relay rider said that there were sixty thousands of the Persians, under the banner of the great Princes Shahin and Rhazates. He saw no elephants."

"Excellent. Well done, Abu Kabir. See to your horse and tell no one else of what you have told me."

The Tanukh, flushed with pleasure that his captain remembered him, bowed again and left. Mohammed turned to Ahmet, who was still surveying the board with a puzzled look on his face.

"Arethusa is ninety miles north of here, my friend. The Queen's battle is very close. Shahin could be upon us with six days, less if he hurries."

Ahmet nodded, then shook his head in disgust. His position on the board was untenable. He stood and gathered his bag and staff. "You'll inform the Queen?"

Mohammed nodded; he was almost hopping from one foot to another in excitement.

"Good," Ahmet said. "You should send some of your riders out on the road to Palmyra and see if they can find Vorodes and his army. She will not want to give battle until we are reinforced."

The Arab paused at the door and looked sharply at his friend, who was buckling his belt around his waist. "So, you're a general now?"

Ahmet smiled, a brief thing, and shook his head in negation. "No, you've that gift. I have heard something of her thought. I go to see to the state of the hospital. You must see the Queen at once."

NEAR THE HIPPODROME, CONSTANTINOPLE

"Your friend seems to have collected his last secret, Persian." Gaius Julius' voice was droll.

Abdmachus cursed, muttering under his breath, and scratched his thinning hair. The narrow street, crowded by *insulae* of flats on one side and warehouses on the other, suddenly widened. On the northern side there was a wide gap in the buildings. Smoke-blackened pillars of brick and mortar rose out of a great tumbled heap of masonry and charred wood. In the ruins of the house, local children were picking through the rubble for salvage. The overcast sky and the thin gray smoke that lay over the city heightened the sense of destruction.

"His library will have been buried or destroyed in the fire," Maxian said, his voice level. He held Krista close to his body, his arms crossed over her chest. Her hands curled around his forearms. He was wearing a broad leather hat that kept the drizzle off both of them. She was wearing a dark-green cloak over a russet tunic and laced-up boots. He had adopted a dark gray and black for himself, something that matched his mood.

"Perhaps not, Lord Prince," Abdmachus said in a low voice. "It will have been in the basement and well protected, both by stone and wood and by unseen forces."

"True." The Prince felt grim and determined. He had spent a long time thinking, during the swift voyage from Ostia to the Eastern capital, and had come to some conclusions about his adversary and the strength he would need to overthrow it. Any concerns about the propriety of looting the cellars of a dead antiquarian were of little interest to him. "There are no guards set to keep scavengers off, so any family that might have inherited it must be absent, uncaring, or nonexistent. Gaius?"

"Yes?" the older Roman said, turning away from his survey of the nearby buildings.

"Ask around—see if the property is for sale and for how much. If we can afford it, purchase it. Also, we will need lodgings nearby. Secure these. Krista and I will return to the port and see about getting our baggage ashore and dealing with Captain Ziusudra."

Gaius Julius watched in interest as the two youngsters hiked off down the street, arm in arm. He put a finger alongside his nose and sighed, thinking of the lost days of his youth. Water continued to dribble out of the sky. The clouds, if anything, were growing darker.

"Huh," he said, turning to the little Persian, "that leaves you and me to do the dirty work. I expected no less . . ."

Abdmachus looked back up at him, his eyes filled with concern. "How will we acquire the building? If there are relatives, it might take months to resolve a court case."

Gaius Julius smiled, fingering a heavy bag of gold *aureus* strapped to his belt. "No matter, my friend. I once worked with a man who made his living off burned buildings. I think I remember a thing or two. Come along, my fine foreign friend, and I will show you how the city fathers of Rome dicker over the ruins of someone's dreams."

"A substantial sum was owed on the property," Gaius Julius said in a pedantic voice, "in *taxes*. Some six thousand *aureus*, to be precise."

Maxian, sitting in a backless chair in his cabin aboard the *Nisir*, flinched a little at the sum. The elder Atreus had taken great pains to impress a traditional Roman penuriousness upon his sons. As a result, Maxian was loath to spend money, particularly large sums of it.

"And so? Will we have to dig in secret then?"

"Not at all," Gaius Julius said with a grin, "I was able to purchase the entire property for only four thousand *aureus*, not counting, of course, a substantial gratuity to the secretary of the city records. It seems that the house had a poor reputation when occupied and is positively unsalable now that it was destroyed in such odd circumstances."

"Those being?" Maxian had also heard a little of the story from the custom's office at the port. "That a dragon woke underneath the house and burst forth, spitting flame in all directions before flying off to the east?"

Abdmachus coughed, then covered his face with his hand. He seemed to be laughing.

Gaius Julius glared at him and put a leather satchel on the edge of the table. "Not a dragon, my lord, but rather a wizard, I believe. I spoke with two young men who had been servants in the house, and they agree that a mysterious visitor from the East had been a guest of their master, this Bygar Dracul, right before the explosion and fire. I suspect that our Persian ally's friend had been negotiating with the enemy . . ."

Maxian stared at the roof of the cabin for a moment, collecting his thoughts.

The little room was warm with the heat from an iron stove built into one wall. Krista had packed all their belongings and was just finishing folding all the blankets and quilts that made the bed built into the opposite wall. He was distracted for a moment, watching her fold and stow the bedding. Her hair was tied back and fell to the small of her back. Her hands were quick and sure. He realized that he did not feet the heavy pressure against his mental defenses that marked his time in Rome.

"These servants, where are they now? We will need to question them."

Gaius Julius smiled again and stepped to the door of the cabin. He rapped sharply on the frame. "I understand from them—they are foreigners and a little hard to follow, but I managed—that they sort of *come with the property*. So I told them that they have a new master. Really, they are quite happy about it, though not so happy as the land secretary. When I told him that a priest of Asklepios was moving into the house, he was ecstatic. I think he had put too much credence in all this talk of a curse."

The door opened, swinging out on polished brass hinges, and two young men entered the room, stooping to pass under the low frame. They were lean looking, with long stringy dark hair and bushy eyebrows. They wore dark tunics the color of freshly broken slate, with bracelets of silver on their left arms. The taller one, with deep-set dark brown eyes, stood a little forward. His fellow looked nervously around the cabin, hunching down a little, his pale white hands clasped in front of him.

"Master," the tall one said, kneeling on the deck and bowing his head to the floor, "we are overjoyed to enter your service."

Maxian sat up a little, a feeling tickling at the back of his head. The eyes of the two young men were marked with pain. He could feel, as he had felt the agony of men in a military hospital, some anguish upon them.

"Welcome," he said, standing from behind the desk. He walked to the side of the first servant and lightly touched the long shank of hair that fell down the man's back. "You are in pain?"

"Yes, master," both servants said, bowing to the decking, their breath a soft hiss.

"Perhaps I can ease it," the Prince said, feeling the eddy and current of their disease brush against his outstretched hand.

"What are your names," he asked, "and where do you come from?"

Krista finished packing the last of the blankets away and sat down on the bed, yawning.

THE GREAT CAMP, SAMOSATA

)•(

Dust puffed from under his feet as Dwyrin settled himself a few yards from the archery butt. His skin was a deep brown under the peeling scraps that remained on his arms and neck. Six thin gashes lay on his back, still swollen a little. A constant itching ran at the back of his mind. Like Odenathus and Eric he wore a plain white cotton tunic, stitched only at the hems, and plain tan wool breeches. His hair, now pale rose-colored straw under the sun, was bound back at the base of his neck and held by a thin dark band of leather. He squinted against the wavering sky. Two weeks now had passed under the heavy sun of the alluvial plain. Of Zoë's "five," in truth there were only four.

War was in the wind, though no Persians had been sighted anywhere near the city or the camp. Dwyrin had not left the inner camp, but he had heard Blanco and the tribune discussing the extension of the great ditch that bounded the encampment and the raising of many new tents. The senior wizards' faces grew longer with each heat-filled day. Yet the trainees were told nothing. Instead Blanco had drilled them in minutiae.

Before light the four rose each day, and Blanco ran them for an hour around the inner camp in endless repetition. Each had to match the centurion's stride, no more or less. Dwyrin's legs were barely long enough, but he knew that Zoë and Eric struggled to make the pace. Needless, Zoë never spoke of it, and always finished in her place as file-closer behind him. Her rasping breath she kept to herself. Eric moaned theatrically after each run and would often fall to his knees at the entry to the mess tent, begging for water. Blanco ignored him while he did not shirk but was quick with a fist or hobnailed boot for any who fell behind.

Days passed in stick drill; Blanco disallowed them bladed weapons.

"Swords are not for children," he would opine, smirking, and ignore the venomous glances of Zoë. "Better that you master the simple shepherd's staff than the gladius."

Regardless, Dwyrin fell into bed covered with bruises and aching to his bones. Colonna came by seldom, but when he did, his tongue was as sharp as ever. Here in the camp, he seemed to Dwyrin larger, less etched by fear, but the Hibernian's senses were dulled with fatigue and constant pain.

Blanco ordered them to the archery range set on the north side of the inner camp, just under the ramped embankment and palisade that marked the edge of the sorcerer's domain. Here a fifty-foot-long strip was cleared and marked at the eastern end by a mound of dirt and a stack of hay bales. Before each bale a stout wooden frame stood, banded with heavy wood. As Dwyrin had approached, he saw that the wood was deeply scored and riven. Glints of metal flashed at him from deep in the boards.

Sweat beaded his brow and he turned a few feet from the boards and faced the end of the archery throw. At the far end, Blanco raised a simple short bow, no more than a curved stave bound with gut and sinew.

"Hai!" the centurion called, and drew a raven-fletched arrow to his cheek. Dwyrin stood still by the butts, eyes unfocused. Two days now, the four had watched the flight of arrows for hours. Flicker-quick, the arrow snapped from Blanco's hand, hissing a foot past Dwyrin's ear. The Hibernian expanded his sight, seeing all things with equal acuity, and felt the shining trail of presence that the arrow left behind.

Blanco drew back another shaft to his bearded cheek. Dwyrin could feel the tension in the string, the clenching muscles in the centurion's hand. He backed off, seeing, feeling less. The centurion's voice echoed behind his ear. *Seeing everything is worse than seeing nothing, you must only see that which is important.* The hand released and copper-headed death blurred into enormity. Dwyrin flicked it aside with a brush of curling cyan, hot morning air given shape and power from the swirling currents of smoldering power in the air and stones.

Odenathus clapped his hand on his shoulder at the far end of the range. Blanco drew again and loosed. The arrow blurred in the air, but Dwyrin could catch the fletching spinning as the shaft leapt toward him. Again Dwyrin flexed the rivers of power that spun between him and the arrow, driving it into the soil four feet away. He grinned, and flinched back as Blanco drew and fired four in quick succession.

The Hibernian skipped aside, cursing, as three of the four whipped through the space he had occupied. One lone shaft he had deflected into the posts of the guard tower at his right. He was sweating worse now.

"Again," Blanco called from the shooting stand, "and Eric will stand with you."

At night, one of the Hippocratii bound their wounds and patched the nicks and cuts drawn during the day's training. The tribune and Blanco, by turns, drilled them on the myriad details of the Legion. Dwyrin fell asleep each night exhausted and worn. Around him a growing host of tens of thousands of men also fell into their cots and blankets blind with fatigue. The two Emperors were not letting idleness dull the edge of the gathering army.

NEARBY THE HOUSE OF THE
BYGAR DRACUL, CONSTANTINOPLE

Smoke still curled up from fires hidden deep in the rubble. A wasteland had been cleared around the ruined building, the fire-damaged *insulae* torn down and the entrances to adjoining buildings bricked up. Gray clouds hung low over the city, sending down a fine mist of rain. The wind from the north was chill and blew the trails of smoke away. Three hooded figures in long dark woolen cloaks climbed over the rubble, careful to test their weight on any new footing. Behind them a few civil guardsmen looked on momentarily but soon lost interest and passed away into the narrow alleys of the city. The lead figure, shorter than the others, halted and stared down into a stairway choked with fallen beams and ash.

"Here! I feel something below, some pattern out of joint."

The other two scrambled across the cracked brick and tortured stone. A great heat had crushed the concrete pillars that had supported the house to grainy white ash. The footing was treacherous, but they reached the side of the first figure without incident. The second figure knelt by the side of the pit and ground the gravel of the flooring between gloved fingers. The edge of a blue and green mosaic peeked out at him, but when he touched one of the tiles, it disintegrated into powder. Another edge of the floor was warped and translucent, almost like glass.

"Find workers who will not tell any stories," the kneeling man said to the third figure. "Excavate this stairway. There are tunnels and rooms underneath that may have escaped the destruction. I trust you will be as discreet as you can."

The third figure nodded and turned away. The two at the stairhead watched him go. When he was out of earshot, the second man turned back the cowl of his robe and looked up into the gray, troubled sky. Rain spattered on his face and he welcomed it. The cool rain was a blessing. Water trickled through his short beard, newly grown in. He wiped it from his eyes.

"You have done well," he said to the first figure, which bowed deeply. "My servants tell me that you and your people can be discreet. I have great need of discreet men to help me. Also, they have explained your precarious situation to me. If you are loyal, this too can be alleviated."

The first figure bowed, folding his gloved hands before him. "These are fine words, Prince. If they are true, we will be greatly in your debt. Forgive my bluntness, but our history is filled with betrayal and treachery. We do not trust easily."

The Prince nodded; he had expected no less. He reached into the pouch at his belt and drew out a gold coin pierced by a chain. He held it out in his open palm. "Trust must be earned by both sides. Give me an opportunity to earn it of your people and I will not disappoint you. Tell this to your elders."

The first figure nodded again. Its gloved hand passed over the Prince's palm and the coin and the brass chain were gone.

"If they wish it, I shall come to your lodgings and bring you news. If they do not, you will not see me again."

The Prince made a half bow and the hooded figure climbed off over the ruins, its step light on the tumbled piles of rubble. After the figure was gone, Maxian drew his hood back over his head. He was tired and the rain was beginning to chill. He sat down on a nearby block of scarred marble. In the air around him he could feel the incredible rage and the staggering efflorescence of fire that had destroyed the house. Something mighty had walked here, albeit momentarily, and wreaked great destruction. His fingers twitched at the thought of that kind of power. Then he sighed. A vaster power was arrayed against him; the thing that had transpired here had been the conflict of men, not the doings of something so enormous it might as well be a god. He buried his head in his hands. He was so weary.

Krista crushed a handful of shiny leaves, green on the top and gray on the bottom, in the bowl of a mortar. A sharp aromatic odor rose from the bowl. Satisfied that they were well bruised, she spilled them into a pot of hot water that was hissing at the edge of the fire. The smell bloomed in the boiling water and filled the little kitchen. She smiled at it; it reminded her of Thira on a cold morning. She assembled a platter of fresh heavy bread and soft cheese while the leaves steeped in the bubbling water. Outside, a cold rain continued to fall, filling the central garden of the house with pools of water.

Maxian was in the back room, christened the "study," for it was filled with spoils from the ruined house across the street. Renting the whole building had been easy, since the disastrous fire and the strange doings that had preceded it, the entire neighborhood had fallen under a pall. Many of the local people had moved on, leaving an unanticipated windfall of cheap housing for the secretive band of Westerners who had moved in.

Of all the things that Maxian had commanded of the little Persian, the excavations of the smashed house of the Valach merchant pleased Abdmachus the most. Once given a free hand, he had fallen to it with a will, showing off skills learned as a boy in the ghoul-haunted canyons of Petra. Even now, in the rain, he was down in the tunnels under the ruin, driving his men onward. A steady stream of messengers trickled back across the street at odd hours, bringing blackened crates, boxes, and unidentifiable scraps to be piled in the ground-floor rooms. Tiny old women—Krista knew not where Abdmachus had found them—picked through the detritus, gently prizing apart melted glass and burned paper.

At the sight of the Persian's energy, Gaius Julius had laughed. "Once a grave robber, always a grave robber!"

Maxian barely looked up from the pages of the ancient scroll he was poring over when she came in. His face was paler, as he spent nearly all of his time inside or in the black pits across the street. His features were more sharply defined, his bones rubbing against the skin. She placed a cup of the infusion next to him but away from his elbows, for he had developed a tendency to bump into things with-out looking. She settled into the couch by the window and peered out into the gray day. The other buildings, even the great bulk of the palace to the southeast, could barely be made out. The city was wrapped in fog nearly all of the time. The fires of the Avars besieging it did not better the air; even on a clear day there was a haze cutting the sun.

"Lord Prince, you should drink something hot. There is a chill in the air."

Maxian blinked and looked up. It took a moment to focus on her, but when he did, he smiled and leaned back in the high-backed chair. "Oh! Thank you. Is there any . . . oh, and cheese!"

Now that he had realized that he was hungry, he fell to with a will, eating all of the bread, cheese, and olives in oil. When he was done, he looked around again and sighed. He sipped at the infusion. It was tart to the tongue and stringent to the nose. He felt his head clear and only then realized that he had been working in a muddled daze.

Krista had come to stand by him and was turning the pages of the scroll. "Is this important?" Her voice was dubious.

Maxian looked over and laughed. "No, most likely not. It is an account of a Chaldean architect named Varus Trisgesene. He was fond of mechanisms and clocks. These diagrams are those projects he hoped to build when he had the time, no more than notes, really."

Krista turned one of the pages upside down, then right-side up again. "He wanted to build a bat?"

Maxian peered at the page; parts of it were smeared where water had spoiled it.

"I think," the Prince said, turning the page sideways, "that he was dissecting bats to see what they looked like inside."

Krista scowled at that and returned to the couch.

"Have you found what you were looking for?" Her voice was even, but Maxian knew that this life of hiding was wearing on her. There was little for her to do. He paused, thinking. *She is a spy*, he thought, *but who do I have to spy on?* He suddenly felt as if he were on the verge of making a dreadful mistake.

"Ah," he said, putting the thought aside, "no. We came here to seek passage into the East; to try to find the hiding place of the Conqueror's bones. I had hoped to find some clue to the workings of this Sarcophagus before we departed. This Dracul, who owned the ruined house, was an avid collector of old books and artifacts. Abdmachus hoped that he would be able to help us discover if the work-men who built the casket left any record."

"Was this Trisgesene one of the workmen?"

Maxian flushed. "No. I just came across his *Meditations* while looking through all of these books and began reading it. A waste of time . . ."

Krista frowned and stood up. The whole side of the study was lined with boxes filled with books, scrolls, and parchments recovered from the tunnels. Fire or water damaged many; others were in languages that no one recognized anymore. She put her hands on her hips and turned to look at him. "You'll have to read through all of these books before we leave?"

Maxian nodded, his mouth turned up at one end in a wry grin. "At least enough to see if they are pertinent to our search."

"Are they in Greek or Latin?"

Maxian was nonplussed. "Why?" he asked.

Krista pulled a box off the top of the center stack and carried it to the couch. She took the first book out of it.

" '*Seven against Thebes*,' " she read out loud, "by a Greek, Euripedes." She glanced up at the Prince, who was staring at her in amazement. "Get that silly look off your face. Of course I can read—both Greek and Latin. I'd be no good to my mistress if I could not read and write."

She tossed the play on the floor and took the next book out of the box. Maxian slowly folded up the *Meditations* and put it back in its scroll case. He didn't need a spy; he needed to think *clearly* again.

" '*The Second Book of Atlantis*,' " she continued, " 'or *A Cautionary Tale for the Credulous*, by Plato. Not, I believe, a goldsmith, carpenter, or embalmer."

Krista sighed and tossed another scroll into a big wicker basket that she had purchased in the market of the Bull. She dragged a heavy copper tube out of the next crate, wiping a thick slurry of ashy mud off the mottled green surface. The scroll was heavy and she shuddered when the weight sloshed from one end to the other as she hefted it. Rain had fallen heavily in the days since the fire, and many of the pits and cavities under the ruined house were deep with black water. She deposited the tube into the basket with a sickly look on her face. When she turned back to the window couch, she paused.

Abdmachus and eight of his workers were hurrying across the street with a large wooden crate on their shoulders. She could hear his voice echoing up from the street below. The workers passed out of her sight.

"Lord Prince," she said, turning to Maxian, who was in his accustomed seat, laboring to translate a long text inscribed in blocks of tiny hash marks. "The Persian has found something. They are bringing it into the house."

Maxian paused and rubbed his eyes. He focused enough to reach out and touch the Persian through the mark he had placed upon the Easterner. The little man was afire with excitement, even giddy. Maxian stood up and broke the linkage. It was disconcerting to feel the emotions of another flooding into his own thought.

The downstairs kitchen had a stout oaken table with massive legs. The workmen, grimy with the black ashy soot of the tunnels and pits of the ruined house, groaned with effort as they hoisted the heavy crate up onto the table and let it fall with a massive thump.

"Master! I think we've found something very interesting!"

Abdmachus was almost fawning, pulling at Maxian's sleeve to hurry him to the side of the table. The Prince frowned down at the little Easterner. Since he had put the mark on him, the personality of the Persian had begun to subtly shift. His aloof manner had completely disappeared, to be replaced with an almost unctuous servitude. He worked endlessly to execute the wishes of his "master," but

Maxian found that he now spent more time guiding the little man than he had before. He wondered if he could revoke the mark, but found to his distress that he did not know how.

The crate was almost seven feet long, made of clapboard and pegs. Maxian recognized it as the detritus of some deliveries that had been made the week before. A lid had been tied to it with hemp ropes.

Abdmachus pulled a chair over and stood on it to begin untying them. "Master, if I am not mistaken, our efforts have borne glorious fruit! The man who owned the ruined house, the Bygar Dracul, was a man of many secrets—not least of which is friendship for Persia!—but among the treasures that he was said to have gathered to him is a most amazing construction." Abdmachus grunted with effort, but pushed the top off the crate. Looking inside, under the light of the lanterns hung from the heavy wooden beams of the ceiling, he hissed with delight.

"Oh, yes! Look, master, upon a masterpiece of the art!"

Maxian leaned over the table and peered into the crate. Within, still half encased in a matrix of sand, ash, and charcoaled wood, was the body of a man, or something that looked like a man. The Prince touched the side of the corpse's neck and was surprised to find the skin still flexible and even soft. Then his fingers touched a ridged line along the thing's neck and he whistled in surprise himself.

"Oh, yes, master—a work of marvels!" Abdmachus rubbed his hands together.

"What is it?" Krista stood on the other side of the table, with Gaius Julius. She looked upon the body in the crate with ill-disguised revulsion. It was not pretty. The skin had become a sallow yellow-green with dark patches and bruised traceries in the translucent skin. The hair on the head was matted and plastered to the skull. The remains of a dark-colored cloak and tunic clung to the limbs and torso, or such that was visible within the crumbling mud that still cradled it.

"Lady, it is a homunculus!" Abdmachus' voice was breathy with delight. "The most useful of conjurations! A man made of the limbs and organs of the dead, but given new life by sorcery. See, his skin . . ."

"Stitched together," said Maxian, who had broken the right arm free from the earth and extended it. His face was close to the mottled skin, so that he could make out the fine lines of skin that had been sewn together to hold the organs of the creature. "It must have taken months to construct such a thing." He laid the arm down, and it hung limply over the edge of the table, the fingers still clutched into an agonized claw.

"Gaius, Abdmachus, help me remove it from this clay and ash. Krista, bring warm water from the fire, and cloths." Maxian began to break the clods away from the body.

An hour later the body of the homunculus lay naked on the table. The charred tunic and tattered boots had been cut off it, and Maxian and Gaius Julius had washed the remainder of the dirt away. The body was of a man with craggy features and a high forehead. His arms were long, and his legs a little short for his torso. The trunk of the body showed the signs of ancient wounds, long ago scarred over. Its hair was lank and dark, not quite coming to the shoulder.

"It must have been on one of the upper floors of the house when the explosion came." Abdmachus was sweeping the dirt up and piling it back into the crate, which had been pushed to one side of the kitchen. Outside, night had fallen fully on the city.

"We found it when we broke into the bottom of a chimney. It was there, packed into the bottom of the shaft, with rubble above it and deep in mud. I could feel it, though, even through the brickwork, like a dying flame. It might have been able to crawl out, if its master had not died in the fire."

"And," Gaius Julius said, "why do we care that the household was frequented by a walking pincushion?"

Abdmachus glared at the Roman. "Such a creature is well made for discreet errands, friend. It would be privy to many of the secrets of the house. If it could speak again, it could tell us much of its master's business—perhaps even what we want to know. It may be centuries old. Ah, the things it has seen . . ."

Maxian leaned over it, his hands gently exploring the face, the throat, the rib cage. Gaius Julius sat down on the steps leading up to the rear kitchen. Krista was sitting there as well, her face pale. She moved away to the other end of the step. The dead man affected not to notice. The Prince began to hum a little tune, and in a moment there was a basso response from the stones of the floor. Then it stopped. Maxian looked up, his eyes unfocused. When they cleared, he cocked his head at Gaius Julius.

"I can restore this thing to life. Bring me blood, fresh blood. At least a gallon."

The dead man's eyes widened. The look on the Prince's face was inscrutable, a mask.

"Ah . . . blood? What kind of blood?"

Maxian smiled at the fear in the eyes of the dead man. "Pig's blood will do, Gaius Julius. But be quick, there is much work to be done."

The dead man left, taking a copper bucket from the little kitchen. Krista disappeared upstairs. Maxian sat down on the step and wrapped his cloak around him. It was cold in the ground-floor room. Abdmachus sat on the chair, staring at the homunculus, muttering to himself.

A fat blue spark jumped from Maxian's fingertips to sizzle on the cranium of the homunculus before it seeped into the flesh of the dead thing. The air wavered in a heat haze around the Prince as he bent over the body on the table, his hands held a knucklebone's distance away from the head. He chanted under his breath, an ancient invocation to steady the mind and guide the thoughts. Abdmachus was his anchor, kneeling at the base of the table within the circle that they had hastily drawn in chalk and silver dust. Blue-white lightning rippled in the air between the two sorcerers, wrapping the body of the thing in a corona of light. Its limbs twitched and spasmed. Maxian's voice rose into a shout as he funneled the power inherent in the air and bricks around him into the trembling form that he was drawing forth in the body of the dead man.

Suddenly, as that immaterial form coalesced into a shining perfect geometric shape, the body convulsed and the eyes, a bright yellow with red pupils, fluttered open.

"Aaaahhh!" The throat of the creature was dry and clogged with soot. It hacked and gasped for air. Maxian's gaze darted to Gaius Julius for a second, and the old Roman, his face a mask of disgust, leapt to the side of the table and turned the body over. Soot and water dribbled out of the thing's throat. Lightning crawled across the tabletop and burrowed into the body. With each burning entry, the thing howled and twitched. It began to breathe, its airway clear at last.

"The blood," Maxian snarled to Krista as Gaius Julius turned the body back over and held it down. It had begun to thrash and its strength, even weak from near dissolution, was immense. The old Roman's veins stood out in his forehead as he struggled with his full weight and strength to hold it down. Krista hesitated but then stepped to the edge of the table. She held a heavy bladder in one hand, bulging with liquid, and a hose made of pig intestine in the other. Her hand darted out and speared the tip of the hose into the thing's mouth. The head whipped from side to side as it screamed in agony.

Maxian's hands seized the sides of the head, holding it still, though the neck muscles bunched and he was nearly thrown aside. Krista, her face an impassive mask, shoved the hose deeper into the thing's throat. It bit at her, and Maxian's fingers dug into the corners of its eyes. It shook again, its feet frantically beating a tattoo on the tabletop. Krista squeezed the bladder under her right arm and the hose filled with a thick red fluid. The blood surged into the mouth of the homunculus and filled its throat. Its screams were cut off by a horrible gargling noise, and blood spattered out of the mouth. Krista lunged in, her face twisted in disgust, and snapped the jaw up with one hand, while the other kept the hose from flying out of the mouth. Gaius Julius cursed; pig's blood had sprayed across his face and chest.

The Prince's fingers danced in the air above the corpse, and the flesh around the mouth suddenly crawled together around the hose, fixing it tight. Krista put her hand over her mouth and staggered back, overcome at the sight. Gaius Julius, lying fully athwart the corpse, gagged and turned his head away. Satisfied that the hose would not come loose, Maxian's fingers sank into the bone and sinew around the skull, and the thing, with one last convulsion, lay still. A white-hot glow spilled from the thing's eyes for a moment, and then the Prince withdrew his fingers, the bone melting back into place where there had been gaping holes a moment before.

Gaius Julius rolled off the bloody body and fell heavily onto the stone floor. He began retching in great heaving motions. Against the wall, Krista was huddled, her face in her hands. Only the Prince and Abdmachus still stood. Maxian laid a hand, gently, on the side of the homunculus's throat. The flesh peeled back away from the hose and it slid out onto the tabletop, dribbling a last bit of blood. The creature breathed then, in a great shudder, and its eyes flickered open. Red pupils stared up, meeting Maxian's calm brown eyes.

"Greetings," the Prince said, the ghost of a smile on his face. "I am your new master."

The thing threw its head back against the tabletop, but this time no sound issued from its mouth, only a long dry hiss of despair.

· · · ·

A light tapping came at the door of the kitchen that led out into the garden at the center of the house. Gaius Julius looked up from where he was tiredly mopping up the pools of coagulated blood and offal that covered the stone floor. The tapping came again. He could barely make out, through the mottled glass pane that was inset in the door panel, a white hand. He looked around. Everyone else was asleep upstairs, save the Prince and the Persian, who were questioning the homunculus in the study.

The dead man loosened his dagger in its sheath and walked to the door. He reached for the latch, but stopped.

There's no gate in the back wall, he thought. *How did they get into the garden?* Then he shook his head and laughed softly to himself. *I'm already dead, what do I have to fear?* He lifted the latch and swung the door open.

Three figures stood in the doorway on the pale-blue hexagonal tiles that covered the arcade around the garden. Their faces were shrouded in deep hoods of dark-green wool. A second cloak lay over their shoulders and dropped to their feet. The one in the middle leaned on a staff of pale-white ivory as tall as a man. A delicate white hand circled by thin bracelets of dark metal held the staff. Gaius Julius licked his lips in sudden unease. The fingernails of the hand were long and tapered to sharp points. The nails were a deep blue-black, like the carapace of an Egyptian scarab beetle.

"What . . . what do you want?" His voice was faint and he rallied suddenly. *Who was he to fear phantoms in the night? He, who had destroyed the power of the Druids? He, who had built an Empire?*

"We wish," the central figure whispered in a low, husky voice, "to have words, friendly words with the lord of the house. He has spoken to one of our friends. He gave a token."

The hand vanished into the deep folds of the robes and when it reappeared, it held a gold coin wrapped in the links of a brass chain of fine links. Gaius Julius nodded, his eyes narrowing. He took the coin and turned it over. The front was stamped with the image of the Augustus Galen, the obverse with a crude depiction of Maxian himself. *A commemorative*, the dead man thought.

"I'll take your message. Wait here."

The old man climbed the flights of stairs up to the third floor. Butter-yellow light spilled out of the study onto the landing. Gaius Julius stepped into the doorway. Within, the homunculus was seated on a stool at the center of the room, clad now in a simple tunic of muddy brown wool. Its shoulders were shrunken and its body seemed compressed in on itself. Maxian sat on the edge of the table he used as a desk, and the Persian was prowling around behind the creature. Krista was bundled up in a quilt and blankets on the window couch. Her eyes were closed and she seemed asleep, though Gaius Julius did not credit it for a moment.

"Lord Prince, there are . . ."

"We are here," came the husky voice from behind him, "as the Prince requested."

Maxian looked up in surprise, hearing the strange voice. Gaius Julius had jumped away from the door and spun, the dagger in his hand. A woman stood in the doorway, and the old Roman backed up as she entered. Two other women followed her. Maxian stood up, stepping away from the table.

The woman was tall, almost as tall as Maxian, with pale-ivory skin and deep-red hair, almost black, that fell behind her to her waist. A delicate net of silver held back the hair from her high forehead, and shining drops of ruby glittered at her ears. Her cloak and hood fell back from smooth white shoulders and revealed a black silk gown with buttons of white bone. She was as thin as a reed. Her lips were pale rose, and the beauty of her face was the more striking for the strength of her features. The Prince met her gaze and saw that her tilted eyes were so pale a blue that the iris was almost invisible in the white.

"You gave a token and a promise, O Prince," said the woman, gliding into the room. Under the hem of her gown, her feet were bare. "We have come to speak of it."

Maxian stood, his hands clasped lightly behind his back. The other two women still stood in the doorway, each possessed of a lush distracting beauty. One had hair like flax, golden and long, the other like a raven's tail, glossy and black. Their robes were slightly parted, and the Prince glimpsed the edge of white thighs and the curve of full breasts under tightly fitting silk. Beside their mistress, they seemed faint reflections of her full radiance. Pale stars to a moon bright in a night sky.

"So I did. Did the one carrying the token speak of my proposal?"

"That one did." The woman drifted to the table, her long fingers languid as they touched the scroll that was open. "You seek assistance in a mighty endeavor. We can give it, if I ken your purpose."

She turned back to face Maxian, her face lit from within by a slow smile. The Prince nearly shuddered at the promise radiating from those eyes. His breathing slowed and he flexed the power that was coming more easily to him with each day. In the unseen world, barriers rose around him, Krista, and Gaius Julius. A whirling sphere of unseen fire already surrounded Abdmachus, who had backed up to the wall next to the window couch.

The woman laughed, a sound of delicate crystal tinkling in a breeze. "O Prince, you seek alliance, or mastery. We will not fight you. You are too strong. If we cannot be friends then we will disappear, water before a blade. If we wish it, none can find us. That one who spoke before mentioned trust to you and you to that one. Do you wish to gain our trust? Our friendship?" She stood close to the Prince now, who had turned to keep her in full view.

"Can you earn my trust?" Maxian's voice was clear and steady, though the room had grown steadily darker. The two women at the door had entered now and stood on either side of it. The fire in the braziers had died to coals. Behind him, the Prince heard Krista move slightly in her blankets. "Can you earn my friendship?"

The woman bowed, her hands spreading in obeisance. Curls of her burgundy hair spilled over the white of her neck. "What is the price of a Prince's friendship? What would please you, O Prince? Gold? Jewels? Murder? Me?"

Maxian laughed softly, just enough to cover the sound of Krista hissing in anger behind him.

"I am not Antony," he said in an amused voice. "Trust and friendship are a long road, O Queen. A first step must be taken to reach the end. I will give you a gift, and you shall reciprocate. If each finds the gift appropriate and worthy, we will take a second step."

"Well said." The Queen's voice was mellow and filled with honey. "What will you gift us?"

"Respite from pain, O Queen."

The woman stepped back, her eyes flashing. Her lips curled in anger, revealing perfect white teeth. "What do you mean, man? What do you know of pain?"

Maxian stepped to the table and picked up a small black box that had been sitting next to the candles. He snapped it open, the only sound in the deathly quiet room, and drew out a small glass vial. In the light of the candles, the contents of the vial gleamed a murky red.

"I am a healer, O Queen, and know many arts. I felt the sickness in the one who spoke with me. I feel the pain that seeps along your bones like acid. This, if taken in moderation, can ease your pain for a full moon. In time, if we come to trust one another, I will provide you with the method of its manufacture."

The Queen stared at the vial with a cold expression, then turned away and paced to the door. "Friendship cannot come of slavery, O Prince. We will not walk that path with you."

There was a flutter of dark robes in the doorway, and Maxian caught a glimpse of the face of the blond one as they departed, looking back in sorrow.

The room was quiet, and Maxian felt the three women depart through the garden door. When they were gone, he breathed a long shuddering breath and leaned back heavily on the table.

"They have departed," he said to the room. "Gaius, go and close the garden door."

Abdmachus sat down on the floor and curled his arms around his knees. "Lord Prince, that was . . . that was a very close thing."

Maxian looked over at the Persian and one side of his mouth twitched up in a tiny smile.

"We are strong enough," he said. "We could have held them off for a little while. Gaius and Krista would not have been affected by their power."

There was a clicking sound behind him. As Maxian turned, he saw Krista sliding the spring gun back under the coverlet. She met his gaze with a solemn look, and then suddenly a smile lit her face.

"If you fancied her, Lord Prince," she said, "I would have killed you."

Maxian nodded and turned back to the homunculus, which had sat immobile in the middle of the room throughout the entire affair.

"So," he said to its impassive face, "you are the creature called Khiron . . ."

Slowly the head of the thing turned up and its yellow eyes met Maxian's.

"I am Khiron," it said in a rusty, dry voice.

"Who is your master, Khiron?" Maxian's voice was patient, as if he were speaking to a small child.

"My master is the Bygar Dracul," it said, though its features seemed puzzled.

Maxian leaned closer, staring into the flat reptilian eyes.

"The Bygar is dead," he said. "I am your master now. I am Maxian Atreus. I have given you life; I can withhold it as well. You serve me."

"I serve Maxian Atreus," it repeated back to him. Suddenly it twitched and stood up. Maxian backed away, folding his arms over his chest. He seemed pleased. The corpse man looked around, apparently aware for the first time. It surveyed the room slowly, pausing when it saw Abdmachus and Krista. Its gaze returned to Maxian. "You are my master."

"What do you remember, Khiron? What was the last thing that you saw?"

The homunculus paused, the muscles under the translucent skin bunching around its jaw. The sight of them sliding under the gelid skin filled Krista with a particular revulsion. This thing was like a skinless snake, abominable to look upon. She stole a glance at the Prince, but he seemed filled with a great good humor to see his power at work, reviving this corpse from the dead. Under the coverlet, her index finger curled around the trigger of the spring gun. She knew that she could put the six-inch-long steel bolt through the side of his head, perhaps even straight through his ear. He would be dead in an instant. She knew that Gaius would die, a puppet with cut strings, and this Khiron creature as well. Only Abdmachus would be left to deal with. Her eyes slid to the Persian, but the sight of the dead thing walking and talking held him enraptured.

We have left the Western Empire, she thought. *Perhaps we are far enough away to escape the curse of the city. No, I must be sure that I will live.*

"I remember fire." The dead thing's voice was hollow and echoed with pain. "My master was speaking in the garden room with important visitors. I brought a boy for them to see; a precious little boy with hair of red gold. The dark one, he found the boy pleasing, he wished to purchase him . . . Then there were lights in the sky, and then fire, like the sun rising. Everything was aflame; I leapt into the dumbwaiter to escape. It was cold and dark there. Then the house shook and I was buried. Things fell and I could not move. I could not breathe. Water filled the shaft. It filled my mouth. It was dark."

The head of the creature slumped onto its chest. Its hands twitched with palsy. Maxian tipped its head back that he might see its eyes. They were half closed.

"Khiron, you have life again. You live. You walk, you talk, and you see and hear. I am your master, I command you to live again." A dark-blue gleam shimmered on Maxian's hand and faded into the side of the homunculus's face. The eyes opened, aware.

"Your old master knew many secrets, Khiron. You must have learned many things in his employ. Tell me these secrets and you will live. Tell me these things and you shall have blood to drink, fresh blood."

The head of the thing rose up, a hungry look upon its face. The yellow eyes were filled with fire at last, no longer dead and pale. "Blood?" it whispered. A hand clutched feebly at Maxian's sleeve. "Blood for me?"

"Yes," Maxian said, his voice soothing, "blood. Hot and still pulsing with the fever of life."

Khiron collapsed to the floor, bowing his head before the prince. "O master, please, give me blood and I will serve you always! Ask of me, and I will tell!"

Maxian looked down, his face lit by a kind smile. He caressed the knobby skull of the thing. "Did you ever hear your master mention something called the Sarcophagus of the Conqueror? An old thing, long thought lost."

Khiron twisted his head around and smiled up at the Prince, his teeth sharp and black. "Yes, master, many times. My old master desired it greatly—it was this thing, this coffin of gold and lead, that brought the dark one to my master's house."

Krista felt Abdmachus tense and looked over at the little man. The Persian was staring at the homunculus with a dreadful look on his face.

"Say on, good servant," Maxian said.

"O master, the Dracul knew many things—he was a strong wizard—but he yearned for great power like a Roman for gold. He collected secrets and sold them for things that would make him stronger. The dark one came desiring a boon, and the master, O he would give it. The dark one had the secret the master wanted. The dark one had seen the coffin of gold and lead. They had come to arrange the exchange when the fire came."

Maxian held the homunculus's head between his hands. His voice was soft. "Where is the Sarcophagus, Khiron? What did your master learn?"

"O master, they sent me from the room! I only heard a snatch, only the tiniest bit of the speaking! Please, may I have the blood?" The voice of the creature was abject, begging. Maxian shook his head slowly.

"You must tell me," the Prince said, "then you may have blood, if I will it."

Khiron laid his head low and wept in anguish, tears of dust trickling down his cheeks. "Please, master, only a tiny sip, only a finger's worth!"

"What did you hear as you were leaving the room, Khiron?" Maxian's voice was harder now.

"I heard them only mention a place, master, some terrible place where no one could go and live. A city in the uttermost East. The dark one spoke of it, he named it Dastagird."

Abdmachus hissed in quiet surprise. To Krista's eye he seemed more fearful than ever.

"Good, good, Khiron," the Prince said. He drew the homunculus upright. "You shall have blood. Abdmachus, fetch more of the pig's blood from the kitchen."

Abdmachus did not move, staring instead at the corpse man with a dreadful expression on his face.

"Abdmachus?" Maxian stepped toward the Persian, concerned.

"What . . ." Abdmachus' voice quavered, "what name did this 'dark one' bear?"

Khiron turned, slightly crouched behind the Prince. He smiled to see the fear in the living man. "My old master named him, fellow servant. He named him Dahak."

Abdmachus turned utterly white and his legs quavered and gave way. Maxian was at his side in an instant, holding him up. The Persian clutched at his arm with clawlike fingers.

"What is it?" Maxian was anxious, for the old Easterner was in poor color. "What is this Dahak? Krista, is there any infusion left?"

Maxian lay the old man back gently on the floor and put a pillow of rolled cloth under his head. Krista brought the last of the hot infusion over from the table and knelt, brushing her gown behind her, to pour a cup. The Prince tipped the thin porcelain cup to Abdmachus' lips. The old man drank gratefully. His veins stood out on his forehead and his skin was chalky.

"O master," he whispered, "that is a terrible name. The name of an old demon, steeped in centuries of evil. In the books of the dead, he stands high in the councils of the lord of all darkness, Ahriman. A man who would take such a name for his own must be a powerful sorcerer. I had begun to fear that something very strong had been in the house across the street. Echoes of it are in the broken tile and bricks of the center of the house, like a foulness had taken root there."

Maxian looked down on the little sorcerer, his face tender. His fingers pressed the side of the Persian's neck, feeling his pulse race intermittently. "Fear not, my friend, you will not die. You need rest, though, and sleep. You have been working far too hard. I will complete what you have begun. Tell me this—where is this Dastagird? Is it far away? How long would it take to reach this place?"

Abdmachus sighed, his voice faint with pain and exhaustion. "Dastagird is the stronghold of the *magi*. It lies along the banks of the great river Tigris, barely twenty miles north of the Persian capital of Ctesiphon. It is a closed city, entered only by the mobehedan and their servants. Once, when I was very young, I was taken there to be initiated into the order, but all I remember are towering buildings of black basalt and green soapstone."

"Ctesiphon . . ." Maxian stood up and motioned for Gaius Julius and Krista to bring blankets and quilts for the old man. "Still very far away. We must make haste." He scowled. "Curse this war of my brothers! If there were peace upon the land, we could travel swiftly." He began muttering to himself.

THE HILLS ABOVE SAMOSATA

"Left!" shouted Eric, ducking away from a spinning disk of blue fire. The disk caromed off the rocks on the hillside and crashed into a scrubby tree. The juniper burst into flame, throwing long flickering shadows across the twilight-shrouded hill. Dwyrin, following the other boy's lead, weaved uphill between the boulders. His right hand tugged at the air and the juniper roared higher, burning to a white ash in moments. Fire, curling into spheres, darted away from the skeleton of the tree and hurtled downhill at the half-seen figures of the other cohort.

White light vomited up, briefly outlining a sphere of glittering green. Dwyrin felt a shock through the working he had sent out and stumbled against the crumbly stones. Eric halted, his young face drawn in concentration. The Hibernian clutched at the sharp-edged rocks, feeling blood ooze from his fingertips. With the pain came focus, and he could suddenly see the jagged byplay of powers that rippled and strobed in the air over the hill. Downslope, three separate groups of lights moved, darting from stone to stone. As one group moved, another laced the air above them with invisible lightning. Jagged white tendrils leapt from rock to rock, covering the advance.

Eric staggered, his shield taking the side blast of one burst. Dwyrin gulped, remembering that he was supposed to be covering too. Furiously he tried to calm his mind and add his own intent and will to the ragged, incomplete shield that the Northerner was sketching between them and the onrushing attackers. It seemed agonizingly slow work, not like drawing power from the flame of the tree. Bit by bit the Shield of Athena wavered into being between him and the men scrambling through the field of volcanic debris.

Another flare of light lit the sky, and a twisted flute of spongy black rock blew apart not fifteen feet from them. A cloud of fragments scythed out, smashing the delicate web of the shield Eric had thrown up. Dwyrin gasped in pain, feeling a sliver of rock slash across his cheek. He leapt forward in front of Eric, arm thrown up, and the hail of stones suddenly crashed to a halt against a shimmering wall of fire. Bits of broken rock rained down, smoking and bubbling, to clatter on the ground.

"Up! Up!" He dragged at Eric's arm, throwing it over his shoulder. The other boy was bleeding from cuts on his face and arms. Dwyrin jogged forward with the Northerner stumbling behind. The air hummed with power. More tiny stones pattered down out of the darkening sky. They had been about these exercises, as Blanco was fond of terming them, since the sun had risen over the grimy, fly-infested plain. North of the camp, a long low row of hills rose up. They were only barely covered with scrub and cactus and spindly trees. The stones and rocks were crumbly and porous. Some you could crush into dust with your bare hand. Others cut like flint, showing deep-green colors in their serrated surfaces. They were an evil place.

The tribune, then, was fond of sending his troopers out to exercise their powers among them. Today, starting with the dawn, Zoë's four had been sent out as prey for the journeymen in the other cohorts. It had been a long-drawn-out affair. The four youngsters had flitted among the dry washes and narrow, boulder-choked canyons for hours. At Zoë's order, they had damped their powers down to a mute whisper. Zoë and Odenathus were at home among the spiny plants and sandy drainages, flitting invisibly from draw to draw. Eric had suffered in the heat, and Dwyrin had not done so well himself. The air itself drained them, hot and dry. Still, thanks to Zoë, they had eluded capture for a long time.

Now they had run out of places to run. The night air trembled with a dull rumbling.

Dwyrin pushed Eric ahead of him, feeling the hair on the back of his neck stand up. They staggered down a gravelly slope, their feet slipping and sliding. Pale ghost images followed the movement of their pumping arms and legs. Dwyrin's ears hurt. The sky lit with blue-green fire.

•   •   •

"Let's take a walk."

Dwyrin rolled over on his bunk, his stomach seething with a horrible burning feeling. Zoë stood over him, her dark hair falling over her shoulder in an open-weave pattern. He squinted at the coarse canvas wall of the tent, feeling bile at the back of his throat. The leader of their four had a grim look on her face, enhanced by the bandage tied with twine to the side of her temple. Groaning inwardly, the Hibernian tried to roll back over, his forearm thrown across his face.

Zoë hissed in anger and rapped his knees sharply with the short wooden baton she carried as part of her equipment. Dwyrin flinched and turned over, coming up onto his feet. Zoë stared up at him with her head a few inches below his own.

"We walk, barbarian, and we talk." She pushed him ahead of her out of the tent. Behind them, Eric continued to snore, his arms swathed in gauze bandages soaked in honey.

The camp was busy. The sun was well set over the curve of the world and the heat of day was past. A cool dimness lay over the long rows of tents, and nightjars and bats filled the air, feasting on the swarms of insects that thronged around the lanterns hung from tall poles along the beaten dirt avenues. With the deadening heat gone, everyone was out and about. Voices filled the air. The streets were filled with men coming and going. From the far end of camp, there was a sound of drums and flutes coming from the encampments of the *auxillia*.

Zoë walked quickly uphill from the tents that the thaumaturges maintained. A low hill butted against one end of the camp, surmounted by a watchtower of fieldstone and wooden uprights. Dwyrin walked behind her, his mood sullen, dragging his feet. At the tower, there was a gate of wooden slats. Zoë nodded to the trooper standing watch. He unlatched the gate and she slipped out. Dwyrin swallowed and followed after her.

The hill was rounded and covered with scattered rocks and thorny bushes. The Palmyrene girl wound her way down the far side, far enough to escape the light leaking from the camp, but not so far as to be beyond sight of the top of the tower. She found an outcropping of stone and sat down. Dwyrin remained standing, staring off into the darkness, his hands clasped behind his back. Zoë sighed and leaned back on her hands, looking up at the dark sky. It was filled with eddies of stars, a scattering of twinkling jewels. The night air was cool and clean against her face.

"You trouble me, MacDonald." Her voice was clear and level. Dwyrin flushed.

"You're strong—as strong as Odenathus or I, yet you haven't the control of a first-year apprentice. You're quick, but quick to make a godless mess. You can summon fire from dead stone, but you take an age to draw the simplest ward. Never have I seen someone work so hard at this and fail so miserably to master their craft."

Dwyrin stumbled a little at the biting tone in the girl's voice, and then he sat down too.

"In single combat, you can give the journeymen and even some masters a run for their money—but fighting in a five, as we *must* if we are to survive on the field of battle—you're a menace or worse. You and Eric were dead a dozen times today—all because *you* cannot seem to get the concept of teamwork through your fat barbarian head."

Zoë paused, pursing her lips and then letting out a slow breath. There was a *tick-tick* sound on the rocks as she absently drummed her baton against the stone. "Centurion Blanco asked me today, after the tribune was finished grinding my head off with a mill wheel, if I wanted to send you to another five. Some capricious god must have stolen my thought, because I told him that I would take care of the problem."

Dwyrin shivered, feeling the smooth cold surface of the baton come to rest on his neck.

Zoë leaned close. Her could feel her breath on his forehead. "You're a donkey, MacDonald, fit only for simple tasks. But by Hecate, you are *my* donkey and I will see how much weight you can carry. You will learn to fight with us. You will learn to be effective. If not, then I will dispose of you myself. Do you understand me?"

Dwyrin nodded, then felt her move away in the darkness. The sound of her sandals crunching on the soil and gravel of the slope stayed with him for a time. He stayed on the rock, feeling the night close around him. Tears dripped down his face and he fought back a sniffle. He was sixteen years old, old enough to take this. Stars wheeled overhead, full and bright in the clear desert air.

A wagon wheel trembled in the air. Unsupported, it wavered back and forth in the clear space in front of the cohort tents. Dwyrin and Eric stood on either side of the wooden disk, their eyes closed. Sweat was streaming down the Hibernian's face, matting his thin tunic against his chest. Eric was not doing much better; his chubby fists were clenched hard at his sides and he was breathing heavily. The wheel rose up another three handspans, then began to rotate drunkenly. Dwyrin felt the heavy wood and iron slipping from his mental grasp. He bit his lip, putting forth his will, trying to stabilize the disk.

It swung back toward him as he took on the weight of it himself. Eric staggered forward, one hand rising. The wheel suddenly sped up and whipped through the air at Dwyrin's head as the Northerner lost control of it.

Dwyrin cried out, seeing the wheel spin at him, and *pushed* back hard, trying to keep it from him. The wheel reversed course, flipping over in midair, and shot back across the little square. Eric leapt aside, arms windmilling and his eyes wide in fear. The wheel tore through the row of tents behind him with a ripping sound and smashed into the side of a wagon. Dwyrin sat down heavily, sweating, and buried his face in his hands. He was trembling.

"So," said a grim voice from above him. "No luck with the wheel exercise either."

Dwyrin scrambled to his feet and stood up, facing the centurion. For a change, Blanco did not have an expression of furious anger fixed on his face. Instead, there was a resigned look tinged with something close to pity. Zoë stood behind the centurion, her head barely coming to his shoulder. Her eyes were very grim, and her face was drawn. Dwyrin swallowed but said nothing.

"Lad, you've got to learn to work with another sorcerer." Blanco's voice was even. He motioned to the wrecked tents and the soldiers peering out of them in alarm.

"This exercise is simple, very simple, not much more than doing the weave. Just lift it up together and make it spin. It's a wheel, for Mithra's sake, it *wants* to spin."

"The, ah, the weave, sir?" Dwyrin felt like his head had been clubbed with a hammer.

"Yes, MacDonald, the weave—you know, like in school?"

Blanco stopped, his eyes narrowing, watching the incomprehension on the boy's face.

"Like, say"—he paused, searching for the right word—"like *platting the twishers*? Is that what they call it in your homeland? Or—ah, what do they call the weave in Palmyra, Zoë?"

"The weave, sir. Just the weave." Zoë's voice was clipped and biting. She was not pleased.

"I don't know, sir, I've never heard of that." Dwyrin felt a little light-headed.

Blanco leaned close, taking a good look at his newest recruit for the first time. He realized that he had been lax, leaving the newest sorcerers to their five-leaders. He had seen the Hibernian boy for weeks now but had never taken the time to find out the boy's background or any details of his life at all. The centurion pulled at his ear, scratching at a scar that ran along it. Considering the boy now, he seemed younger than he had first thought. He hadn't even reached his full growth yet. He was muscular in a wiry sort of way, but he still carried a little baby fat. Blanco put his heavy fists on his hips. He had seemed a troublemaker when he first showed up, what with losing his horse and all, but . . .

"Tell me about your schooling, MacDonald. Which school, which master, everything about it. Which circle have you reached, what techniques did they teach you?"

Dwyrin gave him a sickly grin. No one had asked him anything about how he came to be in the Legion. They had just accepted his appearance and put him to work. Now, faced with the prospect of being turned out, he realized that he wanted very much to succeed here, to earn the respect of Eric and Odenathus, even Zoë. He squared his shoulders unconsciously and summoned the courage to look the centurion straight in the eye.

"Well, sir, a witch-hunter found me when I was eight years old . . ."

Blanco sat down heavily in his folding camp chair. He was a thickset man, with beefy thighs and arms like tree roots, so the bronze and wood chair squeaked alarmingly under his weight. The waxed cloth roof of the tent admitted a pale fraction of the sun beating down outside, but Zoë could see the other chair. She sat down too, though her weight did not test the fabric of the camp chair. The centurion's face was closed and she could not read his thought in his eyes. He seemed to be looking very far away. While she waited, Zoë tried hard not to fidget.

She had a terrible desire to start twirling the loose end of her hair around her finger. Despite this, she remained seated, her hands on her dark-brown thighs, waiting.

After nearly an hour, Blanco blinked and moved a little in his chair. He scratched the stubble on his chin and opened a wooden trunk at the base of his bed. He pulled a heavy skin out and uncorked it. Two battered tin cups followed, which he placed on the little map table, and he poured a measure of watery red liquid into each one. After stowing the skin, he downed one cup.

"Have a drink," he said, pushing the other toward her with a thick fingertip.

Zoë grimaced and downed the shot of flavored vinegar in one gulp. Her throat stung at the passage of the tart liquid. She put the cup back on the table. "Thank you, sir."

Blanco made a *humph* sound at that.

"So," he said, "what are you going to do with your troublesome recruit now?"

Zoë shrugged her shoulders. "I don't know. We'll have to start all over with him, I suppose. He hasn't received half the basic skills I thought he had—he hasn't even been exposed to things that the rest of us take for granted." She sighed, picking the cup back up and turning it over.

"It seems more than a little cruel to send him to the levy without any skills. I wouldn't have expected it of one of the Egyptian schools—they pride themselves on taking good care of their students."

Blanco nodded. "It could be worse—he could be missing a hand or an arm or even a thumb. Then, of course, we'd have had to take two of him . . . I think, five-leader, that the schoolmaster did send him to us to protect the rest of the students—the good ones, or the ones who are paying a pretty *aureus* to be trained in whatever fraction of the Skill they have. They thought they could spare this one."

"I suppose—he's just a kid, though! I shouldn't have been so hard on him."

Blanco laughed, saying, "Happens all the time, five-leader, so get used to it. The question now is what are you going to do with him?"

Zoë looked up, meeting the centurion's eyes. She didn't know what to do, and she was loath to admit that to her superior officer. After a tiny struggle, she shook her head. "I don't know. Have Eric work with him through the basics and hope that he won't be such a liability if we get into a fight."

"Why Eric?" Blanco squinted at her, his thin eyebrows crawling together over his nose.

Zoë looked back in confusion. "They're already a pair. Why should I break them up?"

"Because," Blanco said slowly, "Eric isn't a very good teacher. He's the second weakest of your five. He's the second most inexperienced . . . You should pair Dwyrin with your best thaumaturge. That way he'll learn faster and his weaknesses won't be so exposed."

Zoë grimaced. She had considered that and immediately rejected the idea. She and Odenathus were too good a team to break up.

"I can't spare Odenathus," she said, "we're comfortable together—we're close to feeling how the other thinks!"

Blanco guffawed. "Ha! I wasn't thinking of Odenathus—*you* need to take the Hibernian under your wing. Odenathus and Eric are like brothers already—they won't have any trouble meshing up. You're the five-leader, you take the responsibility and the work."

The centurion's voice was firm. Zoë knew that he had already made a decision and it was an order.

Eew! she thought. *Hours of tutoring the barbarian . . . he smells!*

"Yes, centurion," she said meekly.

You'll pay for this, MacDonald, she thought.

THE PALACE OF BIRDS, CTESIPHON

"The Great King comes! All bow before the *Shahanshah* of all Persia!"

Trumpets pealed, sending echoes fluttering down the vast hall that marked the center of the Imperial palace. There was a rustling like the wind over the sea as two thousand attendants, ambassadors, and noble lords knelt along the sides of the chamber. Long stripes of sunlight, falling through the windows set high above the floor, banded the multitude. The crowd was a gleaming mass of gold, red silk, brilliant azure feathers, and rich brocades. At the end of the hall a high seat rose on a pyramid of enameled bricks. The seat had a high back of lustrous pearl and a thick cushion of dark-purple velvet. Above it, suspended by silvered chains, was a heavy gold crown, set with pearl and emerald and Indian ruby.

On the second step of the four-stepped pyramid that housed the Peacock Throne, Kavadh-Siroes knelt as well. It was difficult, in the stiff brocade and heavy silk robes, but he managed. He did not like the ceremony that insulated his father, but there was little hope of changing it. The King of Kings loved the ceremonies and rituals like a child with a new toy. Anything that enhanced his glory and majesty pleased him.

The tramp of a hundred feet sounded from the far end of the hall. Siroes glanced up, peering out from under the brim of the heavy ornamental hat he was forced, by ceremony, to wear. A phalanx of dark-skinned men, each no less than six feet tall, preceded the King of Kings. They were dressed in burnished gold-scale armor, with helms of brass and silver that hid their faces. Their arms and legs were bare, showing mighty sinew and muscle. Each man held a tall staff before him, surmounted by a pennon showing the crest of the House of Sassan.

Behind them three lines of attendants gowned in linen and samnite advanced, alternating those who bore the cupped fire of the Lord of Light, Ahura-Mazda, and those who held small copper pyramids of smoking incense. Behind these, at last, came the wall of guardsmen—swordsmen from the Hindic kingdoms of India—in ornamented armor of interlocking plates that covered them from head to toe. Their metal shoes rang on the azure and crimson tiles of the floor. Each armored plate was scribed with signs of defense and victory in gold inlay. Tall plumes bobbed from their helmets. Only dark slits revealed the hidden presence of eyes. Each guardsman bore a blade of watery steel, held before him in a scabbard of tooled leather.

Siroes flinched to see his father. The Great King, Chrosoes, King of Kings of Iran, Shahanshah of the Persians, was carried forward on a platform raised on the shoulders of sixteen massive Ethiops. He wore a mask of gold, as had been his custom for the last nine years, exquisitely carved to emulate the features of the ancient Achaemaenid King Darius the Great. A beard of gold curled at his chin, and his eyes peered out from under cunningly crafted eyelids. His robes, a dazzling midnight purple in the finest silk, fell from broad shoulders. He wore a close-fitting tunic in gleaming white beneath them. He lounged on a smaller throne of ivory that sat amid a platform strewn with fresh-cut flowers. As he passed, the assembled court rose, filling the air with the rustling of their gowns, tunics, and robes. Behind the rear rank of guardsmen, four slaves in short cotton kilts walked, holding great palm-shaped fans that stirred the air for the King of Kings.

As the royal litter approached the dais of the throne, Siroes, like all the other great ones assembled on the steps, pressed his forehead to the floor. The attendants who accompanied the King of Kings peeled away as they approached the throne, until only the finest of the guardsmen ascended the steps and took up positions on the second step, each facing outward. Two pageboys scurried out from behind the pedestal and carefully unrolled a carpet from under the massive onyx-, ame-thyst-, and jewel-studded throne. The special carpet held dried, aromatic flowers within its roll, and the King of Kings stepped down on rose petals and the hearts of lilies. Chrosoes mounted to the throne, where he carefully arranged his robes and sat.

The trumpets pealed again, and there was the rattle of hidden drums. Gun-darnasp, the commander of the *gyanavsyar*, the Companions of the King, stepped forward on the lowest step and raised a cone of enameled brass to his lips.

"The King of Kings has come," he proclaimed, his voice echoing from the trumpet. "Great Chrosoes, he who bestrides the world like a Titan of old, receives you. Stand forward to seek his judgment, his mercy, his love!"

Siroes groaned inwardly and picked at the stiff collar of his raiment. It chafed and always gave him a rash. He hated to spend hours in the court—and there was no day of court that did not involve six or seven hours of standing, as still as could be managed, at the side of his father. He thought longingly of Barsine and the other concubines waiting in his quarters to ease his fears and while the time away.

Below, the embassy from the Prince of Samarkhand approached, swarthy men with deep blue-black-colored robes and hair swept back like a raven's wing. Siroes sighed; *this would take forever!* The vizier Khomane nudged him from behind, and the Prince straightened up, keeping his face impassive. The appearance of the court and the endless ceremonial that it engendered consumed a great deal of the Prince's time, yet all the wise heads agreed that it was absolutely necessary to reassure the people and the subject nobility of the strength and permanence of the Empire.

There was a final clash of cymbals and the last troupe of dancers fluttered off the raised platform at the center of the dining chamber in a cloud of feathers and trailing, translucent silks. Servants entered and began clearing away the silver and gold platters from the long tables that surrounded the platform on three sides. The fourth side fell away from the dining room through a wall pierced by many arches onto a long series of terraces. The gardens led down to the reflecting surface of the great square Lake of Paradise that Siroes' grandfather had ordered built. Now it was the domain of birds and fish and a thousand reeds. The gardens that occupied the terraces that marked the northern side of the palace were redolent with orange and jasmine and rose. The smell, when the wind turned over the lake, was heady and thick in the rooms along the border of the garden. Siroes drained the last of the wine, a Luristani vintage, and discarded the goblet—silver and ruby on bronze—under his couch. He smiled weakly at one of the serving maids as she passed, her arms laden with the heavy platters and goblets.

She failed to smile back, her attention focused on keeping the crystal glass and heavy gold flatware from toppling onto the floor. He frowned after her, then dismissed her from his mind. There were a thousand more women, each more beautiful than the last, at his disposal. He could choose as he pleased. He picked at the sweet grapes and sliced fruits garnished with sugar and honey that were on the low table before him.

"Bring the map of the world!" The gold mask lent a strange echo to his father's words. Siroes glanced up, his long dark eyelashes covering his eyes. He sniffed. His father was mounting the steps that led up to the platform of the entertainers. The heavy purple robes had been cast aside, showing the strong shoulders and forearms of the King of Kings. From behind one could see the leather straps that held the gold mask onto the King's face, that and his thinning hair. Siroes snapped his fingers and a slave, a Greek by his look, was quick to bring him a fresh goblet of wine.

Chrosoes looked up, his arms akimbo.

Above him, the ceiling descended—a vast disk of mosaic tile. Winches and pulleys groaned in the background and ropes squealed as they slithered through the workings of the apparatus. The center of the room, dominated as it was by the elevation of the platform, was matched in a stair-stepped ceiling with a circular center. Now that center descended and, as it did, it began to swing down until, at last, as it reached the level of the floor, it stood vertical, a great round disk thirty feet high. Above, the ceiling was revealed to house a hidden chamber filled with ropes and chains and diverse mechanisms. On the face of the disk, illuminated by many candles and lanterns that the other servants had quietly rushed forward to install, was a map of the entirety of the world, picked out in tens of thousands of tiny colored *tesserae*.

The great map was centered, as was held proper by the Lord of Light and man, upon the city of Ctesiphon, where the court of the King of Kings now sat. It stretched west to the rim of the known world, the Island of the Dogs on the endless ocean that the Roman named the Atlanticus. South, the wild coasts of Axum and Canoptis were lined with tiny pictures of terrible beasts and strange races of men. East, beyond India to Serica and Sinae, the map faded out into wastelands and jungles. North, high above the head of the King of Kings, the vast steppes of Scythia and the Hunnic lands ended in endless forest and snow. But at the center, where Chrosoes stood and spread his hands wide, the thousand cities, towns, and fortresses of Persia were carefully laid out.

"We stand on the verge of victory," the Great King proclaimed. "The Roman enemy has been defeated again and again. Our armies stand within sight of his capital. Our allies besiege his walls. The great Prince Shahin and the Lord Rhazates will soon sweep the coast of the Levant and seize Egypt from him. Without the grain of Egypt, Rome and Constantinople will starve."

A servant in the pale-tan robes of a scribe mounted the steps with a long pointing staff in his hands. He went to stand behind the Great King. Chrosoes paused, his hidden eyes sweeping the assembled generals, viziers, and Princes. His gaze paused for a moment on Siroes, who looked up guiltily from where he had been nibbling at a slice of candied meat. The Prince flushed, meeting the stern eyes of his father. The Great King's attention passed on and Siroes slumped back in his seat, relieved. *What can he want of me?* The Prince was constantly confused by the expectations of his remote and forbidding father.

"The harvest has been gathered, noble lords, and the enemy has at last moved against us. Recent reports from Shahr-Baraz at Chalcedon . . ." The servant raised the pointer to indicate the shore opposite the Roman city of Constantinople in the upper left quadrant of the map, where the Sea of Darkness and the Mare Aegeaum met in a narrow strait. ". . . indicate that the army of the thrice-defeated Emperor Heraclius, he who will be my vile and insensate slave, has departed with a fleet to the north, to cross the Sea of Darkness to land, doubtless, at the city of Trabzon." The servant moved the pointer east, along the long coast of northern Pontus to the eastern end of the Sea of Darkness.

"From this place the Roman dog can slink south through the mountains to attack us from the north. The Boar, most beloved of my generals, has already marched his Immortals east to the new city of Tauris on the lake of Matian." Now the pointer moved to the southeast, to where a lake had been depicted in blue and white, amid high mountains. A tiny symbol stood on the eastern shore, a city with red walls and domes. "Any advance of the Romans east from Trabzon must force a passage through Tauris. The Boar and his army wait for them."

"There are rumors that a Roman army has landed at Tarsus on the plain of Cilicia." The servant scurried to the left, moving the pointer to a bay on the eastern end of the Mare Internum, north of the Roman-held island of Cyprus. "My spies in the capital of the enemy suggest that this is a small army of Western Romans, led by the Emperor Martius Galen Atreus."

Chrosoes stopped, a bubbling chuckle escaping his lips and then thundering from the roof as he threw his head back in great humor and howled with laughter.

"Two Emperors will attend me," he shouted, "and be my slaves! There will be no ransom for them; they will live at my side, sightless, tongueless, for a hundred years! When they die, they will be decorations of the court. Embalmed by the finest craftsmen, their bodies shall be stuffed with spices and salt. They will bow before the throne of the King of Kings for all time! So shall all traitors and kin murderers be treated."

In his couch, Siroes shrank from his father's outburst. The King of Kings had been more and more given to fearsome display of late, leading his son to sequester himself more and more in his private chambers.

He is insane, Siroes thought mournfully. *My father is mad. How can I love someone who has become inhuman?*

"I see your eyes, I know that you are afraid! We have never held Rome so close to utter defeat. Never, even under the glorious reign of my ancestors, have we been poised to recapture everything, *everything* that the cursed Greek took from us! Three armies stand against us, but they are small, and weak, and widely separated. We have every advantage and will crush them each, one by one, and line the boulevards of my city with a forest of Roman skulls!"

Chrosoes paused and the echo of his shouting died in the high alcoves of the great room. The generals and viziers gathered before the platform stirred, their robes rustling. The Great King looked down upon them, and they were silent and looked away. Siroes looked up again, afraid, as his father's gaze settled to rest upon him at last.

"Great King," the Prince mumbled as he struggled to stand up. His knees were watery and he clutched at the heavy velvet of the couch arm. "O King of Kings, how . . . how will we defeat them? Only . . . only two of our armies are in the field. The Boar is far to the north, while Shahin is far to the south. If this Emperor Galen strikes from Antioch against the capital, there will be no one to stand against him."

The King of Kings, the light of the torches glinting off his golden face, gravely descended the steps of the platform. The nobles and viziers drew away from him silently, leaving a clear aisle to the figure of the Prince, who trembled slightly as he stood by the couch. Chrosoes stopped before his son and looked down upon him. Siroes felt pale and weak compared to the mighty figure of his father. Chrosoes was taller by a hand, and his shoulders were broad and his arms corded with muscle. Only the pale glimmer of his mask detracted from his physical presence. In his youth, his face had matched his clean-lined body. Now unwinking eyes stared down at the Prince.

"The Great Prince Shahin could march back to the capital, son of my first wife," the King said. "But then the rabble of the desert that stands against him would advance in his wake and find easy prey amongst the cities of the northern plain. The Boar could ride down from the north, with his ten thousand Immortals, and crush this invader, but then the Romans in the north would ravage the highland provinces." He laid his hand on his son's cheek. Under the permanent smile of the mask, his own lips stretched gruesomely to form a matching expression.

"Is not Persia the greatest empire in the world?"

The Great King turned, his gaze lashing the nobles, who shrank back from him. "Is not Persia the greatest Empire in the world!" His voice was a shout.

The nobles bowed, falling on their knees before him. Their voices echoed off the glassy smooth marble floor. "O King, Persia is the greatest empire in the world!"

Chrosoes nodded and chuckled. "Loyal subjects . . . raise a new army, the greatest army that the world has seen. Forty thousand Romans march from Tarsus—let four hundred thousand Persian warriors meet them! When these things are done, the enemy will lie in rows, rotting under a Persian sun. Gundarnasp . . . loyal guardsman . . ."

The commander of the palace guard rose from the floor, his broad face impassive. He was the most loyal of Chrosoes' men, a devoted tool to be used at the whim of the King of Kings. He smiled in anticipation of his master's wishes, the black bristles of his beard framing a mouth filled with teeth of gold. Scars lined his face, old memories of years spent in the fighting pits of the city. The fish-scale armor of the Immortal Guard clinked softly as he stood. A full helm, with only a narrow eyeslit breaking its smooth golden surface, was tucked under one arm.

"Command me, Great King." His voice was a growl, ruined by years of shouting over the tumult of battle and the screams of the dying.

"Gather me this army," the king said, pacing back through the assembled nobles. "See that all, even the lowest or the highest, give their due in men and weapons and gold. The harvest is done, the canal walls are strong, and the storehouses are filled with grain and olives. This victory shall be so great, even the least specimen of Persian manhood will stand on the field of victory and raise his spear in triumph!" He mounted the platform steps again.

"Any man who does not stand with us on that field will be base, stripped of honor. He shall be driven from his house and his wives taken from him. His lands will be given to those who have honor, those who shall stand with us against Rome. Let this word be known! Persia's honor will not be tarnished by cowardice."

Siroes sat down heavily on the couch and gestured weakly for another goblet of wine. A servant, head bowed low, crept up to him, the cup trembling in his hands. The King of Kings remained on the platform, staring up at the great disk of the world, his back turned to the nobles. They stood quietly for a time, then slowly realized that the Great King was done with them. Gundarnasp moved among them, smiling like a shark in a school of minnows. Many of the nobles crept out, hoping to go unnoticed by the guardsman. In time, all of them were gone, even Gundarnasp, and Siroes was alone with his father.

The torches had burned out, and even the four great braziers that surrounded the platform and lighted the disk of the world were ebbing when Siroes woke suddenly. His father had ignored him, and the Prince had drifted into a nervous sleep filled with strange dreams. Now he came fully awake, his hands and feet touched by an unexpected chill. Cautiously he rolled over.

His father still stood on the platform, his hands clasped behind his back, but he no longer studied the disk. Instead, he looked out into the darkness of the garden. Siroes peered that way too, into the gloom. Though the moon should have risen over the ornamental pools and cast a silvery light upon the fruit trees and acres of flowers, the space beyond the arches was black as pitch. The braziers suddenly flared, casting his father's shadow huge and swollen across the face of the world, and then died. Only a single flame burned in the brazier farthest from the arches. A chittering came from outside, and the light sound of boots on marble tile. Siroes lay utterly still, for a cold draft now blew over him and rustled the curtains behind him.

"Lord Dahak." Chrosoes voice rumbled low, seeming distant and faint.

"My King" came the answering whisper, and a figure resolved itself out of the darkness that pooled between the fluted columns of the garden. A tall thin man glided forward, his pale skin glowing in the faint light. A loose robe of dark silk fell around his thin shoulders, revealing a white hairless chest mottled with a tracery of shining skin, puckered and twisted over terrible wounds. His face was sharp, though it too was horribly marked by a spiderweb of scar tissue and glassy flesh. Chrosoes hissed in alarm at the sight, a strange whistling sound from beneath his mask.

"Oh, yes, my King. I emulate you too well now. My visit to the city of the Eastern Romans had an abrupt and rather unfortunate end." The thin lips curled in a sardonic smile, revealing fine white teeth. A long thin finger traced the scars along the dark man's neck and chest. "Some presents are best left unopened."

"What happened . . . are you unimpaired otherwise?"

Chrosoes' voice held an edge, the sound of a man that is faced with an unexpected flaw in a well-used tool. Unbidden the Great King's hand rose to his own face.

The lord Dahak bowed, his long hair falling over his shoulder like a wave of ink. "My power is, as ever, yours to command. Fear not, dear King, I will suffice for your efforts. I can still pay my debts."

"Good." The King's voice ground like a stone. "Your debt to me is heavy and still not paid in full."

"Do I not know this, O King? You reproach me with your smile, but my sin is my own. Command me and I will move the earth to please you."

Chrosoes grunted and toyed with the frozen golden curls of his mask. The dark man stood before him, quiescent, though to Siroe's eye, he seemed only an instant from frightful motion.

"Your swiftness is necessary now," Chrosoes said. "The Romans come at us from three directions and I have but one Boar to toss them on his tusks." He paused, seeing a flicker of motion on the face of the sorcerer. "What?"

The Lord Dahak had climbed the steps to the platform, and now he too gazed up at the disk of the world. From where he crouched, the sight of this terrible thing and his father, standing side by side, struck Siroes with foreboding. Though the King of Kings was taller and broader than the slight night visitor, there was a sense of familiarity between them that bade ill.

"My King, there are but two armies that face you. I took some small time, while I made my slow way back from Constantinople, to look upon the doings of your enemies. The movement of the Roman fleet to Trabzon on the Sea of Darkness is but a feint. The whole of the enemies' strength is thrown from Tarsus . . ."

The tiny depiction of a town on the plain of Cilicia, at the join of the Levantine and Asian coast, burst into a green flame.

". . . east, to Tauris, in the passes of Albania." The green flame licked right, eastward, across the northern fringe of the plain of the Tigris and the Euphrates, through high mountains and north, curling, into a broad valley dominated by a lake of blue and white.

"He strikes against Tauris and the Boar is already there. Baraz will have great joy of that meeting . . ."

Chrosoes stared up at the disk of the world, now lit by the line of flickering green flame.

"The Roman does not seek battle," the King of Kings growled, "he seeks to break into the highlands of Media and destroy the lands that have always been the backbone of the Empire. Wretched Roman! He fights us like a tax collector. A base man, an honorless man . . ."

The Lord Dahak inclined his head, smiling at the rage swirling in the mind of the King of Kings. He tucked his hands into the folds of his robe and stood at ease.

Chrosoes turned to his ally. "Could you transport a single man the length of the Empire in a day?"

"Of course, my King. Is it not the least of my talents?"

The King glanced out into the darkened garden, then back to the Lord Dahak.

"Find the Boar at Tauris; he is to send his Immortals south to meet me and the army that Gundarnasp is raising. Tell him to place the defense of the city in able hands—it must withstand the Romans for at least a month! Take him, then, to Shahin in the south. The Boar must find the army of the desert tribes and destroy it. Then he must return to me in all haste. Shahin's army must press on Egypt as soon as possible once the whore Queen is dead. Aid him if you can, to a swift conclusion."

Dahak bowed again, his features calm and composed. "As you say, my King, it will be done."

The green fire faded from the map, and the shadows slithered out of the room as Dahak glided down the steps and out into the darkness under the arches. Siroes ventured to peer over the edge of the couch in time to see the pitch-black night in the garden shift and fold around the wizard before it lifted and the sound of mammoth wings echoed from the tiles. The moon shone through then and gleamed from the marble floor. The Prince slumped back down, breathing at last. On the platform, Chrosoes looked one last time upon the disk of the world and then walked out, his boots making a hollow sound on the floor.

THE ROAD TO TAURIS

}{

Dwyrin drank thirstily from the waterskin, his parched throat eager to drain every last drop from the sweating leather bag. When he wiped his lips, his hand came away caked with yellow dust. He spat and handed the bag off to Eric, who was sitting on the tumbled pile of stones below him. The German was almost unrecognizable under a thick coating of the same clinging yellow dust that afflicted Dwyrin. Eric nodded his thanks from under a broad-brimmed hat and turned the skin up to drink from it as well. Dwyrin rubbed his nose, red and peeling again from the unrelenting sun.

Below the cairn of rocks upon which they sat, the road up the valley of the Rawanduz echoed to the tramp of tens of thousands of booted feet. From his vantage, Dwyrin could see the long glittering steel snake that wound up the side of the valley, stretching back—it seemed—to the broad plain of dried mud and grass that had deposited so much of itself on the two boys. Dwyrin had heard that the combined armies of the two Empires numbered sixty thousand men, a number larger than he could conceive. They seemed endless, a constant stream of *cohorts* and *banda* and *alae* that tramped past below the outcropping and its stacked flat stones. A Legion century swung past, their shields and packs slung over their backs, their helmets hanging from straps, feet moving in unison like a steel millipede.

"Oh, there was a birdie with a yellow bill," they sang in deep voices as they marched past, "it sat upon my windowsill . . ."

These men were clean-shaven and their gear was in good order, their shirts of mail glittering in the hot sun. Nearly all wore the same kind of woven hat that Eric always carried with him, to give a little shade. The spears they carried on their shoulders danced past, a forest of iron reeds. Their hobnailed boots clattered against the flinty stones of the roadway. A stocky man with short white hair paced them at the rear, his bull-roar of a voice carrying over even the massed noise of a hundred men. He glared at Dwyrin and Eric as he passed but made no move to disturb them.

Wagons followed the Western troops, towed by oxen and mules, filled with rolls of canvas and lengths of wood. The drovers walked at the head of the lead teams, the grade too steep to put any more weight in the bed of the wagons. Above the road, a long tumbled slope of sandstone scree rose up, merging with the vast bulk of the mountain that towered over the valley. Dwyrin turned, shading his eyes against the fierce sun. The road continued up, into a vast wall of mountains capped with snow and ice. Beyond those peaks, he knew, lay Persia itself.

A fist rapped his ear and he cursed at the sharp pain. Zoë stood over him, staring down at the two boys with slitted dark eyes. "Get up, you lazy brats. We're to move forward to the next station."

Dwyrin squinted up at her; she was only a dark shape silhouetted against the sun. The Syrian girl continued to ride him hard, though she no longer showed him the fierce anger she had before. She was only a year older than he was at the most, but he did not dare question her authority. Her fists and lightning-quick reflexes in the hidden world were more than a match for his. Too, she had been taking more pains with him of late, showing him the weave and the other exercises that she and Eric and Odenathus took for granted.

He had realized, to his dismay, that his training at the school had been cut short drastically, leaving him with only the rudiments of the necessary education. In its place he had a scattering of meditations and invocations that must be, had to be, the province of more experienced masters of the art. Dwyrin felt a hollowness in his chest; the skills he did possess were tremendously dangerous, as his period of hallucinations had shown.

"Come on, barbarian." She held out her hand, brown and strong. He took it and she grunted, pulling him up onto the top of the cairn. Eric scrambled up behind him, puffing at the effort. Weeks of hard labor and constant physical abuse had not improved the pudgy German's physique. Odenathus, who was uncoiling himself from a seated position on the rocks, Zoë, and Dwyrin had all become wiry and stronger than Dwyrin had expected. He slapped his thigh, feeling it hard and corded like a carved log. He could barely recall the softness of his life at the school.

Dwyrin followed Zoë down the slope, his eyes drawn to the sway of her long hair, braided into three dark ropes that lay back over her bag and bedroll. There was a fierce beauty about the girl that reminded him very much of his sisters back home. He tripped on a slab of rock and skidded down the slope. Luckily he crashed into a solid boulder within feet of falling. He got up, brushing more dirt off of him. Zoë had stopped and was staring at him.

"I'm fine," he said, picking up his hat.

"Good," she said, "you go first. And run—we have to take up the next watch in twenty grains." She did not smile, but Dwyrin flushed—he knew that she knew he had been paying more attention to the shape of her ankles than where he was going. He slid the rest of the way down to the edge of the road. A mass of archers in pale-yellow cloaks and copper arm bracelets were marching past, the tramp of their feet raising a cloud of more dust around them. Dwyrin shrugged his pack tighter on his back and then jogged up the road, keeping to the outer edge where there was a little clear space. His calves reminded him that he had run the day before, but he ignored it. Zoë was right behind him.

At night they crowded around a tiny fire, barely kindling smoking down to coals. Eric had gone down to where the cooks had made fires in iron baskets and come back with fresh bread. Dwyrin tore into the partially burned loaf with strong teeth. Until they had set out on this march, he had not realized how good bread could taste when you only got it every three days. Clouds had come up, covering the stars and it was cold. Zoë, wedged in next to him and Odenathus, poked at a battered iron pot sitting in the embers with a stick.

"Not ready yet," Odenathus muttered, his face half covered with a woolen scarf. "Those yellow beans need to cook for at least two glasses. Otherwise you'll get no sleep."

Zoë ignored him and continued to stir the beans. When the army had halted an hour before sunset, she had told off Dwyrin and Eric to find some spot out of the way of the mass of the other regiments and pitch their tents. Then she had taken her bow and jogged off into the mountain canyons. The army was sprawled along a narrow tongue of rising land in a barren valley. In the next days they would cross the high pass and enter Persia. But now, above the last scraggly trees, they rested in a wasteland of huge boulders and cracked stone. Snow lay in the shadow of the larger stones and the mountain peaks that ringed the valley held eternal caps of ice.

Dwyrin and Eric had scavenged for heavy stones to hold down the ropes of the tent and had looked for a sheltered spot between two of the monoliths. The rest of the army, particularly the cohorts of the Western Emperor, had taken the flatter ground by the sides of the narrow track. The sun was setting as the legionnaires began cutting a shallow ditch in the hard ground and raising the rough outline of a travel camp.

Shaking his head, Dwyrin had climbed among the boulders and slabs of stone until he found an alcove with fire markings on the southern wall. He, Eric, and Odenathus had dragged their gear from the wagons up there and set up camp. The looming rocks, brittle and worn by the caress of winter, made a fine windbreak. The army of the Eastern Emperor was still staggering into the valley and falling asleep wherever they found themselves.

"What do you think will happen when we come to battle?" Dwyrin said, after washing the grit of the bread from his mouth with a draft of sour wine. "It seems like we are two different armies, cast together by mischance."

Zoë snorted, peering at the wild onions and dried apricots she had mixed in with the yellow beans. She looked up, catching his eye, her own reflecting the red gleam of the coals. "If *you* can learn to work with us in the hidden world, barbarian, then the two armies can fight as one."

Eric choked with laughter and Odenathus leaned over to thump him hard on his back. Dwyrin made a face at him and passed the *acetum* over. The Northerner took two long swallows and breathed easier.

"Five-leader, I'm serious!" Dwyrin spread his hand in dismay. "You see how they march—a shambling disaster. Stopping and starting as they please, fouling the water of any river we cross, a mob of disorganized bands and personal retinues."

"They do lack discipline," Odenathus said from the other side of the fire. "But they are here, and they will fight. The Legions of the West are the core, though. If they stand firm, we will have victory."

"Nicely quoted." Zoë sniffed. "I think these beans are done. Give me your bowls."

A glass after dark, Zoë had appeared at the edge of their camp, a sour look on her face. The sky behind her was lit by the fitful glow of the encamped army. She still had her bow, but no game, only some gathered herbs and the onions. She had been pleased that Dwyrin had found kindling, for they had not had a chance to gather wood on the lower slopes. Her quiet word of thanks had lifted his spirits tremendously, though it was no stretch for him to ferret out the hidden stockpile left by whomever had been using the alcove as a camp. Any shepherd at home would have done the same.

The beans were sour and tough, but to Dwyrin they tasted divine after the long day of trudging up the steep road. Salt pork and mutton also paled after weeks on the march. He crushed an onion and felt its sting on his tongue. It felt good to be here, with his companions, around the fire under the dark sky with weary feet.

"The first battle will be the test," Zoë said, cleaning out her bowl with a long finger. "If someone panics and runs, or we lose the barbarians to a stratagem, that will put paid to us. But if we can win one with this circus, we'll be invincible."

Eric rattled the pot, looking for more scraps. It was empty. He frowned and put it down. "What will we do? I mean—we're the weakest five in the *Ars Magica*—will they have us do anything? I don't want to hold horses again . . ."

"No," Zoë said, "we'll be in front. Colonna tipped me off yesterday. The tribune has decided to put us up with the skirmishers. We run forward with the slingers and archers and harass the enemy lines while they deploy. He thinks that we can spook the enemy while they're still getting their thumbs out. Oh, we look for elephants too."

Dwyrin stole a glance at Odenathus, who had turned quite grim at this news. Zoë did not seem happy either, staring moodily into the fire. Ramifications tumbled around in Dwyrin's thought until some of them slid queasily together.

"Ah," he said tentatively, "that would mean that we'd draw the attention of the other side's heavy hitters first, wouldn't it?"

"Yes," Zoë said, her full lips twisted into a grimace something like a smile. "We're bait for the big fish. As a condolence, if they slam us down, the tribune promises to make them pay a heavy man-price for us."

THE SKIES OVER SYRIA MAGNA

Shahr-Baraz shouted aloud in joy, though his words were instantly torn away by shrieking wind. He strained against the heavy leather straps that bound him to the back of the *byakhee*, leaning forward into the wall of wind that howled around him. Ahead of him, also strapped into a web of leather and metal clasps, the Lord Dahak grimaced at the foolishness of men. The sorcerer leaned to the left and blue-black light flickered around his hands, driving the vast creature to wing over and sweep at tremendous speed across the face of the world.

Baraz looked down as the creature tilted, its bifurcated wings a blur under the light of the moon. Vast expanses of empty desert rushed past below them, though he could see, to the north, a dim cluster of lights that must be the cities of men. The land far below was marked by long sinuous silver trails, like the backs of thousands of snakes. They passed over a wide expanse of mottled black hills, then a scattering of tiny lights.

We land soon, echoed the bone-brittle voice of the sorcerer in his mind. *The valley of the Orontes lies just ahead.*

Baraz peered forward, leaning close over the shoulders of the Lord Dahak. Suddenly they passed over a city—no more than a crowd of moth-lights under the moon and the glint of a lake lay off to the southwest. Baraz scanned the rushing countryside under them, looking for any sign . . .

There! He exulted at the sight—a great camp of men, lit by hundreds of fires. Tents glowed from lanterns and long lines of torches marked the streets of the encampment. Then the creature rushed on and the camp fell away behind them and they passed over another range of hills, dark and brooding in the night. Baraz stared back, over the long snakelike tail and maneuvering wings.

What? Shouldn't we have landed?

He turned to look forward again and the creature spread its great wings and slewed into a corkscrew dive. The barren top of a tall hill lay below them. There was a blast of air that scattered leaves and dust in a wide pall, and it landed delicately on long thin feet. The vast creature danced a little to the side, folding mountainous wings back against its rugose, tentacular body.

The Lord Dahak relaxed a little in the harness and looked back over his shoulder at his companion. Baraz was already unfastening the buckles that held him into the framework. The big man threw a heavy bag over his shoulder and tossed down two more wicker baskets that had been secured behind him. The sorcerer followed suit, though with less eagerness, his hands shaking a little with exhaustion. The big man slid down the hairy flank of the byakhee and thumped heavily to the ground. Then reached up and dragged down a bundle of weapons that he had been sitting on. Baraz paused.

"Lord Dahak, why are you unbelting yourself?" His voice was puzzled.

The Lord Dahak sighed and rose up to stand on the enormous shoulder of the beast. Under him, it quivered slightly, feeling the lessening of his control. He was weary from the effort of maintaining his mastery over the promethean thing and resigned himself to climbing down to the ground, even as Baraz had done.

"Get back," he snapped at the Persian. "It will make a great wind when it goes."

The mammoth wings unfurled and blotted out the stars and the moon. A wind rose, like a gale, and lashed the two men with small stones and twigs from the trees that surrounded the top of the hill. The thing gave a mournful call, like an unguessably vast hound, and vaulted into the air. The hilltop shook with the pressure of its flight, and then it was gone, swallowed by the darkness between the stars. Baraz picked himself up off the ground and spat out a mouthful of sand.

"Lord Dahak, don't take this amiss, but why are you staying with me?"

Dahak's face was unreadable in the darkness, but he said, "The King of Kings commands, and I obey. He commands that I assist you in this campaign."

Baraz stared at the sorcerer. But then he caught the grim expression of the Lord Dahak, and instead he turned his mind to plan and action and thought. *A wizard to help me, every advantage to my hand! The Romans will suffer greatly with this turn of events.*

Dahak wrapped his robe around him, and drew the hood up over his lean head.

"The camp of the Great Prince Shahin," he said, "is beyond these hills." He walked off into the trees to the north. Baraz looked up at the moon and then back to the south, whence they had come. He tugged thoughtfully at the bristly mustaches that gave him his popular sobriquet, and then he trotted off into the trees after the sorcerer.

The Boar, now dressed in a heavy cloak over his armor of plate cuirass and mail of iron scales, strode up to the doors of the massive tent that lay at the center of the Persian camp. Around him acres of tents glowed with the light of lanterns and torches. His head was bare, and he had combed his lush curls out to lie on his shoulders like a carpet. His beard was groomed as well, though it had been difficult to do in the dim night beyond the sentries of the camp. With some coaxing, Dahak had conjured a pale-white light so that Baraz could see himself in the lead-glass mirror that he carried. The massive sword that he favored jutted over one shoulder in a sheath of wood wrapped with leather. The Lord Dahak limped behind him, his mood bitter. The sorcerer had turned his ankle as they had negotiated the slope of the hill in the darkness. Luckily, he leaned on a tall staff of rowan wood. Still, those men awake in the camp looked upon the two of them and quickly returned to their duties or tents.

Baraz ignored the two guardsmen in light chain mail and russet robes at the entrance to the tent, striding past them with his head held high. The two men controlled themselves, for they recognized the one-time commander of the army. They did not meet the flickering pale eyes of Dahak as he passed, limping. Within the tent, which was divided up into many chambers, a sudden hush fell upon the main room.

"Lord Shahin." The general's voice was blunt, like a heavy axe striking meat.

At the center of the chamber Shahin rose, a stoutly built man with a long face and curly beard. The Great Prince, the cousin of the King of Kings, was richly attired in green robes of linen and silk. He wore a small circlet of gold around his head and many rings on his fingers. He carefully put down a crystal goblet filled with wine and bowed in greeting.

"General Shahr-Baraz, welcome to my tent. May I introduce my companions?"

Baraz snorted, sounding very like his namesake. Shahin's eyes, artfully outlined with kohl, narrowed. The Great Prince was accustomed to being treated politely, even by rivals, and here—surrounded by his supporters and his own army—he was not disposed to be slighted. "There is no time for pleasantries, Great Prince. Summon your commanders and allied princes, there is much to be done before the night is out."

The courtiers, who had remained sitting until it was clear who held the social superiority, tittered a little, laughing behind their hands. Baraz spared them a glance and saw, to his disgust, that the tent was filled with gorgeously attired men in perfumed silks and rich clothing. His heavy brows beetled over his eyes; the number of pleasure slaves who languidly ornamented the arms of the nobles present told him a tale of a leisurely advance into enemy lands. The general turned back to Shahin, who was gazing at him with a tilted head, much like a swamp crane viewing a tasty frog.

"Your presence is most welcome, Baraz," the Great Prince said in a smooth and cultured voice, "but it is late, and I was about to retire. Do you bring some news that must needs be relayed before the sun rises?"

"Aye," Baraz said gruffly, "but first a simple question—do you know where the army of the desert tribes is this night?"

Shahin was taken aback by the odd question.

"Sadly, no," he replied, smoothing the lay of one of his sleeves. "We have made good progress advancing into enemy lands but have yet to see more of the Romans and their rabble than a few tracks upon the road."

The Great Prince returned to the divan that he had been reclining upon. Two of his slaves, clad only in the barest silk, attended to him. Apparently he had been interrupted in the middle of a manicure. The one on the right, with her lush red hair piled up on her head like a stormcloud, eyed Baraz fearfully but bent over the Great Prince's outstretched hand with her tiny file.

Baraz growled in anger, then spun on his heel and stalked to the entranceway. He noted, in passing, that Dahak had entered the chamber behind him and was now sitting in the corner, unnoticed by the assembly, save for one slave who had brought him a bowl of crushed ice. Outside the tent the general rapped the sentries sharply on their helmets. They spun, outraged, but stopped when they saw the looming shape of the Boar.

"Quick about it, lads, find me the commanders of the cavalry, the light horse, the infantry and anyone else with a plume and half a wit about them. Double-time!"

The two sentries saluted and trotted off into the darkness. Baraz watched them go and grunted to himself. *Well*, he thought, *between Dahak and I, we might yet win . . .*

When he returned to the tent, the courtiers and the Prince had resumed their conversation as if he had never interrupted. A quartet of musicians had taken up a tune in the corner, and the flute player was trilling a light air that sounded like birds in flight. Baraz reddened and strode across the room to the drum player. The man looked up in time to scuttle aside as the general snatched up his heavy instrument and laid into the surface with a heavy hand.

"All right, everyone out! Out! Out! Out!" Baraz punctuated his bellowing with a mighty thump on the drum. He shoved his way through the courtiers, who had leapt to their feet in fear.

"Out! Everyone out!" The Boar punctuated his shouts with his boot. Tables overturned and the musicians fled. Baraz threw the drum out the front door of the tent, braining one of the poets who had run out into the camp street. The man dropped like a pole-axed cow and lay still in the dirt. The Great Prince had leapt to his feet as well and was shouting at Baraz at the top of his voice. The other nobles and slaves scattered. Baraz sent the last drunken man on his way with a boot to the fundament that sent him sprawling into the sand. The general turned and a fist ornamented with heavy rings flashed at his face.

Baraz's meaty hand snapped up, catching the thrown punch, and his fingers squeezed like tree roots digging at a mosaic floor. The Great Prince gasped in pain and crumpled to his knees. The Boar released the crushed hand and stared down at the Prince in undisguised disgust as Shahin struggled to his feet.

"By the order of Chrosoes, King of Kings, I am assuming command of this army."

Baraz's voice held the finality of millstones crushing grain into meal. "If you care to discuss the wisdom of this with the Great King, then I suggest to hie yourself to Ctesiphon and take it up with him." He leaned close to the Great Prince's pale face. "But," Baraz said, "he is in a foul mood of late. I would not advise it."

"I . . . I do not believe you!" Shahin stepped back two paces and drew himself up. The Great Prince was a very powerful man in the Empire; his estates were as vast as those of the King of Kings. He could raise armies of his own, and he was closely related to the House of Sassan. "The Great King has entrusted this campaign to me! To me, you ignorant backwoods farmer! What proof do you have of this order from the King? I have received nothing to indicate this!"

Baraz laughed at the red face of the Great Prince. "A messenger brought me this news only tonight, and now I am here. You will command the left wing of the army—this too is the wish of the King of Kings, that you should have a place of honor. But I command here, now, Prince Shahin, and you would do well to heed my commands."

Shahin spat on the thick rugs of the floor. "Where is this messenger? Is he known to you? An Imperial courier? Do you have a written order?" The Prince's face turned sly as he thought he spied an advantage over the Boar.

Baraz chuckled again and turned slightly. "Here is the messenger, O Great Prince. Do you dispute him?"

Shahin stepped past Baraz, angry words on his lips, but then he saw Dahak leaning back in a chair with one foot wrapped with cloths. The dark man smiled and the lanterns of cut crystal and glass that illuminated the tent flickered and went out. In the sudden darkness, there was the soft sound of crickets, and a slow dull-red glow flickered into being around the sorcerer. Fire burned in two sharp points where the man's eyes should be.

"The King of Kings speaks," Dahak said in a deep basso voice. "Will you deny his will?"

Shahin stepped back, speechless, and ran into the solid bulk of Baraz. "No! No, great lord, I obey!" The Prince fell to his knees and bowed three times, prostrating himself upon the carpeted floor.

Flame leapt back up in the lanterns and the tent was filled once more with a warm light. Ominous silence was replaced by the sound of men shouting in alarm and the slap of running feet on sand and gravel. Dahak turned his face away from the two men in the center of the tent and seemed to fade into the rich brocade of the wall.

Seven or eight men, half dressed, with bared swords and spears, rushed into the tent and drew up sharply when they saw that the chamber was empty save for the Great Prince and the Boar. All had come running at the shouts of *assassins!* and *riot!*

"General!" The commanders of the army were surprised to see a man they last knew to be no less than seventy leagues away. The Boar gave them a wide smile, all bright-white teeth. He casually tipped one of the tables back over, though now the candied fruits and jugs of wine were smashed and scattered on the floor.

"Well met, my friends. Where is the commander of the light horse? I see the cataphracti, the spearmen, the engineers represented here . . . is it Tahvaz who commands the scouts now?"

The captains shook their heads, and sidelong glances at the Great Prince, who was now sitting in his chair once more, a slave daubing at his forehead with a cool cloth, made Baraz turn, his eyes slitted in suspicion.

"Great Prince? Where is the commander of the light horse?" Baraz's voice was polite.

Shahin looked up, his dark kohl-rimmed eyes glittering with hatred.

"The miserable Tahvaz was sent back to Ctesiphon a month ago. He was reckless and insubordinate. We are well done of him."

Baraz pursed his lips; something that had bothered him during the hike down the hill was becoming clear. He turned back to the captains, now joined by many of their officers, who were crowding into the tent to see what had caused all of the fuss. "Khadames . . . you command the cataphracts—are there any light horse in this army?"

The commander of the heavy horse shook his head sadly.

"Then," the Boar continued, "you've no scouts out at all, only pickets of spearmen around the camp. And it has been so since the army left Antioch in the north?"

The captains shrugged and Khadames squared himself and met the gaze of his former commander. "No, Lord Baraz, we have advanced in close order, with only some of my horsemen in light armor as flankers. We have not seen the enemy . . . they may still be at Damascus . . ." His voice trailed off as Baraz folded his hands behind him and gave him a steely glare. The other captains shuffled their feet and cast their heads down.

"The enemy," Baraz said in a conversational tone, "is bare miles away, beyond these hills to the south. Given that he commands a host of bandits, you can be sure that he knows your every move, the number of your men, and the temperature

of the gruel you ate for breakfast. I have seen his camp and his numbers are as
great as ours or better."

A bitter laugh from behind him interrupted the general. Shahin rose, his
robes once more neatly arranged and his makeup restored to some semblance of
order.

"His *numbers* do not matter, General. Our heavy knights will smash whatever
formations he places in the field against us. He does not have the weight of metal
that we do, he cannot possibly stand up to us in an open battle!"

Baraz barely spared a glance for the Great Prince. "You have not seen him
or brought him to battle, my friends, because the tribes are laying a trap for you,
one that they hope you will blunder into headlong, unthinking. When this enemy
chooses to fight, then he will fight. Until then he will content himself with bug-
gering your sheep and stealing your women. What happened to the Lakhmid archers and lancers that Tahvaz captained? They can still serve to scout . . . what is
it?"

Now the captains were openly uncomfortable. Khadames sighed and squared
his shoulders again. "There was a dispute over pay, General. The Lakhmid aux-
iliaries are no longer with the army. When last I saw them, they had made camp
at Arethusa."

Baraz's fists clenched and he finally turned to face Shahin fully. The Great
Prince stepped back but then halted, standing his ground.

"The Lakhmid chiefs have not been paid?"

"They demanded twice that which they agreed to serve for! I will not let
dirty tribesmen extort the Empire of good heavy gold! We do not need them, they
are a trouble and a nuisance to us! I bade them return home, and this they did."

In the corner, where Dahak sat tending to his sore ankle, there was bitter
laughter. The captains and officers turned, startled, to see who was there and then
shrank back in open fear. The gaunt, dark shape of the wizard was well known in
rumor and whisper.

"No tribesman ever went where a perfumed dandy bade him go, Great Prince.
If you left some thousands of Lakhmid tribesmen behind you, you can be sure that
they have taken their pay, and more, from lands you counted a fine prize." Dahak's
voice was a whisper, but every man in the tent heard it full well and felt a chill
upon the hearing.

Shahin flushed, but there was little he dared say to the dark man.

"Enough." Baraz growled, thinking furiously. "Khadames, send for your fastest
riders. Take the pay that the Lakhmids were promised and three times that on
horses. Send a man that you can trust and get him on the way to Arethusa. Tell
the chiefs of the tribes that I, Shahr-Baraz, the Boar, call upon their honor to help
the Empire. Tell them . . . tell them that when there is battle, the Tanukh will be
theirs. Tell them that I, Shahr-Baraz, promise it!"

"It shall be so, General. I shall send my nephew Bahram to treat with them."

The captain of the heavy horse bowed and strode quickly from the tent, his
voice raised to call his lieutenants and banner leaders to him.

The Boar turned to the other men and gestured for them to come closer.
"We must fall back, and quickly too. The tribesmen will be lying for us in ambush,

and we must regain some room to maneuver. Every man in this army must be on the road back north, with his kit and arms, before daylight. It will be a near thing, even so, but if we are swift, we can evade the noose. Take only those things that are necessary . . ." Baraz paused and a crafty gleam came into his eye. He turned and faced Shahin.

"In particular, Great Prince, this tent and all that is in it must stay. Not one item may be removed, nor will the tents of your companions and confidants be taken north."

Shahin sputtered in rage but fell silent when Baraz raised a broad hand.

"You have led an army of the Empire into a dire place, Great Prince. Now you must pay amends for that recklessness. Go, 'you lead those horsemen who Khadames' trusted officer did command."

Shahin looked around, but the faces of his captains and their lieutenants held no support for him. At last, with an angry snarl, he strode out, his robes fluttering behind him. With him gone, Baraz sighed in relief. There was business to be done, and quickly.

"You, lad. What is your name?"

One of the couriers who had been attached to Shahin's staff stepped forward nervously. He was very young, barely sixteen and with the look of one of the desert tribes. For a moment Baraz wondered what had brought him into the service of the King of Kings. *No matter*, he thought, and pushed the distraction away.

"Khalid, Lord General."

"Khalid, three things I need of you, right away—first, Shahin's horse. Secure it for me and bring it here. If the stablemen give you trouble tell them that the Boar demands it. Second, the Great Prince's banner and tabard. These too I need. Third, despite what I just said, we will take one wagon north with us—a well-sprung one, with high clearance and enclosed. This is for my friend, who cannot walk at present."

Khalid looked over his shoulder, to where Dahak was sitting quietly, observing the bustle of men going about a hurried business, and swallowed. "Yes, Lord General! I will see to it immediately!" The boy sprinted out of the tent.

"You others, tell me of the condition and organization of the men . . ."

Dahak idly watched the boy run out. Though he seemed sleepy to those around him, he had already settled within his mind to a calm center. While the camp was aboil with activity, with thousands of men rushing about to gather up their gear and arms, the sorcerer stretched out his will and covered the encampment with a seeming of peace and nighted sleep. To the Tanukh watchers who lay hid on the hillsides above the camp, all seemed as it had been before. It was difficult work, and Dahak fell into a light trance as his full attention was devoted to this deception.

THE ARMENIAN QUARTER, TAURIS

"There, mistress, it is as I said."

Thyatis ignored the wiry little man with the pox-scarred face. She crept around the corner of the dome and peered over the lip of the ornamented roof. The red tiles under her hands were hot from the noonday sun. A narrow street was thirty feet or more below her. On the other side of the street a white wall of stuccoed brick rose up a good twenty feet. It was unbroken, save by a battlement at its top, pierced by arrow slits and a fighting embrasure. From where she lay she could see down into the hanging garden behind that wall. The garden had been built on the roof of the massive building that had once served as the residence of the governor of the city. It was filled with small fruit trees, rosebushes, and a hundred kinds of flowers. A small fountain trickled at one side of the open space.

The Roman ignored the ornamental flowers and the garden. Beyond the rosebushes, a second wall rose, just a few feet high, below which lay the central courtyard of the building. It was a barren area, paved with the omnipresent red bricks. All of the walls around it were bare, though the outlines of arches and windows on the first two floors could be made out. They were bricked in now and plastered over. Only a single door could be seen, leading into the courtyard. A man was standing next to the door, his head in the shade of the building roof, with his hands held in front of him. Metal links glinted between his hands.

"Nikos!" she breathed. She had not believed Bagratuni's cousin when he had come to them with this story of a Roman prisoner in the Old Residence. But there he was. She watched for twenty or thirty grains, until two guardsmen came out of the doorway and led the man back inside. Thyatis crawled back away from the edge of the roof then and scuttled across the barren roof to the airshaft. She had climbed up from the cellar to reach the dome on the Temple of the Lord of Light. The little Armenian crept along after her.

At the airshaft, she tugged twice on the rope that snaked down into the darkness. Even with the sun nearly overhead, the angle of the shaft kept it dark and cold. An answering tug came and she motioned for the poxy-faced man to climb down. He was quick to slither down the rope and Thyatis waited, sweating, until another tug came. She could hear the chanting of the priests of Ahura-Mazda coming from the windows of the temple. It was her great hope that the acolytes did not take their ease from chores on the deserted roof of the building. She rolled over the edge of the airshaft and then braced her feet on the inner brickwork. She leaned back against the rope and then walked her way down the wall.

Above, the sky became a square of blue that shrank and then disappeared as she descended below the ground level of the temple. Damp darkness surrounded her and the sound of sluggish water reached up with a foul smell. Her boots splashed into a rivulet of water and she stood in a small space surrounded by moldy brick walls. She crouched down and duckwalked along a low tunnel with a triangular apse. At its end, she gagged at the smell, but crawled out through a place broken in the wall of a larger tunnel. Strong hands assisted her out of the narrow crevice.

She patted Jusuf on the arm and hand-signed that he should lead. The Bulgar nodded and crept off down the tunnel along a narrow ledge. The main body of the tunnel was filled with a gurgling stream of dark water, its surface clogged with a thick crust. The smell was truly horrible here, but Thyatis closed her nostrils and followed Jusuf. Soon she would be able to breathe easily again.

Her Bulgars crowded into the little attic that Thyatis had been living in for the past week. The house was a big one. The lower floors were crammed with the Boar's Immortals, who had been billeted in the Armenian quarter. The owners had been forced to move upstairs into a partially completed floor and the attic. The Persians downstairs spent most of their time drinking and carousing, so the gradual disappearance of the original family and their replacement by Thyatis, the Bulgars, and Bagratuni's cousins had gone unremarked. There was a new entrance, broken through a wall of stiff-fired bricks, from the rooftop into the attic. Thyatis and her men moved mostly by night, save for the activities of the nominal owners.

The ceiling was low, and crossed with beams made from unfinished logs. Thyatis squatted at one end, near a small circular window that allowed some breath of air to enter the stifling room. Outside, the sun was setting and the Bulgars were rousing themselves for the night's work.

Thyatis scratched a map in the dust of the floor. ". . . the prisoner is in the building on the other side of the garden. I intend to get him out, alive, before anything happens to him. Unfortunately, he is privy to my Emperor's wishes, and if they break him, then the jig will be up for all of us."

Jusuf sighed and leaned a little toward his brother Dahvos, who was squeezed in beside him. "See?" the taciturn Bulgar said in a wry tone. "She *will* get us all killed . . ."

Sahul spared a short glare for his brother, then spread his hands to Thyatis.

"So," Thyatis continued, "I have a plan to get him out, alive, without—if the gods smile on us—anyone noticing."

Thyatis laughed at the sour expression on Jusuf's face. She expected disbelief from them. She had conceived the plan during the hours she spent lying on the rooftop opposite the old palace. It had a very low chance of complete success, but she repressed her dreadful urge to attack the palace from the square and slaughter everyone within. By Bagratuni's latest count, there were nearly two thousand Immortals in the city, and she counted only twelve men to her hand.

"There are three things that we need to make this work, however, and all three will be difficult to acquire. First, we need to know the layout of the inner building. Bagratuni?"

The dapper little Armenian shrugged and then scratched his nose in sorrow. "Lady Roman, my cousin's sister's daughter risked plenty to bring us word that a Roman was held in prison! If we ask her for more, her nerve will fail. She is young and not as strong-willed as my cousin's sister." He paused, thinking.

"Maybe," he said slowly, "we could find a guard or servant, and bribe or threaten them? . . ."

Thyatis shook her head. "No, there isn't enough time to find one who is weak enough to take a bribe and malleable enough to keep from getting greedy or betraying us to his superiors. We need to move within the next four days." She sighed. Without some idea of the guards and rooms, the chance of success dwindled to almost nothing.

"How tall," she said, "is your cousin's sister's daughter? Does she wear a veil when she is in the building?"

Bagratuni smiled lopsidedly and shook his head in negation. "She is almost a foot shorter than you, Roman lady. Her hair is brown and she wears a veil. You are not her!"

Thyatis rapped her knife on the floorboards in frustration.

"If only Anagathios were here," she muttered. "No matter! Speak with your niece, Bagratuni, and gently, gently, see if she would help us just one more time . . ."

"Who is Anagathios?" Jusuf's voice was quiet, but Thyatis snapped her head up at the tone. Jusuf stared back at her with hooded eyes. Inwardly Thyatis groaned—all she needed now was suspicious jealousy on the part of her confederates.

"A friend," she said, her voice clipped. "A mute Syrian with a talent for the theater. He was short enough, and slim enough, to pass for a girl with the proper paints. He died on the road here. Satisfied?"

Jusuf bowed his head and did not meet her eye.

Sahul tapped on the dusty floor for attention. His face was quizzical.

Thyatis stared at him. "What is it, Sahul?"

The Bulgar signed to his brothers, though only Dahvos was paying attention. Thyatis watched his fingers flit into foreign patterns; she had been trying to decipher the signs that Sahul used for days.

The youngest brother looked puzzled and then a smile flickered over his face like sun through the clouds. "My brother says, Lady Thyatis, that he has seen a mute actor in the marketplace by the northern gate. He juggles and does tricks. He never speaks but is quite accomplished. He says that this fellow is a foreigner and only came to the city within the last nine days. Sahul says"—there was a pause while Dahvos followed the flickering procession of hand-signs—"he says that the fellow is very pretty and could pass for a girl."

Thyatis whistled, a long soprano note. *Could it be? No, that would be too much to ask. But perhaps this foreigner could act the part as well as her friend . . .* "Find this actor and bring him to me. Bagratuni, take your cousins out for a walk."

The little Armenian grinned, his teeth flashing in the dim room, and then crawled off to the trapdoor that led down into the living quarters on the unfinished floor.

Thyatis motioned for the three brothers to close up the space around her. "Sahul, you have the most critical task. You will have to go out of the city and as far away from here as practicable. I need a . . ."

Each brother was entrusted with a task, and Sahul in particular gave her a long look before shaking his head and leaving through the entrance onto the roof. Dahvos was equally puzzled with his assignment, but he went willingly anyway. Jusuf was the only one inclined to argue.

"This won't work," he said. "To put it mildly, you're insane to think they won't notice. Chances are exceptionally good that every man you take into the old palace will die or be taken captive, and then the rest of us will follow."

Thyatis smiled at him and gestured out the window with the twig she had used to draw on the floor with.

"In five days," she said, "the moon will be fully dark. According to Bagratuni, the fire priests of the Persian god have a great ceremony then. All of the important men in the city and the garrison will be in the temple. The guard on the prisoners will be lax, without the commanders to keep them on their toes. It is our best chance. If it works, and I believe it will, then we will have greatly improved our situation in the city."

"And you," he shot back, "will have gotten your *friend* back! How much is he worth to you? Is he that good?" Jusuf's face was flushed.

Thyatis' lip curled in anger at his insinuation. "Nikos has been my second for almost two years. He's like a member of my family. If it were Dahvos or Sahul in that cage, what would you do? Hmm? Would you let the Persians put Dahvos on the rack, or put red-hot irons to the soles of his feet? If that happened, you would be here, now, in this attic, tearing your guts out with worry that delaying four days might mean his life."

She slid forward on the floor and was nose to nose with the Bulgar. He had a sharp, musky smell about him, redolent of horses and sweat and iron and blood. He matched her gaze, tremendously angry himself. Thyatis' hand snaked out and grabbed his hair, turning his face from her.

"Would you let your brother," she softly whispered in his ear, "die in that square under the axe to preserve your precious skin?" He shuddered at her closeness and pushed her away. Thyatis rolled back on her heels and laughed bitterly. The Bulgar turned, his face a mask, and crawled away to the trapdoor. Thyatis drummed her fingers on the boards, staring after him, and then squeezed out the opening onto the roof. The sun had vanished over the mountains to the west, leaving only long streaks of orange and purple in the sky and a gleam on the ice that capped the peaks.

Clad from head to toe in a layered black gown, headdress, and veil, Thyatis stood in a recessed doorway on a side street near the northern market of Tauris. It was cool and dim, for much of the street was blocked from the sun by hundreds of wash lines strung between the buildings. Bagratuni, dressed in the pantaloons, shirt, and vest of a lower-class Armenian, sat on the steps at the entrance to the building, a blanket covered with cheap copper trinkets laid over his knees.

"Well?" she said, her voice muffled by the heavy garment.

"It's not such a good view from here, you know—a bad location! I can only see down the street when there are no people in the way." His voice raised. "Bracelets! The finest to be had! Bracelets!" A pair of Armenian women bustled by, their laughter echoing down the close walls of the little street.

"Ah!" he continued, "I see now. He acts a play of some kind—now he is a seaman, or so I'd say from the roll in his walk; now a maiden on the blush of womanhood. Say, my lady, this fellow is rather good! The seaman is giving the girl some kind of bracelet. Ah! He is quick to toss the bracelet to himself like that! I don't see either of my cousins, though . . . Ho, some kind of a miser has made an appearance, he wants the girl to come with him!"

Thyatis tapped her foot impatiently. The play, much slowed by the actor having to play all of the parts, dragged on. Bagratuni kept up a running commentary throughout. His cousins did not make an appearance.

"If this is Anagathios, I'll skin him myself . . ." Thyatis' patience was wearing thin. All she needed now was for some nosy *aedile* to come snooping around and find her in this getup in an alleyway. She'd be locked up for prostitution for sure . . .

"Roman lady, I think that he's done. Yes, the people watching are giving him a few coins. He bows, he does a flip, he bows . . . there are my cousins. Oop! He's a quick one all right, but they have him by both arms. Here they come."

Bagratuni slid to one side of the step, keeping the blanket on his lap.

"Which play do you suppose it was?" he asked, looking over his shoulder at Thyatis.

"Eyes front! Sounds like the *Girl from Miletus*, which is about right for Anagathios. Just the kind of play to get him thrown in jail by some straitlaced Persian garrison on the edge of nowhere."

The actor was hustled into the doorway by Bagratuni's two cousins, who bounced him gently off the right wall a few times to settle him down. The actor, free of the arms of the two heavily built men, brushed off his tattered motley and produced, with a flourish, a knife with a serrated edge. Thyatis stepped forward and raised a hand. The man in front of her crouched down and found the wall behind him with the heel of his foot. At the entrance to the doorway, Bagratuni moved back into the middle of the steps.

"So, actor, do you have anything to say to your critics?"

The man's head jerked up, showing a dusky olive skin, a fine-boned nose, high cheekbones, and liquid brown eyes with long eyelashes. The knife wavered in his hand. Thyatis unhooked the veil and demurely drew it from her face. The Syrian's face split with a huge grin and he bowed his head to the flagstones without bending his legs. The knife disappeared into a sleeve in the process. Thyatis wrapped him a huge hug.

"Hello, old friend," she said in a warm voice as she sat him down. "I was afraid that you were dead." Anagathios shook his head no, but his eyes were sad. His fingers sketched in the air and Thyatis sighed. *I was separated from the others and hid in the bushes until the soldiers were gone. I did not see them take any prisoners. Sorry.*

No matter, she signed back. *Time is short. I have work for you to do.*

The Syrian smiled again, his perfect face glowing in a smile. Thyatis smiled back.

Stripped down to only a loincloth with a cotton bandeau twisted tight around her chest, Thyatis stood thigh deep in the rush of the sewage tunnel. Jusuf and two of the other Bulgars, clad only in short kilts, were just downstream of her, a stout log slung on their shoulders. A flickering light illuminated them from a lantern hung on a hook set into the ceiling. Thyatis caught the end of the log with her right hand, halting them. Sahul peered around his arm, then turned and gave a sharp whistle. Behind him, in the long tunnel from the river, the whistle was repeated.

The sound of thirty men moving in the tunnel was drowned by the rushing passage of foul water down the sewer. With the logs stopped, Thyatis reached above her head and found, by touch, a heavy leather collar that was dangling at the end of a long rope.

Sloshing through the muck that swirled around her legs, which left them coated with grease, she dragged the collar down to the level of the log. She knew that up above, in the clerestory of the temple, Bagratuni and his cousins were anxiously watching the upper end of the rope slither through the pulleys that they had embedded in a heavy wooden framework at the top of the shaft. A heavy leather bag slapped at her waist, filled with iron rods. Reaching the log, she dragged the collar over the end of it, which had been cut out into a cross shape by a hand axe and adze.

"Isn't this a bit much?" Jusuf wheezed, his muscular shoulder straining under the weight of the log. "A ladder over the wall would do as well to get us in."

"A ladder in the street would be seen by a passerby," she said, shaking her head. "This way gets us in and out unseen. With your brother's package safely delivered, it could be days or weeks before the prison guards realize that anything is amiss."

Once the collar was past the cutout, she fumbled in the bag and drew out an iron rod. One end was bluntly pointed, while the other was flattened into a mushroomlike cap. She pushed the blunt point into one of a pair of matching holes drilled through the cross-section of the end of the log. It stuck partway through, and she cursed under her breath at the delay. She tapped Jusuf twice on his shoulder and stepped back to the little ledge on the edge of the sewer tunnel. The water was cold, even with the steaming offal that drifted past, and her legs were beginning to go numb.

"You don't believe in keeping it simple, do you? Really, just a plain old ladder . . ."

Thyatis ignored him and picked up a mallet with a cotton cloth wrapped around one end and returned to the log. The three men carrying the log braced their feet against the wall of the tunnel, and she used the mallet to tap the rod through the hole until the cap end was three or four knuckle bones from the wood. The blunt end stuck out about the same distance on the other side of the log. Once done, she stepped under the log and drove the other rod the same distance through the cross-section at right angles to the first. She tugged at the rope and high above her Bagratuni unshielded a lantern over the edge of the airshaft. Thyatis saw the light flash twice up in the darkness.

"Ready!" She hissed at the three men and they walked forward a bit, until she stopped them, just as the log was about to pass beyond the opening in the ceiling of the sewer. She tugged on the rope again, three times, and then felt it go taut.

"Lay it down," she called over the sound of the rushing water to the three men. Jusuf motioned to the two others and they laid the end of the log down into the water. The rope and the collar drew snug against the bolts driven through the end of the log and the rope kept the one end high, while the other end was now in the water. Far above Thyatis thought she heard a creaking sound, and she leaned forward, both hands on the log to guide it. The rope groaned a little as it took the full weight of the log, and then the log began to rise. Thyatis and the three men guided it into the center of the shaft and watched as it rose up into the darkness.

"Prepare the others," she said to Jusuf, handing him the bag of iron rods and the mallet. "If you think about it, my fine Bulgar friend, we can use these pylons for more than just this one purpose."

Jusuf stared at her in something verging on horror. "We're going to move them *again* after this?" His whisper climbed near to a shout.

Thyatis gave him a look that could have melted bronze and pointed off down the sewer.

He shrugged and splashed away into the fetid darkness to prepare the other nine logs that had been pushed in darkness across the river and dragged by the Bulgars up through the water gate of the city and into the sewers. The creaking sound continued to echo above, and Thyatis began to worry that the sound of the pulleys could be heard in the temple. Her fingers itched for the hilt of her sword, but it was in a bundle with her other clothes up at the top of the shaft.

There was a noise above her, and she suddenly skipped out of the way as a cloth bag filled with sand dropped out of the darkness and splashed into the water. Thyatis cursed and wiped slime off her face.

"Quick on the hook," she said, reaching up to grab the rope. It quivered under her fingers, still stretched taut. "Wait for it!" The other two men had splashed forward and grabbed the top of the bag, where a hook was snagged into the rope bag that surrounded the cloth. "There!"

The tension slackened on the rope and the two men were quick to slip the hook out. They immediately dragged the bag, which was soaking with water at a terrific rate, upstream. With the hook gone, the end of the bag spilled open and sand poured out to vanish in the current of the tunnel. Thyatis felt the sand brush against her ankles as it whipped past.

Better than rats gnawing, she thought. She let go of the rope and hoped that Bagratuni's man at the top thought to let the rope with the collar down slowly, or she'd be brained as it fell sixty feet down the shaft. A moment later it descended jerkily and she grabbed it.

"Bring the next," she whispered. Another log, already sporting the cross of iron rods, appeared out of the darkness on the shoulders of the next three men. "Closer," she said, holding out the collar. The numbness in her feet crept higher, into her thighs.

"Any sign?" Thyatis spoke softly, though the black veil wrapped around her face muffled her voice. Sahul, who was crouching next to her on the rooftop, shook his head. The Roman woman grimaced and eased back from the lip. The street below was quiet and deserted. Two of Bagratuni's nephews had run down it a few minutes before and had doused the lanterns halfway down the street. Most of the street was pitch black. Thyatis sighed and squared her shoulders. She beckoned across the dark rooftop for Jusuf and Bagratuni. They crawled quietly over to her and Sahul.

There was no moon, and the sky was clear, showing only a vast expanse of glittering diamonds and twinkling emeralds. On the rooftop it was almost impossible to see the men crouched on it, dressed in dark clothing and their faces wrapped in dark gauze. Only their hands betrayed them, pale blobs in the darkness. The Armenians had smeared soot on their hands as well.

It was very quiet on the rooftop, and Thyatis could hear the chanting from the ceremonies in the Temple of the Flame clearly. Earlier she had watched nearly two hundred Persian notables and their wives, concubines, and children file into the temple. The snap and roar of the great fire on the altar at the center of the temple echoed out of the little windows set high into the walls of the church. Her squad leaders crouched in a circle in front of her, only their eyes showing.

"Anagathios," she whispered, "has not returned from his foray into the old palace. There has been no sign that he has been discovered, so either the Persians are cleverer than I think or something has happened to hold him up. Tonight is our best chance, so we're going to go ahead."

Jusuf shook his head in dismay, but stopped when Thyatis glared at him.

She turned to Sahul. "Is the first pylon complete?"

The elderly Bulgar nodded and rolled up onto the balls of his feet, his fingertips resting on the roof tiles.

"Good," she said, "send it forward."

Sahul scuttled away across the rooftop, keeping to the trail of blankets that had been laid out to muffle the sounds of men moving on the plaster roof. He reached the men at the first log and signed that they should move forward. At the edge of the roof, two men who had been waiting patiently for the "go" signal swung up a heavy frame of wood with a half circle cut out of the top. The man on the left reached into a waxed leather bucket at his side and scooped a huge glob of grease out. He smeared this around the inner part of the half circle. While he prepared the guide, a team of twelve men had lifted up the first pylon from the rooftop. Sahul moved along the thirty-foot length of the pylon, checking to see that the iron rods securely fastened each joint.

The pylon had been hauled up from the sewers in eight-foot-long sections and then slotted together on the rooftop only minutes before. Each cross-section had been cut in such a way that it slotted into the cross-section on another log.

The rods had then been driven into the socket holes with padded mallets, forming a joining cross-brace. Thyatis swore that the logs, cut of average-quality cedar, would hold the weight of a man. Sahul was not so sure, but then he didn't think that they could have hauled ten logs into a hostile city and assembled them on the roof of a fire-temple without discovery either.

The lead end of the pylon slid into the brace guide and slithered across the grease. At the back of the pylon, a metal ring had been screwed into the end of the last pole. Sahul held his hand up to halt the forward movement of the pylon while two of the Bulgars tied two heavy ropes to the ring. The ropes ran down from the end of the pylon to another, heavier ring that been drilled into the plaster of the rooftop.

This, from Thyatis' viewpoint, had been the most dangerous part of the operation. The heavy ring was screwed into a foot-thick roof beam under the plaster. It had taken two nights of careful work to bore into the beam and set it without alerting the priests in the temple below. Still, without the anchor, maintaining control of the pylon would be impossible. Sahul, seeing that the ropes were secured and all personnel on the rooftop who were not already holding up the pylon or manning the guide were in position on the anchor ropes, signed to begin running the pylon out.

The man at the wooden guide raised his hand, and the pylon slid out through it three feet. He dropped his hand and the pylon halted. The second man reached down into a large wicker basket by his side and took out an eleven-inch-long wooden peg with his left hand. His right hand already held another mallet, this one with a very well padded head on it. He slid the peg into a hole bored in the side of the log and drove it home with one sharp rap of the mallet.

The first man scanned the street below, and everyone paused, listening. The chanting from the fire temple continued, rising and falling in pitch. No one moved in the old palace or on the street. The guide man raised his hand and opened his fist. The men on the pylon spun the pylon a half turn. The man with the mallet drove a second peg in, offset six inches from the first.

Pegs were driven into the pylon at two-foot intervals. From her position at the end of the pylon, with half an ear cocked for the sound of discovery, Thyatis worried the grains of sand in the hourglass away. The pylon was thirty feet long, needing thirty pegs. It took a half-grain to rotate the pylon, drive a peg, rotate it back, and advance it another three feet. Fifteen grains dripped past with infinite slowness. She had thought at first to have the guide frame possess a slot, to allow the pegs to be driven in during the assembly of the pylon. Efforts to build a frame strong enough had failed, so she sweated out the fifteen grains. It seemed to take forever.

As the pylon slid out over the street, each man carrying it trotted back on the trail of blankets to the anchor ropes as his section disappeared through the guide. Ten feet of the back of the pylon would remain on the higher roof end, just long enough to allow the anchor ropes to guide it down. Thyatis moved to the front of the roof, next to the guide. The pylon had begun to wobble as it reached farther and farther out over the street. The end of the pylon began to flex back and forth in a semicircle. Thyatis held her breath. Behind her, nearly all of the men were dug in on the anchor ropes, trying to keep the pylon steady. Seeing its wobble, Thyatis realized too late that she should have had anchor ropes on the sides of the pylon as well as the back end. *Too late now*, she thought. The pylon slithered to one side and the guide frame gave an alarmingly loud creak as it took the pressure.

"Drop the pylon." She hissed at the men on the anchor ropes. "Slowly!"

The men on the rope began to release it, an inch at a time, and the pylon dipped toward the roof garden across the street. The pylon was out far enough now that it was actually above the garden. It trembled lower and Thyatis hissed in alarm as the end suddenly angled to one side and slewed through an immature orange tree with a crash. She and the lookout stared each direction in the street in alarm. Thyatis whirled, motioning for the anchormen to lower the pylon the rest of the way.

The pylon settled to the rooftop with a crunching sound as it crushed the little tree into kindling. Thyatis checked her sword, which was securely strapped across her back, and knelt to check the lacings on her boots. They were tight.

"Sahul! Jusuf! Follow me with the bag." The two Bulgars trotted forward with a large hemp bag, easily big enough for a man, over their shoulders. The bag was securely wrapped with ropes, but it twitched feebly regardless. Thyatis stepped up onto the edge of the roof and waited for a moment, poised over the thirty-foot drop while the two men at the guide lashed the last set of pegs to the frame. Thyatis swallowed to clear her throat and then took a deep breath.

She stepped out onto the pylon, her left boot on one of the pegs. The pylon tried to twist away under her, but the lashings stopped it. Her leg trembled as she balanced, but the pylon stopped turning. She hopped up, her right boot landing on a second peg, two feet ahead of the first. Behind her she heard Sahul and Jusuf hold their breath and a low exclamation from one of the men on the guide frame. Thyatis smiled, her blood afire with adrenaline. The moment of balance passed and she ran down the pylon, her feet skipping from one peg to the next. Wind rushed in her hair and then, suddenly, she stumbled off the end and had to tuck herself into a ball as she rolled up from the rooftop. The garden was alive with the smell of oranges and jasmine. Her sword rasped out of the scabbard over her back.

On the roof of the fire temple, Sahul grunted as Jusuf strapped the bag onto his back. It was heavy, but he was strong enough to carry it. With it secured, he backed out onto the pylon and began descending it to the garden, using the pegs as hand and footholds. He prayed to his god that the pegs would not snap or the pylon give way. He would not admit it to the Roman lady, but he was squeamish where heights were concerned. His forearms and calves burned with the effort of supporting over two hundred extra pounds of weight.

In the garden, Thyatis had run lightly to the inner wall and had peered down into the courtyard. It was a black well, unlit, seemingly bottomless. She listened carefully. No one seemed to have heard the crash of the falling pylon. She ran back to the end of the pylon in time to help Sahul and his burden off. Then she unwound a rope from her waist, tied it around the lowest pair of pegs, and strung it out as she walked backward to the inner wall. Checking the courtyard one more time, she dropped the rope over the side. It made a rustling sound as it hit below. A grain later she had swung over the side and crabbed down the inner wall. Sahul followed immediately down the rope, and then Jusuf, who had also run—cursing under his breath—down the pylon to get to the garden faster.

On the roof of the fire temple, Bagratuni breathed out a long, slow sigh of relief. The crazy Romans had done it! When the Roman woman—Bagratuni had begun to think of her as Diana the Huntress in his private thoughts—had proposed this mad scheme, he had been utterly sure that they would all be discovered and slain within hours of beginning the attempt. Even finding the cedars and getting them into the city was a feat to boast of around the hearth fire for a generation! This, this was even bolder. He smiled in the darkness and shooed his men back to their positions on the ropes. The Bulgars had taken up watch all around them. All they had to do was wait, and hope that no priest or noble decided to take a turn under the stars on the roof of the temple.

Thyatis crept up to the door in the far wall of the courtyard and carefully pressed her ear to it. There was a faint murmur from the heavy oaken panels, but it did not seem to be very close. Sahul and Jusuf arrived and paused, panting faintly from the effort of the last minutes. She scratched her nose and then pulled a thin, flat piece of steel out of her belt. The door was secured by what from a distance had seemed to be a heavy lock. Now she fished around in the keyhole, trying to find the mechanism. To her disgust, it had none. She pressed against the panel of the door with her shoulder and felt it give a little before stopping.

"There's a bar on the inside," she whispered into Sahul's ear. "Be ready. If I can get it up, there will be a noise." She began probing with the steel rod at the edges of the door and in the panel, looking for a crevice. There was nothing. Thyatis cursed mentally. This was very bad. She tested the strength of the door. It was stout and they did not have time to cut the lock away.

"Jusuf, we're not getting through this door," she said softly. "Step out and see if you can spy one of the windows on the upper floor. Maybe we can get in through one of those . . ." She paused, thinking she heard something, and then froze as the door rattled slightly. Sahul and Jusuf faded back, away from the door, disappearing into the gloom. Thyatis flattened herself against the wall, feeling the cold plaster surface tickle at her neck. There was a scraping sound from beyond the door and then a latch clicked. Thyatis slid the sword in her hand quietly back into its sheath and then drew a long knife.

The door opened, spilling a pale-yellow light into the courtyard. A shadow obscured the light and then a woman in a tattered gown and headdress peered out, blinking, into the darkness. Thyatis swallowed a breath and then darted around the corner of the door. Her knife was at the woman's throat in an instant and a gloved hand over her mouth. Pretty brown eyes, edged with kohl and glittering sapphire dust, widened and the woman raised hands with long, delicate nails in surrender. Behind her Sahul and Jusuf had slid past into the room on the other side, knives in hand. The room was empty, more a hallway filled with big pottery jars than anything else. Thyatis walked forward and hooked the door closed with her foot.

"So," she breathed, "I see you're having a fine time in the lap of luxury."

Sahul and Jusuf turned and saw Thyatis sheath her knife. The woman shrugged and dug her fingers under the back of her hair, peeling off the heavy brown tresses with a popping sound. Anagathios shook his own hair out and stuffed the wig into a bag under his dress. Jusuf gave a soundless whistle.

"A better-looking woman than a man," he said, his lip half curled.

Thyatis ignored him and signed to the actor. *Have you found Nikos?*

Yes, Anagathios answered. *There is a cellar, with holding cells for the prisoners of the garrison commander. He's down there, but he's not alone.*

What do you mean? she answered, but the Syrian shook his head with a rueful smile.

You'll see. What's in the bag?

Thyatis smirked back at him. *Take us to the cellar and you'll see.*

"The gods have cursed me." Thyatis grunted as she peered around the corner of the cellar hallway. "Cells, with thirty or forty people in them. At least they're asleep—for the moment." She turned and grimaced wryly at Sahul, who was still carrying the heavy bag. "Why did the Boar have to take so many 'special' prisoners?" Jusuf refused to look at her, but Sahul swung the bag off his back with a grateful sigh and rubbed his shoulders.

Anagathios, she signed at the actor, who was crouched right behind her. *Who are all these people?*

Locals, he gestured back, *mostly hostages for the good behavior of the headmen of the town and the surrounding villages. What are we going to do?*

"Victory," she said aloud, "is to the bold. Forget the original plan. Jusuf, Sahul, go back up the stairs and block all of the doorways that lead into this hall or our route back to the courtyard. Then, Jusuf, you go all the way back to the fire-temple roof and tell Bagratuni that we're going to try to bring all of his relatives out. Tell him to pull the pylon back and break it down into the logs and send it down into the sewer. We're not going out that way now. Tell him that in about twenty grains, we're going to need a diversion on the other side of town, something noisy.

"Sahul—go back to the garden and drop more ropes into the courtyard and tie them securely. Then we need more ropes for the outer wall—but not yet, not until we need them! We'll try taking everyone out that way. Anagathios, start tearing your dress into strips, each one about two feet long."

Thyatis stood up and hitched up her belt. Sahul and Jusuf stared at her for a moment, standing there in the glow of the torches that lit the corridor, her face partially in shadow. Then they sketched a hurried bow and ran back the way they had come, their sandals slapping on the stones of the floor. Anagathios stripped down and started tearing the ragged gown into pieces.

Thyatis crept forward, hoping against hope that no one would wake up before she was ready. The men were in a set of cells on the left, while the women and children were opposite them on the right. Each cell was no more than a big room carved out of the thick river clay that underlaid the whole city. They were partially bricked in, with stout doors of oak with windows covered by bronze bars at each entrance. From the door, the entirety of each cell could be seen. Thyatis glided like a ghost along the front of the cells holding the men.

Nikos was in the third cell, leaning against the wall, asleep. Thyatis snarled silently. He was really asleep, not just shamming. She knelt and cut off the tip of one of the leather thongs that bound her boots to her calf. It was a hard little nub of well-cured leather. She flicked it through the bars, and it hit Nikos in the right eye. He started and his eyes flickered open. A piece of sharpened copper was in his right hand. Warily he looked around, his eyes widening in utter surprise when he caught sight of Thyatis peering in the window. She put a finger to her lips. He nodded.

Gently she raised the bar on the outside the door, easing up the slip-latch that held it down. Once it was off, she laid it flat on the floor next to the door and slowly eased the heavy panel open. Nikos was waiting on the other side, having stepped lightly across the sleeping bodies of his fellow prisoners. Thyatis signed for him to step out. She closed the door behind him.

For a moment they stood staring at each other, and a parade of emotions passed over Nikos' face like a triumph in the Forum. Thyatis just grinned hugely and then hugged him close to her hard enough to make him *oof* in surprise. He broke free and rubbed his arms in chagrin.

Which way is out? he signed.

A question, first, she replied. *Do any of these others have level heads?*

He looked at her dubiously, then his fingers danced, saying: *What do you intend, foolish one?*

She mugged an innocent face, then: *We're getting everyone out if we can. If we do, the local tribes will owe me a favor for every head. I need them to take the city for Caesar.*

Nikos started to look sick. Then he noticed the bag on the floor behind her. *What's in the bag?* He asked.

Oh, nothing . . . just your body.

NORTH OF EMESA, THE THEME OF SYRIA MAGNA

"Empress!" One of the Tanukh riders, his *kaffieh* streaming behind him in the wind of his passage, galloped into the command camp. Nabatean spearmen, guarding the entrance to the camp, dashed out of his way. His horse was lathered and coated with dust from the road. Zenobia, her hair still undone, stepped away from the cluster of sleepy officers who surrounded her at the doorway of her great tent. With the army on the march, she wore hunting leathers—a pair of soft kid trousers with a stout vest over a loose cotton shirt. Her hand, quick as a hawk in flight, snagged the bridle of the horse and the man drew to a halt. The horse blew, heavily, and Zenobia patted its long nose.

"The Al'Quraysh sends his greetings on this fine morning, Empress, and says that the Persian army is athwart the road to the north and is deploying for battle."

The Queen flashed a brilliant smile. Her camp had been made on a low hill beside the main road north from the Roman city of Emesa, now some three leagues behind them, to the smaller town of Arethusa on the Orontes River. A copse of trees marked the crown of the hill, and the brightly colored tents of her servants and commanders were settled among the junipers and scrubby pines. Curlicues of smoke rose from their campfires. To the north, other hills blocked her view of the long slope down to the Orontes. Behind her, a fine view of Emesa and the fertile valley around it could be seen. The morning sun, just over the eastern horizon, bathed the land in a pale-pink light. The air was still quite cool from the night and the horse's breath was a cloud in the air.

"It is a fine morning. Tell the Al'Quraysh that we will be with him presently."

The man reined around and cantered away through the line of trees in a swirl of dust.

Zenobia stared north with a sly grin on her face and slapped her thigh with the riding stick she favored as a pointer for staff meetings. The Persians had turned to face her at last. Today was the day that she would equal her distant ancestor and set her people free of both Empires. She turned and strode back to the gathering of her men. At one side of the cluster of officers, Ahmet sat on a camp stool, calmly eating his morning porridge. He glanced up as she passed into the tent. The Queen was in a good humor.

Ahmet jounced up and down, his tailbone complaining bitterly, his hands around Zenobia's slim waist as they trotted up over the last rise. He had added a *kaffieh*, a loose headpiece of flowing cotton and a band of corded rope to hold it on his head, to his usual robes over a loincloth. In previous days he had walked alongside the wagons carrying Zenobia's personal effects and her household, but today the Queen made haste, so he rode behind her.

Beyond the rise, the hills had dropped away and a broad plain, shaped like the head of a spear, pointed to the northeast. A stream ran along the farther edge of the plain, where another range of low hills rose up. The Emesa road cut at an angle down the near slope, crossed the stream at a ford, and then rose up into those hills. The ground in between was littered with rocks, small boulders, scrubby grass, and low gray bushes. Zenobia surveyed the terrain with a glint in her eye.

"Overgrazed," she said, turning to the east on the great black stallion that she favored and riding along the line of the crest. "Firm ground, good traction for horses and men."

"A pity the Persians turned back before they stumbled onto your gift at Lake Bahrat."

Zenobia glanced over her shoulder at the Egyptian, her eyes smoldering with anger.

"The first stroke of good sense the Great Prince Shahin ever had in his life!"

Ahmet nodded and clung tighter to her as they crossed some rough ground. Zenobia's army was disgorging onto the southern side of the plain from the main road and several other tracks that Mohammed's scouts had found leading through the hills. The Palmyrene and Nabatean heavy cavalry was trotting out in oblong formations, five and six men deep, their lances raised like a forest of steel reeds. Banners rose and fell over the formations as their commanders attempted to coax them into a line of battle. Bands of Syrian and Nabatean infantry, *arithmoi* to the Romans, spilled out of the trails on either side. Black-skinned men with tufts of feathers worked into their hair, carrying bows and javelins, ran past the command group down the slope. Zenobia was heading for a bluff to the right side of the main road. A band of men in red armor was already deployed on the height. *Aretas and his priests*, Ahmet thought.

"You're sure that Shahin still commands the Persian host?" His voice was quiet, though the clatter of the horse's hooves on the rocky ground was sure to drown out anything but a shout.

Zenobia nodded, though she frowned in concentration.

"One of our scouts must have been discovered," she said, "to make them abandon the camp in such haste." She snarled in anger, striking her riding boot with the crop. "Just one more day and we would have had them on the plain at Bahrat. Ha, we would have had him already if Mohammed could have kept those Tanukh bandits from looting the Persian camp. Ah, it is as my father always said— the time of battle is never chosen and the field is never favorable!" She pointed out at the plain they were facing.

"This is almost perfect for him, though, the Persian eunuch! His *clibanari* and *cataphracti* will have a fine day against us if we are not aggressive."

She stopped talking for a moment as the stallion surged up the side of the bluff and she rode into the midst of Aretas' guardsmen. The Nabatean's servants had already thrown up an open-sided tent and the Prince, clad in enameled red armor composed of overlapping metal lozenges secured with leather bands, was seated on a stool at the front of the tent. Around him, his servants were busy preparing small tables laden with bowls of water, twisted pieces of metal, and a wide range of curious artifacts. Behind him, in the shade of the tent, the twelve hooded men who accompanied him were seated, a tremulous hum coming from their cowls.

"Lord Prince," Zenobia said, deftly bringing the stallion to a halt. Small rocks thrown by the horse's hooves skittered into the tent. "Are you and your men prepared for battle?"

Aretas looked up from the scroll he was studying, his face bland and his kohl-rimmed eyes languid. He was freshly shaven, and his beard was now only a sketch of dark hair along his lip and cheekbones. A trapezoid had been painted in a dark-red ink on his forehead.

"Of course," he said in a polite voice. "I am prepared, as are my assistants." A hand wrapped in a glove of fine steel links over soft leather indicated the hooded men. "My *tagma* are riding into positions even now. The infantry *arithmoi* are soon to follow. Is there ought else you require of me today?"

Zenobia frowned but controlled her temper. "Can you repel the efforts of the Persian *magi*? Can you master them and their powers?"

Aretas smiled, a wintry thing that touched only his lips and did not crawl up to his eyes, which were cold and dispassionate. He opened his right hand, the fingers uncurling like a claw. A dark light spilled from between his fingers, rippling with lightning.

"I think that I will do as honor demands," he said, and banished the glamour. "Rome will prevail this day, I think. The Persians did not expect us to field such strength of men."

A dangerous glitter entered Zenobia's eyes at the mention of Rome, but she let it pass.

"Then, if all do their duty, we shall have victory this day," she said, and saluted the Prince. "Tell your *dekarchoi* to await my signal before they commit to the battle. We must prepare our Persian guests for such a meeting first!"

Aretas inclined his head and stood. Zenobia nodded back, turned her horse and galloped away. From the bluff, as they rode down onto the field, Ahmet could see that the army of the desert cities had managed to reach the plain. The bluff formed the right wing, with Aretas' cavalry *tagma* clustered in a dull red mass at its foot. In front of them, a hundred yards down the slope, the Nabatean infantry *arithmoi* formed a line of blocks of spearmen, archers, and slingers reaching to the west. More cavalry, these lighter armored, trotted past behind the infantry to take up positions at the far right end of the Nabatean line.

Zenobia and her officers, including a pack of Tanukh, rode along the length of the line. Her Bactrian guards, now kitted out in furs and heavy armor, rode in a block around her, their lances socketed into cups at their right stirrups. At the center, two great blocks of infantry—one of the Palmyrenes who had joined them at Emesa under the command of Zenobia's brother Vorodes, and the other formed of the cohorts of the cities of the Decapolis under Akhimos Galerius—were slowly gathering. Zenobia rode past and shouted instructions at Galerius, the commander of the Decapoli *arithmoi*. He waved back at her and then resumed his argument with the commanders of the various bands of city militia.

Behind the gangs of infantry, clad in shields and carrying spears, was a motley collection of mercenary horsemen—the expatriate Persians in full lamellar mail from head to toe and cone-shaped helmets, the Indian knights in bright tabards and glittering chain mail with long bows that stood from their saddles. Another band of Axumite javelin men ran past, down the road, heading for one of the avenues that had been left between the blocks of infantry. Zenobia took up a position on a rise to the left of the road, fifty or sixty yards from the mercenary horse. Ahmet was pleased beyond measure that they had stopped for a moment, for it gave him an opportunity to relax against the constant fear of being thrown from the horse.

Farther to the left of Vorodes' infantry, a great block of Palmyrene knights stood at the ready. Clad in half-armor for the riders and felt barding studded with metal plaques for the horses, the assembled nobles of Palmyra, Damascus, and the other cities of the Decapolis anchored the western, or leftmost, end of the line.

Beyond them, the Tanukh light horse was a haze of small bands of riders screening the knights and the flank of the army.

Zenobia stood up in her stirrups and stared out over the battlefield. Unobtrusively Ahmet supported her legs, her thighs firm and strong under his hands.

"That is Shahin's banner, all right, and his usual flock of pretty birds are with him."

The Persian army had drawn up on the near side of the shallow stream in a shallow crescent. From the greenery along the banks at the eastern end of the plain, it seemed that there was a marshy area along the streambed. The Persian line began on the far right with a wedge of medium cavalry. From where he sat astride the stallion, Ahmet could barely make out a thicket of lances strapped to the backs of the riders, their tips gleaming in the morning sun, and dull armor. The horses seemed unarmored, and the men were holding bows at the ready, resting on their pommels.

Next, the center of the Persian line was composed of four blocks of infantry—first a rank of spearmen with wicker and leather shields, then archers, then more spearmen. Though the bands of men were not as precisely ordered as a Roman army, there were sharply defined breaks between each block. Behind the infantry, almost at the ford where the road crossed the stream over a broad wooden bridge, there was a great green tent, and before it, mounted on a shining white horse, was the small figure of the enemy commander. His armor reflected the sun with a golden glow and around him his companions were brightly attired in silks and jewels. Behind him, a great standard with a white wheel on it had been hung from a tall pole. Two parasols shaded the enemy commander, each of green silk.

"They seem better suited for a hunting party and picnic than battle," Ahmet mused.

Zenobia snorted. "At Nisibis, when the Boar smashed the army of the Eastern Empire and opened the road to Antioch, Shahin had command of the right wing—it is said that he and his cronies spent the day in a pleasant feast while ten thousand men died on the field of battle. He is the King of Kings' cousin, and well beloved of Chrosoes, but he is a poor leader of men. While he holds command, we will win the day."

To the left of the Persian spearmen, there were two large wedges of heavy cavalry—and these men, Ahmet could see, were clad in mail from head to toe, as were many of their horses. Many banners danced in the air above the Persian horse. Finally, a hundred yards in front of the Persian army, many lightly armed archers in kilts and metal caps were deployed in a long line. The black men, the Blemmenye who served Zenobia, had also advanced before the line of the Palmyrene army, and now the air between the two hosts was briefly marked by the sparkle of arrows in flight. A few men fell, but Ahmet could see no great purpose in their action.

"Odd . . ." Zenobia whistled and one of the Tanukh couriers pushed his horse through the throng of Bactrians deployed around the Queen. He grinned saucily when he pulled his horse alongside Zenobia's.

"Gadimathos, I see no light horsemen to screen the Persian line from our archers. Where are they?"

The Tanukh shrugged easily, his lean brown face wrinkled in a smile. "The Lakhmids are afraid to face the true men, the Tanukh. They refuse to fight."

Zenobia shook her head in dismay. "Go to ibn'Adi and Al'Quraysh and tell them to watch for the Lakhmids. They must be somewhere about—send out scouts to cover the flanks. They may be trying to ride around our line."

The Queen reached back and squeezed Ahmet's leg as the command troop cantered forward. "Worry not, priest, soon the battle will begin in earnest and you'll forget your fear of riding!"

Ahmet held her a little tighter and she laughed, her voice gay. They turned and rode back along the length of the Palmyrene line at a slower pace.

"Why is the absence of these Lakhmids a cause for concern?" Ahmet was confused.

Zenobia frowned again and pointed back to the west, where the Persian knights were lined up. "Without their own horse-archers to protect their heavy cavalrymen, our Tanukh will spend the day shooting at them with arrows. The heavy horse cannot catch these desert raiders, so they'll do nothing but bleed! I had heard that Shahin had employed a tribe of the Lakhmids to provide him with light horse for scouting and such work in battle. Another mistake. If they are not here, that will cost him dearly."

Ahmet nodded.

"What is happening in the unseen world?" she asked suddenly. It took Ahmet a moment to focus; the ether had begun to crackle with invisible forces.

"Aretas is putting forth his strength," Ahmet said, his voice breathy. It was sometimes difficult to breathe and speak and see in the world of the unseen all at the same time. "The Persian *magi* have raised a shield to protect their men from anything we might send against them. He is probing it, seeking weakness or a crevice. The Red Prince is strong!"

Zenobia nodded and looked quizzically out over the battlefield. There was a tang in the air, like before a storm, but the sky was clear and blue. Trumpets rang out, and there was a rattle of drums among the Persian battalions. The Persian center, to her surprise, began to advance at a walk up the slope. Their spears moved in a shining wave, falling forward. She stood in the stirrups again and looked east and west. To the right, on the east, opposite the Nabateans, bands of light infantrymen—wearing no more than woolen kilts and carrying long spears— had run out between the end of the infantry line and the cavalry at the end of the Persian front. These men, too, advanced up the slope toward the Blemmenye skirmishers. Arrows were flying a little thicker now.

To the west, the two wedges of Persian heavy cavalry remained at rest, though their banners and flags were dipping and rising in response to those of the main command group at the bridge. Along the center of the line, the Persian archers began to fire over the line of Palmyrene slingers, ranging for the blocks of infantry behind them. Zenobia considered the movement of forces.

"This is strange," Ahmet whispered from behind her. "The Persian shield is proof against Aretas, even though the air boils with his power and the strength of his priests. And, it advances in concert with their men."

"Why is that strange?" Zenobia said absently. She whistled again and called out to her own officers. "Send the Tanukh against the Persian *cataphracti* and *clibanari*!" One of the couriers spurred his horse away and pelted off toward the west. At the same time, two of her banner men raised a dark flag with a white symbol on it and dipped it twice. Soon afterward, the bands of Tanukh on the left coalesced into three big groups and rode off toward the Persian lines at great speed.

Ahmet began to sweat and hum a focusing meditation under his breath. The light shield that he had raised around Zenobia and himself as soon as the word had come in the morning that the Persians were near surged with power in the unseen world, becoming a complex series of geometric lattices around them. The lattices separated, becoming shells of light that counterrotated around him in dizzying array. The hidden world was afire to his eye. The Persians continued to advance, and the flickering dark shield that protected them advanced as well. Aretas and his priests hammered at it with increasing ferocity, their sendings cutting sizzling tracks through the universe of forms and patterns whose reflected shadows were men and stones and the sky. Ahmet could feel the power drain like a tugging on his sleeve as the Nabateans began leaching the currents under the earth and in the sky to power the cyan bolts they hurled at the dark shield.

"Lady, the Persian sorcerers are very strong. Unless this defense is taxing their full strength, which it may, Aretas will not be able to withstand them if they choose to counterattack."

The strain in Ahmet's voice caught Zenobia's attention and she half turned in the saddle to look at him eye to eye. "What does this mean? Will they be able to defeat my army with magic?"

Suddenly the Nabatean attack ceased, and the boiling fury that had been building to a breaking point faded. The dark shield remained, impenetrable, over the Persian lines.

"No, now they've stopped. I think Aretas has realized that raw strength will not unravel this puzzle. My lady, while each coterie of wizards remains there is a balance on this field—but if one should gain an advantage, there will be a terrible slaughter."

Zenobia nodded fiercely and raised her hand. One of her command banners matched the movement of her arm. Looking down the slope, the Persian center was continuing its advance. The Tanukh had galloped, on the left, to within arrow range of the Persian heavy horse and had begun lofting arrows into the middle of the formation. Zenobia chopped her hand down, and there was a peal of trumpets from her banner men. The war flags slashed the air. Ahmet stared down the Palmyrene line to the right. It began to move.

"Attack!" Zenobia screamed, and she goosed her horse forward. She and her guardsmen trotted east along the length of the line, watching as the *arithmoi* of infantrymen leveled their long spears and began walking forward, downhill, toward the Persians. Behind her the Decapoli heavy cavalry that had been screened behind the Tanukh horse began walking forward, angling towards the Persian heavy cavalry, which was suffering under the arrow fire. The entire Palmyrene force was in motion. Ahmet stared around him as they rode past the mercenary horse that was mounting up, a shiver of movement across the lines of horses. There was a terrible majesty about it.

Baraz scratched at his ear. The grand brocade hat that he was wearing, along with Shahin's armor—as ill-fitting as it was—was rubbing against his ear. He felt half a fool in the opulent costume, but as long as it served his purpose, he would suffer it. It was hard to move his head, though. The desert tribes were in full advance along the length of their line now, and the courtiers that he had "borrowed" from Shahin were beginning to mutter nervously. He smiled and nodded to the Luristani guardsmen who had attached themselves to him. The hulking infantrymen edged up behind the pretty birds to make sure that none of them took flight.

The skirmishers who had occupied the space between the two armies scattered back through his lines now, as the advancing Romans closed to within a hundred and fifty yards of the Persian front. He could see, though his angle was not good, that the tribesmen had committed their heavy horse on his right as well, and there seemed to be an advance of infantry on his left.

Baraz nodded to one of his signalmen, and the man raised a black banner with a skewed cross on it. Behind the group of riders, men crouched over great hide drums began to beat a sharp marching beat. Ahead, the blocks of Persian spear, axe, and swordsmen began to advance up the hill at a walk. Within instants of starting their advance, the clear avenues between the formations disappeared as the men at the edges of the infantry battalions spilled out into the open space to avoid hitting the men in front of them. Baraz grunted. *Just like foot soldiers—no discipline!*

A dispatch rider rode up, his helmet askew. "Lord Baraz!" The rider was one of Khadames' youngsters. "Lord Khadames requests that he be allowed to charge the enemy wing—his casualties are mounting from arrow fire."

Baraz laughed grimly and shook his head. "No, lad, tell Khadames that if he so much as budges, I'll have him beheaded and his whole family sold as slaves in the great market at Ctesiphon. He holds for my order, and no other!"

The youngster put spur to his horse and pelted off back to the right. Baraz smiled, noticing the queasy looks on the courtiers around him.

"Worry not, friends!" he called out in his battlefield voice, so that all could hear. "Soon we'll see action aplenty! Are your swords loose? Are your bows strung and taut?" Then he laughed, for fear was beginning to creep into their eyes. The Luristani grinned and fingered their weapons.

The Persian infantry was only fifty yards from the Romans and the center of the field was about to become a charnel house. Baraz gestured to his drum men, and they beat out a long rolling tattoo. The banners flourished in the air. Two hundred yards ahead of his position, Lord Rhazates began screaming orders at his infantry commanders and the Persian advance halted, raggedly on the left, skewing the line slightly, but it halted. The front rank of men went down to a kneeling position, their spears thrust forward horizontally and their large shields grounded.

The second and third ranks crowded up, and a forest of longer spears and pikes sprang into being along the front.

Baraz sat astride his white horse, drumming his fingers on the high saddle horn. Dispatch riders crowded around him, relaying information to his lieutenants. He ordered the skirmishers, now that they had fallen back through the lanes between his blocks of infantry, to gather and swing to the left end of his line, where a regiment of swordsmen and unarmored spearmen were screening the Great Prince Shahin and his household cavalry from the advance of the Nabatean infantry. Dust rose in a great cloud in the center of the field where the spearmen and swordsmen were now at close quarters. The Boar summoned one of the dispatch riders.

"Lad, find the Lord Rhazates in that cauldron in front of us and tell him to hold his own, neither to advance nor retreat. Just retain the attention of the enemy."

The sky growled like thunder, and Baraz jerked around, staring up into the bright blue sky. There was nothing there, but now an uneasy feeling prickled at his back and he turned his horse, staring across the shallow stream at the covered black wagon sitting by the side of the road. A troop of Uze horse was sitting around it on the ground, seemingly oblivious. To Baraz's eye, it seemed that the air around the wagon shimmered with an unhealthy color.

On the Palmyrene left wing, where Mohammad and his horse archers had been dashing toward the Persians, firing a black cloud of arrows and then swerving away in fine style, the Palmyrene knights had ridden up at last and had dispersed into a line nine ranks deep. Mohammad rose up in his stirrups and waved the green banner that ibn'Adi favored in a slashing circle. His horsemen, seeing the signal, broke away to the left and right from their latest sortie, clearing a lane for the Palmyrenes to charge down. Mohammad galloped past the front of the Persian line, the last of the Tanukh to abandon the attack, seeing the dead and dying Persians transfixed by black-fletched shafts—many still on their horses, milling about in the closely packed formation.

Still the Persians held their ranks and did not charge. Mohammad shook his head at their bravery and discipline—no Arab contingent would have been able to stand the slaughter. He galloped back up the low hill, his bannermen following close behind.

"Regroup! Regroup!" Mohammad shouted, his voice carrying across the field. The Tanukh, scattered across the northern end of the plain, began riding back to him, gathering around the green and white banner of ibn'Adi. And still the Persians refused to move from their ranks. Al'Quraysh wheeled his horse, now that his subcommanders had the horsemen in hand, and trotted up to the line of Palmyrene knights, who had not budged from their positions once they had broken out into a wedge.

"Lord Zabda," Mohammad called across the ranks of armored horsemen. "The

Persians are still stunned by our arrows, you must attack immediately! Their backs are to the stream, you can drive their horses into the soft ground."

Zabda turned his horse and trotted through the ranks of his men. He was clad in a long chain-mail shirt under a breastplate of metal strips tied together with leather lacings. A heavy helmet, cone-shaped like the Persian *spangenhelm*, covered his head, save for a narrow slit for his eyes. A pennon fluttered from the sharp tip of the cone. The shoulders, chest, and head of his horse were covered in thick leather barding with iron scales woven into it. The general pulled up next to Mohammed's winded horse and put a gloved hand on the Southerner's shoulder.

"We are outnumbered by two to one, Quraysh! I'll not send my men to their deaths for nothing. Look, the Queen has dispatched the reserve to support us." He pointed back toward the main Palmyrene positions. Mohammad looked over the man's shoulder. Sure enough, the mercenary cavalry was trotting at an easy pace across the field to join them. The center of the battle had devolved into a massive cloud of dust, momentarily broken by bands of men with swords and spears rushing to and fro. Mohammad could not see Zenobia's banners.

"They'll be here too late for the initial charge," he snapped at the older man. "My Tanukh will charge with you, our numbers will be greater then!"

Zabda laughed, a hollow sound coming from within the metal helmet. "Your desert bandits? There's no way they can stand against the Iron Hats! No, we will wait for reinforcements."

Mohammad cursed luridly and spurred his horse away. As he rode back down the hill, he shouted at his bannermen. "Flag the commanders! Regroup and prepare to charge the Persian lines!"

Zabda called out from behind him, but Mohammad did not hear him.

Baraz finally discarded the ornamental hat and tore the silk tabard and cloak off his shoulders. The rich green material fluttered to the ground and was quickly churned to nothing by the hooves of the horses. The Roman infantry charge had slammed the Persians back to their original positions, and now the melee was beginning to bow the Persian infantry line in the center. The Persian formations had dissolved into a confused mass of men, but the Boar could see that the Romans were holding their line and grinding forward, their short blades flickering in the air. Baraz and his Luristani guards cantered to the west, the general trying to see what was happening on the right wing. The Palmyrenes seemed to have gathered their heavy horse in preparation for a charge—but they had not done so yet. He looked back to the left, seeing that the Roman infantry was fully committed to the center.

"Dispatch rider!" One of the youngsters swerved to join him. "To Khadames on the right, now he must attack! Flags! Signal an advance on the right."

The general rode up to a band of archers sitting on the ground, well behind the clangor of the melee. Their captain leapt to his feet, seeing the banner of the Great Prince fluttering behind Baraz. "Captain, take your men to the left. The Nabateans have engaged our wing. Support the infantry and Shahin's household cavalry there. Go!"

The archers shouldered their bows and quivers of arrows, their bare chests slick with sweat. They wore only short cotton kilts, now drab with mud and dust. The captain saluted and began shouting at his men. They jogged off to the east in a column of twos. Baraz shaded his eyes, staring at Khadames' horsemen on the far right. The banners of the horsemen dipped in acknowledgment of the order. The shining mass of men began to shift and disperse as they formed up into ranks to charge up the hill against the Romans.

Baraz grunted and waved his men to follow him. He turned back and rode toward the center of the line. Khadames would carry that wing or not; it was out of Baraz's hands now.

"What do you mean, they refuse to advance?" Zenobia's eyes flashed in anger.

The courier bowed, saying "The captain of the knights says that he moves upon Aretas' order, not yours."

Zenobia was dumbfounded. She stared up at the bluff where the Prince and his priests were still conjuring in their tent. The Palmyrene right wing had swept down the hill with a combined force of Nabatean infantry and her archers and slingers. They had clashed with a smaller force of Persian light infantry and pushed it aside, fouling the flank of the main Persian infantry. There had been a large force of Persian *cataphracti* behind the spearmen, but it had withdrawn, leaving the spearmen and now bands of archers to fight it out with the Nabateans in chain mail, longswords, and shields at close quarters. The more heavily armored Nabateans were slaughtering the Persians, many of whom only had a wicker shield and spear for arms.

Over the roar of battle—men screaming and dying, the clash of arms, running feet, the whistle of arrows—Zenobia shouted louder to make herself heard to her bannermen. "Send a dispatch rider to Aretas. He must order his cavalry to advance on the right! We can turn the entire Persian flank if they charge now!" Two of her riders galloped off.

"Curse him!" Zenobia wiped sweat out of her eyes. The day had grown hot and she and her command group were in constant movement. She had changed horses twice, keeping a fresh mount beneath her. Ahmet nodded absently, his vision focused inward. The slaughter on the field was seeping through into the hidden world. Eddies and vortices of hatred and fear and the flash of the dying were forming in the unseen world around the battlefield. The Nabatean priests had halted their attack on the black sphere, and even it had begun to flake and fade away under the disrupting stress of the battle. The Persians, though, had begun to attack in turn, sending traceries of ultraviolet stalking invisibly across the field. Now Aretas and his minions were hard pressed to hold back the strength of Persia.

One dark tendril whipped out toward Ahmet and Zenobia, its tip sparking with green lightning. Ahmet's will crystallized and the shield of Athena flared into almost visible brilliance. The ultraviolet lightning struck the sphere and slithered across its face, burning fiercely. Ahmet gasped at the strength in the blow and struggled to draw more power from the land around him. The stones and rocks had already been leached dry by Aretas. Furious, he snatched at the emotion in the air, and the blue geometries of his defense flared up long enough to hold back the lightning. It snapped away, leaving him exhausted.

"The enemy wizards are incredibly strong, my Queen," he whispered into Zenobia's ear. "Aretas cannot aid you, his whole attention is upon the enemy."

"Then I will move his men myself! Ha!" The stallion leapt away and Ahmet clung for dear life as the Queen stormed up the slope to the bluff.

Mohammed spun his horse and cantered to the left of the massed Tanukh. His banner men hurtled along with him, wither to wither. He leaned forward and slashed his hand forward. As one, the three thousand Tanukh wheeled with him and launched themselves forward, a long curving line, like a scimitar blade, against the Persian horse that was advancing at a walk up the hill. Mohammed felt a fierce burst of pride at the responsive movement of his men. The chestnut mare flew across the rocky ground, and he raised his voice in a long ululating scream of battle. Three thousand throats answered him and the Tanukh thundered down the shallow slope, their lances flashing down to face the Iron Hats. Mohammed had never felt so alive and focused in his life. The Persian ranks, still separating into charge intervals, swelled in his vision.

Zenobia's head snapped around as the distant sound of a terrible war cry reached her, attenuated by the dusty air and the distance. She had almost reached the blocks of Nabatean *tagma* who were still sitting ahorse under the eaves of the bluff. She rose up, and dimly, though the clouds of fine dust, she saw a line of horsemen slam into the advancing Persians on the far left wing of her army. She blanched at the dull crash that echoed across the field to her. Her fist clenched until the knuckles were white.

"Dispatch rider," she whispered, then shouted. One of the Tanukh rode up, his face pale. "Find Zabda on the left wing and tell him, by Hecate, to charge the Persian line!" Her voice rose to a shriek. "Find the mercenary knights and tell them to ride to Zabda as fast as they can." There was a sick feeling curdling in her stomach. Regardless, she tore her attention away and back to the small group of Nabatean officers who were standing next to their horses in the shade of a pavilion.

Zenobia's face was grim and set as she walked the dun horse up to the Nabateans.

"I sent orders for you and your *tagma* to advance in support of the infantry fighting on the right wing," she said, her voice calm and controlled.

The middle officer, a plump man with Aretas' nose and tightly curled hair peeping out from under his helmet, bowed to her. "My lady, we are under strict orders from our Prince and King to stand ready to move on his command. He made it quite clear that we were to move on his order, and his order only."

Zenobia turned the horse and stared down at the Nabatean officers. "Your precious King and Prince is well occupied in his own battle, my lords. He cannot spare the time to give you orders. I *am* giving you orders. You will attack on the right in support of your own civil infantry *arithmoi* and turn the Persian line. Is that clear?"

The plump officer stuck out his chin defiantly and his eyes hardened. His people had been powerful on the desert frontier for centuries before a quirk of the Twin Rivers made Palmyra rich and elevated a motley collection of tribesmen into a principality. Too, the man was sure of the favor of his king.

"We ride on the orders of Aretas, Lady Zenobia, and no other!"

"Fool!" Zenobia snapped, losing her temper. "The battle hangs in the balance and you dawdle here and posture! You *will* advance your men, or I will remove you from command!"

The plump officer's hand snaked to the hilt of his sword, but Ahmet suddenly spoke harshly. "Something is happening! Aretas is beset . . ."

In the hidden world, the Persians had finally tired of the game and had sent forth their full power. Aretas and his priests screamed in fear, the sound echoing in the confines of their tent. Their servants rushed forward, but then staggered back in utter horror. The Prince stumbled out of the tent, clawing at his eyes, which had suddenly filled with blood and then burst, spewing red gelatin on the first servant to rush to his aid. Aretas screamed again, clawing at his face, his fingers tearing long bloody strips from his cheekbones. His body convulsed and the servants cried out to see his flesh ripple and bunch, as if thousands of worms or snakes were trapped under his skin. Aretas stumbled forward and then spread his arms wide and stepped off the edge of the bluff.

The falling body, seen by all of the horsemen crowded below, fell for what seemed to be an eternity, and then it was suddenly wrapped in flame and struck the ground with a thudding shock. It shattered, sending burning fragments of the Prince in all directions.

Zenobia and Ahmet flinched back from the explosion, raising their arms to protect their faces. The Nabatean officers stared up at the cliff, jaws agape, the blood draining from their faces. Ahmet reinforced his shields, dimly perceiving that some vast form had stalked across the battlefield in the hidden world and had reached into the tent to tear the patterns of the priests and the Prince into tiny scraps. Now it raised its head in triumph, bellowing a vast roar of victory. Even in the seen world, the dim echo of it could be heard, rising above the tumult of battle like the shriek of the damned. Ahmet shuddered at the shape that he saw flickering in and out of perception. Tripartite wings flexed on the back of the towering figure and tentacles writhed where arms and hands would be. The thing turned then, and a single burning cat-yellow eye swept the field.

Ahmet clenched Zenobia tight, his mind gibbering in atavistic fear as that gaze passed over him. Feeling only an incredible sourceless dread, the Queen quailed in his arms, burrowing her head into his chest. But it did not remark them and it strode away, the earth shaking at its invisible passing. Ahmet breathed a little easier, his eyes wide in fear. He stared across the field and for the first time was aware, like a hunted creature is suddenly aware of the stalking cat, of a distant black shape, like a wagon, behind the Persian lines.

"Oh, my Queen, the enemy is surpassing strong. It must be one of the great ones, the *mobehedan mobad*, come against us."

Zenobia shuddered one more time and then pushed herself away from Ahmet's broad chest and the sanctuary it offered. She wiped her lips and rapped the plump Nabatean sharply on the side of his head with her riding stick.

"You command now, Obodas. Get these men moving right now, or I'll kill you where you stand." Her fingers rested lightly on the saber she carried slung at the side of her saddle horn. Obodas stared up at her with blank eyes. Then he focused and, after taking a shaky breath, nodded. The Nabatean officers ran to their horses and began saddling up.

Zenobia turned her horse; she had to get back to the center and see what had happened on the left wing. Ahmet clung to her like a sailor clinging to a spar in a storm-tossed sea. He was shaking and dripping with clammy sweat.

The Lord Dahak sagged back into the rough horsehair cushions with a long gasp. His hands trembled and for a moment he could barely focus his eyes on the flickering candles that surrounded him in the perfectly dark confines of the wagon. The muscles in his arms and legs twitched involuntarily, the nerves brutalized by the staggering power that he had channeled through his will only moments before. Wearily he leaned over and fumbled at a copper cup beside the pillows. After two tries he managed to raise it to his lips and drank greedily. Red fluid, almost clotted to a gel, spilled in a trail along his cheek. He shuddered again, but the draft restored some of his strength.

The sorcerer crawled to the door of the wagon and rapped on the panel. After a moment the door opened a crack and one of the Uze tribesmen peered in, his eyes wide with fear.

"Drive." Dahak croaked, his throat raw from the effort of forming the words of summoning. "Make for the camp of the Boar. Send one of the men to him with a message."

Baraz scratched his full beard, twirling one of the ringlets around his mailed finger in absent thought. The Uze messenger squatted on the ground, chewing on a grass stem.

" 'This is a matter of men, now.' That is the Lord Dahak's message?"

The Uze spit sideways on the ground and nodded his head.

Baraz curled his lip, and then shook his head. "Go. Make sure that the Lord Dahak reaches the camp safely."

No matter what the wizard thought he had accomplished, the Boar could hear the tenor in the riot of noise around him changing. The Nabateans on the left flank had finally charged down from the slope under the bluff and the entire Persian left was falling back before their lances. Baraz had thrown the last of his spearmen and archers into the fray, but his entire left wing was now being ground backward. Soon the heavy horses of the knights commanded by the Great Prince Shahin would be driven into the marshy ground along the streambed.

"Ready my men," he shouted at the Luristani guardsmen. He smiled, his face creased with a wild grin, at the courtiers who were still held close to him, like bright feathered birds in a cage of steel. "We are needed on the left, so we are going to charge against the junction of the Red Men and the Romans. Their line is weakest there!" He heeled his horse and the entire band of seventy or eighty men surged forward. The courtiers began to weep and scream in fear, but the Luristani troopers crowded them with their horses, driving them forward. He still had no news from the right wing. Last he had seen, the Roman light horse had charged Khadames *clibanari* behind a volley of arrows.

Mohammed slashed overhand at the Persian knight, feeling his light cavalry saber ring like a bell as it smote the Persian's heavy longsword. The Persian knight hacked at him again, and Mohammed kneed his horse away in time to see the stroke part the air where he had been a moment before. Around him there was a confused swirl of men, horses, and ringing steel. The Tanukh charge had taken the Persians by surprise and had shattered the first two ranks of the Iron Hats. But once that momentum was spent, the heavily armored Persians had waded in, swords flashing. The Tanukh, despite incredible personal bravery, were being butchered.

Al'Quraysh spurred his horse away, trying to break out of the melee. Another Persian swung his horse around, its armored head butting against his own. The mare whinnied in pain and fear and reared. Mohammed angled her away from the Persian, hacking across her head at the man. His blade rang on the attacker's armored arm and slid away. The Persian hacked at him overhand with an axe, and his shield splintered into fragments as the blade bit through the roundel. Mohammed shoved the ruined shield at the man and slapped his horse hard. It bolted away, carrying him past the knight. Suddenly a lane opened in the fray and he galloped into it.

A tight knot of his men appeared out of the battle ahead, charging through two Persians in only half armor. A lance slammed into one of the *cataphracts* and speared through his lower belly and out his back, slick with gore. The man screamed and toppled off his horse, taking the lance with him. The Arab whooped and drew a curved longsword from a sheath over his back. Mohammed was among them in an instant.

"Sound the retreat," he yelled, his voice hoarse from shouting. "We fall back to the main body. Gather the men!" Trumpets began to shrill and the sole remaining bannerman waved his standard in a figure-eight pattern. Mohammed and his men charged uphill, their fleet horses stretching full out. Behind them the other Tanukh struggled to fight free from the mass of Persians, but most were surrounded and hewn down. Al'Quraysh turned his horse as the Tanukh broke free, waving his saber above his head to rally the remaining men.

An arrow, fired from the Persian footmen screening the edge of their infantry battalions, whickered out of the air and smashed into his side. He staggered and stared down at the broken shaft hanging limply from his armpit. A cold rush of sickening sensation filled his right side. The saber fell from nerveless fingers. Two of his men, one of whom he dimly recognized as ibn'Adi, closed their horses up on either side, supporting him.

"Fall back on the Queen," he whispered. "She will command us . . ."

Having fought free of the swarm of desert bandits, Khadames rallied his household men to him. The two blocks of Persian heavy horse were disorganized by the melee, and he began shouting orders to regroup them. The general struggled against a terrible desire to scratch his nose, but that was impossible under the heavy helmet that he wore. His splendid armor, carefully buffed and polished by his servants the night before, was spattered with dark-red gore and dinged from a hundred blows. His arms were incredibly weary and he did not think that he could raise his sword one more time. He peered out of the narrow eyeslit and saw that his men were regrouping quickly.

And still the Palmyrene heavy horse across the field had not charged into them.

"Form up! Form up!" he shouted, and spurred his horse forward. "Prepare to advance!" He still had the strength to raise his sword high and wave it in the direction of the enemy.

Zenobia, despite her urgent desire to reach the left wing, had only reached the road at the center of the field when there was a roar of men's voices to her right. She wheeled her horse and peered down into the confused mass of struggling men that marked the right wing of the Persian line. Once Obodas and his knights had charged into the fray there, the Persian wing, already pressed almost to collapse by the Nabatean infantry, had given way. Now the Persians were streaming back from the line of battle, heading for the bridge and the crossing over the stream.

"Mars and Venus!" she whispered, and Ahmet jerked his head up at the strange tone in her voice. A band of gaily attired men had charged out of the Persian rear, led by a giant of a man with a flowing black beard. He was bareheaded, and even from two hundred yards, Ahmet could see that his face was lit by an unholy joy in battle. He swung a long mace with a spiked head. As the Egyptian watched, he and his armored horse plowed through three Nabatean knights and the mace lashed out, smashing the helmet of one of the Petrans into bloody gore. A great shout went up from the Persian lines.

Zenobia's face had gone utterly pale. "It is the Boar, Shahr-Baraz . . . I've been tricked!"

Ahmet seized her arm and shook her. She snapped from her stupefaction.

"The battle is not done," he hissed at her. "We have the upper hand. You are winning."

She stared back at him with a lost expression on her face.

"He has never lost a battle," she whispered. "He has slain his thousands, and his tens of thousands . . ."

Before them, down the slope, the giant and the bear like men who formed a wedge behind him were wading through the Nabatean lines like butchers. Many of the red-armored men turned to flee at the sight of the Boar, and the entire Palmyrene advance suddenly stalled.

"You must rally your men, O Queen. They will believe in you. Your legend is stronger than his!" Ahmet stared into her eyes, his will fully bent upon her.

She stared back and then fire kindled in her and she turned away, rising in the saddle, her clear high voice ringing over the battlefield. "Palmyra! To me! Palmyra and Zenobia!" The stallion leapt forward as she dug in her heels. A wild scream of rage flew from her and the entire battlefield froze, men staring up in shock as she and her Bactrians hurtled down into the melee like a stroke of lightning.

Baraz whirled around, hearing a great cry go up from the Romans, and he saw a black stallion rushing toward him with a solid block of lancers at its back. A slim figure in golden armor and a winged helm stood in the saddle, a silver sword raised in one hand. The Boar blinked twice and his vision focused enough to see that it was a woman.

Zenobia! His heart raced with surprise. He had heard rumors that the Queen of Silk was wont to lead her men in battle, but he had not believed it. Around him he felt the tide of battle shift again; the Romans had almost broken when he and the pretty birds had charged, but now they had taken heart again. Arrows fell around him like rain. He spun the heavy charger and pressed back through the struggling horsemen around him.

"Zenobia and Palmyra!" The shouts of the Romans rang over the clatter of steel and iron, and the screams and moans of the dying. The Romans pressed forward again, their front a bristling thicket of spears and swords. The Persian courtiers and the Luristani guardsmen were overwhelmed and went down fighting, axes and maces biting at the shields of the infantry to the last.

Beyond the battle Baraz gathered the remains of the horsemen who had been fighting on the left wing. One of them, to his disgust, was the Great Prince Shahin, his magnificent bronze and gold armor dented and muddy. The Great Prince's face was haggard, and blood seeped from a cut on his forehead. The withers of his horse were caked in blood. Baraz counted heads; only fourteen horsemen remained to him. He looked to the right, up the Persian line, and saw to his horror that the fighting in the center had gone worse than before. The infantry had fallen back almost to the bridge and he was close to being cut off.

"Fall back to the bridge," he shouted over the din. The Persians trotted west as fast as their weary horses could carry them.

The earth shook with the thunder of thirty thousand hooves. Dust billowed up from the rocky ground, rising in a great cloud behind Khadames and his knights as they stormed up the low hill at the western end of the battle. The Palmyrenes who had been sitting for the last hour and a half on the hillock were at last beginning to gather into a wedge to charge, but Khadames screamed in delight, his arm strong again. They were too late. They had waited too long for their reinforcements, and now he had the momentum against them. The sacrifice of the bandits had been for nothing. The Persian commander's face split in a terrible grin. The ground sped by under his charger as eight thousand Persian heavy horse rushed up the hill in a great crescent.

Zenobia thrust with the point of her saber. The silver blade danced off the Persian knight's noseguard and then slid into his eyeslit. His whole body jerked convulsively and the Queen, screaming with delight, whipped the blade out, the first five inches sluicing blood into the air in a spray. Ahmet looked away as the knight toppled off his mount. Zenobia wheeled her horse and galloped out of the fray to the west. Ahmet's white headdress was gone and his long dark hair blew free. His face was spotted with blood. The Queen trotted up the hill toward the road and her command tent. Half of the Bactrians who had ridden with her into the fight rode out again, hurrying to rejoin her. Only two of her messengers remained.

The field was clouded with dust, making it hard to see either end of the battle. Zenobia resettled the winged golden helmet that she had been wearing on her head. One of the wings had been sheared off and it was unbalanced. It still would not sit right, so she pulled it off her head with a gasp and wrenched the other wing off. The heavy gold struck the ground and stood there, impaled on the wingtip in the broken earth. Zenobia uncurled the braid that she had woven of her hair that morning and let it fall across her back.

"Report!" she rasped to the messengers who had rejoined her. "What is happening!"

One of the dispatch riders, a Tanukh, bowed his head wearily.

"My Queen," he said, "the Lord Mohammed was struck down on the left and has been carried back to the camp. He lives but is sorely wounded. The Emir ibn'Adi commands the remainder of the Tanukh, but . . ." He pointed helplessly off to the west.

A great roar echoed through the dust, and everyone turned to stare in that direction. A heavy crash, like a thousand cast-iron pots thrown into a gravel pit, echoed out of the tan clouds, and then, suddenly, the ground to the west of the road was filled with Palmyrene horsemen, knights and lancers alike, in flight. The silver shapes of Persian heavy horsemen loomed out of the dust in pursuit, their banners fluttering.

Zenobia groaned and crushed her fist into the mane of her horse. Ahmet gripped her shoulder hard, but some sound behind him made him turn.

To the east, downstream, beyond where the Nabateans had advanced to smash the right wing of the Persian army, a column of horsemen had appeared, riding hard up the valley. Their robes were black and their banners were a long snake on a field of sable. Ahmet's eyes twitched left and right. To the right, the bluff where Aretas had planted his tent was abandoned, only a scattering of bodies and the forlorn banners of the Prince of the Rose Red City. To the left, the

Nabatean horse and spearmen were still fighting, hacking their way into the right flank of the remaining Persian infantry. There was nothing between the riders in black and the unprotected rear of the Palmyrene army.

"Zenobia," he whispered, "the missing horsemen—the Lakhmids—what color are their banners?"

"A red snake on a field of black," the Queen said, turning, and then she saw them as well. Her pupils dilated for a moment, and then she raised her head. Fire still burned in her eyes, but with it there was a realization of the extent of the disaster she had led her men into. She gestured to the lone remaining trumpeter. She put the mouthpiece of the trumpet to her lips and blew a long single note. Across the field of battle, the weary commanders of the Roman army raised their heads, staring behind them. Some could see the Queen, shining golden amid her officers, others could only hear her.

"Fall back," she cried out, a mournful sound on the suddenly quiet field. "Fall back!"

THE GATES OF TAURIS

The night sky over the city was lit with a sickly green glow. Odd lights burned and flickered on the battlements of Tauris. A mile downstream from the city, the Emperor of the West, Martius Galen Atreus, stared north across the swift waters of the Talkeh. The river was running deep here, and the far bank was only dimly visible in the moonlight. Where he stood, on a flat-topped hill overlooking the river, surrounded by his guardsmen bearing torches and lanterns, the wind rustled in the leaves of the sycamores and aspen trees that crowded the bank. At the Emperor's side, one of the Eastern scouts raised a hooded lantern and flipped the stiff leather shutter up and down, then up and down again.

In the darkness on the far bank, there was an answering flare of light: flash—flash—flash. The men around the Emperor murmured softly; no one had expected their allies to be where they had promised to be. Who expected such things of barbarians? Galen raised a hand and the noise stopped.

"Send a man across with a rope," he said to the centurion standing next to him. The twenty-year man turned and muttered gruffly into the darkness. A moment later two men climbed up the hill, stripped to the waist, with heavy leather belts. The men were well built, with thick chests and arms like wrestlers. Their dark hair was cut very short and their skin gleamed in the torchlight. Galen looked them over and nodded.

The centurion growled at the two. "There's a band of horseflies on the far bank. They have an emissary to speak to the Emperor. Take a line across and bring the fellow back." While he spoke, other legionnaires had snapped a waxed line of heavy cordage onto hooks built into the backs of the leather belts. The two legionnaires saluted and scrambled down through the reeds that lined the water.

"Batavians," the centurion rasped, "swim like eels." His breath puffed white in the cold air. Galen nodded, drawing a heavy wool cloak around his shoulders. Winter was coming. There was a quiet splash, like a frog jumping into the water. The rope began to spool out from the hands of the legionnaires that were holding it.

The Emperor waited patiently in the darkness.

Galen rubbed his eyes wearily. It was late and he had been up since before dawn. Luckily, he sat in a chair a pace back from the heavy goldplated monster of a throne that Heraclius' servants had been lugging over mountain and valley for the last six weeks, and could indulge himself with a yawn. The great tent, fully the size of a villa, was warm too, with hundreds of beeswax candles to light the audience chamber at its heart. The Eastern interpreter was listening intently to the words of a wizened old man in a bright blue shirt with heavy stitching around the collar and embroidery at the cuffs. The old man, with a wisp of white hair around his head and pale-yellow pantaloons, reminded the Western Emperor of a mummer in a traveling show. He smiled a little and turned his attention back to the notes that his secretary had given him of the numbers of wagons that were still sound, of the number of bushels of wheat and barley that remained in stores.

Long ago, when Galen had first opened discussions with the new Emperor of the East, they had struck upon an arrangement by which precedence could be resolved when one of them was in the lands of the other. By Imperial fiat, each had declared the other his *magister militatum*, an old title reserved for the official in charge of the armies of the state. Each Emperor had then agreed to the appointment of a *strategos* who actually performed those functions when the *magister* was absent from his post. Now, with both of them on campaign, Galen found that Heraclius had been serious about his fellow Emperor fulfilling his duties. In truth, it worked well, for Heraclius spent nearly all of his time unraveling political difficulties among his warlords and the local tribesmen, leaving Galen to tend to the army.

The little old man stopped speaking, and the interpreter turned to the Eastern Emperor, who was beginning to fidget on his golden throne.

"*Avtokrator*," said the interpreter, a nobleman from Tarsus that had joined the army at the behest of Prince Theodore, in heavily accented Greek. "The headman blesses your house and your sons and welcomes you to the land of the Armenes. He says, too, that the Persians have many men, many thousands of men in the city. But he knows that the arms of the Rhomanoi are the strongest and that all the land will soon be free of the blight of the Iron Hats."

Heraclius nodded and smoothed his beard. He was weary; the day had been very long. "Tell him, good Proculus, that the Emperor is pleased to receive his friendship. Tell him that he and the other headmen hereabouts will receive many fine gifts from my hand if they are good friends to us. Ask him if he knows who commands the defense of the city across the river, and—more to the point—if there are any other bridges across the river than the one at the city."

The Tarsian nobleman related this in turn to the old Armenian and then the two dickered back and forth for a time, until Heraclius raised an eyebrow at Proculus and the noble bowed deeply to him in apology.

"Great Lord, pardon me. The headman says that it is said that the Persian general known as the Boar commands the defense of the city, and that the men who stand upon its walls wear coats of red and gold. By this I take it that they are Immortals."

Galen looked up at this; he had been listening with half an ear while he made notes for his lieutenants to deploy the men and begin building a fortified camp. The other Eastern officers had stiffened at the mention of the Boar. Pursing his lips, Galen wracked his brain and then remembered: The Boar was the nickname of the foremost Persian general, Shahr-Baraz, a giant of a man who was rumored to have never lost a battle or a fight. The Roman remembered, too, that Heraclius had sent three great armies against the Persians when Chrosoes had begun this war and that the Boar had smashed each in turn. Galen rubbed his jaw, feeling sandpapery stubble under his fingers. *How do these Easterners manage with those beards?* he wondered. The name of the Boar was something to conjure with for the Easterners: the enemy who had never been defeated by their arms.

"Ask the headman," Heraclius said, "if any new men have come to the city of late or have left. Ask him if he has seen the General Baraz or if he has only *heard* that he commands here."

Another long session of muttering went back and forth, then Proculus said: "Great Lord, the headman says that three seven-days ago, many of the horsemen left for the south in haste, but that the Boar was not with them. He says that the Boar has been seen often, stalking the battlements of the city with his banner men. He says that he has seen this with his own eyes. No other men have left the city, save for strong bands of the Iron Hats to punish the villages around the city."

Galen looked over at Heraclius at this last. The Eastern Emperor stopped drumming his fingers on the armrest of the throne. "Punish the villages? What occurred that they had to be punished?"

Proculus spread his hands in dismay. "The headman does not know, only that two seven-days ago there was a great clamor in the city. The next morning the Iron Hats rode out in strong companies and raided all of the villages in the valley. Many of the villagers had fled already, hearing strange rumors from their kinsmen in the city, but those who remained were taken hostage and their dwellings burned."

Heraclius raised an eyebrow at this and glanced over at Galen, who shook his head a little.

"Since that time the Iron Hats make a foray each day and take prisoner any of those who are foolish enough to be caught in the open. The headman says that nearly all of the villagers have fled into the hills. No word comes from the gates of Tauris."

Galen frowned and scratched off a line on his wax tablet that read: *native laborers?*

The Emperor of the East listened for a little while longer and then dismissed the headman, though the old man was given many gifts of cloth and jewels. Heraclius stood, groaning, and divested himself of the heavy jeweled robe and crown. His servants took these things away.

"What do you think?" Heraclius asked.

Galen looked up and then put his tablets and notes to one side. "I think that my engineers can put a bridge across the river in five or six days, one strong enough to carry horses and wagons. If we're lucky, there's a solid footing well away from the city walls, outside the shot of a heavy engine. The Khazars can cross the river and we can ignore the city."

Heraclius rubbed his nose and frowned at the suggestion. "That would leave a Persian garrison right on top of our line of retreat. They would play Hades with our communications back to Constantinople."

Galen nodded.

"If we have to take the city, brother," he said, "we'll have to build a bridge anyway, to move the army to the other side of the river so that we can invest the walls and begin siegeworks. That will take even more time, and as you've doubtless noticed, the nights are beginning to chill."

Heraclius sighed and pursed his lips in thought. He signaled to one of his servants for wine.

"The Persians," he said slowly, "built a fine stone bridge across the river, with a bed of bricks and mortar."

The Western Emperor scowled at the Eastern Emperor. Heraclius gratefully accepted a brass cup filled with dusky red wine.

"A fine stone bridge," Galen said, "that runs into a double towered gate at the center of a city occupied by several thousand veteran men as well as militia, and perhaps—just perhaps—this general who has taken down your breeches and given you a whipping three times before. If—if, mind you—we were to try to take the bridge and the gates by assault, it would be my men who would bleed for it."

Heraclius nodded somberly and drained his cup.

"You've the heavy infantry," he said, raising the empty cup in salute, "and the experience. How soon can we make the attempt?"

Galen settled back in his chair and thought. Heraclius downed another cup. The Western Emperor sat forward again and began making notes on his tablets. "I'll need six days to prepare. Then we'll see. I shall need all the men you can give me, or find, for the preparations."

There was a note in his voice that made Heraclius look at him quizzically. Galen arched an eyebrow, but said nothing. A predatory look had entered his eyes. He had the beginnings of a plan. He pulled one of the tablets over to him and made a quick notation, *grease.*

"The rumors are true," Nikos said, sitting on the edge of one of the rough stone crypts. "A Roman army is on the south side of the Talkeh, and it seems to be digging in to stay. At least, they've gone beyond a night camp. From the top of the grain silo, I could make out some kind of big effort east of the city, up the river. I'd guess a bridge, or maybe some kind of diversion canal to lower the waters."

Thyatis nodded and turned around slowly in the circle of space in front of the crypt wall. She met the eyes of the assembled Bulgars, Armenians, and towns-folk one by one. In the wake of the disappearance, the Persians had enforced a very strict martial law upon the city. No one was allowed out after nightfall, and gatherings of more than two people during the day were forbidden. Twenty or thirty people were crammed into the lower vault of the crypt of the Sesain family. It was the only hidden place left that was large enough for them to meet in.

"The Roman army is very fond of siegework," she said, stopping next to Nikos. "In other circumstances, they would bridge the river and surround the city with an earthen rampart on all sides so no one could break out. Then they would really get to work. This army is in a hurry, so I fear that they have a more drastic effort in mind."

Thyatis reached behind her and dug around in the open coffin. Some of the Armenians began muttering among themselves, but Jusuf and Sahul, who were standing by the trapezoidal doorway, glared at them and the locals quieted down. Thyatis pulled out a handful of bones and two skulls, hooked on her fingers through the eye sockets. Nikos brushed aside some of the dust on the floor with his boot.

"The key to the city, to the whole situation, is the bridge over the Talkeh." She laid a pair of thigh bones in parallel and then two femurs across them at right angles. "Wide enough for two wagons, and the only crossing in the area. It runs into the center of this city, through two octagonal towers." She placed the two skulls at the end of the femurs and laid a forearm splinter across the crowns. "Behind the two outer towers is a courtyard, and then two more towers. There are three gates, one at each end and a gate of iron bars in the middle."

Ribs were placed behind the skulls to mark the inner walls, and then shattered jawbones the gates.

"Most of the Immortals remaining in the city are in that bastion. Our work in the sewers tells us it has its own water gate, so unless the Roman army diverts or poisons the river, they'll have plenty to drink. Doubtless there are food and arms as well. Inside the inner towers . . ."

Another pair of skulls, these markedly smaller than the first, were placed to mark the final two towers.

". . . is another open yard. Right now it gets used as the winter market and to hold caravans when they are assembling to go south. A fine use, but in this siege, it's fifty feet of open pavement between the nearest building"—Thyatis moved Nikos' boot over to demonstrate—"and the inside wall. The bridge has only a low retaining wall on either side, the plaza is wide open. Each is a fine place to die, skewered by a Persian arrow."

She stood, sighing, and brushed her hands off on the long dark dress she had recently taken to wearing, along with the headdress and veil. Jusuf had finally had to appeal to Sahul to convince her that she had to hide her looks. The Persians were offering a heavy bag of royals for the heads of those responsible for the disappearance.

"The Roman army only has one option that I can see—to launch an assault across the river in boats or rafts and try to scale the walls in a rush. If they can seize the rest of the city, then they can bring up siege engines and hammer the bastion to rubble. We must be ready when that day comes. You have all said that you will fight Persia."

There was a muttering of agreement. The harsh policies of the Boar had made him no friends, and since the Disappearance, the threat against the families of these men had faded. Thyatis had been listening to the Armenians while they talked at night, in the darkness, and knew that they counted Rome's presence in these high and distant valleys to be brief, like a summer snow. If the Persians were driven out, they would be the kings of their own land again. She noted that Sahul and Jusuf listened too, and she wondered how the Khazars would like to trade their snowy lands in the north for more temperate valleys closer to the sun. But she said nothing; her mission was simple and straightforward.

"Well," she continued, "we will see our fill of battle. My plan is to split our men into two forces. One force, which friend Jusuf has volunteered to command, will hide close to the Dastevan, or northern, gate. When the Romans attack, he and his men will rush the gate even as the Romans reach it. With luck, Jusuf will be able to open the gate and the Romans can enter. The second, larger force, which I will command, will see about the southern bastion."

Thyatis smiled in the gloom, her eyes bright in the light of the few flickering candles. "Friend Jusuf has expressed to me his concern about my chances of capturing the bastion. I will tell you, as I told him, that I have sworn to deliver the city to my Emperor, and I will."

Nikos eyed her surreptitiously. His commander was growing very bold.

Full night was passing, stealing away into the west at the rumor of the sun. Two Persian soldiers, Immortals, in their gold and red cloaks, stood on the southeastern tower of the city wall. The river gurgled at the foot of the tower, washing against the stones. The land was still covered with darkness, but the air began to change a little with the hidden touch of the rising sun. The older of the two soldiers, his head covered with a furry leather cap with long ear flaps, stared out into the darkness. The land around the city was desolate and swathed in midnight. His companion shuffled his feet, holding his hands out to the lantern that illuminated the wall below their post.

"Quit doing that," said the older man, his voice muffled by the woolen scarf he had wrapped around his lower face. "You'll ruin your night vision."

"Huh. What is there to see out there? Nothing. Not even the light of a farm."

The older soldier shook his head and returned to watching the river.

Almost invisibly, a chill mist rose, curling off of the water like steam, then climbing the banks. The older soldier, for all his vigilance, did not notice it until the first wisp obscured the lantern. Then he cursed, for the cold had grown worse. He turned away from the battlement and stomped across the icy flagstones of the rampart to the brazier filled with coals. His companion was already there, rubbing his hands over the little fire. They did not see the mist creep along the wall, rising higher and higher like a tide, until it spilled through the firing slits and embrasures of the battlement like pale water. The mist was heavy and where it drifted the sounds of night faded.

Zoë crouched in the bow of the skiff, her fighting staff laid in the bottom of the boat, peering out from under the sycamore branches that hung down almost to the water. The mist had thickened into a soupy fog, reducing vision to only a few strides. Eric and Dwyrin were at the back of the boat, their hands resting lightly on the poles that would drive the skiff across the river. Odenathus lay in the bottom of the boat, wrapped in woolen blankets and a mangy hide that Eric had stolen out of the tents of one of the Gothic auxillia. He was breathing shallowly, though his eyes twitched back and forth. Zoë raised her right hand and clenched it into a fist.

Dwyrin and Eric picked up their poles and rose up into a crouching stance. The skiff rocked gently from side to side. Somewhere out in the darkness there was a signal and Zoë dropped her hand. The two boys dug the poles into the muddy bottom of the little inlet and the skiff, soundless, darted out into the river. They poled furiously, feeling the bottom drop away unevenly under their poles. The skiff slid out over the water, turning first a little to the left and then to the right as they alternated strokes. In the bow, Zoë stood up, her staff held crossways to her chest, her legs braced against either side of the little boat.

Dwyrin kept a weather eye ahead and slackened his stroke as the bottom vanished entirely. He kept the pole in the water long enough for the drag to keep them on course when Eric staggered, his strongly thrust pole finding nothing. Dwyrin grabbed the collar of his tunic in time to keep him from falling into the river. For all the imperfections that Zoë found in him, Dwyrin had grown up in fens and marshes. A boat like this was second nature to him. Eric, trembling from the effort, sat down in the back of the boat. Dwyrin remained standing as they slipped through walls of fog. Zoë looked back at one point and Dwyrin met her eyes with a smile.

She nodded and turned back to her watch. Utter quiet surrounded them as they drifted downstream in a universe of dark clouds and damp, clinging mist. Suddenly the skiff tipped a little to the side and began to crab. Dwyrin raised his pole, peering downstream into darkness. The water smoothed up into a curve in front of the skiff and Zoë caught sight of a standing wave. She struck out with her pole and caught the edge of the bridge piling.

Dwyrin saw it too, and he too pushed away with his staff. The skiff spun away from the looming brickwork. Their staves scraped across the mossy surface as each put his full strength behind the poles. The wave around the piling raised them up and then they shot down the other side. Dwyrin immediately turned to the other side of the skiff and dragged a heavy rope with a large bronze hook at the end out from under the rear seat. Eric ducked down and squeezed behind him to get out of the way. The current was running faster now, and to the right. Dwyrin felt a massive shape in front of him, and then the wall of the city appeared between parting veils of mist.

The Hibernian closed his eyes and felt perception jar around him as the flickering shape of the wall swam into view. There was very little time, but he had proved to the centurion's satisfaction that of the five, he could drop into the second entrance the fastest. His control was still very poor, but now they needed speed most. A shimmering ring of green and yellow blazed to his right and he hurled the hook with all his strength. In the front of the skiff, Zoë had dug her pole into the river bottom. The skiff rotated at the back end, around the fulcrum of the pole, and the back flank of the boat crunched into the wall.

Dwyrin's hook clanged soundlessly into the ring and he whipped the rope around a stay in the back of the boat. Zoë felt the skiff shudder to a halt and grind up against the city wall. The current continued to press at the boat, driving it into the bricks. Eric and Dwyrin began hauling on the rope, and the skiff inched back against the river. Finally they reached the ring and the narrow walkway under it. Zoë pushed past both of them, her long braids piled on the top of her head, and clambered up the slippery stones onto the walkway. Eric handed up the blankets and two lumpy cotton bags. Dwyrin knelt in the bottom of the boat and slapped Odenathus gently on the cheeks.

The Palmyrene boy's eyes flickered open and he groaned, the first audible sound since he had settled into his trance across the river.

"Quiet!" Dwyrin whispered, holding his hand over the boy's mouth. "We're right under the gate." The Hibernian helped Odenathus to his feet and they managed to struggle up onto the walkway. Zoë and Eric had already disappeared. Dwyrin gave Odenathus a moment to catch his breath while he carefully unhooked the bronze grapnel from the ring. Sighing at the waste of a good boat, he lowered the hook into the water and then let the rope slip from his fingers. The skiff, no longer moored, grated on the wall once and then spun away on the current.

"Come on, let's find the others." Dwyrin breathed in Odenathus' ear. The other boy nodded and stood up, his frozen hands tucked into his armpits. It was particularly cold down by the water. They crept off along the walkway. Dawn was less than an hour away.

Thyatis' eyes opened, her mind clear and free of the confusion of sleep. She reached over and found Nikos' ear by touch. Her pinch woke him, though he too remained quiet. Deep night was on the city, but something was happening. It seemed that the air itself had grown heavier. Thyatis rose and gathered up her sword and the long knife. She was already wearing a thick cotton doublet and leather leggings. Over this she had a shirt of iron scale mail that Bagratuni had excavated from some ancient hoard in the countryside. To complete it, he had found an ancient helmet with an iron strip along the top of the helm and flaring cheek protectors. She pulled this over her hair, her braids coiled into a cushion at the top of her head. The leather strap snugged tight on her chin. Beside her, Nikos had also risen and moved among the men, waking them quietly.

Thyatis climbed the steps out of the cellar and carefully pushed the door open into the ground floor of the shop they had taken over the day before. The shop was still deserted, all of the goods packed away. Piles of wooden ladders filled the space, leaving only an aisle between them. She glided to the front, where heavy shutters were closed and barred against thieves. A small spyhole was set into the center of the shutter, and she swung the little iron flap up from it and peered out. The southern square was empty and dark, but by the light of a single lantern hung from a stone wall where the main thoroughfare of the city emptied into the square, she saw that a heavy fog was filling the air.

There was a faint sound behind her, the *clink* of armor. She turned and Nikos was standing there. Men were filing into the room behind him.

"Fog," she breathed. "We couldn't be luckier. Send the word to the other shops. We attack as soon as everyone is in position."

Nikos gripped her shoulder with a gloved hand.

"Are you sure?" His voice was faint and filled with worry. "We've had no word from outside . . ."

"Victory to the bold," she said, her teeth white in the dim light. "It's the hour before dawn and there's a heavy fog. Regardless of what the Roman army does, we have a chance to capture the bastion by ourselves."

The Illyrian regarded her for a moment more, then shook his head slightly and moved off to prepare the men. Thyatis turned back to the spyhole. Within the next ten grains, they would be ready. She felt a familiar thrill of expectation. Hundreds of men were preparing to move at her command, like a strong swift horse responding to her will. They would live or die upon the strength of her planning and courage. Her fingers curled around the wire-wrapped hilt of her sword, feeling the grooves worn by long use. Even the borrowed helmet felt right on her head.

Galen stood in the mist, his gilded armor shrouded by an even heavier cloak. A servant stood by him, holding his plumed helmet and sword. Around him he could hear the quiet movement of thousands of men. Just to his left, on the hard-packed mud of the road, a tortoise rolled up through the darkness, the squeak of its huge wooden wheels swallowed by the liberal application of all of the pig grease that Heraclius' foragers could steal. He strained to see forward through the mist that swallowed the bridge. There was nothing there, only shades of black. He rubbed his nose, feeling a tide of apprehension rise in him. For a brief moment he wished that he were his brother Aurelian. Aurelian had never felt the slightest fear in battle or any concern for his own safety. He wondered how Maxian was faring, buried under scribe-work in the palace. Galen pushed thoughts of his brothers away. The river rolled past, silent in the fog.

Moisture beaded on the massive beams that formed the gate of the city. The fog licked against the black stones and water puddled on the pavement. Dwyrin and Zoë crouched at the base of the gate, a dull gray cloak thrown over them. Under the wool it was still bitterly chill, but their shared warmth made it a little more bearable. The Hibernian was on his hands and knees, concentrating on the join between the two halves of the gate. The left valve of the gate was faced with a nine-inch-wide strip of iron that overlapped the right-hand side. Zoë was holding the cloak up over them in a tent.

Dwyrin shuddered, feeling the vibration of the spells etched into the oaken panels, and breathed out slowly to settle his mind. He descended again into the second entrance, and then the third. Perception folded away from him like the leaves of some infinite flower, each layer revealing ten thousand other layers. The cold receded as he did so, and the gates rose up, glittering with hidden power. A complex geometry held them closed against an attacker, delicate traceries of power and form a hundred levels deep. The boy was stunned by the work that had gone into the defense. He quailed for a moment in the face of that complexity.

Zoë, who had also descended into the hidden world with him, though slower, whispered: "Ignore all that, look at the stones."

He looked down, dragging his gaze away from the subtly shifting patterns of the gate. The heavy volcanic stones of the roadway and the gate were dull and inert, sullen black lozenges. No power crept through them like an infinite number of glowing worms. They were stolid and well worn by the passage of thousands of feet. Dwyrin's concentration focused. His fingers dug at the cold stones, and his perception flowed into the pavement, seeking for even a tiny spark of fire.

At last, deep under the gate, in the foundation of the tower platform, he found it. A small thing, only a whisper of fire, trapped in a great slab of basalt that had been laid to form the base of the gate itself. His spirit hand wrapped around the little flame and his unseen breath blew on it. It dimmed and then flickered brighter. He drew on the power of the other stones, weak as it was, and slowly it burned hotter and hotter.

Zoë shivered under the cloak. The cold from the river and the mist was creeping up her legs and thighs. The Hibernian was still in a trance, his fingers trembling on the pavement, working in the deep stones. She rolled back and forth from her left foot to her right, trying to keep some circulation in them. Dwyrin suddenly shuddered and looked up.

"Let's go." He croaked. Zoë pulled him upright, startled at the hot flush in his skin. She carefully folded the woolen cloak aside and pushed him down the walkway at the side of the gate. The boy stumbled ahead of her, his skin steaming in the cold air. Behind them, the stones under the gate made a popping sound.

The sound of hundreds of running feet echoed back from the dark wall that towered over the southern square. Thyatis jogged through the darkness, following the dim shapes of her men running in front of her. The first rank of men were carrying long ladders, scrounged from the city in the previous weeks, and the pylons that had so vexed Jusuf. The wall that rushed toward them was twenty feet high on the city side, and the ladders were a good thirty feet long. Their uppers were wrapped in wool or cotton or hides to deaden the sound of their slapping home on the rampart. The mist continued to hang around them, and the Roman woman realized, as she ran, that it was swallowing the sound of their mass rush across the square.

The lead men reached sight of the wall, only five or six strides ahead of them, and halted. The men behind continued forward, pushing the ladders above their heads while the lead men swung the base of the ladders to the ground and put their full weight on the bottom rungs. Thyatis slowed, raising her sword to signal the men behind her to slow as well. She heard them pause, and she slid the blade back into the sheath slung over her back.

The first ladder rose into the air and then swung over to land with a clatter on the embrasure at the top of the wall. Thyatis was already springing up it, her hands and feet on the rungs. She shinnied up the ladder like a monkey, but even before she reached the top, she heard the ringing of alarm bells within the citadel. She screamed in rage and hurled herself over the battlement.

"Roma Victrix!" She bellowed and the sword was in her hand in a rush. All along the wall, a hundred ladders clattered home and men were already swarming up them. The top of the wall was empty and she sprinted left, toward the nearest guard tower. There was a great commotion in the bastion as hundreds of voices were raised in alarm. Lights began to flicker on in the fog, casting strange shadows. Ahead of her, a door opened and she saw the shapes of men spill out.

The first Persian had only a spear, his armor forgotten in his rush to reach the wall. She whipped out of the fog, her sword a horizontal blur that hewed through his exposed neck in a spray of blood. He was still gasping for air, his hand raised to his oddly constricted throat, and she was past him. The spear clattered to the stones. The next man was in half-armor with an axe, and the men behind him had spears and shields. Thyatis felt a tremendous rage bubbling up inside her and as it crested, she howled and was among them, her blade a spinning wheel of destruction.

Her knife hand trapped the axe head swinging at her from the right and the sword in her left hand licked out, sliding between the Persian's ribs. She kicked him away, the blade coming free with a popping sound, and spun into the next man. His spear stabbed at her, but she was past the point and the long knife was buried in his throat. Blood spewed and her hands grew slick with it. The edges of her vision faded to gray and the world around her seemed to slow. Her sword blurred overhead and the blocking spear of the man on the right split in half with a crack. A sword stabbed from the left and she twisted sideways, taking it on the scaled shirt, where it slid aside, sparking against the heavy iron leaves.

She hewed at the swordsman's arm and the blade cut deep. He screamed, though the sound was very distant, like the clangor of arms behind her on the rampart or the howling that rose from the courtyard. She smashed the injured man in the nose with her forearm, bowling him over, and whirled to the right. The spearman had thrown his broken weapon away and dragged a dagger out of his girdle. He lunged and she caught his blade on the knife in her right hand. Her wrist flexed, twisting the dagger away, and she punched him, throwing him backward. The spearman's foot slipped off the edge of the walkway and his other hand clawed at empty air for support. Thyatis grinned wildly through the blood streaking her face and snap-kicked him in the chest. He disappeared backward into the mist, his mouth a round O of surprise.

Time suddenly snapped back into focus and her awareness expanded to encompass everything around her. The bastion was alive with running men and blazing lights. Something had happened to drive the fog back, a stiff wind swirling off the main tower of the gate complex. Her men were still pouring over the wall, but now Persians in the courtyard below and in the other towers were filling the air with black arrows. Armenians clambering over the wall were pincushioned. A hundred feet away Nikos was firing back with his own bow. An arrow spanged off the wall next to Thyatis, and she dodged through the door the Persians had rushed out of.

The room was square and cluttered with the personal effects of the Persian soldiers. She overturned a table to block the far door and skidded to the top of a stairwell that led down into the tower. Some of her Bulgars reached the tower through the rain of arrows outside, panting with effort.

"Downstairs," she snapped, pointing to the narrow circular staircase. "Clear the other floors so that we can get down into the courtyard." They rushed past her, wolfish smiles on their faces. She stepped back into the doorway.

The rampart was littered with the bodies of the dead. Men continued to come over the wall, but the Persian arrows were taking a heavy toll. Nikos had disappeared. She stepped farther out, desperate to see the positions of her men. She opened her mouth to shout for her second.

The sky to the south lit up, a terrific flare of white light that blew back the remaining tatters of fog and was followed, within an instant, by a blast of heated air and a tremendous thundering roar. Thyatis was knocked back against the outer wall, her arm flung up to shield her eyes.

At the end of the bridge, Galen paced among his guards. They loomed over him, hulking Germans in armor of iron rings sewn to a heavy leather backing. Below that they wore furs and sheepskins. Helms with cross-shaped eyeslits covered their heads, and their shields were heavy oblongs of wood faced with riveted leather. Galen was a slight figure among the Northerners, but no man moved save at his command. The last runners had reached him, bringing him word from along the banks of the river. All cohorts stood ready.

The silence, at first welcome, now seemed oppressive. The mist was beginning, almost imperceptibly, to lighten in the east. Galen felt the grains of time dropping one by one, crushing his plan. He raised his hand, and a man raised his bronze trumpet to his mouth. Galen stared into the mist. Nothing moved across the bridge. He sighed, preparing to order the attack.

A bell rang, dim and muffled in the fog. Galen started, his hand hanging in air. Another bell rang, and then there was a shrill of whistles and shouting men.

"We are discovered." He groaned and motioned to the trumpeter. "Sound the attack!"

The trumpeter took a great breath and then sounded his horn. A clear ringing sound blared across the riverbank, cutting through the mist and its strange deadening effect. The trumpeter blew again and now other trumpets answered from the left and the right. Around the Emperor thousands of men were suddenly in motion. The Germans drew themselves tight around him, their shields interlocking to form a wall of sinew and wood. The tortoise creaked and then rumbled forward onto the bridge. Inside it a hundred men in heavy armor strained against the stanchions, pushing the massively heavy thing forward on its twelve wheels.

Archers ran past the hide-covered walls of the tortoise, their bows in hand and arrows at the ready. They sprinted across the bridge, looking up into the mist. The river echoed with the splashing of hundreds of boats and barges being rolled down the bank on logs. Men shouted as century after century scrambled onto the rafts and began poling them forward across the water. Boats and skiffs, gathered from the river and the marshes, scudded out between the rafts, packed with men.

Somewhere behind Galen and to his right, there was a sharp snapping sound as a siege engine released, its trunklike pivot arm slapping up into a hide-covered rest. A thick sphere of mottled green glass whistled through the darkness to smash against one of the towers on the river side of the bastion. The tinkling sound of the impact reverberated through the darkness, and then there was a *whoosh* of flame and the tower lit up with incandescent phlogiston. Screams reached the Emperor's ears then, as the guardsmen on the fighting platform jutting from the tower were wrapped in consuming fire. A lurid red-green glow stabbed through the murk.

The tortoise rumbled forward, legionnaires crowding onto the bridge behind it.

Galen stared into the murk, his nails digging into his palms until blood seeped around them.

Another glass sphere sailed overhead, unseen, but marked by the *thrum* of its flight.

There was a rush of wind from the bastion, and Galen covered his face as something howled past him, tearing away the veil of fog and mist that the Roman thaumaturges had raised to cover the preparations of the army on the near bank. Green light sputtered at the tops of the towers in the city, and suddenly the entire bridge and river were lit up. The river was black with men and boats and rafts, the first of which had only just managed to reach the far bank. From the battlements of the city there arose a great shout, and Galen could see that the walls were thronged with men. Arrows began to fall in a whispering rain onto the men packed into the boats below. Screams rose.

The second glass sphere burst on the battlement above the gate and blossomed into white-hot flame, clinging to the stones and hissing off the slate tiles that covered the towers. Persians wailed, writhing in flame, and plummeted into the river below. Along the battlement on the city side there was a red spark; a waterfall of red flame rushed down the side of the wall, spilling into a raft packed with Roman legionnaires below. The raft rocked as men rushed to leap from it into the water, but more were trapped by the bodies of their fellows and screamed horribly until the red flames filled their mouths and they fell silent.

Galen cursed, seeing the snarl of rafts on the river. The tortoise was too slow!

It had not even reached the gates yet. He turned to order the retreat sounded on the bridge.

Something filled the world around him with blazing white light, and the Emperor felt himself slapped to the ground like a reed crushed under the foot of an ox. The Germans cried out in fear and then a massive *boom*, so loud as to fill the whole world with its sound, rushed over them on a hot wind. Galen was buried under the bodies of his guardsmen as they threw themselves down to protect him from whatever demon had raged into the world.

The stone walkway along the river rippled with the shock of the stones under the main gate rupturing in a blossom of white-hot flame. Zoë was hurled aside into Dwyrin, and the two of them fell into the river in a tangle of limbs. Eric, who had happened to be looking toward the gate when Dwyrin's foundation stone erupted, was blinded by the flare of light and then spun around and thrown, afire, into the river. He wailed once as the dark waters closed over his head with a slap and then he was gone. Odenathus, who had been crouched at the very end of the walkway, felt a hot wind rush over him, and he clung tenaciously to the stones at his back.

The valves of the gate rose up in the air on a blast of white fire, torn from their hinges like impossibly large leaves. They tumbled over and over and then arrowed down into the river like giant axes, punching through the sides of two of the barges, spilling stunned Romans in heavy armor into the dark, crowded waters. The two towers on either side of the gate shook with the force of the blast but stood firm, though the men inside them were deafened by the shock of the sound. The inner courtyard behind the gate was filled with the shattered bodies of men wrapped in flame. The archers who had run forward to cover the advance of the tortoise were incinerated where they stood or smashed to the ground or thrown off the bridge into the river. The tortoise was blown back twenty feet, crushing the men inside to a pulp and then sliding another ten feet on the bloody grease that they made.

The men behind the tortoise were bowled over; many were killed or maimed. The gruff centurion, half blinded by a wood splinter that had spun out of the tortoise and slashed the side of his face open, staggered up out of the mass of tumbled men.

"Advance!" He bellowed and loped forward over the corpses of his friends. The cohorts of the Third Augusta picked themselves up behind him and rushed forward as well, though their hobnailed sandals slipped and skidded on the blood and bodies of the dead men. "Roma Victrix!" they shouted as they ran, a great basso roar.

Dwyrin struggled in the icy water. Darkness surged around him, the current dragging at his body with chill fingers. He clung to Zoë fiercely with his left arm wrapped around her midriff, while he kicked strongly and clawed at the water with his right arm. The river spun them around, and suddenly the darkness broke as Dwyrin's head shot above the water. A red glare lit up the surface of the water, and Dwyrin could see the flanks of boats all around him. The bow of one rushed toward him from the left. The Hibernian kicked sideways, rolling onto his back and pulling Zoë onto his chest.

His legs, filled out with muscle over the past weeks, kicked hard, pushing him through the water. The boat surged past, huge and black, with the pale faces of men staring over the side. Dwyrin gasped for air, nearly swamped by the wake. It passed and he continued to kick.

He found the bank with his head, ramming into a stone in the shallows downstream from the walls of the city. He cried out in pain but did not let go of Zoë, who was a dead weight in his arms. Dwyrin staggered up, dragging her out of the river through a torn-up cluster of reeds. Around him the night was alive with the shouts of men, the red glow of the burning citadel, and running figures. More boats were piling up against the shore, and legionnaires were climbing out into the muddy shallows. He lay Zoë down once he found ground firm enough to hold her. She was not breathing. Dwyrin felt a chill.

He rolled her on her side, wrapped his arms around her abdomen, and squeezed hard. Her body twitched and water dribbled out of her mouth. He squeezed again and there was a burp of muddy water. Dwyrin, his motions quick, rolled her back over and tipped her head back. Fighting back tears, he leaned over her and breathed into her mouth. Soldiers ran past in the murk and centurions bellowed, trying to organize their men. Zoë coughed, spewing water and bile into Dwyrin's face. He wiped it out of his eyes and leaned back. The dark-haired girl coughed again and he rolled her over. She spit up more liquid but now she was breathing.

Dwyrin held her close, trying to warm her cold body with his. There was a rumbling sound from the city, and new flames shot up. In the ruddy light, Dwyrin could see lines of men trotting off through the brush toward the walls. Zoë trembled in his arms. Fire gleamed off the water like a stain of living blood.

THE IRONWORKS, CONSTANTINOPLE

A long rod of white-hot iron, gripped between pincers held in hands gloved with a triple layer of leather, plunged into slick dark water with a tremendous hiss. The forge man stepped back, raising the iron rod from the quenching bath. It hissed and steamed, water sluicing from it. The forge man turned and laid the rod on a massive block of steel where another man joined him, seizing it between his own pair of pincers. A hammer, massive and solid, rang down on the glowing bar. Sparks flew, joining thousands of others clouding the superheated air of the forge.

Maxian stalked through the darkness, his hollow cheeks puddles of shadow. Abdmachus drifted behind him, his clothing stripped down to a pair of trousers and sandals. Sweat slicked his skin, muddying the tracery of inked symbols that covered the little sorcerer's body. The roaring fire of the forges and crucibles gleamed off Maxian's face, highlighting his nose and cheekbones. The noise was so great from the hammers and spitting cauldrons that a man could barely hear himself think. Around the Prince, dozens of men in heavy leather aprons labored, their muscled bodies slick with sweat. The air was thick, charged with fumes and vapors. Maxian climbed a stairway of stone to a platform that rose from one side of the great chamber.

Below him he could see the whole floor of the ironworks. A great apparatus was rising amid the open space between the rows of forges and pits of molten iron. Sparks showered from hammers bent to the task of welding iron to iron. Men carefully raised the bones of a great skeleton high, helped by a dizzying array of winches and pulleys that were suspended from a ceiling lost in smoke and fumes. The outline of vast jagged wings arched over the chamber, high above even Maxian as he stood on the platform, feeling the roar of noise beat on him like the ocean tide. His eyes gleamed in the ruddy light.

Ah, Aurelian, he mused, *you would love these works more than any man . . .*

"You have done well, my friend," Maxian said, turning a little toward the Persian.

Abdmachus bowed and then met the Roman's eyes. The little sorcerer's face split with a grin. This construction was his greatest work. Maxian smiled back, pleased that his friend had found a true purpose at last. Without him and his skills, this effort would be impossible.

The men on the floor did not look up, though they felt the gaze of their master upon them. The Prince looked up into the face of the creature, cruel and fanged, enormous, a tilted head with a long snout and deep-set eyes.

Soon, the Prince thought, *you will live.*

The great head, wider than a man was tall, gazed back at him, soulless, eyeless, only pits of darkness lit with flames. Maxian turned and stepped through a heavy circular door raised up on hinges of dark corroded iron. Beyond the portal the noise ceased, becoming only a dull background rumble of hammers and gears and spitting metal fire. Abdmachus wiped his brow and then stepped lightly down the stairs. Work was beginning on one of the wing joints, and it needed his delicate hand at the casting.

Krista was waiting in the room of documents, her long hair tied back behind her head, though it flared out first and then spilled over her shoulders. She wore a smock stained with dark pinpoints and a blousy shirt with heavy sleeves that were tied back from her wrists. There was a smudge of sooty ink on the side of her nose. Maxian's ears were still ringing from the cacophony of the forge. Her lips moved, but he could not hear anything for a moment.

He held up a hand and his eyelids fluttered closed as he concentrated. He was becoming almost gaunt, though the work had begun to raise ridges of muscle on his arms, shoulders, and torso. He opened his eyes when he could hear again.

"There is someone waiting to see you," Krista said, her voice even and polite. Maxian caught the hint of ice under the genteel tone. An eyebrow arched.

"One of the handmaidens of the dark woman. She is in the anteroom."

The Prince nodded and went to the other door, weaving around tables thickly strewn with parchments and papyrus scrolls. Every space on the walls and floor was covered with drawings, books, and tiny models crafted from wood and clay. At the center of one wall, a great drawing, painstakingly etched by Krista on a sheet of copper with a steel needle and then rubbed down with charcoal, showed the apparatus in all its feral glory. Maxian smiled when he looked upon it.

What might men achieve, he thought with a sense of deep satisfaction, *if they could but raise their heads up and dream?*

He paused at the door to the outer rooms and looked back at her. She still stood by her drawing table, leaning on it with one long-fingered hand. She was looking away, staring at the papers and long scrolls. To his eye, attuned to her nature and moods, he could see deep anger in the line of her head and shoulders.

"Do you still have your spring gun?" he asked quietly. Her head turned slowly, her eyes heavily lidded and opaque.

"Yes," she said.

"Let me see it." He held out a hand turned dark by coal dust. She paused for a moment, then it appeared like magic in her right hand. Maxian raised an eyebrow again and took the heavy metal tube. He had never seen it up close before, and he turned it over in his hands. It was eight inches long, with a copper central tube and wire grips welded to the outside. There was a slide on one side that had a thumb-sized ring on it. The ring, currently, was at the top of the tube. Inside the tube was a ring of folded steel that ran in two grooves. He could barely make out the shape of a spring inside the central tube. The grips were well worn with use.

"Can I see one of your darts?"

A dart—six inches of burnished steel with a point shaped like a cone at one end and three small fins at the other—appeared in her hand as well. It was heavy, lying in his hand like a lead weight. He handed the spring tube back, but kept the dart for a moment, cupping his hands around it. There was a flicker of light between his fingers and he muttered something to the missile.

Krista took the dart back without expression or comment. She slotted it into the tube and slid the ring back with a practiced motion. The dart sank into the tube, and there was a clicking sound as the ring locked into a snap at the base. The whole assembly disappeared into her sleeve again. Maxian watched carefully but could not make out how she had secreted it.

"I'd like you to come with me to meet this person."

"Why?" Some interest leaked through in the cast of her eyes.

"I trust you at my back," the Prince said, ruefully, "particularly with one of these women in front of me." Krista shrugged and untied her sleeves, letting them fall to her wrists. When he turned away she smiled, a secret thing that suffused her face for a moment and then was gone.

. . .

Maxian entered the room, bending his head a little to pass under the lintel. He had put on a new shirt, this one a deep-green cotton, and had made some attempt to get his hair, grown ever longer now, back under control. There was more color in his face too.

The woman rose, her dark robes falling around her like the wings of night. It was the blond one who had looked back over her shoulder. Her hair was loose and very long, a shimmering cascade down her back. The cloak covered her shoulders, but her breasts, creamy white, threatened to spill out of the tight leather bodice that contained them in criss-crossed leather ties. She bowed deeply as he entered, allowing her dress to slither away from a long smooth thigh and firm calf. Her sandal straps oozed up and around her leg almost to her knee, snug to the flesh. Her eyes were a tremendously deep blue, a clear winter sky over bare trees and fallen snow.

"I am Alais," she said in a husky voice. Maxian's nostrils twitched; there was a musky smell in the air around her like a waiting noose, filled with the rich smell of spring and freshly turned earth. Her lips trembled, a dusky red like dying roses, showing tiny white teeth. The Prince could feel his body quiver in reaction to her. Behind him there was a very quiet laugh from Krista, who had drifted silently into the room. The sound was an anchor for him, keeping his thought from drifting to Alais' smooth thighs and breasts.

"Welcome, Alais." His voice was even and quiet, though it was a struggle to keep from stepping even closer to her. "What brings you to our house this night? A message from your mistress, perhaps?"

The blue eyes flickered and the pouting lips firmed at the mention of the lady in black. "I come on my own accord, my lord. Though we all hold the Matron in all honor, she is not our master. I heard your generous offer when she spoke to you. Would you offer another the same trust?"

Maxian cocked his head to one side and regarded the woman. He was centered again. The balance in the room changed, and he felt it. For all her glamour, the woman was an echo in an empty room. "You desire respite from pain?"

She bowed her head, the long tresses falling around her face. "Yes, lord. I and others will serve you and earn your trust if you will give us the elixir." Her voice trembled, a ragged edge creeping into it.

"You understand that until you have won my trust, I will not reveal to you the mechanism of its manufacture?"

"Yes, lord. I . . . we . . . understand."

"You will swear an oath to me, to follow my will and accept my protection? To do my bidding and to execute my desires in exchange for surcease from pain?"

"Yes." She knelt on the floor at his feet and the air in the room subtly changed. Krista felt the hairs on the back of her neck rise up. The lamps flickered and dimmed, casting an odd gold light into the room. Her skirts and cloak puddled around her like a lake of ink, broken only by the long white trails of her hair. "I will be oathbound to you." A hand crept out, trembling, to touch the toe of Maxian's shoe.

The Prince stared down at the woman. He moved his boot and the hand withdrew.

"Your Matron has withdrawn her favor from you." The statement hung in the air.

"Yes," the woman whispered. "I . . . some of us protested her decision in the matter of your offer. We begged her to accept your patronage and let us be free of the pain. She refused to see reason, content to maintain the ancient traditions and usages of the people. She says that our freedom in pain is worth more than a delicious servitude. I protested too much, and she declared that I would be without her favor."

"You are an exile, then. Without a home, without what protection she could offer you. In pain. Denied the Hunt. Suffering from the affliction that is upon your people."

"Yes." The woman sobbed, still kneeling, her head pressed to the floor at his feet. "Please help me, the hunger is like acid . . ."

"Then rise, swear to me, and you will know peace and ease and there will be no more pain."

Alais rose, her face turned up to Maxian. It was pale and vulnerable, her eyes haunted. The Prince took her hand and helped her up. Her face was thinner now, touched by gauntness. Krista pursed her lips, seeing the fabrics of the cloak frayed and thin in places. Maxian folded her hands together on her breast and tilted her head up a little. A capsule, swimming with ruby fluid, was drawn from inside his shirt. He raised it above her forehead.

"Close your eyes, Alais."

The long eyelashes fluttered closed and her lips parted, the tip of her pink tongue visible. Maxian made a mark on her forehead, though nothing remained after his fingers had passed. The woman swayed and Maxian steadied her with a hand. Krista quietly stepped to one side, where she could see both of them clearly.

"Do you swear to abide by my will and desire? To execute my commands and to serve me in all honor? In exchange for this I offer you the protection of my house and my servants."

"I swear, my lord. We are strong and we can serve you well."

"Then I banish your pain."

The wax plug on the capsule came loose under his thumb and he dripped a little of the red fluid into her open, waiting mouth. Her tongue licked up to capture the drops. Maxian stepped back. Alais shuddered and crumpled to the ground, her limbs suddenly weak. She began gagging as her throat convulsed and her skin flushed. The Prince rubbed his chin in contemplation, watching her twitching at his feet. Krista slowly slid the spring gun out of her sleeve and leveled it on the woman on the floor. Alais groaned, a terrible sound that swelled until it filled the whole room. Then she shuddered one last time and lay still.

Maxian touched the top of her head lightly, and Alais turned her face up him. Krista hissed in surprise. The gauntness was gone, a flush obvious in the woman's cheeks. Her blue eyes were liquid and alive. Her red lips pressed against the Prince's hand in a kiss.

"My lord, your blessing fills the world."

The Prince smiled, his eyes narrowed in calculation. "Alais, rise up. Stand by me. You say there are others that feel as you do among your people. Bring them to me and I shall give them the same blessing, if they will swear to me."

The blond woman curtseyed, her smile slow and languid, filled with promise.

"So you command, lord, so shall it be done." The husky purr was back in her voice.

Krista, unseen by the Prince or the woman, rolled her eyes in disgust and slid the spring gun back into the leather sheath strapped to her arm. Maxian released Alais' hand and the woman gathered her cloak around her. Bowing once more, showing a flash of firm high breast and smooth throat, she left. The Prince stared at the doorway for a moment, scratching at the stubble along his chin. Then he turned to Krista, who was standing by the inner door, her face a calm mask.

"Ah, well," he said, "each tool to a purpose. I think that I shall give them to Gaius Julius as a diversion. He is jealous, I think, of Abdmachus and his works."

"Jealous?" Krista raised an eyebrow. "Bored is more like it . . . you keep him mewed up in here, while you and the Persian labor on your creation. He wants to be out and about, putting that long nose of his where it does not belong, sniffing after the intrigues of the city."

Maxian frowned, feeling the same sense of missed opportunity that he had felt before, when Krista had revealed her talent for languages. *I had put him to work as my spymaster in Rome* . . . "You are right. It is a waste to have him loitering around, drinking too much and trying to seduce the servants. I shall set him to work more to his liking."

"Good," Krista said, turning away, back to the tables filled with drawings.

PALMYRA, THE CITY OF SILK

Towers of pale-gold sandstone rose from the desert floor on either side of the road. Ahmet stared up them as his camel padded past on the hard-packed road. The towers were square and built of heavy blocks of stone. At a height, windows and doors leading into empty air pierced the walls of the towers. One stood near to the road as they passed, and the Egyptian stared with dull eyes at the carvings of men, camels, and fat-bellied ships that adorned its sides. A familiar smell reached him, leaking from the close-fitting stones.

The smell of dead men laid to rest, embalmed with spices and salt.

The forest of tombs was scattered across the valley floor and climbed the shoulders of the hills. Their shadows, gaunt fingers in the light of the setting sun, stretched away across the rocky ground. A hawk circled high in the sky. Around Ahmet, the rattle and creak of the army echoed off the tomb walls.

No one spoke. Weary lines of men behind them, on horses or camels, rode with heads down. Dust covered them, dulling their battered armor. Zenobia rode at his side, and beyond her, Mohammed. The Southerner sat stiffly on his horse, favoring his right side. Bandages, crusted with dried blood and sweat, wrapped his midriff. His color was poor. The long retreat from Emesa had told on him, though he was very strong. The queen had veiled her face the day after the debacle at Emesa and now met no one's eyes. Her voice, when she spoke, was faint and hoarse.

The road swung wide around a cluster of the towers and the city, at last, came into view.

Ahmet raised his eyes to the cyclopean walls, a vast expanse of golden sand-stone, and the strong towers that flanked the Damascus gate. Forty feet or more high, the walls of Palmyra reflected the ancient wealth of the city, slightly sloping, constructed of massive blocks. They seemed playthings of the Titans of old. A stream lay between the marching army and the city, bridged by a broad span of wood with stone pilings. The ramparts of the city, still distant, were lined with thousands of figures. There were no bright colors there, only gray and black. The Queen had sent riders ahead with the news of her defeat.

Zenobia nudged her horse to the side and Ahmet turned as well. The Queen rode down off the road and into a wedge of flat, sandy ground. When Mohammed made to follow her, she made a slight gesture, pointing to the city.

"The army enters first," she said, her voice faint. "I shall enter the city last of all, when my men have found sanctuary."

Mohammed nodded, his bleak eyes rimmed with dust. He angled his horse back into the center of the road. The men continued their slow march. Zenobia sat on her horse, with Ahmet at her side, watching them trudge past. Their com-panies were small and many men were wounded. There was little infantry and no wagons. All of that had been lost in the mad flight from the field where the Boar had crushed Zenobia's dreams of freedom in a vise of steel.

At last the rearguard had passed, the remnant of the Tanukh that had sur-vived Mohammed's mad charge against the Persian knights. The desert men bowed in the saddle to the Queen as they passed, though their scarred faces were gaunt with weariness. Ibn'Adi was the last to pass, his old face grim and drawn. He raised a hand in salute and Ahmet was shocked, in his tired way, to see that the sheykh had lost two of his fingers. The old man's hand was bound with a dirty bandage.

The dust settled and quiet returned. A hawk continued to circle in the twi-light sky. Zenobia reached out a hand and Ahmet took it. They sat there on their mounts for a time, holding hands. The sun was swallowed by the western hills and darkness crept over the land. Then the Queen squeezed his hand and let go, unclipping her veil.

"Those few who survived will have entered the city now," she said in a dead voice. "I must go and face the grief of my people."

She turned to him, her eyes bruised and darkened by tears and fatigue. Her horse stirred restlessly, but she laid a hand on its neck and it quieted.

"You could go. The trails to the south will still be open. You could make your way to Aelana and home, home to Egypt."

Ahmet shook his head, smiling quietly. "I will remain in your service, my lady. There is nothing left for me in Egypt."

Doggedly she continued. "If you stay," she said, "you will doubtless die when the city falls to Shahr-Baraz. If you go, you will live. Is that not better than death?"

"If I go, my lady, will you go with me?" He struggled to keep his voice level.

A look of despair and longing flitted across her face. "Oh, Ahmet . . . I cannot. I have duty and honor to discharge. My hubris has led my people into disaster. How could I face my father in the House of Bel if I abandoned them? Please, my friend, go. There is nothing you can do here."

Ahmet shook his head again and twitched the bridle. The camel snorted and ambled forward. The Egyptian looked back at the lonely young woman. "Come, the city waits for its beloved Queen."

The Damascus gate was flanked by two huge towers, each rising seventy feet or more to a crenellated battlement studded with triangular teeth. Above the lights at the gate, the tops of the towers were lost in the night sky. A long passage, thirty feet across and open to the sky but walled on either side by the bulk of the towers, led up a ramp to the gates, which stood wide. They were stout panels of Lebanon cedar, each twenty feet high. The crest of the city, the sigil of the God of the Desert, was inlaid in each panel in brass and silver. Guardsmen, attired in silver mail that reached from head to below the knee, stood in ranks on either side of the portal, arms presented. A hundred torches flickered, lighting the entrance. Zenobia rode through with Ahmet at her side, her head held high, her long hair loose, flowing down her back like a wave. She was covered with grime and her eyes were hollow pits, but no one could have mistaken her for less than a Queen.

Beyond the gate they rode down a short ramp into a square. More guardsmen stood in lines on either side of the paved road, their arms held wide to hold back the crowd. Beyond the mass of dark clothing and pale faces, great pillars rose up, making a colonnade around the square. Fires burned on the top of the colonnade, casting a shifting light upon the scene. The avenue before them arrowed north into the city, and it too was lined with mighty fluted columns. Between the columns, platforms rose up above the crowd like marble islands in a sea of quiet, waiting people. On the platforms, statues of kings and gods rose, their painted faces come alive in the firelight.

Zenobia rode forward and Ahmet fell slightly behind her. She stared straight ahead. The sound of the hooves of her horse on the pavement and the jingle of its tack were the only sounds. Even Ahmet's camel was quiet. They rode down the aisle of the city in utter silence. The snap of logs in the fires atop the columns was muted. Tens of thousands of people lined the arcade, staring with desolate eyes at the Queen. Ahmet slowly realized that the entire city presumed that it was now doomed to desolation. Still, they came to look upon her and share her grief.

A thousand feet into the city, the avenue turned to the right at a sharp angle and Zenobia entered the great colonnade that formed the heart of the polis. The avenue widened and Ahmet swallowed a gasp at the sight that met his eyes. Now the columns were even higher, soaring thirty or forty feet into the air, and the press of people occupied a wider street. Tens of thousands of torches blazed, filling the avenue with light. The men of her army had fallen out and now stood in formation at either side of the pavement. As she passed, they raised their arms in salute yet made no sound.

They passed through a circular plaza that surrounded a great house of four parts, each faced with four massive pillars. Hundreds of priests in robes of white and pale yellow stood on the steps that led up to the house. They bowed, a rustling wave, as the Queen passed. Beyond this, Ahmet could now see that the avenue sloped upward toward a great platform that dominated the eastern end of the city. A vast building, with white walls faced with marble, rose up behind walls of its own. Great carved friezes lined the walls, showing men marching, hunting, sailing the seas in swift ships. A pair of mammoth winged lions flanked the entrance ramp to that building.

Three men stood on the ramp, halfway up, in their tattered robes and armor. The firelight gleamed on their helms and from their eyes. Zenobia halted her horse at the bottom of the ramp and stared into the weary eyes of her brother.

"Welcome, Zenobia, Queen of the city." His voice was hoarse but clear, and it carried across the ramp and to the mass of people who had filled in the avenue behind Zenobia's passage. "The great god Bel welcomes you in the name of his people. Enter your palace, O Queen, with his blessing."

Zenobia sagged forward in the saddle, then, with a trembling hand, slid down to the ground. Ahmet dismounted as well, the camel kneeling to the stones of the plaza that faced the great building. Surreptitiously he touched her shoulder, and she jerked slightly as a spark of pale-orange light passed from his outstretched finger to her. She nodded and straightened her back. Head high, she walked forward to where her brother, Mohammed, and Ibn'Adi waited.

They bowed, Vorodes first, then Mohammed and the old sheykh. The Prince of the city fell to one knee and extended a circlet of pale-white gold to the Queen. Zenobia stared at the tiara for a moment and then took it in both hands. While she did so, Ahmet led the horse and the camel away to the side. The Queen turned, raising the crown above her head. There was a great murmur from the thousands and tens of thousands who waited in the avenue below.

"While one Palmyrene lives, the honor of our city shall not die."

Her clear voice, high and strong, rang off the pillars and walls.

"We have gambled with Mars and lost, but our city will withstand the Persian storm. Rome will come to aid us, as they have always done, and then the Persian will perish in the sands, of thirst and the merciless sun. Palmyra will stand, free and strong, as it has always done."

She placed the crown upon her head, and it laid heavy, winking white amid her raven curls. Then the Queen turned and mounted the ramp, slowly and alone. When she reached the top of the ramp, where all could see, she raised her slim white arms to the sky.

"Bel bless us and stand with us. The love I hold for my people will sustain all."

Then she turned and entered the citadel, and the people in the streets and the avenues raised a long slow wave of sound, the prayer of Bel. Then they bowed as one toward the great building and the Queen who symbolized their city. Ahmet stood at the base of the ramp with some of the palace guardsmen, staring out upon the throng. A strange power was in the air, and the small figure of the Queen, now gone, was its focus. He tasted the air and felt some promise there.

Two figures stood on the crest of the escarpment, staring down into the valley. The moon had not yet risen and the land was dark, but they could see the blaze of light from the plaza at the center of the city. Fires burned on the walls, showing many men watching the approaches to the gates. A faint sound reached them in the quiet night air, the rumor of thousands of voices raised in song. The taller figure scratched at the grime in his beard.

"Little water," he said in a voice made harsh by the dust. "Our men are nearly dead of the heat and sun."

The other figure stirred and peered through the darkness. Narrow fingers wrapped around a staff of pale bone. "Dam the stream and make a reservoir. Cut the aqueduct. We shall have plenty and they none."

The taller figure nodded, rocking back on his heels. The city lay in the night, safe behind strong high walls and the vigilance of its protectors. "This will take time, time that mires us here, leagues from where we should be, at the gates of Damascus."

The smaller figure smiled in the darkness, his sharp white teeth flashing. "She would fall on your flank like a leopard and claw you again and again until you bled to death in the sand."

"Yes." The taller man laughed. "She should not have mewed herself up in the city. An error made by a tired mind. Now she cannot maneuver or escape into the desert. We can destroy this enemy utterly. Then there is nothing between us and Egypt."

Dahak turned away, his staff making a tapping sound on the stones of the escarpment. He felt something in the air, a trace of familiar memory; he raised his nose to catch the scent. The general remained on the ridge, his eyes taking in the lay of the ground, the height of the towers, the banks of the stream. It was a strong place, but he had broken strong places before.

A puzzle, he thought, *a problem of walls and towers and the wills of men. A man may make such a puzzle, and man may solve it too.*

After a full glass had passed, he turned and picked his way down the slope in the darkness. The wizard was already gone, back to his wagon with the army that had halted beyond the hills at sunset. Baraz walked alone, under the cold stars, and realized that he was almost happy. Then he laughed, a full rich sound that echoed off the rocky walls of the defile, for it was not the fate of men to be content with their lot.

· · · ·

Servants showed Ahmet to a small room, no more than a cell, though it boasted a fine soft mattress on a bed of cedarwood. He laved his face and hands in a pewter bowl that stood on a three-legged table by the side of the bed. He was terribly weary, but he took the time to calm his mind and recite the prayers that let him sleep. He fell asleep under a thin cotton quilt, his eyes tracing the painted patterns that adorned the walls.

Very late in the night, as the Egyptian slept, the door to his chamber opened and a figure in a long dark cloak entered. It stood over him, face hidden by the depth of the cowl, for a time, watching him breathe, and then it left, quietly closing the door behind.

Ahmet woke to a sharp rapping sound on wood. He stared up at a white plastered ceiling crossed by wooden beams. Sunlight fell on the wall to his right, illuminating bands of geometric patterns in black and red and white. The rapping came again.

"Holy Father," a man with a shaven pate said from the door, "your presence is desired in the Queen's chambers."

Ahmet rose, throwing back the thin coverlet. His thighs ached from the long trek on the back of a camel. He rubbed his face and frowned at the stubble he found there. His things were laid on a chest of light-red wood next to the opposite wall. He dressed and washed his face again. An ewer of pale porcelain sat on the table, filled with fresh sweet water. He drank his fill, then settled his tunic and headdress. He fingered his chin again but decided against shaving. It was late, the sun, seen through a narrow window in the wall, was high in the sky.

The Queen's chambers were opulent. Ahmet stared around in undisguised wonder at the wealth represented in the silk hangings and tapestries that adorned the walls. Rich carpets three and four layers deep covered the floor, obscuring the vast expanse of marble tesserae. Fluted pillars crowned with stylized acanthus leaves held up a soaring domed roof. Light fell in pale columns from circular windows set into the sides of the dome. It was cool and light. Many men were gathered around a cluster of couches and chairs at one end of the hall. Ahmet walked slowly toward them, his eyes taking in the richness of their brocaded robes and tunics. No man there had fewer than three rings on his fingers, of heavy gold and adorned with glittering gems.

The Queen sat at the center on a great chair of carved sea-green porphyry. She leaned on one arm that curved under her into a foaming wave. Her usual garments had been replaced with long robes of pure white samnite over a rich purple shirt, and her hair was almost hidden behind a heavy gold headdress. Bracelets and armbands of gold adorned her arms and tinkled at her wrists. Her face was a smooth white and her eyes were artfully anointed to hide the signs of fatigue and weariness that had marked her so harshly on the road from Emesa.

Ahmet stopped at the side of the cluster of men, who were talking in low tones, and bowed deeply to her. Zenobia inclined her head slightly and her almond-shaped eyes slid to the side. Ahmet looked and saw that Mohammed was sitting on a low stool behind Ibn'Adi at the edge of the circle of chairs. He sat down next to his friend.

"Lords of the city, please, sit with me and partake of wine."

Zenobia made a small gesture and servants came from openings behind the tapestries with plates of cut fruit dusted with sugar and honey. Others bore flagons of wine. The richly dressed men milled about for a moment and then seated themselves. Some took wine, but many did not. When they were settled, the Queen made a small gesture toward her brother, who sat at her side.

"Welcome, friends," Vorodes said, raising a cup of beaten gold. He took a small sip.

"A difficult time has come upon us," he continued, setting the cup down. "Morning has come and brought with it the sight of a great host of Persians encamped in the hills and their riders circling the city. As has happened only twice before in our long history, the city is besieged."

There was a muttering among the noble men, and Ahmet saw that some of them cast curious or angry glances at the Queen. She remained quiet, staring at some point above the heads of the men she ruled, her expression calm.

"Persia, as we feared, has come against us. Now the Boar waits outside and will soon begin works against us. Already the flow of water out of the aqueduct from the west has slowed to a trickle. Soon it will be dry. Given time, the Persians will build a wall around the city and pen us in. But, my lords, you know the strength of our position. Our cisterns are deep, our storehouses filled with grain. We can wait a long time while the Persians are reduced to eating their camels and horses, then their shoes, then nothing. Even water will be short for them—the streams are not reliable."

The Prince paused, surveying the faces of the clan lords and the great merchants. Ahmet studied them as well and saw men who had eaten too well for too long. He wondered if they had the stomach for such a battle. The city had grown mighty on trade and goods. Now there was no trade, and no goods flowed from east to west and back again.

"The Queen has decided to stand firm," the Prince continued. "We will not negotiate with Persia, nor will we surrender."

One of the magnates stirred at this, his long face marked by many days under the desert sun.

"Lord Prince," he said in a deep gravelly voice. "forgive my impertinence, but we are far from aid. The unfortunate setback that the army has suffered has removed our Nabatean allies from the field as well as the militias of all of Syria. As there are no Imperial Legions to succor us, we seem to have few options save . . ."

"Rome," the Queen said in a quiet voice, "will not abandon us."

The merchant turned a little, meeting the calm azure eyes of the Queen. His face was grim. "My lady, please, we are not children. The Roman army has withdrawn to defend Egypt. We are abandoned. The only hope of the city's survival is in negotiation. We have been strong allies of Rome; we can serve Chrosoes as well."

Zenobia made to rise, her perfect mask beginning to crack, but she restrained herself and remained seated.

"Chrosoes," she said in the same quiet voice, "will destroy us all. He is mad. He traffics with foul powers. Rome will win and will return. Our hope is to stand until that day."

The merchant shook his head in dismay. His dark eyes were filled with sadness. "If that is your will, my lady, then we shall honor it, but there is no hope for the city. There will only be the long horror of a siege and then death, or slavery."

Zenobia looked around the circle of faces, seeing the same despair in the eyes of the other lords of the city. Of all the men seated there, only the desert men to her left were unbowed. Ibn'Adi's old eyes flashed with the same fire that had ever filled them. The Al'Quraysh looked positively eager. She glanced at Ahmet. He smiled, just a little, and she took heart from it.

"There is hope, my lords," she answered. She reached into the folds of her garment and drew out a heavy bronze scroll case, well worn and dented. One end unscrewed and from within it she drew out a heavy piece of fine white papyrus. A purple string tied it up. She removed the string and smoothed out the paper on her lap.

"This," she said, "is a letter from the Emperor of the East, Heraclius. It was sent from Constantinople by courier soon after our army marched north from Damascus. It reached us on the road from Emesa. We have told no one of its contents until now."

She paused and took a breath.

"Daughter,
"Lady Zenobia, Queen of Palmyra, dux Romanorum Oriens
"Greetings from your Imperial Father, Heraclius, Augustus Caesar
"Know, O Queen, that the legions that were promised to the defense of Damascus and the eastern lands under your protection have been delayed in Alexandria by plague. When the foul disease has run its course, the legions shall march to your assistance."

She stopped, rolled the scroll back up, and carefully put it into its case. She looked around at the men seated before her. She smiled, and the smile was a fierce one, filled with anger and bitter fire.

"The Boar is trapped here, unable to abandon the siege that he has committed to. Thirty leagues lie between him and the nearest water. Soon the armies of the Empire will close the trap behind him, and then it is he that will be annihilated. His bones will bleach in the sun, like so many of our enemies' have done before. This is why we will stand fast and bleed the Persian on the walls of the city. Help is coming, my lords, and if we are patient, we will have victory."

The lean merchant frowned, but he held his peace. The others, Zenobia saw, were heartened and began whispering among themselves of the stories they would tell their grandchildren of the defeat of Persia before the golden walls of the city. The Queen nodded slightly to Ibn'Adi, who presumed to wake from his nap.

"In the matter of the defense of the city," she said firmly, interrupting the murmuring of the nobles, "we have decided to entrust the matter of command to the noble sheykh, Amr Ibn'Adi, who has long been a good friend of the city. My brother, Vorodes, shall command the walls as his second, and the noble Mohammed Al'Quraysh shall have the matter of harassing the enemy and making his stay with us as unpleasant as possible."

Some of the nobles looked around, their faces filled with questions, but then they saw that the Lord Zabda was not among their number. The general should have held command of the city if Zenobia or Vorodes did not take it upon themselves. They wondered if he had fallen at Emesa, for none had spoken of him since the return of the army.

"Then, if there are no objections, let us concern ourselves with matters of detail . . ."

Ahmet considered the beauty of the room and relaxed into a state of light meditation. Many hours would pass now in discussion.

The sun was setting again, and once more Baraz looked upon the city in twilight. On the great walls, lights twinkled on as the sun began to dip beyond the western hills. He sat on the summit of the tallest of the tomb towers west of the city, the sun at his back. His legs dangled over the edge, kicking idly at the crumbling bricks and masonry of the upper story. A hot wind ruffled his long curly hair, leaching the last bits of moisture from his skin. The bulk of his army remained in the hills, building a camp and laboring to dam the stream. The horses needed a lot of water.

The Lord Dahak sat beside him, cross-legged on the flat stones that made the roof of the tomb. As was his wont, the wizard had drawn his cowl over his head. With his long limbs and ragged cloak, he seemed a great raven perched on the height. Only part of one hand was visible, curled around the bone staff.

"Are you strong enough to break the city by yourself?" Baraz's voice was contemplative.

Dahak shifted and the Boar felt the cold eyes of the sorcerer on him. "Have you not an army? They must do more than eat and sleep and shit."

Baraz looked sideways at the wizard, to see if he was angry. If he was, then the Boar would not live long, not in this tiny space circumscribed only by darkening sky and a drop of thirty-five feet on every side. He could not make out the sorcerer's features in the shadow of his cowl.

"My men are exhausted from the trek across the desert. The horses are nearly dead. Our supplies are low, and there is precious little in this wasteland to feed them with. The longer we wait here, the weaker we will become. There is little wood here, and what there is will not suit for siege engines. My King bids me make haste, so I must consider every stratagem, every . . ." He paused. ". . . every weapon."

Dahak stirred, then said: "The King of Kings bade me assist you in all ways, Lord Baraz. It is my duty to obey. What would you have me do?"

Baraz grunted and stared back at the looming walls of the city. Throughout the day he had made a slow circle around the city, viewing its walls and towers and defenses from all sides. It was a long city, running beside the stream, with each narrow end coming almost to a point. At the eastern end, a low hill bore the great palace—an imposing bulk of golden stone and many pillars. At the western, by the great Damascus gate, there was another sizable building. Within there must be markets and gardens and storehouses. Tens of thousands of people must live inside the walls. And all around, on every side and facing, towering walls of vast blocks of stone. Thirty feet was the lowest wall, and that above a deep cleft where the stream ran along the base of the walls. Fifty feet in the other places, with regularly spaced towers.

"It is strong," Baraz said. "But as necessity directs, the gate is the weakest point. We have no ladders, no siege towers, precious few mantlets. We must storm the gate if we are to carry the city. Some rams we could fashion, given time. Can you break it? Can you sunder the gate and let us into the city?"

Dahak seemed to stare out at the distant walls, though it was impossible to tell. "There is a power in the city, Lord Baraz, something that I felt before on the field at Emesa. It is strong, though not as strong as the Red Prince that I slew."

"Another sorcerer?" Baraz was startled. He had thought that Dahak had murdered all of the wizards the Romans could gather. "How did he escape your sending?"

"He did not put himself against me," Dahak mused, his voice almost inaudible. "He only watched on the fringe of the struggle. Perhaps he is clever, this one. Perhaps he wanted to gauge my strength in the unseen world. Then again . . . he may be weak, or a captive. No . . . Something held a ward around the Bright Queen through the battle and shielded her from harm. It must be this one."

"What does this mean?" Baraz asked, pulling one leg up and resting his chin on his knee.

"The city is not without barriers and wards unseen," Dahak said. "The gate is no exception. They are strongest there, in fact, as it should be. Many priests and wizards have labored over them for many years. Yet—a gate's purpose is to open. If I have time enough, and the strength, I can make it yield to me."

"But?" Baraz could hear the question in the wizard's voice.

"This clever one, he might have will enough to hold it closed against me. If he can be removed from the board, then the city will be yours. If not, then the sun is fierce here and your bones will bleach quickly under it."

Baraz snorted and turned his attention back to the city. After a time he said: "In the world of men, it is easier to defend than to attack. Is it so with wizards as well?"

"Yes," Dahak said. "What do you intend?"

"If this sorcerer were to come forth and test his strength against you, man to man, could you destroy him?"

Dahak laughed, a sound of falling stones crushing limbs and bodies. "If he were to come forth, I could best him. But how would such a thing be contrived?"

"Honor," Baraz said, a grim smile on his face. "Mine against that of the Queen of the city."

"Honor?" Dahak sniffed, rising easily, like a serpent from the stones. "Honor brought us here—honor and duty to a dreadful King. I spit upon honor. But if it will serve us here, then let it."

. . .

Rich red light fell across the marble wall of the Queen's garden room in broad slanting beams. The setting sun glowed through rice-paper panels set around the western edge of the garden. Zenobia sat on the edge of a couch with a plush velvet cover, her gowns and robes discarded. She wore the purple shirt loose around her waist and had pulled on long cotton pantaloons, so finely woven that the outline of her pale legs could be seen through the fabric. The couch was on a raised platform made from a pale-tan wood. Around the platform the rich earth of the garden was filled with flowers and herbs. Slim white pillars, delicately fluted, with flaring capitals held up a dome of wooden slats over the platform. The Queen was peeling an orange and watching the sun set. She idly tossed the peels in a bucket of chased silver. Her hair was loose and fell over her shoulders in a wave. She bit down on an orange slice.

Ahmet sat behind her, his long brown legs straddling her to either side. His fingers kneaded her back, finding the knots of tension that were hiding among her muscles. The Queen gasped as he found a particularly tight spot. The Egyptian smiled and eased it out with deft hands.

"That was clever," he said, "producing the letter today."

Zenobia glanced over her shoulder, eyes reflecting the setting sun in gold.

"An exiled teacher should not mock a Queen," she said with some asperity.

Ahmet shook his head and gathered her into his arms. He had put aside the tunic and his broad chest was bare. She sighed and leaned back against him, her fingers curling around his forearms. The western horizon was a glorious display of orange and red and deep blue-purple.

"I was not mocking you, O Queen. They took heart from it, and how shall they know different? By the time it becomes clear that Rome will not come to our aid, it will be too late."

"True," she whispered. "They will fight to the last for the city."

"And for you," he said into her ear, "and for you."

She clutched him close and buried her face in his shoulder. The sun slid down beyond the western hills, and the sky alone retained its memory. The garden, built out from the top of the palace, fell into darkness. Below it the lights of the city brightened, ten thousand fireflies in the night.

TAURIS, PERSIAN ARMENIA

Heraclius and Galen picked their way through the rubble of the gatehouse. Their guards stalked through the ruins beside them. Smoke and fumes rose from the wreckage of the bastion, fouling the air. Beneath their boots the bricks of the inner courtyard steamed and cracked as they passed. Legionnaires with cloths bound over their mouths and noses were dragging bodies out of the buildings and piling them into wagons. The great middle gate had been torn from its hinges; it lay across the entrance to the city at an angle. Heraclius climbed up over a drift of fallen masonry and saw that there were several Romans standing in the shade of the gatehouse.

One of them was the tribune who had commanded the Third Augusta in the attack. He saluted the two Emperors as they strode up, ignoring the scattered bones and rotting limbs that were washed up against the wall like driftwood. The tribune was a heavyset man, with a short salt-and-pepper beard. One side of his face was badly burned and a raw red color. He saluted smartly, though his left arm was bound across the front of his body with strips of cotton cloth.

"Ave, Augustus. The citadel has been secured and the city as well. Most of the Persians are dead, though many surrendered and are being held in the square beyond the gate."

"Good," Heraclius said, his sharp eyes roving over the others who stood behind the tribune. None of them was familiar to him. "And these men?"

"Our . . . allies, Augustus. They broke through to the middle gate when my men were trapped in the central courtyard. If they had not driven the Persian archers off the wall, we would have all been dead men."

Heraclius nodded sharply. The assault on the gate, even with the destruction wreaked by the thaumaturges, had been a near disaster. Though the cohorts of the Third Augusta had rushed past the first gate, the inner yard was a trap, covered on all sides by Persian archers. Over four hundred men had died in a struggling mass, unable to retreat due to the pressure of new cohorts crossing the bridge. The Eastern troops had failed to carry either of the outer walls, suffering heavy casualties in the attempt. Only the unexpected appearance of friends had broken the trap.

"Good work, men," the Eastern Emperor said to the soot-stained and bedraggled men who stood behind the tribune. Their armor was battered and dented. Their swords were nicked and dull. All five were coated with black ash and the ragged remains of cloaks and leather armor. None seemed to have escaped injury. Heraclius' eyes narrowed, focusing on the leader, the tall red-haired man in the middle. There was something familiar about him . . .

The red-haired man stepped forward, favoring his left leg, and made a military salute. Heraclius' eyebrows raised, for the man had faced Galen, to his right.

"Ave, Augustus Galen. Thyatis Clodia of the Sixth Victrix reporting as ordered. I am sad to report that nearly all of my men perished in the effort, but the objective was secured."

Galen, keeping a smile to himself, returned the salute. "Well done, centurion."

The red-haired man turned smartly to face Heraclius and saluted as well. "Augustus Heraclius. If I may, it is my pleasure to present to you our ally, the Prince of Tauris, Tarik Bagratuni. Without the aid of his clansmen, our effort would have failed."

Heraclius frowned at the short man who stepped forward, his chain mail torn from many blows. The little man grinned, his teeth bright in the sooty darkness of his face. The Armenian bowed and hitched his thumbs into the broad leather belt that supported a profusion of knives and a stabbing sword.

"Well met, Bagratuni. We shall have to speak . . ."

Thyatis turned back to the Emperor of the West. He was smiling lopsidedly, his hair cropped shorter than she remembered. His armor was immaculate, the gilded eagle emblazoned on the front glittering in the sun. Germans with great swords and suspicious eyes crowded behind him. He reached out a gloved hand and wiped some of the grime from the side of her face.

"I did not think to see you again, Clodia. I am sorry about your men. Get cleaned up and a messenger will come and fetch you to my tent. We have things to discuss."

The Western Emperor surveyed Nikos and Jusuf and Dahvos. They looked worse than Thyatis, ground down and exhausted from fifteen hours of battle. Nikos had taken an arrow in the arm and was nursing a slowly clotting wound. The Bulgars looked like they had crawled out of a muddy sewer behind a butcher's shop. Dahvos looked particularly good; his right eye was oozing yellow pus from between crude stitches.

"Centurion!" Galen shouted back through the hovering ranks of his guardsmen. "Take these men to the baths and then the healer. See that they are well treated."

Thyatis sagged into the wall, and the Emperor was there, holding her up.

"I am very proud," he said quietly to her. "I will not forget your service."

The gruff-voiced centurion bustled up with several men in tow. Thyatis allowed herself to be led away, through the shattered gates and across the bridge. It was fouled with reddish-brown mud that clung to their boots, and fogs and mists still hung over the river. Behind her parts of the city were still burning, filling the sky with trails of black smoke.

Steam hissed out of a copper pipe, filling the wooden bathhouse with a delicious fog. Thyatis sank into the water with a groan of pure pleasure. A Greek manservant stood by, carrying a kettle filled with hot water. She motioned for him to add more to the tub. He tipped the kettle and very hot water joined the steaming water in the wooden-sided bath. She closed her eyes and submerged, luxuriating in the clean water. The manservant left the kettle and some soap behind, along with a curved bronze strigil. She spent an hour in the bath, scraping herself clean.

There were towels too, though the cotton weave was a little bare. It did not matter to her; to be clean and have her hair free of grease for once was reward enough. She sat in the little wooden room for a long time, toying with the strigil and thinking of the dead. In the steaming room, no one could tell, should they enter, that she was crying.

Finally there was a polite knock on the door and Thyatis looked up. She sniffled and blew her nose, then scrubbed her face vigorously with the towel.

"Come in," she said, wrapping the towel around her thighs.

Jusuf ducked into the room, then saw her, naked from the waist up, and blushed a bright red.

"Pardon." He gasped and stepped back out hastily, closing the door. Outside he slumped back against the wall of the bath, his breath a white puff in the chilly air. He closed his eyes, still flushed with the sight of Thyatis almost naked, and then they snapped open again. He ground his fist into the wooden planks of the wall. Whenever he closed his eyes she was there, her breasts dewed with steam, rich red-gold hair tumbling around her pale freckled shoulders.

"Well?" Thyatis' voice was querulous from inside the bathhouse. "What is it?"

"I'm sorry, my lady, I had no idea you were naked. My apologies for barging in."

Thyatis laughed and poked her head out of the door. Her hair, undone, fell in a long cascade almost to the ground. In the cold air, it began to steam and wisps of white vapor curled up around her. "I'm not naked," she said, still laughing, "I have a towel on."

Jusuf looked away, out over the canvas awnings and tent poles. The trees the camp was set among were beginning to turn color. Soon snow would fill the mountain passes. "My lady, among my people it is customary for women to remain fully clothed unless in the presence of their husband. I meant no disrespect."

Thyatis frowned and closed the door. Her good humor was fading slightly in the face of this barbarian's peculiar customs. "You'll have to wait, then, until I'm *properly* dressed. Tell me. Did they fix Dahvos' eye?"

Jusuf swallowed and turned to face the wall, arms outstretched, palms flat against it.

"Yes," he said, "they fixed his eye, he can see out of it again. He says that it's blurry, but he'll still be a whole man. He can still . . . he's fine. The others are eating now, and everyone we could find is fine. There's only one man still unaccounted for. My lady, I don't . . ."

Thyatis stepped out of the bathhouse; her hair tied back with a green ribbon, in dark-gray leggings with laced-up leather boots and a heavy woolen shirt dyed a cobalt blue. Her belt, sword, sheath, and knife hung over one shoulder. She eyed him from under her bangs while she finished tying her hair back. "Who is missing, Jusuf?"

He turned, seeing her face set and grim. "Sahul is gone, my lady. I can't find him anywhere. No body, nothing. He always stays with us, save if he needs to go—then he would tell at least me! Or Dahvos—someone!"

Thyatis nodded, her face a mask, but she was stunned. The thought of the quiet older brother gone was numbing. He was so reliable that she had begun to take him for granted. "He was with you at the northern gate? When did you see him last?"

Jusuf spread his hands, shaking his head. "I don't know. We attacked the gate, and then it was dark and we were fighting . . . I can't get anything out of the Armenians either. Bagratuni just shakes his head and says it's the fate of battle."

Thyatis gripped the young man by the shoulder and met his gaze. "Jusuf, I will believe that Sahul is dead when you bring his corpse before me, cold and stiff. Until then, at least in my mind, he lives and will be with us. He probably met some girl . . ."

The Khazar nodded, staring at the ground. Thyatis cuffed lightly him on the side of the head and pinched his ear.

"Go," she said. "Find any of the rest of our band of brothers and make sure they're at our tents in a glass. I'm off to see the quartermaster about horses and equipment. Oh, and if you see a messenger from the Augustus, send him on after me."

She stared after him as he made his way along the muddy path between the tents. She thought of her own brothers, but then pushed the memory away. That was too painful. She sighed and snugged the weapons belt around her waist and made sure that nothing was loose. Around her, the camp was gray and the trees seemed shrunken with the onset of winter.

"Centurion. Please, sit." It was well past midnight, and Marcus Galen Atreus had finally put aside the piles of wax tablets and papyrus scrolls that filled his days. Thyatis looked around and, at the nod of the Emperor, cleared off a winged wooden stool and sat down. She had changed into a plainer tunic and had carefully restrained all of her hair. Galen looked her over; the girl he had sent out from Constantinople on a wild throw of the dice had come back to him leaner and grimmer.

Almost a woman, he thought, *but one out of legend . . . a Roman Boudicca, standing triumphant in the back of a war chariot, her armor flashing in the sun.*

Still, even knowing that she was his tool, a dart to be thrown at the heart of the enemy, he still felt a queasy reluctance to use her. It seemed dreadfully foreign to assign a woman the rights of men—to bear arms in the service of the state—even, to use a damning word—*oriental.*

"This Prince of the city, he speaks well of you. He was surprised to see a woman in arms for the Empire. He calls you—what is it?—ah, he calls you Diana the Huntress."

Thyatis smiled politely. The harried general she had last seen in the drafty palace room in Constantinople was gone, replaced by a languid man in pale robes, at ease in his tent. Something about Galen had changed, she thought. He seemed more Imperial somehow, a sense of power was apparent around him. Odd, that it would be so, here in the back end of the world, but perhaps victory brought such changes. She only felt drained and worn out.

"That was very good work that you did. Heraclius did not believe that it could be done—it cost his purse ten thousand *denarii* on a foolish bet! A pity that so many of your Romans were killed. But . . . you seem to have found new men to replace them. These Bulgars—fierce as Sarmatians, they say. Do you trust them?"

Thyatis' eyes narrowed. The Emperor was fishing for something. "I have trusted them with my life, Augustus Caesar. They did not fail me, and they paid in blood for that service. Yes, I trust them."

Galen nodded and idly rubbed his ear. He thought for a while, staring off into one corner of the field tent he was living in. He turned back to her, and the Imperial presence was gone. "Can you do it again?" His voice was honest, without the echo of a disputation in the Forum. "Can you take a band of men into hostile lands again and do what you have done here?"

Thyatis stiffened in her chair, and her head turned a little to the side as her eyes narrowed. "What do you mean, Augustus Caesar? You have more work for me?"

Galen nodded ruefully.

"There will always be work for you," he said with a wan smile. "You are a rare leader, even among men. If I have you in my quiver, should I not put you to the bow and loose? The Easterners are still astounded at my daring and at your success. Do you know, they still think you are a man? It surpasses their comprehension for you to be a woman! Fools."

Thyatis grinned a little. Then she frowned, considering what he had said. "Augustus Caesar, I am a soldier, you are my commander. Command me. It is my honor to obey. Those men who followed me from Rome will follow me still—the others? I cannot say. I will put it to them, but whether they come or go? That is their decision."

Galen pursed his lips in consideration, but then rose and walked to the worktable he inflicted upon his household servants to carry from Rome to the Eastern capital to Tarsus to here. It disassembled into manageable pieces and was cunningly fitted together with wooden pegs. He ran a finger across the worn varnish on the top. Once it had been in his father's study, in Narbo, when he had been a child. When Galen had left Hispania with his Legions to fight against the pretenders and to claim the purple for himself, it had traveled with him. For the last decade, the office in the Palatine had housed it, and now it was here. He pushed aside a pile of tablets and dragged a parchment map up from under the other debris on the table.

"See here, Centurion, we are at Tauris, in these mountains . . ." His finger began to trace a path on the map. Thyatis came to his shoulder and leaned over the table herself, listening to him speak, following the finger. "And here, here is Persia proper. Our intent now is to move north into the valley of the Kerenos River, which runs from these mountains down to the Khazar Sea—the *Mare Caspium*—and join the army of the Great Khan Ziebil."

The *Mare Caspium* was a large oblong of blue, slanting from northwest to southeast. The map showed a rampart of mountains rising at its southern end.

"There is a pass," Galen continued, his forefinger resting among those mountains, "through what the Persians call the El'Burz, and beyond it the highlands of Parthia. These lands are rich beyond counting—the heartland of the Sassanid realm. With our combined army—Roman and Khazar—we will wreak great havoc upon those lands."

Thyatis looked up, seeing a grim smile on the face of the Emperor.

"No Roman army has ever penetrated into Parthia itself," he said, answering her unspoken question. "It has always been their surety, their fortress we could not breach. It is the purpose of this campaign, but the prize—ah, the prize—is Ctesiphon."

His hand drew her eye back west, and south, across the mountains that bounded the land of the Two Rivers and the sweep of the plain of Mesopotamia. Hundreds of small notations marked cities, canals, roads. At the south, where the Euphrates and the Tigris drew together, almost touching, was a golden symbol.

"The capital of Persia. The residence of Chrosoes, King of Kings, *regnum parthorum*. The heart of his realm. A city of nearly a million people, housing all the mechanism and artifice of government. This is your target, if I am to draw you to the bow again."

Thyatis measured the distances on the map. It was a long way to the enemy capital. "And you desire that I deliver it to you, a neat package wrapped with twine?"

"No," Galen said, shaking his head, his eyes dark with worry. "For all its importance, Ctesiphon is not well defended. Rome has higher walls and it is nothing to match the defiance of Constantinople. It is a city that can be defended only by a field army. If we reach it, it will be ours. I want you there, within the city, in secret, when our armies arrive—as insurance."

He paused, his gaze settling upon her. Thyatis straightened up. There was some odd emotion behind the eyes of the Emperor. After a time he sighed and looked down at the map again. "You are well capable of seizing an opportunity, should it present itself. You cannot do that if you do not know what an opportunity is. This is little known, centurion, but the first wife of the King of Kings, Chrosoes, was a Roman princess—Maria, daughter of Emperor Maurice of the East. Yes, Maurice who was murdered by the usurper Phocas, whom Heraclius then slew. The sons of Chrosoes are claimants to the throne of the Eastern Empire. Indeed"— the Emperor of the West stopped and drew a breath—"with a better claim than Heraclius himself, should the matter be argued in the court of law."

Thyatis let out a low, soft whistle. Then she clasped her hands behind her back and waited.

Galen rolled the map back up and slid it into the tube of ivory. He met her eyes with a level gaze.

"Law has nothing to do with this," he said. "This is a matter of strength and the contest between empires. We will win, because our victory means peace over the whole of the world. I want you, and your men, in Ctesiphon when our armies arrive. If fortune smiles, I want you to take any advantage offered to ensure that the children of the Princess Maria either"—He paused—"do not survive the fall of the city or come into *my* protection."

Thyatis felt a chill pass over her. A reckless political mission with almost no chance of success. Death seemed to hover at her shoulder, whispering in her ear. The Emperor looked away.

"Ah . . . Augustus, do you mean that the children are not to fall into the hands of the Eastern Emperor or his agents?"

"Yes," he said, still looking away. "In my hands, or none."

"Very well." Her response was toneless and clipped short.

Galen turned back to her, his eyes haunted.

"We will reach Ctesiphon," he said in a low voice. "I will look for you in the ruins."

•   •   •

Thyatis sat on a boulder, huge and gray, half covered with dark-green lichen. Pale morning sunlight fell across her, making her red-gold hair glow. Below her, below the huge trees that surrounded the boulder and its clearing, there was a rumbling sound. The Roman army was crossing the bridge at Tauris, heading north with a long train of wagons. Between the giant boles of the trees, she could see regiments passing up the road to the Araxes and the north. The sun, even through the scudding clouds, sparkled on their spear points and gleamed from their helmets. Behind her a roan horse cropped contentedly on the little white and yellow flowers that grew in the clearing. Among the trees, uphill, Nikos and her men were sitting on a mossy slope, sharpening new weapons or repairing armor or mending clothes.

She looked back down, to the valley. The outline of the great camp was still visible, but all of the tents were gone; even the bathhouse had been disassembled and the great copper kettles loaded up on to wagons. She picked at the lacing on her leather leggings. One of the laces made a corner, and she absently played with it, rubbing her forefinger over the sharp edge. The *clip-clop* sound of a horse came through the dim greenness under the trees. Dahvos, his eye still covered with a patch, rode up.

The young Bulgar looked older, much older than the day Thyatis had found him and his brothers hiding in a thicket. His face was still drawn with the memory of pain, though the wound to his eye would not disfigure him. He seemed to have grown within himself. His armor, a shirt of iron scales chased with silver and cunningly worked to fit like a skin to his broad chest, sat easily on his shoulders. The horse followed his lead, and his eyes were wary, watching the forest.

Thyatis sighed and raised her hand in greeting.

Dahvos pulled up close, looking up at her perched on the boulder. He wore fine kid leather gloves and had acquired a heavy furred cape with a hood to go with the armor and the profusion of weapons slung on the saddle of his horse. His long legs were wrapped in dark-green woolen pants stitched with burgundy thread. He was wearing his hair in a long braid. His face was troubled. "My lady."

"Lord Dahvos," Thyatis said, her expression sad. "Is there news of your brother?"

Dahvos shook his head, looking away. Thyatis noted that his jaw was clenched.

"And you? North with the army to meet the *Khazars?*"

He looked back, his eyes filled with pain and an unexpected anger.

"Yes, my lady." He sighed ruefully. "My people think that I've done well enough to command for 'real' with the host of the *Kagan* Ziebil. An *umen* of ten thousand lancers is my reward for seeing half of my friends die."

He turned in the saddle and pointed down at the long lines of spearmen and archers and horsemen crossing the river. "We all go north, to the Araxes, and then down the white river to the land of Albania on the shores of the *mare Caspium*. There Ziebil will be waiting and the armies of the People."

He looked up at the sky, only a narrow strip of washed-out blue peeking through the green roof overhead. "Winter is close. Both armies may winter in rich Albania. In the spring, Rome and Khazar both can strike south, into the Persian highlands. A daring campaign . . ."

Thyatis stood up, brushing her hands off on her woolen leggings. She stared down at the young man on his swift horse. "Command will suit you well, Dahvos. Be well. If, by chance, you should find your brother, tell him that he owes me for giving me such a fright as to think him dead. We must go too, and we will see you in the spring." Her lips quirked into half a smile.

Dahvos smiled back. "Ha! By the time that we reach Ctesiphon, you will have torn down the Empire of Sassan and made yourself a Queen on Chrosoes' throne! Take care of my brother. I only have only four left now and would begrudge another to the Crow Goddess."

Thyatis shook her head as she climbed down from the boulder and swung up onto her own horse. "Jusuf is a fool to come with us. The Emperor is fond of brilliant stratagems that either fail utterly or are spectacular successes. He should be with you, watching your back and carrying your banner in battle."

Dahvos shook his head, all light gone out of his face. "He is too devoted to you, my lady. Be careful of him. He is often moody and given to reckless action. I think . . . well. It is not my place to say. Good hunting and a clear sky!"

Thyatis stared after the Bulgar as he cantered away down the slope, deftly weaving his horse through the great mossy boulders and massive trees. She missed him and his irrepressible humor already.

"Enough!" she said to herself, and turned the horse to walk uphill to her men. Spring would come soon enough.

Nikos rose as she reached the men. The others remained sitting, weapons or clothes or tack in their hands. Thyatis turned her horse, looking down at the lot of them. Two of Bagratuni's sons had shown up, bristling with knives, axes, and spears, the day before. Efforts to run them off had failed, and now they were sitting together near the horses. Jusuf had brought four of his men, survivors of Tauris and the battle at the gate. Anagathios made ten.

"Mount up, lads. We've a long journey to make before the snow comes."

Jusuf and Nikos both nodded sharply and turned to deal with the men. Each noticed the other and stopped, staring. Thyatis almost laughed—they were bristling at each other like barnyard dogs! Neither spoke, glaring at the other.

"Jusuf," Thyatis said in a calm voice, "I am used to Nikos being my second. When I am not here, he leads."

The Bulgar met her eyes with barely repressed anger. For a moment she thought that Jusuf would test her will, but then he nodded and turned away. Nikos looked at her, his brown eyes filled with worry. Dissension among such a small group was a quick ride to disaster. She shook her head, signing *I'll talk to him later.*

Nikos shrugged and turned back to the men. "Check your gear, check your horses, check your water! We ride out in ten grains!"

·   ·   ·

The wagon rattled over the bricks that paved the bridge, and Dwyrin bounced up and down, clutching at the planks of the bench seat to keep from being thrown off. Squeezed in next to him, Zoë grinned a little, though her dark eyes were somber. Dwyrin matched her smile with one of his own, wedging his arm in behind her to get a good grip on the backboard. Odenathus was crammed into the back of the wagon with bales of hide tents and other supplies. He did not bother to disguise his morose expression. His battle partner was gone, swallowed up by the dark river and the flames at the gate. Now he seemed the outsider.

"Hey-yah!" Colonna snapped the reins, and the four mules yoked to the wagon snorted and flicked their tails from side to side. The speed of the clapboard wagon picked up, and they trundled forward through the streets of Tauris. The *ouragos* was heavily bundled up, with two shirts and a heavy cloak wrapped around him. Zoë huddled in an equally thick bundle of clothing and a fur-lined robe. Dwyrin was still in his linen shirt, with dirty blue leggings.

At last, he thought, *some reasonable weather!*

His breath puffed a little, white in the chill air. Despite the numbness that he felt for Eric, he smiled broadly and grinned at the other two passengers. Zoë was not amused and turned her face away. His fell—the day was beautiful but he could see that it made no difference to her.

The Roman army wound through the streets of Tauris like a steel snake. The buildings echoed to the stamp of thousands of booted feet, all marching north. Ahead of the wagon, Dwyrin could see the helmeted heads of a troop of infantry, their spears dancing over their shoulders. The Westerners were singing, a rude song about the bathhouse maiden. A few of the townspeople watched from the shelter of the deep doorways they favored in this land. The women were veiled and the men watched with closed faces. Dwyrin frowned at the ill-concealed hostility.

"They are not angry," Zoë said in his ear, her breath warm on his cheek. "They are patient, waiting for us to be gone. Then the city will begin to come alive. But they have as little love for Rome as they did for Persia."

"Why?" he said, turning to face her. She drew back a little. "These people, like my own, have been a prize for the great Empires for centuries. First they are a Persian province, then a Roman, then a Persian again. Never ruled by their own King. Who is free of Rome? No one."

Dwyrin demurred, saying, "My people are free, under their own Kings. Romans come to trade and barter, true, but not to conquer."

Zoë frowned at him, then lifted her fine nose in the air.

"That is because you are barbarians." Then she sniffed. "Who would want to rule you?"

Maxian closed the door carefully, making only a slight rasping sound. In the great bed, Krista continued to sleep soundly, her arm curled around a heavy pillow, her dark hair tousled around her head. The low light of an oil lamp lit the hallway for him as he padded to the window at the end of the floor. Around him, the house was deep in slumber. Even the homunculus, which often sat up in its room, unsleeping, its pale-yellow eyes staring at the wall, was abed. The Prince pushed the window open, feeling a fresh breeze on his face, cold and smelling of the sea.

One hand on the frame, he stepped up into the window itself. The moon rode low over the roofs of the city, illuminating a hundred towers, domes, and buildings with silver light. Taking a deep breath, Maxian felt a quiet peace steal over him. Beneath his feet, the garden court at the center of the house was completely dark, even the light in the kitchen window having died. Nimbly he swung out and caught hold of one of the lead drainpipes that carried water from the roof to the flower beds below. Centering his thought, he scrambled up the wall, feeling his toes dig into the crevices between the stones.

Alais was waiting, smiling. The Prince walked gingerly along the edge of the canted roof, one foot carefully placed in front of the other. The Walach woman bowed to him and held out a pale-white arm. He took her hand in his, feeling the long nails bite into his wrist. Alais was clad in a tight shirt of silk dyed with squid ink and leggings of soft cotton. Her long hair was tied back behind her head, a long, lashing tail that reached the small of her back.

"My lord," she purred. "Are you ready to learn the night?"

"Yes," he said, his pulse quickening. She bowed again and turned, running lightly along the bricks of the cornice. He swallowed and shrugged his cloak off of his shoulders. Exhaling, he followed, the rooftop and the buildings fading into a blur as they flashed past. At the end of the house, Alais sprang forward off the ledge, her hair flying out behind her as she vaulted over the dark canyon of the alleyway that separated the house from the next building.

Maxian, too, leapt out into darkness, hitting the end of the ledge at a flat-out run. Wind rushed past, and then there was a sharp thudding under his feet as he landed on the warehouse roof. A flicker of liquid light flared away from his boots and his knees flexed with the impact. His blood seemed afire with delight. The blond woman ran on ahead, her laughter floating back to him in the wind of her passage. The Prince picked himself up and sprinted after her. At the far edge of the warehouse roof she sprang up into the air. Maxian's breath hissed between clenched teeth, seeing her vault up onto the side of the next building.

"O lucky cat." He snarled, gathering himself for his own leap.

"How long have your people been in the city?" Maxian's voice was a little raspy. His legs and arms were leaden weights from the effort of following Alais across the rooftops. He leaned back against the legs of a great bronze statue, his head in shadow. Moonlight fell across the valleys and mountains of the city that lay below them. Alais sat close by, her arms wrapped around her knees, which were drawn up to her chin. At their backs, the summit of the towers that adorned the Temple of Apollo formed the highest point in the city. Only a bronze of the god rose above them, his crown of gold gleaming even in the near-dawn darkness. Broad expanses of tiled roof and more statues ornamented the temple below. The entire city slept.

"Long?" she said dreamily. "No, I suppose not. I have only been here for seven years. The Matron, she has always been here. Even when crude men first put stone upon stone for shelter, I think she was watching with her cold eyes from the darkness. This is why she rules, she is the oldest."

Alais flexed her hands, seeing the long nails flash in the moonlight. "I am quicker, and stronger, fleet of foot. But she is the oldest and she rules here."

"Where did you come from?" Absently he reached out and ran his hand across her smooth back. She stretched under his touch, arching her back, and slid closer to him. Under the silk, her skin was hot, warming him in the cold night air.

"I came," she said, leaning her head on her hands, wrapped around his knee, "from the north. From high mountains crowned with ice and snow, from highland valleys filled with bright flowers and deep stands of great green trees. My family lived in the high places, above the abodes of men, hunting as we have always done. The air is so clear there, free of the stink of fires and so many men. It was a delicious time. I miss it."

"Why did you leave?" Maxian rubbed the skin behind her ear and she turned her head, making a low rumbling sound at the back of her throat.

"War came. The Night Kings and their blood-drinkers came up the long valleys with bright spears and fire. My people fought and lost, even when the humans in the villages rallied to us. The Dragon-lord and his crimson banner could not be defeated. All of my brothers and sisters died, fighting at Súreánu fort. The humans thought it was our one chance for victory—but it was only a trap and a feast for the Dragon."

Alais looked up at him, her pupils expanded in the darkness to fill her whole eye. "My people did not have someone like you, my lord. There was no one to lead us, to command us, to understand that victory must be paid for in blood."

"Do you think," he said, his voice raw with doubt, "that it is worth it, to pay for victory in blood, to spend the lives of some so that some greater purpose might be achieved?"

She sat up, turning to face him, her hand on his thigh. "Listen to me, my lord. You are a Prince of your people, not some common man. It is the duty of a

Prince, or a King, or a chieftain, to see the greater good for his whole people. The lives of individuals must be weighed against the lives of a whole people." Her voice was strong and sure. "In desperate times, some must be spent to save the tribe."

"Have I done that?" Maxian's voice was distant, his face troubled by evil memories. "Have I saved anyone? Everything that I have touched, trying to save, has died so far, and those who remain are so close to death with each day . . ."

"You will save them," she said, digging her claws into his leg. "You will save the world. You are strong enough, my Prince, to pay the cost."

Alais stood, her hair swinging out behind her shoulders. She took the Prince's hand in her own, pulling him up. "Come, my lord, the sun will rise soon. Time for one more race."

THE VALLEY OF THE ARAXES, PERSIAN ARMENIA

Dwyrin bent close over the surface of the stream, the round disk of the sun glittering up from the waters into his eyes. The water was cold, born in high mountain springs and melted snow. He was stripped to his waist, his pale freckled skin dewed with sweat. Each hand he held just above the water, drifting this way and that like the shadows of the few clouds that marred the otherwise perfect blue bowl of the sky. Around him, spreading out on either side of the stream, was the army of the Emperors. A camp was rising on either bank, the armies segregated not by race or nation but by the order of their march.

Soon, within days, the Romans would meet their allies for the first time. At the moment, however, Dwyrin shut out the sound of axes on wood, the shouting of centurions eager to see their men complete the raising of their tents, and the preparation of cleared lanes among the brush and stands of trees. He focused on the flickering shadows of fish in the stream. Old experience, from when he was only a lad, taken in hand by the great paw of his father, told him that fat-bellied fish, their flanks stippled with pink and gray and black, were waiting.

His hand dipped into the water slowly, without making even a ripple on the fast-moving surface. He ignored the chill in his feet, clammy dampness of his trousers. His hands nestled between a pair of rocks, matching the current. He waited, his breathing steady and even. A fine fat trout swam into the channel among the rocks, brushing over his hand with its supple skin of tiny scales. A grin flickered for a moment on his features, and his fingers moved gently, caressing the flanks of the fish. It shivered at his light touch, but he continued to tickle it gently.

Then Dwyrin's hand darted and the fish thrashed in his grip, but it was too late. The Hibernian laughed and strung it on a line of cord that hung from his waist, sliding an arrow of bone through its gills. It joined six of its fellows on his belt. Dwyrin turned at a sound.

On the bank, clad in a simple white gown and half cloak of pale green, a young woman was clapping her hands in delight.

"Oh, well done!" she called out, shading her eyes with one pale white hand. Dwyrin flushed and, remembering his manners, bowed. The woman bowed back but then sat down heavily. Dwyrin splashed through the stream, weaving his way among the rocks, to the bank. The lady, for the quality of her bracelets and hairpins marked her as one, was a little pale. The Hibernian could see, too, that she was very pregnant.

"Domina," he said, his voice concerned, "are you all right? Should I call your servants?"

"No!" she said, though she was short of breath. "They cosset me to death. Here it is, a gorgeous late-summer day—the sky like the sea, the air freshened by wind. I refuse to sit inside and listen to the natterings of my maids. We are in uncharted lands, filled with savages and Persian spies—I should like to see something of the land I travel through."

Dwyrin nodded sympathetically, though the thought of being cosseted by white-limbed maids with golden hair was distracting. Still, it was far better to be out and about than stuck in some sweltering hide tent, in the dark, wondering what was going on. "True words, my lady, though in your condition you should take care."

"Feh." She snorted. "My condition is held up to me as a fine example of all the things that I should not do. I am tired of it. Tell me, young man, where are you from and where did you learn to beguile fish so?"

She smiled at him, her green eyes merry, her perfect complexion like lustrous pearl. Dwyrin felt a little faint, but somewhere in the back of his mind he realized that she was barely older than he was. A young woman, being carted around by some rich husband—doubtless one of the grandees of the Eastern army—well with child. Distantly, the great brass gong of the school sounded in his head. He looked around furtively.

"Ah, my lady, shouldn't you have a chaperone, or a maid, or someone with you? Your fair skin and soft hands mark you for a noble's wife! I'm only a soldier in the Legion—I'm not supposed to traffic with the likes of you. No disrepect meant!"

The lady sighed and looked around as well. The line of her neck did not match the classical beauty of the Greek sculptors, and her nose was too pert and rounded for the image of Athena, but her good humor and ready wit had already captured Dwyrin's heart. She made a moue and pouted, putting her hands on her cheeks. "Oh, I hate a chaperone! And look at you, a soldier, brave in the face of the enemy, doubtless noted for your daring and courage—looking like a schoolboy caught with an extra pastry! I will be driven mad by this . . . I am sure of it."

Dwyrin forbore telling her that he was, in fact, a schoolboy.

"I should go," he said, mumbling and trying not to look at her. She frowned and patted a rock next to her.

"Sit," she said with asperity, "and tell me of your life in the Legion. I see so many soldiers, but I never know what they are doing! If you do not, then I shall cry out, making a scene, and you will be punished!"

"I will be killed!" he blurted, then covered his mouth. The lady smiled sweetly at him and patted the rock again. He sat down, though he was not in the least pleased by it.

"Now," she said, pulling a waxed tablet out of a pocket sewn into the inside of her cloak, "tell me about the life of a soldier in the army of Rome. Spare no detail—the sun is still high."

Dwyrin sighed and arranged himself cross-legged on the rock, the hooked fish carefully laid in the stream. They twitched, trying to escape the line through their gills, but could not. He felt much the same.

Well after nightfall, Dwyrin trudged up the hill, through stands of birch and cedar, to the edge of a meadow where his five had made camp the day before. He scratched at his shoulders, sunburned again, and muttered darkly to himself about the nosy nature of young Greek ladies. He had retained the fish, at least, and that would make dinner far more palatable than the hardtack and salt pork they had lived on in the mountains. He passed through a sentry line, giving the password of the day to two long-bearded Armenians leaning on their spears. The tents of his five were couched under tall red-barked trees, and a little fire was going in front of them.

Zoë looked up with a murderous expression as he shuffled into camp and flopped down next to the fire. Odenathus looked guiltily at him too, making him surmise that the five-leader had been holding forth upon his unprofessional behavior and the extent to which it merited punishment. He smiled weakly at them.

"I found some fish," he said, mumbling. A cooking stick was near the coals in the fire and he began gutting his catch. "A noble lady saw me in the stream and called me over—then she pestered me with questions all day! I couldn't leave, it wouldn't have been polite . . ."

Zoë, her expression thunderous, toyed with a knife, one of the several that she carried in her belt or thrust into the uppers of her boots. The side of the blade caught the glow of the fire, shimmering with red and orange.

"A noble lady . . ." The scorn in her voice cut at him. "A poor lie. A penny-hatiera in the baggage train, more like. Did you bring her fish too, to pay for her time? Was it worth it?"

Dwyrin stiffened at the vitriol in the five-leader's voice. Unconsciously he sat up straighter, his eyes narrowing. "She was a noble lady, well mannered and she could write. She asked me all about our lives in the service of the Emperor—what we eat, how we march, who carries the axes to fell trees, everything in the world, it seemed! In my country," he finished, glaring back to Zoë, "we are polite to strangers and accord them honor."

Zoë half sat up, her face stilling at the implied insult, the knife in her hand sliding forward toward him. Dwyrin felt the air chill, but he did nothing, keeping his balance—though it was hard! Part of him, some thing that lived in his gut, wanted to jump up and smash the Palmyrene's face with his fist or call fire to burn her. But he did nothing. He knew that he was telling the truth.

Zoë breathed out, calming herself, and sat back down.

"I suppose that she was very beautiful," she said, her voice weary and bitter.

"Well, no," Dwyrin replied, accepting the olive branch—if that is what it was. "Very pregnant, though! My mother would guess only a few weeks before she births, I imagine."

Zoë's eyebrow crept up at this, a procession of unreadable, but marked, emotions crossing her face. She slid the knife back into its sheath and put it away in the back of her belt.

"Pregnant?" she asked, her voice a study of innocence. "A noble lady, you say?"

"Yes," Dwyrin said, now suspicious that she believed him. "Richly dressed, though the paints not overdone, with green eyes, long brown hair, and soft skin."

Odenathus hissed in delight, leaning over the fire, eager to catch every word.

"Did you touch her?" His voice was touched with a lurid amusement. "What else happened?"

"Nothing, Macha be praised!" Dwyrin said, making a sign for good luck. "We talked by the stream is all."

Zoë curled her arms around her knees, watching Dwyrin over the light of the fire. "Your noble lady, did she have a name? A house perhaps? A bevy of maids? A glowering chaperone? Bands of guardsmen?"

"No." Dwyrin sighed. "More's the pity—if she had, I would have made my escape much easier and been back here hours ago. Why should anyone care how the spearmen lace up their boots, or that we have sour wine one day in three?"

"Well," Odenathus said slowly, unable to contain himself, "did you kiss her?"

Dwyrin turned a freezing glare upon the Palmyrene boy, which made Odenathus sniff and poke industriously at the fire.

"I think," Odenathus said, when Dwyrin said nothing, "that our barbarian friend was too polite to take such advantage—among his people it is not done, or so I surmise . . . this is why there are so few of them!" He laughed, but Dwyrin laughed with him too. It was good to sit all around the fire like this, sharing the events of the day.

"And, you say, this noble lady was pregnant too." Zoë's voice cut in from the side. "You did not say whether she had a name or not?"

"Oh," Dwyrin said, scratching his head, trying to remember if he had managed to get a question in amid the flurry of hers. "Yes, Martina—if my memory serves. Her husband is an officer from Africa—from Carthage, I think. I'm not a bard or druid, you know, to remember every little thing that happens . . ."

Zoë shook her head, then stood, staring up at the stars peeking through the crown of the trees above. She hooked her thumbs into her belt and turned, warming the backs of her legs at the fire. The nights were growing colder, even down here, out of the mountains. "I suppose that you *were* polite to her."

"I was on my honor," he snapped back, bridling at the implication of poor behavior in her tone. "I treated her as one of my aunts, or my mother—though she is neither so young nor so nosy as that one."

"Good," Zoë said, looking over her shoulder for a moment. "The penalty for such familiarity, you know, is blinding, I believe, or perhaps just torture and death. But still, I suppose that the tribune will understand. He is a caring and forgiving soul."

"Do you think trouble will come of it?" Odenathus tapped a long stick on the rocks at the edge of the fire, watching Zoë carefully. "I have heard that she is rather wise, even for her young age. Surely she saw what a lackwit our Hibernian friend is . . ."

Zoë cut him off with a motion of her hand, turning back to the fire. Dwyrin looked from one to the other, a damp chill percolating in his stomach.

"The Empress is not my concern," Zoë grated, "but rather the temper of her husband."

"Empress?" Dwyrin squeaked, feeling dizzy and faint. "What Empress?"

Without sparing him a look, Zoë continued: "The Emperor of the East once had a man cut to bits and fed to swine for insulting her. Granted, he was an enemy of her house and a lying fool, but still . . . Or the matter of the usurper Phocas—there was a grisly death! He is a man, with a man's rages. He loves her too much, I think, to be as good an Emperor as he might be . . ." Zoë's voice trailed off.

"Lady Martina is an Empress?" Dwyrin lay down on the cold pine needles. He felt quite faint.

"Yes," Odenathus said, sighing as he removed the trout, now crisping in the heat of the coals, and slid them off the stick onto a wooden platter he had stolen from the ruin of Tauris. "I fear so. The only pregnant noble lady in this army would be the Empress Martina, the young and scandalous wife of the Emperor of the East, Heraclius of Carthage."

"Scandalous?" Dwyrin perked up, leaving off from nervously chewing on the end of his thumb. "I didn't hear! What did she do? Did she cavort with stableboys? With gladiators, shining with oil?" *Maybe she talks to young barbarians all the time!*

Odenathus cuffed the Hibernian gently on the head. "No, you idiot . . . she is his niece. These Greeks are beside themselves with outrage that the Emperor should follow his heart—it *is* said that he loves her, and no less because they have known each other for years. Some odd concept that they should spread their seed afar . . ."

"That," Zoë said, her voice serious, "is not the issue. The problem is that fisher-boy here has poked his nose into a political hornet's nest. We are more likely to be screwed by something political than killed by the Persians. You"—she stabbed a finger at Dwyrin, still lying on the ground, feeling overcome—"are not going anywhere without someone to watch you." She grimaced. "Me, I suppose."

Well, Dwyrin thought, watching the moon slide across the sky, *it was a good day after all.*

THE WALLS OF PALMYRA

)⋅((

Zenobia stood on the battlement of the Damascus gate. Above her the sun blazed, a giant brass disk in a bone-white sky. The valley was filled with terrible heat, raising shimmering waves from the stones and sand. The Queen was garbed in thin silk robes that fluttered around her in the forge-hot breeze, clinging to the curve of her body. Her hair was loose, a dark cloud cascading around her shoulders. She had forgone the heavy crown of the city in favor of a thin band of silver set with a single ruby the size of her thumb. She looked down upon the Persian embassy with narrowed eyes.

"I am the Queen," she said, "if you would speak to the city, you speak to me."

The Persian herald, a thin brown man with a long nose, returned her gaze amiably. He was comfortable in tan and white desert robes and *kaffieh*, though the men behind him were red-faced and dressed in heavy, ornamental robes and armor. Zenobia guessed that at least one of them would faint from dehydration and the sun if she kept them there long enough. She looked forward to that with a small malicious pleasure.

"My master," the herald said, "bade me bring you his best wishes on this day. He inquires if you would consider yielding the city to the might of Persia and receiving his clemency and gratitude."

Zenobia sneered, her full lips—outlined with dark henna—twisting into a semblance of a smile. "Give your master my condolences for his imminent death. Assure him that after the buzzards and vultures have picked his bones clean, I will see that his widow receives the remains in a fine burlap sack. I will give honor to his family and grind the bones to powder myself! The city does not desire the clemency of bandits and thieves. Tell your master that we will not bow our necks to him. He, however, may come to me and beg forgiveness of his trespasses. My mercy is well known throughout the whole of the world."

The herald nodded, taking a moment to fix her words in his memory.

"My master," he replied, "the great General Shahr-Baraz, he who is known as the Royal Boar, the favorite of the great King Chrosoes, the King of Kings, is well known for his mercy, O Queen, and for his honorable word."

Zenobia cocked her head to one side, staring down at the brown man. "And what, pray tell, does his honor have to do with murdering my people and looting the tombs of the fathers of the city?"

Overnight there had been odd cracking and thudding sounds from west of the city. Mohammed's men, having slipped out of the city at dusk, returned before dawn with news that the Persians had been looting the tower tombs and carrying off their contents to the Persian camp in the hills. Zenobia had been forced to isolate the scouts in the basement of the palace to keep the word from spreading. If the people of the city learned that the honored ancestors were being violated in such a way, they would have thrown the gates wide and charged out themselves with kitchen knives to take revenge upon the Persian army.

"My master's honor is unimpeachable, O Queen. He has no quarrel with you or your city. His quarrel is with Rome and the murderers of his great and good friend, the Emperor Maurice. He does not desire to cause you harm—he desires only peace between the great and noble realm of Persia and the renowned city of Palmyra."

"He expresses his friendship," Zenobia said, her voice languid, "in a strange way. Thousands are dead in this 'peace,' and many more will die here in the dreadful heat before his peace is done."

One of the Persian nobles began to breathe heavily, leaning sideways on his horse. The other nobles glanced at him out of the corner of their eyes, but no one moved to help him. The noble began to flush a bright red and his breathing became more labored.

The herald ignored the soft noises behind him, continuing to watch Zenobia with a mild expression on his face. "O Queen, if this disagreement is pursued to its conclusion, you and all of your people will be slain or driven into the desert. Your city, if it resists, will be utterly destroyed. No stone will remain on stone. Its name will disappear from history, buried by the sand. But peace . . . peace and friendship with Persia will make you mighty. The entire world will hear of the glory of Palmyra and wonder at the magnificence of it. Do you not chafe under the auspices of Rome? That mean, gray old man who clutches at you with greedy fingers? That miserly father who demands that you pay and pay, without hope of a return? Where is the investment in this? Where is Rome now? You stand alone, brave and glorious, against the might of Persia. None can say that you have not done your duty—the honor of the city is satisfied. Why continue to fight?"

Zenobia leaned forward, resting her palms on the hot ashlar stones of the battlement. "Tell your pig master, this Boar, that Zenobia will not be foresworn. His master is a whoring pustule of evil and his honor is worthless. Palmyra will stand against him."

The herald nodded, his face creased by a slight smile. "Be it so, O Queen. My master makes one final offer, then, though if you call him faithless, then it bears no weight on the balance of your judgment. He will send a champion forth, one man, to face the champion of the city. In single combat, here on the plain before the gates, they will fight. The man who stands the victor will carry the day. If your champion triumphs, my master will withdraw and his army with him. Palmyra will remain free. If my master's champion triumphs, then Palmyra will accept the friendship of Persia and open her gates."

The herald bowed deeply in the saddle and then turned his horse about. The Persian nobles turned as well, though the red-faced man had to be helped by two of his companions. The embassy rode away, seemingly small under the white glare of the sun. Zenobia remained on the wall, watching, until they disappeared into the dun-colored hills. Then she turned away and, surrounded by her guardsmen, descended the broad stone stairs to the courtyard below. Her face was pensive with worry.

"All rhetoric and disputation aside, my lady," ibn'Adi said, his face grave, "I have never heard that Shahr-Baraz was faithless. He has always served Chrosoes with honor, even when the King was a prisoner in his own keep. Did he not go into exile with the young King to Rome, leaving behind all lands and family? If he swears this, he may well mean it." The sheykh leaned back in his chair, stroking his long white beard in thought.

Zenobia looked around the gathering, gauging the reactions of the men she had assembled in her study to advise her. Her younger brother, Vorodes, and the Southerner, Mohammed, were eyeing each other, seeing who would offer first to bear the honor of the city. The high priest of Bel, old Septimus Haddudan, was sunk in deep depression. Though in his youth he had been a firebrand and a kingmaker in the politics of the city, now he was tired and withdrawn. Once the General Zabda would have sat at her council as well, but since his failure at Emesa she would have nothing to do with him. Ahmet she looked to last. His eyes were troubled, but his face was calm.

"The fate of one against the fate of the city," she said slowly. "I too have heard that the Boar is an honorable man. His position is tenuous, trapped here in the desert at our gates. Men in such a place often look for a bold throw to give them victory at little cost."

Her fingernails, long and carefully shaped by her handmaidens, tapped on the smooth surface of the table by her chair. Ahmet watched her, seeing something of her thoughts in her face.

"I shall accept the challenge," she said after a moment of reflection. "Mohammed, send one of your rascals to the Persian camp, under truce, to carry word of my acceptance. Tell the Boar that my champion will meet him on the field before the city tomorrow morning, at dawn."

Mohammed raised an eyebrow in surprise. "You think that he will stand forth himself?"

Zenobia smiled, saying: "Has he ever lost a fight, man to man? No. Or so his legend holds. He is not the kind of man to send another to defend his honor for him. It will be he."

"Then," Vorodes said, breathlessly, "his defeat would wound Persia twice—once in their failure to capture the city and once in his death, for he is their strongest arm!"

A grim look passed over Zenobia's face and her lips thinned to a harsh line. "Yes, that is the prize."

Ahmet woke in full darkness. Zenobia was curled up in the curve of his body, her head tucked into his shoulder. Her breath whistled softly at his ear. The room was dark; even the narrow band of eastern sky that was visible through the windows was as black as pitch. Gently, he eased out from under her, leaving her among the pillows and quilts, frowning in her sleep. In the faint light, she seemed more beautiful than ever, a perfect alabaster statue among the dark blankets. He pulled on his breechcloth and tunic, smoothing back his hair. He did not bind it, but he did find his longer robe. The door opened silently on well-greased hinges and he went out into the passage.

The wall that girdled the palace formed the southeastern point of the city. Ahmet walked along the parapet in the dim light of torches placed in iron brackets along the battlement. Two of the city guardsmen followed him at a discreet distance, keeping an eye on the shadowed hills to the west. The Egyptian walked slowly, tasting the air, trying to divine what it was that had waked him. There was something, some pressure in the air, that raised hackles along his back. He dimly sensed forces gathering the darkness, out among the narrow canyons and ravines that edged the fertile plain around the city.

He stared out into the night, seeing only the faint light of watchfires among the Persian tents. Soon dawn could come. He shook his head, still uneasy, and went back inside.

Pink and amber streaked the sky in the east. Zenobia came to the Damascus gate, riding on a stout-chested mare with Ahmet and Mohammed at her side. Vorodes and the royal guardsmen were waiting, torches held up to banish the lingering night. The Prince was unhappy, and he did not bother to disguise it as he looked up at his sister.

"Peace, little brother," she said. "I am the better swordsman. I should not have to prove it to you again before you open the gate."

The Queen was clad in dull dark armor; a breastplate of iron, worked with the signs of the city, wrapped her torso. Her shoulders and arms were covered with a lamellar mail, a supple coat of iron rings that flowed with her motion. The broken wings had been restored to her helm, and it was snugged tight under her chin. A long sword lay across her saddle, cased in a metal scabbard ornamented with lions and elephants. An inch of the blade peeked out, showing a watery surface that caught the light of the lanterns and held it, glowing like a jewel. Overlapping plates of iron covered her legs, tucked in against the sides of the horse. Tough leather riding boots and gloves protected her hands and feet. Another sword, this one plain and well worn, was clasped behind her on the side of the saddle, and she balanced a long, slim lance with a steel leaf-shaped blade on the right side of the horse.

Vorodes had a sick look in his eyes, and he grasped his sister's stirrup fiercely. "Please, let me go instead. If you die, then the city will lose its heart. If I die, then you will still stand. The Boar has your reach; he outweighs you by a hundred pounds! He is a giant, and though you are faster with a blade than any man I've seen, he will crush you with sheer strength."

Zenobia smiled and ran her hand through his hair. "I love you too, little brother. It was my folly that brought us to this day; it is my responsibility to make amends for it if I can."

The Queen looked around at the faces of the men, their faces somber in the flickering light. "My friends, it has been an honor for me to stand with you in battle and in peace. I have bent my thought to this moment for a day and a night. I am a better swordsman than my brother. You, ibn'Adi, are too old, though I see in your heart and in your tears that you would go forth if I asked you. You, Mohammed, you I might send if you were of the city—but you are a stranger here, though Bel bless us that you have come. Without you and your bravery on the field at Emesa, I fear none of us would have escaped alive. And you, Ahmet, dear Egyptian, have you ever held a sword in your life?"

Ahmet laughed, seeing the sparkle in her eyes, and the other men laughed as well. The dreadful tension was broken, just for a minute, and Zenobia looked around gaily, her face lit with great happiness. "Open the gate. Let us be done with this."

Vorodes gestured to the guardsmen arrayed on either side of the gate. There was a clanking sound and then a grinding as the huge iron bolts that secured it were withdrawn into the rock of the towers. Windlasses creaked as men labored in hidden rooms to turn the wheels that withdrew the foot-thick iron bars. When they had receded, the guardsmen put their shoulders to the heavy cedar doors and the gate swung wide.

Zenobia urged her horse forward and it trotted out onto the sloping ramp. The sky had lightened, revealing the plain and the looming shapes of the tomb towers that marked its border. Light grew and Zenobia waited under the torches and lanterns, alone before the gate of the city.

The sun peeped over the eastern rim of the world, and the road between the funereal monoliths was at last illuminated. A single figure waited—a dark shape on a black horse. There were no Persians in sight; even their scouts had withdrawn. The light of the sun touched the top of one of the towers, and it glowed like a pearl in the dawn.

The dark shape rode forward slowly, and a dreadful chill touched the Queen. The sun continued to rise, touching each of the tomb towers in turn, creeping down their sides with a wash of golden light.

"It is the one I felt at Emesa," Ahmet said from the shadow of the gate. "The terrible power that struck down the Red Prince."

He stood forward, his shoulders square, and put his headdress and robe aside. A tremendous calm had settled over him, and his heart was suddenly light. He knew why he had come to this place. "This is for me, my lady, not for you."

Zenobia turned her horse, staring at the priest with stunned eyes.

Ahmet made a half smile. "The Boar desires only victory, not the honor of the world."

"No . . ." she whispered, but stood frozen as he walked past her, his staff held under one arm.

Ahmet turned at the bottom of the ramp, his bare feet digging into the sand. "Close the gate and set a watch upon every wall. This is a little deceit; it may grow larger."

Ibn'Adi and Mohammed took Zenobia's reins from her nerveless hands and led her back into the city. Vorodes stared out at the barren field, where Ahmet walked alone, and put his shoulder, with the others, to the great gate to swing it closed.

Sand crunched under his feet as Ahmet crossed the bridge at the foot of the wall. The dark shape remained, sitting on the horse under the shadow of the tombs. As he walked, the Egyptian was calming his mind, settling into the fourth entrance of Hermes. Though the plain appeared flat and smooth to the eye, hollows and rocks made it uneven. Footing would be poor, and he could not afford to lose sense of his physical body. Perception unfolded, the sky falling away in a riot of blazing lights and swimming with patterns of force. He focused on holding his physical sight and senses together.

The figure moved, the black horse walking forward a few paces. Then it stopped and the robed figure dismounted, his cowl falling away from a pale head. Ahmet stiffened, seeing the vulpine line of the skull. The shock of perception was like a blow to the face. The enemy sent his horse away. Then it turned, arms held away from its body, and Ahmet saw its eyes blaze with subtle fire.

A dead thing in the shape of a living man, he thought in amazement. *What hell did it crawl forth from to learn the usages and speech of men?*

Ahmet's shields flickered, growing stronger and more complex with each moment. The Egyptian spoke words to himself, things half remembered from the chanting of the masters of his order, keys to unlock the powers and patterns of the ancient gods. The air around him trembled and mortar in the towers that bounded the field of battle on two sides began to fray.

Seventy feet separated them. The dark shape bowed its head and Ahmet felt the earth echo with some dark thought. He balanced on the balls of his feet, his mind quiet. The thing looked up.

I am Dahak, echoed in his thoughts, a caress of ice. *Bow to me and you will live.*

No, Ahmet responded. *Between the race of men and you there is no compromise.*

Then you will serve me in death.

The plain of sand erupted in fire, the dark man's hands raised in invocation. Ahmet danced aside, his shields ringing like an enormous bell as bolts of incandescent flame raged against them. He began to sweat, but his own hands danced and a shockwave lashed through the ground, hurling the dark man aside like a doll. The earth shook and bricks and mortar toppled from the nearest tower. Dahak struggled up and Ahmet raced across the sand, his voice howling like the wind. Lightning lashed out from him, savaging the thing, tearing great blackened gashes in the desert floor.

The thing stood and its fist clenched. Ahmet's shields fractured and crumpled under the blow, hurling him back thirty feet to smash flat onto the sand. He shook his head clear and rolled up as a line of white-hot fire scorched the ground where he had lain. The Egyptian rotated his right hand across the front of his body, and the air between him and the thing wavered glassily. Dahak's second bolt spattered across the invisible barrier, etching it like acid. The sand under the wall of air boiled, fusing to mottled glass.

Ahmet snarled and swallowed the power in the stones of the nearest tower. Stones cracked like a bowstring and the entire edifice, thirty feet of sandstone blocks bigger than a man and thousands of pounds of brick and mortar, toppled slowly over. Dahak scrambled aside then made a prodigious leap into the air as the tower smashed down where he had been. The booming sound of the collapsing tower washed over Ahmet like a wave, and the sand jumped at the impact. Dust billowed up, obscuring the field. The Egyptian dashed to his right as fast as he could run.

The ground convulsed behind him, bulging upward like a mushroom with frightening speed. Then it burst, spraying sand in all directions, and something enormous and writhing with green-black tentacles was exposed for a split second before it all collapsed into the ground with a *boom!* Sand fountained and the ground groaned as a deep pit was carved out. Lightning stabbed from Ahmet's hands into the pall of dust that had billowed up from the tower, searching for the dark man.

A hammerblow threw the Egyptian to the ground and his shields flared like the sun, a hundred layers disintegrating in an instant. Through a blur of sweat and falling sand, Ahmet saw the dark man standing on the pinnacle of a tower on his left. On his knees, the priest screamed in rage and punched in the air at the distant figure. The tower exploded, erupting with shattered rock and brick from every window and doorway. It crumbled majestically, each floor shattering in succession and the whole thing toppling to one side. The dark figure staggered on the summit as it slid sickeningly toward the ground. Then Dahak sprang up and flew through the air to the next tower, his robes streaming out behind him like the wings of some enormous raven.

Ahmet wept in rage. *The creature can fly!*

The Egyptian staggered to his feet and drew his hands, palms facing, together before his chest, his face a mask of concentration. Around him the sand and rocks within a dozen paces flashed a bright blue-white and collapsed to ash and smoke. Snarling, his hands flexed outward, palms facing the figure of the enemy hurtling toward him through the air. He shouted, his voice enormous, filling the whole valley. In the city, windows of rare glass shattered, spraying the streets with a cloud of tiny knives. People screamed, their faces drenched with blood. The walls of the city shook and men stumbled back from the ramparts, stricken deaf by the sound.

Dahak slewed wildly to one side, trying to avoid the blow, but it was not enough. Something enormous slammed into him and his own shields blazed up, radiating tongues of flame in all directions. He cartwheeled through the air and smashed into the side of another tower. The edifice trembled and cracked, parts of the upper stories sliding down in slow motion, dust bursting out of the far side. The dark man pulled himself limply out of the crushed bricks, his right hand making a sign in the air before him.

Ahmet ran across the sand toward him, leaping over fallen pillars and broken statuary. Lightning danced from his hands, slashing across the face of the tower. Dahak wiped a pale hand across his mouth; it came away streaked with blood. A heavy bolt tore into his shields and the top half of the tower blew away in a cloud of bricks, dust, and bones. Heavy stones crumbled onto the sorcerer, smashing him to the floor of the doorway he had been blown into.

The Egyptian paused, panting, a good distance from the tower. It trembled and then collapsed in a roar of agonized stone and mortar. Ahmet struggled to rebuild his shields, now only a tattered wisp of their former strength. His hands were shaking and his nerves were an agony of brutalized tissue. He staggered, barely able to think. The Fist of Horus was more debilitating than he had heard.

Dahak rose up out of the rubble, a dark flame flickering around him. His face was a ruin of blood and broken bones. His mouth opened, showing sharp canines, and he screamed, a long dreadful cry of rage. In the city, men fell to the ground, mindless with fear. It was the sound of a great beast, hunting in the night beyond the light of the cave fire. On the wall Zenobia, her face streaked with tears, gripped with bloody fingers at the stones of the battlement.

Wreathed in a corona of ultraviolet fire, Dahak sped toward Ahmet, his mouth howling inhuman words. The sky darkened and Ahmet felt the sun grow dim. He clutched at the earth under his fingers, leaching the deep blue-green rivers of power that he felt under the land. The dark man raised a fist and then his hand flashed in a circle, describing a sphere filled with black light that he clawed from the air. His fist stabbed out. Ahmet surged up off the ground, wrapped in green fire of his own, then there was a brilliant light and the earth shook.

In the city, Zenobia wept to see the huge billow of flame that erupted from among the crooked towers. It blossomed like some infernal flower, rushing out in a blast that tore at the funereal pillars, turning the sand to glass around it. The hills rumbled with the sound of the blast and a hot wind flew before it. She turned away, shielding her face with her arm, still clad in the stout armor. Smoke shot into the sky, forming a pillar a mile high. When she turned back, nothing could be seen but desolation among the ruined towers save a single figure, black as night, stumbling among the shattered stones.

Dahak could barely see, his mind blinded by incredible pain. His skin smoked and his hair was burned away. He ran into something solid—the remaining fragment of a wall—and he slumped against it. He was exhausted, trembling with fatigue. His fingers, withered to clawlike talons, scraped at the stone for purchase, but there was none. The rock was very hot and it burned him as he slid down it. The sky wavered overhead and he moaned. All around him the air was filled with the creak of stones cracking and snapping as they cooled from the incredible heat. He crawled away, instinctively looking for some hole or pit to crawl into.

Fifty yards away, his skin caked with fine gray ash, Ahmet lay senseless in the center of the destruction. A fine dust rained out of the sky, powdered brick and stone, settling over him like a funeral cloth. His clothes had been burned away and long burns scarred his face and chest where his failing shields had ruptured. His breathing faltered and then stopped.

A thick pall of smoke and dust hung over the valley, drifting slowly to the south.

. . .

On the ridge, Baraz nudged his horse forward with his knees and looked down upon the city. Nothing moved. He motioned for his standardbearer and trumpeters to advance. His own long banner now flew, the stylized head of a tusked boar on a field of dark green. He wore his own armor too, old and battered and nicked by a hundred battles. He rubbed his hand across the greasy iron rings. *This is as it should be*, he thought. *Men will do this work and win this victory.* He waved to the banner men behind him.

"Signal the attack!" he shouted, his voice ringing like a bell. Below the lip of the ridge, tens of thousands of Persians rose from a crouch and began moving forward. Those few engines that his engineers had been able to cobble together from the wagons rumbled forward on the road. The Boar turned his eyes back to the walls of the city and a fierce exultation filled him.

"Persia!" he shouted, raising his sword to catch the sun. "And victory!"

THE OUTSKIRTS OF KAHAK, NORTHERN PERSIA

Nikos stood in shadow, his broad face dimly lit by the bonfires and torches in the street below. The shutters were thrown wide, but the room itself was dark. The Illyrian was just inside the window and standing to one side, leaning against the poorly plastered mud-brick wall. A racket of horses neighing and men shouting rose from the street. Thyatis sat, cross-legged, on a thin cotton pallet against the far wall of the room. Her sword, gleaming with oil, lay across her knees. There was a sliding scrape as she honed the blade with a whetstone.

"What do you see?" she said, not looking up. Her voice was quiet.

"I see," he answered, "more than a hundred men ahorse. Their mounts are burdened by half-armor of leather with broad rings of iron stitched to it. The men are bearded and fierce, with long lances and curved swords. Their helmet plumes are of many colors, and the banner they follow is the head of a tiger on a field of yellow."

"That is the crest of the King of Luristan, Kûrush of the House of Axane." One of the Armenian boys had spoken, his voice soft in the darkness. "Those are *dihqans*, knights in your parlance, from the far South. They have traveled many leagues to reach this place."

Thyatis nodded. Her thumb ran along the spine at the core of the length of Indian steel. It was a good sword; it had been a gift of the Duchess after her first successful mission. Holding the scabbard with her right hand, she tipped the blade in with the left and then ran it home among the silk lining. "It seems odd that such a pimple as this place should be so popular this late in the year."

Jusuf, also sitting against the wall with the Armenians, nodded. "The King of Kings knows that the snow will be late," he said.

Thyatis considered this, then spoke. "Will the snow truly be late? The air is chill already."

Jusuf shook his head, his eyes upon her, hard over the barrier of his folded arms. "It is growing cold, but there has been no rain. It is a dry year. Snow may not close the passes to Albania and the north for another month or more."

"Then," she replied, "there is time enough for the King of Kings to gather an army and send it north against the Emperors and their army."

"True," Nikos said, gliding from the window and squatting next to her. "This is the third company of *dihqan* that have passed while I've watched today. By the conversation of the innkeeper and the merchants at the midday meal, there is a great road junction to the north."

"Yes," the other Armenian boy added, looking to his brother for support, "a great highway runs from the south to the shores of the *Mare Caspium* and the Persian city of Dastevan. They built it in the time of our grandfathers, when they were fighting the barbarians on the steppes north of the Araxes."

Jusuf coughed and glared at both boys. They blanched, suddenly reminded of where he came from.

"Then we should leave this place soon, tonight, before someone thinks to mention a party of foreigners from the north to one of these nobles." Thyatis looked at the two Armenian boys. "One of you, and . . . say, Menahem, will ride north to carry word of this to the Imperial army. The rest of us will continued south."

The Bulgar, Menahem, looked up at the mention of his name. He was a short fellow, blessed with a very thick, bushy beard and curly brown hair. He rarely spoke, though he was not as reticent as Sahul. He slid a long knife with a toothed edge out of his belt.

"I have to nursemaid some milk-sucking boy back to the Araxes? What if he soils himself, do I clean him up?" He grinned evilly at the Armenian, who half stood, his young face pale in anger.

"Save it," Thyatis snapped, her face serious. "The boy knows the trails between here and there; you can scare off anyone that you meet. Just make sure that the word gets to the Augustus Galen as soon as possible. Go, get ready."

After the two men had left, Thyatis motioned for Jusuf and Nikos to come sit by her. When they had, she spoke softly: "We leave right away, and we don't continue southeast. If there is a Persian army in the field, we want to avoid stumbling on it. We're going to cut back to the west and make for the land between the Two Rivers."

Nikos made to protest, but Thyatis raised a finger, stopping him. "The Emperors expected to spend the spring wrecking these highland villages and the farmlands to the east, with the help of our eyes and ears. I wonder if they will grow bold after they face this army. We are going to Ctesiphon as quick as we can. There is something in the air. Chrosoes is taking a risk to try to smash our army so late in the year. He is weak."

Nikos shrugged. Thyatis' feelings and hunches were her own and had rarely turned wrong. He slapped Jusuf on the shoulder and went to roust the others. The Bulgar remained squatting by the Roman woman, his expression pensive.

"What is it?" Thyatis said, her voice low and soft. "Are you thinking of Sahul?"

An odd, guilty look flitted over Jusuf's fine-boned face. He shook his head. "No . . . I was thinking of Dahvos and his command. There will be a great battle and he will be in the thick of it without me to stand by him. I fear for him."

"Do you regret coming south with us?"

Jusuf looked at Thyatis, his face a rigid mask. "With you? No, I never regret that. How could I do anything else?"

He stood up, angry with himself, and left the room quickly. Thyatis considered his words and then stood herself, scratching the tip of her nose in thought. *Men!*

THE ROMAN CAMP, ALBANIA, THE *MARE CASPIUM* SHORE

A thin wash of clouds covered the face of the moon. They were rushing to the west, trailing long gowns of white and gray. A shepherd sat on a high mountainside, his back to the comforting bulk of a slab of granite bigger than the Temple of Zeus in his village. Two black and white dogs slept at his feet, their dreams filled with running prey.

One of the dogs twitched in its sleep and growled. The man looked out, over the sleeping sheep, and saw nothing. He listened, stilling himself. He heard it then, a high thin scream, like a baby roasting on a spit over a hot fire. Looking up, he caught a glimpse of something, huge and winged like a titanic bat, rushing through the higher air, obscuring the face of the moon.

Then a shriek of sound came from above, piercing down from the heavens, and the man, who had leapt to his feet in alarm, cowered on the ground in fear. A long wail echoed off of the rocks, and there was a booming sound that reverberated through the air, passing away into the east. The dogs whimpered at his feet and the man stared, seeing demons in the dark. The sheep turned their faces to him, frozen with dread, their eyes reflecting the pale light of the fire.

It is strange, thought Maxian, *to hear the rough dialect of my city under these foreign stars.*

He stood in the shadow of a copse of trees, looking down a grassy slope toward the fires of a great camp. He could hear laughter and singing. There was a familiar tang in the air; the wind out of the east was bringing the smell of a salt sea. The night air was cool but not chilly, and he had thrown back the heavy cowl of the cloak he wore. Firelight gleamed on his cheekbones and in his eyes. Four legionnaires passed by, coming within feet of him, on patrol. The Prince smiled in the darkness, feeling his strength subtly filling the air and ground around him. No one could see him if he did not wish to be seen.

He walked down the hill, smelling the thick aroma of flowers and fresh grass. Winter threatened in the mountains, but here, on the flat plains by the shallow sea, summer lingered. The night was heavy with the smell of orange blossoms and jasmine. Even the stars seemed kind, twinkling down with a cheerful fire. He came to the ditch around the camp and stopped. Brush had been cleared hastily away from the verge, and sharp stakes, carried by the legionnaires for such a purpose, were driven into the soft earth at the bottom of the trench. Beyond it, a palisade of logs had been raised.

He brought the woman Alais to mind, a vision of strong white legs flitting across a rooftop in the Eastern capital. Frowning in concentration, he sprang forward. His boots slapped hard against the top of the log wall and he swayed, teetering over the trench behind him. Then he calmed his racing heart and stood upright, finding his balance. The camp lay spread out before him, hundreds of canvas tents in neat rows glowing with the light of lanterns and candles. He could hear a dim murmur of voices now, coming from thousands of conversations. From the height where he stood, a slim black shape melting into a dark sky, he could see that a great tent, well lit, had been raised at the center of the camp.

He dropped silently to the ground within the walls. A sentry walked past, on the ledge built up behind the wall of logs. Maxian wrapped his cloak around him and moved off between the tents.

Martius Galen Atreus, Augustus Caesar of the West, sat at his folding desk in a pool of yellow light. Beeswax candles, taken from the nearest village by one of the foraging patrols, burned brightly at the edges of the worktable. Neat piles of wax tablets and stacks of papyrus scrolls covered the tabletop. The Emperor leaned back in his chair, rubbing his eyes. He was very tired, but then he did not remember a time when he had not been exhausted, or buried in detail, since leaving the Eternal City. It was late and he had sent his secretaries to their bedrolls thirty grains before. He reached forward to pick up a tablet bearing a roster of the lamed and injured horses in the army. His eye caught a thin dark shape standing just inside the doorway of his tent.

Galen looked up, surprised that someone would be admitted without his guards announcing him, then stopped, his eyes widening, the tablet frozen in midair.

"Brother." Maxian's voice was raspy and thick.

Galen rose, his lean face filling with a slow glad smile. "Maxian!" Then the Emperor paused, seeing the dreadful pallor of his brother's face, grasping his utterly unexpected presence. "What is it?"

The Emperor leaned forward on the table for support. His mind was a cataclysm of fears. "Aurelian? The city? What has happened?" His voice was tight in anticipation of disaster.

Maxian stepped forward, his black robes furling around him, and slid his thin body into one of the camp stools in front of the desk. The Prince shook his head, a half smile dancing on his lips. "Oh, fear not, brother. The city stands. The Empire stands. Aurelian, when last I saw him, was well."

Galen sat down heavily in the chair, sighing in relief. His brows furrowed and he glared at his younger brother. "Good . . . You gave me a fright, barging in all unexpected, looking like a shade out of Hades. You're the last person I'd ever expect to see here. What is it? You must have left Rome only weeks behind us to get here now—you didn't travel alone, did you? Ah, of course you did! Why should a healer fear in this dark world . . ."

Maxian looked up, seeing the concern in his brother's face. He realized that he had missed his brother tremendously, difficult and judgmental as he was. Both of his brothers. Of late, in the pressure of building the engine and making haste to come here, he had begun to think of Krista and Alais and the others as his family. Now, sitting in the warm confines of a campaign tent in the light of plain candles, he remembered a thousand other times when he would sit in the back of just such a tent while his brothers plotted and planned their quest for Empire.

He missed that, the closeness, the days on the march, the tight community of the army. A sad look came into his face and the Prince looked away from his brother, feeling very lonely. Tears threatened to well up as he struggled against a flood of emotions. He treasured those days, now long gone. He thought of leaving; this was too painful.

"I traveled with friends, brother. It was very safe, safer than your journey."

Galen nodded, his face marked with a wan smile. "What is it? Wait, you must be starving from the look of you. Eat first, then tell me."

The Emperor rang a small bell that sat on the side of the table, and a moment later one of the household servants entered. The old man, a Greek, smiled to see Maxian and bowed deeply to the Emperor.

"My brother has had a long journey. Bring something hot to drink and whatever is left of the dinner. And warm too, not cold."

The old Greek scurried off, calling out to the other servants as soon as he left the tent. Galen stood and walked around the table to his brother. Maxian stared up at him, his eyes dull with fatigue. The Emperor reached out, clasped his brother's hand, and drew him to his feet. Maxian stared at him, filled with an odd dread. His brother wrapped him in a fierce hug. Maxian looked away, blinking back tears.

"I missed you and Aurelian," Galen whispered. "I . . ."

The servants bustled in, laden with platters and jugs and a bucket of coals. Maxian stepped aside from his brother and greeted the cook and the other house servants. He had known them for as long as he had lived. They laid out a feast: roast pheasant, lamb stew, grilled fish, hot rolls with butter, a thick gruel of chickpeas and spices. The cook pressed a mug of hot wine into his hand. Maxian drank deeply, feeling the heat flush through his body. He sat again and stared in amazement at the platter of food in front of him.

"Eat," Galen said. "I'll wait."

• • •

The engine was quiescent, its fires banked, midnight wings folded in against the serpentine body. It crouched in a defile a mile or more from the Roman camp, hidden by evergreens and a thicket of gorse bushes and thorn. Krista sat on the huge head, feeling the heat of the metal under her, her legs on either side of the long pointed snout. She had adopted woolen leggings and a heavy shirt under a half-tunic of lambskin with fleece on the inside. One of the Valach who now served the Prince had shown her how to make it, his thin fingers quick with a heavy needle to stitch the fleece to the leather. It was warm, a little too warm now that they had come to this temperate land. But when the engine was in flight, high among the clouds, the wind bit with teeth of ice. She gazed mournfully off into the darkness in the direction of the Roman camp.

She would have to make a decision soon, to go or to stay. To fulfill her duty or to hang on, seeing what more she could learn. A soft giggle distracted her, and she drew her legs up, folding them under her. Two shapes moved in the darkness under the shoulder of the engine. White skin flashed in the dim moonlight, and a deeper voice answered. Krista curled her lip in disgust. For a dead man, the old Roman had not lost any taste for the pleasures of the flesh.

And Alais is all too willing, seeking some advantage of it.

The dynamic of the small group had changed markedly with the introduction of the Valach girl and her "friends" to the circle. The other Valach, pale and quiet, had proved invaluable in the completion of the engine. They were tireless, once Maxian had graced them with the elixir, and the dreadful haunted look that had filled their eyes was gone. Some, like the boy Vladimir, were even kind in their own way. He had spent hours stitching the rich image of a curling serpent that adorned the back of her half-tunic. But Alais? She was poison.

Krista smiled, caressing the shape of the spring gun snugly tied to her left arm. Someday something would happen in some confused moment, and the Valach woman and her soft full breasts, overgrown like some lush flower left in the dark for too long, would be a corpse. Laughter filtered through the trees. The old Roman and the woman had gone through the brush and up the hill. Moonlight fell in long slats in the passages of the wood. Krista stood, shrugging the half-tunic into place. A little ways away, she could see them.

Alais was dancing in the moonlight, her long hair slowly swirling white around her pale shoulders. Her dress clung to her like a spiderweb, sheer and fine. Her long legs flashed in the silver light as she turned and spun. Gaius Julius leaned against the trunk of a tree, his face in shadow. She danced closer to him and his hand flashed out, capturing her arm. Krista turned away and climbed down off of the great engine. She stooped to enter the dim, hot chamber at the center of the device. Night would proceed. Maxian would return soon.

Galen watched his brother closely while he ate. Something had happened to the youth he had left behind in the capital. He had somehow become a man in the past months, a man with a haggard face and secrets hiding behind his eyes. His clothes, too, were strange. Dark rich robes and a mottled gray tunic underneath. The Prince finished the platter of food and pushed it away from him. The Emperor put down his own cup of wine and motioned for the servants to leave them.

"What troubles you, Maxian? Something important must have transpired since I left the city. Has something happened to you?"

Maxian nodded, his head heavy. He had just eaten more than he had in the last week and his body was seized with lethargy. For the first time in days, he thought of sleep. Something about the old familiar tent, the narrow, concerned face of his brother, the smell of the candles and the horses, made him feel safe and comfortable. He yawned, then blinked and rubbed his face fiercely.

"Do you remember the night that you, and I, and Aurelian were at the Summer House? You were telling me of your plan to invade Persia. I felt something that night, something I had felt only two times before. Brother, it frightened me. You know that I am a healer, that I have power in the unseen world."

Galen nodded, his attention fixed on his younger brother.

"Like a sorcerer, or a wizard," the Prince continued, "I can see the invisible powers. That night, in the little temple under the moon, I felt something powerful. Something inimical to men. It piqued my curiosity, so I started to ask some questions . . ."

Maxian continued for close to an hour, his even voice recounting nearly all that he had done and all that he had seen since that night. He left out only the details of his companions. When he finished, he sipped from a cup of wine the servants had left when they cleared away the dinner plates.

Galen stared at him, his face pale and drawn with horror. The Emperor looked away suddenly, and when he looked back, his eyes were angry. "Fool of a brother! How many times could you have died in this? Without anyone knowing? And your curse . . . if it is true, then my life is forfeit if I return to the West. I will die as surely as your friend the shipwright, or these weavers."

The Emperor sprang to his feet and began pacing, his face a mask of concentration.

"No," Maxian said, staring in surprise at the agitation of his brother. "You, of all men, are safe in this thing. Such a construction needs a focus, some point from which all else springs. You are that focus, as the Emperor is the focus of the state. I know that you are safe. It may influence your thought and your intent. But so too does it protect you and shield you. Of all the men in the world who do not count mastery of the hidden world among their skills, you are the only one who can know this thing."

Galen turned, fists clenched in anger. "What would you have me do? Throw down the state I have sworn to defend? Wreck the Empire that, for all its faults, brings peace and protection to the people of half the world? I cannot do this thing. I will not do this!" His voice had risen, almost to a shout.

Maxian stood as well, his voice anxious. "But, brother! We can be free of it—and the Empire will still stand. All I need is a lever that is long enough and a fulcrum firm enough to dislodge it. I know where I can find the lever—I am sure of it. Help me do this thing, and a new world will come, one of freedom for all men. Our poor citizens can be strong again, Rome mighty again without the affliction of this curse."

Galen stared at Maxian's outstretched hand and stepped back. His mind whirled, filled with strange images and the words of his brother's trek across the Empire. It came to him that there were things missing, things left unsaid, passages only hinted at.

"How did you reach me so quickly?" The Emperor's voice was low, controlled. "By your accounting, you left Constantinople only days ago. What power brought you here?"

Maxian started to speak, but then closed his mouth, shaking his head.

"Tell me. Something must have carried you here—what is it? Where is it?"

"No," Maxian said, his voice clipped. "I see that you will not help me, so I will go and trouble you no more. There may be another way to break the curse. If there is, I will find it."

Galen's eyes narrowed in suspicion.

"I have heard," the Emperor said, sliding sideways around the table, "that the *magi* of Persia command powers that can carry them great distances swiftly. Do you have allies in this? Allies you have failed to mention?"

Maxian drew himself up and moved toward the door. "Friends have helped me. Friends who see clearly, unfettered by your fear. But I am my own master— you cannot command me, nor can anyone else."

Galen stopped him, a stiff hand on his chest. "Chrosoes King of Kings would laugh to see the Empire stripped of this protection."

Maxian stared back, his face taut with anger.

"I care not," he hissed, "for the King of Kings. Your war is an inconvenience to me, no more. Something to be taken into account. You forget, with your dream of Empire, that the common people pay for your glory in blood. I have had enough of it. It is the nature of man to learn and to grow, to seek out new things. If the Empire cannot stomach that, then I do not care for the Empire either. Stand aside. I will take my leave of you, brother."

Galen shook his head, whistling sharply. The Germans outside, already aroused by the sound of voices raised in anger, crowded in through the doorway.

"My brother," the Emperor said, "is weary and full of anger. Take him to my tent and keep him there, safe, until the morning. Sleep will restore his good humor."

Maxian did not speak, eyeing the broad chests and thickly muscled arms of the Germans. There were many of them, and he was tired and only one. He nodded, smiling weakly.

"It may be so," he said, and when they led him from the tent, he did not resist.

Galen, troubled beyond measure, leaned against the pole at the door of the tent, watching as the Germans took his brother away into the darkness. He scratched the back of his head, feeling the short stubbly hair, then turned away. There was still work to be done. He would sort things out with his little brother in the morning.

.   .   .

The Prince lay amid soft cushions and pillows on a fine bed. It was soft and yielding under him. Weariness washed over him in slow waves, dragging him closer to sleep. A lantern of cut-crystal facets gleamed at the top of the tent. Rich dark fabrics formed the walls and it was raised up, above the ground, on a platform of boards. It was warm and close. Maxian smiled wryly, remembering the disgusted faces of the two concubines who had been hustled out into the cold night by the Germans. He yawned.

Despite the comfort, sleep did not come easily to him. Dreams of fire and great wheels turning in dark places haunted him. In one fragmentary moment, he saw himself on a high place, surrounded by pillars of cold marble, hearing a great roaring sound, like the sea crashing against cliffs. He saw vast wings blotting out the sun and felt joy at the rush of hot wind in his hair. He saw Krista, her face pale and drawn in concentration, facing him, her arm outthrust toward him. At last he slept, but sounds and images of places he had not seen and people he had not met troubled even that. A woman looked down on him, maddeningly familiar, with eyes as gray as a northern sea. The sky behind her was red with burning clouds.

A touch woke him, feather-light. He slowly opened one eye and saw that the lantern had failed, leaving total darkness. A pale face hovered over him, seemingly lit by some ghostly pale-blue inner light. Long pale hair fell like gossamer on either side of the face. Rich dark lips moved.

Master?

"Alais," he said, his voice fuzzy with sleep. He raised a hand and touched her cheek. She turned, kissing his hand, the contact shockingly hot. Her tongue moved wetly against his palm. He stroked her hair back, away from her neck. She trembled at his touch.

"Master, we must go." Her voice was an electric whisper in the darkness. "The Romans are searching the woods, looking for something. There are hundreds of men with torches."

"Ah, my brother is keen for something he can only guess at. So, even a brother cannot trust a brother. Help me up."

Her hands, strong as iron, raised him up. He gathered his clothing and let her dress him. Her hands were very warm on his stomach. The Prince smiled in the darkness. If he had to go alone, without his brothers, he would go alone. The citizens were more important. Saving the innocent from unseen, unstoppable death was more important.

Alais drew back the curtain at the door, her voice whispering in the night. The guards outside sat at their posts, unmoving, and did not look up as the Prince exited the tent, closing the drape behind him. Together he and the pale Valach woman walked away through the camp, she a pace behind him.

)•((

The boy ran through the forest, blood trailing from a cut on his scalp. He gasped for breath and ran crookedly, his right leg moving in jerks. The ground rose, becoming thick with low brush and saplings. He crashed through the bushes and fell to his knees. Without the breath to swear, he scrabbled at the ground, finally finding purchase and rising again.

Behind him there was a whistling sound and the shouts of men. Hooves thudded on the loamy earth, growing closer. The boy staggered up the side of the hill, bent nearly double, trying to keep the brush and trees between himself and his pursuers. Near the crest, his right leg gave out and he tumbled to the ground, rolling back down the slope. Blood oozed out of a deep cut on the outside of his right leg and he lay there, wheezing, unable to move.

The hunters began climbing the hill, their voices quite close. He could hear the horses blowing and the rattle of armor. Through the canopy of trees above him, the boy could see blue sky streaked with high white clouds. He rolled over, biting down on a cracked lip to keep from crying out. On his hands and knees, he crawled along the side of the hill, away from the crest. The ground was rough— rocky and covered with small stones. There was little grass, for these hills were dry and covered with stunted trees with sharp thorns.

He came to a rock outcropping and hauled himself up onto a shelf. Leaning heavily on the stones, he managed to limp around the corner of the rocks. For a moment, as he swung around the side of the boulder, he was silhouetted against the sky.

The boy spun around, losing his grip on the crumbly granite. A black-fletched arrow stabbed out from his shoulder, blood welling around the exit wound. For a moment he stared at the sky and the slope below him on the backside of the hill. Then his knees became terribly weak and he slid down to the ground. His body rolled off the ledge and bounced, arms and legs flailing, down the slope.

Gordius Falco, *equites* scout of the Third Augusta Fretensis, stared in shock as the body of a young man in dirty tattered clothing bounced down the slope above him in a spray of gravel and smacked into the bole of a thick juniper tree. He kneed his horse to turn it around, halting his slow trot up the hill. Gordius stared around, his eyes wide, but he saw no one. He walked the horse forward to the boy and leaned down to shake his shoulder with a meaty hand.

The boy's eyelids fluttered and he turned his head a little. There seemed to be some dim recognition in them. Gordius probed the arrow wound gently, but blood was spilling out of the boy's back and puddling on the ground under the tree. The boy tried to say something, but his lips moved and there was no sound. Gordius leaned closer, feeling the faint flutter of a pulse at the boy's throat.

"The Iron Hats . . ." was all he heard. Gordius looked up sharply, scanning the ridge above him. Off to the right, where a dip in the line of hills made a saddle, his eye caught on movement. He squinted and saw, there in a clearing of tufted grass and scattered rocks, five men on stout bay-colored horses with colorful peaked caps and long coats over their armor. Curved bows were slung over their backs and longswords hung from their saddles.

"Mithras," Gordius breathed, pushing away from the tree and the dead boy. "Time to be going!"

He turned the horse again and calmly rode away down the hill, being sure to keep trees between himself and the dip in the ridge. After a mile of walking the horse, he kneed it to a trot and hurried north, hoping to run into the rest of his patrol.

Heraclius was standing on a log platform, looking out on a field south of the Roman camp, when one of his dispatch riders scrambled up the ladder behind him. The Emperor turned at the sound of the boy huffing and puffing for breath.

Theodore laughed, catching the boy by the shoulder before he pitched off the platform. "Hold, lad, before you break your neck!"

The dispatch rider fell to one knee before the Emperor, having caught his breath. "A patrol has come in, Great Lord! Persian horsemen have been sighted seven or eight miles south of the river, moving north. The centurion in charge sent a man ahead to warn the camp."

Heraclius traded a glance with Galen, who had ordered the patrols south, and with the third King on the platform, Ziebil of the Khazar khanate. The Western Emperor was tired looking, but this news did not please him either and he met it with a frown. The Khazar, a short, broad-shouldered man with sandy hair streaked with gray and a very short beard, shrugged and returned Heraclius' look with a bored expression. Ziebil spoke seldom, preferring to listen and watch. Heraclius had heard that he was a very demon in battle, though he seemed almost unnaturally calm in the short time they had seen each other face to face.

"Is this what you expected?" Heraclius had turned back to Galen, who shook his head sharply.

"Winter is close," the Western Emperor said. "They must have sent men north to keep us from sneaking over into the highlands before the passes are closed by snow. Shall we drive them off?"

Heraclius nodded, his mind made up. It was time to see how well his Khazar allies performed in the field. "Great Khan? Would you care to do the honors?"

Ziebil pursed his lips and idly pulled a thick-hafted knife from his belt. He tossed it from one hand to the other, then slid it quickly back into its sheath. He nodded, and there was a flicker of a grim smile on his face. He leaned over the side of the platform and whistled, a piercing sound. Out on the field, two bands of horsemen detached themselves from the crowd of men maneuvering about and galloped over to the platform.

Ziebil turned and gestured to the dispatch rider. "Boy, take these men to find the patrol." He pointed south and shouted down to his men, "Iron Hats!"

There was a fierce cheer. The Khazars had been late reaching Tauris and had not blooded themselves on the walls or in the fighting in the streets. They were eager for battle. The dispatch rider climbed down and swung up on his own horse. Together they trotted off to the south, the Khazars whooping and yelling as they passed through the picket lines around the camp.

Heraclius snorted and turned back to his compatriots. Galen was still worried about something but had volunteered nothing save a desire to have the lands around the camp thoroughly patrolled. Heraclius put the worry away, doubtless it was nothing more than a runaway slave or nerves.

THE HILLS ABOVE PALMYRA

Darkness crawled across the rocks, fanged and red-eyed. Skeletal wings fluttered on its back. Moonlight fell across the sandstone. It stopped, hissing at the sight of the moon, its head raised. Dull red fire leaked from its eyes. A long black tongue darted, tasting the air. The creature was afraid, and it slunk across the stones on its belly.

Taloned fingers flashed and seized the thing by its scrawny neck, dragging it out into the moonlight. The winged creature hissed and scrabbled at the air with its claws, but it found no purchase. The fingers, stronger than iron, squeezed, and the thing gave a mournful bleat and hung limply in the withered hand. The Lord Dahak drew a bag from within his robes and stuffed his captive into it. After throwing the bag over his shoulder, he limped down the hill. The moon gleamed on a vast tumult of boulders, stretching in every direction. The sorcerer vanished into deep shadow between two monoliths.

Baraz dreamed. He dreamed that he was walking on a battlefield, littered with heaps of corpses. Only he remained alive, his sword coated with gore, his legs splashed with blood. Tens of thousands of dead carpeted the field, rotting and covered with ants. The horizon was a wall of snowcapped mountains, blue in the distance. A sun hung overhead, a pale disk of white. Banners hung limply, askew and tattered. The air was still and quiet, though he was sure that, a short time before, it had been filled with a stunning noise. He was alive, amid all the dead, and his heart was filled with a fierce joy at his survival. He raised his arms to the sky, shouting, his voice echoing across that dreadful valley.

Something touched his shoulder and he was awake, one thick fist wrapped around the hilt of a thin-bladed dagger. His tent was dark, but he could feel the chill presence of someone standing by his cot. The general sniffed the air and then cursed. "Lord of light, Dahak, can't you let me sleep?"

Baraz fumbled for the lantern by the bed and, after a moment of work with a flint, lit the wick. Dim light spilled out, showing the sorcerer sitting at one of the stools next to the planning table.

Baraz squinted at him. "What is it? They trying something in the city?"

Dahak laughed mirthlessly.

"No," the sorcerer said, his long, lean, face slashed with shadows. "A message has come."

Baraz sat up, his thick chest and massive legs painted with warm light from the lantern. A thick black pelt of tiny curls covered his chest and stomach, though his arms and legs were shaven bare. He reached under the cot and dragged out his riding boots. Absently he turned them upside down and knocked them against the side of this cot. A translucent scorpion fell out of one, tiny and pale yellow. It bounced, then flipped itself upright and scuttled off into a dark corner of the tent.

"What does it say?" Baraz pulled a tunic on over his head and closed a thick leather belt around his narrow waist.

Dahak reached into the folds of his robe and pulled out an ivory cylinder, no more than three inches long.

"It is for you," he said in a raspy voice. He was slow in recovering from the wounds he had taken in the fight on the plain of towers. "I have not opened it."

Baraz frowned and took the cylinder. He grimaced, feeling the stickiness clinging to it. He put it on the table and raised the lantern up to better light the tent. The ivory was coated with partially dried blood.

The general made a face. "Isn't there some other way to deliver these things—clean, perhaps?"

Dahak said nothing, sitting quietly, a pool of shadow at the side of the room. Baraz shook his head in amusement and unscrewed the cap on the end of the cylinder. There was a rolled-up piece of parchment inside, which he teased out with his finger and uncurled. It was covered with slanted letters in a strong hand.

Baraz looked up, meeting Dahak's glittering eyes. "It is from Chrosoes. Gundarnasp's army has cornered the Romans in the valley of the Kerenos, in Albania. The King of Kings bids you send me there, that I might command our armies in victory over the Two Emperors. He bids me make haste."

Dahak sighed, a thready sound, wind among gravestones. He seemed very tired. "Does he . . . As the king commands, I obey. That fop Shahin will command here, as we will be gone?"

Baraz raised an eyebrow at the bitter tone in the sorcerer's voice. "He would have the rank for it, though Khadames would be a better choice. Yet if I leave them both here, without you or me to keep Shahin in check, it will go poorly."

Dahak steepled his fingers, his eyes glowing the light of the lantern.

"I could send you by yourself . . ." he mused. "Such a thing can be done, if you've the stomach for it. I could remain and see that this business here is finished."

Baraz caught the eagerness in the sorcerer's voice and smiled. "You want the Egyptian, don't you? You think that he is still alive, in the city."

Dahak snarled, a low animal sound. "No one showed me his corpse. He still lives. I will have him. He owes me a great deal of pain. I will collect upon the debt."

The general turned the scrap of parchment over and smoothed it out on the table. There was a brush and a block of ink close to hand. He wrote quickly on the paper, then blew on it gently. Finally he sprinkled fine sand over it and rolled a blotting stone across the paper.

"Here, I have told the King of Kings that I will be with Gundarnasp presently and that the siege here will continue. Make your preparations. Need I do anything to ready myself?"

Dahak rose, the cylinder in clawlike fingers. "No, only keep a brave heart."

Mohammed stood in an arched doorway, his face grave. He was dressed in heavy armor, like that favored by the Persians. A long shirt of scales fell to below his knees and a long sword hung from his belt. A heavy helm was under his arm, dented and scored. A cotton tabard hung over the mail, bearing the crest of Palmyra. He had grown thinner in the face and had trimmed his beard back to his chin. His eyes were filled with a slow anger.

In the room, Zenobia was curled on a bed with cedar posts. Heavy quilts and blankets covered it, and a thin silk drape hung from the posts, making a tent. The Queen lay close to the body of the Egyptian, Ahmet, her white arms clutching his bronzed body to her. A low murmur of chanting filled the room, interrupted only by Ahmet's irregular breathing. Each day Mohammed came to the room, buried deep in the palace, and looked upon his friend. Each day the priest was the same, comatose and close to death. The Queen rarely left the chamber.

Mohammed turned away and walked down the hallway. His boots rang softly on the blue and green mosaic tiles. As he mounted the stairs, he pulled the helmet on, closing out all the world save the narrow slit before his eyes. There would be battle today, as there was nearly every day now. The Persians pressed hard against the city.

Cold stone pressed into Baraz's back. He lay on a great slab of sandstone that formed the rough peak of one of the hills humped along the western edge of the plain that held Palmyra. The Lord Dahak crouched at his feet, hands held between his knees, muttering. Baraz looked up, seeing the dark vault of heaven wheeling slowly above him. Cool wind blew out of the desert, ruffling his curly hair. The moon had just risen in the east, still huge and red-orange over the endless plain of sand dunes that stretched behind the city. Dahak's dark shape moved, and his long head bent back, staring at the dark gulf that held the stars.

Baraz shivered. He was dressed only in a cotton kilt and shirt. His feet were bare and there were no metal fittings or items anywhere upon his body. Even the pins that held back the mane of his hair had been pulled out by the wizard and tucked away in a bag. His forehead itched where Dahak had incised some unknown sign with a small silver knife. The general lay still.

Dahak's voice became almost audible, a low guttural growling that rose and fell to no rhythm that Baraz could identify. Finally the dark man rose up to stand with his legs straddling Baraz's feet. His hands flashed white in the darkness, reaching for the dark sky opposite the moon. He shouted something unintelligible. Then he squatted again, crossing his legs under him. He took a thin silver pipe out of one of the pockets in his robes and, with a breath, began to trill on it.

The sound made Baraz's skin crawl and he felt unaccustomed fear creeping into his blood like acid. The silver pipe chirped and tittered. The wind picked up and Baraz closed his eyes to keep blown dust from them. The sound of the pipe rose and rose, until Baraz almost screamed from the deafening noise. Then it stopped and there was silence.

Almost silence. A noise came, a slurping noise that seemed to come from all around. A chitinous rustling, the sound of a million crickets squirming in a great vat of stone. The air became very cold. Baraz screwed his eyes shut and dared not open them for fear of what he might see, looming over him, enormous, blocking out the sky and the moon.

Dahak's voice came, or something that sounded like the dark man's voice. Low and indistinct, but filled with power. Then, startling, recognizable words filtered through the rustling and slurping sound.

"Sleep now, mighty general, and when you wake, should you wake, you will be in the north, where battle waits for you. Sleep now, and dare not dream."

A dark cloth settled over the general and he twitched violently at the touch. But then he slept and did not dream, though he rose up, carried in ten thousand faint translucent tentacles across the sky, under an unseeing moon.

Mohammed spurred his horse hard, goosing it up the side of the *wadi*. Gravel and sand spurted from under the red mare's hooves and she flew up the slope. At his back, thirty of the Tanukh and an equal number of men from the city, swaddled in dust-brown robes and pale-tan *kaffieh*, surged after him. Al'Quraysh galloped across the sandy flat, his sword sliding out of its sheath in a flash. Ahead of him, Persian soldiers stared up in horror. The slab-sided shape of a thirty-foot-high siege tower loomed behind the Persians. Many of them were stripped to the waist, hauling on the ropes that dragged the wooden behemoth. Others had been trotting alongside, shields in front and spears over their shoulders. Now they were shouting and pointing at Mohammed as his horse flew across the hardpan.

Men ran, scattering before the charge of the desert horsemen, dropping the long ropes. Mohammed stormed into the thick of the spear men, who had hastily run around to the back of the tower and were trying to form up into a line. His saber lashed out, cutting at the face of one of the spear men. Blood fountained and the man fell, clutching at his ruined jaw. The rest of the Tanukh smashed into the engineers, swords flashing in the sun. More men died and then the Persians were running. The Tanukh whooped with delight, their voices raised in a high-pitched yell that echoed across the desert.

Mohammed spun his horse, checking the sweep of his men. The city was two miles distant, its gold walls rising above the date palms that lined the farmlands around it. The Persian army had established a crude earthwork a hundred yards from the walls. They thought that their engines would be safe here, miles from the city. He rose up in the saddle, shouting at his men. "Sideways! Pull it sideways!"

The spearmen were dead, scattered across the ground, or fled toward the palms. The other laborers had also scattered. The Tanukh wheeled their horses around the tower, shooting arrows into the fighting platforms inside it. As Mohammed watched, a green-robed Persian engineer toppled from the highest platform, his torso pierced by three arrows. He hit the ground with a sharp slapping sound and bounced once before lying still. The Palmyrenes were tossing torches into the lower chamber of the tower. Mohammed's horse trotted forward, obedient to the pressure of his knees.

He leaned out of the saddle and scooped up one of the tow ropes. With a deft hand, he wrapped it around the horns of his saddle and waved for the others to do the same. The Palmyrenes, with their heavier, four-cornered, saddles, caught on and snared the rest of the ropes. Once they had each acquired a rope, Mohammed slashed his hand down and they moved, as one, to the east.

The tower trembled as the ropes drew taut, then the Palmyrenes whooped and put their heels to their horses. The beasts strained against the lines, their hooves kicking up dust. The whole tower suddenly groaned and began to tip. Mohammed shouted at two Tanukh who were still staring up at the wall of wooden slats that was bending toward them. The tower creaked and then toppled over, slowly, and smashed suddenly to the ground with a flat booming sound. Dust and sand billowed out from under it. The Palmyrenes cheered and Mohammed grinned at his men.

"Now the torches," he cried. Some of the Tanukh who had held back darted in, throwing ceramic jars of heavy olive oil and burning sticks into the collapsed tower. A thick black smoke began to rise. Mohammed wheeled his horse away and the whole band followed him, howling like banshees. Clouds of dust marked their passage into the desert waste.

"Enough," Dahak said sharply, his hand cutting off the rambling excuse. "These barbarians come and go as they please from the city. This will stop. Complete the earthwork within the next two days. Lord Khadames, I want every man we have digging. You will work in shifts, day and night, until it is done."

Khadames bowed stiffly, watching the pale face of the noble who had commanded the siege engines. All three, laboriously constructed over weeks of careful work, had been destroyed in the space of two days. The precious wood that they had scavenged from wagons and farmhouses and from the few suitable trees in the area was gone, wiped away in clouds of dirty smoke. The man was a cousin of the

Great Prince Shahin, an honor enough to get him a command, but nothing to protect him from the wizard's icy anger.

When Baraz had left, he had given orders that Khadames would command the army, with the "able assistance" of the Lord Dahak. Shahin had barely waited a day before challenging the lower-born Khadames, and many of the nobles in the army had supported the Great Prince. But Dahak had no patience for such bickering and simply declared that *he* would command. Against his glittering dark eyes, no one was brave enough to protest the usurpation of authority.

Since then the siege had pressed ahead at a wearing pace. Dahak was, as far as Khadames could tell, tireless, and he assumed that his followers were equally iron-willed. Baraz had led by example, exhorting his men to greater feats than they had imagined. Dahak commanded with a clear and icy fear. Failure was not tolerated if it sprang from incompetence.

"Your task was simple, and had you heeded the advice of the Lord Khadames, you would have been successful. But you ignored his advice and my command. I will not tolerate this. We press ahead with the attack, though now I will grant another day to see that the circumvallation is complete. And you, Lord Pacorus, have exhausted my patience and mercy."

Khadames flinched from the bleak expression on the face of the sorcerer. A silence fell on the nobles and captains assembled in the tent. The Lord Dahak rose from the plain wicker chair that had been Baraz's and stared down at the nobleman, bent before him in the proskynesis usually accorded to royalty. The sorcerer stared around the tent, forcing the men before him to meet his eyes. They were cold and Khadames realized with a shiver that the sorcerer's pupils were vertical and narrow, flecked with gold in green.

"This is a lesson. Learn it." Dahak's hand clenched into a fist. Dark-red light spilled out of the cracks between his withered fingers. On the ground, Pacorus suddenly moaned and tried to rise. Dahak's boot, a supple black leather with blood-red lacings, crushed down on the back of his neck, pinning him to the carpet. The nobleman began to tremble and his limbs twitched spasmodically. Khadames turned away when Pacorus' skin began to crawl and squirm with something moving under the surface, something like ten thousand worms.

"We attack at sunset in two days, with the sun at our backs. Understood?"

Pacorus whined in terrible pain under the dark man's boot, his flesh beginning to flake away from liquid that had once been bone and sinew.

)•((

Dwyrin shuffled his feet, his breath puffing white in the chill predawn air. He stood next to Zoë, at the end of the line of their cohort, at parade rest. Quietly he checked his kit, making sure that all the straps were snugged tight and that nothing was hanging loose. The sky was pitch black—he guessed that clouds had come up in the night and covered the stars. Fitful light cast by lanterns and torches illuminated him and the other thaumaturges clustered around him. They stood in four rows, their backs to their tents, grouped by rank. In the front row, the senior thaumaturges stood at ease, surrounded, to Dwyrin's inner eye, by soft patterns that said *warm* and *comfortable*.

In the privacy of his mind, he cursed the priests at the school for neglecting to teach him anything *useful* like the so-obvious spells for keeping warm on a dark morning like this. Still, he was better off than Odenathus and Zoë, who were tightly bundled in every scrap of cloak or fur they could find. On the other side of the Palmyrene boy, one of the Gaulish wizards was almost grinning, blowing frosty breath up into the air. He didn't think that it was that cold. Zoë he could feel trembling right at his side. For a moment he considered putting an arm around her, but then he thought of the knife at her side and rejected the idea.

"Soldiers, attention!"

The tribune, with all four centurions at his back, paced along the front of the assembly. The odd pieces of glass that were suspended in front of his eyes on wire frames glittered in the light of the torches. Like the centurions, he was clad in a heavy wool cloak and a doublet of furred leather. It looked warm too.

"Soon," the tribune said in a carrying voice, "there will be battle. The armies of Persia advance upon us in haste. The weather will turn soon and close the passes to the south. This King of Kings, this Chrosoes, desires to decide the contest between his treacherous Empire and ours now. He hurries toward defeat. Some of you have never been in battle before. I will say this to you! If you follow orders and keep the men of your unit around you, if you obey the commands of your five-leader and your centurion, if you hold your place in the line of battle and do not run, you will live and we shall have victory."

Dwyrin straightened up a little more, for the tribune and the centurions had come to the end of the line closest to them. Zoë stared straight ahead, over the heads of the men in front of them. Dwyrin wrenched his eyes aside.

"Some of you," the tribune continued, walking behind them, "will not be fighting in the line of battle. You will be deployed forward of the main army, to

harass and threaten the march and deployment of the enemy. This is a new strategy. It has not been tested in battle. It may fail, but I believe that it will succeed.
I believe that we, the thaumaturgic arm of the Legion, will be decisive. Our success
in the coming battle, operating in teams, will make all the difference."

Once more before his men, the tribune turned, surveying them. "The Emperor
is watching, and through him, the city and the Senate and the people. Do not
disappoint them."

Dwyrin felt a chill in his mind and throat, but it was not from the air.

"Do you think there will be battle tomorrow?" Dwyrin's voice was soft in the
darkness. With Eric gone, they had taken to sleeping in one tent, even though it
was crowded. The nights were cool enough that the warmth of the three of them
filled the hide walls. Even by morning it was not unpleasant—at least until you
had to go outside. He knew that Zoë was awake—he could feel her moving under
the woolen blanket. She was thinking, as he was, wondering what would happen
in the next day.

"No," she said, turning over to face him. Even in the very dim light filtering
through the small opening in the front of the shelter, he could make out the
planes of her face, the darkness of her eyes. Dwyrin wondered if Odenathus were
awake. *Probably not*, he thought, *he sleeps like a stone.* He struggled in his own
bedding and managed to free a hand to scratch his nose.

"The scouts," she continued, "are still coming and going from the command
tents. When the enemy is close enough, we will march. Then we will know that
battle is close."

"Have you been in a battle before—one like this, not like the city?"

"No." Dwyrin stopped rubbing his nose. It seemed that Zoë was unsure—a
strange emotion for her. They had worked together for weeks now, practicing
together, learning to fight as one. Eric's death had wrecked their original plan to
fight as two pairs. Now they were learning, again, to fight as a three. In some ways
it was much easier this way. Both Zoë and Odenathus were quite skilled, though
they lacked the raw power that Dwyrin could summon. They could bind a shield
of defense far faster than he could, but while they covered him, he could bring
fire or cast it with blurring speed. Colonna, watching them train, had commented
that they reminded him of the old Thebans, who would fight in pairs, each with
a different, specialized weapon.

"I have never seen a great battle." She paused. "Before Tauris, I had never
seen battle at all. No struggle to the death, no corpses piled up like sheaves of
wheat beside the road. No friends die." Something caught in her throat and she
turned her face away from him. Dwyrin felt a rush of pain too, thinking of what
it meant to lose their friend.

"Zoë," he said, touching her hair, "I miss Eric too. It was just bad luck that
he was thrown into the river."

She mumbled something, but he could not hear what it was, her face was
still turned away. He stared up at the ceiling of the tent, feeling his own tears well
up in his chest, clenching at his heart. But, like her, he did not cry out loud,
letting them trickle down his cheeks instead. Finally he slept, his fingers still
touching her hair.

)·((

A cold wind blew out of the north, driving sheets of dust before it. Nikos and Anagathios huddled in the lee of a tumbled mud-brick building. Their horses clustered in front of them, tied to stakes driven into the loose sandy soil. The sky was dark, the sun only a dim circle through the howling wind and dust of the storm. The yellow-brown grit got into everything, even when they were, as now, bundled up tight in their robes with scarves over their faces. They sat, not bothering to speak, waiting for the storm to pass. The wind hissed and wailed around the building.

A figure appeared momentarily in the dust, between flying sheets of sand. The figure was wrapped up too and leaned forward into the wind howling out of the north. Nikos made to rise, but Anagathios grabbed his arm and sat him back down. The approaching figure continued to battle against the wind, but finally reached the poor shelter of the wall and sat down heavily next to them. Nikos and Anagathios leaned close, straining to hear.

". . . a city of . . . there." The figure pointed off into the brown murk.

Nikos shook his head—he couldn't make it out over the sound of the storm. The figure shouted again but was still unintelligible. Finally the other gave up and settled back against the wall. The horses continued to stand, heads down, and the sand began to pile up around the feet of the three waiting travelers.

The storm passed and the stars came out in a deep blue velvet sky. The sun had begun to set while the trailing edge of the sandstorm had passed. The travelers shook the dust from their cloaks in clear red-gold light. There was still a high cloud of thick dirty brown and the rays of the sun slanted in under it, painting the desert with rich full colors. Jusuf, Nikos, and Thyatis stood at the edge of a canal a hundred yards from the tumbled-down wall. Across the gurgling water of the canal, beyond a belt of date palms and greenery, a great city rose around a broad, flat hill. It had no walls, only a gate that they could see. A huge building rose at the center of the city, a stepped pyramid a hundred feet above the flat roofs of the houses. Sand had invaded its precincts, burying the streets and agora. Pillars thrust from the dunes, leaning at odd angles. The windows of city were dark, the only light a dull orange flame coming from the top of the ziggurat.

"That place has an odd feel to it," Jusuf said, scratching at his beard, which had finally recovered something of its usual fullness. "There should be lights, noise, something."

"And walls," Nikos added, peering through the night, trying to see if anything was moving in the silent city. "The Arabian desert is not far off—there might be raiders."

Thyatis felt something too, a prickling at the back of her neck. She looked up and down the canal. The water was a black pit holding the stars, wavering, in its heart. There seemed to be no bridge or crossing.

"Some things," she said softly, not wanting to draw attention to herself, "do not bear investigation. Get the men mounted up—we press on down this canal. We need a bridge if we're to get to the Tigris . . ."

Dawn was close when the dark engine descended out of the sky. A wailing high-pitched roar and the rush of flames shattered the quiet of the night. Ruddy light scattered over the dunes as it touched down, limbs flexing as they settled into the sand. Flames hissed and then died, leaving the desert quiet again. Molten sand bubbled and popped where the talons of the engine had touched. A door, hinged at the top rather than the side, swung open and pale-yellow light spilled out onto the dunes. Figures climbed out, stretching and groaning after the long flight from the north.

One, taller than the rest, strode to the top of the nearest dune. Two shorter figures followed, one on either side. Beyond the dunes, across rippling white ridges, the shape of a buried city rose, dark and desolate. Behind them other figures were busy unloading supplies and tents from the belly of the engine.

"So," the first figure said in a conversational tone, "this is the city of the *magi*."

"Yes, great lord," the shortest figure said, a tremulous note in its voice, "the forbidden place. Dastagird of the Kings of old. Once it was the residence of the King of Kings—a city of marble palaces and beautiful gardens—but the priests coveted it and made it their own. Now the gardens are buried in the sand and the palaces are filled with shadows."

The Prince pulled the cowl of his robe back and shook his shoulders out. He was nervous, but there was little to fear. He had powers on his side too, strong powers.

"Gaius?" He turned to the other figure. The old Roman stood at ease, his hands clasped behind his back. "Suggestions?"

The dead man nodded, his leathery face creased with the smallest of smiles. "First we take a look around, and see what there is to see, Lord Prince. Then we show ourselves. With your permission, the Valach and I will go out tonight and find the lay of the land."

Maxian nodded sharply, then turned around and descended the dune. The others were still unloading crates. He was tired and hoped to find sleep soon. Behind him the little Persian took one last look at the darkened city and then hurried after him. Gaius Julius took his time, watching the silent buildings and the empty steps of the great ziggurat for a long time. Two other figures joined him, squatting in the sand at his back. When at last he turned back to the engine, he found both of them waiting for him.

The dead man smiled, looking upon his little army.

"Alais. Khiron. Are we ready?"

"Yes, lord," they whispered. "We are ready."

"Good." He checked the shortsword at his hip and the fit of the bracelets on his arms. "We go."

Dust blew in the street, and steppe thistle bounced past out of an alleyway. Gaius Julius strode down the middle of the pavement, feeling the edges of the bricks under his sandals. The sun had just risen when he and his companions entered the city through the eastern gateway. Pale-pink light fell on dark bricks and stone and was swallowed. Beside the wind and his shadow, sprawled out before him on the street, nothing moved. Alais paced him on the right, shrouded in a voluminous black cloak and cowl. Even her face was hidden in the depths of the cloak, only a pale-white shadow peeping out. The creature, Khiron, was on his left, garbed in dark-brown wool and a thin desert robe over that. Khiron's face, too, was hidden; he had wound his *kaffieh* around his head, hiding everything but his eyes.

Gaius alone showed his face. He wore only a simple tunic and kilt, with his thick leather belt cinched tight and his sword slung over his shoulder. His leathery brown face was set and his nearly bald head gleamed in the sun. The buildings narrowed, hanging over the street, but then fell away to either side. At the center of the city, a plaza was open to the sky. On the western side of the square, before them, the ziggurat rose up in mighty steps. Gaius Julius halted, the thin fringe of white hair around his head ruffled by the hot breeze. The city was quiet, but Gaius felt that its tenor had changed since they had come into the heart of it.

"Eyes are watching us," the *homunculus* said. Its voice was still raspy and harsh. Even great quantities of pig and calf blood had not restored it to full health. Gaius Julius nodded absently. He felt a familiar tickling sensation at the back of his mind. A brief memory surfaced: a deep-green forest and blue-painted warriors creeping, their long red hair thick with grease and mud. The others made to move forward and mount the flight of steps that led up the imposing side of the ziggurat, but he raised a hand and they stopped.

Gaius Julius stood, waiting, his hands clasped behind his back, his eyes narrow slits against the light. Khiron, as was his wont when action was not required, froze into immobility. Alais drifted closer to the dead man, close enough for him to smell her perfume. It was a bitter scent, reminding him of rose petals that had withered and died still on the thorn.

A man appeared on the second level of the ziggurat. He was elderly, with a long white beard and bushy eyebrows. His skin was very dark and shone like a polished walnut burl. Gaius could feel the power in him. The man was wearing a long dark-blue robe and leaned heavily on a tall staff. His head was bare, allowing his snowy mane of hair to flow behind him.

"You are not welcome here, dead man." The booming voice emanated from the ziggurat, filling the square and echoing off the blank faces of the buildings. "Begone."

Gaius Julius hooked his thumbs into his belt and squinted up at the elderly man.

"My master bade me come," he shouted back, his voice clear and strong, though not the overpowering volume of the other, "and I came, doing him honor and you as well. My master bears you no ill will. He does not come with armies or with fire. He comes openly, seeking knowledge. Will you admit him to your precincts? Will you treat him with hospitality?"

The elderly man did not respond, the hot wind ruffling his robes out to the side. Two more men appeared, one on either side. They seemed equally ancient.

"No," came the booming voice. "We felt the passage of your master in the night. He is not welcome here, as you are not welcome, corpse man."

Gaius Julius, having taken the measure of the empty town and the men on the ziggurat, bowed deeply, held the pose for a beat, and then turned on his heel. Alias and Khiron fell in behind him. The wind escorted them out of the city, whistling through empty doorways and barren windows. The watching eyes followed them too, until they were well past the gates. On the first dune ridge, the old Roman turned, his eyes measuring distances and elevations.

"What is it, Gaius?" Alais' voice was sweet and only for his ear, not that Khiron had the slightest interest. He turned and his mouth stretched in a smile, but it did not reach his eyes. "Nothing, only a fancy. We must apprise the Prince of our welcome."

Maxian nodded, unsurprised at the news. He stood in the shade cast by one of the wings of the engine. It made a broad canopy, though it cast an odd jagged shadow on the ground. Krista stood at one shoulder and Alais at the other. Gaius Julius and Khiron leaned against one of the massive iron claws that dug into the sand. The Valach boys squatted on the ground under the curve of the belly. Beyond the shade, the sun beat harshly on the sand.

"Khiron, what did you feel?"

The eyes of the *homunculus* opened and turned to the Prince, swiveling like the turret of a siege engine. "Master, three men we saw, standing on the platform of the ziggurat, but others watched us in secret. Some were not men, though none were as I or as Gaius Julius is. Nor the Lady Alais. I smelled fifteen or twenty in the buildings. They were afraid."

"Alais?" The Prince barely turned, keeping the old Roman in his sight.

The blond woman moved forward and curtseyed deeply, as was her wont. "My lord, all the town stank of abandonment. It is the residence only of dogs and crows. Only in the ziggurat are there living men. Too, my eyes saw vents high on the side of the pyramid, vents that billowed hot air. My thought leads me to suspect that the domain, the residences, of the *magi* are beneath the ziggurat."

Maxian turned to Abdmachus, who alone among them all was sweating heavily in the heat. "My friend?"

"Master," the little Persian choked, "it has been so long . . . I barely remember any details!"

Khiron moved at some unseen gesture from the Prince, swift as a snake, and his mottled hands were at the Persian's throat in an instant. Abdmachus gobbled in fear as the cold fingers tightened around his larynx. Maxian smiled pleasantly. Behind him Krista frowned slightly.

"Abdmachus, please, this is important to me. Khiron and Gaius Julius will help you remember. Alais, assist them. Make sure that we have as good a map as can be drawn."

The three escorted the little Persian, gently but inexorably, into the belly of the engine. Alais' white face appeared in the doorway for a moment as she swung the hatch closed. Maxian looked away and sighed. Krista remained in the shadow, her face a serene mask. He went to her and bowed slightly, drawing a small frown.

"My lady, would you care to join me on a short walk?" His phrasing was very formal.

She nodded and drew part of her scarf over her head. The sun was fierce.

The Prince led the way, up over the huge dune that rose above their little camp. On the other side, the slope fell steeply away and it was slow going to descend. Beyond it there was an area of rippled sand and—incongruous among the waste-land—a ruined circle of marble pillars, fluted and crowned with acanthus capitals, rose from the sand. The Prince led Krista there and sat down on one of the fallen pillars. Krista remained standing, her hands demurely clasped in front of her, look-ing down upon him.

"Tonight," he began, "there can be a pair of horses here, with water and food and supplies. The riding horse will have a bag of Persian eagles on the saddle. Five or six hundred *aureus* worth, I guess. I borrowed an invocation from Abdma-chus—the shoes of the horses will leave no trace in the sand. These are my gift for you, this and one other thing."

He reached into his robes and drew out a heavy roll of parchment, sealed with rich purple wax. He held it out to her, and after a moment Krista took it.

"You are a free woman now, free of any obligation to the Duchess. This is an Imperial writ with the stamp of the Emperor upon it expressing that in no uncertain terms."

"Why?" Krista's voice was even, though her mind was afire with concerns and questions.

Maxian smiled, a brief, wan expression that quickly fled his face.

"This business of the city of the *magi*," he said, "will be a cruel one. I see myself embarking on a path edged with darkness. The excision of this corruption . . . it will require blood to be spilled. I would not see you on that same path, regardless of how much I might desire you at my side. Go east, to Taporobane or Serica. Build a new life for yourself, free of the past, free of the curse, free of me."

"It is a kind gesture, Lord Prince."

"Then you will take it?"

"Perhaps," she said. "I would not care to give the white witch the satisfac-tion."

Maxian's eyebrow quirked up. "Jealous?"

"Competitive," she said with a slow smile. "I have seen enough to know that you may be right. My mistress' duty—my duty—is to sustain the Empire in the face of constant disaster. So I will stay."

Maxian stared at her for a long time, his face troubled. He wondered, briefly, if she knew of his excursions into the night in the company of the Valach woman. Finally he stood up and brushed the sand out of his kilt. "So . . . very well. Thank you."

She shook her head, saying: "Thank me when this is done, if you are still alive."

THE KERENOS RIVER, ALBANIA

Surrounded by a thick wall of red-haired Varangians, their round shields turned outward, the three Emperors conferred. Beyond the stolid Germans and Scandians, tens of thousands of men were marching past, raising a choking cloud of clay dust from the dry road. Eastern and Western regiments jostled on the road, trying to keep their order of march open. Galen had dispensed with his servants, bidding them remain in the camp five miles behind them. Three of the Western Emperor's staff officers clustered at his back. The Khazar, Ziebil, as was his wont, was alone. Heraclius, half clad in his battle armor—a solid breastplate of welded iron with a pair of eagles emblazoned on the chest—had ten or twelve servants, officers, and dispatch riders crowded around.

"Augustus Galen, your Legions have the center."

Heraclius gestured toward the open fields to the south of where they stood. The Romans pouring past on the road were fanning out into the rocky flat by cohort and century. Their standards jogged up and down as the bearers trotted across the field. Only one good road ran south from the camp across the river and into this dry upland. Ziebil's scouts had returned the previous night from their latest foray south of the river with news that the Persian army was, at last, in striking range. The Romans had broken camp well before dawn, the Khazars riding out in complete darkness to secure the road and the northern edge of the plain.

"Khan Ziebil, your horsemen are on the left, though keep a strong reserve behind the line of battle. The woods are thick there, and I fear the Persians may try to send men through the brush to attack the flank."

It was almost noon now, and the majority of the army was still backed up on the road, trying to reach the flats. Galen's Western legions had made the best time, forming up in the camp on schedule and marching out in orderly fashion. The Sixth Gemina had reached the field at sunrise and had deployed to screen the arrival of the following elements. Galen, pushing his horse and his guardsmen, had arrived soon after dawn to find the legionnaires loitering around under the trees. There had been no Persians in sight.

"Theodore." Heraclius turned to his brother, attired much like him, down to the red boots, in heavy armor and chain mail under the solid plate. "You and I will command the right, with the Eastern knights and the Anatolikon thematic troops as reserve. Once we have shaken the line out and there is proper spacing between the *tagmata*, we will attack. If the Persians are still in confusion, we will advance along the entire front and drive them back into the trees. If they have formed a good line, then the Khazars"—Heraclius nodded to Ziebil—"will feint on the left and then we shall attack on the right."

The Western Legions were on the field by ten o'clock. The archers and slingers Galen had sent forward to screen the assembling legions had reported back that an enormous Persian army had begun to spill out of the tree line on the southern edge of the fields. The Khazars began arriving in bands and companies, generally congregating to the left of the Roman positions, and the Eastern knights were still clogging the road from the camp. After receiving reports that estimated the size of the Persian army in excess of a hundred thousand men, Galen had ridden forward himself and stared in awe at the multitude of Persians on the southern side of the plain.

Thousands of banners already fluttered in the morning breeze and still more bands of men were coming out of the forest. The enemy army was a riot of color— yellow banners and green, red surcoats on some mounted men and bright blue on others. Each band seemed to have a different garb, or even different styles of dress. It was hard to tell at this range.

At eleven o'clock there had easily been a hundred twenty thousand men in the enemy lines, jostling and milling about in apparent confusion. If the reports of the Khazar scouts were to be believed, the enemy forces who had reached the field were peasant levies armed with wicker shields, spears, and other light arms. While he watched, some contingents of horsemen in furry vests and round caps had arrived, trotting out in front of the ragged Persian line. Galen had shaken his head and ridden back to his own troops, who had taken orderly positions and were standing ready, leaning on their spears and swords, waiting.

"Any questions?" Heraclius glanced at Galen, who had a pensive look on his face. "Augustus Galen?"

"Yes . . . it seems that we are likely to be outnumbered by almost two to one at the rate that the Persian reinforcements keep arriving. The enemy seems confused, however. I propose sending our thaumaturges forward to attack the enemy formations with sorcery while they are attempting to form up. The longer they stay at the tree line, the more room we will have to maneuver."

Heraclius scowled, for Galen had not discussed this notion with him the previous night when the plan of battle was laid out. He glanced at his officers, one of whom was a wizard himself. "Demosthenes?"

The elderly man coughed in surprise and rubbed his long nose. "*Avtokrator*, the primary role of thaumaturges in battle has always been one of defense, to protect the army from the sendings of the enemy. The will and sinew of men has always been the deciding factor for Roman armies, not the strength of our magicians. Speaking plainly, my lord, my brothers and I are not skilled in the arts of attack, not like the Persians are. Now, a siege . . ."

Heraclius cut him off with a look. The Eastern Emperor glared at Galen.

"Some of my wizards," Galen said, calmly, "*are* skilled in the arts of attack. I will send them forward with the skirmishers to disrupt the enemy ranks. It will buy us a little more time to deploy."

"Very well," Heraclius snapped. "They are your men, use them as you see fit. Gentlemen, to your commands. We will have victory this day, or perish."

The Khan Ziebil yawned and pushed his way through the crowd of men. His horse, a sleek lustrous black creature, was waiting. He vaulted easily into the saddle and kneed her forward, disappearing into the flow of men and horses on the road. Galen looked after him, a puzzled look on his face.

"What is it?" Prince Theodore had come up alongside the Western Emperor, his young face flushed with the anticipation of battle.

"I still fail to understand why the Khazars stand with us this day. This is little affair of theirs. The risk of defeat is far higher than the reward of looting some hill towns."

Theodore laughed and slapped Galen on the shoulder. "My brother is a shrewd bargainer. He offered the khan many fine gifts, not least his own daughter in marriage. And, the Khazars will gain much booty from this and the friendship of Constantinople. Friendship in gold and arms and training for their men weigh heavily with the khan."

"His daughter?" Galen was outraged—he had heard nothing of this, but he had met Epiphania while in the Eastern capital. She was a shy girl with long dark hair and an interest more in music and books than politics. She and the Empress Martina got along very well, though Galen was not sure if Martina had replaced Epiphania's dead mother or had merely become an unlooked-for older sister.

"Oh, yes." Theodore's eyes twinkled in delight at the discomfiture apparent on the stern face of the Western Emperor. "My brother always used to carry a picture of her with him in a cameo. He sent it to the khan months ago with the first embassy. Apparently the old man was quite taken with her."

Galen turned away in disgust. To his Western sensibilities, it was revolting. He mounted up, pulling his helmet on. His own guardsmen gathered around him in a solid block, keeping a space clear in the mob of men that were milling around behind the lines. Theodore rode off to the right wing of the army with his coterie of young nobles thronging around him. Galen surveyed the ranks of his men. For just a moment he allowed himself to wish for Aurelian at his side and to wonder where Maxian had fled to.

Are you over there? he thought, feeling sick at the prospect. *Did Persia listen to you?*

"Lord Baraz! Your banner, Great Lord!"

The Boar turned in his saddle, seeing that one of the dispatch riders had managed to make his way through the ocean of infantrymen that had surged around them. The boy was carrying a furled banner across his saddle, though it was hard work keeping it from fouling in the thicket of spears and wicker shields milling past.

"Oh, Ahriman take that damned thing." Baraz spat, his patience at an end. "The King of King's standard is well enough for me. Get rid of it."

The boy blanched at the naked fury in the lord general's voice and turned away. Baraz did not give him a second thought, turning back to trying to force his own way through the press of feudal levies that hemmed him in on every side. Over the heads of the press of men, he could see a river of knights, their lances a waving steel forest, and beyond them the banner of the Lord Rhazames. He spurred his horse and it surged forward, pushing men aside. Cries of outrage rang out around him, but he did not care.

After the turmoil of the past five days, Baraz remembered his time in Syria with fondness. There, despite the poor leadership of the Great Prince Shahin, he had commanded an army of experienced men. Many of them had served with him before and knew how to march and fight. This mob was another matter. When Chrosoes had sent Gundarnasp out to raise the "greatest army in the world" they had taken him to mean numbers, not quality. Every landowner with a spear and a nag from Nisibis to Tokharistan was jammed onto this road, along with a vast number of wagons, mules, and men on foot. Baraz managed to break out of the stream of men clogging the road and sent his horse up the side of a low embankment.

The general guessed that the army numbered almost two hundred fifty thousand men. Yet he feared that for all its size, it was near useless. The ten thousand Immortals he had commanded for so long were the only reliable troops in the entire vast host. They, at least, would follow command and advance or retreat as he directed. The rest . . . He shook his head in dismay. For the first time since Chrosoes had launched his war of revenge nine years before, Baraz was afraid that he faced a hopeless fight.

Among the few bright spots in this canker sore of an expedition was the presence of two bands of Ephtathilite Huns, mercenaries hired by the governor of the Eastern city of Balkh. The Huns were the very devil on horseback and made superb scouts. The news that they brought him from the north was disheartening, but he was fairly sure that it was accurate. The army of the Two Emperors was just over a hundred thousand men, about half infantry and half cavalry. Had numbers been the only deciding factor, Baraz would have just pointed north and howled a command to attack. The Persians would have swamped the Romans with sheer numbers.

Unfortunately, and this was the spear that twisted in Baraz's gut, the enemy was composed of veteran troops, well drilled and disciplined. It seemed unlikely that they would panic in the face of the Persian numbers, and that meant that the King of King's "greatest army" would run right into a meat grinder. His one hope was to pin the enemy with his levies for long enough to bring the Immortals and the bands of heavily armored knights to bear on a flank of the Roman army, bend it back, and crush it.

He reached Rhazames' banner and found the young nobleman and his coterie of officers shouting in confusion at each other.

Baraz bulled into the center of their conversation and raised his voice in a bellow. "Shut up! Everyone, quiet. Tell me what has happened so far."

Rhazames cleared his throat and nervously stroked the long mustaches that spiked out from the sides of his face. He wore an open-faced helmet with an ornamental dragon enameled on its crown. He could not have been older than eighteen. "Lord Baraz! The army is still gathering and the Romans have sent their sorcerers forward. They are sending fire and lightning against the front ranks of the infantry. Many men are already dead or fleeing toward the rear."

Baraz grimaced at the thought of the peasant infantry stampeding back into the companies of men still trying to reach the battlefield. Things were dicey enough already.

"Where are our wizards?"

Rhazames shrugged, his face a mask of confusion. "I do not know, Great Lord. I thought I saw their wagons some hours ago, by the side of the road, but . . ."

Baraz controlled his temper with a supreme effort of will. The boy was very young, and it was quite likely that he had never commanded in battle before. His father had served Baraz in the first campaigns against Syria but had been killed in a duel at Antioch. He spurred his horse through the collection of nobles and officers, finally reaching a low mound where he could see something of the battlefield. He cursed then, for a long time and with great feeling. The entire Roman army was already on the field and in motion. He looked back, past the pale, frightened faces of his commanders, and saw that the roads were still clogged with men and animals. Not even half of his army had reached the area of battle yet. He gestured at the nearest dispatch rider, his hand chopping at the air.

"You, lad, ride like the wind to the right flank and find the *Kagan* of the Huns. Tell him to charge the Roman lines and spoil their advance. Then find the Lakhmid light horse I saw loafing around earlier and send them to deploy before our lines. They can drive off these magicians with javelin and lance."

The courier put spur to horse and pelted off down the hill, dust swirling behind him.

"You, you and you . . . get down there into that mess and send the infantry forward and the knights to the wings. I don't care how, just get the road cleared. More men are coming and half of the regiments I see down there are standing around wondering where they're supposed to go."

More men galloped away from the hilltop, banners bobbing behind them in the breeze.

"Lord Rhazames, take your household troops and form up in the center of that mob of infantry. One of your men for each five of those peasants. Spread them out and get them facing forward. Any man who has lost his spear, sword or axe, back a rank. They can pick up fallen weapons."

The young man bowed in the saddle and then was gone in a cloud of clods and dust. His banner men hurried after, pale and frightened. Baraz sighed to see them go. He desperately missed his officers in Syria. This army was too green to stand a full day of battle against professionals unless they were very lucky. A booming sound echoed over the field. Baraz started and peered down the hill. A column of black smoke rose from before the ranks. Blue flashes of lightning rippled up and down the front. He saw men fall, burning like torches.

He turned and began, "You . . ." then he stopped, surprised beyond measure. "Salabalgus! What in the Corrupted World are you doing here?"

The stocky man smiled back at him, most of his face covered by the iron plates of his helmet. He wore a deep-green cloak over a battered shirt of ring mail. A bronze boar's head was pinned at his shoulder. "Greetings, nephew. The Great King's messenger came and ordered a new levy, so I came, bringing the lads from the estate. We're down there, at the bottom of the hill."

Baraz stared down through the brush and saw, to his horror, that he knew nearly every one of the young men clustered there in their motley armor, antique weapons, and earnest expressions.

"Oh, Lord of Light," Baraz breathed, turning to his uncle in dismay. "Is there anyone left at home?" Salabalgus shook his head silently.

Baraz ran nervous fingers through his beard and twisted a curl around his thumb. Nine years ago he had left his highland estates in Bactria with a troop of two thousand men, answering the summons of his King. There were, when last he had counted them, a few hundred left, all officers or sergeants in his Immortals. Behind them, he had been careful to leave a smattering of veterans and all of the youngsters. Someone had to guard the herds and farmland from raiders. Now Salabalgus was here, not at home, and all of those youngsters, grown up, were at the bottom of the hill.

He looked out across the vast host of men on the field and those still coming up the road. They were all too young or too old. He felt a chill. *How many of us has Chrosoes killed in this war?* Then he pushed a flurry of seditious thoughts aside. Battle was at hand.

Zoë ran forward through the short grass, her brown legs flashing in laced-up leather boots. Dwyrin and Odenathus ran right behind her, flanking her on either side. Armenians with bows and quivers of arrows ran before them. The grass was burning ahead of them and to the right, sending trails of white smoke across the plain. Arrows whickered overhead in both directions. The Persian lines were only a hundred paces ahead. Zoë stopped, going down on one knee. Dwyrin ran up behind her and halted as well, his breathing heavy with the effort of dashing the two hundred paces from their own ranks. He did not feel tired, only exhilarated.

"Loose!" the leader of the Armenians cried. The archers stopped in a ragged line and let fly with their stout bows. Their arrows arched high and then fell, flashing, into the tightly packed ranks of the Persian spear men in front of them. There were cries of pain and a wave of angry shouting. The Armenians reached back over their shoulders for fresh arrows.

"Loose!" Zoë shouted, her forehead creased in concentration. Dwyrin had already shed the prison of flesh. He clenched his fist and whipped it through the air in front of him. Power built in it, leached from the sky and the hot stones under his feet. Pale-blue flames danced around his fist, and he flung them in a whirling ball at the spearmen. The sphere leapt from his hand like a sling bullet and shrieked across the intervening distance. Persian axemen scrambled to get out of the way, but they were pressed too tightly together. The flames were searingly bright when the sphere smashed into the chest of one of the spearmen.

The man vanished in a white-hot burst of flame. His companions screamed horribly as their flesh caught fire and the green flames leapt from man to man. Lightning danced from Zoe's hands a moment later and lashed across the front rank like a terrible whip. More men died, their flesh crisped black and their leather armor burning merrily. Odenathus' hand chopped down and the earth shook, toppling their ranks. Spears wavered, tangling with those behind them. Somewhere a horse screamed in pain.

Dwyrin grimaced for a moment, seeing the wailing men die, falling to the ground. He felt an odd detachment. Here, at a distance, they did not matter to him. If he had seen Eric die again, he would have felt sick, disgusted, filled with revulsion. Instead, a thrill crept along his skin as his power smashed at them again and again.

More arrows flew, turning the sky dark. The Armenians emptied their quivers into the Persian lines, then ran back toward the Roman army. Dwyrin sent one last bolt of brilliant orange flame cutting into the Persians, then he too trotted off after Zoë. A vast, angry roar rose from behind them. He looked over his shoulder and saw that the surviving ranks of Persians were beginning to jog forward.

Galen swayed in his saddle as the horse cantered along the length of the Roman lines. He had deployed his legionnaires in a double-depth frontage. The front line, five ranks deep, was comprised of the veteran Third Augusta at the center, with the Second Triana on one side and the Sixth Gemina on the other. Behind them was an interval twenty paces deep and then another line of five ranks. These were the Second Audiatrix on the west, the Imperial Bodyguard in the center, and the Third Gallica on the east. His banner men kept close to the Emperor, riding no more than an arm's length away. Men wearing conical felt caps ran off the field between the armies and down the avenues cleared between each Legion.

Galen completed his circuit and surveyed the field. The Persian army had filled the far side of the plain with a solid mass of men and was beginning to move forward. He could not tell if it was an ordered advance or the simple pressure of more reinforcements entering the field. He saw that the Armenian skirmishers and the thaumaturges he had sent forward had finished retiring behind the stolid lines of legionnaires.

He looked to the west and saw that two huge wedges of Eastern knights had fanned out at the end of his line. The sun sparkled from twenty thousand lances, blinding the eye. Red Imperial banners fluttered at the center of the mass of men and horses. To the east, the Khazars had swung out in a long curved line, stretching from his anchoring cohorts to the tree line at the edge of the field. They were in constant movement, bands of horsemen galloping here and there in apparent confusion. Within the swirling screen of horse archers, Galen picked out Ziebil and his heavily armored lancers, a tight knot of fifteen thousand men.

Trumpets blared in the Roman ranks, and bucinas shrilled. The Legions advanced at walk, their great rectangular shields angled in front of them, each man carrying a javelin at the ready in his hand. The Western Emperor rode through the ranks, angling for the block of red cloaks that marked his bodyguard and the hulking shapes of the Varangians. As he passed, the men raised a cheer and he smiled and picked up the pace, his right arm thrust out in salute. Eight thousand voices rose up around him, a great booming shout:

"Ave Caesar! Ave! Roma Victrix!"

Galen smiled, his blood afire with the prospect of battle. The roar of eager men filled his ears.

"Ahriman's three-pronged lingam!" Baraz was beside himself in fear and rage.

The front ranks of the mass of spearmen and swordsmen at the center of the rough line he and his officers had barely managed to form had suddenly broken into a run toward the Roman lines. The rest were wavering, some pushing forward, still pressed by men behind them, others trying to move back. Snarling, he glanced up and down the rest of the line. The blocks of horsemen on the right and left wings were still sorting themselves out by banner and clan. The unexpected advance of the infantry in the middle was unsupported. Hunnic horse archers scattered out of the way as sixty thousand men stormed forward, heedless of the slowly advancing lines of Romans to their front. Baraz felt sick. He wondered if the untrained peasants in front of him even knew what they were doing.

"Dispatch!" One of the lads spurred up to ride alongside him.

"To Salabalgus and Doronas on the right; tell them to wait for the mob in front of us to lock with the Roman lines and then charge if the Khazars attempt to take them in the flank."

His uncle and the other Eastern lord had all of his heavy cavalry—the *clibanari*, or oven men, so named for their body-length metal armor—under some vague sort of control. If the Khazars on the Roman right wing took the opportunity of the exposed Persian infantry to charge, his countercharge could demolish the entire Roman right.

The boy galloped away. Baraz chewed on his thumb, watching the center of his army rush headlong into waiting, steady, disaster.

The *Kagan* Ziebil, khan of the Khazars and overlord of the Bulgar tribes, sat easily on his horse. It had been awhile since he had been in the saddle, and he found that his body remembered better than his mind did. He rubbed his stubbly beard and peered with watery blue eyes off to the right, where the lean-faced Roman king, Galen, was advancing his men at a walk into the teeth of a vast black mob of screaming Persians. Unlike the Persians, who were rushing forward in clumps and without the slightest possibility of organization, the Romans were moving forward in step, their front rank a gleaming wall of interlocking shields.

With barely fifty paces between the two armies, the Romans came to a halt, closing up the interval between their lines. The front of the line rippled as men brought javelins to their cheek and then, at the hoarse shout of bull-voiced centurions, let fly. The air was filled with a cloud of silver-tipped darts, and the running Persians suddenly staggered as the rain of iron slashed at them. Ziebil smiled, seeing the leading edge of the Persian line disintegrate into a red welter of dying men.

He gestured to one of his banner men, who dipped the long black dragon banner once, then twice.

His own long line of men, lances pointed to the sky over the distant Persian cavalry, rippled with movement, and they moved forward at a slow walk. The Khazar light cavalry commanded by Prince Dahvos had already driven off the Huns and Sacagatani archers who had been harassing them.

At the center of the field, the Romans in the first rank drew their shortswords as one, the sound of four thousand blades scraping from scabbards cutting across the tumult of the field. The second rank let fly with their javelins as more Persians rushed over the bodies of their first wave. Then the third rank let fly. The Persian infantry slowed, tangling with men trying to run back from the edge of battle and clambering over the bodies of the dead. The Romans stood firm.

The main mass of the Persians slammed into the Roman lines with a dull crash of metal. The Roman ranks staggered back three steps and then stopped. Ziebil could hear a chorus of screams rising above the din. Thousands of iron swords flashed as the legionnaires waded into the press of spearmen who had surged against them. The Kagan smiled, thinking of the bloody brawl at close quarters that unfolded along the long lines of Romans. At arm's reach, the short stabbing swords of the Romans would have no lack of targets for their thirst. More Persians swarmed into the fray, heedless of their fellows dying in droves in front of them.

Ziebil motioned again and two flags dipped and rose. The horsemen on the right-hand side of his wedge trotted forward toward the flank of the battle. As the front of the Persian lines ground against the Romans, the men running up behind began to spill around the edges of the Roman formation. The Khazars galloped in, rising up in their stirrups, bows at the ready. Two quivers were slung on the side of each saddle, packed to bursting with triangle-headed arrows. The lead Khazars, their horses thundering across the field, drew and let fly into the flank of the Persian formations. The air clouded with black arrows. Men began falling, pierced by the long shafts.

Salabalgus could barely see out of the narrow eyeslit of his helmet, but he could see enough. The right flank of the infantry was melting away under the rain of Khazar arrows. His commanders were shouting at him, urging him to charge into the midst of the wheeling Khazar archers and drive them off. He ignored them, watching the hilltop where the banner of the King of Kings fluttered in the air. The elderly man had fought beside Baraz for as long as the boy had been able to lift a sword. His nephew had excellent instincts for battle. Salabalgus was in no hurry to die today. He waited.

Thousands more Persian infantry poured into the center of the field. The front ranks, locked in melee with the Romans, could not bring their bows to bear, and the ranks behind could not see the enemy. The Roman legionnaires continued to slaughter them methodically, but now they were getting weary and the center of the Roman line began to bend inward.

On his hilltop, Baraz's quick eye caught the flex in the enemy lines and saw too that the enemy right wing had continued its slow advance, leaving it only two or three hundred yards from his own right wing and the heavy cavalry there.

"Signal Salabalgus," he shouted at his banner men. They raised the lurid green banner of the House of Lord Rhazates and waved it in a figure eight. He looked to the left where the Roman *equites* and *lanciarii* were still sitting patiently, waiting for the outcome of the infantry melee in the middle of the field.

Heraclius must be there, he thought. *Being unusually patient too.*

He waved a dispatch rider over. He leaned close to the boy. "Message to Lord Gundarnasp on the left. Tell him to send his Lakhmids and Huns forward against the Roman horsemen. When they are distracted, he is to charge in behind the archers."

Baraz looked back to the right. Salabalgus' formations were aswarm with activity as they shook out in preparation to charge. The Boar smiled, long teeth flashing in the midday sun.

The Khan Ziebil saw the waving banner too, and his eyes caught the movement among the Persian *clibanari*. He whistled, a piercing sound that cut the air like a knife, then pointed forward and chopped his hand down. Fifteen thousand Khazar lancers put spur to horse and leapt forward as one. The earth shook as they charged forward, their horses lengthening stride to keep up. As the charge sprinted forward, it folded out into three wedges, each one led off by a tightly packed band of heavily armored men. The ground flew past under the hooves of the horses.

At the head of the middle wedge, Ziebil at last cut loose with a long shrieking cry. *Ah-la-la-la-la-la!*

As they galloped forward, Ziebil's men drew their bows, fitting shaft to string, and at a bare hundred paces—let fly. Their arrows arced up, a hungry dark cloud, and then whistled down, slashing through the ranks of the Persians. Behind the arrow storm, the horsemen continued to charge forward. Now lances rasped from their wooden sockets and were held overhand, ready to strike.

Galen felt the rumble in the earth like the soundless echo of a great drum. He rose up, shading his eyes with his hand. The banners of the Khazars on the left wing were in full flight, plunging forward into the Persian right. He wheeled his horse and shouted for his trumpeters.

"Signal advance, Third Gallica and Second Audiatrix, by ranks, forward on the flank!"

The blare of the trumpets drowned the rest of his words. Dispatch riders pelted off for each wing of the Roman reserve. Galen slapped his thigh with a glove, staring to the west.

Where are you? he wondered, thinking of Heraclius.

Ahead of him, the two Legions that he had held back from the butcher's work at the center of the line picked up their shields and trotted forward in column, swinging wide around the backs of the legionnaires already locked in battle.

Baraz watched in mounting fury as the confused mass of cavalry on his right wing finally sorted itself out in preparation to charge. Precious minutes had been lost as the bands of horsemen jockeyed for the front rank and snarled each other over matters of clan honor. He could make out Salabalgus' banners, and the old man had held his position, waiting for his commanders to beat their men into position, but it was too late. The Khazar charge had sprung forward like a pack of well-trained hounds. Baraz could only look on in sick admiration at the smooth flow of the attack.

The first wedge slammed into the Persian horse at a gallop, right at the junction between Salabalgus' formation and Doronas'. The Persians had barely begun to move forward at a walk when the Khazar charge tore into them like a heavy axe into a lamb. The clang of the impact echoed over the whole field, and Baraz winced as the shining wedge of Khazars plowed through his right wing.

Then the second and third wedges struck home and the entire right wing collapsed into a swirl of men fighting for their lives. Salabalgus' banner vanished under the wall of Khazar lancers and did not rise again. Baraz ground his fist into the saddle. The helms of the *clibanari* were bobbing silver islands in a sea of Khazar horsemen. Long hooked poles stabbed at the Persian knights, clutching at their armor and helmets. Lassos snaked out, snaring their throats.

Another sound caught Baraz' attention, and he turned back to the center of the field. The Roman lines in the middle had suddenly unfolded like a steel flower. The thick line of Roman infantrymen had unfurled its wings and was swinging around to compress the huge throng of Persian spearmen and levies in the center.

The Boar drummed his fingers on the saddle horn. There were only two dispatch riders left. He beckoned them over.

"You," he said, jabbing a thick finger at the first one, "ride back along the road. Find every commander and tell them to stop coming forward. We need maneuvering room, not more problems. When you run out of bands of men to hold up, get them moving back to where we camped last night. Form up there. I fear I'll be along presently."

"And you," he said to the second one, "get after Gundarnasp on the left wing and countermand the order I sent before. He is not to attack, repeat, *not* to attack. He should regroup his light horse and fall back to this hill behind a screen, protecting our left."

The boys dashed off and the Boar sat for a moment, brooding. He still had his Immortals, patiently waiting at the bottom of the hill. The center looked like a complete loss, but it would keep the Roman infantry busy for a while. The right wing was a more severe disaster. He could commit his reserve and rectify the situation, or he could wait for more troops to form up . . .

• • •

A thin man with a sallow face leaned close to Heraclius, whispering in his ear. The Eastern Emperor smiled, delighted at the news. He pressed a bag of heavy coins into the priest's hand and smoothed out his mustaches. The day was proceeding in a better fashion than he had expected. He kneed his horse and it trotted forward through the ranks of waiting men. Twenty thousand heavy cavalrymen were arrayed along the right wing of the Roman army in two echelons. Heraclius reached the front rank of the echelon he commanded and wheeled his horse. His voice was amplified by the design of his helmet.

"Men of Rome! The enemy is in flight. Advance at all speed!"

The Eastern nobles picked up the cry and urged their mounts forward. Slowly at first, but picking up speed, the mass of horsemen rode forward. Within moments they were thundering over a shallow rise, bearing down on the Persian flank at full tilt.

Heraclius was in front, his great tan stallion flying over the ground. He leaned forward, reveling in the rush of wind over his face. He held his longsword back, parallel to the horse, waiting for the moment to strike. Persian light horse, Huns by the look of them, scattered out of the way in front of the thundering charge. Some turned in the saddle and shot arrows back at the Eastern knights, but far too few to do any damage.

The Persian horse loomed, almost at rest. They began to move forward, lashing at their horses. Heraclius could see their faces, frightened by the sight of the twin wedges of *cataphracti* storming toward them. The line of horses and men flew forward, legs blurring over the ground. He straightened up, his sword flashing out.

"Rome!" he shouted at the top of his voice. "Roma Victrix!"

Ziebil coughed blood onto the ground, feeling the earth under his hands shake with the thunder of hooves. Somewhere on the field of battle, a cavalry charge was going home. He staggered up, his long knife in his hand. His helmet was gone, smashed off by the blow of a Persian war mace. Blood streamed into his right eye and he blinked furiously, trying to keep it clear. Horses and men rushed by him in the swirl of battle. His horse was gone, as was the small round shield that had been strapped to his upper arm.

A Persian in half-armor spurred toward him, cutting overhand with a long curved sword. Ziebil ducked aside, slashing at the horse's legs. He missed but felt the tip of the sword cut across his shoulder. Fresh pain blossomed and he felt cold wetness on his arm. The Khazar jumped at the next horse that thundered by but missed the saddle horn and was knocked down hard. Gasping for breath, Ziebil caught a glimpse of a long spear flashing in the sun, then there was a stunning blow to his stomach.

He cried out, but there was no breath left in his lungs. Men were shouting, and dimly he heard a voice calling his name. Darkness clouded the sky and he saw the spear rise, thin red blood sluicing off of the leaf-shaped blade. He was very cold. Men struggled over his body, but he did not care. He closed his eyes.

• • •

Baraz howled in delight, his huge sword spinning above his head. He rushed three Khazars trying to pull one of the Immortals from his armored horse with a lasso and hewed into them from behind. One head flew off, shorn clean from the man's neck, and the other two screamed as he mauled them. The Boar and his men pressed on, wreaking terrible havoc on the more lightly armored and armed Khazars. The Persian right flank began to re-form around the solid core of the Immortals.

The remaining Khazars fell back behind a flurry of arrows. Baraz did not pursue. The Boar rallied the men who had followed Doronas and Salabalgus, both of whom were dead, to him and fell back toward the hill.

Galen and his staff watched the Khazars fall back in disarray on their left. The red and yellow banners of the Persian Immortals waved amid the heaps of dead that were left in their wake. The Western Emperor frowned and made a quick count to himself. The Third Gallica was locked in a fierce struggle on the left wing of the Persian infantry, trying to turn the line and roll it up. A scattering of Khazar archers were all that stood between his exposed infantry and the Persian heavy horse.

"Caesar!" One of his staff officers was pointing to the west. Galen turned.

Heraclius' charge had slammed home, brushing aside the remains of the Hunnic archers and crumpling the entire Persian right wing. Persian horsemen were fleeing south in ones and twos, but more were being hewn down by Heraclius' men as they surged across the Persian flank. Galen smiled grimly and signaled to his trumpeters.

"Sound retreat, ten paces and stand," he shouted. The trumpets blared again, a sharp staccato. The buccinators wailed. "Signal the guard to swing right and cover the flank of the Third Gallica."

Behind him the Varangians and Germans ran forward, their axes and longswords at the ready. Galen turned his horse, watching the Persian line. His legionnaires backed off, their front re-forming where their ranks had been eaten away by the melee. Fresh men rushed in to fill the holes in the line. The Persians staggered forward and then stopped in confusion. The relentless pressure that had been forcing them forward had stopped. The Roman front was solid again, a bristling wall of shields, spears, and swords. Men shouted at the rear of the Persian formations. Many men turned, staring to their rear. Heraclius and his knights swept down the hillside toward the spearmen. The Persians began to mill about, shouting. Then a man on the left wing started running. Within moments the entire mass, still at least thirty thousand men, was in flight.

Heraclius' knights, screaming their battle cry, plowed into the running infantry. Galen closed his eyes for a moment, but the din filled his ears even so. A great wailing rose up. It was enough. He spurred his horse forward.

"All Legions, advance at a walk!"

The Western Legions surged forward, closing the trap.

. . .

"Lord of Corruption, I commit my soul to your keeping . . ."

Baraz shook his head. The Immortals had collapsed into a broad arc around his position at the eastern end of the plain. Scattered bands of Persians—horsemen, archers, spearmen—accreted to his banner like salt around a string suspended in brine. The rest of the field was a disaster. Tens of thousands of Persians lay dead and many more staggered south, heading for the chaos of the road, their formations scattered and broken. He could not make out Rhazames' banner in the middle of the field, and he was sure that Gundarnasp and all of the entire left wing of the army had been destroyed.

Now the Romans were redressing their lines. From where he sat upon his horse, he could not tell if any of the Roman cohorts had been destroyed. Soon they would march against him. Baraz beckoned his officers to him.

"This day is done. Send the men on foot ahead. Then the horse. The road south will be a charnel house. We will strike due east, through the woods to the shore of the sea and then south, back to Persian lands."

Baraz stared out over the field, his mind ignoring the windrows of dead, the wandering, riderless horses. The Roman army crouched in the middle of the field, a scaled and plated creature with myriad sharp spines. He shook his head, wishing for a fleeting moment that the King of Kings had not seized so greedily upon Dahak's power. If he had come to this field by horse, the advance of the Persian army would have been delayed into the spring, giving him time to flog the inexperienced men into some kind of army.

No matter, he thought. *Chrosoes has made his throw of the dice and lost. Now if only I can escape this debacle with my own head intact!*

He did laugh then, for the game of wits and skill that he embarked upon pleased him. The Immortals near him shuddered—the sound of such gay laughter in this place was madness.

THE ZIGGURAT OF THE MAGI

Maxian and his followers entered the buried city by a hidden path. The Valach, at the bidding of Gaius Julius, had found a trail made by goats and sheep that entered the city from the north, winding its way through fallen palaces and ruined temples. The old Roman had been more than usually smug, noting that even wizards had to eat sometime. Maxian took his time, walking slowly, most of his mind submerged in the hidden world. Strange patterns and geometries filled the spaces between the buildings and even the sky above the city. The dead man had been right to counsel stealth.

The stock trail crossed a cracked mosaic floor, exposed to the sky by the collapse of the building that had once housed it. The Prince walked for a space on clouds and a brilliant blue sky filled with wondrous birds. Two of the Valach boys preceded him, slinking low to the ground, sniffing and smelling everything that they encountered.

Krista shadowed the Prince at his right shoulder. The homunculus followed, carrying the unconscious body of the Persian magician. Abdmachus had been a long time in yielding up the secrets of the ziggurat. Gaius Julius had emerged from the body of the engine with a sour, drained expression on his face and a carefully drawn map in hand. Khiron, though his chest and arms were covered with a network of fresh scratches and bruises, was unmoved. Alais had fairly glowed, her hair thicker and richer in texture, almost the color of molten gold. Krista wondered if the Prince had noticed.

The lush blonde and the rest of the Valach followed behind the homunculus, as quiet as fallen leaves. Krista moved as quietly as she was able, but anger simmered in the back of her mind at the effortless skill the barbarians exhibited. She felt heavy, weighed down by a light shirt of chain-mail links that she wore strapped around her torso under the dark colors she had lately favored. The Prince seemed to move with the same grace now, though he had never shown an aptitude before. She stole a glance over her shoulder at Alais.

The Valach woman was watching the Prince with ill-disguised avarice. Despite the threat of imminent violence, Alais had chosen to dress herself in a tight-fitting leather top that revealed just enough of her figure to excite the imagination, silk leggings, high leather boots, and the heavy dark cloak. Krista sneered inside, ignoring the fact that she had worn similar outfits herself, though in slightly more fitting circumstances.

This isn't a summer party on the Seven Hills, she thought, *someone will be dead soon . . . maybe a fat woman with no sense of style.*

She missed the Duchess. Anastasia was so skilled with this kind of thing that were she here, the barbarian woman would have already fled in shame. The Roman woman smoothed her sleeves over the hidden shapes of the spring gun and her knife. She still had some small consolations.

The lead Valach stopped, raising a hand in warning. Silently he pointed to the left, into a dark recess. The stock trail turned away to the right, into a high barrel-vaulted building made of thick courses of stone blocks with bricks laid in between. The smell of sheep and goats tickled the nose. Krista watched the Prince advance carefully and confer with the two Valach boys.

"Soon," Gaius Julius said in her ear, "there will be some blood spilled."

Krista nodded, turning around to keep the old Roman in view. The others had stopped, the Valach squatting, Alais drifting up to the Prince, her hand resting lightly on his shoulder. Gaius Julius met her eye and winked, his face holding back some suppressed amusement.

Krista's left eyelid flickered in anger and then she made a small smile. "You must be pleased, seeing battle again . . ."

Gaius Julius grimaced and shook his head.

"No," he said, "I never miss war. I miss the disputation in the Forum. I miss testing my wit and voice against others. This escapade has some intrigue, but little else . . . I used to say that war was the recourse of the defeated or the barbarian who knew no better. If you had to fight, you had already lost your case, you see?"

The Prince hissed at them and they turned. Maxian gestured toward the dark recess. One of the Valach boys was disappearing down the flight of brick steps hidden within its shadow. Krista nodded but then held back until everyone else had gone ahead. She took one last look around, starting with alarm when a white face appeared at the doorway of the barrel-vaulted building. Then she smiled and nearly laughed aloud.

A puzzled-looking goat stared after her as she turned and descended the stairs.

Krista hurried down the stairs. At last the staircase wound to a stop and a narrow corridor split off from it. She had to bend down to keep from bumping her head against the triangular roof. The Prince had stopped ahead, his face illuminated by a pale-green light. The others were kneeling on the dusty floor.

"Ahead of us," the Prince whispered, "is a wooden door. It is not locked, but there is a pattern on it. Khiron, take our Persian friend forward and use his hand to open the door." The Prince smiled, his green-lit features corpselike in the darkness.

"Beyond that door is a hall. I can smell smoke. We go to the right and head for the center of the chambers. The priests will come to me, or I will go to them. Then we will settle this dispute. Remember, we need to find the Sarcophagus—so take anyone that you find alive!"

He glared at the Valach and Khiron in particular. The homunculus met his eyes with an impassive stare. The Valach boys bobbed their heads in acknowledgment. Alais smiled, her lips softly moist. Krista checked the lacings on her boots and the tightness of the leather harness she wore around her slim waist. Fingers touched each weapon and tool in turn, ensuring that they were still in place. Khiron moved ahead to the door, the body of the Persian held limply in front of him.

There was a clicking sound and the door opened, flooding the dark passage with warm orange light from some hidden fire. Khiron cast the Persian's unconscious body aside and blurred through the opening. The Valach boys bolted into the chamber on its heels. Maxian moved forward but stopped, holding up a hand to prevent Alais and Gaius Julius from entering.

There was a savage howl and sudden screams from beyond the door. Men shouted and there was a clatter of metal and ceramics falling. The Prince, silhouetted in the doorway, raised his hand and thunder spoke, shaking dust loose from the ceiling of the corridor.

The caverns under the ziggurat were ancient broad brick-lined passages with triangular ceilings. Maxian stormed forward through them, wrapped in smoke and fire.

Khiron's fingers dug into the dark wood of a door fifteen feet high in a wall of sandstone blocks each bigger than a tall man. Ancient oak splintered and snapped as his fingernails dug into the surface. The Prince stood back, his cloak furled around his shoulders, his eyes dark. The panel groaned as the homunculus put his shoulder and leg into it. Iron bolts quivvered and then screeched in agony as they pulled out of the wall. The muscles in the creature's back bunched and strained under his mottled translucent skin. The bar that held the great door closed creaked. Blood, thick and black, seeped out of the deep holes that the homunculus had gouged in the oak panels.

The bar snapped with a sharp report like an amphora dropped from a great height onto a marble floor. Khiron cried out, an animal shout, and tore the door out of the wall. With a heave, he cast it aside, crashing into a pottery statue of a long-dead king. Blue-white fire blossomed in the doorway and the homunculus staggered back, covered with licking flames and screaming soundlessly.

Maxian's face contorted into a grimace and he flared his hands out from his body, palms facing forward. The blue-white flame snuffed out, a candle plunged into deep water. Khiron collapsed to the ground, a puppet with strings suddenly cut. The Prince clenched his right fist and punched in the air at the door. The remaining panel boomed and then sheared out of the wall, sending fifteen-inch iron pins spinning across the chamber. The Valach boys ducked as the bolts flashed past. The oaken door spun away into the vast room beyond with an echoing roar and smashed into a flight of steps that occupied the far wall.

Krista picked herself up from the brick floor and shook her hair out of her eyes. Kneeling, she hurriedly rewove the braid that had come loose. The Valach boys had loped forward into the great chamber, but Gaius Julius' whistle had brought them back to heel. The Prince stood in the doorway, his arms held away from his body. Alais had moved to place the Prince between her and the room. Krista slid the long water-steel knife out of her forearm sheath for the first time. The metal gleamed in the ruddy light spilling through the doorway.

Flame roared and hissed in the great room, rushing up from two rows of pits along the walls of the chamber. Between each pit, statues of frowning men in long robes rose up to the murky roof. The men on the right-hand side were clean-shaven with high foreheads. The men on the left were scarred and ugly, their faces distorted with rage. The floor between the rows of statues gleamed with polished hexagonal tiles. The shattered door had sprayed wooden splinters and chunks of oaken panel across the space. At the far end, the entire wall was a staircase rising up to some other level, currently unseen.

The three old men who had confronted Gaius Julius on the ziggurat stood on the steps, the hot wind from the fire pits ruffling their beards. A few servants were arrayed at the base of the steps, though the scything door had pulverized two of them, leaving a bloody smear of limbs and intestines on the floor. The Prince descended the short flight of steps inside the shattered door, his own followers spreading out in an arc behind him.

Krista stepped through the door and slid to one side, vanishing into the murky shadows at the fringe of the room. While the Prince advanced slowly across the broad floor, she flitted through the space behind the statues, feeling her way through the darkness between the bands of illumination. The rumble and roar of the flames was constant, filling the entire vast room.

"We bade you leave this place." The voice of the walnut-hued man rumbled out above the hiss of the flames. "Yet you come against us with steel and claw."

Maxian stopped, looking up at the old men. In the unseen world, each was a haze of brilliant, coruscating geometric forms. Patterns flowed into almost definable shapes and then contorted again. They were strong, but he could feel their fear through the barriers and shields they had raised against him. He wondered that there were so few of them. The chambers through which they had passed to reach this place, the sanctuary of the Fire Temple of Ahura-Mazda, were rich and vast. Hundreds of priests could have labored here, not merely three.

Your brother's war drew them away, whispered his memory. *They are fighting in the north.*

The Prince smiled.

"I sent my messenger in open embassy," he replied, voice echoing from the looming figures of the statues and the unseen, distant roof. "He was refused, and rudely too. I will not be denied, for what you hold you hold as thieves, stolen from its rightful place. I would look upon the face of the Conqueror with my own eyes. You cannot gainsay me."

The shock in the three men was visible even to Krista, who had reached the end of the room. A hidden stair rose up behind the last statue and she crept up it, her hands outstretched in the dark, feeling across the dusty bricks.

The eldest man sagged for a moment, then stood forward, his shoulders stiff. "It is our charge to protect that thing of which you speak. Many have attempted to divine its secrets and all have failed. You shall fail too, but we will deny you even the attempt."

The old man struck the stones under his feet with his staff, a sharp cracking sound. The others raised their hands and a buzzing moan echoed from their mouths. Maxian felt the hidden world convulse and quake around him. The floor trembled and the fire in the pits suddenly died. The Prince raised his hands and spoke three words.

Lightning leapt from his hands, curling and snapping through the air. Alais and Gaius Julius, who had run forward to stand beside him, screamed in pain as the chain of lightning rushed over their bodies. The Valach boys screamed in panic and fear and bolted for the door. Ultraviolet fire crawled over the Prince, sparking from his eyes and open mouth. Behind him, at the doorway, the little figure of Abdmachus, forgotten since the kitchens, cried out in fear. The ring of lightning had leapt to him too, including him in the whirling arc of power.

The floor fell away as a series of great pits opened under the Prince and his two servants. Fire raged below, leaping high and sending streamers of flame high into the air. A molten pit seethed and bubbled below them. But the Prince did not fall. Blue lightning trembled in the air around him, raising the three of them up. The tiles had rotated away, leaving narrow walkways honeycombing the floor. The three old men cursed violently as the Prince and his servants alighted on the nearest one.

Maxian laughed and drew the seething power in the dead man, the animal woman, and the Persian into his heart. A wind howled into being around him, lashing his hair, and a sphere of pale-violet light sprang up. The old men raged, their ancient fingers stabbing toward him, but the torrent of flame they called forth was swallowed by the sphere or splashed away from it to fill the air with a hideous burning fog.

Krista fled up the stairs as the air behind her incandesced and was consumed. Wind blew past her in a rising shriek as the atmosphere of the great chamber was exhausted by the conflagration. At the top of the stairs there was a flimsy door of cottonwood panels that flew apart in the rising wind. She shoved the broken door aside with her shoulder and darted ahead. The room at the top of the great stairs was the temple itself, a great hexagon around a single pillar of fire that twisted and burned. Altars ringed the tracery of pure white flame. Six pillars circumscribed the room, and rich silk tapestries hung from floor to ceiling between them. The floor was slippery and she skidded to one side, fetching up against one of the altars. It was very smooth, almost slick to the touch, under her hand. She stared around in amazement.

The floor was glass, a surface as still and smooth as a forest pool. The altars were polished Minoan marble, so well cut that it seemed to be translucent. The tapestries were woven with gold and silver wire, each one depicting a shining being with golden wings. Krista ignored all of that, though later she could remember the room as she had first seen it with complete clarity.

The floor jumped and there was a vast *boom*. Krista rolled across the floor into the shelter of one of the altars. One of the old men flew past from the entrance to the greater room and struck a pillar with a bone-snapping crunch. The body slid to the floor, leaving a glistening track of dark red on the marble fluting. Another of the priests staggered back, his face bleeding from tiny cuts, the air around him flaring with shock after shock against the half-seen geometries that protected him. As Krista watched, holding her hands over her ears to try to shut out the thunder and lightning crack, the air sparkled, and a fluid twelve-sided lattice crystallized out of the air. Then the lattice broke apart, raining pale-green fragments to the floor. The priest shuddered, clutching his chest. There was a liquid popping sound and he fell bonelessly to the tiled floor.

The air around her trembled and Krista risked peeking over the top of the altar. At the top of the steps to the great room, a wall of darkness shot with flickering blue lights had sprung into being. The oldest priest skipped back from it and then turned to run. Krista rose up off the floor, her left arm arrowing out. As the priest ran past the altar, her forearm caught him across the chest with a jarring shock. His eyes widened in complete surprise as his feet flew out from under him and he slammed onto the floor. In one movement Krista was down, her knee at his throat and her right hand reversing the knife. The old priest was gobbling with fear when she rapped him hard on the side of the head with the pommel. His eyes rolled up and he went limp.

Silence suddenly filled the temple room and Krista's ears were ringing. She dragged the old man's body aside and tied him securely with cord from a pouch on her belt. Her fingers tore a strip of his robe off, and she wadded it up to gag him.

The wall of darkness cracked open soundlessly, but as it faded away, the roar of flames from the fire pits inundated the room. Maxian staggered through, his face haggard. Gaius Julius held him up, his wiry arm around the Prince. Alais stalked ahead of them, her face lit with an inner fire. Her cloak was gone, torn away in the violence of the struggle against the priests. The red-orange light of the great room outlined her, raising highlights on her legs and arms. She danced forward, her spear whirling around her.

Krista brushed her hands off and stood up.

"It's over," she shouted, over the hiss of the flames. "The last priest is here."

Maxian grinned out of a soot-stained face, then his eyes rolled up and he fell heavily against Gaius Julius' side. The old Roman eased him to the floor, the glare of the flames casting his lined face in deep relief. Alais swung the spear to a stop, pointed at the floor. She slide sideways up to Krista, who met her feral gaze with a slight smile.

"Oh, my dear," the blond woman purred, "I thought that you had fallen to your death. It's so good to see you alive."

Krista smiled back, baring her teeth, white and sharp, though not so long as Alais'. "It's good to see you too, have you fed well today? Not so feeling so . . . ancient?"

Alais snarled at the snap in Krista's voice. The spear swung up off the floor, but Krista stepped forward, inside the weapon's reach. The knife had reappeared in her hand.

"You know what the Prince wants. He won't be pleased when he finds that you've slaughtered most of the inhabitants of this place . . ."

"I know what the Prince desires," Alais shot back, her voice low and filled with a palpable chill, "and unlike you, I give it to him."

"I've no time to time to discuss your fantasy life," Krista said, her eyes glinting. "We have work to do." She pushed past the blond woman, suppressing her surprise at the corded muscle she felt under the lush flesh. The prince was on his back and Gaius Julius was chafing his wrists.

Krista squatted beside the old Roman. "What is it?" Her voice was even, but concern leaked through.

The dead man looked up, his eyes filled with fear.

"Breaking the last barrier was too much for him," Gaius Julius whispered. "He is cold, too cold . . ."

Krista frowned and took the Prince's head in her hands. He was cold, like ice. She cursed and felt for his pulse with her fingertips. "It's like the time before, when he carried too much of the power through his body. We've got to get something hot into him, some broth or soup." Krista stood, staring around in dismay. The great room was a sea of fire, cut only by the narrow honeycombs. Carrying the Prince out that way would be very dangerous. The temple room offered nothing. Her forehead creased in concentration. *The priest was running away*, she thought, *heading for something* . . . She spun around.

Alais was rising from the body of the old priest, her face flushed, her eyes glittering. There was a streak of blood on her cheek, dark and smoky against the pale cream of her flesh. Krista snarled, feeling a hot rush of rage suffuse her. She took two swift steps and her hand, stiff, lashed out, clipping the Valach woman on the ear. Alais' head snapped sideways and she skidded into the nearest altar.

"Fool!" Krista snarled. "He was the only one who knew the secrets of this place!"

Alais sprang back up, her face contorted in anger. Her long white teeth gleamed in the firelight. Krista dropped into guard, her knife dancing in the air in front of her. Alais blurred forward, quicker than any cat, curved claws snapping out from her fingers. Krista blocked right, chopping down with her hand, and stepped into the charge, her left elbow smashing into the Valach woman's face. Alais howled in agony and rolled away with the strike.

Behind them, as they circled, Gaius Julius strained to drag the Prince away, into the shadows.

Alais lunged, her claws gleaming ivory in the ruddy wine-colored light. Krista skipped back, her knife still waving in the air. She felt a pillar behind her and leapt into the air, her left leg snapping out at Alais' head. The Valach woman ducked and her claws slashed at the inside of the Roman's thigh. Krista came down out of the kick and her right hand, the knife pointed downward, caught the blow. Alais howled in pain as the steel bit at the webbing between her fingers.

Krista sprang away from the pillar at her back, hitting the ground and rolling up, facing the way she had come. Alais sidled to her left, crouching low, firelight gleaming off her sweat-slick breasts. Krista lunged in, feinting with her knife. The Valach woman danced aside and uncoiled a kick of her own. A steel-tipped heel grazed Krista's head as she whipped away. The edge of the sharp metal tangled in her hair for a moment, cutting the leather fillet that held it back.

Krista danced aside from another lunge, her hair spilling out behind her in a dark waterfall. Her foot found the top of the steps. Alais suddenly fell back and Krista advanced a step, away from the steep slope of the stairs. The Valach woman snatched up her spear from the floor. Krista felt a wash of chill fear, but she had time to snake a curved iron hook from her belt. It was attached to a length of twisted, wire-cored rope wound around her waist. Alais advanced, the spear whirling in her hand, whistling through the air.

Krista skipped back, furiously unwinding the rope from her waist. The Valach woman shrieked a hair-raising yowl and leapt ahead, the spear blurring in the gloom. Krista swayed sideways, the leaf blade cutting the air where she was. She jumped forward, whipping the iron hook out and snapping it back. Alais ducked the flying hook but screamed in pain when it buried its head in her shoulder as Krista dragged it back to her in one motion. Blood fountained and Alais roared in rage. The Valach woman snapped the spear sideways and caught Krista in the chest.

Breath exploded out of her as the ironwood shaft cracked two ribs and flung her sideways into the pillar framing the steps. Krista's head rang like a gong and her nerveless fingers dropped the knife. The wire rope was still curled around her right arm, and it tangled the Valach woman. Alais, weeping with pain, dug the hook out of the flesh under her shoulder blade. Her hand gripped the rope like iron. Krista struggled to rise, but her vision was blurred. Two, then three, blond women with bare skin slick with blood wavered before her.

Alais yanked on the rope and Krista flew toward her. The Valach woman's right hand caught the Roman girl out of the air, her talons digging into Krista's throat. The Roman gagged, feeling cartilage crunch under the incredibly strong fingers of the barbarian woman. She clawed at Alais' eyes, but the Valach held her at arm's length, feet kicking fruitlessly at the air.

Alais laughed, her voice thick with rage, watching the Roman struggle in her grasp.

Krista's fingers dug into the Valach woman's shoulder, trying to pinch a nerve, but the corded muscle was like granite under her nails, shrugging aside her pitiful efforts. There was a roaring sound in Krista's ears and darkness seeped into her vision. The barbarian woman, her pale face split with a terrible grin, receded into a tunnel of swirling gray. Krista flexed her left arm and the spring gun was in her palm. She thumbed the catch.

A six-inch iron dart suddenly sprouted from Alais' left eye in a fountain of blood. The burnished metal crackled with green fire as the spell that Maxian had placed on it so many weeks before discharged. Green light flooded out of the Valach woman, blazing in her eyes and mouth. Alais seemed to be screaming, but Krista couldn't hear her. She felt herself falling and then the marble floor embraced her with a sharp *crack*.

Gaius Julius approached the two bodies tentatively. He had dragged the Prince out of the way and had watched the remainder of the fight with a calculating eye. Krista lay sprawled on the steps, halfway down. Alais, curled into a tight ball, was at the edge of the platform. The green fire had faded, leaving her eyes hollow. The dead man knelt at her side and brushed the shriveled hair away from her face.

"Too greedy, little cat," he whispered. "Too much cream . . ."

He walked down the steps and knelt by the Roman girl. She still had a pulse, though swelling purple bruises marred the smoothness of her neck. Gaius Julius shook his head, wondering what to do. He thought of the Prince and his own fragile mortality and then stood up.

Alais was light, her body boneless and limp, as he carried her down the steps to the edge of the pit of fire. The roaring flames had been dying down since the walnut-hued man had perished. Still, the nearest pit was filled with sullen coals and a fierce heat. He raised the body over his head and then threw her forward. The blond woman plummeted down and was enveloped by the fire. Smoke billowed up in a dark cloud. Gaius Julius watched the smoke rise to the ceiling and then turned back to the living.

Behind him the fires guttered down, casting long shadows over the shattered statues. Heads peered out of the darkness, lying sideways amid a rubble of arms and stones. At the far end of the chamber, beyond the honeycombed pits, Khiron stood silently, waiting for the command of his master, holding Abdmachus by his neck. The Valach boys, cowed and whimpering, crouched behind him. The eyes of the homunculus were dark pits filled with guttering flame.

NEAR THE TOWN OF GANZAK, NORTHERN PERSIA

)•((

The cohort was sitting at the side of the road, their wagons pulled over onto a verge of stubbly brown grass. Most of the veterans slept. Zoë, Odenathus, and Dwyrin were perched on a wall made of fieldstone, their backs to the yew trees that had grown up behind the wall. Behind them a fallow field stretched off to another line of trees. Behind that the valley rose into low rounded hills capped with terraces and green bands of trees. The air was heavy with dust and it was hot in the bare shade of the yew trees. In the mountains behind them, to the north, snow was falling and the air bit like ice. Here, in the sheltered valleys of what the locals called Azerbaijan—the land of fire—it was still a warm autumn.

A troop of *clibanari* trotted past in single file, their helmets slung over their backs on leather thongs, lances drooping from slings, raising more dust. The three young mages were coated in it and had been for weeks as the army had wound its way down out of the mountains. They had heard that the armies of East and West had split into two great columns that were advancing south along the axis of the valley, each army taking care to leave nothing useful in its wake. For his part, Dwyrin had seen nothing but an endless succession of burned-out towns and looted villages.

The horsemen passed, leaving the road empty for the moment.

Dwyrin, who was twisting two soft reeds together for lack of anything better to do, looked up. He heard the swift clatter of a running horse.

"Someone . . ." he started to say to Zoë, but the rider cantered around the curve of the lane, ducking his head under low-hanging branches. ". . . is coming."

The dispatch rider slowed down, stopping his horse by the front of the resting cohort. The young man was streaked with mud and pasty with road dust. He had the riding leathers and broad-brimmed hat of an Eastern Empire courier. A long sword was tied to the side of his saddle and a quiver and bow were slung over his back with crisscrossed straps. He bent over, speaking to Colonna and Blanco. From where Dwyrin sat, he was sure that the centurion and the *ouragos* had not gotten up. The fellow on the horse did not outrank them, then.

Dwyrin went back to plaiting the reeds together. Zoë was dozing, leaning against his side, and Odenathus was flat asleep, snoring a little. The army had pushed south fast after the victory at the Kerenos River. The Persians had scattered in front of their advance, making little effort to deny the Romans the passes above Dastevan. There had been little rest for the thaumaturges, and less to do. Just march, fall down in a temporary camp, get up and march again. Two of their wagons had been lost in a stream crossing and no time had been taken to build or steal new ones. Dwyrin had been keyed up all day, unable to sleep like the others. He kept his hands busy with the reeds.

"MacDonald!" Blanco had roused himself from his nap. He waved the boy over. Dwyrin scrambled down from the rocks and jogged to the end of the line of sleeping men. The dispatch rider had dismounted and was stretching his legs, leaning against his horse. The courier was young looking, though like everyone in the army of the Two Empires, his eyes were getting older and older each day. He seemed exhausted, with deep lines of exhaustion marking his face. Blanco jerked a thick thumb toward the Hibernian as Dwyrin reached the three men.

"Here's your specialist," the centurion said. "Just put him back where you found him."

"Centurion?" Dwyrin tried to look unconcerned. Blanco lay back down, pulling the hat over his face. Colonna winked and leaned back against the wall as well. Dwyrin, without an option, turned to the courier. The young man was scratching furiously at his beard.

"Ah . . . sir?"

The courier looked Dwyrin up and down. He frowned. "You're a thaumaturge?" The courier seemed too tired to sneer.

"Yes, sir. Dwyrin MacDonald, third of the third, *Ars Magica* cohort."

"Good enough, I suppose. You're to come with me back to headquarters. Get your kit. They need an expert and I guess you're it."

The courier didn't even get Dwyrin to headquarters, wherever that was. Two miles back down the road, at a bridge over a swift stream, they met a troop of Varangians in their red cloaks and shirts of ring mail. A young Greek with a thick red beard and piercing eyes was in command. The courier handed the Hibernian off and sat down at the side of the road to watch them ride away. Dwyrin was confused, but he urged his horse forward and fell in behind the Greek officer as they took a side road off the main line of march.

Silently the troop of men cantered up into the hills along the side of the valley, passing through vineyards and orchards that had been heavy with olives and oranges. Now many were scorched and burned. The manor houses between the fields seemed empty—not even dogs yapped at them as they passed the gates. At the end of the day they came up over a hill and Dwyrin whistled silently.

A great building rose on the side of a terraced bluff. Three broad decks thrust forth from the flank of the mountain, each twice as high as a normal building. Rows of pillars bounded each floor, tall and white. In the twilight they gleamed like white candles. Vaulted roofs covered the first two floors, but the third rose to a peak and was surmounted by a great circular tower. A red glare blazed from the height of the tower, illuminating a drifting cloud of smoke that hung over the great building. Ablaze with light, it seemed eerily abandoned and quiet.

The Greek officer pulled his horse, a gorgeous red stallion, up next to Dwyrin. The man leaned close, resting his arms on the saddle horns.

"This is the Shrine of the Living Flame, young lad. It is the holy of holies for the Zoroastrian faith. Do you know of their god, Ahura-Mazda, and his prophet, the man called Zoroaster?" The Greek spoke fine Latin, with barely an accent.

Dwyrin met his eye and felt an almost physical shock. The man at his side was *someone*. Someone used to the exercise of power and a decisive nature.

"No, lord," he replied, pulling his horse around. It was shying from the stallion. "I have heard that they worship a living flame and sacrifice to it."

"Babies, no doubt," the Greek said with a wry tone, "thrown alive into a maw of iron . . ."

Dwyrin flushed and shook his head. "I have not heard that, sir. But I do not know much of their faith."

"Well, lad, this is the crux of it—that building, yonder, now held by Imperial troops—by men under my command—is the focus of their faith. Every fire temple in all this land, even in the great cities of Ctesiphon and Selucis, has a living flame drawn from this, the first flame of their faith. In that building is a fire that has never died, not since their great man, this Zoroaster, lit it to drive back the darkness and corruption of the world of woe."

Dwyrin looked back across the valley, seeing the vast size of the building, the rich gleam of the marble and woods that formed the walls and floors. Monumental reliefs and carvings decorated its surfaces. The sky continued to darken and the faint roar of the fire in the cylinder could be picked out among the sound of night birds and the muttering of the troops around him.

"Why am I here, sir? The courier said you needed an expert, but I know nothing of this god or these priests. My talent is to call fire . . ."

"Exactly," the Greek officer said. "Come, and I will show you what you must do."

A great ramp of steps rose a hundred feet from the bottom floor of the building to the entrance at the base of the cylinder on the top floor. Marble panels decorated with bas-reliefs of religious acts lined the corridor. Red-cloaked guardsmen with axes and spears stood along the stairs, holding torches to illuminate them. The Greek officer led, his long legs taking two steps at a time, and Dwyrin trotted along behind him. The man seemed tireless, though Dwyrin guessed that he had been spending long days in the saddle. At the top of the stairs, there was a great vaulted archway, leading into a long arcade that stretched off to the left and to the right.

The pillars of the arcade were carved into the semblance of flames licking up from stolid bases. The round supports at the floor were further carved with figures in torment, lashed by demonic creatures with cruel faces and men without eyes. Above, at the capitals, winged figures with beatific expressions looked down, helping the figures of men and women rise up in the draft of the fire. Dwyrin shivered. There was something odd about the air in this place. He felt a strange sense of memory crowding around him. They walked forward on floors of red-veined marble, through two more doorways, each more massive than the last, past squads of Germans and Sarmatians. The barbarians seemed nervous, and their eyes darted to the shadows as the Greek and Dwyrin passed. It was very quiet, with only the distant roar of a fire filling the air.

The hallway opened out into a vast round room, filled with a stepped platform like an amphitheater that led down to the edge of a great pit. Around the circumference, more great pillars, each thicker at the base than a tall man, rose up to support the round ceiling. That ceiling was painted with a night sky, filled with constellations and moons and planets. The stepped platforms were lined with seats, enough space for thousands to sit, facing the pit and the flame.

Behind the fire a statue rose, crouched on bended knee. Its face was the face of a dreadful king, majestic and wise. Its limbs were mighty, like the sinews of Hercules, thick with muscle. On its back it bore planets and the heavens, cast in bronze and cunningly painted. Its thews were covered with a kilt of pleated metal. Dwyrin had never seen such a gargantuan work of art.

"They worship Atlas?" His voice seemed faint and small in this place.

"No." The Greek laughed, looking aside at him, "that is Chrosoes, King of Kings. He does not lack ambition, I will warrant."

Below the figure of the godlike king, in the pit lined with black-faced obsidian, a fire roared. It was white-hot and radiant, yet it did not fill the great room with a terrible heat. Dwyrin stepped forward without thinking, to the edge of the top ring of seats. The Greek officer followed him, one hand resting lightly on the hilt of his cavalry saber. The pillar of fire did not touch the bottom of the pit; it was suspended a dozen feet above the floor. It leapt up, unquenched, fuelless, to roar in the cylindrical opening in the top of the domed room. Rings of mirrors filled the inside of the opening, reflecting the light of the eternal flame upward out of the temple. The clouds above roiled in the draft, glowing, a sight to be seen for miles and miles.

Dwyrin felt his perception peel away, and this time he did not resist. The flame filled his sight, his entire perception, everything in the universe. In his sight, it expanded to fill the room, then the world. He was suspended at the center of a whirling maelstrom of fire. A great oblate sphere filled his sight, seemingly far away. Long tendrils of fire lurched across its surface, some licking out in long, soaring arcs that sprang away from the surface of the sphere and then plunged back into the unguessably vast surface. The thing, this sphere, this universe of light, was alive. He could feel the incredibly complex pattern of forms and energies that boiled and smoked at the center of the light.

He rushed toward it. Where before he had been consumed by fear and had felt that he would be destroyed by the attenuation, by the dissolution in something so vastly greater than himself, now he accepted it. He entered the outer shell of the burning light, feeling some etheric wind rush past him. The surface of the sphere contorted, opening before him like an unfolding lotus blossom. Something bright was inside. He rushed closer.

He snapped awake, feeling a heavy hand shaking his shoulder. Dwyrin looked around, blinking dizzily. The face of the Greek officer was close to his.

"Can you make this fire die?"

"What?" Dwyrin shook his head. It was hard to hear the man; he seemed far away, his voice echoing as if he stood at the bottom of a deep well. Dwyrin realized that his ears were ringing.

"You can call fire from dead stone—I know, I was at Tauris. Can you send it back as well?"

Dwyrin stared at the man, then back at the pillar of fire, then he looked around, seeing for the first time the grim-faced guardsmen and soldiers that loitering among the pillars. He did not see a single priest. The Greek shook his shoulder again, turning Dwyrin to face him squarely.

"Can you do this thing?" The brown eyes were intent and focused. "It must be done."

Dwyrin felt a tightness in his chest. He could feel the will of the officer beating upon him, driving him to obey. At the same time, the beauty of the infinite flower called to him, singing in his mind. Here was a thing that he had long sought but had not realized he craved like water in a desert. He stared back at the officer, only peripherally aware that the German guards were edging closer, their faces bleak and terrible. The thought that such a thing as this could die, be put forth from the world, tore at his heart. *What will happen to the light?*

"Can you do this thing?" The officer had a hand on either shoulder now, his eyes fixed on Dwyrin's. "Tell me, boy. It is incredibly important."

"What will happen?" Dwyrin had trouble speaking, but he managed. "What will happen when the fire goes out?"

"Then," the officer said, straightening up, "the will of the priests of Ahura will die with it. We are a long way from home, MacDonald, in a hostile land, surrounded by enemies. Their faith, their priests, give them the will and focus to resist us. If we show that our power, our gods, are stronger than theirs, then many will bow down before us. Others will lose heart. The Emperors need every advantage that can be crushed from rock and stone. This is one. Can you kill this fire?"

No! cried part of Dwyrin's mind, grappling for control of his tongue, his voice. *This fire cannot die—must not die! Should it fail, darkness will creep across the land, unleashed from the chains that Zoroaster bound it with!*

"Yes," he said, though he blinked in surprise to hear it. Other powers crept through his mind. His left shoulder burned with a cold like rotten ice. He tried to force words, his own words, out, but they did not come. "I will kill this fire."

The Greek officer smiled, taking his hands away. The guards drifted off, talking among themselves once more. Dwyrin turned, though inside his mind he scrabbled to find some control. There was nothing he could grab hold of. His body descended the stairs, one at a time, with steady, even steps. At the bottom of the steps, a broad ring of marble tiles surrounded the edge of the pit. They were cool and slippery under his feet. He walked to the edge and raised his arms.

Before him the pillar of fire hissed and roared, twisting within the confines of the cylinder. He looked down, seeing only the flinty bricks that made the cavity and the floor. There were no logs or charcoal. The fire sprang forth from the air, burning first a brilliant blue, then this tremendous white. He looked up again, seeing the far circle of night that hovered overhead. The clouds boiled and turned over the temple.

"Fire, come to me," he said, crossing his hands on his chest. He closed his eyes.

In his self, there was a struggle. The cold surged across him, raising a chill and then a sweat on his face and arms. Another fire echoed the pillar, curling in his center, flickering at the base of his spine. Ice leached across it, killing the embers one by one. Finally there was only a pure burning point of flame settled just above his stomach.

Distantly the sound of men crying out in fear came to his ears. Wind blew against him, a fierce gust, and he felt a blow to his stomach. Dwyrin's eyes flew open in alarm. Living flame had leapt from the side of the pillar, a streamer of white-hot fire that burrowed into his chest. He staggered back, but the current did not let go. He began screaming in fear, but the fire did not consume him. The incandescent point in his diaphragm spun and whirled, drawing in the pillar. A molten stream of flame sizzled down into a great depth, all hidden in a single point. Ice raged around it, and Dwyrin lost sensation in his fingers and toes.

The pillar shrank suddenly, rushing with a great noise down into the pit. The room shook with a booming sensation and without warning there was complete darkness. Dwyrin collapsed on his hands and knees to the cold marble tiles. Frost had formed on his eyebrows and skin. He shivered uncontrollably. All through the great room, a light ashy snow fell out of the clear air. It was terribly cold. Above, on the deck at the top of the room, the Greek officer and his men clambered to their feet, stunned and horrified in the darkness.

Dwyrin curled into a ball, trying to warm his limbs. It was so cold. His body shuddered, filled with a bone-deep buzz of delight and pleasure. Dwyrin felt sick; he had never felt like this before. The snow continued to fall, carpeting the floor and the rows of seats with a pale-white coverlet. Flakes settled onto his face, dusting his long braids.

The bloom of late summer was gone now, the cold air that had been held back from the valleys curled along the stream bottoms. The Roman army marched southward in bitter cold fogs and intermittent rain. Dwyrin bent his head, feeling chilly rain patter on his straw hat. A woolen cloak hung over his shoulders, and over that a cape of raw fleece. His boots slipped in the muck of the road—the rains had begun to turn the tracks that wound south toward the Euphrates into muddy rivers. The weather reminded him of home, though he was sure that his mother was not waiting at the end of the day, in a warm firelit house with a big bowl of mutton stew thick with onions. Instead, it would be a cold camp by the side of the road and moldy bread with a bit of salt pork.

Dwyrin was last in the column of thaumaturges, even behind Colonna, so he did not notice that they had entered a village until he had passed two or three ruined houses. When he looked up, he saw that the column ahead was turning left down a lane bounded by whitewashed houses and garden fences. The windows of the houses were barren and open, with smoke stains marking the walls above them. Their roofs were gone, or only a jumble of beams with charred ends. The mud in the street was thick with soot and ash, making a black muck that stuck to everything. The Hibernian shivered in his cloak—not from the cold, which was not nearly so biting as in his homeland, but from some unseen chill that seemed to fill the spaces between the houses.

At the little crossroads, where one road started up the side of a hill to the left and the path of the army wound down to the right, heading for the bottom-lands of the river, he stopped. He heard a *ting-ting-ting* sound, like metal on stone, from the left-hand road. He looked ahead, seeing nothing but the backs of his comrades hunched under their hats, slogging down the road. The sound came again, a hammer or a pick it seemed. Rain continued to spatter out of a dark overcast sky. He hitched up his leather belt and adjusted the straps that held his bedroll and bags of sundries on his back.

Dwyrin hurried up the left-hand road, finding cobblestones under the sheet of mud that covered the path. At the top of the hill, set aside a little from the other buildings, was a solidly built square house with a peaked roof. Two dirty-white columns flanked the door, which had been broken and pushed aside. Unlike the houses on either side, it did not show signs of being burned, but then the roof was slate tiles. He paused in the doorway.

Within there was a central room, bounded by an arcade of columns. At the center, in a stepped depression, was a circular pit lined with dark stones. Dwyrin felt a chill on the back of his neck. He rubbed his arms. Weak gray light filtered in from a hole in the peaked roof. An old man, bent with great age, was sitting at the edge of the pit, striking two stones together. Below him, in the bowl of flint, there was a little pyramid of twigs and grass. Beside the pit a few lengths of wood had been gathered. In profile, Dwyrin could see that the old man had a strong, almost hooked nose and thick bushy white eyebrows. His cheeks were sunken, the skin stretched tight over the bone. His beard was long and parted into a fork.

"Are you cold, old father?" Dwyrin's voice echoed a little from the domed roof.

The old man looked up, his eyes dark in the dim light of the ruined building. "Everyone is cold, lad. The fire has gone out. See?"

Dwyrin stepped to the side of the pit, seeing that old coals still remained in the bottom in a thin layer of rainwater. The water was glassy and swirled with the shimmer of oil. The old man continued to strike one stone against the other, trying to bring a spark to the little pile of tinder. Dwyrin leaned over and slid the gear from his back. It clattered on the tiled floor.

"Let me," he said, rubbing his hands together. "I can make it go."

The old man looked up, his eyes bright under the ridge of his brow. He shook his head.

"No," he said in a gravelly voice, "this is my fire. I will take my time in lighting it."

Dwyrin sat, wrapping his arms around his knees, facing the old man. "Aren't you cold? The roof is broken, the rain . . . winter is coming."

"Yes," the old man said, nodding his head, "it will be a harsh one. Much rain, snow in the mountains. It will be difficult for all the people. But it is my fire, I need to take the proper time of it."

Dwyrin frowned. Fire was not something that took time. He saw that the old man's hands were trembling from the effort of striking the rocks together. He sat up, leaning closer.

"I've a flint . . ." he started to say, but the old man glared at him and moved to put his thin body between the pile of tinder and the Hibernian.

"This is *my* fire," the old man said, his voice even but insistent. "If you desire your own, make your own. Mine is not to be rushed or hurried. Fire will come at its own pace, in its own way. I make fire with two stones—one from the mountain of Ormazd and one from the mountain of Ahriman. In this way, the world is lighted."

The old man turned his back on Dwyrin. *Ting-ting* came the sound of the rocks. Dwyrin swallowed a curse and stood. Rain dribbled down his back from the hood of his cloak. He snarled. It would take the old man hours, or even days, to start his fire. Through the round hole in the roof, he could see the clouds lowering. They were heavy and dark—it might even snow. Ignoring the old man, he stepped to the edge of the pit and looked down into the filthy pool at the bottom.

The slick of oil was spattering out in rings as raindrops fell into it. The old dead coals were almost submerged. Dwyrin thought of the pillar of flame in the temple, now days behind. That whole valley had been dark when the Greek and his men had ridden forth. Dwyrin had not looked back, feeling ill and weak. The ancient building was pitch black, without even the light of the moon to illuminate it.

Dwyrin raised his hand, feeling power bubble up in him, rushing and quick, like a spring stream. The coals in the bottom of the pit began to hiss and the water to steam. *This is so easy*, he thought with a grin. One of the coals turned a ruddy orange and the sludge of water began to bubble and boil. Steam curled up from the surface as another coal caught, burning under the water. Raindrops spattered down, but they hissed away into more steam before they could touch the fiercely bubbling water.

"See, here is your fire for winter!"

Flames roared up, wrapped in scalding steam, and the room was suddenly hot. The water hissed away, leaving burning coals and a bright fire in the pit. Dwyrin turned, silhouetted against the flames, his face cast in red-orange relief by the hot light. He was grinning.

The old man had stood as well, his face dark as a summer thunderstorm. His eyes flashed in the firelight. "I see nothing. The way is finding the flame that is hidden and allowing it to come forth of its own volition. You are a crude boy, without restraint." The old man's voice was muted thunder.

Dwyrin stepped back, suddenly sick at the reproach and pity in the bright eyes.

"Flame that comes quickly dies quickly." The old man stepped forward and Dwyrin stumbled back over his bedroll. "A flame to light the world takes a long time to come, nutured, steady and slow, it might take years or decades or centuries. This witch-light is nothing, a passing fancy."

Dwyrin scrambled up in a dark room. The fire in the pit had guttered down to nothing, only some cracked stones and a faint hissing as more rain spattered in through the hole in the roof. A sense of terrible shame pressed at his heart. He gathered up his baggage and ran out into the street. The rain was heavier now, and the air colder. He slid down the cobblestones toward the other road.

Ting-ting came the sound, faint in the patter of the rain.

THE PALACE OF BIRDS, CTESIPHON

Despite the hour, late after the rising of the moon, the halls of the palace were filled with light. Thyatis, following an unusually ebullient Jusuf, glanced sidelong at grand colonnades of marble pillars, slim and topped with acanthus capitals. On every pillar lanterns burned brightly. The broad floors, a pale azure color, were clean swept and the walls were covered with incised murals of the victories of the kings of Persia. Thyatis was garbed in a delicate silk gown under a supple dark robe. Only her slate-gray eyes, edged with kohl, showed amid the headdress. As befitted a woman of her station, she kept a pace behind Jusuf and a step to the side.

In turn, he was gorgeously appointed in blue and green linen with a silk scarf draped around his neck. His shoes were jeweled and curled up at the pointed tips. The afternoon had been spent carefully waxing his beard and sharpening the points of his mustaches. Now he cut a dashing figure, one that was completely in place, and thus invisible, in the palace of the King of Kings. Far more demure in her dark cloak and robe, Thyatis was also invisible, though her nerves had been on edge since their carriage had been admitted to the grounds of the stupendous palace. The servant who was escorting them paused before a tall doorway with a pointed arch. He bowed to the two guards, massively built black men in leather and iron, and whispered to them.

The guardsmen, somber in a dull red and black, returned the bow and opened the door behind them. Soft music drifted out and Thyatis forced herself to remain behind Jusuf as he bowed to the room and entered in stately fashion. The servant sidled up to the Bulgar and Jusuf bent his head to listen. A bag of heavy coins was pressed into the eunuch's hand and the plump little man bowed again before closing the doors behind him as he left the room.

Thyatis balanced forward on the balls of her feet. Raw boldness had gotten them this far, and the last of their gold had bought entrance to this room, but now she fretted at the prospect of Jusuf carrying off the last of his little stratagem.

Three days before, sitting on the mud-brick wall of a second-rate caravanserai on the outskirts of the sprawling Persian capital, Thyatis had frowned at the taciturn Northerner.

"My friend," she had said, "do not take it wrongly, but as a matter of course, you are a gloomy fellow. You are brave and quick with a sword or bow—true—but you do not, as a rule, have a sunny disposition. In fact, you have the demeanor of a lemon."

Jusuf, grinning smugly, had remained before her, brown arms crossed over his broad chest. He was grinning particularly at Nikos, who was eyeing him with his usual distaste.

"Well?" Jusuf said. "Here we are, but there are no Armenians to raise up in revolt. Any good we might do to help the Emperors must come from being properly placed in the city when, at last, their armies come before the gates."

The Bulgar turned and pointed off across the roofs of the city. Thousands of whitewashed mud-brick buildings rose up on a low hill at the edge of the Tigris. Above the tenements, on a great raised platform of brick terraces, stood the palace of the King of Kings. Actually, one of three palaces. This one shone in the hot sun like a beacon, its roofs plated with gold and the delicate architecture of its towers and dome a sharp contrast to the crowed narrow streets and dark bazaars of the city.

"What better place to be, when that day comes, than within the Palace of Birds?"

Nikos coughed and made a face at the barbarian. "Thyatis has an unusual fondness for underground places, friend Jusuf, but it does not seem likely to me that the sewers of the Imperial Palace are going to be unguarded. How do you propose getting into the palace, much less at the proper time?"

Jusuf rocked from one foot to the other. His grin, if anything, grew wider. "Because, my good Roman friends, I know someone in the palace. Someone important."

The disbelief on Thyatis' face must have been obvious, for the Bulgar snickered.

"Who?" She did not believe it. There was no way this steppe-rider had a contact in the second biggest city in the world, or within the palace of an Emperor.

"You'll see," Jusuf said, still smiling that big grin. "How much gold do you have left?"

The round chamber was softly lit by tall lanterns of copper and amethyst. Deliciously thick carpets covered the floor and spilled through the doorways. No bare wall was visible, save at the edges of the doorways, for heavy tapestries and hangings covered them. Brass chains hanging from the ceiling held more lanterns and the air was touched by the sweet smell of incense. Somewhere, through one of the doorways, a lyre played, a haunting sound pitched low enough to permit quiet conversation.

Jusuf stopped and stood waiting, the richness and subtlety of the furnishings making him seem garish and clumsy in his costume. Thyatis counted doors—three—and eyed the rooms beyond. If anything, they were more gorgeously appointed than this entryway. A severe-looking dark-haired woman dressed in dull gray entered through the doorway on the left. Amid the soft luxury of the rooms, the matron's harsh figure was a shock. She frowned, her face clouding with anger when she saw them.

"You must leave," she said in a clipped voice. "My mistress is not entertaining visitors at this hour." Her voice, though thickened by anger, was naturally melodious and her Persian flawless.

Jusuf bowed, his hands at the sides of his thighs.

"Please, my lady," he said in his best Persian, his voice quietly sincere. "I come from the north and have urgent news for the Lady Shirin. I beg you, let me speak with her. My news is for her ears alone."

The woman paused, halting an incipient tirade. Her head cocked to one side. Coupled with the pile of deep black hair pinned up on her head, she reminded Thyatis of a raven eyeing a shining stone. Her eyes narrowed and she nodded. "Very well. I will convey your message and see if the lady will receive you. Wait here."

When the matron had gone, Thyatis whispered: "What news, O mysterious one?"

"You'll see," Jusuf answered, still smiling.

A moment later the matron returned, a trace of puzzlement on her face. She stood in the doorway and motioned them to enter. Once they were past, she drew closed a curtain behind them. Thyatis listened, but could hear no footsteps on the thick carpets.

"Most gracious lady," Jusuf said, bowing deeply, "we are honored by your hospitality."

Thyatis bowed as well, her eyes canvassing the room. The lyre music had stopped.

Half the chamber was walled with glass doors open to a garden of lush flowers and a sward of short-cropped grass. Paper lanterns hung in the trees, and their light reflected from an ornamental pool set among mossy stones. The delicate placement of the flowers, bushes, and rocks made Thyatis' eyes widen. The gardens around the house of the Duchess seemed poor and ill-made in comparison. This room, these chambers, the garden, all seemed to shimmer with a luxury she had never realized existed. It struck Thyatis that the lanterns, the carpets, the couches, even the goblet of wine on the side table were all the finest that could possibly be acquired.

The woman who had risen, sylphlike, from a pool of warm light and linen pillows matched the room and made it complete. She was of medium height, though her slimness made her seem taller. Gorgeous brown eyes dominated a face of perfect curves and planes. Sleek upswept eyebrows and long lashes framed them. She smiled, her graceful dark lips suggesting laughter and merriment. Wavy dark-brown hair with russet highlights cascaded over smooth olive shoulders and down her back. A rich red gown with a scoop neckline that accentuated her full breasts clung to her body. Thyatis felt a bright spark of jealousy flare in her heart, but then it faded. The woman who returned Jusuf's bow, laughing, her eyes sparkling with joy, could not be hated or reviled, only adored.

"Uncle!" She laughed, her voice husky. "I never thought to see you here, or in such a costume!" She looked upon Jusuf in amazement, and he turned slowly, arms outstretched, showing off his robes. "What could possibly have overcome you to don such frippery?"

Jusuf bowed again, beaming. "I could not come to see my favorite niece without dressing for the occasion! Besides, they would not let me into the palace dressed like a ragamuffin."

A slim-fingered brown hand covered the lady's face as she tried to stifle a laugh. She failed, but then her eyebrows rose in surprise, taking in Thyatis for the first time. The woman stepped past Jusuf and made a graceful bow to the Roman woman, a single lock of her long wavy hair falling in front of her face.

"Uncle, you are remiss! You promised to write me but you never do and now I do not know the name of your wife!"

Thyatis grunted in surprise and touched her face. She had forgotten she was veiled in traditional garb. Jusuf laughed, seeing the movement. The woman spun on her heel, little golden bells tinkling at her ankle.

"Uncle! Do not laugh at me!"

Jusuf held up his hands to ward off the spark of anger in his niece's eyes. "Wait, wait! Your mother has not married me off yet! This is a traveling companion of mine. Please . . . may I introduce you in the proper manner?"

The niece turned away, her face haughty, her arms crossed under her breasts. "I suppose."

Thyatis grimaced under her veil and tugged at the cloth. It didn't want to unwind. She bent over and untucked the tail of the scarf from her neck.

"My dear, may I present the lady Thyatis Julia Clodia of the House of Clodia?"

Thyatis threw her head back, long golden-red hair spilling out, and brushed the tangle of locks from her face. She breathed a great sigh—it was suffocating in those things. The niece's eyes widened in surprise. Thyatis grinned, her even white teeth flashing in the light of the crystal lanterns.

"Thyatis, my niece, the Princess Shirin, the junior wife of Chrosoes, King of Kings. Our host here in the Palace of Birds."

"Pleased to meet you, Princess. Nice place."

Thyatis made a sketchy bow, trying to remember what the Duchess had taught her about foreign royalty. The only thing that came to mind was Anastasia's voice saying *and stay out of their bedrooms!*

Shirin took a step backward, amazement and anger warring in her face. She placed her hands on her hips and turned to Jusuf, her brow clouded with dismay. "Dear uncle, this woman is a Roman!"

"Yes," Jusuf said with an innocent expression on his face, "so she is."

"You can't bring a Roman into the Palace of Birds! If you hadn't noticed, my husband is at war with the Empire of Rome!"

Jusuf rubbed his chin, looking thoughtful.

"Why," he said slowly, "I believe that you're right. We are at war with Persia."

Shirin, her finger raised and poised for a tirade, stopped, her mouth open. Fear crept into her expression.

"*We* are at war with Persia?"

"Yes," Jusuf said softly and took Shirin's hand, leading her back to the couch. "We left Tauris weeks ago, but the Roman Emperors and the Kagan were in accord. Even now they may be marching on this city."

Shirin sat heavily, a bleak look on her face. Thyatis looked away and wandered to the doorway to the garden. Behind her, Jusuf also sat down on the couch, holding his niece's slim little hand in both of his.

"The Emperor of the East," Jusuf said, "made an alliance with the Kagan. Ziebil brought forty thousand men into the south with him. The best forty thousand of our warriors. That is why we are here."

"Oh, Jusuf, how could Sahul do this? He promised Chrosoes peace at our wedding! How can he be allied with murderers?"

Thyatis looked around and pinned Jusuf with her gaze. "So . . . friend Jusuf, you want to explain how our missing companion fits into this?"

Jusuf met her stare but then looked away. Shirin stared at Thyatis with concern.

"Sahul is missing?" Shirin's voice was faint. "Is he dead?"

"No," said Jusuf, slumping back into the couch, "he was as hale and hearty as ever when last I saw him in Tauris." He raised a hand to ward of the explosion about to erupt from Thyatis. "Please, my lady, the Kagan asked me to say nothing to you until he saw you again himself."

"That's a pretty low trick, friend *Khazar*, to let me think he was dead for all this time!"

"I'm sorry," Jusuf said. "My brother found it relaxing, I think, to be one of your troopers for a while. He didn't want to make your task more difficult in Tauris."

"Surely!" Thyatis spat, "kings usually give the orders to centurions, not the other way around!"

"Wait!" Shirin said, holding up both of her hands, jeweled platinum bracelets tinkling. "Tell me the entire story, then the two of you can bicker like crows in a farmyard. Where did you meet and why? Then what happened?"

"And then," Thyatis finished, "your uncle got a wild hair and decided to bust into the palace and see *someone important*." She swirled the wine in her porcelain goblet and then took a long drink. Storytelling was thirsty work. The wine was a joy on her tongue, like rich velvet. Shirin, curled up around a velvet pillow with her small feet tucked under her, stirred under the quilts she had dragged out of a closet.

"You really made Sahul follow your orders," she said sleepily. "And Dahvos and Jusuf? They always ignored me when I was little. He was the worst," she muttered, pointing a long lacquered nail at her uncle, who was sitting on the floor, cross-legged, his back leaning against the end of the couch. "He picked on me all the time and put frogs in my hair."

Thyatis smiled, remembering her own brothers. "That just meant he loved you."

"Maybe." The Princess yawned. "Can I see your sword?"

Thyatis nodded and sat down next to the Princess. She had carried the blade with her into the palace, strapped to her back under the heavy robes. Now it gleamed in the lantern light as she slid it slowly out of the silk-lined sheath. The metal shimmered, the watery surface seemingly filled with glowing light. Shirin traced the patterns with her fingers, but she did not touch the surface of the blade. She fingered the leather hilt, her fingertips tracing the grooves worn by Thyatis' hand.

"It's sleeping," Shirin said, "and warm. Have you killed many men?"

Thyatis returned the blade to its sheath and tugged the leather strap over the hilt to hold it snug. She turned to the Princess, her gray eyes distant and shadowed.

"I've killed men," she said simply. "I take no joy in it."

Shirin hugged a pillow beaded with tiny pearls to her chest, peering over the top at the Roman woman. Thyatis felt a tingle in her arms and stomach when she met the Princess's eyes. They seemed bottomless, a liquid brown, swimming with vulnerability.

"Are you going to kill my husband?"

Jusuf hissed in alarm and began to rise from the floor. Thyatis waved him back down.

"Shirin," she said, "my lord, the Emperor of the West, sent me into Persia to prepare the way for his army. Your husband and my nation are at war. I am beholden to do everything I can to help win this war for my lord. But . . ."—she paused—"I am not here to murder your husband."

"What will you do, then?" Shirin's voice was even, though Thyatis thought there was a tremor of fear or panic hiding behind it.

The Roman woman shrugged her shoulders at Jusuf. "He's the one who wanted to come see you."

Jusuf levered himself off the floor and knelt by Shirin, holding her hand. "Little bug, I know you love the King of Kings, but the stories I've heard made me fear for you. I came here, and, yes, Thyatis, I came because of Shirin, not because of your mission, because I thought you might need help."

Shirin stared at her uncle and took her hand back. "My husband has not been well since Maria died." Her hand crept to her face. "He thinks that he is ugly now, scarred and disfigured by the fire."

Thyatis shook her head in puzzlement, saying: "I don't understand. What fire? Who was Maria?"

Jusuf sighed and sat back down. He looked up at Shirin, but she saw only her own fears.

"Maria was the first wife of Chrosoes," he began, "the daughter of the Emperor of the Eastern Empire, Maurice."

"A Roman!" Thyatis said slowly, remembering Galen's words in his tent at Tauris. "How . . ."

Jusuf glared at her and she shut up.

"Please," he said, "let me tell the story.

"When Chrosoes was a very young man, younger than you, his father—the great king Hormazd—was murdered by one of his generals, Bahram. Chrosoes himself was set up as a puppet king for this warlord, but in time he escaped from

Ctesiphon and fled into the north. He would have died in the wilderness, even with the help of his good friend, the Eastern lord Shahr-Baraz, but he had the good luck to stumble upon a camp of the Khazars.

"My brother was the leader of that band of men and took Chrosoes in. When he learned who the boy was, he decided that he would help him. Chrosoes and Baraz traveled with us for a winter and we took them, Sahul and I, to Constantinople. Sahul thought that Chrosoes would find safety in the court of the Emperor Maurice.

"At first, we told no one who the Persian boy was, but Sahul gained a private audience with the Emperor's son, the Prince Theodosius, and convinced him that with the Empire's aid, a grateful Chrosoes could be restored to the Persian throne. The Prince convinced his father, who became good friends with Chrosoes, and together, they overthrew Bahram."

Jusuf stopped and shook his head in sorrow. "That was a good time. We rode with Chrosoes and Sahul stood at his side when Bahram was killed in the battle outside of Dastagird. That was when Chrosoes met Shirin, in the tents of our people. The boy had already agreed to marry Maurice's daughter Maria to seal the peace between the two empires, but anyone could see that he loved Shirin from the moment he saw her."

The Princess's hand crept out of the covers and Jusuf took it in his own.

"And there *was* peace," he continued, "until Maurice and all of his children were murdered by the usurper Phocas. That turned Maria against the Empire, I think, to hear that her father and mother and all of her brothers and sisters had been hewn down and their heads paraded in the streets of the capital before cheering crowds. Even when Heraclius overthrew Phocas her mind did not change."

"It is true," Shirin said, her voice muffled by the quilts, "she urged my husband to war upon the Empire and restore the true Emperor to the throne. She had great influence over the King of Kings."

"True Emperor?" Thyatis was careful to seem puzzled.

"Her son, Kavadh-Siroes," Shirin said, "is the only remaining male descendant of the Emperor Maurice." Thyatis' eyes widened.

"He has always held me first in his heart," Shirin mused, her voice sad, "but Maria bore him a son first and was very brave, coming with him to live in a foreign land like she did. She was a strong woman."

"What happened? A fire in the palace?"

Shirin shrugged, her face a mask. "No one knows, save Chrosoes and the dark one. The Queen was furious with the lord General Baraz for not having smashed the Eastern Empire in the first year of this war. She struck upon some stratagem with the connivance of the black priest. There was a fire and the River Palace was destroyed. Chrosoes tried to pull her from the flames but it was too late. He bears the scars to this day . . . my poor husband."

Jusuf smoothed her hair back over her ear and stood up.

"It is very late," he said. "We should all sleep."

"Oh," Shirin said, "you must be tired from your journey. Please, there are couches in the other chamber. You will not be disturbed."

The Princess rose, shedding quilts and pillows. She yawned, stretching her lithe body, and bowed to Thyatis. Jusuf gathered her into his arms and held her close for a long time. Shirin put her head on his chest. Thyatis slipped out of the room into the garden. The air was soft and filled with a heady scent of blooms. The moon rode low in the western sky, but the silver light fell among the trees like dew. It was very peaceful.

The glassed-in doors of the sitting room closed with a *click* and Thyatis felt Jusuf step into the garden. She turned around and said, "You niece is very lovely, both inside and out."

"Yes." Jusuf sighed. "We all wished her nothing but happiness."

"Why did Sahul break his treaty with the King of Kings?"

Jusuf shook his head. "I don't know. Shirin always wrote to him regularly, he must have divined something from her letters. Last year he began speaking seriously with the embassies of the Eastern Empire. They gave him many presents, but he spent all of the money on armor and weapons. He feared something, but he never said what. Dahvos and I were very surprised when he declared that he would go to war against his son-in-law."

Thyatis put her hand on Jusuf's shoulder, feeling him start in surprise at the touch.

"My friend," she whispered, "when the time comes, we'll get her out."

Jusuf looked down at his feet. It was hard to tell in the darkness if he was blushing, but Thyatis was sure that he was.

Two little brown-skinned children ran past, giggling, their white tunics in disarray and splotched with grass stains. Thyatis smiled, her face shadowed by the broad-brimmed straw hat she wore to keep from burning her nose in the fierce sun. Around her a warm winter day had settled upon the gardens at the center of the Palace of the Swans like a comforting blanket. She sipped from a tall, cut-crystal glass filled with lemon juice in water. It was sweet and tart at the same time, delighting her tongue. She sat in a wooden chair at the edge of the grassy sward outside of the domed building that held Shirin's private quarters. The Princesses's children were playing with Anagathios and Nikos.

The Illyrian was hiding in the rosebushes, making growling sounds like a lion. The little girls were shrieking and jumping up and down, hiding behind their brothers, who were giggling and darting forward, daring the lion to pounce on them. Anagathios was bounding about, turning cartwheels and pretending to be afraid of the terrible beast. As Thyatis watched, a callused brown hand snaked out of the bushes and seized the unwary foot of the older of the two boys.

The boy wailed in surprise and beat furiously with his little fists on the dreadful claw. His sisters jumped up and down, yelling in delight, as the lion slowly dragged their brother to his certain doom. The other boy latched onto his brother's head and began trying to drag him back. The Prince started yelling louder as his well-meaning brother had laid hold of his ears. Anagathios became a mighty hunter and leapt into the bushes. A terrible racket began and clods of dirt and leaves flew up. Thyatis reached behind her and touched the sheath of her sword with her fingertips. It was still there. She leaned back in the chair, content to watch the flight of sparrows above the domes of the palace.

Something moving at the edge of her vision drew her attention. Shirin was descending a flight of steps that led down into the garden from the balconies on the second floor of the palace. The Princess moved slowly, one hand on the marble railing. She was dressed in a deeply cut pale-yellow silk gown, long and sheer—almost transparent—with a flocked bottom. Her hair had been done up into a sweeping cloud, shot with golden pins and sparkling amber threads, leaving her long neck bare. Thyatis got up, leaving the glass on the ground, but swinging the sword over her shoulder. She too had changed clothes, adopting a loose blouse of fine white Egyptian cotton and baggy forest-green Armenian pantaloons. Her feet were bare. The children continued to rumpus behind her, scaring a flight of white doves out of the fruit trees.

Shirin had stopped at the bottom of the stairs in a patch of shade. The Princess leaned against the carved wall, her fine olive hand laid against the shoulder of a bearded archer in shown in silhouette. Thyatis joined her, setting her back to the granite panel. It was cool in the shade. Shirin looked pale and worried.

"What is it?" Thyatis said, her voice soft. The Princess shook her head, though her hands were trembling slightly. Thyatis caught her left hand and turned the Princess to face her. Shirin would not look up. This close, Thyatis could smell her subtle cinnamon perfume.

"Some news of the war?"

Shirin nodded, her hand clenching Thyatis' tightly. She covered her face with the other.

"Bad?"

"There was a great battle in the north." Shirin could barely speak. "The army of the King of Kings was destroyed. All of the captains of the army were slain or captured by the Romans. Even the Boar was killed, or so the messenger said."

Thyatis flinched as the Princess collapsed into her arms, fighting tears. She gingerly put her arms around the crying woman. The Duchess had left this part out of her training.

"The . . . the King of Kings has heard that Khazars rode with the Roman army against Persia. I . . ." The princess stopped, unable to continue. Thyatis held her close, relaxing enough herself to allow Shirin to slump against her. The Princess was solid and warm. It felt odd, holding another woman this way. Thyatis wrapped her arms around Shirin, holding her close. "I have been placed under guard. I cannot leave the palace without my husband's permission."

Thyatis tipped Shirin's head back with a finger under her chin. Tears had ruined the artful makeup around her eyes. Thyatis smiled crookedly and wiped the worst smear away with her sleeve.

"Then, Princess, we will have to spirit you away."

"How can he love me yet not trust me? My children and I are prisoners! We will be hostages against my father . . . why did he do this?"

Thyatis stared at the Princess, trying to decipher which *he* she was angry with.

"Shirin. Shirin!" Thyatis waited until the Princess had focused on her.

"My lady," she said in a clear, even, voice, "abide by the wishes of your husband. When the time is right, my men and I will get you and your children out of the city, safe and sound. But for now, be at peace with your husband. If he suspects you, or suspects that we are here, it will be impossible."

Shirin seemed at last to take notice of what Thyatis was saying and gave her head a little shake. Her eyes cleared and she stood away from Thyatis, wiping her eyes. Her hands lingered on Thyatis' forearms. "Yes, you're right."

Shirin turned and looked into the garden. Nikos was rolling around on the ground with four small laughing figures swarming over him, tickling him. Laughter pealed to the heavens.

"My children will be safe. Thank you, Thyatis."

The Roman woman leaned back against the cool stone, biting her lip. *That was clever. Now what?* She wondered. *Four noisy kids, all of us, plus the Princess and probably a gang of servants in tow as well . . . I should have kept the circus wagon.*

"So," Nikos said in a slow drawl, "our original mission was to whack or bag this boy Prince—Kavadh—but now, in midstream, you want to change horses." He made a wry face and stared at Thyatis. She shrugged, sitting in the cool gloom under the trees in the back of the garden. Her back was to a mossy wall of old stones. Little yellow flowers grew out of the cracks.

"You can see what the Princess means to Jusuf. You heard the same news I did. The King of Kings made his big throw, and it failed. Now the two Emperors are moving south at all speed. Within a month they'll be here and then things will get ugly."

Nikos nodded, but he did not let go of his point either. "Centurion—I think the heat is getting to you. Our *mission* is to bag the kid. Jusuf has done us a hell of a favor, getting us in here on his niece's word, but she is not the *mission*."

"Nikos." Thyatis sat up a little straighter, her hands cupping her left knee. The other leg was out straight in front of her. "Jusuf is our friend. He has stood with us in dark places. We are Shirin's guests here. We owe them assistance."

Nikos was still frowning; he did not like changes like this. They just made more trouble later. Maybe a lot of trouble. Still, his commander seemed set, and there was something about the tightness of her lips that said she had already made up her mind.

"Centurion," he said formally, "are you changing the mission?"

Thyatis sighed and scratched the side of her nose.

"Yes," she said softly, "I am changing the mission. Now the mission is to spirit the Princess Shirin and her children and ourselves out of the palace at the soonest opportunity."

"All right," Nikos nodded, his sense of decorum satisfied. "Good by me."

Thyatis shook her head. Some days the Illyrian gave her a headache.

"The first thing we have to do," she said, "is get the other Khazars into the palace. We need more hands for this, particularly those snaggle-toothed ruffians."

· · · ·

"I will go," said Jusuf, his grim expression clamped back on his long face. He, Thyatis, and Nikos were sitting in the small room that Shirin had given the Roman woman for her own. By the standards of the palace, it was small and cramped, which meant that it was big enough for an entire *lochaghai* of legionnaires to camp in and only featured one window. The window, however, looked out over a rooftop with no view of any kind, which was why Thyatis had gladly accepted it. Too, it was tucked away at the end of the hallway.

The Khazar Prince refused to sit and was pacing restlessly on the tiled floor. Nikos was sitting on the bed, his back against the wall, eating a pomegranate. Thyatis glared at him and the Illyrian stopped spitting the little pits behind the headboard. Thyatis looked up at the Khazar as he passed her again. She had taken the lone chair and was sharpening and oiling one of her daggers.

"And if you get caught?" she asked. "Everyone in the palace will know that you were plotting to get your niece out and she *and* the children will wind up in the pits under the palace."

Nikos spit, the seed sailing through the open window.

"No pits," he said with a finger in his mouth to dig out another seed from between his teeth. "They put 'em in a tower over by the river—they call it the Tower of Darkness—'cause once you go in, you never see the sun again. Grim-looking place, all dark stone and funny-looking stains."

"Then who?" Jusuf snapped, turning back to face Thyatis. "You? *Him?* The same problem applies—if they question the servants, then they'll know that we're the guests of the Princess. We're safe here only while no one knows we're here!"

Thyatis smiled, her best shark-grin. "Silly boy. Of course not. We send an expert."

Nikos looked up, his face pinched in surprise. He had expected to take care of it.

"I'll send Anagathios. He came into the palace dressed as a woman, so no one will be able to match him up with us, and they can't really make him talk, can they?"

"An actor!" Jusuf fairly spit he was so angry. "You'll send an actor to do a man's job? This is ludicrous."

Thyatis stood up, the long knife glittering naked in her hand. The look on her face brought Jusuf up short. "Listen, *Prince*, we do this kind of thing for a living, so why don't you just let us carry on? And another thing, Anagathios is twice the man either of you are, and I should know. So until you can perform as well as he can, stay off the stage!"

Jusuf stepped back from the snap in her voice and the angry gleam in her eye. He raised his hands in surrender. "Pax! Enough, you want to send the pretty boy, send him. I'll tell Shirin what we're about."

"No," Thyatis said in a flat voice. "No one knows but the three of us."

"Hey," Nikos said, sitting up from the bed. "Anagathios is twice the man either of us is?"

"At least," Thyatis said primly. There was a wicked gleam in her eye. Nikos held his thumbs up and looked at them, whistling. Jusuf stared from him to Thyatis and back again.

"What?" He sounded petulant.

Thyatis just laughed.

"You wanted to see me, Princess?"

Shirin looked up and smiled to see Thyatis at the door of her sewing room. The Princess put aside a piece of lace she had been working on and beckoned for the Roman woman to enter. Thyatis sat down on the end of the couch and clasped her hands in front of her.

"Yes. The Lord Zarmihr came to the city yesterday when I was summoned to the presence of the King of Kings. I had never met this lord before; he is from the far eastern provinces of Tokharistan. He had been upon the field of Kerenos in the north, where the army gathered by Gundarnasp was broken by the Two Emperors."

Thyatis perked up, her whole attention focusing on the princess. Shirin seemed oddly at peace, her features calm and her voice light.

"This was the first witness of the battle to reach the capital. He had ridden very hard, killing many horses. It was as had been rumored. The Boar was laid low and his standard captured. All of the great lords and captains were killed or taken by the enemy. Of the two hundred thousand men who marched north, only a few thousands escaped to the south. Gundarnasp fell, as did the Lord Rhazames and many others known to me."

"And the Roman army?" Thyatis held her breath.

"Messengers came too from Nineveh in the north, on the Tigris. The Romans are only a few weeks away. They must have marched swiftly to reach the warm lands before winter closed the passes in the north. The governor of Nineveh has ordered the bridges over the rivers and canals destroyed."

Shirin paused, staring at Thyatis with that same calm look.

"What else?" Thyatis asked, disturbed by the equanimity of the princess.

"No Khazars have come south with the Roman army. Zarmihr saw that many barbarians were in the army of the two Emperors but did not know their banners. The King of Kings questioned him closely as to the presence of my kinsmen, but Zarmihr saw none of them."

Thyatis pursed her lips and considered the Princess, who looked down, her face lit from within by a smile, and resumed stitching. "You are free to leave the palace again?"

"No," Shirin said, looking up briefly, her lips in a moue, "but soon I will be. My husband will soon be at ease. The magistrates and lords who whisper to him will have nothing to say. My children will be safe."

"You see no reason," Thyatis said slowly, considering her words carefully, "to leave the palace in secret, with your uncle and me?"

"Oh, no," the Princess said. "Within the month things will as usual again."

The Roman woman rubbed her nose, thinking, then rose. "My lady, this is excellent news. I will tell your uncle and we will make preparations to take our leave. I am sorry you had a fright."

"Oh"—Shirin laughed—"it's nothing! In a few days you'll be able to leave peacefully."

"Talk to me," Thyatis said, her voice clipped, once more mewed up in her room with Nikos, Jusuf, and Anagathios. "What are the servants and slaves saying?"

Nikos frowned, his broad face grim. He exchanged looks with Anagathios. "It is very bad. 'Gathios saw three of the lesser nobles leave today with their families. Those were the smart ones. More will be slipping out tonight. The word in the baths is that the King of Kings has slipped right over the edge. He declared that this disaster at the Kerenos is only a minor setback. He collared two of the remaining big hats here and sent them off to raise a new army from the citizens of the polis. He wants a hundred thousand men."

Jusuf snorted, shaking his head. "If *two hundred thousand* men were slaughtered up north, there aren't another hundred thousand fighting men in the whole empire. What is this King of nothing going to do, arm the slaves?"

Nikos' face settled into grimmer lines. "Women and children is what I heard. Kitchen knives and sharpened poles. Whatever they can find in the city. Old men too, I'd imagine."

"Will they do it?" Thyatis said, her fingers twitching on the hilt of her sword. "Are they afraid enough of Chrosoes to drive the citizens out into the fields to face Galen?"

Jusuf laughed at her, but his voice was trembling.

"Nikos, are the palace guards and city watch enough to do that?"

The Illyrian met her eyes and shook his head. "No, there are only a handful of guardsmen left—maybe a hundred—and the city watch isn't going to drive their families out onto the swords of the legions. Besides"—and he smiled a little, his lip curling up—"the two nobles set to this task have already bolted. They left everything behind, concubines and all, and shot out of the city like a stone from a mangonel."

"Good." Thyatis stared out the window, her eyes distant. "I promised Shirin I would not kill her husband." She turned to the Syrian. *Anagathios,* she signed, *are you sure about this water gate in your hidden garden?*

The actor shrugged, his hands languid as doves in the close air of her room. *You didn't ask the Princess?* he replied.

No, I was going to ask her today, but now we'll have to do it without her help.

Then I cannot say for sure. It seems that the garden is part of the King of Kings personal quarters and the lower gate must lead down to the water side. But without getting a boat and checking the bank, I cannot say.

Thyatis punched her thigh in frustration. Jusuf and Nikos, who had only caught a little of the quick conversation, watched her in concern.

"Everything is a bad bet." She snarled. "So we go for the Venus throw. Nikos, get everything and everyone ready—quietly—for a quick exit. Jusuf, you have to stick to Shirin like glue. When things finally come loose around here it's going to be very ugly. We don't want to lose her or the children in the confusion. 'Gathios—you've got to find a better way into that garden. I don't think Shirin is going to be able to climb down a drain like the rest of us."

She stood up. The three men nodded. "Good, get to it."

After they were gone, she stood at the window, clicking the sword in and out of its sheath. The sky was turning dusky purple. The rooftops were already steeped in darkness. She sighed, rubbing her nose. *Sahul, why didn't you come south? What happened in the north?*

THE DAMASCUS GATE, PALMYRA

The midmorning air trembled with a booming shock. Dust rose in a great pillar over the rooftops of the city. The sky was very blue, almost pure undiluted color, scrubbed clean of any clouds or impurities. The dust rose up, a bone-colored smear against the deep blue. Mohammed turned from the doorway, his face graven with weariness. His eyes were old in a still-young face. The *kaffieh* that was wound around his head and trailed over his shoulder was dirty and spotted with old blood. His breastplate was scored and marked with dozens of tiny dimples where spears, swords, arrows had been turned aside by the stout metal. His hands were marked with many cuts and stiff bandages were tied between his fingers. Still, his right hand rode easily on the pommel of a well-used saber.

"My Queen," he said to the darkened room, "I must go to the gate. The Persians will come again in strength."

"Is this the last day?" came a murmur from the darkness. There was a slithering sound as silk sheets rustled and fell away. In the dim light, the Southerner could see a pale blur rise up and slowly swim into focus as it came toward him. He bowed and took the hand of the woman.

"It may be," he said, his voice gravelly with the strain of a hundred days of shouting commands. "There is something in the air . . . perhaps the wizard will show himself. If he does, then the gate will fail and the Persian will walk the streets of the city."

Zenobia squeezed his hand, her long fingers firm.

"I shall command the people of the city to retire to the palace," she said. "If the gate falls, then we will fight on here. Mohammed . . ."

He released her hand. Her shift was plain soft cotton, falling to her ankles, and her hair was loose and uncombed, a tangled cloud around her neck and shoulders.

The Southerner raised a hand, his fingers to her lips. "Say nothing, my lady. I choose to stand with my friends. I do not regret it, though it grieves me to see that your dream has died. I was lost for many years. In this struggle I have found purpose, short-lived though it may be, and I am well pleased for it."

The Queen smiled, her eyes sparkling in the dim light. The press of events had finally stirred her from the deathwatch that had possessed her for so long.

"I will be at your back, then, Al'Quraysh."

There was the echo of another boom, louder than the first.

"Go, your purpose is getting impatient."

He bowed again and strode out, his boots clicking on the polished tiles.

When he was gone, Zenobia returned to the bed and crawled across its expanse. Her fingers traced the forehead, sharp nose, and lips of the man lying in it. She bent close and kissed him, though he did not move. She felt only a faint breath on her cheek, but it was enough to know that he was alive.

"Well, my love, sleep in peace. I have duty to attend to."

Zenobia stood up, feeling the leather strapping of the bed give under her weight, and pulled the slip off over her head. She stepped lightly off the bed and ran a hand through her hair. It was a mess and she frowned at the tangles caught in her fingers.

Silly, she thought to herself, *it doesn't matter if my hair is combed and brushed for death.*

But then she paused and turned the silver mirror on her wardrobe toward her. *No*, she thought, *today it does matter.* She rang a small glass bell, summoning her servants to draw her bath and dress her.

Mohammed looked out over the plain before the city. It seethed like an enormous anthill with men and horses and engines of war. The Persians had been coming down out of the hills since the dawn had broken, long lines of spearmen hurrying down the road. Horsemen thundered past, their lances glittering like stars. Four more great siege towers had been raised up and now they crouched a hundred yards from the wall. Stone-throwers couched behind battlements of rocks and raised earth lay behind them. As Mohammed watched, the one nearest the gate released, sending a boulder the size of a small man flying into the air.

" 'ware!" echoed in a shout down the line of the battlement. Men ducked their heads below the merlons. The stone hissed through the air and struck the pinnacle of the left tower at the gate. Stone splintered violently on stone and shards of rock sprayed on the men crouched below. The gate tower stood unmoved, though another pale scar had been gouged from the sandstone facing.

Mohammed stood again, his hand shading his eyes. Hundreds of Persian archers in light armor and quivers full of arrows were running forward toward the gate. Among them, men jogged under the weight of mantlets woven from reeds gathered from the stream that fell away east of the city and leather cured from their own horses. All along the front of the enemy army, regiments and battalions were forming up. Men jostled to raise ladders to their shoulders. Arrows began to fly up from the advancing ranks, a dark cloud of angry birds.

"This is it," Mohammed said to his commanders, stepping back from the fighting slit. "He has come out."

Away, across the plain, behind the engines and the tens of thousands of men, a black wagon drawn by ten black horses had appeared on the road. A solid wall of knights in heavy armor surrounded it. Their banners were dark, long fluttering pennons in the shape of serpents with scarlet scales. Around it, the marching men of the Persian army shied away, leaving a great clear space. Mohammed blinked— the air seemed to twist and shimmer over the distant image.

"Ten serpents . . ." he muttered, pursing his lips in thought. He shook his head, unable to dredge up the memory.

"To arms!" Mohammed shouted, his voice ringing out over the battlements and the shattered buildings behind the wall. Metal rang on stone as the Palmyrenes rushed to the wall. The Southerner looked out over them, a ragged line of men in battered armor and scarred faces. Too few of them were soldiers; most were the men of the city forced to defend their homes. Many had never held a spear or hacked at another man with a sword before these days. Now they were blooded veterans, forged hard in this hellish place. Mohammed turned back to the wall. Arrows rained out of the sky, clattering on the stones. He pressed himself close to the dun-colored brickwork.

Men along the battlement popped up, loosed their arrows into the running mass of Persians heading for the wall, and then ducked back down again. Mohammed drew his saber and checked the edge for chips or cracks. Shouting rose from below the wall. Another great stone caromed off the nearest tower and bounced down onto the wall. Mohammed turned his head and cowered behind his shield. The stone plowed into a knot of men, bakers by the signs they had painted on their shields, and smashed them into a bloody dough of splintered bones and crushed intestine. Arrows fell like rain.

The ladders hit the wall, a long rippling rattle of wood on stone. Mohammed sprang up and raised his saber.

"Up! Up!" he screamed. "To the walls!"

The two Tanukh who shadowed the general stabbed out with their spears, pushing at the slats of the nearest ladder. One spear caught and the man put his shoulder into it. The ladder slid sideways and then suddenly toppled over. Screams and yells of anger filled the air. Mohammed ran back up onto the fighting platform that jutted from the side of the tower. Hundreds of ladders had gone up along the wall and the men of the city were furiously engaged, shoving them back. The city archers fired down into the masses of men swarming at the base of the wall, their arrows punching down into upturned faces. Another stone sailed over the wall and crashed through the tile roof of a building across the street. Fire gouted up from the ragged hole.

The sky above was serene and blue, clear as a high mountain lake.

Zenobia stepped out onto the broad brick platform that was raised before the vast bulk of the palace. The gates were swung wide and a constant stream of women, children, and old men poured up the ramp and into the precincts of the royal family. She walked out onto one of the buttresses that held the great winged lions, her left hand on the muzzle of the beast. Her attendants had repaired her golden armor and polished her silver helm to a brilliant sheen. She had added a long cape of purple with a gold trim as well. The wings that swept back from her face gleamed in the sun. It was heavy on her head and a trail of sweat trickled down the side of her cheek.

The people pushing past below in the gate looked up at her and smiled, though their faces were haunted by the long siege. Many raised their hands to her, seeking her blessing. She smiled down upon them. There was little she could do now, though the sight of her brave figure might give them hope for the hours that remained. She felt cold inside, shaky with apprehension.

The lion trembled under her hand and a moment later the air shook with the sound of a deafening crash. Zenobia's head snapped around and across the city. At the distant embattled gate she caught sight of a vast towering shape out of the corner of her eye, something wreathed in smoke and flame, looming over the towers. Titanic wings unfurled and Zenobia reeled, gripped by a terrible nausea. The sun seemed to dim and the earth grew silent. The shape struck downward and there was a tremendous booming sound. It struck again and towers and stone cracked. It struck a third time and the gate towers crumbled in a huge gout of dust and smoke. The tower to the right side of the gate split down the side and tilted over. Hundreds of tons of sandstone and concrete crumbled down into the street. The thing moved in the smoke and fire roared up. A nightmare head was thrown back in howl of victory and Zenobia fell to her knees, her heart thudding like a dove.

Across the width of plaza, men and women threw themselves to the ground, shrieking in fear. The darkness on the sun choked the sky. Zenobia struggled to rise, her mouth twisted in a feral scream of rage and defiance. The thing at the gate stomped forward, its mammoth shoulder brushing against the second tower. The stone crumbled and cracked, sending screaming men flying from the platform. Zenobia staggered to her knees and raised the sword of her father up. Her mouth struggled to cry out, but the air was chill and cold and no sound escaped her lips.

"Enough," rang out from behind her. "This is a world of men, not of demons."

The thing at the gate seemed to grow, towering over the city, its serpentine legs smashing buildings to ruin. A red mouth whirled open, filling the streets with a howling hot wind. Fires sprang up in the dry buildings. A roar shattered the air, driving all thought and consciousness from men.

Zenobia turned her head, a Herculean effort, for fear and despair beat down upon her like the blows of a blacksmith's hammer. Ahmet stood in the gateway, leaning on a staff of pale wood, his scarred body barely covered by a clean cotton robe. White fire ringed him, a shuddering corona of a thousand rays. She cried out in pain at the light that shone from him.

"Azi Dahak, I name you, dark power of witchcraft and lies." His voice rang like thunder.

The thing at the gate convulsed, steams and smokes billowing from it. A tentacular claw lashed out, sending a jagged bolt of flame licking across the length of the city. Ahmet raised his hand. The flame sputtered and died, falling into the streets as pale white smoke.

"Azi Dahak, the ten serpents, I name you." The sun flared, a white nimbus, and shadows fell upon the ground in opposing directions.

"Azi Dahak, I bind you in the name of the Binder. I compel you in the name of the God that Died and has Risen with the Sun." Zenobia, her ears ringing with a tremendous noise, fell back to the ground, nerveless and without thought. The whole universe around her seemed only to be the ragged voice of Ahmet, shouting against a gale of wind.

The thing that towered over the city reached down and dust spouted up as its claws dug into the earth, tearing aside brick and mortar and concrete like dry grass. Ahmet staggered forward to the top of the ramp. He made a sign in the air, something that flickered and changed and hung in the wind like a glowing star.

"Azi Dahak, in the name of the Lord of Light, the maker of the world, begone!"

Wind rose in a gale, tearing at the clothing of the people lying senseless within the palace grounds. Bricks and tile sheared off the roofs of buildings and flew toward the thing. A whirling storm of wind hissed up off the deserted streets and abandoned gardens. Timbers, wagons, the bodies of men, entire roofs of tile and slate, leapt into the air. The vortex hammered at the thing, raging with fire and crackling with lightning. It shrank, clawing at the air around it, tumbling palaces and temples. The columns that lined the great avenue tore from the earth and arrowed into the heart of the creature. Marble and agate burst into flames and were devoured by the shape. The sun expanded, filling the whole sky. Men screamed and tore at their faces, feeling their skin dissolve and burn away.

An enormous clap of thunder shocked the city, breaking statues of long-dead kings into a thousand shards, shivering goblets and amphorae into dust. The thing that raged against the whirlwind folded in upon itself and then, with a hot spark of black light, vanished.

Silence fell upon the city. The wind died. The sun stood forth in the blue vault of heaven, a solitary disk. Dust fell in a fine rain from the sky, covering everything with a mourners' pall.

Zenobia crawled from under the rubble of the winged lion. A great stone wing had fallen over her, shielding her from the flying debris. The lion's head was gone, torn clean off. The other lion was scattered across the courtyard. Ahmet lay in the threshold of the gate, his tattered robe wrapped around his loins. She touched his face.

It was as cold as any stone. Trembling fingers pressed against his neck, but there was nothing. Tears fell, sparkling like dew on his haggard, dead face. The Queen of the city wept.

The General Khadames raised his head up, shaking broken roofing tiles from his helmet. Around him, before the gate of the city, thirty thousand men were stirring, amazed that they were alive. They rose, by ones and twos, covered with fine white dust, ghosts in a desolate world. Khadames stood and ran his gloved hands over his body. He was stunned to be alive, much less whole. He looked around, blinking his eyes to clear the grit from them.

The ladders had been torn from the walls, leaving hundreds of men writhing on the ground injured or dead. The siege towers were only lonesome great wheels leaning against timbers torn in half like straws. Acres were covered with horses lying dead on the ground, their riders missing or crawling away, crying out in horror.

The gate of the city was gone. One tower had been smashed down into a great ash heap, while the other leaned drunkenly, its top half torn away. The massive doors themselves were nowhere to be seen. An empty street, lined with broken columns like the stumps of teeth, could be seen through the ruin. Men stirred in the rubble or wandered in the avenue, dazed and mindless.

Khadames cleared his throat, but then paused and looked around him in sudden fear.

The black wagon had slid off the road, a hundred feet behind him. The black horses were scattered about it, dead, their corpses withered and desiccated. The host of knights who had surrounded it in such terrible panoply lay in rows, their arms and legs a jumble of cracked and broken limbs. Khadames breathed a short prayer, but it stuck in his throat.

A dark figure moved in the field of the dead. Cowled in sable, limping, one bony hand clutching a staff of ivory bone, his master came toward him. Cold dread crawled out from that figure, pooling in the hollows of the ground and lapping around Khadames' boots with an icy touch. One of the knights twitched, moaning, hand scrabbling at the earth. The dark figure bent over it, ragged robes masking the boy who lay on the ground.

There was a soundless cry. The dark figure straightened, filled with momentary strength. It strode toward Khadames. He fell to one knee as it approached, his fist wrapped tight around the hilt of his sword.

"The way is open," a voice hissed out of the black cowl. "We enter the city."

Khadames nodded but did not look up until the dark figure had passed him.

"Take him away," Zenobia shouted, her face streaked with tears. "Hide him in the cellars, someplace no one knows. Quickly!" Her handmaidens gasped at the weight of the dead man and raised him up upon their shoulders. The Queen clapped her hands sharply and they staggered off at almost a run. Soldiers were trickling up the ramp from the ruin of the city. One of the Tanukh, a crude bandage wrapped around his head, hobbled up.

"O Queen, the Persians have entered the city. There are thousands of them and few of us."

Zenobia nodded, looking around quickly. Scarcely a hundred men had managed to reach the palace. A few more were running down the avenue. The long lines of columns had fallen, or their arches had collapsed. The Queen surveyed the wreckage of her proud city with dry eyes. She had no more tears to shed.

"Any man with a bow to the wall, you others close the gates. You, Tanukh man, did the Lord Al'Quraysh survive the battle at the gate?"

The Tanukh shook his head slowly, bowing it in sorrow. "No, O Queen, I did not see him. Everyone on the wall or in the towers is dead."

"It is enough that he died bravely," Zenobia said, her eyes glittering like steel. Her saber rasped from its sheath. The blade was still true.

"Begin building a wall," she called out to the men who had ground the gate closed. "Here, at the top of the ramp. You and you, run back into the palace and find oil and wood, anything that will burn."

She walked to the top of the ramp and planted her feet, legs wide. The saber gleamed in her hands. She said nothing, waiting, while the few men still at her command rushed to build a wall of fallen stones, bodies, anything that they could find. The Queen's face was cold and filled with hate.

In the avenue of the city, armored men advanced under a dark banner bearing a wheel of ten interlocking serpents. They made no sound, staring around them in horror at the devastation.

THE HOUSE OF THE WHITE SWAN,
PALACE OF BIRDS, CTESIPHON

"My lady?" Princess Shirin looked up from her harp at the sound.

Ara, the dark-haired woman who had come to meet Jusuf and Thyatis their first night in the palace, stood at the door of the music room. As before, she was clad in subdued colors and her face was grave. Thyatis, who had been lying on her stomach on the floor, rolled over to look at her. Shirin put the harp away and folded her hands on her lap. Late-afternoon sun gleamed through the glass windows, painting her profile and the light silk gown she wore with rich golden colors.

"What is it, Ara?"

The lady bowed, motioning to the outer rooms of the house. "It is the Prince Kavadh-Siroes, my lady, he wishes to speak with you. He seems . . ." The lady in waiting paused, her dark eyes flitting to Thyatis, recumbent on the floor, then back to her mistress. ". . . he seems agitated."

Shirin frowned and put the harp back into its waxed leather case. "Send him in, then, but wait just a moment."

Thyatis rolled up onto her feet. She was wearing a pair of dark-amber silk pants—a gift from Shirin—and a deep forest-green shirt. A sash of muted red the color of old wine was bound around her trim waist. She grinned broadly at the Princess, drawing a glimmer of a smile in return.

"Thank you for the song, my lady. I will make myself entirely invisible."

Thyatis bowed to the Princess and scooped up her sword, which had been placed at the side of the couch Shirin had been sitting cross-legged on. The Princess thought it amusing that the Roman woman took her blade wherever she went. Thyatis became nervous if she couldn't touch it at any time. On bare feet, she padded out of the room, drawing a heavy linen drape closed behind her. The tip of her scabbard made a tiny *tinging* noise on the marble floor as she went. In the other corridor, through a screen of carved wood intertwined with flowers, she could hear the sound of Ara's voice and a thin masculine tone. *The Prince*, she supposed.

Thyatis waited at the end of the corridor, her back pressed to the wall in a niche once reserved for a large urn. A few moments later Ara walked past, her face set and serene. Behind her back, Thyatis glided back down the corridor, completely silent, holding the scabbard at the hilts behind her back, out of the way.

"Beloved aunt." The tension in Kavadh-Siroes' voice was marked, even muffled a little by the drapes.

"Nephew, welcome. Please sit and take refreshment with me. There are light cakes and a sherbet." A plate tinkled against glass.

Shirin sounded languid and at ease, comfortable with the affairs of the day. Thyatis eased the edge of the drape aside, gaining a thin wedge of visibility into the room. Shirin remained on the couch, though now she lay along the length of it and she had draped a shawl of tiny knots around her bare shoulders, covering her breast. The Prince was dressed in dark silk, almost black, but with a rich brown highlight. His long hair was in disarray, and he kept trying to push it back behind his head. Thyatis raised an eyebrow—being mewed up in the House of Swans did not allow any of them to mingle with the nobility of the palace. This was the first time that she had laid eyes on the heir to the Peacock Throne.

He was handsome, his features strong, with clean lines to his face and body. A high brow promised a quick wit or lively intelligence. His dark eyes were edged with a little kohl, just enough to bring them out. In all, a very pretty young man. The commanding expression that doubtless marked his father was absent, though, replaced by sick worry and bags under his eyes that no makeup could disguise. A scared young man.

"Aunt, I know that you love my father truly—and have been as a second mother to me since the death of the Empress. I could not ask for more of you, not in good conscience. But I am driven and I must ask—you, who see him most, please, I beg a question."

"Of course," Shirin said, her voice questioning. "What is it? Pray, ask and I will answer."

The Prince bit at his knuckle, looking around the room. Thyatis became very still, but she judged that the boy was so agitated that a cohort of legionnaires could have been standing against the walls and he would not have noticed. "Please, do not take this amiss—I mean no ill will by it—but doubts plague me, keeping me from sleep. I must know . . . is my father insane?"

A shadow passed over Shirin's face. Her folded hands trembled.

"I . . . I do not know, Kavadh. Like you, he has sent me away. He stays in his own chambers now and does not summon me to them. Like you, I am worried. The palace is filled with rumors and strange stories. When did you last see my husband?"

Kavadh bowed his head, staring at the floor. "A week or more . . . he had summoned his advisors to him to discuss the matter of the Romans." Behind the drape, Thyatis' ears perked up.

"Only a few of us were there, not even half of all those he demanded. At first he was in a rage—then he suddenly calmed down and greeted each man with a glad smile. I was in the back of the room, hiding from him, but even I he welcomed as a guest. I saw his eyes through the holes in the mask—they were calm, but his voice was strange."

Kavadh sighed and picked at the gold laces of his high riding boots.

"He asked if the great Prince Shahin had returned from the conquest of Egypt yet. No one could answer him—no word has come from that army since it entered the deserts of Syria months ago. He asked if the Boar had returned from his hunting trip in the North, the bright-bannered Immortals at his back. No one could answer him—few have come from the North save messengers bearing word of the constant approach of the Roman army.

"He asked if the new army had been raised from the people of the city. No one spoke. I looked around and saw only old men and servants around me. All of the great lords have fled—to Ecbatana or beyond, back to their estates. Aunt, we are abandoned!"

Shirin sighed and pulled the shawl closer around her shoulders. Her hair had been loose while she had been singing for Thyatis; now she began to braid it.

"Nephew," she said, her voice soft, "there are many pressures upon the King of Kings. This war does not go well, the people—even the nobles—are afraid. If he shows that fear he holds himself, then there will be a panic and all will be lost. It is natural to feel fear, each of us, man and woman, does. But you must not let it master you. Be strong for your father, stand by his side, bend your bow as he does."

Her voice trailed off, seeing the desolation in Kavadh's eyes. He stood, shaking his head.

"No one is coming to save us. The Boar is dead, the great Prince Shahin may be as well. There are no armies to succor us if we hold out in siege and no one to hold the walls against the Romans. Our only choice to survive is to flee now down the river or into the moutains. This I will say to my father, for there is no other choice."

Shirin watched him, her luminous eyes filled with worry. She held up a hand and he stopped as he would stalk out the door. "Your father honors courage and bravery above all things, dear nephew. Do not anger him when you say these things. He is quick to take offense."

Kavadh made a half smile while one hand picked at the drape of his shirt. "You mean he accounts me a base coward, hiding behind my dead mother's skirts? That he will ignore and revile me if I speak the truth to him? I know, but I am by rights the son of a King. I should speak honestly to my father in this."

He bowed and left the room. Behind him, the Princess stared out the tall windows. Thyatis closed the drape, though she had to restrain herself from stepping in and putting her arms around Shirin. Instead, she waited in the dim corridor, patient and quiet. She wondered if the boy-Prince would be killed by his father in an insane rage.

)•((

Rain fell in sheets, obscuring the road and the lines of palm trees on either side. Thick clayey mud dragged at Dwyrin's boots and caked his legs. The rain was not heavy but it was constant and it had been with the army for days. The canals the road paralleled had risen, lapping at the tops of the dykes that held them back from the endless fields that stretched to the horizon. In the odd times when the rain lifted or the clouds broke, Dwyrin could see towns and cities pass by, raised up on great mounds of earth. The land seemed empty—no peasants, no shepherds. Even the empty walls of the cities were barren of life.

Dwyrin put one foot in front of the other, feeling his boot suck up out of the mire. It made a popping sound as it pulled free, then he put it down a pace ahead. The tan and brown fluid slid over his foot, trapping it again. Ahead of him, the other mages toiled forward as well, their heads low, their hands on the sides of the wagons for support. Riders splashed past in both directions, urging their weary horses forward through the sodden road.

The Hibernian wondered if they would ever seen an end to the mud, if their destination would ever rise out of this endless plain of fields and towns and rows of palms and other trees. The army had come down out of the mountains above the city of Nineveh in a break in the weather. For a brief few days they had marched down firm roads under sunny skies. The air had been crisp and cool, with miles passing away under their marching feet. But past the great northern city they had entered the plain between the two rivers, a vast expanse of mud and deep loamy soil.

Then the rains had come again, and the world had dissolved into endless leagues of gray sky and muddy road. He put one foot, dragging it out of the muck, in front of the other. He was weary, very weary. Zoë looked back over her shoulder, her face drawn and grim. He was falling behind. She motioned for him to catch up. Dwyrin sighed and pushed harder through the mud.

THE PALACE OF BIRDS, CTESIPHON

F ires lit the plain, red and gold under an overcast night sky. The clouds scudded
    past, reflecting ruddy light from bellies fat with rain. Thyatis stood on the
roof of Shirin's house of marble and jade, her nostrils filled with the clean smell
of rain on the desert. She stretched her arms wide, feeling the damp wind ruffle
her hair. A deep breath filled her with a curious peace. The city was dark around
her, with barely a light showing. The Roman army had come to the gates of the
city of the King of Kings, but the populace had not seemed to notice.

Thyatis felt the air move behind her and she shifted her weight. Nikos
climbed up onto the roof next to her.

"Is everyone ready?" Calm settled over her. Violent action was close at hand.

"No." He cursed. "Jusuf had to take a leak and when he came back, Shirin
was gone. Her handmaiden says that a messenger came from the King of Kings to
summon her to his presence."

"Mithras! Where are the children?"

"Anagathios has them in hand. Dosed their fruit juice with some poppy.
They're sleeping hard. The Khazars are with him, though."

"Something . . . maybe enough. Well, we can use the drainpipe then. Take
'Gathios and the Khazars over the rooftops. Jusuf and I will go the other way and
see if we can catch up with . . . what?"

Nikos smiled, his grin a white line in the darkness. "Jusuf already left. Just
grabbed his sword and ran off after the girl."

Thyatis considered wasting a good five grains cursing luridly but put that
pleasure aside for later.

"Great . . . I'd better be quick about it. Get the children to the water gate."

"Ave, centurion." Nikos turned to go, but then stopped and held out a hand.
Thyatis clasped it, feeling his firm familiar grip. The Illyrian's expression was unreadable in the darkness.

"Good luck," he said. Then he hustled down the rooftop to the window to
her room.

Thyatis stood up and slowly turned around, her eyes surveying the city. She
could hear people running in the streets, but there were no fires and no smoke.
People had come in from the farms outside of the city the previous day, shouting
the news that the Romans were upon them. Few heard them, for Ctesiphon had
been emptying for the last two weeks. She wondered who was left in the darkened
buildings. The palace was abandoned, save for the royal guard and a few remaining
servants. No one had seen the King of Kings in days. Had he decided to flee, she
wondered, or simply to die in the ruin of his dreams?

Her room was empty, her travel gear already packed up for her by Nikos. She slung the bag over her shoulder and checked the straps and belts. She laced up her boots, tying the tops off just under her knees. Rolling from side to side on the balls of her feet, she settled the weight on her shoulders.

The door closed under her hand and she forgot about the room. Downstairs, in the common room where she had first set eyes upon the Princess, Anagathios, Nikos, and the Khazars were pulling on their own packs, laden with supplies and food. The Illyrian was sporting a variety of weapons as well.

"You sure you want to haul that bow over those roofs?"

Nikos looked up and smiled, fingering the leather case tied to the side of his pack.

"Never know when you might need it," he said.

Thyatis tested the leather straps that held the four sleeping children to the backs of the Khazars. She clasped hands with the men, searching their bearded faces for signs of fear or dismay. All of them met her gaze with level eyes.

"Kahrmi, Efraim, don't misplace this baggage, you hear? The owner wants it back."

The Khazars laughed, their white teeth sparkling behind their bushy brown beards. Thyatis turned to Anagathios and signed, two quick motions. *Don't wait for me at the water gate.*

The Syrian frowned but bobbed his head in acknowledgment. Thyatis nodded once to all of them and then strode off through the rooms of the Princess' apartment.

Nikos stepped to the door and watched until Thyatis had disappeared from sight. Once she had rounded the bend of the corridor outside, he closed the teak panel and latched it.

Anagathios, he signed to the Syrian, *take the Khazars to the garden and begin climbing out.*

The actor shook his curly locks, his face mournful. *Dear Nikos, why do this thing? Chances are passing small that anyone will find out what the centurion is doing. And if she finds out, it will go badly for you!*

Nikos shook his head in negation. He had already made up his mind.

It must be done, he signed, *otherwise her gamble may be for nothing. This way it will be a long time before anyone suspects.*

You are mad, replied Anagathios, *she would never countenance such a thing.*

True enough, Nikos answered, sighing quietly, *she would never think of bringing unhappiness to the Princess. But we are her true friends, and I will do this thing for her, taking the onus of it upon myself, out of my friendship for her.*

Anagathios shook his head again. He did not believe the Illyrian was right.

Go, I will clean up here.

Anagathios spread his hands wide and signed something about the gods. Then he slipped out of the other doorway into the garden and the waiting Khazars. Behind him Nikos went through the room carefully, checking in the trunks and behind the curtains for anything that might have been left behind. Once he was done he scoured the other rooms as well—the room of glass where music had played, the banquet room, the Princess's bedchamber, the quarters of her maid-servants. In the little room at the back of the servants' area, he found that one of the Khazars had left a copper buckle under a chair. Frowning, he pocketed it. As he left each room, he left the door open, sometimes propping them with the edge of a chair or table.

In the last room, the entrance to the baths, a cool stone-floored chamber, he paused, grim eyes counting the men and women trussed on the floor. Of them all, only the lady-in-waiting, Ara, was awake. She had stopped struggling with her bonds when he had appeared in the door. Now she stared at him with a blazing fury in her eyes. Nikos nodded to her and put down a bundle of clothing he had been carrying on the stone bench inside the door of the room. He slipped an amphora of fine oil off his shoulder and carefully leaned it up against the bench. Ara made a muffled sound, but this too he ignored.

He pulled a knife, long bladed, almost a shortsword, from a scabbard slung over his shoulder. It was a Persian weapon, one quietly taken from the guardroom of the House of the Black Swan where the King of Kings slept. Its edge was keen and the blade itself gleamed in the soft light of the single oil lamp. Nikos knelt and turned the first of the servants over. His thumb rolled back the eyelid of the man—he was still unconscious. With quick sure movements, he cut the simple garments from the man, leaving him naked on the floor.

Nikos looked up, checking the other captives. Ara had rolled over and was watching him with brown eyes wide with fear. The Illyrian looked away and punched the knife under the rib cage of the man with a single strong blow. The man twitched and his mouth opened silently. After a moment his chest stilled and a trickle of blood spilled out of the corner of his mouth. Nikos, his face still expressionless, quickly dressed the dead man in fur-lined boots and the rough homespun trousers and shirt of a Northern barbarian. This done, he rose and surveyed the others.

Too little time, he thought as he stooped over the next man.

In the end, Ara stared up at him, her eyes sightless with fear, as he bent over her.

Thyatis jogged through the halls of the palace. Great rooms, filled with treasures and glorious murals, blurred past. Her boots fell on expanses of intricate mosaic tile, showing scenes of wonder and delight. The crystal lanterns were falling dark with no one to refill the reservoirs of oil. In those places where there were torches, they had already guttered out. She climbed a great flight of stairs, each step carved from sea-green marble in the shape of breaking waves. In darkness, she hurried through a vaulting chamber lined with a thousand pillars containing a stepped pyramid. Atop the pyramid a throne of silver and gold sat in the dark-ness, waiting for a claimant. Behind rich red drapes, she found an open door banded with iron and clattered down a narrow sloping stairway.

Hexagonal rooms passed, filled with couches and wardrobes bulging with clothes. A closet door stood half open, showing rows and rows of jeweled shoes.

Ahead of her, she could hear faint voices, raised in anger. She crossed a bedchamber dominated by a four-poster bed with a canopy of purple silk sewn with diamond stars. The bedclothes were shoved all to one side, a mountain of fine-brushed Egyptian cotton and silk. Water tinkled from a bowl-shaped fountain. The western wall of the room was composed of wooden doors framing hundreds of squares of colored glass.

There was a garden beyond the bedchamber, filled with thousands of white flowers. The sky was very dark, save in the east, where a dull red glow lit up the low clouds. The flowers gleamed, pale and nacreous, in the light of hundreds of rose-colored paper lanterns hung from the trees. The garden stepped down toward a looming dark wall, in three great terraces. A stairway with steps carved from cedar logs descended the length of the garden. Thyatis came to a halt on a circular platform of wooden slats outside of the bedchamber.

Shirin stood in the darkness on the stairs, a pale-yellow flame in the long dress, her hair undone. Below her, on the second tier, Jusuf stood in the path, his blade glittering in the light of the lanterns. His dark-green robes and tunic blended into the grass and bushes, leaving only his long face illuminated by the rosy light. A heavyset man with very broad shoulders and dark curly hair stood behind Shirin, her arms twisted behind her back in his grip. His own blade, a long cavalry saber, was angled toward the Khazar Prince.

"Stand aside, boy." The voice of the heavyset man was oddly muffled, echoing. Thyatis drifted to the side of the platform, her left hand resting lightly on the pommel of her sword. The face of the heavyset man gleamed golden and, with a start, she realized that the smooth features and high brow were a mask of cunningly worked gold.

"No, Chrosoes King of Kings. Leave Shirin be. She does not go with you tonight."

"Jusuf . . . *ah!*" Shirin cried out as Chrosoes twisted her arm, her face grimacing in pain.

"Be still, wife. You, boy, once we accounted each other friends. Now you come to my house in the company of enemies and demand my property of me. I will not countenance it. Stand aside and I will allow you life. If you do not, then you will die, faithless, like your brother."

Thyatis hissed in surprise, but the sound was covered by a growl of rage from Jusuf. "Servant of the Lie! My brothers ride south with an army to end your madness!"

Chrosoes threw back his head and laughed, a long echoing sound. He thrust the heavy sword into the ground, point first, and flipped a length of cord from his pocket around Shirin's wrists. She struggled furiously, but it was too late. Jusuf rushed to the bottom of the steps but did not throw himself up the height. Thyatis began sliding her blade out of its sheath, her breathing even and slow. The sight of Shirin's face twisted in pain excited a trembling in her hands. Anger flared in the back of her mind, a dull red coal growing steadily brighter.

"Your oathbreaking brother is dead," crowed the King of Kings. "He fell at Kerenos, pierced by many spears. His body was carried from the field upon a shield of the House of Asena, born aloft by a hundred lances."

Shirin cried out again in pain and stumbled to her knees, her hands bound tightly behind her back.

"I've no time for a hobble, my wife, but this will suffice."

The King of Kings plucked the sword from the ground and spread his feet wide. "Come then, thief, and steal my property if you can."

Jusuf, his face bleak, moved to launch himself up the steps, but Thyatis called out in a clear, strong voice. "No, Jusuf, I forbid it."

Chrosoes whirled, dropping into a guard stance. His mask gleamed in the lanterns, his eyes murky pits.

Thyatis stepped down off the circular platform and the water-steel sword moved lazily in her hand. "We have no quarrel, Chrosoes King, if you will let the Lady Shirin choose her own way."

"A Latin Roman?" the King of Kings wondered, circling to the left. "And a woman! What strange days are these? Are you Jusuf's pet? He always loved exotic things."

"I am no pet," Thyatis answered, her feet light on the ground, matching the movement of the Persian. "Jusuf is under my authority. Will you let Shirin choose her own way?"

"No!" the King of Kings thundered his voice harsh and metallic. "She is my property, given freely in marriage by her family. Where I go, she goes. Neither you nor this dishonored whelp will steal her. If you desire her so much, come and let us gamble in blood for her."

"I will not kill you, King of Kings. I promised Shirin that I would spare your life."

"You promised her?" Chrosoes' voice was incredulous. "A possession cannot promise another possession! Does the hawk promise the hound? Does the ox hold the sheep to account for its honor? Your words are meaningless." He turned away in disgust.

"Do you think that she would not choose you, if you asked her?" Thyatis' voice was sharp.

Chrosoes stopped, shocked, looking down at Shirin, who had struggled to her knees, the long gown torn off her shoulder, revealing the curve of her breast. Her hair was a tangled mess and mud from the soft earth was smeared on the side of her face where she had fallen.

"Why would she choose to come with me?" he whispered, a thick-fingered hand going to the mask of beaten gold on his face. "Who would choose a monster, disfigured, unworthy to be a king?"

"You *are* a king, my love," Shirin said, her eyes filled with tears. "You have always been a great ruler, mighty and proud. Please, there is no need for more blood to be spilled."

"You would not choose me," he said distantly, his fingers brushing against the crown of her hair. "I am a ruined thing, fit only for dark places."

"No!" Shirin wept. "I do choose you. I have always chosen you. When I look at you, I see the face of my husband, my love, not just the flesh of your body."

Chrosoes turned away, his fist tight on the hilt of his sword. Thyatis stood only feet away, her knees slightly bent, the water-steel blade pointed away and to her left.

"See?" she said, her voice soft. "Ask her! She will choose you. Then Jusuf and I will stand aside and you can go to the water gate. The night is dark and the Romans have no boats. You can get away on the river . . ."

The King's sword rose, its edge glittering. The red glow in the sky was spreading and, very faintly, Thyatis could hear a great murmur of thousands of men shouting and screaming. The Roman army was loose in the city.

"You mock me," Chrosoes grated. "It is a lie! No *Roman* ever spoke truth to me, save one, and he is dead for long years. Only lies and deception and murder spring from your hateful stock."

Thyatis' right foot slid back on the wet grass and her body turned, subtly, into line with her sword. Her mind cleared and she became aware of a thousand tiny sounds in the garden: the soft mutter of birds, the *tink* of Anagathios descending a rope at the base of the garden, the harsh breathing of the man facing her.

The King's sword blurred overhand and Thyatis was in motion, a burst of fire jolting her blood. The heavy saber rang like a bell on the base of her blade and she slammed her shoulder into Chrosoes, locking sword to sword at the hilt. The King grunted and Thyatis sprang back, her upper arm numb. He was like a mountain. She could barely hold onto the hilt of the sword, her fingers were so stunned by the shock of his blow. Chrosoes shouted and leapt forward, sword slashing.

Thyatis leapt back, the tip of her blade flicking his stroke aside. Chrosoes pressed, raining blows upon her like a summer storm. Her defense was a blur of glittering steel, fending off each attack. Her arms raged at her in pain. Every stroke was a hammer blow to her upper body. She gasped for breath, giving ground. Fine cuts welled blood on her shoulders and arms. Chrosoes laughed, a high wild sound.

Thyatis spared a breath to shout. "Jusuf! The gate, get to the gate!"

The Khazar paused at the top of the steps, his hand reaching for Shirin. He looked over his shoulder. The Khazars, precious bundles strapped to their backs, were climbing down the mossy wall of the garden on long ropes.

Shirin hissed angrily at him. "Get my children out, you oaf!"

Jusuf turned on his heel and bounded down the steps, taking them three at a time.

Thyatis dodged sideways, feeling the air part where her head had been. She kicked out, catching the King of Kings' knee. Her boot bounced away, but he gasped in pain and switched stance to put the injured leg behind him. Thyatis gulped air and fell back a step herself.

"A Roman relying on skill in battle?" Chrosoes voice was mocking. "It *is* an age of wonders!"

Thyatis settled her grip on the sword, both hands wrapped around the long hilt. Her palms were slick with sweat, but the wire and leather were like an old familiar glove. She feinted at the King's shoulder, her blade flashing like summer lightning. He beat the stroke aside and bulled in, howling a war cry, catching her in the chest with his elbow. The iron rings of her vest crumpled around the blow, but the leather backing swallowed most of the force. Dampness spread under her armor. Thyatis flew backward into a sapling.

The tree cracked and she spilled to the ground. The water-steel blade slithered out of her hand, and she rolled up off the ground, hands wide. The King of Kings circled around the tree, his boot kicking the gleaming shape of the blade away across the grass. Thyatis crouched down, scuttling to one side. He attacked again, laughing in joy, the heavy blade whirling around his head.

She ducked away from the saber twice, then kicked at his bad knee again and had to backflip away from his counterblow. She found herself balanced on the brick wall that divided each terrace, wavering, her arms outstretched. Chrosoes laughed again and blinked sweat from his eyes. The mask had been knocked askew and he took the moment to tear it off his face. It sailed into the rosebushes.

Thyatis' eyes narrowed, seeing him fully in the glow of the lanterns. He had been very handsome once, with a proud nose and full strong lips. His eyes were dark, with long lashes and his cheekbones would have made many a Roman matron swoon and bat her eyes at him. Now he was terribly scarred, with one eye almost closed by the ravaged tissue. His beauty was marred, shattered by glassy skin and ridges of tormented flesh.

"You see!" He howled, seeing the flash of repulsion in her eyes. "Nothing like a king!"

He leapt in, slashing diagonally, his full weight behind the blow. Thyatis jumped up, high in the air, her legs curling up under her. The sword carved empty air and the King stumbled forward, catching himself on the edge of the terrace. Thyatis stormed in, her fists and elbows smashing at his face. Chrosoes screamed as his nose shattered again. She snap-kicked his sword hand, catching the thumb at the joint. The saber clattered off down the steps to the second terrace.

The King of Kings swung wildly, his heavy fists bunched like tree roots.

Thyatis wove between the blows and spun, the back of her boot clipping Chrosoes on the side of his head. The skin ruptured, spewing blood. Hot rage welled up in her, giving her fists lightning speed. Chrosoes fumbled, trying to block her blows, but he was slowing. She hammered at his face and diaphragm again and again.

The tip of her boot flashed into his groin and he screamed, a high keening sound, and doubled up. Her right elbow cracked on the back of his neck, driving him to the ground. Her fingers clawed into his hair and dragged his head up.

A slim hand caught her raised fist as she pulled back for a strike to crush his larynx.

"No! Thyatis . . . you promised!" The Roman woman turned, the gray tunnel that had focused her entire world down to the bleeding, crushed face of the King falling away. Shirin held her hand. The Princess was muddy, with her hair a rat's nest of dirt and leaves. Her hands, clinging tightly to Thyatis', were streaked with blood and dark bruises where she had sawn the cords away with the water-steel blade. The pale-yellow silk dress was utterly ruined, sopping wet, clinging to her in tatters.

"Leave him be," Shirin said, pulling Thyatis away from the moaning shape on the ground. "He made his choice."

Behind the Princess, fire suddenly blossomed from the roof of the palace. Shouts of excited men echoed from the windows. The low clouds were dark and glowing with the red of fires below. Ctesiphon was burning.

"The gate . . ." Thyatis whispered, suddenly feeling very weak. Shirin slid under her shoulder, her slim arm wrapped around Thyatis' waist. Shirin started to drag her toward the steps, but Thyatis turned clumsily. Rain had started to fall, slanting through the glow of the flames that were licking around the domes of the palace. "My sword . . ."

Shirin cursed and propped Thyatis against the trunk of an apple tree. The Roman woman clung to it, feeling the blinding pain in her ribs and forearms for the first time. The Princess cast about on the grass, swearing like a sailor. The drizzle of rain began to swell, hissing through the leaves of the trees. Thyatis turned her face up to the sky, letting the falling water sluice across her face, cooling her skin.

The Princess ran up, soaked to the skin, her long hair plastered to her shoulders and back.

"Here," she said, pushing the sword into Thyatis' hands. "We must go."

There was a sound of glass shattering and red light bloomed in the upper terrace. Shirin held Thyatis close and they stumbled down the steps. Thyatis looked back, seeing the palace outlined in roaring flame and steam. More glass shattered as the soldiers looting the chambers of the King began throwing things through the glassed doors. At the bottom of the garden Nikos was waiting, water running down his face, at the little gate. He was grinning fit to burst. He loved the wet.

Shirin dumped Thyatis into his arms and he ducked under the lintel, carrying her to the boat. The Princess turned back, wiping muddy water out of her eyes. Above her, the domes of the Palace of the Black Swan were blossoms of fire. Flames roared from the windows and smoke and steam climbed into the clouds in a great column. Helmeted figures capered on the balconies, throwing furniture and rugs into the courtyards below. At the top of the garden, outlined by the bonfire, a heavyset figure staggered. Shouts rang out.

Shirin wiped water from her face, her shoulders trembling. She turned away, pulling the iron door closed and putting her shoulder into the bar that held it closed from the other side. It was rusty and creaked for a moment before it slid home. With the door closed, the screams and crackle of falling timbers shut off.

The boat was a long skiff with a covered cabin at one end. Nikos stood in the stern, his bare toes gripping the planks of the deck, a heavy pole in his hands. Two Khazars reached up and helped Shirin into the boat. The Princess stepped gingerly to the little cabin and ducked down to crawl into it. Thunder rumbled in the heavens above. Lightning flickered from cloud to cloud. The Khazars cast off the mooring rope and Nikos dug in with the pole. The stones of the dock backed away, pooling with water in the downpour.

The boat slipped away into the storm, water pouring down all around it. Nikos, soaked to the bone, began singing a song of his youth as he held the tiller steady. The surface of the Tigris was broad and flat, dimpled with thousands of falling raindrops. Darkness folded around them. The Khazars put their backs into the stroke. The far shore was nearly a mile distant.

In the close darkness of the cabin, Shirin wormed herself into the woolen blankets, gathering her sleepy children around her. They murmured but fell asleep again, smelling her perfume in the night. It was warm, and the blankets were soft. The boat rocked gently from side to side with the stroke of the oars. The Princess drowsed, her babies in her arms, Thyatis' exhausted breath soft in her ear, one scarred forearm curled across Shirin's smooth stomach. Tears leaked from Shirin's eyes, even after she had fallen into a deep sleep.

CROWS OVER PALMYRA

Dahak stood in the ruins of the Damascus Gate, fine gray ash puffing up beneath his boots as he paced. Two stonemasons, their faces white with fear, knelt before him, each holding the side of a black sheet of polished basalt. On the face of the stone, in ancient spiky letters, they had carved an inscription. Only Dahak could read the words graven there, but he found them a fine jest drawn from a memory of his youth. His fingers, clawlike and withered, caressed the surface of the stone. Its smoothness was a thing of beauty. The words read:

I destroyed them, tore down the wall, and burned the town with fire; I caught the survivors and impaled them on stakes in front of their towns . . . Pillars of skulls I erected in front of the city . . . I fed their corpses, cut into small pieces, to dogs, pigs, vultures . . . I slowly tore off his skin . . . Of some I cut off the hands and limbs; of others the noses, ears and arms; of many soldiers I put out the eyes . . . I flayed them and covered with their skins the wall of the city . . .

The Lord Dahak laughed softly to read it and held the hot feeling of revenge close to his heart. It warmed him, he who always felt a chill in his breast. He shuffled back to the steps of his wagon. His men had pulled it out of the ditch, and the loot of the palace adorned it. Plates of beaten gold covered the doors, etched with many symbols. The Lord Dahak had placed them there with acid brewed from the blood of living men. His right hand, almost fully fleshed again, grasped the railing and he pulled himself up.

"Nail it to the wall of the gate, there, above the entrance."

The stonemasons bowed their heads to the stones of the ramp. They alone of all who had lived in the city before the coming of the Persians survived. Soldiers helped them raise the black stone up. Hammers rang, driving bolts of iron into the sandstone wall.

Dahak looked about him, seeing his handiwork. He was well pleased. The long walls of the city lay in ruins, torn down by heat and water and splitting bolts. The houses of the city were empty shells, scooped out by fire. No statue stood whole, no column in that long arcade of columns rested upon its base. The four houses of the gods of the city were shattered piles of cracked stone, brought down by his own hand. Windrows of skulls lay heaped around the gate, empty eyes staring at a brassy sky.

Atop the remaining fragment of the gate, a body hung, its head pinned back by black spikes, its arms flung wide. In death, Zenobia held no beauty. Arrows and spears had torn her body when she had fallen, a raging whirlwind at the last gate. Thirty men had perished, braving the reach of her sword. Archers had brought her down at last, for no man would face her hand to hand. Her body was dragged through the streets, torn by the kicking boots of the soldiers, to Dahak as he sat in the ruin of the House of the Four Gods. Her head had been struck from her body and paraded before the thousands of moaning captives on a tall pole. Her eyes had been plucked out, leaving only ragged pits filled with clotted blood.

All this the people of the city had seen before Dahak had walked among them, a dark shape passing for a man, feasting. When he was done, the withered dead lay in their thousands, skin shrunken to their skulls. Fires had been set, and the soldiers of the army had labored through long nights feeding the bodies to the flames.

Palmyra had died a long and agonizing death.

Dahak laughed, a chill sound that echoed off the walls of the ruined gate.

"Good-bye, O Mighty Queen," he said, bowing mockingly to the corpse above the gate. The head had been sewn back onto the torso, though it was a poor job, done in haste with thick leather stitches.

"Fear not for your beloved. He rests easy under my hand."

Dahak caressed the sarcophagus that was strapped to the back of the wagon. It was heavy gray slate, carved long ago by stonemasons in honor of one of the great nobles of the city. Now its occupant was scattered across the desert, and the body of the Egyptian priest, wrapped in burial shrouds and packed in salt, was closed up inside. A seal of lead and gold filled the cracks between the cover and the base. Dahak climbed over the top of the wagon, his long robes trailing after him.

"Hey-yup!" He flicked the reins and the twenty mules that had been hitched to the wagon twitched their ears and ambled forward. Dahak settled back into the hard-backed wooden seat. In the depths of his cowl, his flesh crept and crawled, pulling his lips into a semblance of a smile. Troops of horsemen trotted out to join the wagon as it rolled west on the long road to cultivated lands. As it passed down the road and through the funereal towers, regiments of spearmen picked up packs heavy with loot and fell in behind. Wagons rumbled onto the road. The Persian army was leaving the city in the desert.

Dahak surveyed his army—for it was his army now, broken to his will by fear and compliance in dreadful acts—and was pleased. His debt had ended with the death of the King of Kings, felt even across many long miles. Now he had no need to restrain himself.

The barren land lay quiet under a dim sun. Crows circled over the city.

CTESIPHON

)·((

The city had burned for three days and three nights before the rain quenched the last of the flames. Now the stones hissed and popped, still cooling, as Galen walked amid the ruins of the great palace that had stood by the river. His Germans walked a fair distance away, a rough circle that traveled where he traveled. It was a gray day, both in the sky, where clouds heavy with rain jostled one another over the river, and below, where a fine coating of ash lay over everything. The Northerners were still chortling with glee over the vast sums of booty they had received from the looting of the city and the palaces. Each man was nearly choked by chains of gold, and rings bulged on every finger. Every man in the army of either Emperor was going home laden with as much booty as he could carry.

Galen frowned as he climbed a broad staircase littered with cracked pillars and burned timbers. The precincts of the imperial residences were coated with a thick slurry of mud made from ash and rainwater. The city was in ruins, its people fled. From the height, he turned and looked back up the river, seeing the broad gray-green surface surging up against the dykes and retaining walls that the farmers and the citizens of the city had labored for generations to build and maintain. The water curled against the top of the earthen ramparts. Soon, if the rains held, it might spill over the top.

The Emperor shook his head, thinking *There's no one left to repair the earthworks.*

Heraclius stood in the center of what had once been a great room. His staff officers were a crowd of red cloaks, muddy boots, and silk behind him, his own bodyguards scattered through the ruins around the platform. The walls were tumbled down, the bricks cracked open by tremendous heat. Great soaring arches had once enclosed the space, and a domed roof had covered it. The dome was gone; only its rocky skeleton remained. A very light rain, no more than a mist, settled down through the gaping holes. The Eastern Emperor was gazing down at an enormous shattered disk of mosaic tile. Galen walked up to him, feeling his bodyguards fade back to the edge of his vision.

"Greetings, brother," he said to Heraclius.

The Eastern Emperor looked up, his eyes bright. His red beard bristled.

"A pity this was destroyed," he said, gesturing to the scattered remains of the world map that had covered the disk. "But a Roman one would be more accurate, I think."

Galen's left eyelid twitched in surprise, but he ignored the comment.

"A pity the entire city has been destroyed," he replied. "It was rich and filled with *fabricae* and merchants."

Heraclius laughed, standing back from the mosaic and spreading his arms wide. "We will build a new city here, even greater, more glorious, but it will be a Roman city! The capital of a Roman Persia . . ."

A faraway look crept into Heraclius' eyes and he took Galen by the shoulder. Together they walked toward the open side of the chamber, where a series of arches had once stood, looking out over a luxurious garden. The rest of the officers and nobles drifted slowly along behind them.

"Persia lies at our feet, prostrate, smashed to rubble. Their army is scattered, the Khazars rampage through the highlands, looting and pillaging. It will be decades before a King rises to rebuild this empire." Heraclius stopped and turned to Galen, his face creased by a broad smile.

"This is our chance, brother, to end the centuries of struggle between east and west. The Eastern frontier will stretch all the way to India!"

"And Chrosoes?" Galen said, his voice wry. "What of him?"

"Here," Heraclius said, his smile that of a cat in cream. He kicked a bundle on the ground, something heavy, wrapped in canvas. "Sviod! Show the Western Emperor what you found."

The Varangian, a mountain of a man with a smashed-in nose and a bald head like a boiled egg, gripped the edge of the canvas and unrolled it. Something slopped out, something black and bloated, crawling with worms and ants. Galen stared down at it in undisguised revulsion. The hand of the thing flopped at his feet, the skin of the fingers stretched tight over rotted flesh like overstuffed gray sausages. The Varangian smiled, showing gaps in his teeth. The Western Emperor held a cloth over his mouth and nose. The stench was tremendous.

"You see," Heraclius said, apparently unaffected by the smell, "the King of Kings is otherwise disposed."

"Where . . . did you find him? Are you sure that this is the King of Kings?" Galen fought to keep from gagging.

Heraclius motioned for the Varangian to roll the canvas back up. He turned away and paced slowly back to the knot of officers by the broken map.

"Some of your men, all unknowing, speared him like a fish the first night. Apparently he was already badly wounded, even bleeding. His body lay in the garden of one of the palaces for two days before one of the surviving Persians found him. I rewarded that servant well, for it was a precious gift he brought me."

The Eastern officers looked up, smiling, at the approach of Heraclius and Galen. One of them was the Eastern Emperor's brother, Theodore. He had his arm around the shoulder of a slightly built young man with a despondent face. Galen arched an eyebrow—the boy was almost pretty, though there was an odd look about him. His clothing, skin and hair were those of a Persian, but his eyes and nose, even his mouth, reminded the Western Emperor of someone . . .

"Ah, my friend," Heraclius said, bowing to the boy. "Theodore, let him stand on his own." The Eastern Prince pushed the young Persian forward. The boy looked up sullenly, his mouth trembling. Galen put his hands on his waist.

"And this?" he said, looking steadily at Heraclius. The Eastern Emperor smiled and ran a finger over his mustaches. He looked back over his shoulder at the bundle of canvas that the Varangians were dragging down into the garden. One of the Scandians had a shovel over his shoulder. The Eastern officers nudged each other and smiled at some secret jest.

"Am I satisfied?" Heraclius said, seemingly to himself. "A nation with which a treaty obtains assails my state. The armies of my enemy plunder my cities, enslave my citizens, loot my farms. I send embassies of peace to this nation, and severed heads, pickled in brine, are returned to me. I send letters, seeking the nature of the grievance against me, and I am called a *vile and insensate slave* in return. I learn, by other means, of the nature of the quarrel between my house and that of Chrosoes. I send the very head of the murderer of the friend of the Persian Emperor as a token of peace!"

Galen looked around the circle of faces. The Eastern officers were grinning, their faces flushed with some secret hunger. The Persian had stopped trembling and his head had come up. The Western Emperor frowned to himself again; this boy seemed terribly familiar!

"I seek to protect myself and the citizens of my state, and armies are sent against me. Tens of thousands die, and more cities are set to the torch. Yet, in all this, though the people of my city beg me to remain in the safety of my capital, I persevere. I come forth, with the aid of my brother Emperor, and assert my authority."

Now Heraclius, at last, met the eyes of the Persian boy. Behind the fellow, Theodore and two of his cavalry officers moved in close. Galen took a step back, feeling the ugly mood running through the young officers with their neatly clipped beards and red cloaks. He signaled his guardsmen. The Germans perked up their ears and sidled closer, brawny hands creeping to the hilts of their weapons.

"I bring ruin and thunder. I break armies. I shatter cities. I stand above the body of my enemy!" Heraclius was shouting, his face red, pressed close to the face of the Persian boy. "Am I satisfied? Am I satisfied? No! I am not. There is blood between your house and mine, Kavadh-Siroes, blood that still obtains between us!"

The Persian boy did not flinch, though now Galen's eyes widened in understanding.

Ah, the Western Emperor thought sadly, *then I did not win the throw.*

"Would his murder sate you?" the Western Emperor said in a voice of steel, his hand on Heraclius' shoulder. "Did Phocas' death make you sleep better at night when you became Emperor?"

"Yes." Heraclius growled, pushing Galen's hand away. "There will be an end to this struggle. A clean break with the past. Only the Queen Shirin will remain, once this sapling is cut down, and she I have promised to Theodore."

Galen's eyes narrowed and he stepped in front of the Persian boy, turning to face Heraclius squarely. The Eastern Emperor stepped back, regarding him with a calculating expression.

"And then," Galen said, "your brother would rule the Persian lands, with a Persian Queen at his side?"

"She is beautiful, I have heard," Heraclius said, hooking his thumbs into the broad leather belt around his waist. "She bears strong sons. But Persian? No . . . she is, what? Armenian? It does not matter. She will be a fitting prize for my brother."

Galen turned, his eyes seeking out Theodore. The young man was grinning, his face flushed with the prospect of a crown of laurels for himself. The Western Emperor's eyes were like flint, and Theodore stepped back, suddenly pale. Galen reached to his belt with his right hand and drew out a short, broad-bladed knife. All around the room, men froze at the sound of metal rasping on metal. The Varangians made to rush forward, their axes raised, but then they stopped in confusion. They could not lay hands upon the Emperor of the West.

"A young man should have a peaceful household," Galen said in a loud voice so that all in the chamber could hear him, "not one stained by blood. This man before you is a Roman, born of a Roman woman. He is the grandson of an Emperor of Rome, he called Maurice, who was murdered by the degenerate Phocas. He is the last of that line, the son of an Emperor himself."

Galen put his left hand on the hand of the Persian boy, raising it up over his head. "By the right of blood, this man should be your Emperor. By the right of blood, he should rule both Persia and the Eastern Empire as one undivided state."

Heraclius made to exclaim at this, but Galen caught his eye and the Eastern Emperor stilled, though his face was thunderous with anger.

"But rule is in the hand of the man who rules. It is the responsibility of the *pater*, the head of the household, to obtain order in his house, to see that civil cordiality is maintained. This, by ancient usage among the people of Rome, extends even to the brother of a brother. I would not have my brother's brother have a household filled with anger and rancor."

Galen's left arm stiffened and the flat-bladed dagger sank into Kavadh-Siroes' side, sliding sideways between his ribs. The boy turned dreadful eyes upon Galen and clutched at the blood oozing around the knife. The Western Emperor pulled the dagger out, the blade making a popping sound as it sucked free. Kavadh-Siroes' eyes grew even wider and he gasped. Galen lay the boy down gently onto the pavement. Blood spattered on the tiny blue tiles. The Western Emperor bent over and kissed the boy on both cheeks. Breath hissed between the boy's teeth, then failed.

"Good-bye, cousin," Galen said, and stood up. He wiped the blood from the knife on the dark-purple hem of his robe. He looked around at the stunned faces of the Eastern officers, at Theodore, at Heraclius.

"This is the duty of an Emperor," he said, his loud clear voice dripping with acid. "Now there is peace, both in your house, brother, and in the world. And your hands"—he held forth his own, spotted with blood—"are clean."

Theodore looked away, unable to meet Galen's eyes.

. . .

Dwyrin sat on a soot-blackened brick platform near the public gardens at the edge of the palaces. A statue had been raised on the platform before the Romans came. All that was left were the stumps of the legs and the head, rolled across the street against the front of an abandoned tavern. The thaumaturgic cohort camped in the gardens themselves, which had escaped the great fire. The sound of axes cutting wood filled the air. The Hibernian's heels kicked at the bricks. Zoë sat next to him, neither close nor far. Odenathus was lying on the bricks too, one leg crossed over the other knee. The day was gray, the clouds had not departed.

"What now?" Dwyrin wondered aloud. He fingered a heavy string of gold coins that he had draped around his neck. Holes had been punched in each coin so that they could be carried easily. He had new boots too, taken from the house of some well-to-do Persian who did not need them anymore. Zoë had acquired so many lengths of silk and linen and fine cotton weave that she had almost doubled in size.

"What now?" Odenathus said with a wry tone in his voice, raising his head up to look at the Hibernian. "Now you go home, to Rome, and another twenty years of this." He waved his hand airily at the ruined city.

Dwyrin grimaced, fingering his identity disk, still on its leather thong around his neck. He turned to Zoë, catching her by surprise. She seemed sad, but she gave him a cynical smile.

"And you, leader of five? Do you and Odenathus stay too?"

"No," she said, shaking her long braids, "we go home to the house of my aunt, in the city of Silk. She sent us to the Legions to learn, not to stay. Now that the war is over, we'll go home and serve in the army of the city."

Dwyrin sighed. He had feared that it would be so. Zoë reached over and squeezed his hand.

"You might be stationed in Syria," she said, her voice hopeful. "Then we can come visit you at the great legion camp of Denaba. It's only a few days' ride from our city."

"I suppose," he said, feeling his throat constrict. "I would like to see Palmyra. It must be beautiful."

"It is," Zoë said, her face lit by a smile. "It is the most beautiful and gracious city in the world."

"MacDonald!" Colonna stamped out into the square, his voice rattling the shutters. "You've duty. Get your lazy barbarian backside over here! And you too, little miss!"

Dwyrin grinned at Zoë and they slid off the platform. Odenathus got up more slowly and brushed the sand and soot off his tunic. Then he clambered down and jogged across the square to join them.

Galen stood in a small stone room, his arms crossed over his chest. Around him, the walls were blackened by fire and the roof had cracked and fallen in. His boots were muddy and his cloak stained with the tenacious black mud that had been birthed from ash and rain. Two of his Germans grunted as they turned heavy blocks of cut stone over.

"Are you sure of this?" The Western Emperor's voice was tinged with sadness.

"Aye, lord," the chief of the Germans said, his blond beard smeared with soot. "One of the palace geld-men we caught knew the ring and the band of silver."

The German reached down and gingerly picked up a withered, fire-blackened limb from among the debris on the floor. A partially melted silver band clung to the arm, and a gob of gold clung to one skeletal finger.

"A woman with dark hair, my lord, wearing the signs of the Princess Shirin. Dead, I think."

The arm fell back onto the muck on the tile floor with a rattle. Galen turned away, looking around the room. The door, too, had burned away, but he could see the bite marks of axes on its outer face.

"There was a struggle?"

The German nodded, pushing one of the other bodies aside with his boot. The body, even burned and withered, showed a thick gash in the sternum. In the mud, the Emperor could see the glint of broken rings of iron mail and the edge of a sword.

"Some fought, but then they fell and the others—the women—were murdered."

"What else?" the Emperor said, frowning at the ruin of the room.

"This." The German dug in a leather pouch on his wide belt. His grubby fingers drew out a disk of tin, pierced with a drilled hole. The fire had scored it, but portions were still readable. Galen took it, turning it over in his hand. The letters, driven into the face of the metal with a hammer and punch, were disfigured but still readable.

"Dardanus Nikolaeus. Nikos. A fifteen-year man." The Emperor felt a brief disappointment.

"This tells me enough. Bury the rest and tell the quartermaster to mark this name and those of any others you find among the list of the dead."

A pity, the Emperor thought as he walked through the ruins, the cowl of his cloak turned up. *She and her men seemed to have the very luck upon them.*

THE NECROPOLIS OF DASTAGIRD

Krista stood in the rain, feeling the heavy drops drum against the thick wool of her cloak. A storm thundered overhead, filling the sky with lurid yellow light. Lightning arced from cloud to cloud, or walked across the fields on the other side of the river with long jagged legs. She stood at the summit of the ziggurat in the dead city, her back to the great stone altar that capped the monument. Thunder growled, filling the heavens. Within the cowl of the robe, her face was dry and pensive.

On the horizon, a red glow stabbed through the murk. In the last hour, it had doubled in size. It pulsed like a great burning heart, visible even through the sheets of rain that blew across the dunes and the fields.

It must be a city, she thought, *being consumed in fire.*

She wondered who lived in the city—were they men like lived in Rome? Were they monsters as she had read in the tales of travelers, with faces in their stomachs?

She sighed, putting the question to herself again.

Is this the time to go? We are at the edge of the world, surely far enough to escape the curse. But where could I go? I spurned the Prince's offer—that at least would have gained me horses and supplies.

Her ribs still ached, though Maxian's touch, when he had grown strong enough to channel the power that healed, had knitted bone and sinew back together. Her bruises were gone and she could walk without limping.

Without him, said one voice, the timid voice, *you would be dead.*

Without him, another answered with asperity, *you would be back in Rome, safe and sound, at a party or in bed with some handsome, well-spoken noble.*

The stones under her feet began to tremble, causing the pools of rainwater to shiver and jump. She sighed and stood away from the wall. The Prince was at work again, far below, and she should be there. Descending the steps of the pyramid, she felt the two Walach boys slink out of the rainswept darkness around her and take up at her heels.

She smiled, her teeth white in the darkness. Among the Walach, the tribe followed the strong. She enjoyed thinking of herself as the Queen Bitch but winced, feeling a phantom of the pain it cost to gain their devotion. At the middle terrace, she turned off the stairs and pressed a stone in the wall. A door opened, steam and smoke curling out of it. A red glare shimmered down below. She went inside, and the Walach boys crept after her.

Days of crawling along dusty corridors and banging on the walls of abandoned rooms had finally borne fruit. A deep cellar, beneath even the furnaces that drove the fire pits of the temple, had yielded an uneven pavement. Under the moldy bricks, carefully prized up by the Walach boys under the eagle eye of Gaius Julius, a circular door had been discovered, set into a floor of chalky limestone. The door was inscribed by seven circles of brass; each etched with a thousand signs. Between the circles of brass, ancient characters had been chiseled in neat rows.

There was no lock, or hinge, only a smooth surface of stone and metal. Minute examination of the stones around the door found that to the right of it, about seven feet away, there was a dimple in the floor, as if a great weight had rubbed there repeatedly.

Maxian had taken the quarters of the high priest of the temple for his own after the battle in the room of fire. The entire camp had been moved into the chambers under the ziggurat. The larders were well stocked, and brick-lined cisterns filled with sweet cold water were buried under the pyramid. Even the great engine had been hauled down into the city by Khiron and the Walach boys, and rested, quiescent, within the walls of an ancient temple. The Prince devoted himself to the books of the priests, searching for the key to unlock the circular door.

Gaius Julius, with a cheerful insouciance and an eye to the desires of his master, looted the temple, loading the engine near to bursting with crates and boxes of scrolls, letters, tomes, tiny odd-looking soapstone figurines, parchments pressed between sheets of copper, flint daggers, and a box of jeweled skulls. Large sums of coin and ingots of gold went into the machine as well. Krista was bored nearly to tears, but she steeled herself to the smell of ancient dust and the feel of dead worms on her fingers and helped the Prince sort through the documents.

"This is too much." Maxian snarled, pushing a diary of some long-dead priest away from him on the tabletop. "During the time of Faridoon the Twelfth, the priests came and went from the tomb on a daily basis, taking measurements, praying, all manner of things. Never once a mention of how the door is opened."

Krista gently put down the motheaten scroll that she had been piecing together. "It seems that it was always so, until quite recently." Her voice was tired. It had been a long day in a succession of long days. "That other diary, the one you found here, said that steps had been taken to prevent the Master of the Lie from gaining entrance to the tomb."

"Yes," Maxian said, thinking, "but who is this Master of the Lie? Why were the priests afraid now—and not before?" He tapped a finger on the side of his skull. "A pity that Abdmachus suffered so cruelly at Alais' hands—if he could speak, he might be able to tell us how to open the door."

"The Lie is the greatest of their sins," said Gaius Julius, who had been sitting on a bench by the door, bouncing a ball of some dark flexible substance he had found in the storerooms on the ground. "One of the temptations sent by their god of darkness to tempt men from the light."

Krista arched an eyebrow at the old Roman. Maxian just squinted at him. "And you know this because . . ."

The dead man hooked his thumb over his shoulder, the ball held between his palm and his forefinger. "They have a list on the wall of the kitchen, for prayers probably. It lists them all, with a nice solar icon of the God of light at the top, and below, under his feet, the God of darkness."

Maxian stood up, stretching, and shook the black robe he wore into place over his tunic. "This god of light, is it the one they call 'Ormazd'?"

"I think so, oh Great Lord," the old Roman said, tugging at a nonexistent forelock. "The rival of the one they name Ahriman."

Krista frowned at the dead man and stood up as well, brushing bits of rotting papyrus from her sleeves. Gaius Julius was fond of playing the rustic, but she knew that his mind was very sharp and though he rarely helped them with the search, he knew Greek, Latin, and Persian better than either of them.

"Then," the Prince said, "lets see what a little prayer will do."

At the invocation of the name of Ormazd, the god of light and the way of right thought, the door gave a great groan and slowly, inch by inch, unscrewed itself from the floor. Gaius Julius' eyebrows went up as it rose. He had suggested breaking through it with hammers and chisels, but the plug was at least two feet thick. The air hummed with some unseen power, and when the plug had backed itself out, it rotated to one side and lay against the floor.

Stairs went down, narrow and dark, roughly carved from the greenish stone.

Lantern light illuminated the bottom of the steps. Krista shed her cloak, hanging it up in the cellar, and stepped lightly down the winding staircase. The tomb was buried in thirty feet of solid limestone. The staircase wound down, uneven and irregular, through bands of white and ochre and tan and finally past a dark layer the width of a man's thumb. The room that contained the sarcophagus was small, barely larger than that required for the coffin itself and space for a man to walk all the way around it. Krista stopped in the narrow doorway, her hands on the walls on either side.

The Sarcophagus was a glory of gold and silver and jade under the light of the lanterns Maxian and Gaius Julius had carried down from above. The air in the enclosed space was already thinning. The coffin was made in the shape of a man, tall and handsome, with wavy hair and a piercing gaze. It was crafted in the manner of the Egyptian pharaohs, arms crossed over the chest, features smoothed and rounded. Signs and symbols, scribed in gold paint, ran along the sides of the coffin in rows.

Maxian sat at the foot of the Sarcophagus, his legs crossed under him. Gaius Julius sat to his right, in the corner near the head of the coffin. Krista slid past the Prince and went to the other corner. She settled to the floor, crossing her long legs. The Prince already seemed to be gone, his face calm and composed, though his eyelids twitched with the movement of his eyes. The dead man, for all she could tell, was sleeping.

The homunculus and the Walach boys waited at the top of the stairs, crouching around the mouth of the tunnel.

Maxian began to speak, raising his hands. His eyes remained closed.

"Give us the corpse hung from a nail," the Prince said in a hollow voice.

There was a pause.

"The corpse, though it is our King's, give it to us."

Pale-blue light sparked around Maxian's hands. Krista felt a hum begin to build in the flat stone blocks of the floor, vibrating against her legs.

"On this corpse, I sprinkle the food of life." The Prince's hands moved in the air before him.

"On this corpse, I sprinkle the water of life." His hand cupped and then turned over, as if to pour some liquid onto the floor.

The pressure in the air of the room changed, crushing down upon her. Her eyes began to water and she blinked furiously. The Prince raised his hands, stretching them out to her and to Gaius Julius. She calmed her breathing and raised her hand, trying to fill her mind with calm.

White light burst around her, filling the entire space, flooding up the staircase. Her whole body trembled as a tingling sensation rushed over her skin. Even though her eyelids were screwed shut, she could see the room in stark detail, each stone, groove, surface, and symbol outlined in a clear white light. Lightning crawled through the air toward her with infinite slowness. She realized that she had stopped breathing. She panicked, but her body refused to listen. She screamed, feeling her blood halt in her veins. But no sound came from her lips.

The burning spark of lightning crept closer, arcing from the Prince's hand to hers.

It touched, and her universe collapsed, every memory, every sensation rushing together in one point just behind her eyes. Every thought, every emotion, every word she had ever spoken flashed past her, swallowed into that one hot point of fire that spun and flickered behind her eyes.

Something clicked, then scraped in the room.

Awareness flooded back into its usual dimensions and shapes. Krista sagged to the floor, her nails skidding across the rough stone. There was a tart smell, like burned pepper, in the air. She looked up, her hair falling around her face like a thicket of tight reddish-brown brambles.

The coffin had folded away. A man sat up from a bed of linen; a strong hand, burned almost bronze by some ancient sun, rubbed a face of noble proportions. He was naked, not a tall man, but well made. His limbs were long and clean, with sharply defined muscles. His hair was long and golden, falling in a wave of curls over his shoulders and broadly muscled back. The man looked around, his blue eyes narrowed in apprehension. Krista remembered to close her mouth. She brushed the hair out of her face.

"Was . . . was I dead?" His voice rang with command, a voice that would inspire men to valor on a field of battle. His Greek sounded strange to her ear, clipped and hurried. Krista felt her throat dry at the sound.

"Yes," she croaked and stood up, forgetting to keep her head low. "Ouch!"

The man laughed, a musical sound, and offered her his hand. She did not take it.

"You've been dead a long time," she said, glancing at Maxian, who was only beginning to recover consciousness. She pointed. "He brought you back."

"Then he is a well-met friend," said Alexander, son of Phillip, standing gingerly on unsteady legs. "I will thank him for it."

Gaius Julius rolled over, groaning and pressing the palms of his hands to his eyes.

"Yes," Krista said, eyeing the Conqueror as he stood up. He *was* well made. "Yes, you will."

)I(

"And the body of the Queen?"

"Laid to rest in the tomb of her father, sheykh. We sealed the entrance with many stones."

"Good."

Mohammed sighed and laid his hand on the mane of his gray mare. The animal looked over its shoulder, speckled with flea bites, at him and twitched its ears. Birds chattered in the palms around the camp. The twenty other men in his band climbed onto their camels and the ungainly beasts rose up. The last man scuffed sand over the firepit with his boot and clambered up onto his mount.

The Southerner felt the side of his face, his fingers tracing the path of the long scar that occluded his right eye and had cut across his mustache, lip, and down his chin. A long arrow of stone, spalled from the collapsing tower at the Damascus Gate, had come within a finger's width of ending his life. He wondered if he would ever be able to see out of that eye again.

I wonder if a priest could heal it, he thought, but then he thought of his friends and their mutilated bodies and resolved to leave the scar. His men looked away, seeing his face marked with a deep and abiding anger. It was not wise to look upon the Al'Quraysh when he was in such a state. The chieftain had already slain a man for speaking ill of the dead; it would not do to press him.

Mohammed adjusted the fit of his *kaffieh* and touched the scabbard of the sword that she had carried into battle. The blade was nicked and badly used, but there were weapon-smiths in his home city who could restore the sword to health again. It seemed that he could still feel the touch of her fingers on his hand, cool and soft, but this could not be so. He nudged the horse again and the mare trotted out of the shade of the palms into the searing light of the desert sun.

At his back a bare twenty Tanukh rode, all that remained of their tribe. With ibn'Adi dead, they had come to him as he had lain up in a cave miles from the ruined city, slowly healing, and pledged themselves to him. The sands opened up before them, long endless rolling dunes that filled the Waste at the center of the world. Mohammed set an easy pace, for they had many many miles to cross before he saw the doorway of his home or heard the welcoming voice of his wife.

His eyes glittered with fury as he rode, thinking of the news that ibn'Adi's nephew had brought, of the defeat of Persia and the capture of their great capital by the armies of Rome. A few hundred miles away they had marched, the legions that could have relieved Palmyra. He thought of the treachery of Kings and the sacrifice of a brave Queen and the priest who had loved her.

Purpose grew in his heart, hot and filled with hate, and the horse, sensing his desire, moved a little quicker. There were many leagues to cross, ere he was home again.